MW01613544

LIZZY PENNINGTON

Kingdom of Beginnings

First edition

Cover art by Joshua Griffin

This book was professionally typeset on Reedsy.
Find out more at reedsy.com

To the readers who watch movies in their heads while their eyes fly across the page.
I hope you find this book to be the escape we're always looking for.

Trigger Warnings

If you want to skip this page and go in blind, then by all means go ahead.

This book is labeled as Adult Dark Fantasy, so please treat it as such. There will be topics in here not suitable for all ages, mental health statuses, or moods. If you need to at any point, take a break and come back later. While not the darkest in this genre, it still leans heavily into the Adult category.

—

Death of family members
Gore
Blood
Sexual Assault - Please note that the sexual assault goes as far as rape being attempted, but not beyond that.
Consensual sexual content
Abusive relationships
Self harm with knives
Assisted self harm with knives
Mentions of racism and slavery
Anxiety attacks

—

Playlist

These songs are fine be listened to over the course of the chapter they are placed with. For a slightly more in depth reading experience, you can listen to them beginning with the exact quotes I have down below. Yes, I recognize that this is strange. But I truly think that playing them at the right moment can add so much color to a scene.

https://open.spotify.com/playlist/6PbblkQ1LPxl3PcvdYn30r?si=b2d4a 513056e4b00

Chapter 34 ("*Don't take this too far…*"): Petrunko by egopium
    Chapter 38 ("What is that…"): Run Boy Run by Woodkid
    Chapter 52 ("Filo swallows…"): She Knows by J. Cole, Cults, Amber Coffman
    Chapter 56: Schubert by Thylacine, Franz Schubert

Please note that there's also a map in the back of the book, but potentially gives some light spoilers if you want to go in blind, so look at it at your own risk.

Pronunciation Guide

Names:
Kali - kahl-ee
Jakir - jah-keer
Senka - sein-kah
Sayah - sigh-a
Aiza - aye-zuh
Filo - figh-low
Mikhail - mick-hale
Janét - jahn-eht
Gallyan - gal-ian
Dominé - dohm-in-aye

Titles:
Samle - sahm-luh
Dronning - droh-ning
Konge - kohng-yeh
Sekund - seq-yun
Kallet - cahll-et

Chapter 1

"I win!" I yell, having successfully grabbed her wrist. This little brat has about three seconds to get into this car before I grab her by her hair and toss her into the back. Somehow an eleven-year-old girl has managed to have so many friends, and so much energy, as I have currently. Clearly I'm failing in the adult phase of my life.

"Carly," I say through clenched teeth, tired of chasing after her. "Lets. Go."

She rolls her eyes and starts moving towards the car.

"Sorry guys, I'll totally see you later. Sister is being totes rude and I can't stand it anymore," she explains dramatically. She finally climbs into the passenger seat and buckles herself in. I cringe at the language she uses, avoiding an argument by breathing deeply.

"I've told you; you can't sit there until you're twelve," I jam my thumb over my shoulder. "So back seat asshole."

"Just be cool for once."

"Oh, I'm so sorry the law isn't cool."

"I'll climb into the back seat once we leave the mall."

I sigh and shake my head, pulling away from the pickup line. Once we reach the first stop sign heading back into the highway, she quickly unbuckles her seat belt and dives into the backseat.

"Thank you," I smile at her in the rear view mirror. She grins back, acting more like herself now that her friends are far behind. She starts her usual non-stop talking that she always does after I pick her up, giving me all the goodies about the drama at VilleTop Middle School.

She pauses after finishing, taking a breath and looking out the window.

"You know, it's not always about acting like you're the most popular girl in school. A lot of those people won't be there a couple years from now."

"Umm, no. We're gonna be friends forever," she rolls her eyes again.

I don't say anything else knowing full well she'll only argue with me, leading to a blow up for our parents to deal with.

"I'm still your best friend though, always," she mumbles. I catch it and reach my hand back to hold hers. I feel a small hand squeeze mine, continuing to hold it until we arrive home.

"Hey, I love you Car" I remind her as she climbs out. "Have fun doing homework."

"Screw you Kali."

"Wow, nice mouth."

I've lost count of how many times she's rolled her eyes at this point.

"Have fun at the beach...*without* me!"

I wink as I back out of the driveway and head over to my favorite spot. A strip of the beach is lined with trees and there are breaks between them. The little spaces allow for each family or couple in them to have their own private paradise.

The palm trees, only slightly bent in the breeze blowing over the sand, offer a few cool spots for some to lay in. Nearby, I catch a glimpse of a group of girls carefully eating their quickly melting ice cream. I smile, thinking about how Carly would be doing the same thing if I had let her come. I make a promise to myself to bring her next time.

A few minutes later after parking and I'm laid flat on the ground, skin already sweating. Not long after, I fall asleep to the sound of waves reaching for my feet.

Somehow the sun seems brighter today, like my eyes have to squint a little harder on my way to the beach. Saturday was supposed to be a cloudy day but the heat radiating from our solar systems center obliterates any chance of that. Still, the waves are big enough for surfers to catch a good ride on, and the humidity is low enough I don't sweat my ass off while laying on the sand.

One of my favorite things about Florida is the absolute madness that it produces just because of the people that live here. The psychos make the headlines so entertaining. Love it.

That's exactly what keeps me from popping my head up and getting back to my car when I start to hear people scream. The sand is soft enough I initially can't hear people running to get inside or the sound of bodies dropping. What does make me pop my head up is the sudden scorching pain I feel all over my body as if I'm being suddenly sunburned in a matter of seconds. In a way, that is exactly what it looked like.

Fucking expired sunscreen.

I jump from my towel and look over the rim of my glasses. I catch a disturbing glimpse of what's happening. My skin is turning red, and blisters are rapidly popping up all over. The adrenaline pumping underneath it through my veins keeps the majority of the pain away. Since the pain is quickly fading in some spots, it's easily a third degree burn that's spreading all over. Spreading faster than a grease fire in a southern kitchen, with nothing stopping it.

I scan around me, trying desperately to figure out if I'm having an allergic reaction, only to realize everyone around is faring far worse than I am.

My body finally kicking into flight mode, I start to move towards the nearest shade I can find just like the others around me. My eyes skim horrors that one would only believe they could see in a movie. People on fire with flames licking at the hair on their heads; elderly people dropping dead before they can swing their foot forward for another step. Kids strain to breathe while their parents struggle to figure out what to do. The world seemed to literally be catching on fire, melting, or disintegrating and there was nothing to stop it.

Palm trees begin to crack, bending under the weight of the heat. Their singed tops tilt toward the ground in slow motion.

The girls with ice cream now only carry singed cones of blackened waffles, the ice cream evaporating from where it's plopped onto the pavement. The palm trees that had provided shade now lay flat on the ground. Their trunks smoke and pop, starting to explode from how hot their interior is becoming.

The heat increases, becoming suffocating.

My mind jumps to shelter.

I try to find somewhere, anywhere, to hide. I look, only to realize there is no shade. Anywhere.

I finally make it to the pavement but my body jerks me back just as I'm about to step on it. I watch the tar melt and shift like liquid. I start to claw at my skin, my very bones burning under the pressure of the intense heat. I open my mouth to scream, only instead able to barely push out a strangled breath. In the distance I see the tires of my car melting onto the pavement and the metal body sagging under the weight of the environment. My body feels like the same thing is happening to it.

With a desperate gasp for air, I sink to the ground quickly and begin to close my eyes. On the spots of my body that hadn't begun to burn yet, I feel the sun causing blisters. Unlike the areas I could no longer feel the burn, these new spots hurt far worse.

People continue screaming, animals drop from the remaining standing trees like paper weights. My eyes, struggling to stay closed from how shriveled my eyelids have become, watch the skin peel off from another woman nearly the same age as me. I watch people sink into the liquid tar, their screams being choked off by the hot air.

I'm dying.

CHAPTER 1

With a groan, I try to bring in one last breath, fail, then watch the world brighten into darkness.

Chapter 2

The first thing I feel as I wake is the sand and dirt covering my body. Confusion settles in as I shift around trying to figure out why I'm being kept warm by the earth instead of by my blankets. Had I sleep-walked out into my backyard? Was my sister playing some stupid trick? That had to be it. Carly would absolutely be the one to put dirt on me in my sleep, even if it meant ruining my sheets and carpet.

"Carly you little shit I swear to god I will make you pay for this," I grumble.

The scowl on my face is quickly wiped away by the sight before me. I'm not in my bed, I'm not even in my own home. I'm sitting on the same beach I now remember burning on, the same one I watched so many others collapse dead on.

I feel the setting sun on my face, and quickly lay back down to try and crawl away from it. I dig, cramming crumbled earth under my fingernails. It's seconds before I realize the sun isn't burning me anymore. Or at least the lower angle has rendered its power mute.

I want so badly to believe that it's a nightmare, some cruel trick being played upon me. There is nothing to convince me of that, however. Looking around I take in scorched bodies of all ages, the little ones being the most scarring. Their little legs either frozen mid-run to escape the mysterious pain or curled up into the fetal position as if trying to shield themselves. Nothing could have shielded them. Not from what I saw.

But something shielded me.

It strikes me like a slap to the face. My body is fine, though naked. I know better than to try and fool myself into thinking this is some strange form of afterlife or reincarnation.

In a rush I brush off the dirt from my arms and legs, checking for any visible injuries. Nothing. Not a single scar, boil, or flaking segment of skin remains.

My thoughts juggle between what's happened to me, and wondering if Carly is safe from the horrors I'd witnessed.

I stumble away from the shoreline back towards where the parking lot used to be. Now, there are sad heaps of plastic and metal that are twisted and melted together. Some of what was once a car is sunken into the re-hardened pavement. Memory flashes to when the massive crowd of people were rushing away, and the bodies trapped in the black tar burns behind my eyes. Figures are still caught there, forever framed by the world-changing event in a setting of suffering.

My head shakes, trying to shake off the intrusion of the history I witnessed only...

No...I don't even know how long I was out.

Mild panic sets in. I could have been out for hours, my chances of being found and rescued slimming down with every passing minute. Was there even rescue? A place that was safe or untouched?

Though guilt racks me for it, I dig through an abandoned duffle bag. A shirt with a few holes in it and shorts is all there is - but I'll take anything to cover my naked body. There's no shoes, but my feet are plenty used to hot pavement from growing up in the south.

Questions begin to bombard my mind, but I swiftly block them. Allowing myself to spiral into an unknown oblivion would only hurt me now. My thoughts turn to my family. My parents, who were supposed to be home with Carly. I mentally prepare myself to begin what might be a long walk to find home.

I continue walking for what feels like hours. Eventually my legs carry the tired body attached to them back to what was once my home. It wasn't even close to that anymore.

It's further, how is it further?

I walk an extra thirty minutes than I normally would have to reach the beginning of our driveway.

To my utter horror, the majority of it is burned, twisted from heat, or melted. It looks like each end had been picked up and twisted in opposite ways like the wrapper around a hard candy. Running closer only speeds up discovery of my mother and fathers body on the porch.

I realize once I'm closer that it's not their bodies. Only the shadow of where they had sat is left on the wall. Even the shadow of their rocking chairs is there too. I gasp, choking on my still raw throat. My hand flies up to cover my mouth.

I stumble away, knowing from chemistry classes and videos of radiation accidents, that there would be no bodies to find

Breathing. It's getting harder with every step.

I have to find Carly. I have to find Carly. I have to find Carly.

Pieces of books, scorched furniture, everything is tossed aside as I look for a sign of my last shred of hope.

Out of the corner of my eye I notice a large hole in the center of what used to be the kitchen. Presently, it's a mangled area of metal and tile. The white of our old bathtub shines in the dimmed sun as if calling to me, the rest of it covered by the shower curtain.

"Car?" I whisper, creeping forward carefully.

Fallen support beams crack under my weight as I make my way towards it, careful not to injure myself. I lean forward and slip down to the level of the tub to pull away the cover.

"Carly?" I call out, louder now. "Car!"

Tears build and flow freely from my eyes as I take in the information laid bare to me. The only chance I had before getting here of not being alone. Of having at least one other person to share the burden of this disaster with, was gone.

"Carly answer me right now!" I sob, tears streaming down my face.

It nearly cripples me as I finally realized how awful it smells. The decomposition was ruthless, making her virtually unrecognizable. The scent burns into my memory.

Her face is nearly unrecognizable, slightly bloated and blue. Her eyes are closed though, her lips parted as though she tried to whisper before her last breath. From the look of her body, either her lungs gave way to smoke inhalation or her body couldn't take the fall from the third floor.

I feel pressured to ensure that Carly's naked skin is covered. The empty shell has to be put to rest. It's the least I can do for her, or maybe myself, since there's a body left to discover. Our parents are a different story from her.

After carefully wrapping her frail body in the mangled shower curtain, I carry her to our backyard. I don't realize I've walked far from the house until I look up to see how open the area around me is. The memories of the past eight years we spent growing up together play like a movie. I don't have the energy to try and decide if it's more painful or comforting.

Doesn't matter, it's happening either way.

Dad's tool shed is gone, so I use my bare hands to dig out the grave. No need for a big one, she was only eleven. Even for an eleven-year-old, she was skinny - just like Mom had been. I didn't get those genes. I got the muscular figure with a soft belly. Something Car had teased about every time Mom tried to remind me that I did at least have a bit of an hourglass figure.

Banter I'd give anything to hear right now.

Enough time passes that the sun sets behind me and darkness takes over. Once I deem the grave suitable enough for my baby sister, I place her gently into the earth.

"I'm so sorry Car," I whimper, my voice reminding me how much pain I'm truly in. How much I'll be in for a long time coming.

Covering her face with the curtain I step back. Unceremoniously my hands and feet begin shoving dirt back to cover her body forever. Occasionally, I pound my fist against the pile as if to take out my anger on it. Nothing seems to calm me, to soothe the ache that my chest keeps captive.

Once I finish covering Carly, I collapse next to the freshly disturbed land. There is no place for me to sleep tonight other than next to my sister one last time. I consider briefly how stupid it is to expose my body to the elements but the survivors' guilt washes over it. Nowhere else will I find peace than being near what once held the soul of the annoying little brat I would gladly trade my life for.

Trade it for what though? For her to try and survive in this awful new land gifted to us by the somehow still-functioning sun? To wake and find my body first thing?

As my eyes shut the tears still fall, feeding the newly forming grass below me.

The early sun seeps through my eyelids, causing them to flutter open as much as they can. I flinch, curling into myself from the sunlight until it clicks that I'm not being harmed. I try to scan my skin for injuries. The combination of the light and my eyes being puffy from crying makes it difficult to really see. My hand provides temporary relief from the sun, allowing me to stand and begin moving away. Soft grass touches my bare feet. Feet becoming sore from walking barefoot so much.

There is no point in me staying here, refusing to leave my old home will only result in my death. Whether that would be from starvation, dehydration, or overexposure I would prefer not find out. I know enough to understand sitting around doesn't equal survival.

When the earth was scorched there was no discrimination in the damage it dealt. Nearly everything was touched in some way by flames that seemed to come from Hell.

That means I was out long enough for the grass to begin growing again?

My brain refuses to process how long that means, because it could be any length of time. The soil would most likely need to recover, and then the seeds would have to germinate and sprout. What didn't seem to make sense, is that I had been completely out of it for the entirety of that timeline.

There is no doubt in my mind that I'm not the only person that made it. The only problem was finding someone else in what was now a wasteland.

Chapter 3

Every time I take a step I consider giving up and laying down. The hot pavement only serves to drain my energy faster but the field next to me is so overgrown that it isn't worth wading through and earning a snake bite.

If there's even any snakes left.

I decide not to take my chances and stick to the hot road.

I had started out my seemingly endless journey going back to the beach, as if I could restart this horrible game and make a better choice. Find Carly alive and well just waiting for me to get home and explain everything. Did I consider that Mom and Dad were gone too? Absolutely, but I just wasn't close with them like I was with my little sister. She was everything, she was half of me. Now she's gone.

What was most confusing to me was that when I returned to the beach, I could see land across the water. Land that wasn't there before when everything was okay. I stare at it for nearly twenty minutes prior to finally pulling myself away. More than the death of humanity had happened.

The very land itself had shifted.

I curse as I lose my footing after stepping in the middle of a dead animal. A raccoon when I look closely; just one that's been melted to the road with only its bones left to show. At this point it's not disgusting, just unfortunate.

A bird suddenly flies in front of me, almost hitting me in the face with its wing.

"Fucking rude," I snap. I nearly startle myself with my first outburst since leaving Carly in that tiny grave.

Oh my god I'm talking to a bird, I realize. My mind starts to follow a rabbit hole of thoughts of how strange the situation is that I'm talking to a bird. A bird.

"So, this is how the end starts," I dramatically throw my hands into the air. "With me talking to a bird that will probably poke my eyes out."

A loud screeching from the bird pulls me out of my thoughts. When I finally look directly at it, I realize it isn't just any bird, it's a raven of some sort. Or maybe a crow. One that had been previously in captivity if I'm right about the tag on its leg. Just as I notice said tag, it leans down and begins picking and pulling at it.

Without thinking I step towards it and reach for the tag only to be rewarded with a hard pinch on my hand.

"Ow! I'm trying to help you! Ungrateful brat."

"Help."

No. Nope.

I'm dealing with a bird that can talk.

Whatever hit this planet obviously did some freaky shit to any surviving animals.

"Help," it states again.

"Kinda hard to do that when you attack me," I mumble.

I reach again, this time receiving no attacks. The bird only stills at my advancement and watches me carefully by slowly turning its head at the same rate my hand reaches for it. Pulling the tag with both hands doesn't break it and seems to only cause more pain. I look around me for sharp objects to help with the cutting.

The only thing in sight worthy of helping is one of the bones from the dead raccoon. Sighing, I glare at both and move to pick up a rib. Feathers flaps his wings, taking off from the ground towards me.

"Help! Help!" He swoops down again and catches my hair in its claws. A slight sting in my scalp repeats as the creature tries to untangle its claws.

Without warning, anger spreads through me like wildfire and I reach up and wrap my hands around its body and yank it down until it's face-to-face with me.

"Calm. Down. Or I will snap your neck and eat you over a fire."

It seems to take the hint and stills completely until I snap the bone, and use it to make a small cut - after quite some effort - and remove the tag from its leg. I release it quickly and watch it fly away to the closest tree branch. The anger in me cools immediately leaving an aftershock of concern.

My emotions were never so uncontrolled like that before. I never had any kind of issues with my temper previously, so this was out of the blue. I brush it off as a result of my stress. Taking a deep breath and starting to walk along the road again, the sound of my feet creates a lull in my mind.

Until the bird flies in my face again.

"That's *it* fucker! I have helped you, threatened you, and left you alone and you have the *audacity* to come after me again?!" I attempt reaching for it as it flies back and forth over me but my weak body only holds me back.

It stops, so the walking continues again in hopes of peace and quiet.

As the sun begins to set, a church reveals itself. Even stranger is that by the position I'm in when in front of it, it's obvious that it is on top of a substantial hill. In Florida.

Dismissing the additional change in land, curiosity propels me to enter it and discover why it was not melted like the rest of the houses in my neighborhood were. All of them had either lost most of their form or had resulted in being a pile of ash and memories. Looking down the side of the hill I had yet to traverse I could see that many houses were untouched like the church. A few of them even seemed pristine compared to the others that had merely suffered a loss of paint or shingles. Perhaps at some point the people in those houses used this church for prayer, or shelter when the sun condemned us all.

I push gently on the door, only to have it fall to pieces below me. Wood was not only burned but beginning to rot away from the moisture and lack of care. The smell of mold curls into my nose only to be worsened by my entry into the building. Even the pews had begun to suffer the

14

same fate. The place where a speaker may have stood remained standing compared to the rest of the furniture. I curl my lip up at the loud symbols that remain standing of what something that clearly hadn't saved anyone. I had been dragged to church and never appreciated it, had it shoved in my face by so many controlling people that it had left a bad taste in my mouth. Now, walking through the destroyed building, there is nothing left but man made symbols.

Car hated it. Hated the idea of all of it. My vision becomes unfocused and I stare off, wondering if she would have grown to love it after getting over the boundless rebel phase she had been in. Oddly enough, the thoughts of what could have been hurt slightly less than they did the previous day when I laid down beside her cold body.

I flinch as wind ruffles my hair from the bird flying over me at an unnecessarily low height. Eyes rolling, I move forward to get closer to the front and inspect. The only thing to be found is another body that was not burned but instead emaciated from lack of nutrition. One hand rests on a bible while the other lays under a gun. Most likely from growing weak with holding it. My breath hitches at the sight causing me to inhale a lungful of dust. Coughing violently for a few minutes manages to clear them and allow focus to return.

The saddest part is that it's the only body anywhere in the church.

He couldn't even pull the trigger. Maybe he was too weak. Or too scared, I conclude silently. *Or hoping for someone to come.*

"Died. He died," the bird screams startling me slightly.

At this point I chose to ignore the feathered annoyance hoping it would convince it to stop following me. Somehow my thoughts alone seem to encourage it, resulting in it flying down to land on the podium in front of me. It looks between the body and I repeatedly until I lean down to grab the gun.

"Gun?"

I pause.

"Yeah, it's a gun."

"Gun good?"

15

"Uh," I pause wondering why this thing is having a higher level of thought that I think it should. "Sometimes, if you use it right it can be."

"Gun good," it answers, and then reaches down immediately to peck it. Even better, it aims right for the trigger.

"No! Do you want to get shot?!" I yell, reaching to turn it away. "If you wanna die that's how you do it bud, so do me a favor and *never* do that again."

I notice that its beak has in fact managed to squeeze the trigger but nothing happens. Picking it up, I try to pull the slide back. An awful grating sound reaches my ears. I look into the chamber, seeing that the sole bullet in it had been melted and warped. The other workings of the weapon are completely rusted, melded together, or damaged in other ways. I look up at the bird in annoyance. Nothing else in the church is nearly as damaged, yet the weapon sustained the worst damage. A flutter of wings and some twitchy head movements is all I get in response. Maybe I shouldn't tell it to be careful.

Gently tucking away the firearm back where it was hidden, I step away from the body and start to move out of the building to continue headings towards-

I stop right as I'm about to step into the sunlight again. It finally occurs to me that I have no idea what I'm doing walking around. I could be wasting energy right now trying to achieve something that will never happen. There was so much to understand about what had happened during my coma that it was possible I was completely and utterly lost. Lost in a place I had grown up in since I was six years old. Lost in a world that had been relatively the same since I was born. Lost on a planet that perhaps I was the only one left on.

Panic sets in.

My breathing stops long enough to make me lightheaded. As my eyes burn more and more with each passing second my vision becomes blurry. I turn, not sure what I'm looking for.

I look at the bird, trying to choke out my thoughts.

"I can't-"

Sobs rack my body uncontrollably causing me to collapse. A worn red rug catches my hands and knees, but the ground underneath it is still unforgiving. Tears cascade onto it making it darker with every drop. My lungs continue to seize up and my heart rate only becomes more frantic. Blood pumps wildly through my ears making it hard to hear anything but my sobs. I feel nothing but fear and loneliness in my break and there is no one to reach a hand over and calm me. No one to pull me up and hold me and tell me that everything was going to be okay.

I lose track of time as I remained curled up on the floor of the church sulking in my own pain. It does nothing to help me feel better and honestly put me at risk if anyone – or anything – hears me and decides they're aggressive enough to make matters worse. Hours pass. I realize that the sun is casting beautiful colors onto the clouds just as it settles beneath the horizon.

"Not good. Not good. Must leave," the bird speaks at an incredibly low tone. It walks up to my face and turns an eye to be level with mine. "Must go now."

My stomach dips slightly at the urgency in its voice. Something isn't right about how nervous or quiet it is as the sun sets. Though nighttime may allow for different creatures to come out, it should never make an animal as nervous as this one is.

Not moving quickly enough for the bird, it pecks lightly at my thigh to rush me. A gut feeling tells me to listen and I quickly stand. Claws dig into my shoulders; feathers ruffle quietly next to my ear as I become a perch for a wildly talkative animal.

My feet carry me towards the houses down the road from the church. I stop when a beak pulls on my hair.

"Okay serious-"

"No. Bad. High. Go high."

A look to my left shows dense forest that looks much worse off than the houses.

"Not happening, that looks like trouble."

I feel anxiety peel off from it as it shifts quickly around while shaking its head. While there may not be the best hiding spot available right now a dark forest is not nearly as inviting as a house with walls and doors.

Reaching a modest yellow house with green trim I slip in through the doorway and look around quickly for any sign of a legitimate hiding spot that I so badly feel I need. Nothing catches my eye, so I move towards the back of the house.

Loud yelling and whooping stop me dead in my tracks. It isn't far, and from what I can hear it is mostly male. My eyes sweep back to hurriedly search for a place to disappear.

"Hurry hurry."

"Ssshh, you have to be quiet," I reach up, not sure if for my comfort or the birds, and stroke its head. Nothing in the house gives me any reason to dive into it but I have no choice when the orange hue of fire becomes clear from the road. The group of men have gotten close far faster than I realized. At the last second, I dip into a storage closet. The group is right outside the house now.

"Clear the area boys! Find some food, maybe some newbies, and if you're lucky..." he pauses as some cheers ring out. "A pretty girl."

Fear drips into my veins causing goosebumps to rise on every part of my body. Boots stomp into the house and begin moving throughout every square inch they can. Glass occasionally breaks, and furniture gets bumped and moved around carelessly. My ears pick up other sounds of searching from what I think are other houses. For a split second I wonder how I can be so sure of hearing things from an entirely different building than the one I'm in.

With luck on my side, or maybe even true understanding, the bird remains quiet. Only barely moving its head when things become quiet for a few seconds. The fear in me tries to close my eyes but the adrenaline has sharpened every sense I have to a needle point. Being aware of my own breathing makes me slow it to lower the chances of someone hearing me.

If this really is just a group of males, and they have gotten to the point of hoping to be lucky enough to find a "pretty girl"...then the gut feeling

18

about finding a hiding place was righter than I thought. By listening to the feet in this house I could guess about three, maybe four people were in here right now. There was no telling how many currently occupied other houses.

More fear explodes in me as a figure passes in front of the closet. Neither of us make a sound as the male pauses and listens to his surroundings. Making it even creepier, he inhales deeply and completely freezes.

There's no way. No. He can't just smell me. Or the bird. There's no way he smells either of us.

Apparently, the low light prevents him from seeing the closet door and he steps away to return to the front of the house. It isn't until I hear the group moving further down the street do I begin to breathe again. A beak gently pulls at my hair, but I brush it away. My eyes shift to the side to meet the black ones, and I shake my head slowly. It seems to disagree but simply tucks itself back into a smaller figure. Possibly half an hour to an hour passes before I consider moving again. Silence surrounds us like a heavy blanket, but I remain in place. Gently sinking down to my knees, I allow myself to sit on the floor with my knees tucked closely to my chest.

The only movement that creates noise slightly louder than my heartbeat are feathers brushing against the wall. My unsuspecting partner in crime settles onto a shelf. It seems we both understand that remaining here for the rest of the night is the best chance we have at surviving.

My head tilts back against the wall at the same time my eyes shutter closed.

Something about that group made the bird uneasy, and in turn me as well. The words of what sounded like some sort of leader only solidified that unease. Rather than risk a confrontation that could result in either a group to lean on or being used for what was between my legs, I decide to play it safe and hide no matter what from them. A thought races to the front of my mind making me feel cold and nauseous.

It might be safer for me to stay hidden, to be alone, than to risk a shot of survival with other humans.

As sleep drifts around my mind, it clicks that I'm not only okay with that, but that I am not crying about it either.

Chapter 4

I probably shouldn't be wishing for solitude. I should be grateful that it saved my life last night. Yet here I am trying to wrap my hands around its throat as it nips and pulls on my ears. It says nothing though it was clear the daylight woke it up, so I should be up too.

Still maintaining a level of silence, I open the door slowly with claws on my shoulder again. Every time a creak rings out, I stop to make sure no one stayed behind from the passing group. Trash litters the floor making it clear that whoever ransacked the place was looking for anything they could take to benefit themselves. My nose wrinkles at the smell of nicotine being blown in through shattered windows and open doors.

Many other houses on the road have incurred more damage to their windows and doors proving just how destructive the group from last night was. The pure will to cause chaos only further solidifies my gratefulness for the bird warning me. The gut feeling I had tells me it most likely either saved my life or saved me from a certain unpleasant fate.

The sun feels hotter than the previous day, making me sweat the second I step into it. My stolen clothes are starting to reek from having not changed out of the miserable long-sleeved sun shirt I'm still wearing from the beach. Stains made it more of an ombré style going from brown to white, so I decide it's time to find new clothes.

"Look at me, already stepping into the new fashion era," I complain to the winged animal on my shoulder. "It's called 'the end of the fucking world'".

I'm hilarious.

"Fucking world," it repeats back to me.

"Oh shit, no don't repeat that, it's a bad word!" I rub my forehead, feeling bad for teaching it that language like I accidentally had my little sister.

"Oh shit oh shit," it lifts off my shoulder and flaps above me while repeating the malicious words. I groan and start working my way down the street in search of a house that doesn't look like it was torn apart. The search is hopeless, leading me to continue in a direction of what I believe to be north but could be any other direction if the entire planet got screwed like this place did.

It only takes me a couple hours to find a pavilion with a Target at the center. Of course, the windows and doors had been smashed to pieces, but the place looks to be relatively okay despite that.

Wind brushes at my hair as my companion flies ahead into the fruit section to pick at some left-over apples on the floor. Some fresh food is either rotting or clearly useless from too much heat. The aisles with packaged foods seem to be the most promising despite how tattered they look.

My mission is clothes first, then food. I grab a military-style backpack that looks like it might hold enough for me to survive a few more days without struggle. Or least without scraping by. The women's section proves to be a challenge itself with how disorganized everything is from the wind and violent heat that destroyed the world. With some luck I find some leggings, and with even more luck they have pockets. Only three pairs are wearable, and all of them long, so capri leggings are no option.

I'll need the long pairs anyway most likely to protect my skin, I rationalize.

The shirt section is a little easier to dig through as it offers up some thin long sleeve shirts with thumbs holes, so they actually stay in place. I pick four of them out in ranges of black, gray, and white.

I make my way back to the food section, but pick up some underwear and a couple compression sports bras before anything else. Having no way to shower, I settle for using some baby wipes to get the majority of the grime off of my skin. Quickly I strip and change into a pair of leggings and one of my new shirts. It's amazing how much clean clothes can change your attitude towards the world.

I hear the bird pecking at food still as I walk through, slinging food into my backpack that I deem to be worthy enough. Mostly granola bars or items that don't perish easily like the fruit might. Even if the food did perish quickly my bag can't hold more than about a weeks' worth of it. If I portion it out correctly.

While snacking on a snack pack I find on the floor I meander to the outdoors section to see if there is anything left to help make things easier for me until-

Until what? I ask myself. *Until Mom and Dad come back? Until someone comes to save you from this obviously horribly played joke? Until you wake up?*

A gloom settles over me and depression weighs on my emotions. Everything seems bleak and useless, as though anything I do right now will only spur me towards either dying from lack of survival or push me to end myself to stop the suffering. The bird returns to me, almost as if sensing my massive mood swing, and walks around on the floor pecking and looking at things. We both move towards the outdoors section – me to find some tools and the idiot to annoy me because he clearly has nothing else better to do.

Like every other desolate place I had seen in the past few days, there is barely anything left. What makes it even worse is that the damage from heat and fire destroyed most of it.

My hope picks up after I find a single water purifier tube and some string in the back of a shelf. A small smile appears on my face stretching my skin in a way that it hadn't been recently. More digging reveals a half useless box of matches, a pocket knife, and plenty of other broken tools. Having found enough to keep me alive, in my clearly professional opinion, I tuck them away in the new backpack and begin to leave.

My hair cooperates despite the millions of tangles in its waves and allows me to put it into a high ponytail on my way out. I give another quick glance before leaving to instill some confidence that I've done all I can here.

And then something catches my eye.

Two somethings.

A small, untouched ax buried under a pile of fragmented tools. The other object is an abandoned and useless shotgun.

I pick up the shotgun first to examine the damage. My hope of finding working technology is damaged as I realize that all the other vehicles and machinery I'd walked by had suffered the same fate. Nothing other than simple tools had survived the sun's damaging flare.

Almost as though it does it itself, it gleams as I turn towards the ax. Pieces slide off of the pile and my hand closes around a metal base. Rust sheds onto my hands from the handles, but the blade itself is somehow unbothered by the damage the rest of it has endured. Turning it over twice I squint my eyes at it while examining its worth.

You don't exactly have to load it with bullets, and it's a lot more threatening than a little pocket knife.

Content with my new weapon of choice, I slip it through the side handles of my pack. The weight takes some adjusting but I quickly adapt.

Days pass in a blur. The only sense of time I truly have is when I suddenly realize that the sun is setting, or that I wake up just before first light. Waking up never seems to be an option since my body simply will not allow me to sleep more than five or six hours. It becomes quickly draining but the tension in every muscle won't allow true rest. Every day I crave my bed that I slept in for twenty years. Every day I miss the easy life I had before. Every day I wish I had the guarantee of survival I did before.

I learn more about this new world with every step taken forward. Plants that seem unreal have become common in the woods, even ones that I am certain never existed before. Flowers have colors that seem fake. Vines seem to actively move as I pass them. Trees are far larger than they ever were. Nature takes over defeated buildings with a vengeance – progress that shouldn't happen for ten months has already taken place far sooner than that.

The few animals I come across just aren't the same. Squirrels have become long and thin like snakes, deer - the few I've been lucky to spot - are typically the size of bears now, somehow a cougar presents itself as well, but its teeth seem overgrown, and fur is incredibly long. It's tail has a spike on the end that drags through the grass.

Half of the food I'd found in the store is gone. I have more than planned due to finding other sources while exploring. The thought causes a cramp in my abdomen so I kneel and pull out a small pack of nuts.

"Sleep, need sleep," the bird says next to me. Its wings seem to give out just before it lands so I take it as a sign that we should both settle for the night.

"Yeah, let's find a tree bud."

Tree climbing only recently became a skill, so I look for a tree that looks the easiest to get up into. Too many creatures move at night for my comfort, so altitude is the way to go. Very little can sneak up on me in a tree.

Except cougars. The cougars with spikes on the end of their tails. They have the biggest balls I have seen so far.

A tree with large branches starting about ten feet up is my pick, so I grab the bird to plop him on my shoulder before heading up. My foot slips a couple times, but I manage to get myself into a good sleeping position about eighteen feet up into the air. The me from about two months ago never would have done something like this, but survival is survival.

The bag serves as a pillow and the bird provides a comforting warmth against my neck. I take my hair down and let him stuff his head into the mess of it.

Sleep quickly takes over on instinct but doesn't stop. Even when I hear a distant yell.

The warmth in my neck from smooth feathers is gone and my bag is now on the ground. Those missing, however, isn't what wakes me.

The sharp pain in my side blooming into shock is what does.

I look down quickly to discover a rusty knife has lodged itself between my ribs. Courtesy of the shiny-eyed males whooping and hollering below me.

"Holy *fuck* y'all, wait until Kent gets ahold of this one," one of them yells cheerfully.

I gasp as I shimmy myself against the trunk of the tree. Something else hurdles by my head and sticks into the trunk

"Oh, you missed buddy," I say wryly.

You shut your goddamn mouth this is NOT the time to be a smart ass.

A guy with curly blond hair steps forward, dressed in ratty jeans and boots clearly meant for work. His long sleeve shirt has holes in it, making it clear this group hasn't had it easy either.

"C'mere darlin'," he smiles. His mouth looks gentle, but his eyes are wild and hungry.

"You just fucking stabbed me," I snap. More burning as I breathe in. I feel the strange burning sensation start to happen in my fingernails as well. I pay it no attention since there's more important things happening in front of me.

"Sorry, my boys get a little crazy at night. We can stitch that up if you just come on down."

He raises his hands like he'll catch me, and he waits. The only sound around the tree is the shifting of the other guys and some heavy breathing. Seconds pass without me saying a word.

Might be rude of me to assume, but the knife in my side gives me a bad feeling.

"Darlin', we don't have much time-"

"Why not?" I ask.

"So why don't you let my boys here catch you and we can take you to camp and get you fixed up?" He continues, not even stopping to consider my question. I finally get a beat on how many are here.

Five. Two behind what seems like the leader, and two more I can hear looking for a way up the trunk of this tree. My thoughts shift away from them as I see a branch bounce out of the corner of my eye. I make eye contact with the bird and as subtly as possible, shake my head in warning. He seems to shift anxiously but remains where he is.

"For fucks sake get 'er down here I want my piece before we have to show Kent."

The leaders' head whips to his left and glares at the one who spoke. The others shrink back slightly and stop shuffling so much.

"I think I'll stay here. How about you go your own way and I'll go mine?" I offer.

I feel my fingers burn even more. I shake my head to keep myself from focusing on a strange detail.

"You first…darlin'."

My stomach sinks like metal as adrenaline starts to pour out in waves.

Unfortunately, that adrenaline makes my hands sweat, and when my grip on the branch next me slips, so do I.

Everything slows to near halt as my body heads for the ground and my eyes track the face of the biggest asshole here. A revolting grin crawls wider and wider the further I fall. The others don't hesitate to move in like a pack of wolves the second the ground shakes with my landing.

"Be careful not to kill 'er. The knife might be a little close to somethin' vital," one of the smaller ones warns.

I scramble to my feet only to be slammed against the tree with a forearm crushing my neck. Nails seem to do nothing or maybe even encourage the one holding me. The one holding me is tall and beefy and he knows it. His weight is completely on my neck stopping air from getting into my lungs. When I start kicking him it makes him lean harder into me.

Panic begins to set in quickly as I come up with nothing to get myself out of this situation. He steps slightly to the side to allow the leader to enter my personal space as well. A hand grabs my jaw and squeezes firmly, then turns my face side to side. Small chuckles begin as I hear a belt come loose.

"Move, I got her," belt guy says. "Let me introduce myself before we get to know one another real quick."

I land a kick to his stomach.

"Mmm," he grunts. "My name is Grant-"

My face stings suddenly. The fucker slapped me.

"Do that again and I'll take my time."

My leggings suddenly get pulled down , along with my underwear.

Suddenly my hearing becomes very acute before disappearing altogether. All I know is that the word 'stop' is coming out of my mouth as rapidly as possible. Nothing seems to make this better, only worse.

Cold thin fingers touch my vagina and draw the last breath out of me. There's still a hand on my neck that has begun to stop the blood flow to my brain. I scramble to grab anything. Anything I can reach. The hand doesn't stop and starts to move towards my entrance that is harshly protesting the action on it.

He's going to rape me. I'm alone and he's going to rape me.

The thought drills through my head over and over and over. I see feathers flap around his head just before claws dig into eyes. I think he screams but I can't hear it. I can't hear anything. The only thing I can think about is how the fuck I can get away from five guys who clearly want more than blood from me.

Finally the hand releases from my throat and I drop to the ground for the second time that night. Vibrations come through the dirt from the chaos behind me as I struggle to my feet. My hands scramble to pull my leggings up – only to allow me to run away.

Air curves around my face as I put one foot in front of the other as fast as I can away from the nightmare. I start to breathe again, thinking I may have gotten away. That bird may have saved me. I suck in a deep breath and move faster through the trees that appear to become thicker the farther I run.

Go go go don't stop

Branches snap behind me warning of the approaching danger.

Run run run run run

I look over my shoulder to see how far they are behind me. Either I'm not running fast enough, or they are running faster than I thought.

Faster faster faster faster

The air stops moving so gently as my face dives towards the ground. A weight pins me down from behind forcing my hips into rocks.

"You fuckin' bitch," Grant growls.

The hand on my neck is from behind now shoving my cheek against the cool soil.

My leggings are pulled down again, and this time they tear.

My underwear is ripped so hard off of me that my groin begins to throb.

Silence.

No hearing.

Just the horror of what's happening.

There's a feeling of something foreign resting against my ass.

Time slows again.

My vision explodes, everything as clear as though someone flipped on a light around me.

The scent of sweat, nicotine, and body odor hits me like another slap to the face.

The bird drops in front of me and the first thing I hear is him scream louder than anything I've ever heard.

Then my world goes black.

Chapter 5

A gentle sound pulls me out of deep sleep. I try opening my eyes but they resist. Cold seeps into my side slowly, enough to make me question why I'm feeling so much solid ground beneath me. I fell asleep in a tree.

No I didn't, the thought snaps my eyes open. A black form- no, it's the bird – stands in front of my face.

"Up?" he asks.

"Yeah, Feathers, I'm up."

The new nickname seems to make him happy; he does a little dance on the branches around us. I push myself up from the fetal position to get a better view of where I am. A tree only a few feet away seems to look like the one I climbed into last night.

A breeze startles me with how sharp it feels, until the realization that I have no clothes on startles me even more.

"What the actual fuck," I whisper to myself when I can't find any blood from the shallow knife wound in my ribs.

Feathers swooshes past me and onto a limb. The same limb, in fact, I could have sworn I fell asleep on last night. My black backpack is hanging from a smaller branch untouched. I climb up as quickly as possible to retrieve it while my mind kicks into overdrive trying to process what happened. Bark scrapes against my skin.

When I reach for my bag the shiny metal of a knife lodged into the bark catches my eye.

"Darlin.'"

I jump at Feathers being so close all of a sudden.

"What? What did you say?"

"Darlin'."

The back of mind stirs, something about the word makes me anxious so I ignore it. Using both hands I yank the knife out of the tree. Examining it does nothing to jog my memory as to why a pocket knife was lodged next to my backpack. Slipping it into my bag, I quickly pull out a pair of leggings and underwear and slip them on. A black compression bra and shirt are next, all while keeping an ear out for motion around me. I close up the bag after pulling out a very small snack bar.

Slinging it onto my shoulder I carefully lower myself a majority of the way back down the tree, before letting go and dropping to the ground. My body is still tense for some reason, despite having had a peaceful night.

"Darlin."

"Stop that, I don't like it," I swat at him as he flies by. "It's freaking me out."

He becomes silent as he lands on my shoulder, the weight of his body making my muscles straight slightly.

One foot in front of the other is all I can manage while thoughts spin around in my head. Nothing around gives any insight as to what happened, and I can't tell if that makes things better or worse.

Leaves, twigs, and dried roots snap and crunch under my bare feet. A couple animals dart from my line of sight when they hear me but nothing else makes itself known. The loneliness is somewhat comforting when all I can feel is tension and stress. A chill starts to settle into the air, making it clear Fall is quickly approaching.

Is it October already?

How would I know? I never thought to keep track of the days and there hasn't been much around to confidently tell me what time of the year it could be.

It doesn't matter. And neither does the small bit of panic my brain starts to feel as I realize there is no contacting someone on a whim, or a person to reach out to me. No phones, no power, nothing. This world had truly been thrown back decades when the sun decided to throw a temper tantrum.

Sickeningly sweet smells start teasing my nose. Not the kind you get greeted by when you walk into a cake shop, but more like the ones when you walk through a forest after hunting season. A tangy odor joins in the further I walk, making my stomach churn.

Something wet beneath my feet almost puts me on my back in the leaves. Looking down, I see thick dark, congealed red liquid speckling the ground.

Blood.

I'm not stupid enough to try and convince my senses that it's not. My body knows.

The blood becomes more prominent the further I walk, making it impossible to smell anything else. Eventually it engulfs me, only pulling me to find the source rather than turn and run the other way.

I used to love surprises. Used to love knowing there was one waiting for me. Whatever it was, I always loved it. They always made me feel like the universe sometimes had enough good in it to make me feel like I wasn't some irrelevant speck.

This though, the scene proudly laid out before me is a surprise I never thought I would find. One I would have gladly gone my whole life without.

And yet, here it is. The universe baring its ugly yellow teeth at me with all the disgust it can muster. This is what I get for surviving some apocalyptic terror that no one I love did. This is how I get to be reminded that my life is just as erasable as anyone else.

I stop to hover over one of the bodies, a male. His neck is twisted so that his face is looking at me. Gouges down his back, so deep they become too dark to see into, are covered in gore. Flaps of skin hang open and loose, muscle and bone are left exposed to the air. His thigh has a hole in it about as big as my bicep that lets me see the blood-soaked ground beneath him. And somehow, that is just part of the damage done to his body. A dislocated shoulder and missing ear tell me that whatever did this to him didn't just want him dead.

It wanted him to suffer.

My mind races trying to imagine what kind of animal – or even person – could have done something like this. How could someone, in a world of scarcity and suffering, cause such pain and anguish to a person?

It doesn't end. I stumble back, my stomach now clenching in fear to the point I dry heave. As my feet carry me backwards, I don't see what's behind me. Butt meets ground, and now my legs are resting over half of another man's body. A silent scream comes to me with shock. More dry heaving batters my throat as I look into his glazed eyes.

A memory crashes into my thoughts now bringing me back to the night before.

I was attacked by them. Faces flashing in my memory awaken a panicked fear within me. What disturbs me more, is that I can't remember anything past falling out of the tree.

I did climb up there and fall asleep. I was in the tree. They threw a knife at my head.

"Darlin'!" Feathers squawks, his beak is pulling at my hair. Instead of smacking him away I listen to his language and stand up, at the same time another memory floods my mind.

"You first...darlin'."

"You first...darlin'."

"You first...darlin'."

Strangely enough my eyes track over the rest of the bloodied area to find his face. The next body I find is another guy that had chased me. His body is hanging on a thick branch. Or rather, impaled on it.

It's too much for me and finally the small snack I had only an hour ago comes right back with vengeance. Bile rises out of my throat, onto the ground, nearly splashing my companion.

"I...I didn't do this," I pant. I don't know who I'm trying to convince. Or even why I would automatically think I had any part in such a killing.

The heaving continues but nothing more results from it as my stomach is now empty. The blurry vision I have left begins to close into a small circle. Fear of the one remaining man finding me spurs me into action.

No, not just a man. His name was Grant.

I begin running, only slowing to launch myself over large trunks or to climb up walls of rock. Feathers stays close to me in flight, never landing.

A part of me reels at how fast I'm moving through the dense forest around me. I had never been a runner, only doing so every now and then with Carly. Tears cloud my eyes at the thought of her.

A sharp chilling wind dries those tears then nearly slows me down. What overcomes that, is the thought that somehow, some way, Grant is nearby those bodies waiting to jump me again.

I almost hurl again despite the emptiness of my stomach. The blood pumping so quickly through my body keeps me from doing so.

Time slows in this panic-induced run. The distance, unclear, is the only thing I can hear is-

Run run run run

Chanting it spurs me forward, further and further until finally my body settles down. I stop at the edge of where the trees distinctly stop. Wet soil cushions my knees when they buckle. Calloused hands stop my face from the same fate. The bird lands somewhere nearby, not even out of breath like I am.

Time doesn't come back to me until the heavy breathing slows to a restful rhythm. The air is still, not a sound to be heard.

Evening has fallen during the past few minutes, quickly rolling into night. As my legs gain some strength back, I begin to take in my surroundings.

The trees stop as though an invisible force won't let them grow any further. Grass continues on but instead of covering flat lands, it crawls over hills, which grow into mountains. Mountains don't start until the further limits of my vision, but the change in landscape still seems too sudden and strange.

Oddly enough, the open air and space calms me to a point of almost falling asleep. Feathers must feel the same since his eyes are closed and body is motionless. With the decision made, I sigh and scoop him onto my shoulder. One last night sleeping near the trees won't hurt. Being in one brings forward too many feelings to allow me any rest. Instead, I settle for leaning against a trunk and nestling into the roots around it.

My sleep proves to be difficult, nightmares plaguing me every time I close my eyes. They don't even wait for me to be unconscious. What makes it worse is the darkness that threatens to drown me the second I give in.

I'm restless until the sun rises to wash away the night. They're horrid, twisted little things that cause me to stop breathing. That results in a rude awakening, or induced hyperventilating that nearly catapults me into a panic attack every time. My body is exhausted from what it had been through, having never gotten a good night of sleep, having always been on guard – so I take sleep where I could get it. So much time living in terror would do that to a person apparently.

I'm awake before Feathers is, already thinking about what I want to do next. There is no going back on my path, the risk of running into that insane group is too high. The way they acted and seemed to be prepared leads me to believe the chances of them going into the snowy range is slim.

Not impossible. Slim. I'll take what I can get.

Finally, the black feathers tucked into my chest stir and ruffle awake to begin the day. Once he moves, I quickly stand and look forward into the blinding white blanket on the mountains. I look down at the bird hopping around, pecking at the ground. Worms crawl from the dirt, only to be snatched up and eaten.

"We're going into the mountains, Feathers" I inform him. His head actually whips around to look at me as if I had just threatened him. I raise an eyebrow and start moving anyway. He complains with a caw and choice words, but follows.

I cover the distance of grass flatland in only a couple hours – leaving plenty of time to begin the adventure into new land. The sudden changes in geography still blow my mind. How grass could stop so suddenly to turn into snow, how trees stretch for miles only to halt like the front lines of an army at war. The end of everything life knew before has changed, even the earth itself.

My days once again begin to meld into one another as my legs carry me further. Three days into hiking I lost track of why and begin to only listen to the gut feeling telling me to continue. Somehow that push is now more powerful than hunger or fear, making me concerned about why I'm focusing on such a thing.

It's good, however, that my hunger is being blocked out by something stronger. Due to the lack of food left in my bag, and the surrounding empty land masses, my ribs have begun to show. During the second day I had noticed, but now as I precariously scale a steep incline I can feel them grating on the sharp edges. My hips drag as well making it clear that this portion of the fun would be resulting in bone deep pain.

Wind begins to tickle my neck and face with a daunting chill. The temperature drops slightly making it harder to grip the stone in front of me.

"Hungry," Feathers screams, swooping past my left ear and up the rocks. He lands above me, stumbling as a pebble causes his foot to slip.

"Yeah, me too fucker, but I don't have wings to get me up this any faster!" I scream at him. He startles at my loudness but makes no move other than pecking aggressively at a rock below him. "I hope your beak falls off."

More time passes but I haven't moved. I realize that I'm stuck with no way other than back down. I let my head sag back and groan at the situation. Back down is worthless, I might as well fall down to the bottom. The only successful way out is up, and that provided no comfort due to my inability to find another ledge to hold on to. My fingers were quickly growing sore and cold from all the climbing.

As I again look at the wall, my eyes track down from the bird above me to the stone he's still pecking at.

I suddenly realize why he's been pecking at it for so long. The ledge is everything I needed to pull myself up. Right below the larger ledge, a ledge that seemed to provide enough flat ground to rest on. One problem making itself painfully clear is how far it remains from my current position.

Such distance means a jump, one that will result in one of two things. Either I make it and grab the ledge with frozen fingers that may or may not hold on, or I miss and begin the fatal fall down the valley below me. Neither option is preferable, but I have to pick one.

A few deep breaths are all I allow myself before getting my dominant foot into a ledge at knee height. With one painfully cold breath in, I push as hard as I can and reach for my one chance. Only that edge seemed to be present in my point of view despite its tiny size. Faith in my movement forces me to let go of every other hold I had and trust in my will power – because that's all I have left.

Gravity snatches at me the second I'm completely free of my position. Seemingly flying for the next one. It is unforgiving, cruel in its reminder of its presence as I feel my body begin to sink. For a moment, I feel the effects of free falling. Rock begins racing upward as my left hand misses the shelf that provided such a warm welcome. Nothing juts out enough to allow my feet to stop me which throws my heart into a panic.

That moment is suddenly thrown into high speed as my right arm swings in a wide arc to catch me before I fall any further. By the graces of the universe surrounding me I'm now holding onto that targeted ledge. My companion lifts himself up and lands on that last platform that I so painfully wish for now. Heavy blood pumping in my ears makes it impossible for me to dally on the mistake that had nearly been my last. With a speed that only comes from someone racing for survival I maneuver up onto the flat ground above me. At last, my body is able to rest, even if just for a moment.

The wind now dangerously whips around the steep inclines and dips of the side of the mountain. I move slowly, trying to keep my footing while moving down in altitude. Snow begins to fall as well making the weather a rapidly rising beast of nature. A wall that blocks me from the direction of the wind gave me barely any cover. However, I take it as a reward for the past six hours of work.

Never in my life had I been able to physically perform at the level I am now. Climbing, hiking, and suffering for six hours should have been impossible for someone like me and yet I somehow manage it. Cruel conditions like this leave no room for celebrating, instead I take a moment to plan my next move.

The feeling in my gut urging me to keep moving on an unknown path suddenly increases with a sickening sense of heaviness.

Break over, I guess.

I pull myself up one more time and am shown another wide spread of land. Like the one a few days back, it's flat with a few rolling hills. This new land presented itself with a few large trees across it and continued up until a cluster of what seemed like buildings in the distance. Many of the trees closest to my position are massive enough to have built a single-family tree house in. My bewilderment drives me forward from a position of being on my hands and knees to a standing one. Frozen hands help to push me up, but they're not cold enough to stop the pain from blooming.

A soft and short groan escapes me when I lay eyes on the nails – or lack thereof – that have been ripped into the quick's and covered with blood. A couple deep scratches stopped bleeding a long time ago, but the swelling hasn't been reduced by the snow and cold. Cracked knuckles continue to crack the more the skin is forced to stretch over bone and tissue instead of muscle and fat. With nothing around me nor on my pack to fix any of it, so I drop them to my sides and start moving forward.

Feathers lands heavily on my shoulder for rest. I don't protest as a sign of thanks for showing me the ledge.

My feet begin carrying me ahead again to the unknown source of need. A pain in my left foot makes me think something might be injured but I steel myself and resist an investigation. It will only slow me down.

Thankfully the snow does not get any heavier as I trek across the tundra of emptiness. Off towards a hibernating forest I spot some sort of animal grazing from the floor. Though its horns are far larger than it should be, and the muscles on it much stockier than I'd seen before, it looks like a deer. Something that could feed me to stop the pains of starving. Could keep Feathers from sagging so heavily even when he flies.

The deer looks up. Its massive eyes that look too large for its head catch me for a few moments. With a graceful leap, it bounds away. I sigh at the loss of food.

Eventually the mountain terrain becomes softer. Hill after hill, step after step, I put one foot in front of the other trying to reach that shuttered goal. I glance back occasionally to see if I can spot figures as they make their way down from the peak I'd already crested. I don't see anything and continue on. What eventually slows me, not stops me, is a distant sound of yelling. The sound of people singing a horribly off key song.

My feet still move me though my eyes have again rotated to look back over the land I had crossed a few days ago.

Figures move in a group wildly with fire sporadically lighting them up in the night. It looks like one big moving mass, but I know better. Know better than to think I could be safe from what it is and to assume that it's an unknown. The mass echoes a faint sound again confirming my suspicions.

The same group my attackers came from are hunting me now. Serious doubt that they want to thank me spurs me to start a light jog.

I jog as long as I can until the stumbling begins. Walking is barely feasible even though the feeling in my gut told me to ignore it. A bright half-moon climbed and fell in the night sky while I still move. I stop solely for an hour and a half of sleep.

One comforting thought is the group most likely hunting me wouldn't be able to move as fast staying together, becoming even slower in the mountains. Some semblance of confidence helps convince me that they would further be slowed by the vertical climb necessary to reach where I am. I have no idea how far they had to go "around" otherwise.

Two cans of food are all I find in the tiny town I finally reach. A can of creamed corn, and one of asparagus. I fucking hate asparagus. Despite my hatred for the putrid vegetable, I have no choice but to down them both even with the water they're stored in. It's the only source of calories I've ingested in 3 days. Stupidly, I don't portion them out to last me for multiple days and simply inhale it all in one go. A little bit is dumped onto the ground to share with my companion. Neither of us are pleased.

As I eat, I process my options for what to do if the cult of idiots ever does catch up to me. I could possibly outrun them but only long enough to find a hiding spot. I'm not confident in that option. Eventually they would catch me in my weakened state if they did chase me, which would only make it harder to fight back. Trying to fight back in the first place could get me hurt to the point I would never be able to run. Not fighting at all would result in other outcomes that are…harsh. With limited possibilities in mind, I toss the cans into a collapsing garbage bin. The clanging of metal against metal slams into my ears causing those bloodied hands to swing up and cover them. Confused, I walk back over and check out the trash can. I search to make sure there is nothing I should have noticed before that would have caused such commotion.

Finding nothing, I conclude that being alone for so long has forced my senses into high alert.

A ridiculous fear fills my chest. One that makes me think that if the noise is loud enough to hurt my ears it has to be loud enough to be carried to the pack following me.

Feathers is watching me. His silence is and has been unending since I had conquered that steep fall to death. It unnerves me but I don't even have the energy to snipe at him about it. Some small part of me wonders if he knows what's happening, deciding to try his best to not push me too far.

Whatever his reasoning, I'm grateful for the peace and patience.

Chapter 6

Even with eye contact, Feathers' silence continues. No questions of any sort or curiosity of any kind came out of that beak. At some points I question if I have hallucinated, and if eventually the bird himself will disappear altogether.

What I know is ten more days passed just as the previous seven had. Food has become scarcer. I'm lucky to find anything that hasn't already been eaten by animals or time.

I find myself considering the end, my mind wanting to stop those thoughts but unable to. That gun I had found in the church but chosen to leave behind. The possibility of a working one ending up in the hands of a group of people that clearly welcome rapists does not escape me. Even though I have a knife I still don't truly want to do anything.

The loud sounds from the group had become closer, and I could now hear them just a few hundred yards away. My legs shake, weakness setting in from everything my body has been through. I push through it, because even with the tug in my gut I still feel an insatiable curiosity at why I had been pulled so far so fast. The pulling only becomes stronger the longer I move in the same direction.

Snow still coats the ground, thankfully having stopped falling at some point though I'm not sure when. I'm just glad my hair has a chance to dry for once.

Any sense of time is now lost on me. I can see when the sun rose only to be chased by the moon in what felt like just an hour. I could feel when the day was warmest at daylights peak. But the minutes and overall hours that slithered over me did not care to ensure I saw them.

That will also be my downfall apparently. Because the men are now here. A small town, some houses to the left and right on a side road is the only possible safe haven. The main road is lined with shops and businesses galore. All made of windows I can see right through, so not an option.

Nothing sufficient enough for me to hide behind so I bounce between walking and jogging around. My shoes make a sound that causes me to wince with every few steps.

I turn to go down a side ally-

My legs suddenly give out and knees slam into the concrete. Finger's fold and snap under the pressure of trying to catch myself. Even with that effort my shoulder still sags into the lamppost I had slowed at. My body no longer could support the impossible agony I've been forcing it through.

The voices come closer, so far yet so close, pounding at my eardrums with their footsteps.

"Go," I rasp out to Feathers. "Go! They won't let you live."

I know it was coughing but it only came out as hissing at the black bird in front of me. For the first time since we had met on that heated street, Feathers is clearly scared. Feet tap on the road as his wings anxiously shuffle. He knows my body truly couldn't make it - even if I dragged myself away. He finally flits into a nearby tree. Close enough I can see him, but not so anyone else would accidentally find him.

The pounding gets closer, and eventually I hear voices calling out the discovery of my pitiful figure. A shadow moves to block the sun, while other shadows dim my already narrow world. Black boots halt in front of me, and a hand reaches down to pull my chin up once knees crouch down. Even with the sun too high making it impossible to see I know the voice from before. The same voice that told his group to find what they could, even a woman to play with.

My stomach curls as his mouth splits into a revolting grin.

"Looks like we found a brand new toy to play with," a southern accent just barely hangs on his words.

Chuckles and eager grunts surround me. Someone picks up a limp piece of hair and pulls it, causing my head to tilt sideways. As the man continues to examine what is left of me, another familiar voice pipes up.

"That's her. That's the one I told you about."

Grant.

Fucking Grant.

I internally wince, realizing I should have hidden myself better that night. Made sure no one would have found me while I slept..

Stupid, stupid choice.

"Oh." A smokers' chuckle. "Guess we'll need to plan something special for her then."

I attempt to spit and only result in coughing hideously in the face of the man still holding my chin. As my eyes drag to Grant my stomach manages to drop even further while dragging my heart with it.

"Hello...darlin'."

My body finally decides to drag me back into some semblance of clarity in the daily hell I live in. Disassociating had given some reprieve for an achingly short amount of time. As my eyes strain to adjust to the bonfire before me, I start to gain my senses back. Night has fallen, something is roasting over the flames. My mouth waters at the smell of cooking meat bubbling over such a hot flame. That feeling trickles down into a painfully empty stomach causing it to grumble loudly. I try to look around, only to fail due to my blurry vision.

Unfortunately, someone is close enough to hear it leading them to saunter over to me. I go to move back only to be stopped by chains restraining my arms in a V-shape over me. My knees dig into the loose rocks on the pavement I'm kneeling on. The blood flow in my feet cut from having my legs bent for so long. The stranger has a beer bottle in his hand and is clearly intoxicated, making me yank at them even more. What stops me from completely losing it is the cold glass touching my chest.

My bare chest.

To my absolute horror all but my worn leggings have been stripped from me. The backpack I had relied on is nowhere to be seen, as is my shirt and bra. My breasts are out for display, making me whimper just enough for the stranger to hear.

"You can cry hun, even scream, but it might get some of us a little excited," he informs me with a shrug. "That's not me telling you to stop though."

I yank on the chains, no give.

Just my luck with thinking I could move them, because now that they've rattled, I've announced my being awake to more people.

Another head near the bonfire turns slowly, almost looking relaxed, to find me. The one that had grabbed my chin when the group found me, who I think is the leader. A slimy smirk spreads across his face.

Some of the guys turn back towards their drinks and the fire, but he rises to start towards me. Anxiety settles into my system quickly. I glance back at the first one who'd walked up to me.

"You should know," a swig of beer clears his throat. "I really like your tits."

He also touches my nipples with the cold glass, only to drop it and replace it with a hand.

"Get the fuck off of me!" I snap.

"No, no, don't start that hun," the second one, the one clearly in charge, chuckles. "You start screaming and I'm gonna have to fight off every guy here, don't get 'em hard so soon," his wink has me recoiling.

"I will fucking *end* you when I get out of this. You won't even-"

The slap stings my cheek. He hit hard enough to draw blood inside my mouth.

"Shut your fucking mouth or I won't even give you the courtesy of waiting until we're alone to fuck you."

Nausea smacks me just like his hand did, harsh and unforgiving. My vision finally starts to clear a little, making me realize the first one to walk up is Grant. Fear slowly leaks into my veins, my memory of what happened before making my throat dry. I grit my teeth against the accompanying rage, knowing it will get me nothing but more trouble.

Calm down, you push anymore and you'll end up in a situation you can't come back from.

I simply breathe in and out of my nose. A few others have gathered around me now. I ignore them, waiting for him to strike again, holding eye contact as he waits for me to talk again.

When I don't, he praises me, "Good girl. Now let's talk."

A motion of his hand directs everyone else to leave. The only person to remain standing behind him is Grant. I pull myself up to stand, releasing the tension on my shoulders. Surprisingly, they don't move to shove me back down.

"So," he starts. His eyes haven't stopped dragging themselves everywhere but my face as he moves to circle me. The fear builds exponentially as his footsteps echo behind me.

"Who the fuck do you think you are," Grant spits.

"Easy Grant, I just wanna talk," the other one soothes as he grabs me around my waist and presses himself into me. "What happened in the woods hun?"

"Your men attacked me, I ran," I keep my sight pinned on Grant, but my other senses are desperately trying to keep track of his friend.

"Mmm, that's not what I was told. Grant here says they were takin' a piss and you jumped 'em." He presses into me from behind, I can feel his erection now against my behind.

Grant had lied to get him riled up. He probably didn't need to with how sick in the head they all are.

"Yeah, fuck you, Grant. I was sleeping, and they attacked me. I have the

46

healing wound in my ribs to prove it," I try to jerk away, it only results in my butt grinding against him.

"Keep moving like that and I'll start to think you want it," he whispers in my ear. Goosebumps race across my skin forcing me to still completely. He lets go and continues circling me.

"She's a fucking liar Kent I saw her change into-"

"Grant if you don't shut your damn mouth," Kent warns, leaving the threat to be filled in by Grant's imagination. His footsteps begin again, stepping away from me and coming around my right side.

He's in front of me again, so close to my face I could almost lash out and bite his nose. His bottle now empty, he tosses it. Glass shatters against the pavement of the road. Grant leaves towards a cooler to get him another one.

"Look pretty girl, if you tell me the truth this will go a lot easier. You hold back, and I won't stop Grant from getting what he wanted in the first place."

I flash my line of sight between the two, feeling my heartbeat increase drastically. Sweat builds up all over me, a drop of it racing from my collarbone in between my breasts. Kent tracks it like a greedy kid watching someone bring him a dessert. Thoughts of unleashed violence ripple through my mind, almost calming me at the thought of making him bleed. Almost.

Without warning he leans forward and licks it from just above my navel to right in the center of my chest. My legs automatically thrash and try to kick him away from assaulting me.

A hard object swings into the side of my thigh, effectively paralyzing it temporarily. Another swings into my ribs and I swear I hear a sickening crack. I manage to see Grant pull away from having hit me. Titters of laughter come from the crowd. I think I hear a groan.

"Enough, she'll learn. I need her alive anyway. I'm not a necrophiliac," Kent swigs from the beer he was just given.

"You're fucked in the head either way," I laugh at him.

His jaw flexes at my words.

"Last warning," he grinds out.

"Fuck you," I sneer.

What am I doing?

I chuckle at the purely confusing wish for both death and violence. Maybe even after surviving for so long it's time to let go. A cruel end is still an end to the weeks of barely hanging on. It practically feels like a reward at this point, but only if I can free myself. Staying in these chains until my last breath is a waste. Even if I'd still be struggling again once free.

I feel hot shame creep over me, only for it to turn into a blind rage. Everything I had done, thrown into a single hope for a quick death. Laughter gurgles from my mouth again, this time I feel a punch directly into my breast that knocks the wind out of me.

As I try desperately to catch my breath my leggings swiftly tear down one side from someone yanking on them. Cool wind whips around my skin as if trying to prepare me for the next thing to happen. Black clouds my vision heavily making it hard to see, and the chains rattle obnoxiously.

Some of the guys have started to gather with hunger clearly in their eyes for whatever Kent is going to do to me. It's going to happen, I may have stopped it in the woods but now I'm restrained entirely by bonds I could not break.

"Girly, I'm not sure what the ever livin' fuck is wrong with you-"

"For fucks sake it's that stupid twang in your voice that's really bothering me," I smirk. I force the smirk to remain plastered to my face as Kent's slips from his. Flicking my eyes down to his empty hand I watch his fingers curl into a fist that shakes with anger. Even before he raises it I know another punch is coming – except this one lands on my nose. Another hits my jaw from the same side.

Again.

And again.

My ears ring from the force of having my head snapped to the side multiple times. Attempts to reorient myself prove futile as everything continues to spin. I feel hot liquid through my nose nearly choke me until

48

I open my mouth to breathe.

"Get me my knife," my assailant mumbles. He says something else, but I don't catch it over the ringing in my ears. The surrounding crowd seems to pulse with my heartbeat, growing faster as Kent receives the knife he requested. He says something to me. Still, I can't hear him. I want to wipe the blood away that's dripping over my lips. Forgetting that my hands are chained I pull on them resulting in irritating the already raw skin. A rough hand grabs my face to force my eyes to meet his. Without control, a gasp leaves me from the new pain that blooms from his grip.

"-gonna listen now. One more time, I'm gonna give you a new decoration for every mouthy word you just said to me."

Searching my face pushes him into further anger resulting in the command, "Take her pants off, leave the underwear."

Two random males step forward and yank my tattered leggings off, their hands lingering in private areas. Disgust coils around my gut. Grant appears again in front of me with his arms crossed.

"You're gonna pay now for what you did to my boys, maybe I'll even rip out those pretty claws of yours. Now that I know you're one of those ungodly demons, it's our job to put you down the proper way."

My thoughts snag on the mention of claws causing that darkness in me to shift as though stirring in sleep.

"I wouldn't want everyone to see my prize first now, would I?" Kent whispers in my ear, his hot breath dragging down my sweaty neck like wet rope. A pained groan mixed with a whimper is all I respond. Despite his sick reason for it I'm glad I've been left with my last shred of decency.

What a situation I'm in, to be glad my vagina is covered while every other part of me is laid bare for these animals' entertainment. Life had gone from laying on a beach taking every bit of living free for granted, to wondering what part of my body was going to be carved into first. It's almost humorous to experience what the bad is like when it becomes ugly. In my mind, I begin to beg to have the ugly back so that I could be away from them.

Reality comes back swiftly like an angry tidal wave more than ready to take down anything in its path. Cold metal meets with the tender flesh on the side of my breast pulling a much weaker gasp out of me than the previous ones. With agonizingly slow speed Kent drags down the blade to slice me open. Warmth quickly spreads down onto my rib cage as a thumb brushes over my nipple. Against my will that nipple hardened in response to all the stimulation. I hiss through my teeth at the incorrect signals my body relays.

"Oh, looks like you might like that hun..." Kent murmurs against my other ear.

Breathing proves to be extremely difficult, yet I'm able to suck in a deep enough one for a response.

"Fuck you," blood sprays with my words.

His upper lip pulls into a pitiful snarl.

"How many Grant? How many pretty marks does she git?"

Grant didn't even hesitate to lash out, "Forty sounds about right."

"Bro," I gasp again. "I had no idea white trash knew how to count."

That was completely worth it in my head.

Another cold draw opens up the skin right underneath the already tender breast. I kept my mouth shut and breathed heavily through my nose. Dragging my eyes up to meet his takes more energy out of me than it should have, yet I do it anyway to prove to myself that I can. Nothing but disgust for my mouth and hunger for what made me a woman comes from those eyes. The brown of them is so murky and bland I almost comment on them. Almost.

There's nothing to do except try to distract myself while still breathing through the next ten cuts. My upper chest now covered in them, only ten out of the forty I was to receive, and I'm exhausted.

Of course, it could only get better from there. Grant steps forward and grins while Kent hands him the knife. His eyes seem to almost shift into something unnatural as he drags the wide part of the blade down between my breasts. Continuing until the tip rested right above the most sensitive part of me.

"Show me the claws," he demands.

Words fail me, so a grunt is all that's released.

"I saw what you are you freak; people don't do that."

Amid the pain, terror, and exhaustion rises confusion. His words don't make any sense. One part of me thinks it's my mind playing tricks on me, the other wonders at what happened when I lost my mind to that blank space of time.

"Show me!" he screams.

My head drops, unable to be held up any longer. All I hear before the knife moves again is his scream of frustration. I watch the brown boots he's wearing move away from me for a moment, then return quickly.

This time, the knife draws out my first scream. It surely wouldn't be my last. The edge is dragged softly from the parting of my labia to my belly button in a deep motion only mustered by pure hatred. Blood begins to flow heavily from the new wound making me woozy and limp in the chains.

Looks like the ugly can get uglier.

Faintly I hear Kent yell at Grant. Something about it being too soon to end me. The last instruction he gives to the other men is to put some dirt or mud on it to stop the bleeding.

I spend the rest of the night considering which of the thousands of things happening to me now would end me first.

Chapter 7

Feathers still hasn't returned. My thoughts of him are sparse, considering the possibility that I'd hallucinated his talking is very strong. A woman with no one to talk to but a bird? And that bird could talk? Right. A part of me is glad when I don't see him strung up anywhere. But the feeling is shallow.

They do give me a break. Let my arms down so I don't lose them, it was interesting knowing they had enough sense to know that limbs could die from lack of blood. However, they aren't nice enough to catch me before my knees slam into the ground.

Two days have passed. I only know because the night is when they get truly rowdy. They stopped using the smooth blade and switched to the serrated one. Even went over the wounds that started to close up with it to make sure they would scar.

I'm washed with freezing water to get the smell of urine and defecation off of my body. Nobody likes their toys to be dirty. I have no choice but to endure the shame of going to the bathroom on myself as I stand for them all to see. I'm fairly certain an infection has crept into my bladder along with the infection in each cut.

Each time night brakes, everyone in the group gathers to drink and watch me be butchered as if I'm an animal. The second set of ten cuts are divided between each thigh, but they use a serrated knife for that. How I don't bleed out and die would have fascinated me if it weren't for my lack of awareness. If I watch the cuts long enough they would seem to start to heal in front of me. Unending pain could do that to somebody.

I want to make everything feel like a hallucination, but the cuts are too harsh. Kent won't let Grant do it anymore, saying he wanted to "do the painting himself". That didn't stop Grant from rubbing himself through his jeans at each scream that rips itself from me.

On the third day, the third set of cuts are also divided. The arms don't hurt so bad since they were numb from hanging. Unfortunately, Grant realizes that and advises Kent to let me go. He even tells him to wait until the numb static feeling is gone. His leader tests for feeling by slowly pushing the tip of his knife down my forearms. When I finally gain feeling back there are three marks in one arm, two in the other.

"I gotta make this even hun," he reasons, that sick grin on his face.

The slicing continues.

I know he passed his original number long ago.

I fall into a disturbing sleep riddled with night terrors that has me thrashing in my chains. Only a handful of males are awake when they happen, so I only receive a handful of slaps and am told to shut my mouth.

Emotions no longer exist for me. I sort of miss them, even with all the suffering I continue to endure. On the other hand, I'm glad they might be gone. I don't want to die with terror in my veins, I want to die with some semblance of peace.

Whatever that fucking means.

Even my inner voice is tired, as if it too, had pieces of it sliced away more than thirty times.

Only ten more times. Ten more times that knife will slice through my skin to let blood spill onto the ground. That's what I tell myself, knowing damn well that Kent would add more whenever he felt like it.

Moonlight comes from the sky for the fourth time since my capture.

Those same brown boots. I would hate those boots with everything left in me if I could feel. Hate who wears them even more.

Death lingers in the air right as the thirty-first cut is finished. My senses at least understand that this body couldn't handle much more. Pitiful excitement rises at the possibility of the release from life. Perhaps today I would finally learn what rest meant.

I could see Car again, maybe even Mom and Dad. We'd be together again after so long.

I wonder if they'd be mad for making them wait for my arrival. Always fashionably late. Just like when we were all alive. Maybe they wouldn't mind, they'd be happy to see me.

Two more cuts. Only seven more to go.

"When I'm done with you, I'm gonna lay you down all nice and gentle on my bed, and I'm gonna fuck you until every single cut opens up again," he told me. The dripping greed in his voice would have made me throw up. If I had anything other than a couple saltines in my stomach. The dryness had lingered for hours after they quite literally shoved them down my throat. Cuts litter inside my mouth from lack of ability to chew with a damaged jaw.

Three more cuts. Four more to go.

"Maybe I'll cut deeper, fuck some of the cuts."

Still nothing. No fear, no anger, no sadness. Just an empty void.

That's okay, it's a good thing that I am now void of emotion. Given some semblance of freedom for enduring these days of torture.

The air had gotten chillier, adding to the list of terrible things happening, my body now shutting down along with the temperature.

I barely register the last cut. All ten are on my back tonight, because Kent wants to look at his newest artwork as he takes the last part of me that's mine away. That last part of me would be gone long before he climbs on top of me. I start letting myself slip into that warm embrace of silence.

Unfortunately, I'm pulled away from that warm place when a crack rings out in my ears. My side burns with new pain, flaring with every new breath I take. Most likely, another rib is broken. Most definitely, some cuts are reopened.

"Wakey wakey pretty girl, you don't wanna miss this part."

I don't actually. I want to know when to push my body to that ledge that dangled so teasingly in front of me.

I'm finally coming down from the chains.

Two lines of animalistic men form a path to the nearest house, with the door as open as a monster's awaiting mouth.

This is it.

Run. RUN.

The small part of my humanity begs, pleads for me to make one last effort. There is just no effort to give.

As the most dangerous person disappears behind me, mild panic settles in. Thrashing gives the feeling of slowing him down but instead just angers him. Two hands on my hips control some of it, also slowing time.

Emotion chooses then and there to start rolling into me.

The fire dances in front of me like a wild animal. I feel that fire embodies me now. Caught in a trap but unable to get out. Even knowing what's coming couldn't give it enough fight. I watch the chains twist and ripple slowly in the corner of my eye as the men around me begin laughing, glaring, watching with hungry eyes. A different kind of fear sets in when I recognize the time this had happened before. I lost a chunk of time to the black hole in my mind that didn't keep memories. I have no idea what happened then, and I wasn't sure if I wanted to know everything that happens now or not.

Time still hasn't picked up speed, my body nearly just as slow. I most definitely begin hallucinating because a glimpse past my hands shows that nails no longer tipped my fingers. The long razor-sharp talons wink in the night, just as suddenly a feeling clicks inside of me. Similar to that first scarring night I could suddenly see everything around me and beyond in the smallest detail. Adrenaline is a hell of a beast.

Grant's voice springs out in a yell. Something about an animal.

The painfully slow sound of a zipper behind me breaks any trace of sanity, and I let out the most feral scream I've heard in my life. It drags just as the time does. In the same slowness as the reality I'm in, people stumble back away and the hand on my hip slips back.

Not too quickly, but just fast enough time returns to normal.

Someone drops to the ground in front of me with his throat torn to ribbons. Actual ribbons of skin lay on the ground around him as blood pools. Another man is tossed so fast in front of me that his head caves in at the force of meeting the ground.

Blood spews everywhere, coating my bruised and battered skin in flecks of blood. My vision quickly becomes blurry and useless. As that fades my hands begin to burn tightly, a limb waking up after falling asleep. Maybe they want me to feel the cuts again for having screamed so loudly.

Chaos spills around me endlessly. I have no spirit left in me to look up and see what is causing it. My legs give out to the weight of my trauma, forcing a shoulder to slip out of the socket.

Another scream. Not so brutal. Not so feral. But still loud enough to shake those too close to me.

Quiet enters the bubble of my mind before my hearing loses most of its capability. A dampened roar greets my ears.

I just want to sleep, I'm so tired, I want sleep, everything hurts

My eyelids flutter to bring me towards that wonderful sleep I now dream about. That ledge that offers a new world.

They nearly close just as I see a dark face with kind eyes dip into my view. Beautifully decorated locs swing gently around that face as the person crouches below my hanging body.

Large hands reach up and find a way to release my dislocated arm, then the other. A cry comes out of my mouth, causing the person in front of me to flinch. I'm still hallucinating since I see his eyes flashing as brightly as a candle being lit.

All I remember is dropping to the ground only to be caught by my strange savior.

True to recent form, I once again lose myself to the blackness of my mind – and lose consciousness.

"Kali wake up!"

"Car...stop it."

The sun hurt my eyes as if I had been trapped in darkness for days.

Carly knew better than to wake me up like this. Her little hands pushed on my shoulder and belly, causing pain to echo through me. Screaming echoes somewhere but I can't pin down the source.

That same memory repeats itself what must be a million times.

My eyes open in between the repetitions, flashes of a tall figure moving around me where I can't see. Blurry film keeps me from picking up any more details.

"Car-" yelling at my sister is cut off by my sharp inhale. Only seconds pass before I catch my breath again. Our breathing matches for just a moment before my mind shifts back to being awake.

Stiffness has settled into my body, rendering me practically immobile. All I feel is my finger and eyelids shift.

Wetness drops onto my cheek. It must have been a tear to be so small and cool.

She wraps one arm under my shoulder, and the other under my knees.

"I'm sorry, I'm sorry, I'm so sorry love."

Carly never called me "love". She would never call me anything again. She also was never big enough to hold me. Or rock me this gently. Such a solid body holding me never could have been female. Fear begins to build in me but the comforting warmth seeping into my body is keeping it at bay. My breaths are labored and painful, each one a struggle when my chest expands and moves my shoulder.

Memories slowly drip into me causing the air in my lungs to halt every now and then. Each time it does, the body holding me squeezes just a bit. It's as if they can feel the memories coming back as well. Time was still non-existent, making it clear that this could have been a cycle repeating itself for more than an hour.

The last memory to slither in is of hands on my breasts, a knife flaying my skin open, and a zipper being pulled down behind me. Then it all stops.

"You're safe. They're gone, they're gone. Never again," the body holding me seems to rumble with the bass of the voice.

That deep bass is what shakes me into being fully awake.

My eyelids fly open, meeting kind eyes made of liquid gold.

The shock on his face doesn't stop me from pulling myself out of his arms and planting a foot firmly in his chest. I lose my balance, weak from my survival and abuse. He merely takes a step back. While he shakes off the impact I begin to wildly take in my surroundings.

I glance around, trying to figure out where I am. We're in a large clearing, one surrounded by trees. Old pine trees stand taller than anything I had seen before. The shade of them stretching as their numbers continue for as far as I can see. Sounds of water echoes from my left and right, with one of them sounding loud enough to be a river.

"Easy, beautiful, I won't hurt you," despite my solid attack on him he stands and stretches his arms out in front of him, palms facing upward. None of the slow steps he takes towards me helps to calm my nerves. His pure size put more fear into me, he easily had to be over six and half feet tall. I search frantically around for clear path through the woods to escape being trapped by another male.

Not a man not a man please not again.

"The last man I hit said the same thing-"

"Those men won't hurt you anymore-"

"He tried to rape me-"

His face falters and those open hands clench into tight fists. My live wire of a brain quickly estimates that those fists could cave in my face if I let them. The part of me that had been damaged from such pain and suffering urges me to run away. A majority of me, for some psychotic reason, tells me to run towards him. Warfare rises in me, my brain battling to figure out not only what to do, but why I would be feeling such things.

"I won't hurt you."

"I have no reason to believe that," I snap. The tips of my fingers begin to burn as the running away part of me starts to win.

"You do, because I know there's a part of you screaming at you to run away at the same time another part of you is telling you to run to me and never leave. I'm telling you right now that you are the safest you will ever be with me."

I wonder briefly why I'm not running, why I'm not feeling instinctually fearful of him. His voice reaches a part of me that had been stomped out in survival mode. Survival meant ignoring the part of me that craves another's presence. That alone had been what kept me from losing my already fragile mind. And an annoying bird entertaining me.

My silence is my only answer.

"Those men won't hurt you anymore," he repeats. "I saw your body when I found you. Saw all of the horrible bruises and marks they forced into your skin."

His face winces at the mention, putting my mind back into those chains. Puts me back into that horrible cluster of buildings I was held in the center of. Puts me back at the mercy of the group of animals that couldn't even be called men.

"They weren't men," I mumble.

"What?"

"They weren't men. They were animals. Whatever you want to call them but do not call them men. Men don't behave like that."

He nods and takes a few steps towards me. I force myself not to run away. What can only be described as a bubble forms around me the closer he gets. It's a warm and gentle bubble, close to the air being blown out from a heater.

"Do you feel that?" he asks, only a couple feet away now.

I nod, still tense to defend myself. My fingers still burn intensely.

"You can put the talons away now."

Instead of dragging my gaze from his face and risking my awareness, I lift my hands in front of me. My fingers are slightly bloody, and there are in fact talons that have busted through the skin. My nails are gone, and thick black claws similar to an eagle remain. They're thick, and long enough to touch my forearm when I close my hand.

Blood rushes to my ears, drowning out everything around me. I know

I'm mumbling, perhaps screaming, something, when I begin to stumble back away. That bubble of warmth and gentle pressure fizzles out quickly as my mind starts to black out.

"Hey, hey, hey, now don't do that. You're gonna be okay,"

"I-I saw it before, but I thought I was hallucinating. Am I hallucinating?!"

"No, this is very real-"

"N-n-no it can't be. This isn't real, there's no way this is real."

Wild panic stirs in me, my fear certainly being the catalyst for it. Suddenly everything is silent, I feel my throat straining every time I open my mouth. It's probably due to screaming since it disturbs a few of the birds in the trees enough for them to fly away.

Just as my nails had, my skin now burns. The intensity is all-consuming enough to force me to my knees. What feels like liquid terror shreds through my organs without pause. My body convulses in as a reaction, the pain starting to build. Screaming stops, but only because the pain is so intense, I can barely get a breath in. The skin on my back hurts, it more than burns. The knife Kent was wielding before is back with its own fury, pulling at my dermis with wild anger.

My vision is shutting down, and everything feels close to a climax about to hit me that wouldn't bring pleasure.

Hands grab my face and jolt me out of the silence. Leaves rustle and wind pushes at branches. My green eyes connect with eyes so golden they practically glow. Everything ceases to hurt, and a snapping feeling whips through me.

The crack is internal but louder than anything I had experienced before.

Electricity ripples through me pulling me towards the strange man that holds my face sweetly. Colors around me brighten and fluctuate. I have no idea what's happening except that the fear that had held me down for so long is replaced with a need so strong I had no choice but to bend to it.

The golden eyes disappear for just a moment as one hand slips from my face. Strong fingers interlace my own and bring the joined limbs into my vision. Out of his own hands were talons that are a washed-out gold. My eyes widen at the sight.

He is the same as me. Even with no knowledge of where he came from or how I ended up in his arms, I trust him. Trust that part of him. A lesser internal snap shakes me, bringing my eyes back to meet those golden ones that promised safety. They promise everything I could ever want.

"You," is all I manage to breathe.

My talons withdraw back into my hands, albeit painfully. No blood spills this time though there is a significant amount of tingling as I watched my nails grow over the empty nail beds. My jaw is most definitely on the floor.

We stay in that position for a few minutes, our breathing evening out until it matches the other. The comfort of that quiet is gone. I don't need it anymore. Everything I need is right in front of me.

"Jakir," he whispers.

I pull my hand away, needing some breathing room to process what just happened.

"My name is Jakir, and you and I are Bonded."

Chapter 8

My thoughts spin like a wildly unstable top. I can't keep one in the front of my mind long enough to truly understand what's happening.

"What? The fuck?" my voice is bland, the words the only thing I'm able to get out.

"You have a foul mouth," he frowns.

"No shit, now try again."

The frown stays temporarily, evaporating when he begins to speak again. I still feel the buzz that has taken root in my spine. It's small, but enough to maintain concern.

"The Bond, you don't know about it?"

"Obviously I don't," I roll my eyes. "I wanna know why you aren't freaking out about having *talons* come out of both of our hands."

The frown is back, partnered with concern that seems to well up in me at the same time.

"You have no idea? Absolutely no idea about the changes in this world?"

"I know something happened that caused a meltdown that killed lots of people, that a lot of life isn't the same on this planet anymore."

A tree branch rustles nearby in the silence. I keep my eyes on Jakir, weary of his intentions.

"Interesting."

"My name is Kali, by the way. I guess I should give you at least that much for saving my life."

"Kali," he rolls the name over in his mouth. A small smile lights up his face. "Fitting."

"Thanks, now please explain everything that just happened."

"That's going to take a while. You just woke up after a very long nap, and I don't want to overwhelm you."

"I can barely believe talons just came out of my hands but low and behold they did, so I'm kind of open right now."

"Friend?" a cracking voice yells. I know that annoying voice anywhere.

"Feathers?!" I call out, whipping around to look for the black animal.

"You call him Feathers?" Jakir asks humorously.

"Yeah, the asshole has been following me from the start. I think his main goal is to make me want to shoot myself. "

"I doubt it, considering he helped me find you."

I whip around to face him; my brows pull together. His smile stays put to my slight annoyance.

"I was with…another group of people, when I met him. He just kept yelling 'danger' and every time I got close, he flew away. I followed him for three days, up until I found you."

Feathers finally flies down from the branch he was in, landing on my shoulder. I reach up and ran my fingers over his head gently. He closes his eyes, enjoying it, then flits over to our mutual friend.

"Seems like he likes you now, good luck with that," I shrug.

"I think patience gets a little more friendliness out of him."

I simply roll my eyes and make my way back towards the campfire he had built, with a large roll-out bed near it. Only one pad is visible.

"Where did you sleep?" I asked over my shoulder.

"Next to you, it's the only way you stopped having nightmares or dying on me," his smile is sad, making my fingers twitch towards him. I resist the urge to and swallow before clearing my throat.

So, someone has been holding me. Stopping in front of the barely lit fire I pull up the loose shirt I have on. Angry red lines destroy my chest, most of them fully closed. My eyes burn at the permanent memory I'll always have now.

"They will heal, but they will scar. You survived, now you need to live ."

63

"They're already healed so well," I mumble. Pressing on them causes heat to rise under the cuts. I ignore the way it brings me back to being Kent's prisoner. "How long was I out? It must have been days for them to be this far along."

He sits down on the pad and offers the spot next to him. When I shake my head, he doesn't push.

"You were down for two days, in and out of consciousness. But the body you had before the Fall is long gone, this one you have now is capable of far more."

I make note what he'd called the apocalypse before responding, "Nothing heals that fast."

"You do," he raises a brow. "As do I."

"And my shoulder?"

"I fixed it in your sleep, nearly died when you grabbed my throat."

"I'm not sorry."

"Neither am I," his voice is soft, but a raised eyebrow shows how little he appreciates my tone.

I freeze. The response to my attitude disarms me.

"Thank you," I whisper, ashamed

"Kali, you need to understand that we're not human anymore. Those days are long gone."

"Okay, assuming that you're not currently spewing lies at me for fun, then explain what exactly you and I are."

"Let me try this, we have our human forms," he gestures between us. "And we have another form."

"That doesn't-"

He raises a hand, "Let me finish, this will take a while so you can ask questions later."

I nod and close my mouth.

"That radiation changed animals too. Horses are two or three times the size they used to be, cows are now the size of pigs, and pigs the size of cows. Deer have antlers so large it looks like their necks shouldn't hold them. That change happened to some people too. Those that weren't in the radiation had minimal changes, maybe becoming stronger or faster."

Jakir's hand flexes in front of him to reveal those golden colored talons that grow out. His nails are pushed out of the way and drop to the ground, allowing for sharp weapons to take their place. I stare at them, until I drop my gaze to my hands. I think of them growing out of my own hands just as they had before. Catching me off guard they do start to grow, a burning feeling growing in the tip of each index as my nails plop to the ground. Once they stop stretching out I force myself to look at Jakir again.

"Keep them out for now, it'll help you get used to it. Plus, you don't want to be regrowing them over and over, it takes energy out of you."

"How do I make them go away?"

"I literally just told you to ask questions later."

I smile with a tilt of my head, not caring about the demand. He sighs the answer to me.

"I'm not telling you that yet because, like I just said, you need to let them be."

I huff impatiently. When I cross my arms and the new body part rests on my skin I shiver; they're cold.

"Let me show you," he starts pulling his shirt off. I startle, stepping back.

"Show me...the other form?"

He nods, pausing at his pants. I still, my thighs twitching in preparation to run.

"You'll need to step back...a lot."

I walk backwards, until he motions for me to stop. I carefully avoid my eyes lingering on his body, not wanting to be creepy. The first sound of snapping pulls my gaze back to him. I freeze.

It happens in a moment. His skin stretches so much it tears, only to reform immediately as his bones break and rebuild themselves. His black skin disappears as a thick, dark yellow hide takes over. His form grows quickly, expanding into the clearing. His back bends, bones being covered by more hide that stretch out into wings. My mouth drops open, hands hanging uselessly at my side as he reaches his full height.

His arms and legs finish shifting into thick, muscular limbs. They bend like dog legs at the elbows and knees. All four end in huge paws with talons tipping the four toes and dew claw on each one.

But that's not the most amazing part.

It's the golden scales that shine like coins glinting in the sunlight.

Horns thicker than my entire body stretch from the crown of his head. A few of the sharp teeth lining his mouth poke out over his lips. His wings stretch upwards above him, so large they seem like they would be nearly impossible to lift.

His body shrinks back down quickly, the stunning gold color disappearing into his deeply dark skin. He pulls on his pants while I walk back towards him.

"That-you're...you're beautiful," I stumble over my words, still trying to process the pure size of him. Just under the height of two school buses stacked lengthwise.

"Thank you," he glances down at my fingers before pulling his shirt back on.

"Judging by your talons you'll be black, or some shade of it."

"I'm not ready," I blurt out, wrapping my arms around myself. "I don't want to yet."

"Then you won't. We need to stay low anyway, avoid attracting more attention than you possibly already have. If you shifted in another Samle's territory, you might have set them off. We'll be walking."

I dip my head in thanks, still blinking through the image in my head of him as a dragon.

"So now you see, that's not the only part of your body that can change. In fact, your entire body can. We're a new species on this planet that is now above humans on the food chain. We have a form that gives us flight with wings. We're covered in scales that protect our bodies. Those claws," he nods towards my hands. "Become larger, just as mine did. You'll grow to have a height of anywhere from six to sixty feet depending on who you are. Maybe more, but I don't know our limitations on that quite yet."

People having wings, talons, scales doesn't make sense. I know it's real because I just watched it, but the *why* isn't making sense to me. Radiation made people sick before. Even if it was some special radiation that shook down the planet, it shouldn't be possible.

"You'll take it slow the first time. The first time I shifted without blacking out I nearly had a panic attack. You'll eventually - when you're ready - shift while fully cognizant, and I'll be there to help."

I take a deep breath, trying to ease the fear of switching into another body and losing control.

"There are a lot of things you will need to learn, but there are a couple points I can give that might help you understand. First off, we can shift whenever we choose but our emotions can make it extremely difficult to control the shift at first."

"Would high levels of fear cause a shift?" I pick at my talons, trying to discern the difference between all the times I'd been within the grasp of those animals.

The time I lost control was the most scared I've been...even compared to the chains.

"Probably, have you had any black outs recently?"

Flashbacks to the woods flood my mind. I keep them quiet and only nod.

"I felt something, it felt like time slowed down. Like I was watching everything in slow motion."

"You shifted; you just don't remember it. The shift most likely happened fast. Your brain takes in every bit of information it can to prevent you from being caught off guard while changing."

"Mmm."

I go quiet again, he watches me thoughtfully.

"When you're ready...I'm here."

"We'll see."

"I suppose we will," he chuckles. "We have plenty of time."

A bag is pulled out from under the padding, revealing a pack of dried meat.

I raise a brow, "How did you have time to dry meat like that?"

"I was living with a group of other dragons before I left to find you. There were only a couple handfuls of us, and we split since they were drawn somewhere else. Left to find their "Samle's", some Norwegian word that got picked up."

"Why Norwegian?"

He smiles, "Something about the first person to shift after everything was living there. Maybe it's just rumors."

I nod, staying quiet as I process things.

"Anyways, certain people are drawn together by a pull."

"So it's similar to a pack of wolves?"

"You could say that - don't curl your lip up at it. I heard from a couple others while trying to find you that there's always a natural leader, the person that makes the connection between every dragon what it is. "

"And that's determined by...?"

"Bonds, like one you and I just formed, I assume. I could be wrong."

"Let's dig into that one, bud."

"You can pretend to bounce back with sarcasm, but I see through you."

I only stare and wait for my answer.

"Not every dragon gets one, but many do. Some people think it's what platonic soulmates are, others believe it to be the universe keeping balance to power. Either way, my time with a Samle has led me to believe that it only forms one time in life. It's unmatched by anything other than finding the love of your life. Once it is formed, well you know the rest."

"No - I don't think I do."

"I beg to differ; you feel what I feel. I feel what you feel. Your healing has already sped up in addition to its previous speed, not having to be scared is letting your body heal."

"That's-"

"Not true? I can feel you still being defensive trying so desperately to avoid giving me too much information. You feel like you could give me every piece of you but refuse to do so."

He lets me catch my breath after finishing the verbal assault on my emotions. I don't like being opened up like a book in front of someone I have no previous connection to. The eye contact between us never breaks, making it more terrifying. A bit of calm enters me, feeling forced in rather than created.

"Okay you've succeeded in making me nervous," I stand again and start to pace.

"When you began to break for it earlier, you felt me before we bonded. You knew that I was safe. That's what calms you down, that calm from both of us is what allowed the bond to snap into place."

"Why did I have to feel calm?"

"The Bond cannot be forced, if any part of you rejects it, it will not occur. It must be freely given, even if you are not completely aware of it."

I stop, consider what I felt right before it all happened, and only find confirmation in my experience. My pacing resumes immediately.

"I will always be a part of your life now, just as you will be a part of mine. From now on, I am the only person that will match you in capability, strength, and power. If you ever start to lean towards poor intentions I will stop you, and as you move forward in life with good intentions I will support you."

"I think I've had enough for one day, just one more question." My fingers play with the green leaves on a nearby branch. The softness is comforting. Feathers is off at another tree swallowing a bug. "Where did you learn all this?"

"I stayed with that Samle for a while, learned from them. Their leader and his Bonded were very gracious. I never became a part of the group, so we all assumed I was meant to be in another Samle. We assumed correctly."

"And now you're here with me."

"And now I am here with you," he smiles while offering out some dried meat. I accept, taking a seat next to him. We both chew for a bit, calming the hunger in our stomachs.

"It seems a bit much for two people who just met."

"If nature allowed the Bond to form later, it would allow for more time for one in the pair to either die or get out of control."

More chewing. Feathers hops around the area nearby, pecking at grubs in the dirt and grass. His feathers were shiny, meaning he had found enough food for himself in the days we were apart.

"Thank you," I whisper. "For saving me. I don't think I would have made it much longer."

"No, I don't think you would have."

The bag with dried meat is put away, as well as two blankets.

"I know you just got comfortable, but unfortunately we need to leave. That group might catch up soon."

"Where are we going to go?"

"Well, we can't build a Samle without a place for people to find us at."

"There's almost nothing left, anywhere."

"We can build, and we can search. There was something telling you to keep moving when you were on your own, did it not?"

I narrow my eyes at him and began to roll up the mat, "So what? We just keep following that feeling until we find a suitable place?"

"I can't think of a better idea."

"I sure fucking could, like finding old homes and using those."

"We need safety, not convenience. Also, you really don't need to use that kind of language."

I clip the rolled mat to the backpack he has, and then show him there are ways I could use foul language without speaking.

Chapter 9

There's no need for rest as we move. Aches and pains never cease across my body despite any break we take. Eventually they aren't worth it, so I push Jakir to just keep going. For the most part he listens to me, allowing the travel to continue. We both sleep for only three hours in that time, only getting what we need and moving forward immediately.

There was a crumbling city in the distance that we now begin to walk through, cautious of the corners we can't see around. Though I know it's not where we need to be, it's the most direct path to the pull dragging me. Most of the buildings aren't even buildings anymore, too decrepit to be safe.

Keeping a minimum pace is crucial to enforce the distance we need between us and whatever is left of the group chasing after us. As we travel north, I continue to question whether or not they would even spend the energy trying to find us. I voice them to Jakir after careful consideration, and he shuts them down gently but firmly.

If they were angry enough for not letting three of them have their way with me, I can't imagine the violence they would play out when multiple had been murdered. Especially when they seemed to believe it was their job to take me out of this world.

Maybe watching them try to hurt you would be at least a little entertaining.

Shaking the thought from my head I clear my throat. He looks at me without turning his head. Curiosity bleeds into my mind, feeling foreign. I realize quickly that it's his feelings and I'm just picking up on them. I manage to gently push back, closing off my mind.

Most of the time we're both silent. Surprisingly Feathers stays silent as well, either flying above us or resting on our shoulders. I repeat the verbal lesson Jakir gave me over and over in my head, trying to decipher how things on this planet have changed so drastically. Or even how humans were now capable of physically becoming something five times their size or bigger. Even the speed they recovered from my own attacks were..unexpected. I could feel something inside me, like a tightly wound ball that's warm and comforting. Every time I consider the idea of shifting I feel that ball start to get warm, eventually it gets so warm I yell out. My partner reacts quickly, turning around and grabbing my face with both hands.

"What, tell me what's wrong," he begs. He glances around at the concrete jungle surrounding us as if some unknown force will appear around some corner and attack.

"There's...there's this ball I can feel in my spine, but I can't tell where exactly it is," the words come out rushed and frantic. The heat builds.

"Ah, take a deep breath in through your nose," I follow his command. "And out through your mouth. Your body wants you to shift because it hasn't done it properly yet."

"So let me shift," I snap through clenched teeth. The pain edges into the territory of blinding.

"Kali, trust me," his massive hands pull my face up so I'm forced to look at him. His eyes seem brighter when I meet them with my own. The odd golden hue is just enough to distract me from the ball growing with heat. "You cannot shift right now, this area is too small. We have no idea how large you'll be and being in tight places might hurt you."

"I'll manage," I still repeat the breathing exercise. Afraid of the pain he warns me of more than anything. I've had enough pain for now.

"Kali if we're in another Samle's territory right now they will either hear or feel your shift and they will strike first and ask questions later. You need to stop it, just keep breathing."

My saving grace was the calm person in front of me, but the fear of being attacked is what completely stops the shift.

"They can sense others shifting?"

A beautiful smile stretches across his face eliciting a warmth in my chest, one that was nothing like the panic I was just experiencing. Happiness edges into me, but this time I know it comes from both of us. He knows my curiosity will distract me.

"The leaders can, once you find a place for your Samle to call home you connect with it. Nothing too detailed – at least from what I understand – but enough to keep you aware of any threats."

"Did I maybe trigger anything?"

"We're going to hope not and keep moving but stay alert in case we do get caught. We may also not be in any territory, but I'd rather not test that out."

I nod and grasp his hands to pull them from my face. Before I drop them, I give them a light squeeze with my own. I turn to focus again on the building surrounding us.

The buildings in the city are a sight to behold. Greenery stretches up some of them, while others had become too weak under the weight of nature and crumbled. It all seems alive around us. Occasionally a rock or piece of concrete breaks off and falls somewhere nearby due to eroded structure. Birds glide high up above, though Feathers went nowhere near them. In fact, he had stayed on Jakir's shoulder since my near-shift moment.

"Feathers, why won't you fly with them?" I whispered. This place feels like a dare to speak any louder.

A pause, then a head tilt.

"Birds kill," he simply states.

As if determined to prove he was right, I hear a screech from above. Looking up I watch as one of the figures plummets down to us. One of its wings are gone. The second it hits the ground a wet slapping sound bounces off of the concrete jungle then finishes with a crack right after. The slap was its body, the crack was its other wing. Louder screeching echoes from above.

Jakir's hand grabs my upper arm and guides me forward. I don't protest.

We eventually reach a small building before the city eventually gives way to a land full of shallow canyons and few plants. Most of the canyons aren't very tall from what I can tell. They were more long ditches than anything, though still distinctly new.

"Despite the concern about being in someone else's neighborhood, and the clearly malicious birds, I think we should stop for the night before crossing that," his cheekbones flex as he clenches his jaw. I agree and start moving towards the building.

It was a church at one point, the cross on the front is cracked, half of it hanging off. Most of the glass-stained windows have remained intact through the cruel days of the new world. Both doors are still on the front of the building giving us the ability to shut out the world. When pushed open, a loud squeak meets our ears resulting in a tense moment of waiting. Nothing happens, so we slip in. Feathers takes off into the rafters, walking up and down beams as he inspects them for spiders to eat.

A lot of the pews had been reduced to ashes, only a few half-burned ones are left. Dust coats the floor, making it easy to spot two different sets of footprints.

"There's footprints, look," I murmur. We both nod and keep an eye out in opposite directions. Nothing moves, making the silence worse than if at least a rat had run across the floor. Some of the windows facing the canyons had some broken areas but nothing too bad.

What is possibly the smallest gasp suddenly sounds off to my left. I whip my head towards it, grabbing Jakir's forearm in the process.

"Hello?" I whispered.

"Kali..."

"I heard you, so I know you're there. Either come out now, or I'll force you out."

My voice hadn't been that strong in a while. It feels good to finally have the advantage. Even if they're the same thing as us, there was no chance they were stronger than the man standing behind me.

74

"I don't have patience anymore," the words come out like a growl. My hand drops and I walk forward with a body ready to fight. The tension made me anxious.

"Wait!" a feminine voice calls out. Slowly, blond hair appears along with a round face. Hands rise up in surrender but don't ease the tension in my shoulders.

"We don't want trouble I swear. My girlfriend and I have been sleeping here for weeks now," a man's voice behind me explains.

I reach out through the bond for the first time, like extending a hand over a door frame. Jakir is strangely calm and collected without a hint of fear. Far different from my braced stance and tight back.

"You're not a threat?" he questions.

The female lowers her hands as her eyes drift past me to her companion. To put both into sight I move up the stage, where obviously a podium once stood. Both have bright eyes, but the similarities stop there. While the female has pale skin and blue eyes that made her look gentle, her athletic build that makes her taller than her companion says otherwise. The man is lean but not muscular, his deeply tanned skin and dark hair suggests he gained the color from hispanic genetics. Warm brown eyes move from my friend to me, suddenly becoming interested.

"Who are you?" he asks.

"Kali, and this is Jakir," I give her the answer, still trying to figure out if they're friend or foe.

"I'm her Bonded."

I turn my head to him with the question in my eyes, *How the fuck are they gonna know what that means?*

"I can sense...you're like us," the woman spoke. "Where are you coming from?"

My mind pauses trying to figure out what she meant by "like us", until it finally clicks they aren't exactly human either.

That answers that question...

"Wait," I stop Jakir before he answers. "What about your names?"

"I'm Harlow. You can relax, I swear we have no intention of fighting you," pale woman reaches out a hand to me. Only staring at it I nod and turn just enough to keep her in sight.

"And you?" I ask the man. He grins, seemingly erred by the clear tension in my voice and body.

"Jacob, pleased to meet you. And please, if you attack anyone, attack her," his joke brings a tight one onto her face.

I don't smile back.

"We're leaving as soon as the sun rises, just need to sleep somewhere secure tonight."

"We would greatly appreciate your hospitality tonight, the three of us are in need of much rest," golden eyes meet mine as a gentle push reaches the bond. Harlow looked up briefly to where Jakir motioned, to see Feathers still in the rafters.

Nodding, I sit down and let out a breath I had been holding. Most of the tension releases out of my shoulders as the feeling of fear leaves me. His calm lets me relax, and my gut tells me there's nothing to be concerned about regarding these two. I'm suddenly uncomfortable with feeling so at ease around strangers. The bird lands next to me with a spider the size of my hand halfway down his mouth.

All four of us gather around a fireplace hidden in one of the alcoves on the sides of the room. So strange to see it in a destroyed church.

"We found it in a hardware store nearby. Not everything was salvageable but this was. We've used what we could," Jacob explains. A small smile on his face. So, others had scavenged to survive just like I did.

Maybe I wasn't as alone as I had been before. Or ever would be again.

Cans are cracked open, soup for each of us. Jakir pulls out some of his meat so as not to be rude and ask for more. Water would have been nice to thin out the jellied mushroom soup, but one couldn't be too picky when it came to apocalypse food.

Jacob does most of the talking at first since Harlow is more reserved. She seems content in listening to him while watching us new people.

"We were both in the city when it happened, underground thank god. When we found one another it was quite the meeting, killing each other seemed like top priority. And was out of our control."

Harlow laughs at that. Her food isn't gone yet, taking her time eating was probably the smart thing to do. Not inhale it like I did.

"We tried to be around one another, always wanting to fight but never seeming to be able to get rid of this feeling of *need*. It was a pull. Not just to fight but to fuck too," Jacob continued. Jakir frowns at the language, the frown turning sourer when I raise an eyebrow humorously.

Their bluntness is refreshing, but their story confuses me. Something about how casual they are when it comes to being violent to one another doesn't add up.

"It seemed like everything we did to go our separate ways only drew us nearer to each other more and more," Harlow adds. "Did the same happen for you?"

"No," I sigh. "Jakir got me out of a very messy situation after being led to me by that stupid bird."

Feathers takes a jab at my thigh a couple times before I push him away.

"You stupid. Not me!" he screeches.

Harlow's eyes widen, "It...it talks?"

"Fuck!" his beak opens wide for that one.

"You didn't," Jakir gives me the most disappointed dad look I've seen in a while.

I return it with a bored look, "Oops."

"Well, ravens could mimic before all of this. He just seems to also be able to process what we say. He seems nice."

"Oh he can, and he'll make you want to hug him so hard you break his neck," my cheeks strain at how hard I smile. Jacob notices the sarcasm and laughs instead of being put off by it.

Glancing at Harlow I notice she's staring at me unabashedly. Her eyes are filled with curiosity. She says nothing, so I continue the conversation.

"I was in Florida, not sure where that is anymore since the land has changed so much. I started moving north, picked up the feathery idiot on the way. Got into a bit of trouble. Jakir and I met. We connected. Walked here. You know the rest."

Jacob inquires further, "What kind of trouble?"

"None that you would want to get into."

He gets the message, backing off into a different conversation, "Well, Harlow and I aren't Bonded like you two are."

"We've heard of it from people passing through here, some coming from Samle's, others looking for one," she flipped her blond hair back over her shoulder. "Everyone we met was just another person. With you two, we can actually feel it."

"Agreed, not sure what it is but you feel familiar," Jacob seemed to taste the words on his tongue.

"It's hard to explain but...from what I've heard, when you find where you should be you develop a connection. Perhaps..." Jakir's pause is evidently for him to consider his next words. "Perhaps you two are supposed to be with us."

His words are heavy in the room, none of us willing to admit we couldn't quite trust the others yet.

I look between Jacob and Harlow, realizing that having them at my back is far better than the hand I've been dealt so far.

"You're both more than welcome to join us," I invite.

"And you're heading where?" she crosses her legs slowly.

"North, to find home."

"I doubt you'll find anything."

"We don't really have a choice. But let's say our little group does get bigger at all - being nomads isn't going to do us any favors."

She doesn't argue, the men remain quiet. I wonder if they've had any previous interactions with the same horrors I did.

"Jacob and I will decide in the morning."

I don't push any further, wanting to sleep. Jakir and I move to one side of the church opposite Jacob and Harlow. He rolls out a thin pad for us to sleep on, motioning me over once it was to his satisfaction.

The feeling of him curled against my back gives me a sense of calm I hadn't felt since I'd last seen Carly. Warmth seeps into my skin from him lulling me into a gentle sleep.

I wake up screaming - or attempting to - while a hand covers my mouth. My body thrashes against the body at my back violently. Throwing my head back into my captors' nose gives me just enough time to scramble out from under the blanket. There is no time to stop, I need to get away.

"Don't let her get out those doors!" the one holding me whisper - yells. Another figure, a male one, stands directly between me and the only exit around. Creaking has me snapping my head to my right. A female.

Holy fuck another woman

Who is she

Can't trust her

I don't recognize her, which makes me stumble backwards. The fear of being restrained again pushes me to move towards the woman to fight instead of flee. Her stance makes it clear she's willing to fight too. Her extreme height makes it threatening.

"Kali, what are you doing?" the woman asks.

"How the fuck do you know my name?" I snap. Her face turns into cold shock at my question. Instincts tell me to fight her now while she's vulnerable. I launch at her keeping my weight low to avoid being tossed. Her hands grab at me in odd places and throw me past her.

"What is wrong with her?" another male asks, the one blocking me from the main door.

The one who held me previously disregards the question while sprinting at me, "Let me handle this," is all he says before I push through the doors into a long hallway with no windows. There's just enough light for my eyes to see that the end has another set of doors. My legs pump as hard as they can, carrying me towards them as fast as they did in the forest.

He feels familiar but all I can remember was being trapped in chains. I need to escape.

Dammit run faster!

Don't stop don't stop please

Splinters rupture my skin as I slam into doors. They open up into a massive lobby causing me to falter at where to run next. That moment of hesitation gets me slammed into by a massive weight.

"No!" I scream. "No get the fuck off of me!"

"Kali!" he whispers harshly back. He knows my name too. "Kali enough, it's me!"

I'm wrestled onto my back, panic filling me at being so vulnerable. Nothing around except pieces of glass too small to even pick up. My eyes go wide as what feels like a little push touches my mind.

"What the fuck," I whisper. Golden eyes that appear to glow catch mine. Suddenly I'm jerked into reality as I realize the man above me isn't an enemy. A moment of calm passes between us – until the panic sets in.

Everything my brain had attempted to wipe clean walks itself back into my memory.

"They cut me," I sob out. Breathing is quickly becoming harder and harder. Black edges seep into my vision, slow but very present. I claw at Jakir trying to get him off of me. It does nothing but worry him. "They had me hung up like a toy and cut me Jakir. They were going to rape me, he was going to-"

Tears well in his eyes, brought on by the grief that echoes through our bond. It's pulled back suddenly, most likely him trying to keep from adding anything to my panic attack setting in.

"I know beautiful, you have to breathe though. Please breathe for me.

In through your nose, out through your mouth," I try my best through the shaky breaths. Tears roll freely down my face. My hands stop their assault on the man comforting me only to begin shaking so bad I can't function. As the shaking travels up my arms, he pulls me up and leans back so that I'm straddling him. He gently guides my legs around his torso and puts my arms around his neck. I hold on to him as tightly as I can without choking him. The intimacy should have scared me, but it didn't, only gives me something real to feel.

"That's it, hang onto me. You hang on as tight as you need to," his body moves again, this time standing up to walk. We don't head back towards the doors, which I think I catch two people peeking out of. The strong body I'm wrapped around moves further into the lobby, stopping near a couch. I drop my legs from him and nearly collapse at how weak I feel. All of the cut's flare at once with pain, probably due to my excessive movement. I look down, seeing some red bleed through my shirt.

Fear deepens, I need to get these clothes off. They're choking me.

"Get it off, get it off! I can't do it, I don't want to feel it!" I beg. There's pressure through the bond, as if he's trying to hug my conscience. It only stops the attack from getting worse, doing nothing to lessen it. I turn away from him, embarrassed by my behavior and unsure of what to do.

A large mirror leans against the wall across from us, perhaps one day long ago meant for the people who walked by to admire themselves. For now, it only lets me see the marks on my body. I rip through my shirt, my talons having made an appearance earlier in the panic attack. Bloody lines with puffy skin cover me; burning underneath the clothing that remains. My torso is hideous, makes me choke on tears as I look at myself for the first time in months.

Little fat remains on my body, everything leaned out except my chest. The only parts of me I recognize are the broad shoulders that had once gotten me into swimming, the high cheekbones I'd gotten from my mother, and the brown hair that looks like a mess. Everything else is foreign. My eyes aren't just green, they're deeper and brighter. Thin muscles are built up from the physical exertion they were forced into so many times now. This body has been starved of calories.

My brain picked up all the new pieces about me, put them in a box, and kicks that box into a dark corner. It wants to see the permanent reminders of abuse I now carry. For everything being so fresh, it can't see past what's carved into me. Those reminders would never just be physical, they would never be as deep as the emotional ones. Having these scars just meant I would never be able to hide my past. The bastard who thrived on doing this wanted me to feel it if I survived, he planned on every person who touched me pulling back and wondering what kind of fucked up toy I had been before. He knew it, now I know it.

Jakir lets me have my moment, both of us knowing that trying to keep me from seeing myself would only delay the reaction. He waits patiently, off to the side where I can't see him. Never moving or speaking, until I start spiraling.

My mind turns into ugly thoughts, ones that make me the one to blame. Thoughts that hurt me even more. My nail beds burn as I raise my hands to touch the scabs.

I deserve this; I should have been smarter. I should have been faster. If I had just been better, it wouldn't be like this now.

Maybe I never should have run in the first place...maybe then they wouldn't have been so cruel.

"I can feel you spiraling, your mind is getting darker," he says gently. His arms come around me to pull my hands away from picking nervously at the scars. The pain from pulling at them is the only grounding thing I really feel. He gently turns me and pulls me into his chest while cupping the base of my head with one hand. "There is nothing that would have changed this. And there is nothing about the marks on your body that make you any less than you are. It's something that happened to you, yes, you will never deny that. You will never deny your worth."

My body still shakes from the memories flashing behind my eyelids.

"Every time I close my eyes, I see them. I see Kent and Grant cutting at me, smirking every time I screamed. They all loved when I screamed, I swear to god some of them made a drinking game out of it," I spit the last

82

words with venom.

He only takes a deep breath and lowers me to the ground; my legs slide under his as we both sit on the floor. We face one another for a moment, looking at the other with utter trust. I'm sure my eyes plead for help just as much as my mind is.

"Maybe I should have died," I whisper.

That's what I get for not fighting back enough.

"And left me to live without you, having never felt this Bond? Right," he gives me an incredulous look, obviously trying to humor me. I still see the sadness in his eyes. I started picking at the scabs, hoping for more distracting and familiar pain. His eyes drop and remove my hands from my chest.

I look up at him, my eyes filled with tears, "Please, Jakir. I need to-"

"No, I'm not gonna let you do that. You're out of control, it's dangerous."

"Please," I feel my face crumple. "Help me. I can't-I can't do this."

I feel my lungs struggle to take in even breaths. The muscles feel jerky every time I try to find a better breathing pattern.

He says something so quietly I have to ask him to say it again.

"I'm going to give you new memories."

"What?"

I track his slow movements as he reaches into his back pocket. It's a knife that's brought back around, being gently opened in front of me. A look over his shoulder to check that we're alone is the last thing he does before pulling me in. My cheek presses into his pectoral muscle that showed from his open shirt, then my eyes close. The need to fidget and pick is like needles pressing up out of my skin.

"Make it stop," I cry into his skin. My breathing begins to pick up again, unable to stay calm for long.

"I can't make it stop, love, but I can make new ones. New memories that overwrite the bad ones a little."

Black talons curl into his biceps, blood being drawn from the pressure I put on them. If he feels any pain, he doesn't show it. My bra is unclasped, allowing the cool air to kiss all of my skin. The knife is cold against my skin, causing me to jerk a little. He waits so patiently until he feels me nod.

"I will always be here," I know he isn't lying. The bond grows every day we're together. I know how much I'm growing to care for him. "We will always have each other."

"I trust you," I breathe out.

The slick feeling of metal on my skin starts at the top of my spine. Not nearly as hard as what I had become familiar with, but just enough to cause every muscle in my body to tense. He never stops.

"You are more than your memories," Jakir continues. Never stopping the repeated motion over the same spot. He moves the edge so slowly I almost forget what he's doing. He repeats the motion, causing my breathing to slow and tears to dry on my face. The fourth time he does it, the Bond opens up like never before.

With my eyes still closed, I feel every emotion pour from him into me, and from me into him. At one point, the blend of feelings becomes a whole piece. Grief, sadness, pain, anger, protectiveness, even love flows like the blood running down my back in tiny little drops. Sometime in that opening he feels the physical pain start to become more present, so he stops the carving. I open my eyes to see the bloodied knife on the floor.

"I'm so sorry," I'm not even sure if he hears me.

"Don't ever apologize for that," he gently guides my chin to look up at him. "Never."

"We only just met and you're having to rebuild some broken person."

"I would do it a million times. Even without the bond, because I know in another life, one where the world doesn't end, we are best friends."

I breathe in deeply, wincing slightly at the stretching of the cut on my back.

"Will it scar?" a part of me is sickeningly hopeful.

"Most definitely, I cut deeply enough."

"What if this happens again?"

"Then I cut again. Every time your mind starts to sink into that dark place, I will pull you up. As long as it is what you want, we will make art from the pain."

"Only you."

"Of course, only me," his forehead touches mine gently.

Chapter 10

Neither Harlow nor Jacob made any mention of last night's events. I was grateful for it. I understood that if they stuck around long enough, I would need to explain what happened. Those memories would not be shared freely, nor would it do any good to share them with people I might be stuck with for a while. Perhaps one day.

Our trip began with the two newcomers questioning Jakir's decision to cross to somewhat desolate land in front of us. It was only fair, considering that it seemed like water and life did not exist for miles past the borders of the broken city.

Feathers landed on Jakir's shoulder, pecked at my cheek and then flitted away.

"Bye fuckers, bye bye," he screamed as he flew off.

"Guess he's tired of us," I shrug.

"Maybe he'll come back, and with a cleaner mouth," the large man next to me says, giving me a pointed look.

I jerk off my imaginary penis towards him in response.

"None of us have any idea when we're going to find a good place to remain for a while," Harlow starts.

"Or where we'll be safe enough to settle permanently," her companion adds.

"Look, I know all three of you have had a bit more time in this new world of..." I struggle to admit the word.

"Dragons?" Jakir pushes gently.

I nod and continue without repeating the strange word, "but all I know is that I have this gut feeling we need to keep moving north. Maybe that same gut feeling will stop once we reach a suitable place."

"She has a good point. Might as well get going," she decides.

"It's an unknown distance, we should shift," Jacob swiftly removes his shirt showing thin but hard muscles on a clearly survivalist body. I glance at him, and watch as Harlow does the same, both of them removing all of their clothes.

"You should turn your face away, and undress," Jakir whispers in my ear. My arms immediately fold over my chest in a defensive position at the notion of removing my clothes – even willingly – in front of everyone. After removing his shirt, he looks to me again and frowns at my lack of nudity, which quickly shifts into realization when the bond shows him my fear.

"There's nothing weird about it, you'll get used to it Kali," the blond smiles at me but it's not returned. Her confusion matches Jacobs.

"Just take off-"

"She will not be removing anything, I will find a way to carry her," my Bonded cuts her off.

My thoughts do not spiral but instead firmly situate themselves into a dark corner of my mind. Flashes of a bonfire and knives occupy me until Jakir's presence leaves my side. The emptiness pulls my head up to look for him only to find him about thirty-five yards away. I immediately move towards him but a huge hand stops me.

"Don't, love, I need the room."

I stop, arms still crossed, and wait to watch the transformation again. His body isn't thin like Jacob's, in fact it's incredibly muscular with some clearly unblemished skin. Muscles move like thick cords as he takes a knee and places his opposite hand on the ground. Even with the distance between us my mind still struggles to comprehend his height.

"Why is he kneeling?" I ask the two flanking me.

"Have you not seen him shift before?" Harlow asks, the concern in her voice causes my anxiety to rise.

"He did but he didn't kneel. I can't even remember my own, actually," I mumble.

She breathes out heavily and wordlessly takes my hand, almost too firmly. When I look down to see it, I hear a loud snap from Jakir. This time, I don't freeze. My eyes snap up to him quickly. Another snap, like bones breaking from a fall. Pain radiates down the bond, obviously muted by him so as not to cause me stress. The next snap is loud enough I flinch, and he groans. Instead of watching in awe like last time, my entire body shakes and pushes me forward to him. I don't go far as Harlow will not release my hand.

"Let me go, he's in pain!" I lock eyes with her and a strange warmth builds behind mine. Her hold falters for a second, but not long enough for me to pull away.

"He's fine, I promise," she attempts to comfort me despite my continuing attempt to escape. "This is part of every shift."

Jacob steps back to begin putting distance between us. Soon enough the sound of bones breaking is coming from both men. Jakir seems to have broken every bone in his body and is quickly expanding. Skin stretches and tears, healing itself every time a new tear forms. I gasp as tiny bits of glitter seem to start pouring out of his skin, quickly growing in size into what I realize is scales. Each of them bigger than my hand they continue their reveal, growing and shifting as his body changes into something new. The talons that came out first are also growing with alarming speed to consistently match the size of his form.

I feel a sharp rise in pain from him as a nub pokes out from right above a shoulder blade to form into a small wing also enlarging rapidly. Everything is happening so quickly I almost forget the pain coming across the connection between us. Almost.

His head snaps around to look at me as I poke at the bond, trying to ease the pain I can feel.

"No," his voice doesn't sound the same, its normal smoothness is replaced by a rough, almost unintelligible rasp. He doesn't say anything else, just groans more as his face contorts and begins extending. His nose quickly recedes into his face, spreading to accommodate the rapidly expanding jaw. Harlow pulls me back as his entire form reaches a height close to thirty feet.

It feels like the air around me is both too heavy and not present, because my breathing switches between labored or rapid. Words refuse to come out of my mouth. Just pure awe, fear, even excitement overwrite the ability to speak.

The next sound to leave him is more of a rumble, bringing me to watch as his throat extends into a lengthy part, and a massive tail whips around behind him nearly too close to my head. Absolutely no fear fills me when it does come close despite there being a solid reason to feel it.

Eventually, it stops. I loose a heavy breath and pull my hand from Harlow's.

Jakir's final form is more than double what I thought it was when I initially gauged his height. Golden scales move like water as he rotates towards me while lowering his head to be in front of me. I take in everything about him, the wings that seemed too big to carry, a tail resting on the ground, muscles that match the physique his human form carries.

A part of me still wants to fight the reality of this new world. Wants to fight the fact that I, too, will be doing this soon enough. I need more proof, to touch what was a fairytale before.

The heat has made his scales warm to the touch, seemingly reflecting most of what the sun was bearing down on us. His eyes close gently when I drag my hand up his face. I can only reach halfway up to his eyes with my arm fully extended.

"Holy fuck," I whisper.

Immediately his eyes fly open and stare down at my small form.

"Bro that was completely warranted, I refuse to take back anything."

His new form is unreal, like the hero of a story that had that beautiful color everyone else wanted. His face was gentle somehow, despite the teeth that probably rested inside his mouth and the size of the tail that could kill me in one blow.

Snapping begins again behind me causing me to flinch. When I turn,

Harlow is going through the same process.

Golden scales come into my peripheral vision as my partner's head hovers beside me. Dust stirs up as his tail sweeps in front of me and gently pushes me into his side. One golden eye flicks down to look at me as if to say "stay put". His head raises and disappears out of my vision as I watch the other shift occur.

As her scales present themselves, they are initially blue along her back but fade into white as the ones on her belly protrude. The ombre pattern becomes much more prevalent as she grows to her full size, something probably close to five or so feet shorter.

Either her shift occurs faster, or the newness of a human changing into a dragon is wearing off. Like watching a video for a second time. The awe never wears off, however, still silencing me as it happens. Her form, despite being the same species as Jakir, varied quite a bit. They were so vastly different I began to wonder how much they could vary across the world.

Actually, it's "we" now...

For the size of Jakir's head he somehow manages to gently nudge my shoulder, pulling me away from staring at the long horns on the blue dragon that sweep back to lay against the length of her head. Turning, I see that he's placed his tail so I may climb up onto his back. Not seeing a place for me to sit without risking falling off I throw my hands in the air at him.

The only response I get is his eyes closing and a small tilt of what might be considered lips.

A dragon's body isn't as slick as one might think, just the tiniest bit rougher than a new leaf. Thankfully that was enough for me to get a leg up on his tail and not slide down. Due to his body being too tall he had to lift his tail to carefully slide me up and onto his back.

The extreme dip between his shoulder blades catches me off guard, resulting in me sliding down into it. It actually proves to be a great place to stay, hopefully shielding me from the wind as he flies, and keeping me from falling off.

"This will be fine, I'm sure you'll feel the panic if I start plummeting to my death, Jakir."

His neck allowed him to just almost turn his face a complete one-eighty from facing forward. After an assessment of where I was and a questioning tone sent down the bond, we nod.

Snorting sounds from behind Harlow, who moves toward us revealing she's completely shifted - and a now dark green Jacob. His wings snap out to begin pumping. With a quick jump, he glides into the air like his size means nothing. The last to leave, Jakir pumps his oversized wings and I jolt in the human-carrying pocket. Nothing to grab onto means simply keeping my eyes open to ensure I know where to lean.

My back presses into his neck allowing me to be wedged between the two massive scale-covered bones moving on either side of me. My feet plant firmly to keep myself from slipping.

The first strong gust of wind as we gain altitude actually has me relaxing instead of hyperventilating. Its strength instills strength in me pushing the anxiety down into nothingness. Every few feet we climb I feel my body ease into the feeling of wind wrapping itself around me, the sight of watching the ground become further and further away. It relaxes me more than I have been since waking up alone.

Once we've leveled out I build the courage to actually kneel. The new view below me proves that Jacob was right earlier, we would have been traveling for weeks if we had tried to walk it. Shame of my lack of ability to shift trickled in. I knew I had shifted before, had felt that surge of power before blacking out. They all managed to learn how to do it, so why couldn't I?

So far, Jakir had not only saved my life, but also killed for me, fed me, and baby sat me. Now it seemed like Harlow and Jacob had been pulled into the same boat. Why couldn't I do one thing to make it so people didn't have to keep helping me?

Right along with my track record, the bond opens up and I feel my emotions being shared between us. I quickly attempt to stop it, but he stops me so he can read everything. The feeling of someone flipping the pages of my mind makes me want to tuck myself into a dark corner. It finally stops as a warm touch brings my eyes back into focus, he was comforting me. A shake of my head tightens the leash on our bond, only allowing him to sense that I'm still on his back.

Pulling my eyes from the desolate wasteland below us I search for our companions around us. Harlow is slightly ahead but off to our right, while Jacob is twisting around in the air to occasionally check behind us. He's a lot easier to see than the woman in front of us who tends to blend in with her surroundings while flying. My mind mentally flips her color pattern, noting that she'd be practically invisible from the ground if that were the case. As a dragon though, having the pattern she does now would protect her from other dragons that might pose a threat.

I want to know in that moment so badly what my color will be, what my form will look like to those around me. Will I entice people to stare, or will I instill a deep respect like Jakir did? I want power, wanted something that would stop people from ever thinking they could touch me again. That want burns deep in my belly, so much I can feel the weight settling in. A weight that I'll let sit there until I have it around me like a suit of armor.

Jakir

I could tell her mind was twisting every which way as I flew silently. The bond let me see that her feelings were mostly dark, probably reviewing the past week's occurrences. The small amount of information she had granted me about her survival up until I found her told me she was very much stuck on an independent track. Slowly but surely I was working my way into her absolute trust. The bond had already done most of the work for me in that regard by opening up the deepest emotional connection I had ever felt. It was both terrifying and exhilarating to know that at any point we could feel one another's truest emotion. Instinct told me to run from that, but my months of loneliness said otherwise.

Quite quickly Kali had learned how to control what flowed through that bond. Trauma could do that – could teach someone how to put up every wall. Even now, she held a tight leash on it so as to only allow me to ensure she hadn't fallen off from between my shoulder blades.

There was something wretched growing in her soul that might become too awful to control if I didn't move quickly to steer it in another direction.

"Jakir!" she screams suddenly, I flinch my head away and shake it. My hearing is good enough she didn't need to yell.

I turned my head slightly so as to see her with a single eye.

"Left slightly, we need to go left," she said a bit quieter. Still hurts my sensitive eardrums.

The others could hear her as well and began tilting their bodies in that direction. We were soundless as we lowered our altitude so she could see the terrain better. The dry brown we had been flying over for a better part of the day was starting to turn into gray rock that slowly built up into mountains ahead. These mountains weren't like the ones I had been through before, in fact they were nothing like I had seen before.

These gray beasts stood taller than fifteen thousand feet, their peaks disappearing into wispy clouds that seemed to wrap gently around each point. Snow covers a large majority of the caps resulting in a distinct change in color on them.

"We're close...just not yet," she says in a level tone. Her end of the bond was as tense as the wall she had put up.

Let me in, Kali, let me see what you feel.

The limitations of being in this form were frustrating, as was her ability to block me out.

Snorting came from my right. Harlow snorted again when we made eye contact and dipped her snout down towards the ground. She wanted to land soon.

With an agreeing dip of my head I push harder with my wings, building speed to fight against the wind that viciously whipped around the mountains. A few caves were present, but I didn't land until I found one deep enough for us to be safe in.

Jacob and Harlow let me land first, my size allowing them to see just how much room there was as well as all of us wanting to get Kali into safety immediately. Every movement around us felt like a threat, the feeling of danger creeping across our scales.

My landing was rougher than intended due to a powerful gust of wind that forced me to tuck my wings in. Fighting it would have dragged me over the ledge that lurked not so far behind my back legs.

"Fuck, a little rougher next time yeah?" my friend complains.

The cursing was really unnecessary.

My back right claws open to drop the back pack I had picked up before we left right as I begin to shift back into my human form.

Kali

The same cracking and tearing sounds happen as Jakir shrinks back to his human form. I feel only the smallest bit of shame staring at him when he was done. His body is in amazing shape and the dark skin that seems to glide over muscles makes him even more of a dare to stare at. Picking up the bag from behind him, he walks towards me into the cave.

"Aren't you going to get dressed?" I ask incredulously. Temperatures here were not forgiving, biting wind wasn't making it any better.

"I will once I'm out of the way so the others can land," he replies.

Harlow and Jacob's landings were much softer, but they still struggled not to be pushed off the edge by gusts of wind. They pick up their small bags as well as they walk into the cave with us. Clothing is quickly put on even though the cold seems to seep into our bones a lot less than when we were human.

"I think our body temperatures are a lot higher now," I think out loud. "Looking at how fast the ice forms and the type of snow on these mountains, as humans we never would have been able to survive this."

Three sets of eyes watch me closely, silently agreeing with my new revelation.

"We've changed to survive," Harlow responded.

"No," I turn quickly and correct her. "Humans changed to survive. We just got moved up to the top of the food chain."

"That's an arrogant way to think," Jakir's voice almost so low I didn't catch him. Something about the cold gave me the strength to respond confidently.

"Not thinking that way will ensure you're *not* at the top. You can choose to think however you like, but I'd prefer to not waste my time around people who'd rather be humble when it is unnecessary."

It wasn't hurt that flashed through his eyes, rather a sign that he was clearly taken aback by my rapid growth from the shy, weak woman he had saved weeks ago. I raised an eyebrow, challenging him to argue against what I knew was the truth.

Tension seeped into the air putting the other two people at a standstill. Nobody moved a muscle until Jakir closed his eyes and dropped his head in concession to me.

"I never liked arrogance, I also never liked dying."

"Then it looks like we're on the same page."

"I will not change myself to become some rabid animal only focused on survival-"

"I never asked you to. All I want is someone that has the confidence to accept they're stronger than humans, rather than ignore it."

His eyes brighten a bit, he understands the point. A small smile appears, whether it was happiness at his new understanding or my new confidence I didn't know. Satisfied with having made my point I turn towards Jacob and Harlow carefully watching me.

"Hey, no arguments I wanna live too," Jacob threw his hands up in mock defense and a dorky smile.

I sweep my eyes to the blond sitting against the wall, dragging a stone across a knife that appeared out of their bag. Her blue eyes seem just as bright as mine feel.

"I think I am going to like our little Samle very much."

The wicked grin that matched mine was all I needed to know she already was.

Chapter 11

"We need a game plan," Jacob brought up, making me break eye contact with Harlow.

My eyebrows pulled together in confusion at his remark, "We have one."

"No, you have one, we have no idea where we're going."

"We're close, I can promise you that. It's my gut, my gut keeps telling me to move north and with every mile we move in that direction the feeling gets stronger."

"So we're effectively playing a game of hot and cold," Harlow sighed. She stopped playing with her knife to slide it back into her black boot. "How do we know when we get there, when we don't have to keep moving?"

"The Samle I was with seemed to kind of just *fit in* with the land they lived on, when I asked the leader – or rather what they called their *Konge* – he said it just felt right," Jakir stared at the ground in front of him. His mouth seemed to be rolling the foreign word around his tongue.

Jacob latched onto the most useless part of that statement by asking, "Konge? Interesting, where did that come from?"

"Doesn't matter Jake," his girlfriend responded, "what matters is if they had to do the same thing we are currently doing. What if this gut feeling isn't right?"

"You have a better idea?" I question.

No one does.

"So did they have to find it?" I started the conversation up again.

"He said when everything burned up, he and his bonded were already

97

together, the connection formed when they both woke up. Did a few days of traveling but eventually felt like he could just stay."

"Sounds like the same thing happening to us, there's no downside to following this feeling."

"Maybe," Harlow added. "We end somewhere safe away from that awful group of boys."

They had somehow encountered them too.

"What was it like?" my voice softens a bit, unsure of what happened to them.

"We never got close enough to find out, just saw them pull another guy and his girlfriend out from a house. They gave the boy an option," Jacob's eyes turned dark with his next words. "Join them or end up like her."

"Jacob-" Harlow reached out to touch his arm. He didn't pull away, but the touch did nothing to ease him.

"Th-they took her clothes off right there and started doing horrible things to her. Harlow and I couldn't run because they would have seen us, so we had to stay an' listen. The boyfriend was a god damn coward, didn't do a thing to save her. She tried running a bunch, the last time she ran they just shot her in the back of the head."

"She died not having to see them" my weak attempt at comfort somehow washed away most of the tension in his body.

"You didn't see how scared she was-"

"I don't need to, because I was in her position too."

Sad brown eyes snap up to mine. Harlow is the tense one now and looks towards me enough to put me in her peripherals.

"I'm sorry I didn't mean-"

I wave my hand, "I know you didn't. I was just offering a position of understanding. I was in her spot too, the only reason I got out was because he found me."

Jakir's head doesn't move, most likely too heavy with the memories of how I looked when he saved me.

"I promise you won't ever be in that position again," she promises me. There is so much weight in her words that my breath whooshes out of my lungs. I had never heard someone sound so sincere.

"Thank you," I feel vulnerable. This vulnerability isn't awful and consuming, I wasn't strung up by my wrists against my will. I was just open, willingly, in front of these new people. Unconsciously I rub the faint scars on my wrist from rope burn.

"We should sleep, it's better to get moving early in the morning," golden eyes stare into me. He motions me over while laying out a blanket.

"Not a very comfortable bed," I mumble.

"You can lay your head on my chest," he whispers back.

I don't hesitate when he lays down on his back and stretches out an arm. Warmth and the sound of his beating heart lull me into an uneasy sleep.

I rise first, before the sunlight even crawls over the peaks across the cave. Pink hues seem to paint the world in a happy color, reminding me of Carly suddenly. She always liked the easy way the sky shifted in the mornings.

Sleep wasn't easy being full of nightmares, ones that ranged from having knives dragged down my chest, to watching people's skin melt off again on that beach. Sometimes I even found myself running through that forest again, the air around me becoming stagnant causing me to fall. Every single time, I fell straight into one of those bodies that hung in the clearing.

Jakir gently eases down next to me, hanging one foot off the ledge while propping the other up. His bicep brushes against my shoulder as he leans back onto his hands. Silence is comfortable with him. It's the easiest thing I had done since this world flipped itself belly-up and died. I broke it first knowing he was going to wait until I did.

"They're deep sleepers."

Only a nod.

"We should wake them up, I want to get moving."

"I'll wake them, we'll need to find food immediately. We can't keep flying in our dragon form without sustenance."

"The only thing we're going to find out here is wild animals and plants, we don't know what's safe and what's not."

He smiles gently, casting his gaze to me, "You'll find that the gut feeling in that form will tell us just about everything we need to know for survival."

My face turns expressionless at the lack of understanding of what it was like to be in that form. I stood at the same time Jakir did but remained at the edge of the cliff pondering when I would finally feel that new body. The new body that hadn't been touched by those foul men that destroyed every inch of my body with both visible and invisible scars.

I'm going to be better one day, I felt my inner voice echo in my head. *I'm going to be better than them.*

My internal planning stops as I hear Jacob and Harlow move quickly. I wait at the edge for them to line beside me, all of them now naked for the shift.

For the first time I notice Jacob's hair length, how the sides of his head were shaved closely but a long ponytail was tied back keeping the hair out of his face. As my eyes drag down to see his ponytail stop at his shoulder blades I feel eyes on me. Warm, brown eyes smile at me.

"I know it's hard to look away when I'm just sitting here like a buffet."

Harlow smacks the back of his head while frowning. He complains playfully with her while grabbing her hand before she pulls it away.

I jerk my chin up at Harlow, "You change first, find something for you all to eat. We'll follow behind."

"I won't mind lookin' at some tail while traveling," Jacob grins like a high school boy in love. Clearly Harlow struggles to bite back the smile.

Jakir wraps a hand around my bicep to gently guide me back, giving the other two enough room to shift. Once they're done he moves forward. I tail him, feeling a need to stay close.

"Kali I need-"

"No, you don't," green and blue blurs dive down into the canyon below. "I know my limits, I'm learning yours."

I don't move, so he begins the process.

I only duck once to dodge the massive wing sweeping over my head. A golden eye meets mine with concern splashed across his face. He's clearly being careful, but so am I.

In a swell of trust I open the bond completely as I continue staring into the only eye I can see. Even in a dragon's face emotion is still slightly apparent, making it easy for me to see the surprise when he feels the Bond open. I let him feel everything, down to the self-hatred, fear, and caution that sits coiled around my spine. He gently prods with his mind to see everything while also pulling me into his feelings.

No, too much. It's too much.

I don't close off the Bond completely, rather I put up a wall that stops me from seeing his side. I wasn't ready to see every vulnerable part of him when I was still so broken. I needed to learn how to carry my own baggage before picking up anybody else's.

A harsh blow out of his nose snaps us out of the tiny bubble we were in. I say nothing as I climb onto his back the same way I did yesterday.

Jacob and Harlow are across the gap sitting next to one another on a ledge. Their tails swish against one another gently in a loving way.

Jakir grunts as his only warning before diving into the wicked depths below. My stomach lurches with adrenaline as he dives towards broken rocks and pillars of stone that could kill if he didn't have wings. Seeing the ground rush up to me was dangerous but it felt so right to have wind scream past my face. A smile pulls at my lips, partially made by the force of the wind, partially made by the happiness of freedom. I feel my nail beds heat up as black talons push out my nails in the thrall of excitement, a part of me happy that they don't just come out when I'm scared.

He doesn't stop when I thought he would, causing a gasp to come out of me. His wings are tucked in tightly around him, almost forming additional walls on either side of me. I lean up to see over his shoulder when he suddenly snaps them out, yanking his head upward. My body weight shifts back, almost sliding me right off of him and down into the ravine below. The only thing stopping me is my talons sunken in between scales into flesh, securing me to him. Our bond doesn't flinch, confirming that he can't even feel it.

A laugh bubbles out of my throat so strongly I don't even bother trying to stop it. It was the first time since being reborn that I felt free and safe. Vibrations come up through my legs and into my chest confusing me until I realize it's practically purring coming from Jakir, though the sound is more like a tiger's chuffing.

A current helps him glide up along the flat wall to meet with the open air of smaller mountains, causing us to slow as we level out. Harlow is a few miles ahead sweeping up and down the sides of gray rock looking for food. Her white belly makes it hard to see when she turns away from us occasionally. Being able to see her every once in a while, is the only thing calming the strange need to protect her in my chest. I rub my sternum, trying to rub away the stress and put myself back into the happy state I was in only minutes ago.

Suddenly the mountains around us seem to drop into silence, marking the same timing of me losing track of Harlow. I silently begin to slow my breathing, hoping to see her pop up again. Jacob glides up next to Jakir and I, having to slow the beat of his wings to stay next to us. His eyes search the range ahead as well as his head tilts minimally listening for sounds of his girlfriend.

The silence continues for a few more minutes stretching us into tightly wound worry.

I see her snap into the side of the mountain before I hear the sound of rocks crumbling. Something strains in her back talons before going limp, just as she drops it, she grabs another form and drops it from a significant height successfully killing it. Jacob speeds ahead to help, using the same methodology to kill four more of what look like goats. Watching the two of them working together is absolutely enthralling, like a dance of two hawks.

Jakir stays back clearly trying to keep me out of potential harm's way, which I don't blame when I watch more rock explode from the side of the cliff as Jacob jams talons against it while grabbing the last creature.

As they settle down on the ground at the base of the mountains where all of the prey was dropped Jakir lowers us – much more gently this time.

"That was a lot more graceful," I comment, slipping from his back. A short growl is all I get in return. None of them shift back into human form. "Oh…you don't plan on eating this as a human."

The couple begin tearing into what I now see are goats, goats that are the size of moose. Another change from the old world.

Jakir rips open his own with a delicate claw never hesitating to dig in.

Content with ignoring the hunger in my belly and just watching them I sit down on the ground to lean against the wall. I hadn't had anything but a few pieces of dried meat and a can of soup in the past two days. My hands and knees were beginning to show signs of malnutrition and starvation. My metabolism seemed to be working a lot faster now. Thoughts drift to the idea of a hot meal that we would all sit around and have. Even if it wasn't delicate dishes spread out in front of us, those eating around me felt comforting.

The sounds of chewing suddenly stop as my stomach groans loudly enough to wake the dead.

"Sorry," I whisper, closing my eyes and leaning back.

A snap breaks the silence followed by my foot being nudged. When I open my eyes, I see Harlow pushing a leg of meat towards me. The hoof is what's nudging me.

I wince at the raw meat and shake my head, "I'm not a fan of raw meat."

Her teeth click and her jaw snaps, frustrated with me. She pulls away but leaves the leg. Jacob nudges her neck with his snout and motions to the meat, then breathes heavily through his nostrils.

The adrenaline of riding with Jakir has sapped the last of my energy. All I want to do now is fall into a deep sleep, one I know isn't just because I'm tired.

Weeks of travel and fear have worn my body down, pushing it to the limit it had now reached. Everything is shutting down, not going to sleep.

Jakir shoves his massive face into mine, sniffing me quickly from head to toe, which honestly doesn't take almost any movement from his head. He groans and swings his head to Harlow, almost too quickly for my eyes to track. Concerned eyes dash between green and blue begging for help. Jacob nudges Harlow harder, now also watching me with concern.

A couple more snaps from Harlow and she takes the leg from me to drag it to the other side of the wall.

"Thank you though," I mumble.

Jakir pushes his tail behind me and wedges himself into a curled position. His body wraps around mine in a protective ball.

"Protecting me won't stop the hunger, love," I whisper. I know now that his hearing in this form was incredibly sensitive, so I needed to be careful.

Jacob stood back hunching down like a cat ready to pounce. I realize suddenly that Harlow is about to do something when I feel a wave of heat crash into me. Two instincts flare up simultaneously, one to run from the similar heat that I thought killed me, another to stare at the magnificent colors.

Blue almost the same as her scales was being blasted at the leg, some parts almost white flame. I only caught half a second of the sight before being covered by Jakir's wing.

"Hey I want to see!"

A loud growl makes it clear that the heat outside of the shell I'm in is too much for my human body. Only another two seconds pass before the cold begins to seep in again. The wing moves away, revealing a burnt leg in front of me presented by a tense Harlow.

"You...you cooked it for me?" Even with the dumb question she nods her head, and uses a talon to rip the meat open. Blackened skin and fur gives way to brown meat that's well overcooked. It didn't matter how overcooked it was, I could finally eat.

My hands grab the now cooled meat and shove it quickly into my mouth. I have to pause and take a deep breath as I eat, almost causing myself to choke on the ball of food stuck in my esophagus. Eating snow seems to help it go down, giving me more room to eat. The others finish the rest of the meat, leaving only vulture-worthy bits on the bones. The heads are untouched, massive horns on all but one.

"Wait," I swallow one of my last bites. "Take the heads with us, we can use the horns."

No one questions me as they each pick up two heads to hold in their claws. Jakir's claws are too big to carry a head, forcing Jacob to pick up his load. Harlow keeps her front paws free, most likely due to the fact that she's our biggest form of defense.

She takes the lead, watching ahead for signs of danger as we climb over the final band of mountain range stretching both east and west. The fog slowly begins to dissipate as a forest of what seemed like dead trees revealed itself below us. A hideous smell reaches us, even this far up. Hoping to block it out, I tuck myself as far as I can into Jakir's back and shut my eyes.

It feels like only moments before I open them again to see the awful smelling forest behind us. Getting onto my knees I look over Jakir's shoulder to see a massive tree in the distance. The wind is carrying us, some current strong enough for him to merely glide on with an occasional pump of his wings.

Excitement bubbles up my chest, adrenaline pumping from my heart not as strong as early in the morning, but still present.

That's it, that's where we need to go.

With every fiber of my being I know that it's what my body had been looking for. A large flat space of land stops at a cliffside, which drops in a slope on either side. It creates a crescent shape around a tree that reaches high enough to touch gentle clouds floating past. That tree, whatever was around it, would be the thing that gave Jakir and I something to build off of. I have to crank my head both left and right to be able to see where it finally flattens into the land.

To the north I see the beginnings of mountains after quite some stretch of rolling plains. To the south, only flat plains with various textures. I begin slapping Jakir's back while laughing, his confusion, then immediate excitement snapped through the bond like an electric shock.

"That's it! Harlow go scope it out," I shout, not caring about the lightly scolding look my ride gives me. She looks between me and the tree off in the distance a few times, before moving as quickly as her lithe body allowed her.

Jakir and Jacob followed suit, only slowing slightly to give her time to do her job. Her excitement is like a new breath into my lungs, as she sweeps down near Jakir looking at him. She gently tips one of his wings causing him to tilt, then smiles as much as a dragon can. It looks more like a snarl.

Sunset begins to settle on the land marking the end of our last day of searching. Anxiety trickles in, making me want to see it all up close more and more. A lake appears beyond the gray and tan rock that make up the perfectly vertical cliffside, though it's a bit further behind the tree by a solid distance.

After what feels like ages Jakir touches down onto soft, pillowy grass that reaches my knees. Harlow lands near the water with Jacob, both of them shifting into their human forms to tentatively dip their toes into it. Jakir swings his head around waiting for me to climb down.

"I'm nervous," I whisper. "I don't know why but…it's so new. I've been looking for this place for more than a year and now…"

He doesn't move, just watches me.

"Now I'm not only here, but I'm here with someone I'm supposed to be emotionally attached to for the rest of my life, an absolute stray neuron of a man, and a woman that I think would kill for me."

He turns his head slightly, craning his neck to look towards them at the lake. A silent minute passes before I slide down onto the soft grass.

It's softer than I imagine it to be, like being brushed against by a cat's tail.

The warm ball in my chest begins to warm as I move towards the tree. Its size is more shocking the closer I get. Just another to add to the possibilities this planet had to offer after being wiped clean and made anew. The leaves are bigger than Jakir's hand, nearly as big as my face. Its exact type was a mystery, especially since I didn't exactly study trees before everything went to shit.

My hand extends out to drag my fingertips along the bark, as I do my chest feels almost too warm. Air leaves my lungs. I don't even notice the overwhelming pain until it's too late. I whip around to Jakir with a hand around the base of my neck.

"Jak-"

A choking sound, more like a wheeze covers my call for his name. Afraid of what was happening I shut off the bond as gently as I can, not wanting to hurt him. He wasn't in dragon form anymore, just standing with pants on facing the setting sun. I collapse to my knees as air stops entering my lungs completely and my talons shred from my nail bed so fast skin tears.

I try to scream, but nothing comes out from my crushed airways. Panic sets in as the same pain I was in once before - in front of so many men - rips through my body. Skin feels like it's tearing and stitching itself back together, a hot itchy feeling.

Everything hurts make it stop make it stop make it stop it hurts

I hear splashing from my right where two people were before.

What are their names I don't know their names

The man in front of me finally shifts, beginning to turn as his face finally contorts into confusion, maybe even fear as he turns to me.

The last thing I see is his golden eyes meeting mine.

The last thing I feel is my hands hitting the ground, black talons sinking into the hard dirt below.

Then my vision edges with black as my first bone breaks itself apart.

Chapter 12

Jakir

I should have known the second my mind went silent. That was the first point I failed her. She closed off the Bond so gently, while I was distracted taking in our new home, that I didn't notice until it was too late. I hadn't expected her to be able to do that. There was absolute silence within me. It's unnerving. Like a candle losing its flame.

I turn my head, time seeming to slow as the Bond wildly searches for Kali. When I meet her beautiful green eyes it is not hope and wonder I see, but pain and suffering. She's on her knees in the grass, almost hidden completely as she falls to the ground. I watch blood drip down her hands when the black talons tear through her nail beds too fast for her blood to clot. The hand around the base of her throat drops to catch her as she falls to all fours.

"Kali!" my voice echoes across the area, causing Harlow and Jacob to cease whatever they're doing. Heads whip in my direction, but I pay no mind as I sprint to her.

My heart stops when I hear the first crack.

The other two are running as quickly as they can towards us, but they have a mile to cover before reaching us.

Another crack reaches my ears, followed by another three that come from Kali's back.

Her eyes begin to glow, that primal power I can feel that makes her Dronning almost bringing me to my knees. I stumble but catch myself, finally reaching her broken form. As I touch her shoulder a low growl rips through her, nothing human about it.

Knowing she could finally breathe I tilt her chin up, "Kali it's okay just breathe, you're fighting the shift. You have to let it happen or it's just going to hurt more."

Her eyes drag up to my face with an empty look. I stop breathing when I see that nothing sits in them but malice.

"She's finally shifting?! This is great, what were you so worried about?" Jacob asks, slowing to a halt.

They both look to her with interest, but Harlow's face falls as she realizes what's happening.

"Kali isn't here," she whispers. Her arm goes in front of Jacob pushing him back, even though she steps forward. I put a hand up stopping her.

"Kali, listen to me," she's still watching me with nothing but anger. "I think this might not be your first time because you're able to fight it so much, so you know how to do this."

While I speak small bones are changing. I pause my speaking, and suddenly the shift rushes forward. Her body convulses causing her claws to shred through the dirt as she hunches into a ball. The bones sound louder than I had ever heard when someone shifted.

"Jakir, you need to move back," Harlow warned me. She wasn't moving either.

"No, I'm staying as close as possible until she's done. You need to shift now in case she lashes out in form; we don't know the extent of her size."

She nods and moves away as Jacob starts jogging back to the water, looking over his shoulder every few steps. Kali's eyes follow yet she does not; too involved in fighting the physical changes slipping through her.

A part of me aches to bend the knee as Kali's skin begins morphing into matte black scales, not shiny like so many I had seen before. They seem to absorb every wave of light around her as her body expands rapidly. Her angled jaw stays sharp as it extends out to stretch into a snout. I watch her teeth become sharp weapons. The long canines that swoop down across her lip would have shaken me to my core if I wasn't so focused on reopening the Bond. Everything she's experiencing in her first cognizant is nearly overwhelming. I can tell she's shifted before from her recounted memories to me of waking up to those bodies in the woods. But she doesn't remember that, and neither does her body.

I push harder, realizing that being gentle will get me nowhere. The animalistic side of her isn't just staring me down, it is pushing me back too.

"Let me in, love," I mumble.

Those bright green eyes connect mine at the last word, causing that wall to crumble. Fear and anger and panic and pain pour out like a dam being broken in a storm. Tears form in my eyes at the depth of each emotion she feels. My own talons began pushing through, demanding my body to shift with her. I don't need to change like she did, I have to fight it so she can see my face every second and know she isn't alone.

I begin pushing the love I've already developed for her into her, all those days on the road and learning every expression or quirk she had that made me want to keep her close. Our Bond causing a true connection to develop quickly. I push the feeling I had when she trusted me enough to drag the blade of a knife into her skin into her side of the Bond.

Her body finally slows to more of a swift change than a jerky one, I relax the tension built up in my shoulders slightly. My eyes drag along her wings, spotting massive claws at the tip of each wing digit. Her tail had already fully extended up to the spike that protruded from the end, allowing the body to play catch up.

Her growth finally reduces its speed, then stops as she extends her neck to her full height putting her at just over a third of the tree's height. I try to come up with some number, and can only roughly estimate a height of nearly eighty feet.

"My gods," I marvel, right as a massive sweep of wind pushes out from us to wash over the land.

Kali

Everything is so much clearer when my eyes aren't limited to the useless human ones. The tree's leaves are now so sharp it causes me to flinch back towards Jakir.

Wait.

I'm not human anymore.

My heart begins to pump harder, still maintaining the rapid pulse it had earlier. All five senses are on high alert, so as I breathe in in shock my lungs surprise me at their depth and smells overwhelm me.

Fear starts to slip in. I don't know this body. This body didn't get me through the past. I feel anger at my lack of understanding of how to operate in this form.

My eyes take in everything I can see of my new self. The huge talons that now match my size curl into the grass and dirt below me. The tail with a lethal spike at the end formed by sharp edges. What appears to be claws at the end of every curved bone that creates the structure of my wings.

My scales are the last thing to grow, then the transformation finally stops.

They don't shine like the others do, instead they soak up every ounce of light the remaining sunlight has to offer. Night is falling quickly and I find it hard to see the edges of myself.

"Kali," Jakir whispers.

I whip my head at him in surprise. I can tell how quiet he had whispered yet I had heard him like he said it directly into my ear even louder.

"You can't speak in this body like we do as humans," the invasion of another voice in my head edges me back towards defensive territory. Despite recognizing Harlow's voice, as well her dragon form mere yards from me,

I curl my lip back in a warning.

She cowers down by lowering her body to the ground and dropping her head slightly. Her eyes still meet mine. I try to make sense of her reaction to me, but I'm too flustered to fully process it.

"I'm sorry I didn't mean to startle you, I just want to help."

"Harlow, don't push too far. Give her a second to adjust," Jakir warns, a warm edge to his tone that states his unmoving command. Him speaking pulls my attention back to him.

"She seems...on edge," Jacob steps back away from us.

My lip relaxes as I let out a low rumble, warning them both to tread carefully. I want to ask so many questions about my new body, why it's taken so long for me to finally change or why my scales are so different.

"I'm going to shift now, love, so I can help you," Jakir begins carefully removing his clothing while keeping an eye on me. "I need you to promise me you won't do anything ridiculous."

I nod my head at him – still very much cautious of all movement around me.

A minute passes while he shifts into a starkly contrasting golden dragon to my mute black one. I turn to Harlow as his body begins changing everything inside of him.

How did you just speak to me?

My thought goes nowhere, clearly not being received. Frustration builds, making my heart rate increase. Harlow's usual bold self is practically bowed under my stare as I take in her body with new eyes. Blue eyes meet mine in question when I finally drag them up to her face. I stare down at her, suddenly pissed when she keeps staring at me. Her gutsy personality is quickly coming into play again, marking my last straw for patience.

I lunge for her, cracking my teeth together once in dominance. Just as I take another step towards her Jakir slips in front of me and snaps back. My unsure feet stumble back slightly, but I manage to catch myself before falling down. I raise my head, just barely able to look down at him at my full height. The muscles in my neck feel strange as they work to move my head like I want. I heave out a furious breath through my nostrils at my Bonded.

"I promise you that you do not want to challenge me," his voice shatters my calm edge I had been keeping. It irks some deep part of me that's thriving on this power flowing through my veins. Making me want to pin him down and rip open his snout.

So, I do.

My maw moves to close around his throat with what feels like lightning speed. He sees it coming and uses the boned edge of his wing to snap my head back. He darts past me, so I'm forced to spin to meet him head on.

Those oversized things aren't just for flying then.

I felt a part of my mind reel back at the violence I'm displaying towards the man who had saved my life. Desperately the two sides within me begin to fight, one acts like a human while the other acts like an animal. I don't stop vying for both sides despite knowing which one should come out on top.

"Kali stop-"

I sling my tail around catching the underside of a scale, allowing me to slice at the leathery skin underneath of his armor. Harlow shouts at me to stop, but I ignore it. A satisfying growl rolls towards me only blowing the flame of violence higher. Surprise rolls through his eyes, most likely at how fast I actually am in this form. Rearing up slightly I put a massive foot into his shoulder. I push off with my back feet, successfully pinning him to the ground. My blood surges at the rush of being on top. In a split-second decision, just as he hits the ground, I begin to close my teeth around his wing.

"Kali enough *already!"* Harlow screams. I begin to swing my tail around, blindly aiming for Jakir. I'm too uncoordinated, so she easily pins me down with her paw. I try to snap it out and nearly lose my balance.

I stop the pressure on Jakir's wing, not removing my teeth, just not fully clamping down. His head is on the ground being pinned by my other foot yet I still see the whites of his eyes as he strains to watch my long teeth hovering at the edge of danger. His eyes whip back and forth between mine and his wing for a few moments until I begin to pull myself back from him. Fear slowly melts into concern for both. Harlow is no longer lowered before me like a scared dog waiting for the hand to hit. I move my head from Jakir's wing to take in her position, seeing that she's prepared to jump on my back to take me down.

Lesson learned, I think sourly.

"*Stop this,*" Jakir grinds his teeth together, the grating sound making me shake my head. "*Stop letting the power control you and pull yourself together.*"

Before I can lash out again, Harlow adds in her own commentary. She's still managing to hold my tail down, but she's struggling with how hard I'm pulling at it. Jakir manages to slide my hold off of him, forcing me to regain my footing so I don't collapse pathetically.

"*You're not weak, Kali. We can all see that, so stop acting like it.*"

The words shock me back into a more humane thought process. I blink rapidly, clearing the fog of my shift until I have full control of my actions. Feeling embarrassed by my temper tantrum, I relax my body a bit. The human part of me is still standing up to dust herself off. Any remaining violence pools into a corner of my mind, waiting to be shaken up, yet keeping to itself. I open my mouth to try and talk, only for a strange rumble to come out.

"*You can speak to us with your mind,*" Jakir instructs. "*It just takes a lot of focus, think of pushing your thoughts to me like you push things down the Bond.*"

I attempt multiple times to communicate with both of them, mostly just receiving waiting stares, or accidentally pushing feelings down the now open Bond.

"*Focus on projecting them Kali,*" Harlow pushes. I slide my gaze over to her and let out a low growl in warning. Jakir keeps his eyes on me as she turns and dips her head to him.

"So...no more angry girl over here?" Jacob grins as he comes around the tree from where he'd hidden during the fight.

"*I am not a girl,*" I bite out.

Jakir and Harlow both attempt a grin at me suddenly relaxing. Pride from Jakir confirms that I have in fact managed to communicate with them.

I take a moment to let my eyes settle at taking in so much information before doing anything else. I can still see the blades of grass below me, even from this high up.

I begin moving away from the tree towards the mountains behind us. Though absolutely no moonlight is offered my eyes are still capable of seeing the outline of the dead forest. Its disturbing stillness invites a curious part of me to go to it to see just how dead it really is. Another day I will.

"We should shift back so we can talk," Jakir slides up next to me. *"This wasn't even close to being your first time shifting."*

"We can talk in the morning."

He doesn't argue as I settle to the cool ground for sleep. Hissing grass gently lulls me into a state of light rest as that forest whispers promises of answers to me. Next to me, Jakir does the same. His tail lays down curled with mine, his wing stretched to rest against me.

I only doze through the night, constantly lifting my head to keep an eye on our surroundings. The intense height of the cliff miles back from the tree stands proudly, even without the sun lighting up the crescent shape that wraps around the tree. The lake behind us whispers as small waves caress the shore of rocks. A few fish pop up at the surface every now and then, making me consider if it could be a source of food for us. There would have to be some reliable source nearby, otherwise I would have to move them again. Even if this land felt like a long-lost limb.

I look down to Jakir, sleeping so peacefully for someone who had their Bonded's mouth around their wing mere hours ago. I uncurl my tail from him to test how deeply he is sleeping. I feel a sense of responsibility for how much work he's done taking care of me. He deserves the rest after all he's done. When he doesn't stir, I remove myself from his side to make my way to Harlow, sleeping under the tree. Checking for Jacob, I see no signs of him and assume he's under her wing.

Not wanting to scare either, I nudge her head and lightly nip at her cheek. Groggy eyes slide open, quickly adjusting pupils taking in as much light as possible. I knew what I was going to ask of her was a lot, but I also knew she most likely wouldn't hesitate.

"I need to see the rest of this land, need to know how much feels like mine."

"It's weird, how you feel that. How we all seem to just...get along."

"You don't like it?"

"It's not that. I'm just wondering what's driving all of this."

She then huffs out of her nose, turning head back to what I think is sleep. Instead, she unfolds her wing and gently slides away from Jacob to leave him covered by the grass.

"Hope Jakir doesn't step on him," I say humorously.

"He'd like it," she says with knowing eyes. I let out what feels like a laugh but sounds more like coughing as I clutch a bag of clothes. She says nothing else, wordlessly following me north. We reach a point where the boys are out of ear shot and pause. Giving each other enough room, we both begin pumping our wings.

She takes off much sooner than me, climbing high in a corkscrew as I gain the strength to do the same. It feels like stretching sore limbs as I pump them harder, using longer strokes rather than short ones. Eventually, my feet lift from the ground as my wings carry me into the sky. I opt to fly diagonally out and up to gain altitude as Harlow keeps a slower pace. The further up I climb the easier it is to glide with the air currents around me. Eventually Harlow meets me at the same level, flying close enough that just a few feet separate our wingtips.

She keeps her eyes and head moving, taking in her surroundings constantly. I do the same, learning from every movement she makes. I pick up on the pieces of movement she ignores, and the ones that pull her attention. It doesn't take long before I'm getting the hang of not just flying, but of how to stay aware.

I'm flying behind her and to the right for a while when I realize that if I stay here, it's far easier to glide on the draft of air coming off of her body. I feel a need to ease her work load.

"Drop behind me, it'll make it easier on you," I direct gently.

She hesitates, then does so with an encouraging nod from me. As she falls behind me to my right her body relaxes, not having to work nearly as hard to fly. A sense of satisfaction settles in my chest knowing she doesn't have to use her body as much.

"What about you?"

I simply turn my head back to look at her, then face north again.

A full day passes - one I feel deeply with the distance from Jakir, and we still haven't reached the end of the lake. My need to explore this land I feel tied to encourages me, as does the knowledge that he's not too far. We stop for a few hours to rest our aching joints. I set myself down near the lake and begin the painful shift back into my human body. My mind feels sluggish as bones snap apart to shrink themselves, my skin too tight as it adjusts to a smaller body.

After a handful of minutes Harlow and I are both at the edge of the water completely nude. I take in her athletic body, not curvy to satisfy someone but instead muscular for fighting. Her thighs were large, clearly built via strength training of some sort to the point her quads curved out over her knees.

"I did a lot of lifting, even after the city fell."

I smile in appreciation, "I can tell. Hope you can keep it up."

We both wade into the water, appreciating the coolness of it coating our skin. Though the temperature had only gotten to around sixty degrees as we headed north, the work of flying was warming. The water remains as clear as it did near the tree having been filtered by some efficient plant. No sand could be stirred up since the bed had been made by smooth, flat rocks. As we dip our head into the water a flash catches my eye. I stand up to keep as much area around us in my vision. Another flash catches Harlow's eye.

"Did you see it?"

"It's why I stopped moving, back out slowly from the water."

We both step backwards slowly, careful to feel around behind us before planting our feet. Nothing else moves for a minute as we reach the shore.

"There," she points out.

I watch as another flash jumps completely out of the water.

"Oh," I chuckle. "It's fish. I've never seen one like them before."

"They could have teeth."

I shrug, "Let's see."

"Kali I don't think we should..." she trails off as I wade back into the water. She stays at the shore tense for action. The fish look like a kaleidoscope of colors as they flash their sides to the sun. I raise my hand to cover my eyes from the sun for a better view of them. As I turn to spot another one it flies up, smacking me in the elbow. I frown at both the smack and Harlow's giggle.

"Not so funny when the damn thing smacks you," I frown. My mind wanders to how Jakir might laugh at my current state, then speak some soft words about how stunning their scales are. I've only known him for a short time, yet I already feel connected with his mannerisms and personality. Just as I begin thinking about his face another one smacks me in the back. The others seem to get into a frenzy jumping out of the water and occasionally hitting me. I cover my head as I run back to shore to escape the onslaught of bruising fish.

"Don't worry, I'm sure I'll regret laughing if I bring you back to Jakir all bruised up," she grins, it reaches her eyes making the blue seem to sparkle. I playfully smack her arm then turn my attention back to the water.

My mind wanders back to him, remembering how murderous I had been towards them both. A gentle tug at the bond shows me only the faintest feeling of comfort. Increasing distance between us seemed to weaken communication through it, never having erased it. When morning had finally arrived after leaving, I felt him reach out in concern - only to back off politely once he confirmed I was still alive. He probably first thought I had taken Harlow out for slaughter.

"I'm sorry about...last night."

I continue to watch the fish fly as she turns to me.

"It's okay, we're not human anymore. That has to mean we have instincts that aren't human either."

I don't argue with whether or not it's okay. A part of me didn't want to apologize, the part that felt I had every right to show just how violent I could be. Another part had screamed for me to be human when I had my jaw hung open, lunging for Jakir, and had wanted me to apologize for a while. Harlow seems to recognize that battle, so I drop it.

We lay down under the sun, allowing our bodies to dry in the cool crisp air. Recognizing the opportunity I might not have for a while, I tell her about what happened to me. Explaining how I ran for so many days from that same group of men.

"They caught up eventually, they were mad. I think..." I speak cautiously, discerning suddenly what happened when I blacked out. "I think I killed a couple of them. I blacked out, everything would slow down for a couple seconds. I'd wake up later completely naked not even knowing what happened. I was sure they got me Harlow, at one point I was so sure they had used me and dumped me."

"If they had dumped you, you'd have been dead," she deadpans.

"I know. I woke up one time and found three of them dead. Shredded apart by something massive. I was so afraid of what could have done that to them that I didn't think twice before running. Even Feathers seemed to be worried. Stupid bird probably knew it was me. I was the one that ripped them apart like that."

She sighs as she brushes her hair out to fan around her head, nearly dried.

"Do you regret it?"

I glance at her, eyes closed, face relaxed as the sun kisses her pale skin. I allow my mind to drift for a moment, critiquing how sharp her jawline is, noting how her thin lips seemed to fit her face well. She was no model, instead she had the kind of beauty that came from someone brutal. A brutal kind of pretty.

My silence has her opening her eyes to look at me. I can't stand to look at her when I finally respond.

"No, I don't regret it. In fact, I think I'd like to do it again."

A little bit of my heart carves out for her when she looks at me not with fear or judgment, but with understanding.

Chapter 13

We silently agree after that conversation to continue our travels. I extend a hand to her and she rises to tower over me by a full head. As we shift, we take painful steps forward during the transition. She had opted to take a knee but changed to mimic me. Moving while shifting proves to be a challenge itself, the bones snapping making it feel like fire is starting in my limbs. I decide then that moving while shifting would be something I regularly do since it would give me an advantage over others who can't.

"Does it always hurt this much?" I consider to her.

"Pretty much, I've been able to shift for about six months now. The pain only gets slightly easier to put up with every time."

I mull over her words from the time we take off until we finally spot massive black peninsulas in the distance. We remain silent even through the next two days of travel, both knowing the other saw the mysterious formations. On the fourth day of travel we both only stop to rest for a moment before continuing through the cooling night.

Flying through the night is making it nearly impossible to see them, if the moon hadn't begun its slow reveal, we might not have seen them again until we were over the formation.

I know both of our bodies were exhausted from flying for so long, aching from muscles constantly working. Harlow moves to fly in front of me at an angle to provide easier currents. At my warning growl she shifts back. I feel some innate need to make it easier on her, despite how weary I am.

Having such a large body is exhausting yet exhilarating. Simply twisting my tail has me pointing the opposite way. Angling my wing up or down is stressful on the joint where they attached to me, though it proved useful for helping lift me when I no longer wish to flap as much.

I'm learning to love my new body more than my human one. The depth of my color makes me feel stronger than I ever had; at night Harlow had to check multiple times to make sure I was still there. She had commented twice about how difficult it is to see me.

I look down to the talons curving out of each toe. Deathly sharp tips seem to tease me to use them, clearly not being made for force or gripping. I would be testing them next time I fought. Curling them to be open and closed multiple times catches Harlow' eye.

"Yours are the sharpest I've seen, like knives."

"You have to meet more than a handful of other dragons," I counter.

"True, but look at mine. More like weapons for blunt force, Jakir's are perfect for him, Jacob's are thin with a soft rounded top."

I realize as she speaks that the sharp edge along the top is in fact different. A part of me envy's hers – meant for pure force or power. The build of her body something that could be used in the future for sure.

At the sun's highest point in the day we reach a distance we can see the black peninsula's far clearer. Like fingers extending from the land, multiple walls of shiny black rock stretch out into the ocean. Their sides are rough, but extremely vertical, forming canyons between each that are menacingly tall. Rough foamy waves slam into the base of these walls.

We fly along the top surface of one of those landmarks, landing close to the point of its tip. Soft grass sways in the breeze, looking as though it's dancing every time the current of air changes direction. I drop the bag in this grass before I land, nearly losing it.

Upon closer inspection, there are remnants of buildings along the beach. Only walls or partially standing structures remain. Even now, they're slowly being worn down by the salty water and air. I walk towards the left edge of the cliff, seeing that the wall of the opposite cliff face has bits of gray swirling within the glassy look of the lava rock.

Harlow shifts at the same time as I, somehow returning to her human form just a fraction of a second slower than I do. We grab a change of clothing we'd brought, and tug it on. She nervously glances at me while we proceed towards the furthest northern point that seems to stretch into the horizon. There, the last outline of some triangular structure is standing. It seems to be only the front framing of a building and stones that's left.

"What do you think this is?"

A metal cross is at the top of the triangular frame. Hanging on to the only thing left.

"It was a church," my voice is low, considerate of the memories left behind here.

Only the front of it is left, not even a door standing to welcome someone. Just a thought left behind to remind somebody of what it was. I stop as Harlow moves past it towards the edge of the land where it drops off. She stands close to the ledge, leaning forward to look down.

"It's definitely not calm water!" she yells. I quickly reach her and see just how awful the current is. Occasionally a wave slams so forcefully into the side of the rock that it sends a clapping noise thundering out.

There's a few clouds in the sky, a calm wind, no storms in sight. Yet the waves seem to attack the base of the rock with a vengeance unlike anything I had seen before. Sharp edges break the waves, not yet smoothed from years of wear.

"At least we don't have to worry about someone coming in by boat this way," she smirks.

"No, not unless they never want to leave again," I match her smile. This part of our home is too wild to be tested.

"Kind of like they were cut with a steak knife. Helps to roughen the wind a bit."

I nod, turning back to the wider part of the surface to shift again. Looking east and west I consider just how far my limits were with this land. How much of this new planet was mine?

I don't kneel again as I shift. I allow groans of pain to escape me, even a yell when a particularly painful snap radiates from my spine. Walking during it was more painful, but I stubbornly still feel it's necessary to teach my body to be able to.

"Kali," nothing more than a conveyance of concern from her. Perfectly reasonable considering the noises coming out of me.

I nearly reach the edge when I finish, my body fresh and tingling with the excitement of flying. I swing my head back to her, gently putting my nose into her stomach. Her hand touches the bridge of my snout. A nod in concurrence is the only response I get before she does the exact same. Her voice becomes raw as she screams more than I did, nearly falling a few times. Every look at me is returned with a firm one, I refuse to allow her to kneel.

Once transitioned I reach out.

"Don't kneel. Jakir and Jacob will learn how to shift while moving as well."

"And the others that come to us?"

"They'll learn too."

We stay along the coast as we move, keeping close enough to see it clearly but far enough to test the limits of my connection to the land. The black walls eventually disappear behind us as the land shifts into low-rolling hills. All of the beach sands are dark, staying nearly black despite how far away the lava rock walls are at this point. Further inland it matches the pictures of various steppes I had once seen in Europe when traveling with my family.

Such a simple thought of my family sends my mind tumbling into memory lane. My eyelids close to allow flashes of Carly's sweet face appear behind them. Her laugh feels distant in the memories of her, my parents face so obscure I can't even recall the shape of them. Pain settles in my heart at the realization that I'm slowly beginning to forget my family. I have somehow survived and the least I can do is remember what they looked like.

"*You okay?*"

"*I think I'm forgetting my family,*" I admit. Harlow is easy to talk to, making no room for hesitation in telling her the truth. She considers my words before responding.

"*I think all of us are forgetting what things and people looked like. It's natural, so don't let it hold you back.*"

"*What was your family like?*" I prod into her past, wanting to know more about the woman I'm beginning to truly care for.

"*Old fashioned. My father believed I should know a little bit about everything so he shoved books and information down my face as a kid,*" she begins. "*My mother believed parents weren't meant for loving, thought it was her job to 'prepare me for a harsh world'.*"

"*Doesn't sound very friendly.*"

"*No, I got my escape out of reading massive amounts of books from their library.*"

"*Fairy tales or biographies?*" I tease. She turns her head to bare her teeth playfully.

"*No, actually it was the history and war books that got me. I had a love for how war changed the world while also changing* with *the world.*"

"*So you were the weird kid at school?*"

"*Oh one-hundred percent. I got the shit beat out of me a couple times by my father for it.*"

Despite the grotesque nature of her past we both laugh it off.

Seagulls the size of bears fly up under us, screeching loudly enough to hurt our eardrums. I whip my tail at one that gets a little too close with its beak. They disperse immediately when my companion spits a thin line of fire towards them, singeing a few feathers. When the blue flame accidentally causes one of the birds to die and fall to the ground she dives after it.

A quick crunch using the molar far back in her mouth and the creature is torn apart, half of it in her front talons. She offers it, causing me to balk at the thought.

"Don't waste food," is all she says. I catch it when she throws it at me. The crunch of bones between my teeth satisfies a wild part of me, the taste of blood satisfies the hungry part of me.

We continue like that for a few more days, speaking occasionally to share our past or discuss plans for our small group. I find comfort in the quiet of flying with her. No pressure to speak all the time, just an understanding that we both enjoyed being around the other.

Harlow frequently brought up random bits of information about war and history that had been stored in her head since childhood. She spoke passionately about how it all worked, what happened, why different people failed or succeeded. Closer to the evening, she expressed her appreciation of my listening and interest. At her thankfulness, I brush a wing against hers.

"I could smell that dead forest when we were in the air, it has to be close," I inform her after shifting back into human form to cool off in the ocean. I leave our bag behind, not bothering to get dressed. She nods, looking towards the south where the smell is coming from. "We don't need to travel much further, something about it tells me that's where our boundaries lie."

"Ours?"

I ignore the question of it not just belonging to me, unsure how to convey the instinctually possessive and protective feeling I have regarding both the territory and my Samle. Instead I move to be waist deep in the water. Moonlight glints off of the surface, making it somewhat easier to see. I don't go past my calves, unsure of what could be hiding in the water.

"The Dead Forest, we might as well just call it that," she suggests, moving with me. "I want to know what's in it that makes it so…"

"Cruel?"

She looks at me seriously, "Yeah, that. Doesn't seem completely dead… or alive. It's something for sure. I hate it."

"Try to appreciate it instead. I mean, think about how we have this other body meant for killing that puts us at the top of the food chain. Yet, that forest might do the same to protect itself."

"You know," she considers, looking down at the water as she walks in to join me. "It might actually be useful for defense. Either people won't want to come, or if they do we can back them into it."

"I didn't think of it that way," my hand drags across the nearly flat surface.

"One of the bonuses of my dad cramming all that war history into my brain," she rolls her eyes.

"Well, thank you General Harlow" I give her a playful smile. She squints at me as she splashes water at my head. I raise an eyebrow, cupping my hand to splash salt water directly at her face. A small movement in the corner of my eye stops me. Harlow tracks my line of sight, seeing the tiniest figure of a boat on the horizon, almost so small it disappears a few times. Even with only the moonlight to help, we can still spot the figure well enough to know for certain that it's there and not just a figment of our imagination.

"I don't know if I can shift right now, I'm exhausted from so much traveling," she whispers, not to keep us hidden, but rather out of innate caution.

"I can," I grab her bicep to pull her to shore with me, out of the refreshing water. "That thing is so far out we should have enough time to rest before it gets to shore."

I drop her bicep and keep moving inland away from the beach. Harlow grabs the bag of clothing, getting dressed before moving forward again.

We walk for a bit, towards the hills that are large enough to mostly cover my full size. As silently as possible I force my body to break itself into the shadow form as we walk. Less noise comes out at the ever so slightly less painful transformation. Once it's talons curving into the grass and not human feet I let Harlow walk in front of me. Turning to walk behind the large mound of dirt and grass I ensure my hearing can still pick up the crabs skittering across the coarse black sand. Confirming that I can, I silently lay down to create a sort of nest for her to sleep. Her naked human body wouldn't be able to take the chilled wind for long without the warmth being produced by my now massive body. She lays down using my back foot as a pillow, which I use to keep her pressed close to me. I fold my tail around adding a layer of protection, then place my wing over the spot.

"You know I really don't need this much protection."

I only let out a gentle growl, successfully ending the argument. Her breathing slows eventually allowing me to hear the world around me. Only grass sways, an owl sings somewhere, and a herd of deer actually walk slowly through the field. They never notice me as they pass through, hesitating slightly when they hear Harlow let out a gentle snore. I keep my ears out for the sound of approaching voices, occasionally lifting my head just enough to see over the hill that blocks the beach we'd walked from.

They can't even see me laying here, so we should be safe if I hear them first.

I internally smile, focusing my attention again on the sounds around me. The body covered by my haunch and wing doesn't move. She had clearly exerted herself keeping up with me. We hadn't truly stopped for real rest for days, only napping for no more than an hour or two before moving on again. My desperation to explore the boundaries of home had made me ignorant to the exertion of Harlow. I feel guilty, then assure myself I'll do better in the future.

I force myself to stay as still as possible, not wanting to disturb her much needed sleep. I rest my head on the ground while making a promise to myself to take better care of her. I sigh contently at the friendship forming between us. She deserves better than her childhood gave her.

Letting myself rest my eyes, I send a feeling of comfort down the bond as strongly as possible. It had strengthened slightly, only to lessen greatly over the past couple weeks. Him and Jacob are most likely doing some of their own exploring. An echo of the same feeling returns a few minutes later.

Dozing for an hour proves to be just enough rest for me, despite never going deeper than relaxation. My scales warm as the sun starts to peak over the horizon in the east. The wind begins to warm somewhat allowing me to peel my wing back from covering Harlow. Sunlight gently touches her eyes, pulling her from a deep sleep.

"Mmm," she groans. Her muscular body tenses as she stretches out. Shaking the sleep off she stands to stretch once again. Pulling my body from around her I stand to also release the stiffness in my body. My head twists dramatically as I lean out like a cat waking from its nap.

"How close?"

I tread silently around the hill, only peeping my head around to see the boat now nearly within listening distance. I pull back, catching Harlow scanning the area behind us. With a large sigh I begin another painful shift as I walk towards her. A small amount of joy fills me when for the first time I don't stumble as I shift. I only pause to get dressed.

"You're getting better," she says, surprised.

"That's the point, I want to be able to shift while running eventually."

"Okay chill the fuck out for now," she says incredulously, turning to face me. I place a hand on her shoulder while taking up the scanning of our rear.

"Are you rested enough to shift?"

"More than enough, how long did I sleep?"

I don't answer, not wanting to lie but also not wanting her to feel guilty.

"Shift, now, before that boat is here. I want to speak to them, but I need you to have my back if they pull something stupid."

She nods, clearly not pleased by my lack of answering her question.

"How much sleep...you got?" she grits out before her jaw pulls forward. Her blue scales slide into existence, bones breaking excruciatingly as she takes slow steps forward. As a small test, I push her shoulder. She catches herself before she falls, looking at me with a small amount of annoyance.

"Just pushing your limits, you're getting better too."

A rumble comes out as her vocal cords reform.

I turn back to the beach to walk towards it, padded steps behind me now, "And enough, I got enough sleep."

The boat is being pulled in by two figures, one standing around six feet and a couple inches while the other stands slightly shorter than me - both very thin in an eerie yet stunning way. Four more figures sit in different places in the boat. It's large enough to be comfortable for their group size, clearly having space below the deck for sleeping. The two figures pulling the boat by its ties lock eyes with me as they near, then look to one another with excited grins. I raise my eyebrow at their expressions. I see Harlow shift her body closer to me, standing behind me in defense and slightly to the side so as not to knock me over if she lunges.

One of the people on the boat stand, their figure masked by loosely hanging clothes. They move forward, gripping the railing up front. When the hull slides into the sand, successfully wedged into it they begin unloading themselves. The two figures seem to move in tandem, never moving without the other. They're the first to move towards us.

The one who had gripped the railing launches herself over the side, moving as fast through the water as she can. She ends up reaching me before the others.

"Hi," she says breathlessly, putting out a hand to shake. "It's nice to meet our Dronning finally."

I draw in a breath at the sudden awareness that these weren't just random people happening upon new land. These people are *my* people now, having somehow found me across an ocean.

Chapter 14

I reach out my hand and firmly grasp the hand of the woman in front of me. Her kind brown eyes meet mine with an excitement I wasn't sure of. I feel Harlow carefully watching our interaction, as well as the last three people approaching. Her breathing is almost impossible to hear as she intakes everything around her.

"My name is Aiza. This is Sayah and Senka-"

"We're twins," they speak at the same time, their voices tinged by a throaty accent. A slim grin spreads across their face.

"They don't mean to seem creepy-"

"They're just excited," I cut her off, already understanding the energy they were putting off. Most of it being like a squirrel on crack, the rest being curious. "Apologies, I didn't mean to interrupt."

She nods, continuing, "We're from a mix of the clans across the pond. Filo and I," she motions to a man with a large build, his face framed by a thick mahogany brown beard. "Originally stayed with the Shadow Samle up north. Ellie and her daughter," her hand swings to a dainty woman with uptilted eyes that pierce towards me. "Came from the Midlands Samle. The twins are from the Hellish Samle."

"I'm assuming none of the land over there is the same anymore?"

"You'd be correct, we lost a lot of the old world."

"Why..." I take a deep breath while dragging my eyes over each of them. Six pairs of eyes looked at everything about me, especially pausing on the scars littered across my torso and thighs. Their stares are a mixture of poorly made attempts at hidden sadness. "Why are you all here?"

130

Filo, Ellie, and Aiza all give me strange looks.

"When you first changed, you called us," Filo explains like it's a known fact.

"I didn't call anybody, I just had my first change about two weeks ago," I grasp my hands behind my back to hide the tiny tapping of my fingers.

"Right," Filo continues. "And when you had your first shift it sent out *kallet* – the calling."

I simply glance back and forth between him and Aiza. They both show concern at my lack of knowledge.

"Has anyone taught you about our kind?"

"I've learned a few terms, everything else I learned from Harlow here," I flick my hand at her. "Or from her boyfriend Jacob, or my Sekund."

"Ah," she bites her lip. Ellie shifts uncomfortably, placing her daughter down to play in the sand. "Well, basically *kallet* is a wave of energy that gets sent out when a dronning or konge shifts for the first time. It tells anybody, anywhere, that their leader is ready for them to come home. It guides us, telling us where to go. Until that point, most unclaimed dragons stay with a samle generous enough to host them. Or, they simply survive on their own."

"What did this *kallet* look like?"

"It looks like a strong compressed wind, but the feeling you get when it hits you is indescribable. If you're looking in its direction, you can see it coming like a shock wave."

I nod, taking in the new information. It wasn't nearly as shocking as finding out dragons existed and I was one of them – still shocking. Something about them felt comfortable, familiar as though I had met them before. What they're saying makes sense while at the same time it doesn't. The twins move between us to get closer to Harlow. She steps back to allow them access to the open beach to our left. I focus my attention back to the three other adults before me.

"There's only four of you?" Ellie asks, her voice soft like any mother's would be.

"Correct."

who leans slightly to push me to the side. Catching myself I feel my black talons shred through my nail beds. Using them with caution I grip his nose with my talons by digging them into the sensitive skin on the inside. With my hand like a bull ring on him Senka opens her maw slightly to go for it. Faster than I had ever moved before I reach out and do the same to her. Whines whistle past my wrists at the stabbing pains going down their snout; but the whines aren't at the pain.

"I might be new to this but I promise you the last thing I will let you do is stupid shit like that," I shove their noses back. "So knock it off."

Harlow wisely stayed where she was, mostly having been busy getting Ellie and Lilly onto her back. She had watched every second of the encounter waiting for me to get violent.

"If you have energy to spend like that," I begin walking back towards the beach. "Then let's find you something to play with."

Snorts come from the twins as they look at one another, realizing I had no intention of dampening their fire. Just needed to guide it correctly.

They all watch, save for Harlow who is looking around for signs of danger, as I begin to walk towards them. I feel no shame in not wearing clothes, rather a sense of comfort at how normal it is. All confidence flowing in my chest moves to support the pain my legs begin to feel as I break. These steps are slightly faster than when Harlow and I had first begun. More of a casual stroll rather than broken, sporadic foot placement. As skin tears to accommodate rebuilding bones I see Ellie place a hand over her mouth discreetly. Aiza takes a step back, her head tilted up to look at my face. Her teeth peeks out from her mouth, too long to fit comfortably should she try to cover them.

Must not be common practice, I think snidely. Basking in the awe doesn't last long as my attention is pulled to ensure I don't stumble through the transition.

Moments later, I'm ready to fly with the others.

Eyes drag down my body to take in the light-absorbing color of my scales. Wearily I keep my eyes towards the twins to catch any sign of hostility.

"We're not little," Sayah snips lightly, treading carefully.

"Whoever told you being little is an insult?" I only move my eyes to look at him past Aiza. His eyes brighten just enough to show me that small phrase makes him reconsider.

"Gallyan, he hated Sayah and I. Was quick to kick us out the second he had a chance," Senka explains with light venom in her voice.

"Gallyan is the Konge of the Hellish Samle," Aiza elaborates. Her eyes tinge with sadness. *"He's an awful person."*

A sliver of violence snakes in at the back of my mind in anger of what someone could have done to the siblings now under my care. Neither of them shows any anger, just keep quiet as they pump their wings to push themselves into the air. I watch as they move sharply up to gain altitude, gaining as much distance from the rest of us as they can.

"Give them time, Gallyan isn't their only horror story" Filo whispers across my mind. His eyes track them climbing above.

"I will give them everything they need."

Gentle brown eyes from Aiza slide to me, conveying some kind of hope I'm not sure I can give. Her and Filo take off as well, using more of an angle to lessen the weight on their wings.

"Go, I'll stay under you until you're steady in case I need to catch her."

Harlow dips her head in response. Her feet lift off the ground slowly, taking her time to not jostle the precious cargo between her shoulder blades. Ellie wraps her arms around the bundle tied to her chest. With Lilly's face protected from the wind she looks to me to watch my ascent. Maintaining close proximity to Harlow without bumping into her proves to take more minuscule muscle control. Muscles along my back twitch in strain as I angle myself to catch them. We reach a comfortable altitude, one not too high so as to keep the two in human form warm. I pull to the front to lead, seeing Sayah and Senka trying to peek behind them subtly.

"Sayah and Senka, cover the rear," my voice pushes out to them. Communication in this form is easier every time I use it. Like learning to ride a bike.

A sound, rather than a thought, caresses my mind from them both. Low humming conveys gratitude to having everyone around them in constant eyesight.

Conflicting feelings roll in my belly. Anxiety about new people being a threat yet supposedly being the rest of my life puts me in circular thought. When we reach the massive tree by the lake three days later, I still wait for one of them to feel stronger.

Chapter 15

"It's a lot, I know."

"Jacob, how many times did you fly back and forth to bring all this here?" I ask, my brows pulled together in concern.

"Four total round trips! After the first two days of y'all being gone I figured I might as well drag Jakir along to start building this place," his grin makes him look so young I can't help but grip his shoulder.

"Thank you, even though a third of this is just books."

"This..." Harlow stands from the circle her, Ellie, and Aiza have formed around the pile of books. "This is enough information to build houses, start farming, maybe even train a damn army."

Every single book is a variety of thorough instruction. Titles boast 'How to Build a Porch', 'Starting Your First Garden', even 'Stocking Up for the Apocalypse'. I snort at the last one. All of them selected to help us learn what we don't know so we can start making an actual home. Aiza gravitates towards three thick texts, I catch the title of one marking it as something related to political relations. As she walks to the tree to begin reading I turn to Jakir.

"You went on your own trips as well?" I nod towards the containers of miscellaneous materials. I swallow repeatedly trying to get out my next words. The emotions feel difficult to convey. "You two should have stayed together-"

"We were just fine. Needed to split so we could get things done faster," he cuts me off gently to end the lecture before it begins.

After returning with six new people Jakir only brushed a hand down my back as they introduced themselves. Him and Aiza began to speak to one another getting along well, until the twins cut in to introduce themselves. Sayah dragged his eyes along Jakir like a jaguar looking at its next meal, Senka smiled wide enough to show teeth. Dragging her tongue along them sends goosebumps along Jakir's skin. Glancing through the Bond I can feel his discomfort making me feel a sense of pride at how they can elicit such a response from someone much larger than them. I rewarded them both with a dark, knowing smile. Neither smiled back, watching me with learning eyes. I don't drop it until I winked at them, allowing them to walk around and explore.

"Fine," I drag my consciousness back to the present. "Then do it again. We can't sleep under a tree forever. We need actual houses."

Jacob perks up, "Let me please, I have years of experience working small jobs on houses. My family didn't have good money so I helped make some extra."

Jacob waits for me to respond. Harlow grabs his hand to give reassurance, turning her body towards him to get closer.

"Make some plans, come up with ideas, come back to me," my attention turns from an excited Jacob to Ellie who has picked up some farming books.

"Some of this is outdated, but it could help greatly with getting used to this area. I can start on it," she sticks out a hand to keep Lilly from hitting her chin as she trips over a book.

"You know a little about farming?" I question, not ready to believe I got so lucky to find people like this. These people could be the reason the samle survives.

"Yes," she brushes her dark bangs back from her eyes. "My parents grew up poor on a family farm. I never worked the farm myself, though I was lucky enough to have multiple gardens where I lived."

I breathe deeply to steady my nerves. So much potential in having Ellie and Jacob, as well as so much luck in them falling into my hands. Jakir reaches through the bond to ease the tension spreading everywhere. Being so close to him after the bond had been taught seems to ease a muscle that had been under severe strain.

Jakir lifts a small bag filled with smaller loose items, "Whether or not we knew how to garden, I picked up multiple packets of seeds. This should be enough to help us get started. I'll start a place on the top of the cliff, where there won't be any shadows cast over it. However, we need something that will provide protein."

I nod, not realizing until now how much work there is to be done just to support nine people. Homes needed to be built, food cultivated, everything just to keep these people alive. I walk around the tarps, untying the last two to reveal four tents and sleeping supplies. Small containers of soap spill out from a large reusable bag.

"You really thought of everything," I mumble to Jakir, now crouching next to me. His wicked golden eyes meet mine. "I didn't think of any of this until now, what would we have done if you hadn't?"

His hand reaches up to grab my chin so gently, "We would've learned, and still gone to get the stuff we need."

I close my eyes to allow myself comfort in his touch. Weight settles in my chest forcing me to continue, "We're going to need much more than this. You and Harlow will go back and get more. I can't leave the others alone."

"Just tell me what you need."

"Concrete, saws, anything you can find that can help build a home. Whatever isn't rusted or broken to help Ellie start the garden. More books on food, building, trapping, whatever we can use."

"Done, we'll leave first thing tomorrow morning. Give us a week, though it should only take four or five days."

"Whatever you need, just don't go too far where I can't feel you," I stand to unpack the tents, turning my face so the embarrassment heating my cheeks at the admission. The need to protect feels unnaturally strong, but I can't help it coming out.

"What's in that direction," Senka speaks next to me, having appeared out of thin air. "We can tell something is there, spans to the south too."

I look to where she is. The excitement in her eyes seems to trickle into me. A scar down her face on the right-side shines in the afternoon sun. It's jagged, clearly having not been allowed to heal properly. It curves down her neck around to her collarbone, barely noticeable unless you're really looking.

She notices my staring, narrowing her eyes at me.

"You're not the only one with scars, don't stare," she snaps. Sayah's head turns towards her away from the book he holds in his hand. My eyes snap up to hers, burning begins behind mine as I feel power push up from my heart. Her eyes falter, casting downward only to glance up at me, then back again.

"I stare because I know that scar is from survival, not mistakes. You saw the scars covering my body on the beach. I hate them as much as you hate yours, but whatever gave it to you had a hand in bringing you to me. For that, I appreciate it."

I feel like some scrap of trust blossoms between not only her and I, but her brother and I as well, then. Despite my hesitance in doing so, I give myself the mental room to let it begin. It's not a leap, just a tender step. Simply a stranger's recognition that what she has isn't shameful but instead of part of why she's alive.

I start to walk away, the twins follow. It gives them the space to let their shoulders drop an inch before I begin speaking.

"I was stripped down and strung up, a play toy for a man that hated me."

"Why did he hate you," her voice thickens slightly with a Russian accent.

"I killed three of his men, as a dragon, and I don't even remember doing it."

Her eyes stay glued to the west.

"Do you wish you did?"

I don't know. Maybe I deserved to be caught since I survived and Carly didn't.

I catch my vision glazing over, and refocus on the conversation at hand.

"Only to watch them die again," that black corner threatens to creep out from the corner of my mind as I recall what their bodies looked like.

"Our father gave me this one, our mother gave the matching one to

Sayah."

I don't push, letting her decide if she wants to speak anymore.

"We got it for not being able to best them that day in training," Sayah now stands on the other side of me. "They did not give birth to us to love us."

I breathe silently. Knowing their trauma was occurring long before the world ended was another weight on my chest.

"There's a forest that spans the western and southern parts of our territory," Senka's eyebrows flick up at the word 'our'. "It smells like death, no sign of color but gray and black. If you want to explore it, go."

The grins they share could shatter worlds.

"We'll be back," they promise.

"I think you should wait," I grab two tents to drag underneath the tree. As I walk away I hear them halt at my words, considering them. They only pause for mere seconds before beginning to shift. I sigh at them leaving, nearly shifting to demand they return.

Harlow calls as she walks towards me, "Walk as you do it, it's hard but it gets easier. Makes you more mobile than others."

They understand, based on their expressions, and start moving as their skin changes to scales. Not a single sound comes from their mouths as they stumble forward in each step. I do a double take when they are fully transformed and they still haven't made a sound.

Harlow grabs the other two tents to help. We walk silently up until we reach the tree.

She tosses down the bags, "They're dangerous."

I unzip the first large tent, "They're mine."

I catch myself nearly apologizing for the sudden claim, instead just sticking with my declaration. She doesn't say anything else as we set up the temporary sleeping places. One tent has two "rooms", allowing four people to sleep comfortably. Two of the tents are long, meant for one. The last tent fits around four people, a simple contraption meant to protect from weather, not keep someone warm. The others join us soon after Harlow and I begin. Once the tents are ready with sleeping bags inside people begin to pick where they'll sleep. Harlow and Jacob stay with Ellie and Lilly, using the middle divider for privacy. Filo elects to sleep on his own, as does Aiza.

"The twins will be back when they feel like it, Jakir and I will sleep in this one for now," my hands flicks at the singular large one. "Jacob and Harlow leave in the morning to go get more materials. The rest of us will stay here to plan things out."

Pleased nods from everyone confirm I've made a decent plan. The rest of the day is spent bathing, washing clothes, or easy conversation. When night falls Jakir and I are the last to go to sleep. I hug him for a long time before sitting down by the water.

"I'll be in later," I assure. He nods and lets me sit alone under the moonlight. The water in the lake ripples occasionally as various fish dart at the surface for food. Eventually they reach the shore, lapping at my bare feet. I wiggle my toes, enjoying the cool feel of pebbles rolling around, my shoes having not moved from the tents when I took them off hours ago.

Moonlight makes it easy enough to see my legs and arms. The edges of my gray shorts fall forward as I fold my legs in front of me. Jakir had thought to pick up some clothes for me since my bag was long lost when he saved me, and the only remaining set of clothes was shredded when I shifted for the first time. Or shifted the first time I could remember it.

I consider the fact that I had most definitely shifted before. There was no other way I could have shredded three grown men in the forest like that. Their bodies were nothing but decoration for Kent and Grant to find. The blackout must have been due to pure terror since my body had no choice but to run. Even with me still having a human side, some dark part of me now had the freedom to wake when it wanted. It blotted out just how bad it could be. If it hadn't the human part of me very well might have cowered, letting me die uselessly.

That pure violence and darkness would get me killed one day. I just needed the time to build a home for them – my new family – before I could let that happen. I realize in my thought process that I have yet to lose total control to it. A part of me remains nearly every time, save for when I killed three people.

It must be the darkest part, I think clearly. *If I ever let go again like that I could kill someone.*

I decide to find someone strong enough to kill me. My gut tells me no one here currently could do so if their life depended on it. Perhaps Jakir, should he swing enough luck. Even then, the memory of how fast and deadly I proved to be when I shifted memorably for the first time courses past on the back of my closed eyelids.

None of them deserve to live in fear ever again.

As if in defiance that dark cloud creeps up my mind. I stomp it down, not wanting to deal with it nor wake up Jakir via the Bond. He needs rest just like the rest of them. More so, they need a home.

Every one of them deserves a home. I choose in my mind then and there to build the most beautiful place they could hope for. Even if it takes the rest of my life.

My constant train of thoughts finally slows as footsteps come behind me.

"I'll be there in a bit, Jakir, I need to think."

Aiza stops, looking down at my tightly folded form. Her face is grim. "We need to talk."

"Can it wait 'till morning?" I sigh, turning back to look at the lake. She gracefully lowers herself, so she is at the edges of my vision. I tilt my head, examining her hijab. "Why do you still wear that?"

"It's part of my religion, my beliefs. Islam did not end when the world did. I still have the freedom to choose, and this is something I choose."

"What happens when you shift?" I realize I never saw her shift since she remained behind all of us at the beach.

"I have certain folds and pins that allow it to slip away when I change. Though I'm not the biggest fan of being in dragon form. I always tear through my clothes because I cannot remove them."

"Hmm, interesting. I appreciate you explaining," I give a small smile to show I genuinely appreciate the explanation.

"Now that we've discussed why I'm still a hijabi, let's talk."

"I doubt it's important-"

"Kali I could not say this until the others were asleep. This needs to be a conversation between you and I," she demands. Her voice changes as she speaks. It becomes something firm and powerful, possibly more powerful than one's dragon form could ever be. It shocks me enough I turn my body and give her every ounce of my attention.

"I don't like the sound of your voice," I caution.

"You're probably not going to like the news I bear either then," her slim face is grim, making her beauty stark. Large round eyes search my face attempting to gauge my feelings. "I told you on the beach I came from the Shadow Samle, which is true. Though I did not indulge everything I came here for."

A fish rolls out in the water catching our attention. Some small break before what feels like bad news, hits.

"Mikhail is its Konge, it's debated which one of the leaders came first but he is most definitely one of the first to shift. There's more than just us who felt your *kallet*, others weren't ready to travel after being so comfortable for so long."

"The others are with this Mikhail guy? We have more coming?" small worry sets in at how I'll feed more mouths than the ones I already have. "When will they be here?"

"Some said they may come later, not all are from the Shadow Samle, others have been waiting for you across the world. No doubt for the next few months people will trickle in."

My eyes search across the water, dragging up to the moon as if I'll find the answer to everything in it.

"Kali you're the last dragon to start a Samle, everyone else has been shifted for two years, what took you-"

Her voice fades out as a puzzle piece seems to audibly snap into place in my head. I had taken nearly a year to travel from the southern coast up to the northern one. When I woke up alone I had no concept of time nor any idea of how long I had been out. Car's body seemed fine, like it hadn't been there for long though now I think about what could have preserved her for a full year while I slept.

What had been so forceful that it took my body a year to wake up, not even ready to shift.

"When do dragons normally shift?" I cut her off mid sentence, not even sure what she was saying.

"I was just explaining, most dragons shifted within the first six months of waking up, many were delayed because they were alone so they had no idea how to do it. Kali, what took you so long? Did you force yourself to not shift?" her concern is genuine despite the sting in my chest.

"I wasn't awake," my voice is rough. "I think I was comatose for probably a year before I woke up, it took me almost another one to get here."

Her mouth parts slightly, the corners of them pulling down the smallest amount.

"How...nobody manages to hide that long as human unless they force themselves – which is exceptionally damaging from what I've heard – otherwise you were stopped by something else."

"Probably the group of men chasing me for months at a time," my voice in monotone, no emotion about my reason except boredom. "I shifted at one point but it was purely out of self-preservation. I don't even remember it."

She wraps her arms around her legs, her loose pants shifting as she hugs herself. Concern flits across her face quickly, just as fear settles in.

"Is that...where those scars came from?"

"All forty of them," my teeth flash at her. Her skin pales, making her seem sick. I school neutrality onto my face as my heart drops a little in my chest. "My pain isn't your pain. I'm fine now."

"Your pain is all of ours to bear, you're the reason we have a home."

"Jakir is the reason, he found me."

"Probably followed the pull of the Bond if you were in any distress-"

"That's an understatement," I murmur.

"Then it practically screamed for him to come get you before it even formed," she continues. "Those things are quite literally a force of nature from what I've come to understand."

"It formed after he found me and let me heal, not before then."

"Bonds have a very simple use before formation, finding the other. After that is when the emotions connect, and it becomes a truly living thing. Allah's will made us dragons strong, the decision to decide the Bonds is even more proof of his presence. He has ordained it, so therefore it is."

I know she speaks from her own perspective, so I decide in my head that it's the universe playing games.

"And you came to know all of this how?"

"I like information, like using it even more," Aiza shrugs. "I was involved with politics before everything changed. Information is the most powerful tool when it comes to people."

"Useful, I'll keep that in mind."

"You'll need me when you go to the Eastern Continent to meet with the other Samle leaders."

My hand freezes over the smooth pebbles. The thought of ever meeting hadn't crossed my mind until now. Such an obvious thing that there were other Samle's out there, yet I had just gotten back from traveling.

"I need more information," I flick my hand at her in dismissal, expecting her to balk. Pebbles roll as I push them around with an open flat hand.

"There are eleven total Samle's including you."

"Dammit woman," I let out a single laugh.

"You're welcome, I believe I was born for this. Three Samle's reside on this continent, three on the south western continent, four on the north eastern continent, and one on the south eastern one. There's some land that's unclaimed, though not for lack of trying."

She continues for a while, dumping information on me to bring me up to speed. Lessons range from what each Samle trades or needs, to how they all interact. Relations remain ever changing, some volatile while others became concrete rapidly. Aiza is even so kind as to slip in some basic information like how no two dragons look exactly alike, dragon forms tend to mimic ones base personality which is why children hadn't been recorded changing until after puberty

"There is yet to be a full meeting between all Dronning's and Konge's, which is why I needed to talk to you in the first place. Mikhail invited you to come stay with him, he's interested in the woman causing such a ruckus," a playfully evil grin winks back at me.

I pause again, feeling like I do so every time she stops talking.

How does he know I'm a woman?

"Where did he get the information that I'm a woman? The only people who have been near me before are Jakir, Harlow, and Jacob," my voice solidifies becoming a bit too loud. Someone in the tents cough as they come out to use the restroom. Aiza pauses as well, breaking eye contact only to look down at the ground in confusion.

"That's a good question," she whispers. "I don't know, maybe someone saw you as you traveled. Word might have spread. Either way, he's not a man frequently denied."

"For that exact reason, now I don't want to go."

"I agree, but not showing up will only isolate us. He wants to set laws and agreements since there will most likely not be another Samle any time soon. We don't have to suck up, but we do have to mark our place in this."

I consider her advice, knowing she has a better handle on how to do this right than I do. With a deep breath I ask, "When?"

"It took us a week to cross the ocean. When I left, he told me we had four weeks to arrive. Warned the meeting would be in six. He wants you there early so he can have a leg up on everyone else," she shrugs, conveying that she isn't surprised at his actions. This Mikhail character is quickly irritating me.

"Fine, we take the next two and half weeks figuring out how to keep everyone situated while I'm gone. You, me, and the twins will go once everything is stable enough," I rise to head back to the tents. "I need to know everything you know before we go."

"Of course," she puts a gentle hand on my arm. Possibly testing the waters of my boundaries, possibly developing a friendship. As we walk back we make a plan to give me lessons every day on the dynamics of the new world. She slips into her tent after bidding me a good night's sleep.

I slip my clothes off and fold them neatly into a pile. I walk out of earshot to practice shifting. Over and over and over again I force myself to walk while my body snaps into a different form. By the first signs of morning, I manage a steady walk while shifting. Not a single step falters.

Each one of us throws our bodies and minds into work for a few days. Harlow uses her dragon body with Filo to rip up a substantial patch of land back on the top of the cliffside. Their claws till the dirt to the best of their ability while tossing large rocks or pesky roots to the side. Ellie directs them as they go, calling out where to stop and start. Once they understand the end goal, she places herself at the end of each row planting the seeds. After reassurance from us all, Lilly is allowed to run around and explore near the tree.

I quickly learn how much a toddler can fit in their mouth.

"A worm, really Lili?" I use her self-proscribed nickname as I pry open what feels like the strongest hand in the world. Giggles are her response so I can't help but smile as she toddles back to the tree.

Jakir smiles at me when I rise. The Bond throbs with happiness from both of us. A wink from me sends him back to cutting up the trees he brought back on the first day. I join him after assuring Lilly is now under Aiza's watch. Picking up a saw I begin to rock it back and forth to help create materials for a fence around the massive garden.

On the third day of nonstop laboring Jacob brings me a pile of large papers with an excited look in his eye.

"I'm so gonna be your favorite after this," he preens.

"That's awfully confident of you," I retort.

He frowns dramatically, "Ouch, Kay-kay. Give a man some credit."

"Stop calling me that," I clench my jaw. My eyes pin him down for a second, before he cracks his neck and lays out the papers before me on our only makeshift table.

"Oops, this one is a surprise," he flings a piece of paper away before I can take it in fully. All I catch is the label. "The Manor? What is that?"

"Nonya," he grins, not even looking at me as he digs like crazy through the building plans. I look over my shoulder at Jakir who shrugs and turns away. I don't miss the small smile on his face.

"Come on Jacob, we have work to do," my arms cross in impatience.

"Oh I know we do, especially with what I've got planned. Okay," he points to a drawing of a small house layout. "I made a bunch of plans so we have them ready when more people start to come in. There's one-, two-, three-, and four-bedroom houses. For now, we can start with the one bedroom plans. Each one has a kitchen with room for dining room, full bathroom, living space, and optional porch. The windows are operated on pulley systems, the bathrooms will mostly be large tubs that we'll have to figure out how to fill later."

"Where do you plan on finding these tubs?" I tilt my head to him, still leaning over the table.

"Uhh...yeah I'll just go steal some eventually. We can bathe in the lake for now."

"Uh-huh."

"Anyways," he draws out. "They aren't huge, but they're big enough to be comfortable. We'll need people to make round trips constantly, but we'll try and use what we have available too."

"Depending on what the twins say when they come back," Jakir wipes the sweat from his temple as he walks up shirtless. I can't help my eyes appreciatively dragging over the well-built body dripping in sweat. I feel nothing in the way of attraction, but his build isn't easily ignored. "We could possibly use the wood from that forest to build most of it."

"I'd be surprised if the trees themselves don't smell like death," Jacob wrinkles his nose at the thought.

"Same," I uncross my arms and shift through the plans. Each house has the same amenities, with increasing numbers of bedrooms and living space. I flick to a new page that isn't a house. "A greenhouse?" I interrogate.

"Yeah, there's these red pinecone-looking plants towards the south just before the mountain range. Jakir and I found them on our last trip. When you squeeze them this stuff comes out that you can use for washing yourself. I remember seeing them on some video one time."

"Can we transplant?"

"Yes, but they need darker soil, which we don't have here. The green house helps keep them in a moisturized environment too," Jakir answers. His voice is rough from a long day of hard work. He rarely took a break when I asked, only mentioning I deserved to eat something other than the mushrooms we found. Deserved to sleep in something other than a tent.

I lied when he asked how I slept every day, not wanting to tell him I spent most of the night expending my body to become faster at shifting. His disbelief echoed down the Bond repeatedly. I ignore it each time.

"Fine, start on a house first. Ellie and Lilly need a better place to sleep more than any of us," I watch my Bonded's face fight against a disagreement. "Then we'll go from there."

Narrowly avoiding an argument with the massive man across from me, I quickly walk back to saw at massive tree trunks.

Chapter 16

"We'll start seeing some growth in at least a few weeks, but the mushrooms won't cut it any longer."

Ellie wasn't wrong. We had quickly eaten the mushrooms we found five days ago when our work had started. A bush producing some type of berries was found across the lake yesterday by Harlow, but their sweetness made everyone a little nauseous after not having premade sugary treats for so long. More discussion between us all results in a conclusion that we needed meat, and not just a few mountain goats, but something we could keep around. Jacob and Jakir bring up a herd of bison they spotted while exploring, but that they seemed aggressive, and had become twice the size they were before. Getting them all the way down here would be no easy feat.

"It's about a day and a half of fast flying, it'll take about three of us to get them up here," Jakir explains, his brows drawn together as a plan unfolds.

"How big is the herd?" I ask, considering how we would keep them here.

"Easily around a hundred," he offers. He watches my face, offering open curiosity down the Bond. I respond with an iota of worry.

"Jacob and Ellie, can you have a small stream dug to let water into a large pond? If we can make it easier for them to live, they'll stick around."

Everyone nods in agreement, either moving to start the work required next or getting ready for orders. After assigning Filo and Jakir to leave with me, I begin shucking off the shorts and loose tank top to change. Out of sight of the others, they both do the same. Filo keeps quiet as usual, only grunting as his body begins the shift while he attempts to move simultaneously. His fiery scales shimmer in the afternoon sun as he begins a trot in full form. The large rudder-like span of flesh extending from the bottom of his tail drags through the grass until those narrow wings pull him up.

Jakir stands next to me as I watch the others, breathing in some peace at the comfort of my small Samle. His fingers brush mine, his cool talons bump into my thigh.

"You sure you can handle that much flying? You've barely slept the past few days," he doesn't look at me as he asks. I feel the Bond being pushed open, that door being widened so he can see if I lie.

"I said I slept fine every time you asked."

"You lie every time I ask. I can see the bags underneath your eyes, I'm sure everyone else can too," those golden eyes swing to me.

"They haven't said anything," I shrug one shoulder, not bothered to shrug both.

"They won't, they know you've been through something. Here's the thing, Kali," his voice drops so low I barely hear it. "You get out your anger when we fly and get these bison back here. But when we get back, I'm not playing friendly with you anymore."

"I never asked you to," I snip. Guilt eats at me. He had done everything, is still doing everything, and I have the audacity to push him away.

"You won't ever have to ask me to watch your back. I just got you, I'm not losing you to whatever this is."

"Well I leave in a little bit anyway," as if that would stop him from trying to fix me.

"Since when? To where?" he pushes my shoulder effectively turning me to face him.

"Sorry," I bite the inside of my cheek. "Didn't want to worry you. You've had to do so much already."

I get a displeased look from him until he sighs and shakes his head.

"Aiza was told by one of the Konge's that I was invited to join him before some meeting. All the Samle leaders are meeting up to talk. I don't plan on hiding."

"I would never expect you to," his fingers twitch towards me. "Let's hope you're well rested and feeling better before you leave, or I'll go in place of you."

"You weren't the one invited," I roll my eyes.

"I don't care," he smiles playfully at me. I frown and smack his arm. "Asshole."

"That language really isn't necessary," he purses his lips as I walk away into my other skin.

All the pain of shifting, even the snapping of my bones, seems distant as thoughts of what could happen soon fill my head. My mind drifts to what Mikhail might look like. A thick, balded man. Maybe even a short, angry teen. Only someone so cocky would have such an extreme shortcoming about them.

Probably has a small di-

"Bye bye!" Lilly yells as I fly upwards. Jakir and Filo follow closely. I look back and down to see her running through the grass that reaches her waist. Ellie waves as well, the large floppy hat obscuring most of her face from this height. My heart squeezes slightly at leaving the others. Comfort ebbs over it, making the trip to these wild bison easier.

Jakir

I know a part of her could probably go forever. I know she's trying to prove that she's not weak and that she can manage everything despite what's happened. Every time I ask how she slept I feel the sting of her lies via our Bond. She thought she's protecting me, or possibly protecting herself. Either way, I know it has to stop.

Something has upset her, setting her on edge the day after Aiza had spoken to her. I nearly joined Aiza when I heard her leave her tent with barely a breath. My feet never carried me, since I understand that Kali needs time with each of them to truly develop her own relationships. To heal with people other than me.

Filo breathes yellow fire into a pile of branches, dried leaves, and some sticks. His flame is so controlled, so small compared to Harlow's wild blue. Harlow still refrains from using it since she roasted the meal we had in the mountains. When I asked, she became serious and explained how difficult it was to control.

We all remain in dragon form as we curl into ourselves for the night. Kali's tail searches for me as she leans against my side. Warmth spreads at her need for comfort from me. I wrap mine slowly around hers forming a twist of gold and sightless black. I don't miss the sigh of relief as she lays her head down next to Filo's. He keeps his distance typically, though can't seem to resist close proximity to his Dronning.

"Sleep, I'll keep an eye out for anything concerning," I offer to them. Filo opens a single, orange eye at me in acknowledgment.

"Don't tell me what to do," Kali sounds serious, but the tinge of sarcasm isn't missed by me. Filo chuffs out a laugh.

Only the sounds are of bison roaring miles away carried along the breeze as they both sleep. I keep the Bond wide open to ensure she actually sleeps. To my relief, she falls into a deep slumber. As the sun rises Filo offers a plan for getting the herd back home.

"We have no idea what their temperament is, so we stay in these bodies. We pick one to share among us for some energy on the way back. Don't let them break off, if one goes they'll all probably follow."

"Sounds fine," I nod, glancing out over the land.

Kali stretches out her stiff limbs. *"Sorry I slept for so long."*

"No problem," I don't let on to how much anxiety I pulled from her end. I'd be keeping it with me to bear only to slowly let her take it on again. Over the days of working and traveling, the joints where my wings meet my body have become stronger. Only a couple full blown

flaps put me into the air. We all power through the distance faster than anticipated, so we reach the edge of a plateau shortly. Our bodies flatten to the ground as much as possible as we eye the massive herd below on flat land. Excitement bubbles up from Kali nearly knocking my sideways. Her tail tip flicks back and forth, unable to sit still while brewing excitement of a hunt.

"They're absolutely massive," she comments. *"Those are closer to the size of a full-grown moose than a bear."*

"Look at the two fighting," I add. *"Brutal."*

Somehow, more excitement pumps out. Two males are headbutting one another,

"Stay here," she rises slightly, preparing to launch forward. *"I'll bring back food."*

Filo looks at me in concern just as she shoves her body off of the ledge with such force the ground seems to groan. Her wings pump hard and fast, carrying her over the plain with vicious intensity. It's too late for the bison to start running as they spot her about a mile out. Dust kicks up as they all turn to run, only for her to disappear while swooping low over them.

Curved horns peak out of the low dust cloud, one catches her back paw. A small kick knocks the angry animal away. They all continue to run, leaving the dazed one behind. It shakes its head trying to regain its balance and coordination. Legs seem weak as they buckle once more, forcing it to stand again. The rest of the herd have begun heading for the incline that will eventually bring them up to the plateau Filo and I still hide on. Our focus swings between them and the hunting ahead. Now steady, the bison snorts while pawing at the short grass below. One bison in the herd slows to turn towards his companion.

Her body tilts at a full perpendicular angle to swivel her back to the one now attempting to catch up. Instead of tucking its tail, the bison begins a full-blown run at her. Those matte black wings straighten out at the last minute, then flare to bring her feet towards it.

A low mooing sound echoes from the prey as her right foot grabs its head. Using the momentum it built up for her, she swings it back behind her into the air. Brown tufts fly when those claws release it. I lean forward in amazement as I watch her whip her head back, quickly followed by her body.

Her tail spears through its head, ending the animal's life before it hits the ground.

Some of the males in the herd have turned back, attempting to save a life of their own. Her tail slides out from the body to whip around in a threat. Five charge at her at full speed. Panic rises, accidentally seeping into Kali. She flicks it away like some bug buzzing around her face. Filo blanches, not at the blood that spilled to the grass, but at the teeth bearing down from Kali's parted mouth. Pure white bones that glisten in the heat and sun, dripping saliva from one of them.

Only a couple hundred yards away now Kali drops her head low, throat hanging over the dry land. With a breath visible from our location, her chest heaves widely. I feel that darkness edge from her, not reaching out to take me hostage, but to push me away. Violence and pain shove me out as if sentient enough to know I'd try and stop it again.

She lets out a roar so powerful, my body forces my belly to the ground. My head dips, though not my eyes. While I watch in awe at her maw opened wide to spill out the sound only she could let out, Filo's body is completely pinned to the ground. His eyes fight to stay open, mostly sweeping the ground in front of him.

I realize, suddenly, that her roar isn't just a claim on her land, it's a claim on her rightful title. The end of the roar cuts off as the bison skid to a halt, turn, and run away. As they rejoin their group Kali throws her head into the air. Her long neck sways as she somehow manages to release an even more powerful one. This time, I bend under it.

Kali

I grip the body, no, the food, between my curved talons. To ensure small shards of bone don't break off I drop it from a couple feet above the ground next to the men.

"You first," I offer. Filo rips off a leg with a wet tearing sound.

"You have to eat too," Jakir reminds me. A look in his eyes gleams with pride. Of what, I don't know. My anger when taking down the aggressive bison was dark, that corner of my mind pushing to be released completely. I wanted to slaughter the whole herd. The only thing stopping me was the faces of those waiting for us to bring these back. We finish the meal before us by splitting it evenly. Rough ridges on our tongues clean the bones of any meat.

Wordlessly we leave only the head for the crows to pick at as we fly away. Three of them are pecking at its empty eyes before we even take off. My mind drifts back to the bird that stayed with me for so long. He still had yet to find me again before returning. I think of his smart mouth. How he acted out save for when I needed to be hidden.

"I can feel you reminiscing," Jakir side-eyes me. *"What are you thinking about?"*

"Feathers."

"He was with you when you needed him, you don't need him now."

Despite the projection meaning Filo could hear the conversation as well, he stays quiet.

"Something tells me he'll be back."

"Then I suppose we shall see."

Filo sweeps out, corralling the herd to head southeast. As we travel we discover wolves, a small pack of seven. They attempt to take out the herd. I take pity on them and let them have an older one that can't keep up as well. Black eyes shine back at me. Perhaps in thanks. Perhaps in respect of another predator.

Forming a triangle at night to keep the herd surrounded proves to be easy. I miss Jakir's tail threaded with mine. He lifts his head drowsily when he feels me missing him. A slow blink calms me down enough to settle into the ground. We trade shifts, though I let Jakir sleep through the last one.

In the morning, the sunlight glints off of Jakir's golden scales. Filo hisses as he is awoken from a light slumber.

"*So grumpy,*" I tease him. A smile pulls at the corner of my scaled lips.

"*You try havin' a beast of gold blind you. I shouldn't be mad cause he's so righteous but it's kind of rude.*"

I chuckle as I nudge my friend awake. He lifts himself up quickly like he wasn't just fast asleep.

The travel back proves to be a workout for our muscles. Quickly burning through our meal as we dive, snip, and guide the herd towards home. Most of it is spent running since they only stop out of tiredness every few hours. They run without bounds. Air itself only minimally necessary as their hooves stampede across the plains.

Home comes within sight off in the distance.

Filo and Jakir surge ahead to guide the sides of the herd away from those tents around the massive tree. Silence falls into my head as I drift back to thoughts of Feathers and where he might be. Light brushing sensations jolt through my wings causing me to automatically pull it towards me and veer away.

"*I could kill you with that sort of unawareness,*" Sayah says with a sneer in his voice. I settle back at level flight next to him.

"*You won't, though.*"

"*Would you like to test that?*" Senka asks, pulling up to the other side of me. I use that rope connecting me to the power I felt when going head to head with angry males earlier. I yank hard like it's connected to my core. With a swell it washes out of me to whip out at the twins. Sayah flinches back, Senka blows air harshly from her nose.

"*No, because I know you don't want to.*"

My ability to enforce my position was capable of much worse. After letting them feel it, rather than inflict it on them like a weapon, I pull it back and stuff it within myself. They both continue to fly next to me with their wings under my own. I flare mine quickly to bring them under theirs. Neither look directly at the motion of me placing my wings under theirs, but I feel the shift to a more relaxed energy.

Our new herd slows down as they head to the waters. Sounds of slurping and drinking begin once their heads dip down to the lake. Both Jakir and Filo have already shifted and clothed themselves. I land with the gray dragons on either side of me, still walking as my human side takes over. My Sekund tosses me a loose t-shirt and jean shorts to put on.

"Herd is yours, Ellie."

She thanks me with a nod. She and the others begin discussing the choice of fencing them in or not.

"Sayah, Senka, come with me," I walk away from the rest of the Samle to a more secluded area. Jacobs hammer echoes as he works on the framework of the first house.

"You didn't have to do that," Senka says. Her voice is small, so unlike her. I meet her eyes with a tilt of my head. Knowing she speaks from a history of never being truly cared for I select my next words carefully.

"You're right. I didn't. I wanted to."

"We don't..." Sayah shoves his hands into his pockets. He doesn't finish.

"Look this Samle is all we have left. Nobody else has come to check on us. Most likely no one will. I get the history, I do. I'm not saying to forget it, I'm just saying don't let it control you." They remain quiet with closed-off looks. "I got the shit beat out of me, was tracked down every day for a year, got strung up for display in front of people probably just as nasty as your history," I throw up my hands and shrug. "But I know nothing about it except you didn't deserve it."

Before I open my mouth again Senka speaks.

"Our parents didn't want kids. We were accidents. *Are* accidents. So instead of having two useless people around they decided we needed to learn about how bad life could be."

"We learned everything we know from them," Sayah continues, his Russian accent peaking through. "We still love them, despite how much abuse they put us through."

"But we're here now," Senka cuts her eyes to him, effectively ending the history lesson. "We just don't want to follow someone around who doesn't know what the fuck they're doing."

"You think you can do my job better?" I raise an eyebrow to both of them.

"Never said that," she crosses her arms.

"Never hurts to test the waters before you jump in," Senka shifts his weight, a cocky grin on his face.

"Fair," I nod my head to the side. "So we're good?"

"For now," they say in unison. I grin with teeth feeling their dark confidence creep back in.

"So, what did you find?"

Most people would pull back at the giddy looks on their faces while listening to the horrors the forest provided. Deer with half a face made of its skull eating at moss that seem to seep black goo. Its antlers had been so large that the muscles in their necks bulged from supporting them. The smell comes from the bark of the trees so if one pulls it away an incredibly dense wood is revealed.

"Then we can use it to build our homes," I nod.

"We tried to use it as firewood but it would never catch," Senka's face furrows in confusion.

"Even better," my eyebrows raise.

"Something about the air is...intoxicating. Like it puts fear into your very bones," I turn to Sayah in doubt and confusion. "I think it wants to keep people out."

"It," I repeat.

"Yes, the forest feels like it breathes. No sounds except for that. You try to scream and the Dead Forest drinks it."

I don't argue against the name.

"I like it," Senka licks her lips. Her eyes grow distant thinking about the lifeless part of the territory. They bounce back and forth like that for a few moments longer, explaining how everything is either made to keep you from eating it or make you sick. Both laugh when they tell of the hallucinations and vomiting that came with drinking the water. After receiving the report I shift topics.

"I'll be leaving in a few days to visit the Eastern Continent," they stiffen at my words. "Easy. We're going to Mikhail's Samle, he requested I grace him with my presence before some big meeting."

"They're really going to do it?" She seems surprised.

"If it's something they've been planning, then I guess so."

"Mikhail wants the upper hand before any of them, wants to know what to make of you before the others do," he thinks aloud. "He can be cunning, but from what we've seen he's not the worst of them."

"And who is?" I pull my hair into a ponytail to go help with building the house.

"Easily Gallyan, stupid man thinks he's a gift to this planet," her brother nods in agreement.

"How much do you know about the other Samle's?" my hands wrap around a large piece of wood to drag it to Jacob.

"Some, we can find out more if you let us," she slides in the question underhandedly.

"Nobody *lets* you do anything. Now if you just so happen to sneak around unheard and unseen, I'd be more than happy to hear what you find," I grunt as we lift the wood. Jacob walks towards us as we carry the huge piece of lumber towards him. "If you just so happened to do so."

We help place the beam where the roof needs it, holding it steady as it's fixed with expertly carved notches to lock it in. Nails are hammered for extra security. Once completed, I walk with the two demons behind me. I grab more wood as they both speak.

"It would be our pleasure."

My skin prickles at the venom in their voice directly not at me, but instead at the freedom I had just handed to them. Jacob catches their last sentence as they pass him with wood to begin closing in the sides of the house.

"What was that about?"

"I asked them to do something for me," I shrug, not looking at him.

He leans on a pile of wood with a smile.

"Oooo can I know?" his hand slips, causing him to almost fall. A blush rises to his cheeks as he dusts himself off. I chuckle, shaking my head.

"No," I continue chuckling as he pulls a splinter out his hand. "You cannot know Jacob."

"I'm like, *really* good at keeping secrets."

"Oh?" I toss a humored look over my shoulder.

"Oh totally. Everyone loved to tell me about their secrets in high school," he nods energetically to emphasize his point.

A loud snap sounds as Sayah and Senka lock a large piece of a wall into place. Jacob gives an adorable thumbs up to them. Senka looks bored at him.

"Hmm, well alright," I lean over to him as I pause, whispering in his ear. Pulling away from him earns me a smile. "Don't tell the twins you know."

He wiggles his eyebrows, "I would never."

Dark haired twins walk past me, Sayah smirking as if he can smell the game I'm playing. I nod imperceptibly to confirm that it is, just in fact, a harmless game. Jacob spends the rest of his time with his chest out like the playful secret I handed him fills his lungs with itself. Framework of the first of many houses is completed just in time for dinner.

Harlow proudly presents the first meat dinner any of us have had in a while, Ellie adding mushrooms in a passable excuse for a side. Nobody complains once our bellies are full for the first time in over two weeks.

"So I checked the females in the herd," Ellie burps incredibly loudly, covering her mouth. We all laugh at the enormous sound that rips from her a second time. "Oh my, excuse me."

Senka laughs so hard she rolls from the log she sits on to the ground, clutching her stomach.

"So tiny," she cackles. "But so loud!"

We all break into another fit of laughter again watching her laughing fit. Sayah fails to fight the small smile on his face. Gleaming strikes his eye as he watches his sister be so happy. I watch intently, wondering when the last time any of them truly laughed was.

My heart swells with the recognition that this would be the first happy memory I have of my new life. No one chasing me. No one hurting me. Jakir watching me from my left as I smile wider than I had in more than two years. Aiza, wiping tears from her eyes. Filo shakes his head as his shoulders shake, stoking the fire in the middle to keep the warmth going.

"You are all so ridiculous," Ellie attempts to act indignant. Only to giggle again. "As I was saying, I checked on the herd with Harlow, and we think some of the females might be pregnant. So the herd should be growing soon."

"Clearly not growing as fast as that belch did Ellie, damn," Jacob tucks his chin down towards his shoulder as he jokes with her. Sayah chokes on his water at the sight of such a face. Senka smacks his back, purposely trying to make it worse. Once everyone has calmed down again Lilly's snores reach us all. Ellie looks down at her with a smile.

"Welp, I'm exhausted so I'm gonna head to bed. See y'all in the morning," Jacob stands to stretch. As he walks away Harlow smacks at his butt. Her eyes turn sultry at him as she stands to follow him.

"Try to keep it quiet 'till you have some walls around you," I call.

The others follow suit, save for Sayah and Senka. They walk off shift, wishing to fly for a couple hours to tire themselves out.

"I wonder if you and them have the same sleeping habits," Jakir nudges my shoulder with his own. "They never go to bed or wake up."

I shrug, "Maybe they just have more energy to burn off."

He hums, "Perhaps. Or they refuse to deal with their trauma like you do."

"Don't," I warn. Heat builds in my eyes. He doesn't flinch at the command.

"I am the last person that will ever bend to you," his words make me stare into the fire. "But I'm also the last that will ever leave you. I'm here when you're ready."

At his gentleness I feel the Bond open up on his side. I don't open my end, just let him fully enter my consciousness. Feelings of dread, or pain, flare up at how open I am.

Chapter 17

"Not now, not-" my words choke off as the darkness starts to wash over me.

No no please not now. I hate this. I don't want to see them again.

Memories I had so carefully boxed up free themselves as I drown. Drown in the memory of my hands above my shoulders with blood crusting on my body. It starts at cut one, slowly replaying like a movie. Tears course from my eyes freely.

It hurts it really hurts. It's happening again is it real?

A deep voice echoes in my ear, only making me dizzy with fear.

Never happiness its not mine I don't get happiness this is what I get I'm so weak I deserve to go back

Movement somewhere outside my memories puts me back at the scene of three bodies hanging in the woods. A strange body cradles me. Lifts me from wherever I am.

Flashes of hanging limbs, shattered ribs, torn bodies, leaves in the dirt soaked red with blood. Someone sobs. Visions of shiny blades slice at me. Now it's my blood wetting the dirt.

Time slows to drag me thoroughly through every step I take in the forest. My feet don't fly like I remember, instead they drag. They catch on a limb that wraps around my ankle. My body freezes, unable to move even a finger as the forest drags me away down some dark hole.

Tingles graze my spine.

Feathers flies hard and fast just as hands drag down my torso.

Pain starts to curl around in a circle on my back.

Cruel faces laugh, throwing beer at me.

For a split second, I see the lake over Jakir's shoulder.

My memory reverses back. Dragging me in reverse through the pain. I'm on rewind.

Warm, dark skin rests against my forehead. The backs of my knees are resting over someone's upper thigh.

Darkness pulls back from my mind. Stuffing itself into a corner again. *Here, I'm here. I'm home.*

A knife becomes present against my skin, warming the longer it stays there. Jakir's arm moves slightly in a repeating motion. I slowly realize that he's drawing a matching symbol to the first he traced out in the city church.

Shuddering a breath inwards, then out, he stops to set down the knife. His well-built arms encircle me. Careful of the new mark, he pulls me in tightly. Hands stroke down my hair gently. Every run down the mid-length hair brings another wave of calm.

I speak the first words knowing Jakir won't push me by doing so first. "Why?"

"I didn't push you at all, just opened up your mind. Your mind was locked."

"I had it like that for a reason," I grit my teeth.

"And it wears on you every day when you do that."

"I don't need to relive it all, I know what happened," I try to shove myself back. He gives me a stern look, making me cease my escape attempts.

"But do you? Have you really faced what happened to you? Have you let yourself feel? I can feel it when you let that darkness take over. Can feel every time you put yourself down," his eyes cloud in hurt. "You think you deserved it somehow."

I remain silent.

His eyes glow a little as he reaches an invisible hand down the bond. Light fingers brush over the fire in my abdomen. I smack at them and attempt to pull away in anger. I don't get far with that, as Jakir grips my emotions that rear up like a coiled snake. I gasp as he crushes it.

165

"How?" I seethe.

"I've been learning to do it on myself. Spoken to Aiza a few times about what she knew of other's bonds. You will always dominate over me in position, but I am always your equal."

My face betrays nothing as I question my capability.

"I'm not exactly some unkillable monster, I'm sure there's plenty of things on this planet that could put me in my place."

"I have opposing feelings on that," the invisible hand pulls back, smoothing out the anger as it falls back.

"Based on what?"

"A gut feeling."

"A gut-" I throw my hands into the air and slap them back down onto my thighs. "God damn how much of our lives are gonna be gut feelings. This is getting ridiculous. Fine I get one, you get one. Then we're done."

"Sure," he fights a smirk.

"Ugh," I toss my hands up again.

"Better than living life blind," his bright smile irks me slightly. I lightly shoulder check him as I pass, tossing him a gentle smile. The tents are far, clearly marking that I was under enough time for him to get me away from the others. His footsteps trail behind me, still staying by my side despite my hot and cold nature.

I curl up into the double sleeping bag with him after changing into loose shorts and a fresh t-shirt. We face towards each other as our eyes flutter shut. My nightmares give me break by only creating a new forest for me to run in. When I gasp awake Jakir tucks me into his chest. His heartbeat chases away the nightmares until morning.

I close the door to the Bond enough so that the tension doesn't wake him so suddenly when I creep out of the tent. I hear him stir, however, beginning to wake up.

Aiza easily sets down a small duffel outside of hers. Her smile appears as I approach.

"I'm going to stay in human form for now. I'm running low on clothes so I need to pick some up while we're visiting Mikhail."

"Does he have enough?" I set down my own bag full of supplies.

"No, but a small untouched town right on shore has a million of them. They don't like dragon-men though."

I stop checking my bag to stare at her. She doesn't look at me for a long time, still not doing so when she speaks.

"I'm not sure about the run-in that occurred, but I know the council of women that govern them can be nasty if the wrong person steps into their village. Better to leave the twins on the perimeter while we go in."

"That's their decision," I argue. I catch Jakir stepping from the tent from my peripheral vision.

"Trust me, the clothing they have – you're going to need it. Mikhail likes fancy dinner parties and anyone underdressed in front of other leaders is at risk for unwanted attention."

"I don't think I've had enough of that yet," my eyebrows raise with my smile. Aiza tucks her lips in to fight the laughter at my dark humor.

"Don't be so proper all the time Aiza," Senka taunts. "Let loose once in a while."

I smack his head lightly, warning him off of teasing her. Four duffel bags are spaced out enough for each of us to grab our own once shifted. I place my advisor's next to mine to make it easier to grab. Ellie waves from her tent, not wanting to leave a sleeping Lilly. My chin dips in response. Aiza waves back sweetly.

"She is not to be alone, at any time," Jakir says as he hugs me. My mouth can't move when it's crushed against his pectoral. Any arguments are therefore muffled.

"We'll know when to be with her," Sayah assures him. I pull away and meet his eyes. Those dark brown, nearly black, eyes match my stare. He has no intention of leaving me to my own devices.

I yank off my t-shirt, wrinkled from restless sleep. Gold takes in my scars, then my face.

"There's no shame in coming back if it becomes too dangerous."

I open my mouth to hand him the retort but Senka beats me to it, "Yes there is."

My mouth pulls down at the corner as I fight a haughty grin. The shorts come off next, leaving me bare to the dropping temperatures.

"I expect each of you in a house when I get back," I point at Jacob.

Near identical bullets of danger wait for me to shift, their tails snapping around in excitement. Harlow offers a hand to dainty Aiza, getting her up onto my back in that safe dip between my shoulder blades.

"My word I thought you were large but from up here," she trails off as she peaks over my shoulder. I shift my weight, the only warning before lifting off of the ground in two swings of the appendages draped in midnight black. Grabbing one duffel in each curved-talon back foot we begin the flight to the boat.

Guess we did end up needing the boat, I mentally consider.

"How comfortable was it with six of you on board?" I ask the other two.

"Only a bit snug," her mouth definitely switches into a devilish look. *"Once they all got over the motion sickness."*

My stomach tightens at the thought of hurling my guts up. Mom and Dad had frequently taken Car and I on boat trips out into the Gulf of Mexico. Car found it hilarious each time I puked over the side on the way out. Queasiness was the effect on the way back in.

"Mmm, we'll see."

I got to see, alright. Got to see every watery blow from my mouth spill down the side of the white boat. The ocean was most definitely out to get me.

"Fucking hell," I moan. I step back so I can rest my head on my forearms, resting on the edge. Rocking lulls eventually, finally giving a break to my poor stomach. Butterflies shoot around inside of my gut like they've snorted a line of crack.

I try both looking at the horizon and at the deck. The deck doesn't help at all since it's covered in scars from the twins fighting hand to hand with daggers.

"You are so much less threatening like this," Sayah claps my back.

I resist emptying my stomach of the sip of water I just took onto his shoes. My vision sways slightly as the starboard side dips close to the water. Another groan spills from my lips. Aiza flits around me like a mother, annoying Sayah enough that he leaves to go spar with his sister again. Her cool hands grab my cheeks to face me to her. I close my eyes against the feel of them.

"No no, don't close them, that will make it worse."

"Everything makes it worse," I grumble.

"Here, try a breathing exercise. In through your nose for four seconds, hold for four, and then breathe out for five."

I follow her instructions to a T. Finally, the dizzying nausea ebbs away to a manageable level.

"I look ridiculous," I shake my head, hair falling in front of my eyes. Aiza drops one hand to her waist, the other to my shoulder.

"No, you look like this is your first time out on a boat."

"Yeah. So. It's not," warmth spreads into my cheeks. She shrugs a shoulder.

"Eh, the waters are not for everyone."

Her poor attempt at lessening my embarrassment might have been humorous any other time. Any other time I wasn't constantly trying to fight the urge to empty my already puny stomach. Eventually a tub of ginger is pulled from a cabinet helping to quell my sea sickness.

Two hammocks swing side-by-side at the back of the boat. I lock my hands behind my head while Aiza quizzes me from the left about politics and what they call "court life". Yawns pull at my jaw at the sheer boredom of remembering each Konge or Dronning.

"Midlans Samle?" she drills.

"Sean, who's Sekund is named..." I drag through my melted mind for her name. "Ah, Beth."

169

"And Mikhail's Sekund?"

"Dimitri, and don't comment on his receding hairline."

"I'm going to regret telling you that," she covers her face with her hands.

"I'll comment on it," Senka calls over from her dagger-throwing practice.

"You can if you stop wearing down the damn mast, find something else to do Senka," I jerk my chin at her in a small motion. She pouts, but changes to stretching.

"It's really not polite to comment on it," Aiza turns her head to me.

"I can't control them, they're their own people."

I know they both hear me say it. Aiza doesn't even catch the microscopic pause in the twins to glance at one another.

"They're nightmares," this time she can't help but chuckle at the mischief they embody. I chuckle with her. "Alright, and which one should you be weary of?"

"Elias, though I see no issue with a bit of harmless flirting."

"It's not harmless. It's hit or miss, mostly miss, when it comes to having a real sense of trust between him and anyone else. Don't feed him anything important about yourself or anyone you care about."

"I don't blame him, these people all sound like different rings of hell."

A vacant look in her eyes irks me into asking her questions now.

"Did Mikhail do anything to you?" I sit up slightly.

"No," she shakes her head vigorously. "He would never do anything unless someone well-deserved it. He has boundaries."

"Clearly someone else you came across did not."

Silence sits between us, for at least an hour. I watch the stars rock gently above me without a single cloud to block the magnificent view. Some of them twinkle brighter than I had ever seen as a human.

"I originally woke up on the Southeastern Continent, where Sebastian is. A couple of my friends and I managed to survive, eventually finding him and the Metael Samle. They do not like people who cover their hair like us. Two of us managed to get away after he manipulated Zarifa into no longer wearing it. Tahera felt the *kallet* when we reached Sean's territory, so she went with the others who felt it. Mikhail took me in until then, managed to protect me when Sebastian came to retrieve me."

"Because rogues fall under those who find them," I clarify for myself.

"Right, I don't know how he managed to pull it off but he did. Thought people like me deserved a better life in this new world."

"So he's not all bad," I lay back down.

She scoffs, "He's hideously inappropriate and overly confident. He has a good heart but he's not all here. Some part of him sits with evil, I know it."

"Interesting take on trauma."

"That's not what I mean!" she curls her fingers in the air in frustration. Tension builds slowly even as Aiza pounds information into my head over and over. She feeds me everything she can, assuring that what I can't hold onto she will be there to fill in the gaps. My mind wars between being excited to escape her lessons or shaking with fear in another unknown step into the future.

By some luck of the universe, we aren't greeted by any Samle or their members once the boat reaches land. Three women, two men greet us instead, their eyes smudged with black coal. Our exchange is quick, save for Aiza's confusion. They offer us as much clothing we need, then lead us to the massive barn holding it all. One of them, the oldest, remains quiet. Her blue eyes stay on my face as we converse with the rest of the council.

We trudge across harshly frozen ground following two of the village members. Rabbit fur swishes as they swing open the doors.

"Who would have thought to make such a collection?" I ask no one in particular.

Aiza keeps searching as she responds, "They did. Smart, too, since people are just now learning to make clothes again. I'm concerned why they didn't ask for a trade."

"Maybe they like us," Senka shrugs.

"Most people cannot afford to trade with them, it's why they still have so many clothes," her eyes are grave. I ignore it, not wanting to drown in fear for once. Especially over something so small.

The twins take only a couple minutes to find their first outfit. Matching sets of leathers. Senka's is a tight fitting one piece that moves with strange ease, lined with warm fur. Sayah's is a thin vest, snug pants, and a long matching trench coat with enough pockets to drive anyone crazy.

Good thing he's already crazy.

We search for more clothing ranging from protective winter gear to cool summer outfits for back home. All of us even manage to find formal attire.

"I don't think we'll need anything that dramatic," I say, unsure of the emerald green dress Senka pulls out.

"Hah," Aiza laughs humorlessly. "Did none of my lessons get through that dense skull of yours, Kali? This is how dragons operate when together, flourishing drama. All the while trying to slit your throat."

"You're so comforting and supportive," I sarcastically gush. She smacks my bicep with the back of her hand.

"Go, find something."

"I'm not hiding my skin, we show it at home, so we show it here," I warn over my shoulder. I pointedly glance at the twins, now grinning like hyenas at the permission to dress freely. Aiza sighs, continuing to search for more of the elegant, flowing clothing that fits her taste.

A sense of normalcy fills me at the search to fill my extra duffel bag with clothes. Without the howling wind outside, or the whisper quiet pull at my gut of being so far from Jakir, it was close to shopping like I did before the end of the world. No eyes on me for once, though ears clearly poised to protect me, I close my eyes and reach for the bond. It's thin and taught like a strained tendon. Touching proves both painful and relieving. Phantom chills thrum around it, only the faintest touch of warmth still there. Our bond wouldn't break, but I know moving further inland would be uncomfortable.

I make careful selections for clothes back home. Things that won't fall apart but remain comfortable. Plenty of dresses catch my eye, so I stuff each one of them into my bag.

I'll have you on your knees, Mikhail, I smile to myself at the thought. I could shove him down if I have to.

End of the world shopping takes a short enough time that we manage to head out before high noon. One of the women stops me as I start to lift myself onto Sayah. Aiza didn't want to risk Senka struggling as we met with Dimitri, explaining that presentation is everything. Even me showing up in dragon form is considered threatening apparently.

"When you find yourself in need again, follow the golden star," her voice carries a weight that settles in my spine. She hadn't spoken since our arrival. "We will help you."

I memorize her face. Her words make it feel necessary.

"What is your name," I breathe, unbreaking of her stare.

"Magda. Follow the golden star, it will bring you to me."

"I doubt I'll ever need to, but thank you," I dip my head in respect. It must be enough, because she lets go of my bicep. My spine still feels heavy as I crawl onto Sayah's back. The rider's dip isn't as deep, forcing me to hold onto his flexible spurs running down his neck.

I don't need to turn to know Magda's watchful gaze bores into my back as we fly away.

Chapter 18

"I know you're probably tired as all hell Sayah, Senka, but I need you to land with as much bravado as you can muster. Stir up some snow for a bit of *flare*."

I drag my hand down his neck as three figures appear ahead. They stay a few feet from one another, preparing for our arrival.

Sayah lets out a low bellow to announce our arrival. My bones shudder at the high keen promising death in it. Senka lets out a matching one that starts just before his ends. Their looks may not be identical but their dragon roar most certainly is. I steel myself for meeting someone new.

They flap in sync as their hind legs stretch out to give balance before landing. Aiza slides off after I do, keeping me in the corner of her eye to ensure I land first. I turn and offer a hand as she slides down Senka's outstretched wing. Her pants billow in the wind, her top doing the same. Her hijab doesn't budge. I make a note to ask later how she keeps it so pristine. Today it doesn't drape over her shoulders, merely a black wrap to conceal her hair as she wishes.

I don't miss the note of loyalty in the color of the cloth.

As she dusts off some snow from her floor-length matching jacket, the twins move forward. I can't help but feel pride as their bones snap in sync to their steps. With nearly as much practice as me, the process had quickened to where they could walk a painfully slow pace.

They stop, don their clothing, and wait for me. Their black stare basks in the fear emanating from the guards behind the tall man.

"Dronning Kali, it is a pleasure to meet you," not a single smile from

174

him. "I'm Sekund Dimitri, please follow me."

He spins to walk away but stops himself.

"Do not shift in this canyon, it may crush you," he adds. I swear I see a smirk pass over his aging face. I trace the pathway ahead, a twisting, climbing trek up to what looked like a drawbridge.

Dimitri doesn't give any warning before setting us off at a harsh pace. My bodyguards split, one in front while the others take up the rear. Aiza stays firmly attached to my side. Heels on frozen stone are the only sound as we all make our way to a castle. Its size grows with each pace, marking itself as grand without a word. Lots of windows keep the front looking open and bright. It's built into the mountain peak we manage to reach, disappearing to unknown depths.

"I'll show you to your room, you'll be staying in the neighboring wing to our Konge," the drawbridge groans down as he explains our sleeping situation. Massive chains bounce at the weight they hold. "Dronning Kali you may decide which rooms your...companions, may sleep in. You have four to select from."

"I appreciate the courtesy," I dip my chin in an attempt to appear more graceful than I am. He does the same in return, not breaking eye contact.

We don't enter the grand doors before us. Instead, we are guided to a door far to the right. One of the guards holds it open for our group without a word. I motion Aiza in first, wanting to get her and the twins out of the freezing cold as soon as possible. Senka puts a gentle hand at my waist to guide me in before her. I don't miss the feral grin she gives the guard as she passes him. Clothing shifting reaches my ear as he shivers.

"Easy little nightmare," I whisper in her ear as she walks at my side through the hallway. My face betrays nothing though, unsure of what emotion I can trust to show. She correctly follows suit.

We climb an extremely wide set of stairs to a large parlor area. Four doors are placed evenly apart along the wall that curves in a crescent shape. Old wood beckons to a comfortable room behind each one.

"You have an hour to prepare before the feast. Please wear appropriate formal attire," he frowns as he scans me. I challenge him to say something.

The twins move around behind me.

"Watch those eyes of yours, Dimitri, or I just might carve them out," Senka warns with a lusty voice. He clearly becomes uncomfortable, coughing into his fist. I don't move to control her, wanting to watch him squirm under her focus.

"An hour," he nods, leaving faster than I thought possible back down the staircase. Aiza tells us she'll be in my room in forty five minutes, needing to wash up from the trip. I turn to the room next to hers to head in. A hand in front of my lower torso stops me. Senka looks at me deadpan.

"We check first," Sayah states. I go to argue, but he's already in my room. He passes carefully into the room, then crosses the length of it multiple times before coming back out. Once given the all clear they allow me to walk in and close the door.

"Lock the handle," Senka suggests.

"And what if you need to get in?" I ask.

"The fact that you think we can't pick a basic lock like that hurts my feelings, Kal," I raise my eyebrows at the new nickname from her. She wiggles her fingers goodbye as she slips into a midnight blue themed room.

Alone for a moment, I close my own door. I take a moment, trying to figure out what greets me first. The silence is. Dull, waiting silence that reaches from my ringing ears. I hadn't realized until now that even in the tents at home there was no true silence. Birds sang, wolves howled, or the lake always lapped at the shore.

This is not my peace.

One king sized bed sits in between two massive glass doors that lead out onto a veranda overlooking the mountain pass. I see a different side of the castle by looking to my right. Its length spans a distance my eyes cannot grasp from here. At the center though, most likely opposite from the gate, is the biggest veranda of any on this side. Glass doors are open letting red drapes billow out into the winds as if reaching for some freedom. I ponder what might lead out onto that huge overlook. Before my eyes adjust to the orange glow of evening I close them. My arms hang loosely at my side, palms facing towards the sky to capture the flurries coming down. Inhaling through my nose brings the crisp scent of winter into my lungs, clarifying any uncertainty. Uncertainty of what, I still cannot grasp. Perhaps having to do with having no stability from the past. I flick the thoughts away as I hurry back inside.

A separate room holds a large tub, I don't pause to think about how it's heated as I quickly yank off my clothes. Once my hair is tied up I ease myself into the copper tub. Heat coats my skin, easing the tired ache in my joints from constant moving. I only allow myself a moment of rest before scrubbing myself clean, then using the liquid brought from home. The massive red pine-cone shaped plants were difficult to find at first, but once Harlow had learned their scent she had managed to find a field of them for us to use. Some sort of liquid spilled out of it, useful for washing every part of the body. I still maintain use of the conditioner that Jakir brought back for the women on one of his last supply runs.

Somehow the water temperature never cools, so the only thing that makes me climb out of the massive tub is a knock on the door.

"A minute!" I call. Toweling off quickly, and throwing on the offered robe on the back of the bathroom door, I pad to my bedroom door. Only a crack reveals Aiza, dressed in beautiful layers of black that wrap around her body. Curves aren't overly accentuated, still managing elegance while dressing her thin frame perfectly. Her head covering is formed tightly to her head with a mock ponytail of fabric cascading down her back in dramatic flair. Loose pants swish around her legs, hiding her feet. I watch as she practically floats in, the cinched cuffs on her sleeves somehow marking her dainty figure even more.

"You look..." I search for the right word. "Absolutely stunning, Aiza."

I lower my eyebrows from the surprise as a warm smile crosses my face.

"Thank you," her dark cheeks turn a hue of red.

I notice the stark singular color of black she's wearing. To others she might be trying to blend in, but I see it for what it is. I walk behind a privacy screen to get dressed. The robe has absorbed some of the moisture left on my body from my bath so I have no trouble slipping into the evening gown.

Cool chains that hold the front and back of the dress slip down my thighs. The material of the dress flows freely over my legs, the double slits leave my thighs free to the cold air of the castle. Snug sleeves that start halfway off my shoulder extend down to the loop over my middle finger. I test the elasticity as I did in the barn, ensuring that it won't snap. The corset-like top of the dress scoops up under my chest, long straps of fabric hold my breasts up. The excess of the fabric holding them ties around my back then cascades over my back in a waterfall of black and silver shimmers. I turn to see how much of my back is exposed. Thankfully the long, thick strips of cloth cover the two scars on my spine. I stare at them, taking in the thin lines creating the two unfinished triangles.

"We should leave soon, it's better to be early than on time here," Aiza reminds me. A pin holds my hair in a loose bun, unable to keep a few strands from falling out, I give up and walk out after strapping on sandals that wrap around my calves. She blinks heavily as she takes in my dress. I lift my chin, waiting for her to criticize how it might be inappropriate for a first meeting. She clears her throat finally and speaks.

"You look absolutely stunning, Kali," her use of my earlier phrase eases some of the tension in my chest. I place out a hand precariously to help her off the bed. Placing a well-polished hand in my rough one I take some of the weight of her standing from the bench at the foot of the bed.

"I'm sure the twins are already standing outside the door."

We both step outside, into a hallway only to see Sayah leaving Senka's room.

"Where is she?" he asks frantically. To the common person, his face looks passive. I see the tight worry in his eyebrows. "Is she with you?"

I frown, anger ticking like a bomb in my chest.

"I thought she was with you," Aiza rubs her chin lightly.

"They couldn't have taken her without her making a sound, and she wouldn't leave you," his gaze locks onto mine. "Without letting me know. Someone convinced her to leave."

178

I say nothing, just take a deep breath into my diaphragm. I reach into my chest, trying to determine if I should be worried or not. As if a leak begins from my throat to my heart, I grow angrier.

"Something is off," I grit my teeth. Some sort of gut feeling, perhaps what a mother's sense might be like, spurs me into motion. A foreign feeling seeps into me, having been there for a while.

"How do you know?" Sayah questions me.

"I can feel it, I thought it was my own tension. I think it might be some kind of sense, like a mother with her child," I have no need to grab my skirts to avoid stepping on them down the stairs. Black streams of flimsy cloth flare out on either side of me while I fly down the steps.

Aiza begins to speak but Sayah hushes her. I make a mental note to ask about that later. Nobody but a sparse number of guards stand in the hallway. Each one of them flinches as I stalk down the hallway.

Anger flares up with every step I take towards the large metal doors at the end.

"Open them!" I snap. Neither of the men hesitate.

"Kali-" Aiza tries again.

"*I* will handle this, the *only* time you may interfere is if you deem it absolutely necessary. Am. I. Clear?"

Her tone is confident, free of frustration with me.

"Sayah, you will stay back and mind your mouth," more people are in the hallway, casually walking in the same direction. I push back the guilt at latching control around his neck. People swing their heads.

"Oh, I plan on it," the danger in that voice gives me the last bit of courage I need.

Darkness swells in my mind, setting my eyes ablaze. Discomfort tinged with fear becomes easier to feel.

I'm coming Senka.

I maintain my pace, knowing too fast would show fear. People stumble back out of my way as I plow forward. Some move too slowly.

"Make way!" Sayah calls, his voice lashing out like a whip. Those still in the way stumble back to escape Sayah's gaze, maybe even to avoid me.

Turning down the winding hallway I spot huge doors that stand taller than a semi. I don't bother to shove the ever-creeping violence down, only grasp it firmly to wield as a weapon. My eyes begin what I know is their dominating glow. Burning unlike I have ever felt spreads from them to my temples. The female guard on the right sees me coming. Her head snaps to other as she issues a command. When her head turns back she refuses eye contact, head bowed. I don't even acknowledge her.

I'm coming Senka, you're okay.

Murmuring sounds sway against my ears once the doors reach their full open position. Calm glowing light spills onto the hallway, nothing too bright. Just enough to put a sensual feel to the room. Room isn't even an accurate description for how expansive the ballroom is. Huge windows opposite the doorway look over a treacherous mountain pass.

Gasps fall from surprised mouths as I slow slightly, allowing a widening path to clear for me. Up on the platform, like something from a movie, is a throne made of shimmering gold. It's carved to look like it's melting into the very ground below it. My eyes drag from the feet clad in expensive dress shoes, up across dark green dress pants that caress muscularly built thighs. Hands hang over the arm rests, veins coursing under pale skin that disappear at the long fingers tapping away to the gold. The torso is draped in a matching green suit jacket that does nothing to hide the broad shoulders under it. My hackles rise under my skin when my flaming eyes connect with hazel ones.

He has a smirk slammed onto his face. Reaching to pull his red hair back out of his eyes I nearly begin a sprint just to slam my hand across his cheek.

A heavy breath echoes in the now silent room. Senka is on a knee below the platform. Pulling myself from the taught energy between me and the Konge I look to her.

"Why?" I demand. My voice drops an octave at the violence straining underneath my hold.

"He told me to," she grits out.

She's being held down by a Konge's command, I realize. Whatever power I held to force the guards to open the doors must be keeping her on a knee.

"Get up-"

"She will stay right where she is-" Mikhail's cocky attitude rakes nails over my skin. I hiss through my teeth, more to ease the strain of that endless darkness slicking itself over my head. Sayah shifts his weight closer, sensing my limited patience.

"Senka, *stand. Up.*"

Breath wooshes from her lungs, causing Mikhail's jaw to drop slightly. Tension disappears from my chest, telling me I've successfully overcome Mikhail's hold on her. He watches her stand, lethal control in every movement of her body.

I reach out a hand, willing her to come to me. I stare down Mikhail as my nails drop, not even hitting the floor before long black talons unsheathe themselves. Hazel eyes follow the drop of blood from my pointer finger to the tile. Senka reaches me, placing her hand in mine.

"You will never," heat flares in my eyes and temples. "Follow an order from him again."

Like a landslide coming down on her the command settles on her. Instead of being chained up by my words, she sets her shoulders back. Her chin is a bit higher.

"You cannot permanently command disobedience, even to your own, Kali," his voice sends goosebumps along my spine. I hold still despite the need to shiver. I let the violence slip a little as he steps down off the platform.

"Try me, Mikhail" I tilt my head to the side. A gentle tug has Senka just behind me, safe.

His eyes flare just as mine do, looking to Senka.

"Kneel," he drags the word across his palette as if he's trying a new wine. Not a sound from behind me.

"Kneel," he says again, light becoming more intense in his gaze.

Senka doesn't say a word, but I feel her smirk coming on. I hold a hand at hip level with my palm down, keeping her at bay.

Mikhail frowns, the light disappearing. As he wipes the disappointment away, he begins to walk forward. I match his steps as we near one another. My thighs sneak out each time a foot comes forward, pulling his rapt attention. Dragging a look down my body and back up sends every message of what he's thinking. Nearing him, my head has to tilt back to meet his. He dwarfs me by almost a foot.

We finally come within arm's reach, both extending hands to shake. As our skin touches, I nearly scream.

I never once enjoyed the idea of killing. I loved it when I found out I killed those men, loved the thrill of taking down the meal for Jakir and Filo.

This is something else. Something that ripped and clawed and dug at the deepest part of me. Need to rip Mikhail's throat out surges forward.

The Bond wraps around my spine in support, I feel calm with concern holding me back from doing something incredibly stupid. At the push of more concern I drag an invisible hand down it in assurance.

I'm okay, Jakir.

Knowing he can't hear my words I simply assure him I'm okay. Opening the Bond on my end allows every piece of him to reach me. It may be weak, but it's better than nothing.

I drop his hand, dragging my talons across the sensitive part of his wrist. A sharp inhale through his nose brings him back to the present as well. All I can do to keep from sinking the black talons into his chest is set them on my hips.

"I would say wonderful to meet you, but I'm afraid my first impression of you isn't a good one," the heat dies out from my eyes giving relief to my throbbing head.

"Perhaps a good party can change that," his high cheekbones shift as his teeth flash.

"Please join me," he sweeps out an arm to a table that has replaced the throne. "Allow me to recover our relationship."

His eyes dart at my body again, not in an oily way. A way that makes me do the same to him. Dimitri stumbles in through a door at the far side of the ballroom, feverishly taking in Mikhail and I. He dusts off his jacket, then walks towards us. It takes him longer as many people reach out to talk to him. Once he finally reaches the table, Mikhail and I have already seated ourselves. Sayah pulls out my chair slightly from where the Konge had pushed it in. I smile gratefully at him, relieved to not feel trapped.

"I assume you've already met my Sekund, Dimitri?" Mikhail implores.

"We have, yes. He was pleasant on the way up," I take a large sip of the wine poured for me. After Senka sniffs and tastes it, of course.

"Excellent, well we're pleased to have you here."

"You, you are pleased," Dimitri corrects. His own wine passes his lips. I look to him for a moment.

"I don't blame you for being protective of your Samle, new people in a new world don't typically spell out safety," I shrug. The statement seems to ease the Sekund slightly, understanding passing between us. Aiza touches my knee under the table, our agreed upon sign that I'm doing well.

"Hm, yes I suppose that's fair. Have you had many people come to your Samle?"

I swallow another sip of wine, "No, I think you know that."

A hand touches my thigh, a foot touches mine. A warning from her.

"It's fine Aiza, I'd rather hear her honesty than politics," those hazel eyes dip to my thigh. Even after my advisor removes her hand, his eyes travel to my hip where the chains lay across my skin.

"My honesty isn't down there," I look out over the room at people. Some dance, some eat, some talk. Not a single one of them is worrying about whether they'll have a room to sleep in or a tent. Mikhail's head pulls up quickly, not even pulling from me.

I reach a hand to brush against Aiza's ensuring her of my capabilities.

"This meeting, what's it about?" I don't hesitate to dive off the ledge of pleasantries.

Chapter 19

"So eager to jump into the boring stuff, why not enjoy dinner first?" Mikhail spins his wine glass by the base, those long fingers moving gracefully.

"I've played enough of your games for now."

"If they were enough they clearly weren't fun enough."

"Perhaps our idea of fun is a little different," I hear Aiza politely cough next to me.

Mikhail's eyes snap to my hands, talons still out, then drag up my forearm. I hate the goosebumps that rise up where his gaze drags.

Pretending to not see my own reaction I sigh.

Mikhail leans into my personal space, his mouth inches from my ear.

"Perhaps we should learn what those definitions are."

His low purr sends a shiver that slow-crawls along my spine, that wicked violence still simmers beneath my skin, begging to be let loose on its target. Something about him is enough to attract me, yet not enough to quell the insane need to rip his throat out.

After an inhale he pulls back. His nails dig into the armrest on the other side. I let out one breath for a mocking laugh.

Aiza clears her throat, "So, Konge Mikhail. Who all has confirmed their attendance?"

"Just Mikhail please, Aiza. And all of them, though I'm not sure of who they'll bring. Gallyan won't risk bringing his Sekund, and most likely none of the others will either, save for Addison."

I place the second name as the Dronning claiming territory next to

184

mine. Again, wondering how far her boundaries reached to have not felt me and Jakir traveling. Raising a spoonful of soup that's been passed to me by Senka I stay quiet. Mikhail doesn't seem to want to stop talking, so I let him give us everything he knows.

"I also asked Addison if she had visited you yet," his head turns in my direction. "She said she hadn't. Did you refuse her company?"

"She never offered it," I shrug casually. Implication of her hostility takes root, making me bristle. Aiza shows agreement with my response in a quirk of her lips.

"Interesting, she usually likes sinking those claws of hers into everything she can."

I don't miss the venom in his voice.

"And the others? Who do they typically bring?" I don't linger on the topic of a single Dronning. Too early to draw attention like that.

"Everyone brings two or three people with them, so you aren't far off the mark. Though I'm sure you can thank Aiza for that," he winks.

"Actually," she dabs her mouth with a napkin. "Kali made that decision on her own, I have yet to tell her what to do."

"Playing background character?" Dimitri adds. "How unusual of you Aiza."

"I simply wish to help my Dronning. Her success is the Samle's success."

"Or it's downfall," the Sekund rolls his eyes.

"Watch yourself Dimitri," I swipe my tongue over my bottom lip. Tension settles at the base of my spine, adding to the tension in my chest from the murderous inclination.

"Yes, please Dimitri, let's have just *one* pleasant dinner."

I tap my talons along the table, considering if I should put them back. At this point, it's beginning to become more comfortable having them out. Aiza speaks softly with Senka next to her, discussing how we could go about trading for more clothes when we make our way home.

"How did you find this place?" I ask him.

Mikhail pushes his soup bowl away, then shifts in his seat to face me. His hips turn easily, but his shoulders seem to not quite fit within the confines of the chair. A smallest hint of crows feet touch his face.

"When I shifted, sending out *kallet*, I flew for half a day and found it. Wasn't much, needed a lot of tidying up. I have no idea how it got here, I think when the mountains cracked it revealed the castle."

"Interesting theory, but doubtful. Something strong enough to crack mountains open should have also torn this castle apart. Especially since so much of it is in the mountains themselves."

"Ahh, but then again, who would have thought people could change into something twice their size," he looks pointedly at me.

I don't give in. I only pull the side of my mouth up and respond, "Yeah, who would have thought."

"You can put those away, I have no intention of harming you," he leans towards me fractionally making me realize I've leaned into his space as well. We probably look like a flirting couple from the dance floor.

"We're going to dance," Senka announces. She drags a blushing Aiza from her seat to the floor.

"Why don't you dance with them?" I ask Sayah.

"I cannot dance with Aiza, not unless I wish to disrespect her which I do not. And Senka has finally found a female that likes her. Let them bond," he only glances to the side at me. Noticing Mikhail in my personal space, his head turns slowly to stare him down. I shift my weight to catch his gaze, shooting him with a look.

"As I was saying," Mikhail continues, that perfect teeth smile gleaming at me. Almost perfect, one of his canines is chipped. "You can put the weapons away. Though they *are* stunning."

"I'm not going to be swayed by weak compliments," I begin to grow bored of his bland talk.

"And what exactly would sway you, Dronning?"

"Let's give you *not* boring me a try."

"Kali," his voice drops slightly. I can't tell if it's in anger or lust. "Knock it off."

"You can fix the boredom, but I'll choose when to stop the bitching," I ensure nearly everyone is busy, sliding to the front of my seat to block

Sayah from seeing how close I am to him. "The next time you decide to threaten my Samle, think about if you want these 'interesting' talons sinking into your spine."

My wine-soaked breath grazes his lips. I know because I watch him breath in gently, changing something on his face. I slip my hand towards his rib cage to press the sharp tips to ribs that gleam three inches from my fingertips. At the exact same time, his hand slips under the material of my dress. His palm is hot, nearly scorching. Lines of fire follow his pointer finger as he drags it around my kneecap. My core tightens in response to both his hand on my bare skin and his gaze on my lips.

Mikhail's tongue darts out to pull his bottom lip in. He drags his lip between his teeth, making it swell slightly. Images of the lips below my waist flash in my mind. I pause to wonder if he somehow sees them, because his hand tightens on my leg. Pain shoots up to my hip causing my anger to flare just as much as the heat in my core does. His nails fall over my skin to the floor as the tips of talons press into me.

"Ease up on the claws, kitten," his eyelids drop as he warns me.

"You first," I smirk, a dangerous, hateful, heated smirk. His talons press into a couple of the sensitive scars. Peering at his hand earns me a small bit of information about his other form.

His talons are red, like a cardinal's feathers. It stands out starkly against his white skin. He presses harder, pulling the smallest inhale from me. We're not close enough to attract attention from the crowd so the partying doesn't stop. That doesn't mean the small distance is rattling for both of us. Unfortunately, I hear Sayah push his chair back behind me to stand. I lift my left hand just high enough to signal him back down.

"I can make this hurt," Mikhail pulls his face back enough to be out of my breathing range.

I laugh lowly, "Please try something that's actually a threat, Mikhail."

Those hazel eyes brighten slightly. Swiftly he leans back against his chair, effectively giving in to the drip of blood that seeps into his shirt. I raise one talon to my mouth to drag it down my tongue. A coppery taste blooms. His jaw flexes.

Mikhail doesn't blush. Doesn't even clear his throat as he watches, pulling a foot up to rest on his knee. I notice the shift of his hips to cover the swelling in his pants.

"No one will judge if you need to adjust yourself," I shrug a shoulder.

"I should slam your fucking face into the table for being so brazen with me," he hisses. Dimitri spins in his own seat, looking confused between us. My eyes warm as light barely flares in my eye at the Sekund. "Keep those pretty eyes off of my Bonded."

"Or what?" I swing them to him.

Let's see just how far I can push this.

"Or I might find a reason to add a few more scars to your collection." My body locks up.

Every scar feels like it's on fire. Terror builds at the base of my skull making it hard to get a full breath in. A satisfied victory smile plasters itself on full display at me. I'm about thirty seconds from actually attempting to kill him before my chair is swiftly pulled back. Firm hands guide me up from the seat.

Sayah begins to guide me away, but not before I lean down. Not before I win this battle. Placing a hand next to his forearm I muster every ounce of sexuality I can into my voice. It isn't hard considering how turned on by him I still am, by the crisp scent I get leaning down to his ear. My lips brush against the shell lightly. Even with the raging hostility something in my body still wants him.

"Still not a threat," I croon softly. I sound like a succubus ready to kill.

Veins shift over tightening muscles as he moves to grab me.

Sayah has me stepping off the platform before Mikhail turns around completely. Slowly, we walk past a table of baklava. I swipe a mini piece into my mouth. Sugar explodes on my palate, making me suck in my cheeks.

"You don't like baklava?" he asks. Those dark eyes glitter as he holds back laughter. I gently smack his bicep, then wrap my hand around it. He turns to grab my hand, leading me to the dance floor.

"I've had it before, love it actually. Go ahead and laugh," I shake my head even though we both laugh. "It's just been so long since I've had something other than mushrooms."

His head tilts back as he laughs. We spend a number of songs dancing as we speak about the things we miss most from the 'old world', as he calls it. He carries me in slow circles, guiding my steps so there's no work for me to do. I catch Mikhail staring at me without an ounce of shame. His head doesn't budge, nothing does. Dimitri speaks to him, but he doesn't even respond. Being turned again brings Sayah face to face with him.

"If I didn't know any better, I'd say he's acting like a Suitor," he whispers.

I have a puzzled look on my face at the old term that drags a shrug from him.

"I have no idea what you're talking about," I say, my lips dragging up a bit even in my confusion.

"Just an observation."

"If I didn't know any better, I'd say you already hate him."

"I've met him before, wasn't a fan."

"And now?"

"I like him even less."

We dance a bit longer until most of the hall has cleared out. A barely tired Senka returns with an out of breath Aiza.

"Did you really need to exhaust her?" I extend an arm for Aiza to begin leaving the room. She whispers advice on how to exit without being rude. Bristling, I turn to the Konge and Sekund now standing at the base of the podium.

"I appreciate the lovely dinner and dancing," I don't dip my chin like Aiza suggested. Dimitri goes to speak, clearly trying to cover his Bonded's next possible verbal lashing.

"I didn't have the time as I was...preoccupied," not a single glance at anything other than my face, but I know where he wants to look. "But I would like a dance or two tomorrow night."

I have to do this again? I internally groan.

I can't read the Konge's face. Can't tell if he wants to sink those red talons into my neck or sink his fingers into another part of my body.

Maybe both.

Aiza makes the smallest of noises to spur a response.

"We'll see," I say. I turn to follow out my Samle members. Eyes sear into my open back as I walk down the hall. I swear I feel the gaze over more than just my back. Winding through practically empty halls puts the four of us back at our guest rooms. The twins bade me goodnight before Aiza follows me into my rooms to speak in private.

"These are his nicest guest rooms by the way. He may be trying to win you over."

"I doubt he wants that right now," the black material slides off of me once I'm behind the privacy frame. A warm robe is hanging for me so I slip it on, not bothering to find pajamas. My advisor isn't sitting this time clearly wanting to go to bed herself.

"What did you do, Kali?" she groans. Her petite hand touches her forehead as she mumbles some prayer.

"He started it," I know playing the child card will bug her. I opt to lighten the mood since I'm still tense with energy.

"He has the biggest Samle to date. This is a huge opportunity for us. He didn't reach out like this to the others."

"There also wasn't a konge or dronning that took forever to basically hatch."

"Fair. Just..." she considers her words, taking a deep breath. "I don't know if slapping your confidence out onto the table will piss him off or interest him."

"My confidence?" I tease her.

"You know what I mean. Be careful. If I were you I'd err on the side of caution."

"Good thing you're not me," I give the response no tone as an attempt to mask my frustration with what is still replaying in my head. A ghost feeling of a hand touches my knee. I see the hurt flash across her eyes before I form the apology. "That wasn't meant to-"

"I know, I saw some of the bickering. He can be a very frustrating man. Trying to form an alliance with someone who wants to sleep with you

190

surely cannot be simple."

"Did any of you keep your noses in your own business?"

"Firstly, it's literally our job to have our *noses* in your business. Secondly, I still managed to pick up some tidbits from the other dragons gossiping on the dance floor."

"Do tell," I pull open the double doors to allow freezing air to slither in.

"Gallyan has made it quite clear that he's on edge about your late succession, not sure what that will entail. Sean, from the Midlans Konge will be bringing his wife, Aliyah. Dronning Janét is apparently *very* interested in meeting you and has mentioned an alliance. That in itself is fantastic because of what she possibly has."

"And she possibly has what, exactly?"

"There are rumors that some dragons have begun to develop…extra abilities to find gems. I've been looking around trying to find why some have them, but any Samle keeps their secrets about that under lock and key."

"Rightfully so," I cross my arms, considering the possibility of dragons moving even higher up the food chain. "Something like that could put a Samle above anyone else."

"Agreed, I would try and speak with her if you can. I will attempt to speak with the advisor she may bring."

"Anything else? Perhaps some information about this Addison lady?"

"No," she sighs at me. "The only thing I heard was questions about why she or Linius hasn't reached out to you."

"Linius never would have felt me in his territory, if we're correct about where it is. Even if I was, I was only on the edge. Might have been gone before he could even get to me."

She nods her head, the gears turning so fast in her I can't keep up. I make a mental note to reach out to Linius specifically. We need all the alliances we can get. With a goodnight, she leaves to get her rest. Breathing out heavily I attempt to release the tension in my shoulders. There's not much to unpack and absorb. Only two weeks to be confident in as much information as possible before the others start to show up.

Heat flushes down my spine. Teasing cool air whispers at my feet begging me to come outside onto the balcony. I let the occasional snowflake touch my exposed shoulders as I run over who is who again and again.

Linius is south of me, most likely only made aware of my arrival after I truly shifted for the first time. I hadn't been home long enough for him to make a trip to me. Hopefully he wouldn't show up expecting Jakir to be friendly while I'm gone.

I calm my nerves about the Dronning named Addison, deciding to only worry about her until I'm face to face. The Slips and Rain Samle from the Southeastern continent flanked Janét, but certainly hadn't made their intentions clear. Close enough proximity to Linius's Samle might prove to be beneficial. Or not helpful at all. Shaking my head at the quickly growing web of messy relationships between everyone, I tilt my head to the sky.

Bits of cold settle on my cheeks. They melt instantly due to the heated temperature from my frayed nerves. Basking in the wonderful feeling of snow brings me into a calm. True winter had never been a thing living in FL. Only a reward from mother nature for going on vacation.

Drapes flap to my left, the same ones from earlier. I walk towards the edge to see if I can determine who's room it is. My foot doesn't even fall on its first step before I see Mikhail with his hands behind his back staring at me. His flaming hair is pulled into a bun exposing his cut jawline.

My eyes drop down like a weight in water to the muscled torso that's exposed to the weather. Every abdominal muscle is cut out from an artist carving granite. Painfully visible lines drag down my attention to the low hanging seam of his pants. With every breath those acutely made muscles contract, making me imagine what they would do over me.

A part of me hesitates at the sexual attraction, afraid to let someone get near me like that again. Unwilling to let those emotions well up while he watches, I shove them back. He's close enough that I can see his eyes dragging over my nearly completely bare legs.

He has absolutely no shame, I consider as I watch him move his arms to be crossed in front of him. The shape of his pants changes when his eyes slide over my shoulders back up to my face. Unwilling to stand there for his appreciation any longer I turn to walk back into my room. He yells something, but a gust of wind carries it off.

I look back over my shoulder as I let the right side of my robe slip down. Two could play this game. Stepping over the threshold is where I let it drop completely, letting him see enough to know that the robe was the only thing I have on.

Cracking sounds wind into my room before a large, winged figure dives down. Red scales flash in the corner of my eye as he puts distance between us.

Chapter 20

Sunlight pools in the room with a blue tint pulling me slowly from an unrestful sleep. Tightening in my gut woke me all night, making it incredibly difficult to fall into any deep type of rest. The Bond continues to flare up in mock cramping as I pull on a pair of warm leather pants provided by my host.

A snug shirt with loose sleeves fits nicely under the matching gray leather vest. I frown at the sleeves, wondering if they will get in the way of any movement. Giving up I open my door to find Sayah the only one awake. His grin helps to ease my mind off of the tightening of the Bond.

"You didn't sleep well," he comments. We begin our walk down the stairs to meet Mikhail and Dimitri in a courtyard, as requested by a note left on my door.

"Do I really look that bad?" I query.

"You look amazing as always, Kali," his hand squeezes my shoulder in a mock condolence.

"I hate you," my eyes roll.

"No, you don't," he pauses, a careful look forming. "I heard you cry out a couple times while you were sleeping."

"Stalker," I mumble.

"Anything you want to talk about?"

I almost tell him no, then consider that he cannot effectively protect me if I hide everything from him. He has already made it clear he is learning to trust me. I need to return the favor.

"It's the Bond," I sigh, brushing hair out of my face that's escaped my braid. "It feels injured, as if it's a muscle that's been pulled."

"I was wondering when you'd start to feel the effects."

My eyebrows pull together. We continue walking, but I look at him for an answer.

"Ah, I'll explain. Just keep in mind this is only what I've heard."

Knowing he hears more than anyone else I eagerly await the information.

"It's very much like a muscle, but also not," he begins. "It can become stronger over time, as long as you don't consistently turn it off. Some dragon leaders and Sekund can only sense the life of the other, others can feel emotion."

"Jakir feels emotion, we can push emotion to the other as well."

"I've heard of that as well, I believe the two from the Gem, Scraper, and unfortunately Hellish Samle, can do the same." His mention of each one is fluid, yet I only remember the last one to be Gallyan. "I know the further you are from one another, the weaker it becomes. Always being together also means you never feel the separation, but you also never make it stronger."

"Stronger as in…?"

"Meaning the next time you're so far apart from one another, it won't be as weak. It's just very painful and draining to get to that point."

"We've been apart quite a bit. I didn't think it would be for the better. It honestly kills me Sayah. I hate every second of not being near him. He's a life-given best friend, I've never trusted someone as much as I trust him."

We reach the room from last night, filled with tables of people eating breakfast. We only grab some boiled eggs before leaving. A guard meets us to escort us through the maze of castle walls.

"Lean into it, he might be the best thing to happen to you."

"Don't have to tell me twice."

Through an archway we're brought onto a large stone courtyard. Large enough for a dragon my size to fight with another, it's much longer than wide. Dimitri is off to the side with a handful of young people, showing them some pattern of movement. The red headed pain in my side is nowhere to be seen.

"I hate him... so wouldn't mind seeing you put him in his place," Sayah puts a hand on my back. "But it would behoove you to ask as much as you can about being a Samle leader, a dragon, a Bonded, while you're here."

"He'll only thrive off of me coming to him, cocky bastard," I clench my fists at the thought of his dark smile.

"He will, but that will only increase the chances of an alliance."

I lean back to look at him, "Look at you being all political, thought that was Aiza's job."

His chuckle puts a dimple on his olive face, "I'm nowhere near as schooled in politics as she is."

Conversation between us ends as Dimitri makes his way to us, hands behind his back.

"Good morning Dronning Kali," he tips his head to me then gives my protection a greeting as well. "Mikhail had some business to attend to but he will arrive shortly."

"Kali, please."

Dimitri seems to hesitate at the lack of formality, though he respects my request.

"Mikhail has extended an offer for you all to train with us. Many of our Samle were either previous military or have trained with them enough to be trainers themselves."

"Gladly," I place a hand flat against the bicep of the tall man next to me. "Sayah has some training of his own he could share with your trainers, should he be willing to offer it."

Black hair falls into his face as he dips his head while looking at me, confirming my offer to Dimitri.

"Let's begin then," he clasps his hands in front of him. Thoughtful eyes look around at various groups. "Sayah, you and your sister may begin with our advanced combat group over there."

Mostly men, a few women, battle one another with staffs. Speed and accuracy using such a seemingly useless object surprises me.

"I appreciate the offer."

With a look that says *I'll be right over there* he walks towards them.

"Senka may join him when she wakes up. Aiza will go with the beginning group, those are our newest trainees."

I look at the group he gestures to, seeing only females do long poses that blend into another.

"If she wants to, and it's at her discretion."

"Sure, but any dragon that can't fight is a weak link."

I grab my wrist behind my back where he can't see, needing to hide my anger.

"Dimitri," I give him a sinister smile that barely shows teeth. "I understand you might have some dislike towards me and my Samle but let this be the last warning I give you. I will not tolerate you speaking ill of them anymore. Snide comments to me are one thing, I don't care. I *do* care about how you speak of them. If I hear you say anything out of line again, I'll carve your tongue out with my talons and eat it for breakfast."

My eyes are starting to burn with a glow by the end of my threat to him. A giggle sounds from behind me. Senka.

"I'll cook it for you," she laughs again, truly finding it entertaining. Dimitri keeps his face mostly composed. Only a swallow proves that that combination of my threat with her violence gets the point across.

"My apologies Kali, it won't happen again."

I don't comfort him, nor do I push further.

"Please, follow me."

I walk next to him, refusing to be behind him. He stops at a circle made of dark stone some distance from everyone else. As I stop with him I feel the Bond strain heavily, almost knocking the breath from me. Nothing changes in body language or facial expressions on me.

Dimitri straightens, "He wants to train with you separately. Believes the two of you being seen working together will allow the rest of us to build trust."

"Maybe the twins can as well."

He agrees, then leaves me alone to stand in the circle. The air begins to warm around me making the outfit feel almost too warm. I take in my surroundings, a rack of various weapons to my right, a rack of cloaks and various clothes to my left. Probably for those who needed them after shifting. The courtyard drops off into a deep canyon, carefully protected by a railing. Behind me I spot Mikhail's balcony. His windows still aren't closed meaning he must keep them open all the time. I'm not the only one that enjoys the cold.

No wind carries into the area making the heat uncomfortable for me. Taking off the warm vest gives some relief. My shirt lets me cool down due to the sheer material of the sleeves. I breathe in deeply, trying to quell the pain that stabs at me again. Counting the time for breathing distracts me, even calms my heart rate. It does practically nothing to help with the increasing agony. I close my eyes, willing my frame to look calm – not shaken – in case anyone watches me. Another breath in. Another out.

Eventually it calms down enough to let me open my eyes. Mikhail is standing just out of arm's reach, arms crossed, watching me.

"You look angry," he raises his eyebrows. I can't help but glance at the veins popping out in his arms. As if knowing what I'm drooling over he shifts so his hands aren't tucked away. Flexing his arms turns my awe into annoyance.

"It's just my face," I wave off the attempt.

"Or is it the fact that you were pissed last night? I've never seen such violence in a woman."

"Scared?"

"No," his arms drop, beginning to move as he unbuttons his shirt. "It gets me hard when a woman can follow through on her promise."

I raise a brow, popping a hand onto my hip, "You have yet to see me get violent Mikhail."

"I know, the anticipation is killing me."

I mentally disregard whatever need he's referring to. No sense in getting myself wrapped up in thought right now.

"Let's get started on whatever it is you have planned."

"How about we work on some self defense, wouldn't want you to have any more scars," he winks at the last word. Anger bristles under my skin.

"Stop mentioning the scars, I'm well aware of them."

He reaches out and grabs my neck. Except he doesn't get a solid hold on it because black talons are flipping his wrist away before he can.

"Those babies come out fast, don't they?"

I don't say anything as I brace myself.

"Tell me the story and I'll stop mentioning them," he demands. Another grab, this time my shoulder. I'm in a headlock before I can speak. He explains how I can stop it from happening, walking me through it. Once I have it down, he demonstrates how to get out of it. I feel my arms start to burn from the exercise after an hour of training.

He reaches for my throat again, this time I swipe away his arm and slam a palm into his chest. The jerk only shifts one foot back for balance.

"Why so many?"

"None."

He grabs for my throat. I can tell his holding back by how he slows down just before reaching me.

"Of."

I dodge another slow grab.

"Your."

I release myself from his hold.

"Business."

He actually grabs my throat this time. I peel back his hand using leverage on his thumb.

"Can I at least know if it was before or after you shifted the first time?"

I don't move. My memory still won't show if I ever did shift in the woods. Flashes of blood and muscles exposed to the damp air filter in. Literally stumbling upon them. Feathers mocking them.

"You first...darlin'."

A finger under my chin pulls me out of memory lane. Back into reality.

"Where did you go?" His voice is soft, personal. While curiosity burns behind the mix of greens, I almost think I see worry.

For a moment, his warmth tickles the sensitive part of my neck. I realize his hands are large enough to cover most of my face if he wants to. Everything disappears around us. Grunts from sparring fade into whispers. I forget the walls around us are literal mountains.

My eyes dart down to his lips as his tongue wets them. His chest moves up a little faster when my mouth opens slightly in response. Pulling my gaze back up to his, I feel heat settle in my core. A private part of me clenches as his eyelids drop slightly. He's just as into this as I am.

The smallest step brings him closer to me. Despite the minuscule smell of sweat, I can still smell the crisp scent of his body. Snow on a fresh morning is the only thing I think of. I bring a hand up to rest on his wrist, lightly tracing my thumb talon over the sensitive skin. Sharply inhaling has his pupils flaring at me. Just as both of our eyes start to lighten, low rolling pain drops out of me.

Instead of being relieved by the pain of my strained Bond going away, I get yanked out of the moment. Senses return just as quickly as the ache does. My shoulders pull in slightly wanting my body to curl up into a ball. I fight the need and square off again.

"That's enough for today," his voice is rough.

"No, let's keep going."

"You're in pain from something, did I injure you?"

"You wish," I snap.

"God, a part of me does," the roughness lingers, hardly making it through his clenched teeth.

I curse myself for not stopping my traitorous body before my hand rests on my midsection. He notices before I yank my hand back down.

"How long were you with your Bonded...?"

"Jakir," knowing he's looking for a name, I give it to him.

"Jakir," he repeats, then waits for my answer.

"About six months, maybe? I don't know, hard to keep track of time when you're busy surviving."

Fuck, I can't pull the bit of my history back now. Thankfully, he ignores it.

"How often were you two separated?"

"I'm not - maybe a total of a week?"

"How far?"

"Mikhail, I don't know," I throw up my hands. "Why are you asking?"

"Such a fresh Bond being put under such stress should cause pain. You should have gradually increased the distance, allowing enough recovery in between. You're across an ocean right now. How are you standing?"

He reaches a hand out as if to steady me. I step out the way with some sass, not needing his help.

"With my legs. Any other stupid questions?"

"Kali I just want to help you-"

"How generous."

"I do intend to help you. You just need to let me."

"I don't need your help," I snap. He barks out a laugh at me.

"Maybe not my help, but my healers help you do," he grabs my arm, pulling me back into his castle. "Most dragons in your position would be screaming in pain, unless your Bond isn't very strong?"

The knowing look over his shoulders frustrates me.

"We feel each other's emotions," we make our way down a fairly narrow hallway. "Sometimes we use our own to help manage the others."

At that he stops immediately and pushes me against a wall. He doesn't reach for my neck, instead opting to use a large hand to push my chest back into the biting stone.

"You what?"

"Did you not hear me? I really don't want to repeat myself," I throw a bored look down the hallway.

"I heard you, I want to hear the last part again," he pushes more into my chest.

"Sometimes we use our own emotions to help the other. He'll be calm, and push it to me to help calm down."

He searches my face frantically as if he can pick some answer out of my pores. I wait only a few seconds before pushing him off.

"Kal," he starts. An eerie calm is weighing on him. I don't miss the use of a nickname.

"Out with it," I suspire.

"I have spoken with many others in our position. A few of us can feel our Sekund's emotions. And theirs, ours."

"Like Gallyan?"

He nods, "Yes. I can too, as well as Janét from the Gem Samle. But none of us, *none of us*, can administer our emotions like some sort of medicine."

I slowly understand why my Bond is so startling. How such a strong one being stretched so thinly should have me on my knees, but I'm standing upright. Learning to fight. If Gallyan wouldn't bring his Sekund, and Dimitri was always in some close proximity, it was more than that.

"What-what happens when one of the Bonded dies?" I murmur.

"The last and only time that happened was when Gallyan killed his neighboring Samle. Slit the Sekund's jugular. The Dronning killed herself two weeks later."

I drag a deep breath in. My internal ones are a long list of confusing emotions, concerns, thoughts.

"I didn't know," I admit, feeling vulnerable. I begin to question my decision on leaving Jakir behind.

"Bringing him is the most dangerous thing you could have done," Mikhail comes so close our chests almost touch. I have to tilt my head back to look him in the eye.

"You have this huge meeting happening in two weeks. I'm not prepared for it, I know next to nothing about being a dragon."

"I can help, on one condition."

"I won't make a formal alliance with someone I know nothing about."

"Fine, then agree to consider one. I'll teach you everything I know. You also let me see your other form, go flying with me," he leans down slightly, making me feel pressured. I press four talons into his side. His sudden hiss of pain thrills that threatening darkness on me. It sits up, wondering if it's time to play.

"That's a long list," I push the violence back down not wanting to start a fight in a hallway we can barely both fit into.

"And dinner. That's the last thing."

"We had dinner last night."

202

"Alone, just you and I."

"Fine," I agree, wanting him away from me before that darkness pushes back and takes over. His surprise plasters itself like a billboard put up next to a highway. "Fool."

The insult brushes over him harmlessly. His shoulders even seem squarer as we walk into a well-lit room.

Plants line every inch of the border making it feel cozy. The glass roof, metal welding keeping thick panes in place, allows sunlight in freely. Random focused rays caress some flowers, brightening their colors.

Tables of various experiments crowd the rest of the room. Before I ask a question, an older woman comes bustling out of a corner.

"Oh!" she squeaks. Her round glasses make her blue eyes seem bigger. "Mikhail what are you doing here I thought you were sparring?"

"Nina, this is Dronning Kali. The newest Samle leader I mentioned before."

He's spoken about me before to her?

"Ah! It's so wonderful to meet you. There must be so much coming at you at once. We're grateful here at the Shadow Samle to have you!"

She reaches out a hand, I only nod. Still smiling with glee she continues to babble.

"What can I do to help?"

Mikhail explains the situation, only that I'm suffering from "Bond strain". He doesn't reveal any of the details I gave him before. A part of me is irked that he explains for me rather than offering me the chance to do so. After Nina hurries away to grab some herbs he leans down to my ear, brushing his lips against it. I feel a shiver crawl up my spine.

"Don't mention a word to anyone other than me about the details of your Bond. Warn your people if you choose to tell them. If that information gets out, especially to Gallyan, it could be catastrophic."

"For you or me?" I turn my head, only a bit more and our lips would touch.

"Both, kitten. I'm here to help, remember?"

Nina doesn't even notice our proximity to one another when she

203

returns. I quickly pull away to follow her to a tall chair.

As she grinds up some herbs while explaining how to use them, I listen to nearly every word.

Only a few of the words escape me as Mikhail uses every minor facial expression and body movement to have me rubbing my thighs together. I can't get out of that hallway fast enough after we're done. He doesn't try anything else.

Chapter 21

D inner is another round of who can irk the other the most. Mikhail actually sinks the tip of a claw into my hip while he dances with me. Instead of flinching, it has me pressing myself into him. His face practically drips lust when he realizes the type of reaction I'm hiding. I can only handle one more dance feeling his hardness push against me before switching to dance with Senka.

"You smell like sex," she grins at me with wicked humor. She leads us in the dance, guiding us around the floor. "And you seem to be picking this up, however horrible we may be."

"You may be called nightmares, but I find dancing with both of you enjoyable," I tell her. She beams with pride at my compliment. "And I do not smell like sex."

"Maybe if you'd give up playing politics with a Suitor, you'd stop smelling like it. Or at least stop dry humping each other on the floor."

"All hell, stop using that word," I groan. Senka looks a bit confused though she laughs at my annoyance. I smack her lower back with my hand lightly, but still can't stop from sharing a smile with her.

"I've never seen someone in your position be in such denial."

"Just so you know, your fighting skills aren't the only thing that makes you a nightmare. Your interfering is relentless."

"I think Sayah and I are really starting to like that nickname," she flicks her thick black hair behind her shoulder, revealing her olive shoulder.

"Nightmare?"

She nods, hanging on to my shoulder and hand as we twirl past Mikhail dancing with a young woman. He catches my eye, then dips down to see my hand resting on Senka's back. I raise an eyebrow asking, *jealous?*

His jaw clenches, lip twitching in anger. My own craving to fight him wells up.

"Yes, Nightmares," she rolls it out of her mouth, some of her Russian accent seeping in a bit.

"Good thing I've already been calling you that in my head."

The dance ends, allowing us to return to the table. I sit next to the Konge, but Sayah scoots my chair closer to Senka. Hazel eyes don't miss the movement. I stare straight at him, daring him to contest my people.

"No need to be so far away," he says a bit loud. His hand reaches for my arm rest to pull me back.

Wood cracks slightly as Senka's gray talons sink into the other one.

"She is not a toy to be tugged back and forth," she growls, her accent growing heavier as her anger grows. I place my hand lightly on hers to rub the back of it. Sayah's nails drop to the ground. His own talons sink into the high back of my chair.

"My Nightmares want me close; they've had little time with me today," I know behind me the twins don't even flinch at the nickname. "Please respect their wishes."

"Fine," his coarse tone makes me bristle.

"How about you share dinner with Aiza?" I look to her. Ever the supportive person, she smiles widely. Sayah moves her chair in between Mikhail and me.

I envy the smoothness in which Aiza begins a conversation with him. The questions she poses forces him to focus solely on her. No other words, much less arguments form between us for the rest of dinner.

I'm blessed to be able to listen to the twins describe their day, watching their faces light up. Senka practically foams at the mouth when she tells me of a female that nearly bested her. She makes it clear she plans on sparring with her again tomorrow.

"You should be absorbing everything you can, I want the rest at home to learn once we go back," I point out. They both nod in agreement.

Back and forth they go, telling me about who they sparred with or what they learned. Watching them speak so animated eases some of the strain still tugging at me from the Bond. Most of the herb mixes Nina had given me were helping, but they couldn't erase it.

I answer their questions about my own day, only giving the necessary details for now. Despite my best efforts, they catch that I'm not giving them everything. Before the prying even starts, I offer calm promises.

"Later, not when we're so public."

They don't argue.

Trust between us is becoming so thick so fast, I begin to worry how far they'd go to protect me. How territorial they might be if a person were to say the wrong thing. Being somewhat territorial seems normal for dragons around their own, a behavior I've noticed being around a Samle other than my own. A few of the men and women eyed me dangerously as I danced with their Konge earlier. Senka and Sayah merely do the same thing for me.

Telling them they cannot be protective over me will only take away freedom, and they deserve every inch of it I can give them, I think to myself.

Willing my concern to dissipate I note the opening to excuse myself from dinner. The twins follow me out, leaving Aiza to continue conversing with Mikhail about some trading agreement. I look over my shoulder as I walk away. Someone comes up to him mid-conversation to whisper frantically in his ear. After they leave he's visibly more tense. I brush it off as his ever changing behavior.

My muscles protest at the movement down the stairs to the main floor. Sparring and dancing is the most exercise my body has had since being on the run. They ache even more at the reminder that I'd be doing intense exercise along with more sparring tomorrow morning.

I pass Dimitri, who gives me a respectful nod. I return the gesture with a small smile. He looks to the twins, only to immediately look away when they give him a predatory smile. Perhaps finding it funny isn't appropriate for a Dronning.

Once at the top of the stairs to our rooms I decide to mention what they wanted to know. Pulling them in close so our faces nearly touch I explain how what I thought is a normal Bond between Jakir and I is in fact not. I don't insult them by mentioning the position it puts me in.

"You can't share this, I wouldn't even share with Aiza," Sayah considers. He looks around again to check no one is near.

"She would never tell anyone," I frown at him.

"No, she wouldn't," Senka agrees. "But her having that knowledge could put her in a lot of danger. The two of us are the only one's who could withstand interrogation or torture."

I flinch at the blatant recognition of where this information could land them.

"Who would go that far to get it?" I look between them both.

"Dominé," Sayah offers.

"Sebastian," Senka adds.

"Gallyan," they say at the same time. A sharp edge at the mention of one their abusers.

"Hendrix," Senka rolls her eyes.

"Addison," Sayah shrugs.

"Any of them would do anything to have control over you," she explains.

"In their minds, you're ripe for molding to ideals right now. I guarantee all they want is control over you, by extension, us," he walks around the area slowly.

"I'm sorry if I've put you in a compromised position," I run my hand through my hair, looking to the ground in shame, realizing that their past with one of those leaders could make things difficult. Her hand brushes my shoulder.

"The only person compromised is whoever tries to get to you. Don't be sorry, we can't protect you if we don't know what's after you," those dark eyes of hers meet mine with steel determination. Not a trace of comfort is there, just pure promise of violence. I reach out a hand to touch hers in thanks.

"I need sleep, the Bond is wearing on me. As is having not shifted in a few days."

"There's no rule against shifting in another's territory, go tonight. Wake us up when you do," Sayah opens his door.

"No," I shake my head. "I'll do it alone. I need the time."

He doesn't argue with me, only walks into his room and shuts the door. Senka does the same after sweeping my room to check for unexpected guests. Leaving me to my own accord I walk to the tub to begin filling it with water almost too hot to stand. Dumping a few oils, as well as the herbs Nina gave me to help, creates a cloud of perfume in the bathroom. Breathing in the steamed scents is already beginning to ease the tension in my gut. Closing my eyes halfway, I step into the copper tub, sinking so that half of my chest is submerged.

Breathing slows greatly as the hot water seeps down to my bones. Lavender is the only thing I can smell now, bringing calm to my racing thoughts. A black shape on one of the shelves next to the doorway catches my eye. Some flower with dramatic petals, a red center surrounded by black is laying down.

Mikhail, I note bitterly. Even with it being his home, I still grit my teeth at the thought that he or one of his own entered my temporary room just to plant the flower.

"At least it's not a rose."

Heat begins to turn to sapping cold so I remove myself from the bath. I only manage to dry myself off before collapsing on the bed. Cool sheets cover my body as I lay down on my stomach, wanting to feel the cold air over my bare skin. Lower temperatures lull me to sleep.

Low moaning escapes my mouth. Pain radiates from my lower spine. Tendrils of fire have wrapped themselves around me in my sleep forcing me upright. I gasp as the Bond seems to scream inside me, begging to be near Jakir again. That pain echoes from his side as well, telling me he's feeling everything I can.

Memory dredges up the fire that I was chained up in front of. Everything about this is just like that. Too hot for a room open to the dead of winter. Practically unable to move, unable to feel anything but the Bond demanding to be released.

"Jakir," I sob out in a whisper. I beg the night that the Nightmares don't wake up. Another wave of pain knocks the breath out of me. I can't even curse it hurts so badly. My only win is remaining silent, save for the clawing at my sheets.

Distantly I hear a knock on the door. Nothing but silence afterwards. I control my breathing to the best of my ability in case it's the twins or Aiza. After a stretch of silence I begin to think whoever is there has left.

Until a short cry pulls from my lips. Akin to every cut being reopened on my body, I lose my vision in another wave of pain.

I forgot to take the medicine she gave me, I realize too late. My bedroom door swings open, pulled partly by the suction of cold wind out of my balcony doors.

One tear rolls down my cheek. I can't even lift my hand to wipe it away. Consciousness almost starts to slip away until the wave of pain settles slightly. I suck in a breath like I've never breathed before. Precious darkness starts to drag itself out from that tight little corner I kept it in so well.

It promises to protect me. A never-ending pit of violence, darkness, blindness to right and wrong.

Red hair falls in a current around my face. Someone is leaning over me. *I don't have red hair.*

Another wave, just as strong as the last, has me arching my back up from the bed. Red hair disappears as some sound – probably words – come from the nightstand. I feel my nipples tighten at both the voice and the cold breeze that drops the temperature of the room.

"God Kali, you should have told me."

I snap to the clear voice. My eyes burn slightly when they meet hazel

210

ones framed by brightly colored hair. I stare at them, wanting nothing but to claw them out. More darkness takes over, halfway completed now.

The door opens again, someone asks what's going on.

"Leave, you have no idea how to handle this, girl," the large redhead threatens. Something about the threat lets those claws in my head pull themselves further. I sit up amidst the pain.

"You have no idea what she's like, Jakir told me what she gets like."

I stand, the tall man in front of me steps back.

I want to see him bleed.

"Kali, lay back down," veined hands open a jar of purple paste. "You're hurting."

I ignore the request. My cheeks tighten as I smile. He smells good.

My thoughts are battling between pulling him down on top of me versus carving a hole into his cheeks. I lick my lips at both. His gaze watches my lips become wet, making his eyes start to glow with heat.

"That's not Kali," the female voice says, a rough accent tinges it. It's familiar enough that it causes me to stop my descent into that bottomless pit.

He doesn't even look at her when he asks, "What do you mean?"

His shirt is half undone, exposed part of his muscled chest. I eye up a vein standing out on his neck that stretches over a sensitive area. I reach my hand up to touch the partly exposed pectoral.

Both is always an option. Dinner and dessert.

"Things happened. The things that were before she sent out kallet, but after she may have already shifted."

"That's a volatile time for a dragon," his voice is so rough, so deep.

"That's my point, it did something to her under the surface."

A deep sigh echoes.

"Mikhail," the female uses his name. I start to slowly back away from the darkness, despite how tantalizing it is. "She doesn't even know who you are. Doesn't even know who I am."

"I doubt-"

"Kali!" she yells. I snap my head to whoever called my name. Irritation begins at the tone of her voice. I start creeping back into the pit. Anger is easier than fear.

"What do you want, bitch?" I seethe.

Next to me, the man drops his mouth open slightly.

"Told you, that's not her," she motions at me listlessly.

Sadness in those black eyes stop my descent again. Anger doesn't leave my face however, as I turn back to examine the one in front of me.

Jaw muscles flex heavily as his mouth closes. Nostrils flare when I flash my teeth at him. I feel heat at the tips of my fingers as my nails beg to be shoved out. I dig my short nails into his skin. Pushing his shirt to the side I start to press my palm into him. The attempt to put him where I want doesn't work. His hand comes up, covers mine, and peels it back to twist it away from the crescent indents on his chest.

"Leave," is the last thing he says before grabbing my hip, bringing his face down to mine to kiss me.

His lips are warm against mine, softer than they looked. Suddenly I forget the anger that threatened to control me. His tongue pushes my lips apart without asking. Everything about his kiss is demanding.

A groan pulls from his chest as my mouth dances with his. His hand still restrains the one of mine that was on his chest. The other grabs my hip. We spin, so his legs are backed against the bed. Tugging me down as he sits on the mattress, I feel my knee get pulled up to nestle against his hip. He releases my hand to grab my other leg, making me straddle him. I thread my fingers through his thick hair as the last bit of darkness balls back up in the forgotten corner of my mind. I don't even have the time to be upset about my behavior as he shoves my hips down against him.

I moan loudly. Through his pants I can feel how large he is. Grinding the apex of my legs over it I whimper against his lips. Something about the sound from me makes him growl. His teeth catch my lower lip, pulling it out as he clamps down. Pain blooms, this time making me clench the muscles in my core. His lips push mine open again to kiss me, using his mouth to drag out more sounds from me.

I slowly grind my hips on him, pushing harder when his hand grabs a fistful of hair near my scalp.

"Mikhail," I say his name in a breathless moan. I take notice of what it does. His hand snaps my head back to expose my neck. An onslaught of sensations has my eyes fluttering shut as he nips at the skin just below my ear.

"Say it again," he demands. I keep my mouth shut, wanting only to elicit more anger from him.

I don't want anything gentle from him. All the tension from just two days is wearing my patience thin.

"I said," his hands tightens against my scalp. A crack sounds as his hand lands on my ass. "Say it again."

This time, I give him what he wants.

I get massaging fingers on the muscle of the area he slapped. My senses tighten as a small wave from the Bond whips out.

I inhale sharply, "Agh."

He stops everything he's doing so suddenly I almost lose my head. In one swift movement, he has me laying down on the bed. Purple medicine is on his fingers after the next movement.

"I'm fine," I reach for the bulge in his pants. He smacks my hand away. "Right, flip over."

I listen but perk my hips up to tease him. His eyes dart to my bare skin. To his credit, he doesn't reach for me. He smears the medicine onto my back, a cool sensation forms everywhere he puts it. I sigh with the relief it puts on the bond. My body relaxes finally, putting the Bond into a muted state.

"I can't feel him as much," I complain.

"You won't. This stuff figuratively puts the Bond into a coma, letting it heal instead of injuring itself with stress."

"How did she find it? The solution?"

"I had my own strain when Dimitri went to meet with Sean. She has a knack for finding ways to heal people. She was a nurse before everything changed."

"I should get me a Nina then I guess."

"You should, and maybe get that other side of you figured out too," he looks pointedly at me. I jut out my lower jaw, then turn away.

"Dragons are volatile when they're first coming into themselves. Whether it's right before or right after your first shift, you're susceptible to whatever happens to you."

I don't say anything, just rest my chin on my hands, facing the headboard.

"Sometimes the things that happen can completely change a person."

He stops rubbing in the salve, informing me I can turn over now. I flip so I can lean my back against the wood. Pulling my knees to my chest I attempt to hide my scars.

My voice is monotone.

"Does it make them violent?"

"Usually they go one way or the other. I haven't heard of a dragon having a darker side that hides like yours does. I think," he reaches to pull my chin up. "That your resilience lets you stay true to yourself. Like your scars, whatever trauma you bear isn't who you are. But it is a part of you."

"I don't have trauma," the last word drips bitterly from my mouth.

"We all have trauma."

"Is your trauma why you want to kill me?"

"No, that's just what happens with people like us," his hand rests on my knee.

"People like us?"

He searches my face, remaining silent for a while. I go to speak, but he does so first.

"We can talk about it later, get some rest. I'll see you in the morning."

He stands up gracefully from the bed. His full height pulls gently at my temptation to touch him again. I loosen my arms around my legs.

"More sparring tomorrow?"

He stops at the door, ready to leave. I get a smirk as my answer. Seconds after he leaves I go to get up again, not wanting to be alone. Grabbing shorts and a long t-shirt I start to walk to my door. A figure my size slips into the room silently, managing to not even let the door make a noise. I watch her close it in the same manner.

Senka turns to me, then offers a half smile.

"Want some company?"

"I guess."

By the look on her I can tell she knew I was coming to get her.

"I'll put the salve on your back if it wakes you up again," she flips the sheets back to climb in. "If I don't die in this freezing room."

"So dramatic."

We fall asleep facing each other, both of us comforted by the presence of the other.

Chapter 22

I walk alone to the training yard. Senka was sound asleep when I left. Not wanting to bother her, I dressed silently in the same outfit from yesterday morning, then left. My walk is quiet, calm. Sayah's room was empty, meaning he'd already gotten up to go train. I consider how little he seems to sleep as I leave the dining hall with a small bowl of pomegranate seeds in my hand.

This time, Mikhail is waiting for me in the furthest circle, shirtless as he stretches.

I bite the side of my lip at the sight of his large back muscles moving under lightly freckled skin. With the lightest steps possible, I set the empty bowl down. Forcing control over my movements is easy with the now minimal pain of the Bond. I reach out to touch his lower back.

He spins, catching my hand before my talons graze him.

"You forgot to calm your breathing. I can hear you huffing like a mad woman behind me," correcting my failed attempt at sneaking up on him puts me in a sour mood.

"Way to ruin the fun."

"If you want fun, I can always show you my room," his thumb draws circles on my wrist.

I snatch my hand away from him. Today the feeling to fight with him is stronger. So is the feeling to rip his clothes off.

"You disgust me," I walk away to take off my vest. This time tight sleeves make it more comfortable for me to move around, even some scars stand out under the material.

"If making you feel that way is what brings out those perfect moans, then I'd gladly do it again."

I curl my hands, not able to fist them because of the black daggers at the end. Instead of starting with sparring, he teaches me various stretches, then works me through an exercise regime that has me sweating bullets at the end.

"What else?" my muscles ache, but still hold a different kind of energy.

"You still want to spar? That workout should have exhausted you."

"I don't care, keep teaching me to fight."

He doesn't even second guess my request. A part of me warms at the idea that he could read my body well enough to know I was asking for a good reason. One beam of genuine kindness breaks through his cocky exterior. I hold on dearly to it.

Starting with the same maneuvers we went through before, we move quickly onto more ways to defend different parts of the body. I have a way to protect myself from every angle at the end of training.

"That's enough for today, practice those movements on your own. We'll be doing the exact same thing tomorrow."

A bucket full of water has towels hanging by it. We each grab one to wipe ourselves down.

"Where did you learn all of this?"

"Little bit of rough life, little bit of the military, little bit of meeting the right people."

His body language says he doesn't want to talk anymore than that. I don't push.

Even though most of the area is empty, I don't dare to ask for more.

"Can I have the area?"

"All of it," both a statement and a question. I nod once. "Why?"

"The Nightmares need training."

"Why do you call them-"

"They like it," I cut him off, not wanting to hear an insult.

"I've heard stories about them, a couple involving people being left for dead nearly because they gave them a nickname."

I turn my head with a shrug, "They're mine. They wouldn't dare."

Looking at me like I'm crazy, I throw my head back in a short laugh.

"Sayah! Senka!" I wave them over. They drop their current activity instantly to come to me. "Shift, time to train. And you know the drill. I want it my way."

Shifts in the air put the few others in the area on alert. All eyes move to me at the end of the pier. Male and female jog far enough away. Aiza reaches me.

"Would you like to shift? I'd like to see it from a bird's eye view."

"I'd love to, just need privacy."

"Of course," I look at Mikhail. He's still weary of the change in me. I feel like a Dronning again. A short conversation has large blankets being brought out by women. They hold them up overlapping in a circle.

"We can have a privacy screen built for her in a day," he offers.

"Thank you," is all I say.

Cracking snaps out as bones break and rebreak, forming into bigger support structures. Skin slips from my Nightmares skin as gray scales sneak out. All around are open mouths dropping in surprise as the twins walk while they shift.

"Why-what are they doing?" Mikhail exclaims.

"Shifting, what does it look like?" I know damn well what he's talking about.

"That's just self-induced pain for no reason."

I simply conjure the image of my end goal. I say nothing. Senka's rounded features shake out as she completes hers. Sayah's angled body takes longer to form since he's slightly larger. They both walk down to me, lowering their snouts to face level in front of me. Mikhail steps close to me, his shoulders roll back. Deep rumbling from Sayah, next to Senka pulling back her lips to reveal her double rows of teeth.

Touching both of their noses brings calm into my chest. Deep invisible connections writhe between all three of us.

Mikhail wisely pulls back to escort himself to the sidelines. A yelp tells me Aiza has expanded enough that the women don't need to hold up towels for her anymore. Blush pink wings stretch up in relief from her small body. Brighter pink scales flash in the daylight. Much less than half my own dragon's height, she still looks regal in this form.

Short legs carry her to me, looking nearly like her longer body is slithering rather than walking. Her head dips low in front of me.

"Honestly, it's just unfair at this point that you're so stunning in both forms," I comment. I look to her for permission to touch her nose. She pushes her cheek into my hand in response. Moments of connection give me enough comfort to turn to the twins.

Others, including Dimitri, have gathered around Mikhail to gossip about the turn of events.

I walk back to the twins, gray heads following my every move.

"I know you know plenty about fighting in both forms, but I think there's a way to do it better."

They look at each other, Sayah darts out a tongue. Senka's head tilts slightly with curiosity.

"You, Senka," I look at her. "Are built for brute strength, fear. The opposite of your human body. Same for you Sayah," I turn to him. "Made for agility and slicing. Try tuning into that more. First to pin the other down with threat of life wins. Harm the other past my boundaries, and you won't spar like this until we get home."

Tails flick around, paws shift excitedly. Knowing my own people tells me they feel freedom with this task, not chains. I grab under their chins firmly, my talons pressing into hard scales.

"Absolutely no permanent damage, I care too much to watch either suffer."

Taking my warning with their noses to the ground, I back off to let them begin. Spreading to either side of the massive area gives time and space for both to prepare. The Shadow Sekund walks up behind me, pausing at my side.

"Pitting two of the worlds rumored most dangerous dragons against one another seems..." Dimitri searches for a non-inflammatory word.

"Careless? Ignorant? It's not. If they can be good enough to best one another, who else could best them?"

"She has a point. I never thought to have us train in dragon form. It's an incredibly obvious point," Mikhail offers his support of my demonstration freely.

I raise a hand, raising tension with it.

"Do not go past the upper boundary of the mountain. Do not leave the courtyard," I get confirmation from both, then drop my hand. "Aiza, if you wouldn't mind, take me up when they gain altitude."

Her wings stretch out, broadly built to carry more with less work.

Two gray bullets slither towards one another, gauging the other's movement. Sayah's tail slowly moves in waiting, Senka's snaps around at the end. Rocks skitter at one of the movements, causing them both to fly at one another.

I watch closely, only seeing the two of them and nothing else. Sayah grabs her throat with lightning speed, causing her paw to come up against his chest. Using her own body weight she lifts herself into the air enough to be over him, neck still in a precarious position. Her body tilts down, putting an immense amount of pressure on his chest. His jaw unclamps, freeing her to reach for his. Just as she gets teeth in closing distance his tail flicks up at her side. The top razor-sharp fin slices her thinly, allowing bluish red blood to seep down her side.

I breathe in, watching them twist around. Occasionally their body pauses to adjust an attack or process a thought that would be natural if they were in human form. Hesitation always allows the other to go for an attack.

"Dimitri, if you wouldn't mind," Mikhail requests his Sekund to shift. "Kal, I'll join you when you go."

"Sure," I don't even look at him. "If you don't give me a nickname again in public."

What should have been anger instead feels like a lustier tension from him.

"I guess I need to make sure we're in private more often."

I look bored as I take in his full frame to me. From feet to eyes I judge every micro-movement. His eyes turn into molten lava as I pull my gaze from him.

The match begins to climb, wings beginning to pump as they climb up into the air. Aiza dips down a wing, pushing up my body with her short tail. Comfortably between her shoulder blades I tap her neck to signal take-off. Mikhail does the same with Dimitri, who's frame stares over my advisor's. I glance over the pale, grayed out red scales of Dimitri. I briefly wonder how similar Mikhail's color is to it.

"You'll see soon enough," that damned wink nearly set me on edge. I chose to maturely ignore it.

With a number of swishing, I feel her tilt under to climb up into the air. Fighting still occurs above us, staying confined as their bodies only separate to get a better angle of attack. Aiza rests us on a thin ledge, her claws easily grabbing on to the slanted mountain wall. Lock in key nearly her body goes still to rest on the rock. I twist in my seat to watch the match unfold mid air just below us. They've stopped climbing, only changing height to drop down or return to this one. Multiple ideas pop into my head as I see how their bodies move.

Giving Aiza a warning before yelling over to Mikhail, she turns her sensitive hearing opposite from the direction I call to him.

"The tails!" I yell. He looks over, tilting his head to the side. "We have to learn how to use the tails!"

When I used my tail to pierce the body of the bison, I felt every movement in it keenly. Being aware of every small movement is one of the parts that makes me ache to be in dragon form again. Having such extensive control over my own body, more than I ever did when I was trying to survive. I consider it a blessing.

Back and forth we spot things to work on, strengths, weaknesses to train into or out of others. I begin to develop some respect for him as I realize he's treating me like a fellow leader. Not a conquest. His boundaries may be skewed, but they're present.

Time passes so fast I don't even notice the sun dropping to begin painting the sky. Starting this match wasn't far from sunset anyway.

Eventually, Senka falters in one of her steps hanging on the mountainside, slipping down slightly. Sayah dives after her, latching a back foot onto the tip of her wing. Grabbing her neck with his front talons he slows down their fall. She desperately slaps his body with tail and tries to rip him off of her. His body can't hold on much longer. I decide to end it.

"Mikhail, go ahead. I'll meet you inside."

He respectfully allows me privacy with them. Aiza controls her descent well. Nearing them, I see the effort suddenly stop. They look to me for confirmation of the halt order. Landing proves to be difficult for all three, though Aiza only struggles with the gust of wind that pushes in suddenly as she reaches the stone.

After shifting clothes are pulled back on. Heavy breathing slows to deep inhales that bring air into the bottom of their lungs. I approach with a large grin.

"You did so well," I fist-bump Senka. Her brother stretches his arms over his head.

"I almost had you," he elbows her.

"And now that you've shown most of the cards up your sleeve, she just might have you next time."

Laughter echoes between all of us as Aiza is covered well again, shrinking back down to her petite human form. She doesn't come out until her hair and body are covered to her liking.

"That honestly isn't so hard to do. If I had somewhere to change privately I'd be in dragon form more often," she comments as she smooths out the fabric across the top of her head.

"I'm already working on it."

Her eyes fill with gratefulness. I get a bit uncomfortable at the emotion, walking quickly back in.

Only enough time left to wash up, I quickly clean off the sweat. Tonight, I pull on an emerald green pantsuit. Only leaving the shirt to go under it out. I button the jacket so that my cleavage is visible though not in danger of being freed. The pants are snug, hugging my narrow hips well. Tightness around my growing thigh muscles make me feel more confident instead of worried. With a shrug, I put on simple black heels to finish the look.

Satisfied with my next attempt at both teasing Mikhail and making a name for myself, I stride from the room.

Round three, I think. I repeat the thought to my party, who also find it just as laughable as I do.

Mikhail isn't his usual self at dinner. Not a single touch between us. In increments he receives messages in his ear that are whispered so low I can't make them out. Looks from me do nothing to goad an answer about what's going on. Trying to make the most out of an uncomfortable situation I ignore what's going on.

Until those red claws sink into the underside of the table. No one else catches it. Except possibly Dimitri since he's his Bonded.

Watching him slowly tense up has me doing the same. Friendships are quick to develop in this world, so I already feel a need to reach out and comfort him.

I reach a hand behind him to pull his shirt out from his pants. My fingers are ice compared to his hot skin, so start by touching only my fingertips to him. At the touch he lets out a heavy breath. One he'd been holding for a while. I slide my finger across his spine, slowly flattening my palm against it. With cautious movements I trace shapes around the area. It doesn't take much for him to be relaxed enough to unclench his jaw. Finally finishing the now cold food on his plate I go to remove my hand.

"Don't," he mumbles at me. Not wanting to give my own emotions away I return my hand to his back. Eventually my arm gets tired. Slowing down has him pulling my arm away from him. I look to him wondering why he does.

Leaning over he thanks me, then leaves the table. With him gone Dimitri has a clear sight to me. I throw a concerned look his way. His lips tighten like he wishes he could say something. I purse my own lips in understanding, respectfully removing the pressure from him to answer me. I finish my own food as fast as I can. Excusing myself prompts Dimitri to do the same.

"I'll be with him," I whisper between the Nightmares. "Keep an eye on Aiza. Don't come looking for me."

"Respectfully, if you don't check in with us in an hour we're going hunting," Senka warns. I stare her down, marking my words as command.

Satisfied that they won't interrupt, I leave the room. Dimitri is hiding in a corner just outside waiting for me.

"Where did he go?" I walk next to him. We turn down a hallway new to me. Small windows let in enough light to see.

"Most likely to his office," is the only response I get. He doesn't tell me to stay, so I assume I'm welcome to join him. A metal door blocks the end of the hallway. He knocks three times. Seconds of silence pass. Then clanging comes through starting from above our heads working its way down the knee level. After a few more seconds of silence, Dimitri pushes me back with a forearm to my collarbone.

Groaning so loud I can't hear myself think waves through the air as metal opens up to an absolutely massive room. Light much brighter than that of the hallway makes me blink harshly. After adjustment I can finally take in one of the most amazing feats of architecture I have seen to date.

Chapter 23

Curved walls create a domed room that ends two thirds of the way around. Directly across from the door that now slams shut behind us is a railing marking the edge of the room. Small, decorated columns that twist from the floor up to the height of my hip support a flat top that runs from wall to wall. A desk is off to the side, made of dark wood that looks aged with wear. Shelves line the walls with books of many languages lining them begging to be read again and again. I try my best to ignore the pieces of glass buried in the floor glinting at me. Each step towards that muscular frame has the moonlight flashing at me as a reflection in those decorative shards. Mikhail is leaning against the rail, his hands supporting his tall frame as his head hangs down.

I stop, allowing Dimitri to go to him first. In a small sign of affection between them he rests in hand on Mikhail's shoulder, speaking to him softly. I busy myself by leaning against the edge of his desk to play with a globe paper weight. My clothes feel too snug right now with the anger simmering in the air. Wishfully I consider leaving to go shift alone, fly into the cold night.

My thoughts of being in a black form are interrupted by Mikhail turning to look at me.

"I apologize for my behavior at dinner tonight."

He's tense still.

I shrug and set the paper weight down with slow, controlled motions.

"Being Konge isn't easy. I'm sure whatever bothered you enough to have you storming out of there is rightfully worth your attention."

He doesn't laugh at the joke about storming away. He doesn't react at all.

"Do you want her help or not?" Dimitri pushes him to speak again.

I wait for him to say something. Mikhail stares me down, looking at every inch of my body. Nothing about it is sexual. It's like he's trying to put me in a place he can see me better in. I only wait for so long before taking the hint.

"I'll see myself out then," pushing off from the heavy desk I make my way to the doors. The four men there have to climb ladders built into the wall and work simultaneously to begin undoing the latches. They weren't kidding about security in this room. Harsh whispers sound behind me before those dealing with the door are told to stop.

"I need your help," Mikhail's voice strains out. I shouldn't, but I turn around with a vicious grin. Part of me thrives on such an overly confident man asking me for help.

Dimitri looks at me pleadingly. I weakly try to fight the look off my face. I don't succeed much. Walking back to stand in front of them both I wait for an explanation. Red hair falls around his shoulder as Mikhail tugs his hands through it.

"We've had a rogue problem for a while now," he catches my narrowing eyes at the use of the word rogue. "Dragons who haven't been claimed by a *kallet*, or their Samle was destroyed."

"So, is it the Samle that Gallyan ended that's here now?"

A humorless chuckle, "There's only a handful of them here if they're from that. Gallyan killed every single one he could. Even the kids."

I only blink. Conveying my own emotions would do nothing to help him right now.

Dimitri coughs to clear the air.

"So why are they a problem?" I push for more information.

"They've banded together in their own group; they infiltrate and destroy. Some of my lone members who prefer to live outside the castle are being killed. Only two of twenty have survived."

"They sound angry," I pick up another paperweight. This one has sharp corners I run my fingers over.

"They're terrorists, I can't decide if they should be put down or forced out."

"Who starts the fight?" I press.

"The fuck do you mean?"

"Do your people chase after them or do the rogues come after your people?"

"I don't know but insinuating my people don't have the right to defend this territory is-"

"That's not what I'm saying. They've been attacked, they're clearly untrusting of outsiders, and trying to survive in an icy tundra."

"And I'm trying to protect my people so they can live in peace."

"I completely respect that, but without having extending them at least some type of olive branch before-"

"You're not understanding-"

"No, I'm clearly not," I cut him off by slamming the paperweight down. "Have you tried talking to them?"

"They know what he looks like," Dimitri answers, watching Mikhail's nostrils flair. "They won't answer him because he killed one of them on an exploratory trip. It was well deserved."

"How so?" I still simmer at the thought that people already handed a bad card of life are still being left alone.

"It was one of the more extreme ones, they saw Mikhail and reacted angrily. We tried to control the situation, but the rogue wouldn't hear any of it. They see red scales and either run or fight."

"How would you feel if your people were under threat from a group of outsiders? Ah, wait, you wouldn't know because you just became a Dronning yesterday," Mikhail whips that title at me like a weapon. His arms fold over his broad chest. "Why are you being so defensive of people you don't know?"

"Because I was them," I bite out. "I just got lucky when Jakir found me before I did anything really stupid."

I pull my lips in between my teeth, pinching them. Stupidly, brazenly, I start to build a plan in my head.

"And now?" I ask, looking at the Sekund.

"They're getting braver, coming closer, being more aggressive. They want their own section of land, and the freedom to move about as they please," Dimitri looks at the floor in worry as he speaks.

"They can't have it," Mikhail grits out, finally finding his voice. I snap my eyes to him.

"You'd rather watch your people die than give those people a small section of land to call home?" I raise an eyebrow in my challenge.

"I'd rather kill them all and have it done with, but there are children there."

"I'm glad you draw the line at children. Real ethical here, aren't you?"

"Fuck you," venom drips off his words. "You don't have to feel the threat of enemies constantly traipsing over your land." Pushing from the railing he begins to stalk towards me. He snarls at my once again present confusion. "You can feel it when something isn't right on your territory. Like a nail scraping over the back of your neck."

Bright red talons shove out his nails as his anger grows. He stops a few feet from me. In response I feel my own need to put his face in the ground. It takes everything in me not to.

Cool, one more fabulous trick about all this.

In the silence, I realize that I'd been wrong to suddenly lash out about a situation I'm new to dealing with. Even worse I'd let my emotions control my response when I'm the only possibility these people get a second chance. I don't dare tell Mikhail to his face that I'm wrong. However, I look out over the open balcony and take a deep breath in.

I push away from the desk, closing the distance between us. I put myself so close to him our chests nearly touch. I fight the urge to run my hand under his shirt.

"Let me speak to them," I offer, tilting my head down slightly to avoid appearing too confrontational.

"No," they both answer. Despite the immediate denial, I can feel the want oozing from Mikhail. I want to give to my wants, but I also don't want an answer being the result of a favor of that sort.

I restrain my sigh to one that's far less annoyed than I truly am.

"I'll offer them a place with my Samle, you've already ruined the chance to talk to them. I'm a new face. If anything, I'm sure they'll stop being a nuisance when they're not even on your land anymore."

Dimitri looks hopeful to Mikhail, watches his face carefully. With an opportunity to expand my own Samle I put all the patience I can into waiting for an answer.

Mikhail turns slowly, placing himself before the open edge of the room again. I motion to his Sekund, asking for a second alone. He nods his approval. I walk over, trying to keep the sound of my heels clicking the least obnoxious I can. Leaning the side of my hip against cool stone I look up at him. He doesn't look at me.

"I know you want to protect them," keeping my voice low to offer a sense of intimacy. "I've been in their similar place before - except I was alone. Let me offer them a home with me. They'll be off your hands, and I'll have more than just a few under my care. I could use the numbers."

"Ah, so when you decide to turn on me you can use them against me?"

I pull back at his sudden aggression.

He's struggling with a soft spot for me and being a Konge at the same time, I realize.

"If I wanted to fight you, you wouldn't be worried about them," I throw the threat into the air as gently as I can manage, letting it hang. His eyes start to glow. "Please, Mikhail. Give them one last chance."

"You haven't even seen what I look like," everything in his voice drips malice in response to my initial statement. I can feel the urge to fight me reaching out over his body – a dark cloud over an already angry man.

"While I love playing the game of who's more confident with you, I don't need to see you to know you won't win the size contest."

I send a silent prayer up to the moon hanging over us that I am, in fact, larger than him in dragon form.

And that he takes it as lightly as I conveyed it.

"We can test that theory out when we both speak with them tonight," he stalks away, hands in pockets after retracting the talons. "Meet me in an hour, kitten."

Having never experienced a combination of lashing violence and uncontrolled lust I nearly stumble as the feelings war within me.

Metal clangs open as massive locks come undone from the door.

"Slamming your dick out on the table like that is dangerous," I raise my voice at him not caring that Dimitri is shaking his head at our argument. "Especially when you don't know if I'll blow you or cut you."

The look over his shoulder puts a full-blown leer on my face.

The Nightmares berate me with questions as I change into a simple slip. It hangs over my arms in billowing sleeves, dropping low in the front and back, secured by a tie around the waist.

Aiza sees my logic without asking anything, only curious about the rogues.

"They've been a problem before, but they only harassed people. Never killed them. What changed?" she asks.

Shaking my head I walk from behind the privacy screen, "I don't know."

Senka follows behind me, clearly ignoring personal space as I change. Her curiosity couldn't be stopped by me stripping off my clothes, apparently. Dark eyes miss nothing over my naked legs, having already scanned me for any sign of misstep from Mikhail or Dimitri.

"Senka, I'm fine. Relax, please."

She huffs, plopping herself onto one of the couches in the room. Sayah leans against a dresser watching me closely. His fingers toy around with a chain of pearls left as options by our host.

"Where will you be?" his matching dark eyes watch me. Thin legs cross over one another.

"I don't know, I'll be fine."

"You don't have an ounce of training to protect yourself with," Senka complains.

"I'll be in dragon form majority of the time. If I'm not back by sunrise you can hunt him down and have your fun," I pull my hair out of its high ponytail.

"Really?" Senka looks like a kid being told they have a puppy for Christmas. Sayah's eyes widen a bit at the offer, conveying his own silent excitement.

"Within reason," I look at them with the best mom look I can muster. Senka mutters her disappointment.

"Aiza, you're in charge while I'm gone."

"Are you serious?" Sayah follows the other two as I walk out of the room.

"Yes."

I leave them watching me at the top of the stairs. Aiza's eyes convey more concern than she cares to say. I know her mind is spinning up all the ways this can go.

"This is an opportunity," I offer.

"High risk, but how low of a reward?" she remarks.

I refuse her an answer by spinning on my bare feet to descend down. My heart aches slightly for the twins, knowing that they genuinely want nothing but my safety. They finally have a home, a family, and now nonstop threats.

And here I am throwing myself into the biggest one so far.

Not even guards are standing in the hallways, it's so late. Reveling in the warm loneliness has me taking longer to reach the courtyard than necessary.

Mikhail is in the center of the yard, a loose cloak covering him from behind. I can tell by the way it opens he's most likely not wearing anything else underneath it. I pause, wanting to see how he changes.

The cloak falls off in a gust of wind, being blown back towards me. I pick it up to hang on a light mounted by the archway. Suddenly a loud snap, shockingly clear, rings out from his body. Legs elongate into hindquarters tipped off with long paws. Pale freckled skin is covered by red scales brighter than I expected them to be. As his back widens to accommodate reforming ribs I inhale at the enormous horns that curve out from his, then sharply angle back in. They're half the size of his neck, making the muscles strain as they grow. His nose extends out to spike up in a raised portion just as his head finishes being covered by thick hide. I marvel at the sheer size, wondering if he's slightly larger or smaller than Jakir. I compare gold to red, unsure who would win that contest. Jakir is much bulkier, more imposing with oversized wings. Mikhail has more muscle definition that wraps around the light bones of his dragon form like vines on a tree.

Thoughts of my Sekund have me sending warmth down the Bond in hopes he knows I'm thinking of him. I get a feeling close to that of a hug back.

I undo the tie on my wrap dress. Small sounds of silk material shifting causes Mikhail to writhe his head in my direction. He doesn't lower his snout to be at eye level. Only looks down his wide nostrils at me in a snide way only he could manage. I let the material drop to the ground. Moonlight catches every scar highlighting just how wrangled they are on my skin. My chest swells with each breath, causing different scars to catch the light. Mikhail's head jerks back as the slits in his hazel eyes widen at the lines on my body. I stand, letting him take in how awfully my body is marked.

Oval pupils look at me, again asking for another explanation.

"One day," is all I give before waving him to move out of the way.

His steps reverberate through the ground as he glides backwards, the spikes surrounding the end of his tail dragging on the stones. Staring doesn't end from him. My muscles tense when a cold gust smacks into me. I nearly lose my breath, but the pain of the cold brings out a comfort for me.

Using the safety of him being near I begin the shift in a fast-paced walk, but don't let the shift occur immediately. Tonight, I hold down the

232

feeling that bubbles up instead of letting it empty out. A hand to block the end of a hose, waiting until more pressure builds up before releasing it. Pain snaps out to different parts of my body as I continue walking. Only making a couple yards before the pressure builds too much and multiple bones snap at the same time. My skin feels too tight when they all snap.

Nothing stops me from continuing to move. Pain feels familiar, nearly satisfying in the way a hand on my ass felt the other night. Sharp inhales come from the red beast behind me as my body stretches faster than I had seen anyone else. All while keeping up a pace close to jogging.

The second my skull aches at the pull of my snout coming forth I breathe in deeply to feel the increase in awareness of scents around me. It excites me so much I feel changes happen faster. Black scales slide out fast enough to make a sound similar to a hand brushing over leather. Finally the edges of mountains turn into detailed lines of rock folding over one another, snow that glistens just as the stars above them do.

Done with letting my other half come out, I breath out heavily. Chuffing sounds tumble from my long neck as I sound off relief at finally being in this form.

I nearly growl as a head pops into my view from my right. Cutting it off immediately I remember that I'm not alone.

"Christ, I had no idea," he admits. Awe fills his voice relentlessly.

"I didn't think you were the religious type," I preen a bit under his wide eyes. He walks around my body, nose coming close to me occasionally.

"I think anyone would be at the sight of you. Or the sight of you shifting."

"Oh?"

"I've never seen anyone with a color like yours, even close up my eyes are having trouble making out where you start and the night ends."

"How poetic," I drawl, unaffected by his words. His tail whips around towards me as he stops in front. Faster than I can even recognize, I slash my own tail forward hard enough to spin myself. So sudden it doesn't even echo, the wicked spike weaves through some of his tail spikes and stops it from moving. Pinned without causing pain I seethe at him.

"Let me make this abundantly clear. I might be a guest here, but I am not

going to take your shit. I'll use your intestines as a necktie the next time you treat me like that. I've had enough of your shit today," I snap my teeth at the last words.

"I do love a woman that can actually kill me," he wiggles his tail, useless while pinned by my own.

"What a surprise, even in this form you can't get your mind out of the gutter," I pull my tail out, but it takes force to pull it from the hole I've created in the stone. Shaking it releases the leftover dust, returning it to its true color.

"Let me fly in lead," his wings expand to lift him up. *"I know the mountains better. Currents here don't play nicely."*

I let him take the brunt of the work as we climb straight up, the tilt to fly through the mountain range. Snow pelts at my scales, more of a cooling system than a force to work against. I appreciate the cool temperatures that ease the heat building in stiff muscles. It takes extra work in certain areas to fight against a current coming around a mountain, less in others where the space between peaks carries us. Soreness lingers from my daily workouts.

Clouds dip low tonight with the temperatures that have cooled just as rapidly as the sun sets. If it weren't for the excessive body heat we produce we might have had frost form on our backs.

The castle's home mountains start to lower, softening into a gentler landscape. Trees become more prominent as we go further from Mikhail's home. I watch various wildlife look up to us, herds running or ducking into alcoves. Some owl tells the night it's here as if it might have been gone. Our figures going over do nothing to stop it from being obnoxiously loud.

Light far off is easily spotted, it flickers as figures pass in front of it.

"A fire?" I wonder how blatant these people are about their presence.

"Every time, they never tried to hide it, the peasants."

I struggle to ignore the name calling.

Beginning the plan I formed earlier takes more confidence than I thought it would. With a nervous look to the red tail in front of me, I speed up suddenly.

"Stay behind for a minute, please," I'm not sure if what I say is more of an ask or a demand. *"I don't want them running before I even get a chance to talk to them."*

Flicking up his wing with the tip of mine to force him into slowing down, I push my body to put distance between us. The thought I let out isn't just for him, but anyone close enough to catch it.

"I'm just here to talk."

"You realize the moment they give me a reason, I'll rip them to shreds, yes?"

I nod my head once in understanding, hoping it won't come to that.

Closing the distance faster than I thought I would, I see a dragon shift back into being human, then race to the fire. Another figure begins to take off its pants. Presumably to change forms.

I hover for only a second over the wide-open space they've found. A couple cabins rest out of the area of possible destruction. Cutting the movement in my wings I drop to the ground, creating a cloud of snow to fly up around me. Small amounts settle on my body making it easier for the people to see me.

"Ready!" a man screams. A child begins to cry.

Stilling my tail so I seem less threatening, I tuck my wings back. More so to keep them from having an arrow shot through them. Lowering my head in front of what might be called their leader I keep my breathing shallow so as not to blow him back. He's older, with a limp in one leg clear as day as he walks towards me. People cower behind him to the other side of the fire, the crying child screams even louder.

"Get out!" He yells at me. "We don't want you here, I know Mikhail is nearby."

"We don't want him; we don't want any of his whores!" a woman adds.

At the insult I imperceptibly move my head. My lower jaw drops slightly as saliva drips from my upper fangs. I stare her down. A low, lazy growl rattles her. Moving nothing other than my head. Still raging in her own fury, she shuts her mouth. I hear her breathing pick up as my eye takes her in.

My body pulls back into itself, forcing me to walk forward if I wish to be in front of the older man when I'm done. Silence as I finish.

Despite their hostility, I'm offered a warm cloak to wrap around myself once my human skin is completely exposed to the elements. The aged male looks furious that I've been offered the nicety.

"She's here to kill us, and you hand her a damn coat?" he snaps at the young male with dark skin backing away from me.

"I'm not here to hurt you, or to kick you out," I explain calmly.

"Are you with Mikhail?"

"I'm a visiting guest, so yes and no."

"Don't play games with me girl," he drags a knife from its holster. Glinting raises my heart rate.

"It will take me about ten seconds to be back in a form that could end all of you," I tilt my head at him, void of emotion. "Be smart and put the knife away."

"Pfft," he raises it.

My eyes glow. It looks like a threat to them, it's my body wanting to do anything to keep it from touching me.

"Ahh," another man says. He's wearing glasses so thick they affect how big his eyes look. "She's a Dronning, she's telling the truth Granpa."

I nod my confirmation at him. The old man puts the knife away.

"What do you want," his voice is snippy.

"You want a home, yes?"

"Obviously, no one likes fighting for their lives like this," his arm sweeps out around him.

"You can have one…with me."

Silence again. Granpa looks at me with disbelief, his grandson looks at me with hope. A familiar feeling echoes in my chest.

"I've been waiting for this," the grandson says, stepping towards me.

A thud comes from behind me, warning me to make my move quickly.

"Again, I'm visiting him. He is not my Konge. He does not speak on my behalf. I'm here to offer a home, as well as try to smooth things over."

"And you have control over him?" an older woman close to the age of Granpa walks up.

I give her a sultry look, "You could say that."

Chapter 24

Wrinkles form in a smile from the older woman. Her hand on the man's shoulder visibly calms him.

"My name is Ginny, this is my husband Mark," she introduces the both of them since her husband has no interest in doing so. "And this is my grandson, Brawn."

Brawn's glasses get pushed up by the corners before he extends out a hand to me. I shake it, still feeling nerves in my chest. He speaks the same thing I consider.

"I-I think you're the one that *k-kallet* came from. I saw it r-r-rush through the trees," his face is excited despite his nervous fingers.

I pull my eyebrows together. Again, he answers my thoughts.

"I-I couldn't leave my grandparents here alone. G-Granpa d-d-doesn't want t-to leave, so I didn't c-come to you."

The sound of human footsteps come from behind me. I glance over my shoulder to see the Konge walking from the trees, having shifted further away before approaching in human skin.

"Mikhail," Mark grits out. "We told you we didn't want to see your ugly mug again."

Mikhail throws his hands up in defense, causing the material of his cloak to ripple.

"I asked him to bring me here, it was that or watch the two of you fight like schoolboys," I cut in. Mark throws me a nasty look. I return it right back. It's enough for him to cut down on the simmering anger towards me. Nothing changes between the two males.

238

"Get on with what you want," Mark pushes. "Then leave."

I breathe in snow-kissed air deeply, willing it to fill me with patience not to slap the person in front of me.

"Whoever wants to, whether you like it or not," I severely glare at Mark to make it clear he could not stop people that wished to leave. "Has a home in my territory. I live on the Northwestern Continent. You all can have your own section of land. You'll still fall under my general jurisdiction, but you'll be left alone if you so choose. Anyone is welcome to live alongside me and the others in my Samle as well."

Whispers carry through the campsite. I see someone head towards one of the cabins nearby. Invisible weights press on my chest as I begin to wonder if coming here was a bad idea.

"Why would anyone trust someone who's dragon is as black as death?" a random man walks up from behind. Mark nods his head in agreement.

"You reek of evil," another approaches.

"Please give me a reason to end your lives," Mikhail interjects from over my shoulder. I don't need to turn to see he's most likely curling those lips into a wicked smirk.

"And how do you know so well what evil smells like?" I cock my head in a way that has them all pulling their lips back in response. Mikhail's chuckle behind me is just as predatory as my gaze. No one answers my question.

"The more people that go with her, the more likely I am to give you your own section of land. Albeit a small one," Mikhail's tone is lighter than when we started. Almost like he's truly making an effort to not be so aggressive with them.

"Fine. Anyone who wants to go with you doesn't belong with us anyway," at that, Mark spins around. In the same movement, Brawn steps forward nervously. "You wouldn't dare, boy."

Brawn's eyes dart back and forth between his grandfather and me. I don't make a move, not wanting to force his decision, only to have him regret it later.

"I w-w-want to be happy n-now," he stutters. I stiffen at his nervousness;

upset about the unnecessary pressure he feels.

"Then go-" Ginny starts.

"Ginny! Shut your-"

Ginny's nails drop to the ground as her talons push out. I notice they're much slower to reveal themselves than mine.

"One more word out of you Mark and it'll be the last thing you say. I'm tired of you taking your grief out on that poor boy. He's done nothing but help you and be faithful. It's time to let. Go."

Back and forth they argue about letting people go. Already others have joined in, trying to control the decision of those who wish to go. Bitter looks pass between everyone as some leave, few remain. I don't bother to ask why people would willingly stay in such harsh conditions.

Sadness spills into his eyes, shame hangs on his neck. No agreement comes out of his mouth, but Brawn seems to take stride in the silence from his grandfather. Ginny places her hands on Brawn's cheeks with a gentleness that makes me ache for my own family.

Conversation meant for only their ears flows between Ginny and Brawn. I notice a group of close to twenty or so people coming forward with a bag over each of their shoulders. They pass me setting the bags down to pick up after shifting.

One of them offers their hand before passing me, "I'm Nelly."

Curls bounce around his face, making him seem young. I reach out my own hand, tentatively wrapping my fingers around his. Even living in a snow-covered area, his olive skin glows.

"Kali," I greet.

"Kali," what sounds like a French accent in his voice, makes my name sound more interesting than my own pronunciation. With a nod, causing his brown curls to bounce more, he walks to my back. I turn back to the group of people left, mostly older people or couples.

"Last chance," I warn. Not a soul moves.

Ginny looks sad but refuses to leave her husband's side. I hand back the cloak to her. Hands aged by demanding work take it slowly.

Mikhail steps past me, his arms crossed over his chest. "You can have the northern corner. There's a town of leftover cabins."

I leave the Konge to offer what he pleases to the rogues, withholding any sign of surprise at him actually giving them land. I feel guilt for not doing more, yet I walk away quickly because the rest of me dismisses those who refuse .

Nelly is completing his shift, the green speckling across his partially white body making him look like a map. His dragon form seems softer, rounded on the edges, compared to the others I'd seen so far. Making him look just as young as his human body does. Brawn is waiting next to an older couple. The women are watching me, holding hands tightly.

"They don't want to be separated, even for the flight back. Neither of them are strong enough to shift," he explains.

"I can carry them both," I flick my hand at him, unconcerned with their size. Even if I struggle, they have other issues to concern themselves with.

"They're full-grown adults, Dronning."

"Kali," I correct. "And did you not see me when I landed?"

"We couldn't, it's why my grandfather was so caught off guard."

In response, I show him just how large I am.

"Oh," is his only response as he looks up at me. His eyes squint, most likely struggling to see me entirely.

Turning, I position my body so that the couple can climb up together. Brawn helps them up onto my back - in the same pocket I'd ridden on Jakir before - as best he can. He then strips off the poor excuse for clothes.

"Thank you," a whisper from my back. I turn my head to look at them, seeing the two women huddled close together for warmth. They shiver, and hope I can fly fast enough without causing them to get frostbite. Slowly closing my eyes is all I can do to show them I'm not something to be feared.

Knowing their stiff bodies won't bode well if I tilt myself vertically, I stay aware of the angle my body takes off at. Careful control of both my tail and head drains me slightly. Shaking it off above the trees I'm finally able to start the journey towards the castle.

I stay low, not wanting to expose them to higher altitudes. Though I want to rush, I keep my speed slow..

Light is just barely starting to wash away the night. I feel the need to rush, especially with the twins waiting to get their hands on Mikhail and Dimitri's spines.

"You coming?" I reach out in hopes Mikhail hasn't begun slaughtering those who chose to stay.

"Clingy already?" he teases.

With two frail bodies on my back, I can't do much except give him a few choice words that would have Jakir wincing.

Our trip back is slower than the one going out. Only the moon is left by the time we land, making it just in time to find Sayah and Senka waiting for me. Aiza walks out from the archway, smiling at my apparent accomplishment.

Red wings flap above us until everyone lands, returning to human form after their bags drop to the ground. Thankfully Mikhail starts to ask some of his own people to begin preparing rooms for the temporary guests as they begin to walk inside. I don't mistake his tone in sounding bitter about it.

Impeccable hearing picks up the twins' whispers to Mikhail as they walk by him.

"So close," Senka says.

"So disappointed," Sayah says.

Mikhail looks to me, confused. I pull my stare from his naked chest before I give my feelings away. Aiza is kind, reaching a hand out to help the couple down from my back. I lock my jaw as the second one coming down stumbles, her body struggling to keep up.

I slam the change through my body, needing to get everyone help as soon as possible.

"Clothing, hot food, and water. In that order."

Aiza nods at my command, the twins follow after I give them a look to help her. Begrudgingly they bring up the rear of the group.

Senka licks her teeth at Mikhail as she smiles.

Alone for the first time in a few hours he walks towards me. His steps are slow, deliberate. He's clearly either ready to argue or fight me.

He stops, chest almost touching my arm. I still don't turn to him.

"Eventually, you're going to look at me."

"Oh?"

A predatory shift in his stance tells me I've done exactly what will make him angry.

"It's like you're practically begging me to make you."

I tamp down the shiver from how close his mouth is to my face.

"What has you in such a sour mood?"

Playing dumb with him isn't my best move so far.

"My sour mood is because of your disrespect in my own god damn territory. Don't ever touch me again if you plan on acting like you own this place next time."

"There wouldn't be a next time if it wasn't for me," I whip towards him, shoving at his chest with the heel of my palm. He doesn't even stumble, just takes a step back. My frustration builds.

This wouldn't even be an issue if Gallyan hadn't shoved them from their home in the first place.

I'm too focused on arguing with Mikhail to stop and think through that though.

"There wouldn't be mongrels on my land anymore threatening my people if you had stayed out of it."

"You're the one who asked for my help, Mikhail."

"Because I thought you'd have the balls to help me get rid of them," he looks down his nose at me in distaste.

"Please tell me what exactly I've done to make you think that?" I choke out.

"I've seen the way you look when you feel the Suitor attraction."

I'm so frustrated I don't even catch the use of the same word the Nightmares had used.

"There is no look, just a constant wish to rip your goddamn spine out and use it as a decorative piece for my next dress."

Describing one of the many twisted thoughts I'd had about him the past nights has that corner of my mind begging to be let loose. Many ideas flitted around, never spoken out loud until now.

"That," him pointing at my face has me considering letting it out anyway. "That right there is what I'm talking about, you want to give in to it so badly I can read it on your face."

I smack his hand out of my face. His other hand flies up and grabs me by the neck. My adrenaline slams my talons through my skin so fast I feel blood fly off my fingers. The freezing air has it caking across my skin as if the wind could tattoo it into my skin.

In one swift move he picks me up by the neck, swinging me around to throw me. The moment I feel his hand start to loosen to toss me away I reach up and sink my claws into his trapezius muscles. A roar sings out of his mouth while the momentum of him trying to throw me instead is bringing him to his knees. Still gripping the muscle joining his neck and shoulder, I sink them in further. Muscle strains around the keratin daggers. Now more than halfway buried into his body I start to feel the pressure of his Konge essence fight against me.

"Let go," he spits.

I wiggle my fingers, damaging the muscle more. Faster than I can catch his left hand reaches up and grabs my wrist, the other goes for my thigh. Red talons sink deep into my thigh muscle just as my black ones stop under his chin. Thankfully he's nowhere near burying his daggers down to his fingertips. My leg almost gives out after his hand stops slicing through me. Fingers pressed tightly together my hand is poised to sink long black daggers into the soft underpart of his jaw. I get a little excited realizing that shoving my hand up will permanently damage him, if not completely incapacitate him.

We stay like that, heavy breathing warming our faces. I look down at him the same intensity in my eyes that he looks up at me with. Glowing orbs throb with the demand to submit to one another's will.

"You first," I pant.

It must be funny for him because he laughs, causing his throat to push into the tips resting below it. Skin tightens over them, threatening to break with just a smidge more of pressure. I see blood well up as his shoulder moves. Thick, red liquid tantalizes that darkness in me.

My wrists hurt.

I flash back, chained up again in front of a fire. Except this time, I'm covered in blood. Nothing is washed away with buckets of water thrown at me. I'm covered in human blood. So warm. It smells so good.

"There it is," Mikhail murmurs.

Blinking away from his shoulder I look straight at those amazing hazel eyes. I breathe heavily out of my nose, trying to shake off the pleasure I find in watching him suffer.

"You look good down on a knee in front of me," my voice sounds nothing like me. It's deeper, rougher. I feel like I'm having an out of body experience.

"This is purely situational," Mikhail isn't so entertained as I am.

"Says the man kneeling in front of a woman," I gloat.

He spreads his fingers out in such a small motion that has a gut-wrenching effect on the pain running through my leg.

I begin to slide out my talons from his muscle, willing the violence dripping off my very being to go back to sleep. Reluctantly it does. More pride swells in me at having more control than ever over that part.

Slowly, black reveals itself. I drag them flat against the open wounds. Blood smears over his bright skin. I'm so wrapped up in bloodlust that I've forgotten his claws are just as buried in me. I drop my hands, one still dripping blood onto the freezing stone.

"I think you'd look better from this angle if you were laying down," those delicious lips curl upward. I open my mouth to retort but am silenced as he yanks out his own talons from my thigh. Clenching my jaw in pain I examine the wound.

"Thanks for the distraction," I sarcastically toss at him. Attempting to walk away proves difficult, making me look up and huff in frustration. Limping back to my room will take forever, but it's better than the other choice of being carried by the man behind me. Sayah is in the shadows under the archway and begins walking towards us.

"You have to be kidding me, call off your guard dog," Mikhail groans, gaining his balance on his own feet.

"He's pissed, but he's not coming for you."

"Fascinating, because he's staring right at me."

"Get over yourself," I chastise.

Sayah reaches me, staring down Mikhail the entire time.

"She can handle her own," he tries to reason with the male twin.

"She can handle you too, apparently."

I bite the inside of my cheek, trying not to laugh at the look on his face. Sayah's arms wrap around my torso. He bends to catch me under my knees, cradling me against him; never breaking the glare.

If looks could kill.

"I'll have medicine sent up to you," he calls after us. I tilt my head back to look at him behind Sayah. Heat flushes through me from the way Mikhail tilts his head to stretch his neck. His tongue slides out, moistening his lower lips as he matches my stare. I swallow hard, turning back to look up at those dark eyes.

"How long did you watch?" I nervously ask.

"I never left."

I blink away the unnecessary correction. My babysitter explains that Senka and Aiza are still attending to the new Samle members. He then proceeds to update me on the status of any injuries, ailments, or concerns, managing to distract me from the blood still seeping from my leg. He continues to talk even after reaching the tub in my room, suggesting how to get us all across the ocean safely.

Bitterly he offers the idea of trading Mikhail our boat for a larger one. I nod, asking him to remind me to bring it up with Aiza.

Once the water is running hot, he fills a bowl, then lifts me into the tub. Before long Nina enters with a basket of various herbs mixed into jellies.

She offers to stay and help, clearly not having heard about the newest guests. Sayah refuses her instead only asking her to send for his sister once all of the new people have been placed in comfortable rooms. I lose myself in the sting of pain while Sayah cleans out my wound. Warm water keeps the washcloth from being so rough. I find comfort in the stinging soap that smells of turmeric, garlic, and coconut oil.

Smells overwhelm most of the pain, giving my brain something better to focus on instead.

"I feel like I have to hurt him every time I'm around him," I speak finally, eyes closed still.

"It's natural, part of the Suitor pull," he drops the washcloth in exchange for tweezers. Two shards of red come out of my thigh.

"Sayah you really need to start using modern words, no one says that anymore."

Callused hands on my skin stop cleaning. After waiting for him to continue, I finally pull my head up.

"How alone were you before Jakir found you?"

I can feel my heartbeat under my chest at the hidden point of the question.

"I had a bird that followed me around. My only 'friends'," I weakly put air quotes around the words. "Where a bunch of boys that wanted to play evil doctor on my body."

His eyes fall like a feather across the open part of my chest the slip had fallen down to reveal. Down, his eyes go, until he reaches my thigh where four holes in a crescent shape now dot over some of the lines.

My heart swells a bit at him not asking for more details. Knowing he didn't need to know them understand is nearly more healing than the carving Jakir does to my back.

Once the wound is clear enough to satisfy him, he begins to run the hot water again. Plugging the drain first, he sweeps me out of the tub.

"I know you don't care about nudity but…you're too much like family. Senka will help you bathe."

"I can stand," I ease him away to stand on my own. Miserably my thigh quakes under the pressure of merely standing on it. Muscles flex, then fail. The natural herbs have helped my body heal faster already, just not enough to function on my own.

"Sure you can," he gives me a lopsided grin. Sitting back down on the stool in the tub I huff. He goes to leave, I stop him. I still need to know what the point is behind his question.

"Sayah, I know why you asked about me being alone. There's something I don't know."

More of a question than a statement.

"Against every fiber of my being," he squeezes his eyes shut, pinching the bridge of his nose. "I am telling you, you have to talk to Mikhail about this. He has experience with it."

"And no one else does?"

"Not that I know of," his eyes flicker.

Hesitation coils inside me – a viper ready to strike out in fear.

Walking out to find Senka leaves me with a moment of peace.

I reel at the events of the day. Going from recruiting a large load of people to nearly burying my hand in a king's head could give any woman a little bit of mental whiplash. Now with more mouths to feed, need for a bigger boat, and the looming threat of information my thoughts are scattered. In circles I try to make plans to properly care for people who have learned to live under nothing but the lowest expectations. They most likely expected nothing but to be moved to a different location with the same story of survival starting over again. That campsite was nothing short of a horror story. Each one of them had to have been no more than a week away from starvation. Jakir would be stressed, yet with every inch of my being I know that he will take in every single one of them. No matter the struggle to farm more or hunt more he'll do everything he can to ensure no one suffers again.

I lean forward to turn off the water before the tub fills too much. Leaning back, I drag my fingers along the smooth surface of the water.

Homesickness picks at me. Pulling images of the lake by the inexplicably massive tree does nothing but make it worse. My feelings devolve into frustration. Six of them sitting on an entirely different continent busting their backs to build homes, create food out of nothing. Here I am, sitting around being overfed while playing games with a leader who already has everything his people could need.

Shame makes me feel so disgusting I'm not even sure a bath could clean me now.

I slam my hand across the water, splashing it everywhere.

"I never should have come," I hiss.

"Bullshit," a Russian, feminine voice ends my pity party.

"You don't even know what I'm thinking."

"I know you feel helpless, like there's something more you can do," Senka helps me stand. "I'm here to tell you that being here, preparing yourself to be amongst all of the other Samle rulers, is the best thing you can do for us."

"How," glowering does nothing to deter her confidence in her answer.

"Isolating us would have put us in a weak position. We'd be ripe for taking control of if we had no connections, no alliances, no name for ourselves. Coming here to help determine every dragon's future puts us on the map."

I take off the slip as she examines her brother's work on my leg.

"And now I'm showing up with more than twenty extra mouths for Ellie to figure out how to feed – how generous of me," I drawl sarcastically.

"More mouths to feed? Sure. That comes with increasing your numbers. Mikhail has a large Samle, Gallyan is the only other one that can match him numbers. If we want to be bigger-"

She wraps an arm behind my back to help me into the tub.

"-badder, we have to start thinking about making ourselves so big no one will come after us."

Nervousness at the possible enemies I know she's thinking of has my feelings about bringing the rogues here doing a full turn around.

"Especially them," I use her arm to steady myself, watching to make sure my injured leg doesn't go below the surface.

She side-eyes me with a grin. We both want opposition to fear me. Fear us.

"Especially them. Now, put your head back. Your hair smells disgusting."

I laugh at her endearing insult, causing her to fully smile. Her fingernails scrubs over my scalp so hard, she manages to scrape off some of my self-hatred with the sweat and dirt.

Chapter 25

I beg time to pass quickly so I can avoid another confrontation with Mikhail. Dimitri doesn't hesitate to give me sour looks at every dinner. I give myself breathing room by making my rounds on the dance floor with men and women of the Shadow Samle. Frustratingly, I have to keep a slowed pace to avoid reopening the tightly bandaged wound on my thigh from yesterday. I'd only been given the freedom from the twins on the condition that I'm careful - or suffer the loss of personal space.

Getting to know the people here lets me learn just how vast the array of history really is now. How people leading such interesting, normal – or anything between – lives, ended up in such a brand-new place. Many of them want to extend their own favors for my calling. Nothing grand, small notes of welcome that make me feel better about being here.

A few others only deign to give me side eye, or a look of disdain at best.

On the third night after our fight, a couple of strong-minded people denote their concern about rogues being in the same walls as them. Concerns about their lives being threatened are eased by my own threats that if harm comes to them, I'll be the first in line to dole out the consequences. That earns me a larger amount of trust than I would have thought.

Red hair catches my eye, just as a hand pulls me close to begin a loop around the room.

"My people like you," he seems surprised.

"I guess," keeping myself detached feels like the only way to avoid another fight.

"Don't be like that, Kali. We have something here and one little fight shouldn't ruin it."

"Little?" I say just a bit too loud. I give my apology to the unsuspecting group caught off guard by me. "We were ready to kill each other for god's sake."

"Please," he scoffs. "If I'd wanted to kill you, I'd have done so before you'd sunk those claws into my neck. Besides," he tilts his head, dragging his gaze down to my neck and back up. "What's a little bit of blood spilled between Suitors?"

I stop to spin him around. In a shadowed corner our voices are just outside of the social bubble effectively making us invisible. Even with his bright hair and my maroon dress no one looks our way.

"We have to talk about this. Now," I cross my arms. My chest gets pushed together as I do, pulling his eyes down. On the side farthest from people's view his hand doesn't hesitate to grab my hip. He jerks me towards him hard enough I stumble forward. I have to place a hand on his chest to stop myself from falling into him.

Touching him shifts something in me.

"Don't play stupid with me," he speaks so low and rough it comes out sounding like a growl. My body loves it, my head finds it to be a challenge.

"Then don't *be* stupid."

"Kali, stop it. You know exactly what you're doing and I'm getting tired of waiting around for you to decide if you want to let it happen."

"To let what happen, you kill me?" my eyes roll away from him. I'm quickly losing my temper by not being taught what this Suitor issue is.

"I don't think orgasms can kill people but I'm willing to test that theory," that perfect smile is so wicked it knocks the breath out of me. Coherent arguments dissipate as I stare at his lips moving. He's speaking to me yet I don't hear anything he says. His fingers dig into the muscle of my hip causing a dull ache. Words slow from him to the point his mouth isn't moving anymore. I slip my hand in between us undoing the perfect tuck of his shirt. Hot skin sears my palm now curved on his waist, matching his on mine. Letting a small sigh fall out of me I draw my stare up at his face. More than a full head taller than me, I have to crane my neck back to look at him. His head dips down to kiss me.

Someone behind me asks for a dance with him. I begin to fall out of the sudden stupor I let myself into. Clarity comes back to my hearing. We're not so invisible anymore. Only one person has interrupted, so others are sure to follow. I start the process of putting on the mask that will get me through the rest of the night.

Mikhail has other plans. Ever the polite leader to his people he weaves us through the crowds to the doors. His Bonded appears suddenly managing to distract everyone so he can slip me out of the room. Hesitation from my conversation with Sayah returns with a vengeance.

Aiza catches my eye, I give her a low enough signal so as not to cause concern. In return she gives me a knowing smile that has me blushing like a teen caught by their parents.

A snag pulls at my body by my arm being pulled down the hall. Mikhail isn't dragging me so he's clearly aware that my leg isn't fully back to normal yet. He's also not using his weak side to do so. A short-lived feeling of haughty pride comes at knowing I injured him just as much. It leaves as soon as it arrives when we don't stop walking.

"Mikhail," I say his name softly. He slows at the first bend that hides us from sight. Once I'm close enough my body's want takes over again. It's as if there is no restraint left because I've struggled so long with not touching him. Between my legs starts to throb at the thought of touching him more.

"We have to talk about this," he closes his eyes, pink tongue slipping out to wet his lips. I watch like a virgin seeing a naked man for the first time. Muscles stretch the thin material of his shirt out with every breath he takes. His breathing speeds up, mine becomes calmer. I'm more focused than I've been since nearly driving my talons through the roof of his mouth. Neither of us move, only stare at the other. Every bit of air I pull into my lungs has the swell of my breasts pushing at the low-cut line of my dress.

His hand starts to shake, still holding onto my wrist. I feel his thumb press into my forearm rendering the whole arm useless. Adrenaline pumps through me from feeling the absolute strength in his hands.

"We're going to go upstairs into my room," a small noise escapes his throat. My head is tilted down slightly so I'm looking past my eyelashes at him.

"We're going to try," I whisper. Again I snake my hand under his shirt, feeling the muscles that beg me to dip my hand behind his belt. I revel in the feeling of goosebumps across his skin.

"And we're going to talk about this, I'm going to explain," his breath catches as my nail lightly scratches his skin. Absolutely nothing about his body language tells me he'll crumple and submit to me. I thrive on the control he's forcing on himself right now.

"So much talk…" I tug outward on the belt a bit, letting the back of my fingers drag back and forth across his lower abdomen. Large ridges stand out from intense training that feel better than I thought they would.

Doing this feels foreign. I consider the fact it's been nearly two years since I've had sex. There's some shame in feeling like I'm so behind everyone else in the world because I took so long to wake up. Nothing about that is enough to stop me from trying to push Mikhail over the edge he's already teetering on.

"Everything about what you're, what *we're* feeling," he breathes out the last part of his sentence.

The last word is my mark to press myself against him as firmly as I can. His head tosses back, muscle and veins straining in his neck. Swallowing hard makes his Adam's apple move slowly up and down. Slowly, painfully slow, his head tilts back down to dominate over me. My own testy behavior gets slammed into its seat by the shift between us.

Long fingers wrap under my jaw, applying pressure enough to make my vision shake for a second. There's no control left for me to play with, so I wrap my hands around the wrist flexing to hold me. My lips part in surprise when he walks me backwards, pushing me into the wall. His leg comes forward to spread mine, making me gasp at the pressure it puts on my clit. My breasts tighten so much the fabric of my dress is making them more sensitive by the second.

He doesn't miss the small detail. Combining the weight of his leg with the rest of his body he presses me into the wall more. I test how much I can move, moaning when I realize I can't.

"Who knew little Dronning Kali would like being controlled so much," his face passes mine, opting to drag his nose from my collarbone to right above my nipple. Warm breath trickles over it. Small sighs fall out of me. Nothing about this is controlled by me anymore. Not even my own reactions.

"Mikhail, please."

I have no idea what moaning out a plea is going to do, but it earns me his teeth sinking into my chest making me writhe under him. Another moan comes out as pain blooms from his bite. Fingers pinch the sensitive buds poking out through thin material. Once my nipple is hardened to his liking, he dips his head further down to bite it. His mouth isn't even on my skin yet and I'm writhing under him as if he has me naked in his bed.

Hand still controlling me by my throat, his other slides over the slight inward curve of my waist down to palm my ass. That doesn't give him enough, so his hand moves to cup the warmest part of my body. More pressure is applied under my jaw causing blood to rush to my head so fast I see stars.

"You like it when it hurts?"

I nod as much as he allows me to.

"I should have known, a dominant personality in public that thrives on pain," his lips brush mine, immediately greeted by my own parting. "Then the complete opposite when you're wearing my hand as a necklace."

Our mouths lock together in a kiss so fierce we both stop breathing. I push my chest into his trying to bring us closer than we already are. The warmth of his body is so different from the ice-cold stone behind me that my senses start to feel like I might orgasm just from them. Craving more of the sensory play I lean my shoulder back against the wall, then tug on his belt to slam his hips into me that had drifted back. His hands switch positions, one grabbing a fistful of hair while the other grabs the muscle of my butt. He massages the muscle out until my injured leg gives out.

Without pause he sweeps my legs up to wrap around his hips to carry me up the stairs. I'm still too busy kissing him to notice the temperature oddly raises as we reach his room at the top. Heat sinks into my skin from a massive hearth on one side of his room.

One of his hands drops from my rear to slam shut a thick door giving me reason to bite down on his lower lip just a little too hard. My reward is getting slammed back into the wall so hard I clench my teeth against the pain.

"Too much, kitten?"

I snap my eyes open, letting them glow at him, "Fuck you."

His eyes glow in response making the tension between us feral. Even more attracted to him now, I thread my hand through his long red hair. Slowly my fingertips slide over his scalp. Trying to push me to make a move he rolls his hips into me forcing the bulge in his pants against the most sensitive part of me. Rolling my head back exposes my neck, gauging his control.

"Kali," his breathing is labored. He's fighting it. "I promise you I'm going to fuck you until the only thing you see is red and the only thing you know is me."

I pull my head back forward, closing my hand around his thick hair.

"Then shut up…" I press my lips against his ear, flicking my tongue out. "And fuck me."

Those words do nothing to tease him because the hand around my throat has talons at the ends. I realize my mistake quickly. I've pushed him to want to fight me.

I suck in my cheeks slightly to keep from making a comment about his fragile ego. Reluctantly I drop the burning glow from my eyes, never dropping the stare between us.

Placing a hand on his cheek sheds some of the intensity of the glowing, informing me I can pull him back.

"Mikhail," my voice is soft, soothing. He blinks once. Twice. Slowly coming back to himself.

I drop my legs to the ground making sure to put all of my weight on my right foot. His eyes close in a sort of meditative state so I step out from between him and the wall. I know I'm not going to be the one to bring him back, I certainly don't care enough to do so.

Nothing about this is done, only on pause.

I take in the ridiculously oversized room, leaving Mikhail to recover himself. The fireplace is huge, bigger than my own arm span doubled. Crackling settles out in dull noises creating a cozy feeling in every corner. Walking past the long couch in front of it brings me to the bed... Somehow the metal frame has been lifted onto the high platform the bed sits on.

"Of course even after the world ends you still find an Alaskan king sized bed to have in your room," I toss over my shoulder. He's moved to a table on the other side of the room littered with decorative bottles filled with various liquids. Ice clinks into two glasses.

The center of the room is open, made its own area by the arches next to one another along the border. More books line one side of the wall so densely I can't tell where some start and end. I walk to them hoping to find something in a language I can understand.

"Are these all in Russian?"

"No," he hands me a carved glass with golden-brown liquid in it. Its color reminds me of Jakir's eyes at night when he looks off into the dark direction of the deadly forest. I frown at the memory, missing having my tail wrapped around his as we sleep.

"Any in English?"

"A few, I can find them if you'd like though I don't think you'd enjoy them."

"You don't know enough about me to determine that," I face him, beginning to feel irked at his assumption.

"Then give me enough to do so, let me be that for you."

Strung tightly at the lack of release my words fly out faster than I can control them.

"Stop trying to be Jakir."

His lips tighten, refusing to fall into the trap I've set. I sigh, frustrated with my behavior yet unable to control it. My own display of unease must offer him some comfort in why I've lashed out, because his face softens again.

"Come here, I still need to explain it all to you," his hand brushes on my back lightly bringing chills down my spine.

We walk out to his balcony where an emerald green couch sits against the wall. The cushions look so inviting I don't hesitate to plop myself on the end, leaning my back against the side. He pulls out a blanket from a chest sitting on the other end to settle over us after pulling the large fire pit closer. Grabbing my feet, he slips off the shoes delicately. I sip at my rum while he tucks the blanket around them. My feet now comfortably in his lap, belly warmed by liquor, and skin warmed by the fire, he starts first.

"How much do you know about Suitors?"

His hand brushes through his hair to tug at the curled ends. I stare him down waiting for the uncomfortable explanation to my behavior.

"I have no idea who came up with the word, but it's used by everyone now," he shrugs. "Mother nature must have decided that making us not human wasn't enough. So - she gave us this."

His hand with the glass in it swings between us slightly.

"And 'this' is...?"

"It's," he struggles to find the right word. "An attraction, a pull between two people. Some argue that it's based on the soul, others argue it's based on biology. Whatever it comes from, it's an incredibly strong pull between two people. The need to fuck can become so...overwhelming, that you might forget you hate them."

I look away from the suggestive glance.

"It also induces a strong urge to kill one another, although *very* few give into that urge."

"I don't see the need to fight it," I smirk at him, he's not amused.

"You wouldn't, twisted little demon woman," a squeeze on my foot has my eyes closing in blissful pleasure. He sets his drink down on the ground to start rubbing my feet. "Either way, something drives people to such frustration they end up fucking. Everyone I've heard of that were Suitors and weren't careful, ended up pregnant."

"That's disgusting," I keep my eyes closed at my comment on his explanation. Fear wants to dredge up an inappropriate reaction to the information. Mikhail ignores my comment on pregnancy as he digs his knuckles into the arch of my foot.

"A few have begun to think it might be a biological pull telling us all to procreate with someone that will produce a better heir. I don't disagree."

I quickly finish the last of my drink, then lean forward and grab his off the ground to finish as well. Emotions threaten to bubble up at the idea that everything in me wanting the man near me was pure nature. Pure drive to produce with a man that I barely know. He smiles at me as I swallow his over-poured serving, cheeks rounding at my gag.

"What? We get this one 'Suitor' and can't have kids with anyone else?"

"No, then yes."

"No what?"

"You don't get just one."

"I need a drink," I mumble, shoving away from him to get one. My lips feel numb making me realize I've entered into some level of feeling buzzed. Pushing me back down, he grabs both of our glasses, returning with them each half full. Sipping more puts a tank full of confidence back into me.

"It could be anyone, doesn't matter how much you like or dislike them," veined hands give my foot a firm squeeze. "Everyone gets focused on how badly they want to fuck."

Nothing comes out of my mouth for a while. I sit, sipping on rum and contemplating the loss of control over my reproduction. Mikhail doesn't push for anything from me. He just watches me look out at the mountain range extending past the castle.

Not a thing about Suitor's sits well with me, but I don't lash out in anger. It's nothing compared to being told I can become an entirely different creature with a thought. Sure, changing into a dragon made sense. How did having what sounded like some loose-lipped version of a mate fit in? I'd read those kinds of books as a teen and college student. Everything about having some assigned destiny with one person for the rest of your life sounded so good then. What changed?

My freedom. That's what changed.

Here I am, able to fly through endless limits of sky, snap the bones of human men, grow talons out of my hands. Yet, here I am, destined to only have children with a predetermined set of men for the rest of my life. My life is already meant to serve those who fall under my care, ensuring they never suffer a day in their life.

"Kali?" his deep voice pulls at something in me. Dual strings are tugged – one to climb on his lap, the other to be held.

I give in, needing some kind of reassurance from someone who isn't naturally inclined to love me. His arms open to me the second I move towards him. My large thighs hug his hips once I manage to fit them around him. I wind my arms over his shoulders to bury my face into his neck. Body heat from him warms my front at the same rate the fire warms my back. Comfort - long since missing once I left Jakir - wraps around my back to hold me close. I breathe in that crisp scent as new as the first fallen snow of winter.

"People can pick a person, like marriage, they can pick someone to spend the rest of their lives with."

He misunderstands what exactly is upsetting me.

"We have that choice, Kali. You and I could give that to each other."

"Could give what?" I pull back to look at his strong face, "Give our freedom? Give our choice? We don't even know how long we'll live. It might be thirty more years; it might be two hundred."

"I can give you the world."

I press my lips softly against his, only to stop the conversation. He doesn't make another offer the rest of the night. Once the moon is high enough, I pull away from him. I stand up with his help since my legs are tingling from being so tightly folded for so long.

We walk back together, mostly him guiding me since I'm starting to become more affected by the alcohol I downed earlier. Hand in hand, we arrive at my room. The twins and Aiza are already asleep, their doors all closed completely.

"Kali," Mikhail's voice isn't gentle anymore. I track his eyes to the skin that's been exposed by my dress strap falling.

"I'm going to make you finish over my hands before they all get here," deft fingers slip down my arm to grab my wrist. He pins it next to my head along with the other one.

"Sure you will," I feel unsatisfied by the promise. His control earlier has convinced me he won't do anything.

"I love proving people wrong," is all he replies before sinking a shattering kiss onto me, then leaving.

I huff in frustration. Not at being left to my own devices, but at being the one left to want.

I climb into bed feeling emotionally tired, but nothing lulls me to sleep. Not even the warmth of the blankets against the cold of the night.

Snow starts to fall, making the most gentle sounds against the glass doors. Unable to sleep, I slip downstairs to walk out onto the training deck. The biting cold helps to numb the pain as I shift from one form and back to another. Over and over again I let pain curl its own claws around my bones to break them. Pain is what brings me back to my grounding, showing me that no matter what happens, I can always control this. I will always have this part of me to bring me back.

In dragon form I walk back towards the archway. I hear a heartbeat nearby. Shrinking down into my frail human body I turn to see Mikhail take a tentative step towards me. Before he can take another I'm jogging away to force another shift. His footsteps leave into the castle.

I slow down as my body grows tired from the repetitive changing. Coldness starts to seep too far into my muscles. Quickly I return to my room, where Senka is curled up in bed with a dagger in hand. She stays with me the entire night.

Chapter 26

My three companions and I are out in the courtyard before the sun crests the horizon. Aiza is in her soft pink form, allowing me to watch over the twins sparring in their gray forms. I make notes to her, wanting to remind myself later about what to ask them about and have them try. Did I know anything about dragons fighting? Not much. Could I at least do something to give us the best shot we have of protecting ourselves? Absolutely.

I sit comfortably on Aiza's back. She's perched at the top of one of the cliff sides that loom over both sides of the training yard. Across the way on the other side, three more dragons watch curiously. Aiza readjusts herself, causing some debris to fall down into the cavern.

I had told the twins we'd be situated past the boundary of the courtyard so as to provide more room for error. Apparently that means slamming one another into the walls of the mountainsides more often.

I watch Senka slam her brother into the ground, then kick away from him with her hind legs. She manages to catch him in the snout, earning a hiss from him.

I roll my eyes at Senka's insulting move against her brother that has him shaking his head. Blood drips from his nostril, sensitive flesh exposed. His sister goes to sink a claw into his neck, only to be swung around with his wing. Her head slaps into the rock putting a divot in the unforgiving stone. Everything about his movements makes my skin crawl. Sayah's slick, but Senka's powerful.

Her double rows of teeth bite down on his back leg hard enough to have him roar, yet light enough to avoid too much damage.

"Good, that's the control I want," I speak low enough only Aiza can hear. She turns to put those warm brown eyes onto mine in acknowledgment.

Commotion down below drags my attention to the courtyard, where Mikhail is waiting with his arms crossed. No distance could ever dull out the intensity he always watches me with. His hand points down to the ground in front of him, expecting me to come. I turn back to my Nightmares determining who can pin the others wings faster.

A yell from the Konge snaps their attention to him. They look up at me and stop without being told, both of them sweeping their wings to return to the area closest to the castle, along with Aiza. Sayah growls out to stop her, coming to hover just below the pink dragon I'm on as she clings to rock. Her teeth click in response, and he stops the growl immediately. I lift a brow suddenly realizing he doesn't want me to go down there without him.

"You expect me to jump that far?" I question.

Aiza swings her head over her shoulder to gently nudge me. A large eyelid bats at me, telling me to let go.

This, this right here is why I'll die, I groan internally before climbing out of the pocket. Twisting so I land on Sayah properly causes my abdomen to tighten - which is sore from the training I'd recently been doing with Sekund Dimitri.

He shoves himself upward to close the distance to nearly nothing. It's enough to still have the breath whoosh out of me.

"I'll be keeping that move in mind," I say, surprised. Crouching down in between his gray scales I hold on to his raised shoulder blades. Senka is already changed and dressed as she lands. Having done it enough, I slip off his back without help. Bending my knees catches some of the impact. It also catches Mikhail's eye.

"Confidence looks good on you, Kali," he walks towards me. Sayah brings his head low between us to stare him down. "Tell your Nightmare to back off. I won't be threatened in my own home."

Tilting my head to the side to see all of his face, which has begun to grow in a red beard, I smirk. His gaze doesn't leave Sayah's stare. I run my hand along his neck as I walk forward to the point his chin touches my shoulder. Blood still seeps from the nasty cut in his nostril.

"Go get that fixed before you shift back," I command softly. He pulls back, still holding Mikhail under a penalizing glare. I smile sweetly to him, assuring him of my safety. Slipping a hand onto the bulky arm offered by my Suitor, I follow him into the comfort of warmed hallways.

I still hesitate at the term, but force myself to use it.

"He wants to fuck you," his jaw works angrily. Short red facial hairs ripple as muscles shift. I drag a finger down the sensitive part of his inner arm, feeling heat build between my legs at the close contact. His eyes slide to me, dropping down to my lips.

"You sound so jealous, it's ugly," I go to pull my hand out from being wrapped around his bicep. A massive hand grips my fingers making them disappear in the depths of his pale skin. I snap my head up to him in anger, only to be challenged by his feral smile. White teeth gleam at me in the dancing shadows. I curl up the side of my lip, about to speak before he cuts me off.

"Two Samle's are here."

Shock rolls through me at the realization of what is happening. I suck in a deep breath through my nose, then let it out through my barely parted lips. Schooling my features back into controlled ones, rather than playful, is like slipping a coat on.

"Who?" I ask simply, my voice monotone.

"You don't need to be different-"

"Who?" I ask again, not wanting to play games with him. I forcefully pull my hand from his arm. He tries to stop me again. "We've had our fun, I'm not your trophy to show off. I'm here for the meeting. Just like the others are."

Mikhail has the audacity to grit his teeth together, then ball his hands into fists.

"Dronning Addison and Konge Elias. They'll be here in an hour."

Marking a mental note about the Scraper and Desert Samle's respective

Dronning and Konge, I leave for my room.

"Kali!" he catches up to me, having to lengthen his strides at my hurried pace. "What is wrong with you?"

I stop suddenly. He has to backtrack from the distance his long legs carry him past me. Anger flares with me at his close proximity, threatening to teeter me to the side of drawing blood.

"I know what you were doing, planning to have me walk out on your arm. Don't get me wrong," I chuckle darkly. He pulls his face away from me at the sinister sounds. "I love this little game." His upper lip pulls up at my mockery. "But I am *not* your plaything."

"They'll figure it out soon enough."

"Not because of me they won't, I'm not the weak one here."

My bitter words leave him staring after me with red talons hanging by his side.

"Fuck you," is all I hear before walking quickly up to the room.

Two shadows flank me on my way up, Senka immediately asking in a bubbly voice what's happening. I quickly explain the situation, requesting the twins to place themselves out of sight completely from any visitors from here on out.

"Now we use the tunnels," Senka squeals. I furrow my brows at her. She manages to give the most overarching explanation of what they'd discovered recently. Sayah only stares at me, his lips twitching.

"Don't make me kill someone. Otherwise, play your games," I sigh, closing my eyes at the chaos building in their matching eyes. Aiza agrees to greet each arriving guest along with me until everyone has arrived. With everything planned, I switch into a snug pantsuit. The dips of my hips make my thighs look bigger, accenting the large angle of my calves. I let the cropped top show a bit of my soft belly while the jacket hides the slight curve of my waist. Satisfied with the relaxed yet powerful statement the clothing makes, I make my way back down with my softly dressed advisor. Her gait is changed slightly. Her fluidity while walking impresses me.

I swear I hear a tap in the wall at the last arch before greeting the still infuriated redhead.

"Careful, Aiza. Someone's mad they have to share," I throw a wicked grin his way, nearly purring at the sight of his face struggling to control the jealousy. Chin held high, I walk past him to find Dimitri outside.

"Kali," he bends his neck in greeting.

"Dimitri," I return the gesture. "Any advice?"

The aged face turns older. I hone in on the weariness of his eyes. I simply stare at him, waiting for an explanation of his face. He looks nervously to his Bonded - now next to him.

"Keep your eye on Addison," is the last thing he offers before five people climb the top of the stairs.

Wild red hair whips around an angled face, clearly dyed despite the lack of available supplies. Her cheekbones are nearly so gaunt I wonder if it's structure or starvation. Bones at every joint press out from under her skin making her seem overly thin. Too much of her teeth show as she smiles at Mikhail. The woman directly behind her has her hands clasped behind her back, dirty blond hair wrapped in a tight bun.

Despite having never met her, I still feel a sense of annoyance. Like that feeling one might get when first meeting someone and instantly disliking them.

"Mm, Mikhail," she slows to a stop in front of him. Light brown eyes drag across his body. The thick coat he has on hides most of his massive shoulders and arms, but she seems to undress him anyways. "You look better when you're bitter."

"Hello, Addison," his words are clipped. I find a bit of entertainment at how uncomfortable he seems. Dimitri also offers the greeting to her and her companion. That granite face prowls quickly over Aiza, then me. I have a hand propped on my hip hoping to convey the god complex coursing through me now.

"You," her lips curve upward. I feel the sudden need for a shower. "Oh you must be Kali."

"I am, you must be Addison."

"Lovely to meet you," her arms open for a hug. I stop her by extending a

266

hand. Distaste flits out of her eyes just as quickly as it comes in. We shake hands, hers feels dainty. I don't relax the firm grip, even as she tightens hers up slightly. "Firm hand, like a man."

I feel deep seeded anger settle in my chest. It feels foreign, like the emotion doesn't belong to me. I happen to glance at Aiza, noticing her jaw flexing, her lips thinned. The reaction is so minor I almost can't pick it up without staring at her for a good few seconds. It's a struggle not to reach out to touch her arm to ease her. I can't risk anything right now. Brushing past the comment seems to irritate her. She continues on leading the conversation anyway.

"This is my Sekund, Alastira," Addison steps to the side so I can see the curvy woman.

Not a second after she finishes her sentence the Konge, Elias presumably, steps in.

"Dronning Kali," he drags out the 'a' in my name with emphasis.

"Just Kali is fine," I return the bright look on his face having already gotten a more positive reading off of him. I can look him directly in the eyes since he only has an inch or two on me.

"Don't mind if I do," his eyes flare open for a second as he looks me over. "Then just Elias with you, gorgeous."

I can't fight the twitch of my lips attempting to pull upwards at the corners. His darkened tan skin is stark against the snow around us, making him look more like a model. I find myself pleasantly staring into his dark blue eyes.

"The compliments aren't necessary...yet," I shrug him off.

"I beg to differ," he shakes his head, still smiling. "This is my advisor and general, Sai."

While shaking Sai's hand I ask, "A little aggressive to have a general when there isn't war, isn't it Elias?"

Mikhail visibly bristles at my low tone as I play along with Elias. Interested in the new leader that flirts shamelessly I walk next to him into the castle. Ahead, Mikhail is silent while listening to Addison try to persuade him to come visit. Hands clasped behind his back lets me see how hard he digs his nails into the palm of his hand at her voice.

That strange sensation of external anger simmers out enough I don't feel it anymore.

"Dear god woman you must be freezing," Elias shivers at the gust of wind. I elbow him lightly.

"Chilled, just not cold. I like this weather."

"I might need someone to cuddle with, perhaps a beautiful, willing participant such as yourself?"

I laugh, genuinely laugh at his outright offer, "Careful Elias, we just met."

"I don't need much from you to know what a woman you are," his hand touches my lower back. I don't shy away from him, actually enjoying the harmless back and forth between us. His callused hands brush across open skin between my top and pants line.

All of us walk into the large archway where warmer air settles our pricked skin. I watch as Addison presses herself against Mikhail's side, seemingly harmless from most perspectives. Except mine, I know she wants nothing but to own him. Her head turns to me as he responds to a useless question from her. Those horribly brown eyes burn into me with malice, lighting slightly in her attempt at dominance.

I stare back, not letting an ounce of light into me. I match her smile, tilting my head to look at her like one might look at a child discovering a new toy. We battle silently, her eyes flaring more before she turns back to Mikhail and Dimitri speaking.

"Nasty work of art," Elias says. I only make a sound of acknowledgment.

Dimitri announces that the new guests have time to settle into their rooms, or we can all head straight to the dining hall. Elias and Addison chose dinner immediately.

"Might I ask if you know what dessert could be?" Elias raises his eyebrows up and down at me. I laugh again. This time, Mikhail snaps his head at me. While Elias begins to tell me about his homeland, I see Mikhail's nails drop from his hands, being replaced with red. A feeling more than jealously etches into his face, replaced with an unforgiving lust as he looks at me. My breathing hitches as he stops on the bare skin beneath my collar bone, then on the bare skin of my stomach.

"Elias tell me you'll do me the honor of sitting next to me at dinner," I turn to him, grabbing his hand. Elias squeezes mine back.

"Anything, anything you want it's yours," he turns his head to look at me in a playfully flirtatious manner that has me uncontrollably grinning. *I like this one.*

I spare the territorial Konge another glance as I walk to the table on the pedestal. Just before entering the hall, something shifts in a hidden corner. I pretend to smile at my dark-skinned new friend, not for the Russian-Arab woman watching from the shadows.

I go to put Elias between myself and my current problem, both of us are surprised when Mikhail pulls out the seat next to him for me.

"Please Kali, have your usual seat."

Addison drops her Cheshire grin at his words. She's fast to pull it back up when she catches me watching her. Bored of her pained attempts to play nice with me I sit down. Mikhail scoots my chair in at an angle, closer to his awaiting seat.

"Oops, someone needs to learn how to push in a chair," the playfully scolding tone from me gets a red claw pushing at my shoulder.

"My bad, kitten," he whispers in the ear closest to Elias. Elias narrows his eyes slightly looking between us. I lean away to speak to him.

"Elias, you were telling me all about how your homes are built underground."

"Ah my dear, asking about my home is going to get you a nice dinner," he waggles his finger at me.

I place a light hand on his thigh, "Please don't tease me with such a dream."

He leans his body towards me, the two of us pressing into the other's personal space like best friends, "I would never tease you."

Wood cracks from Mikhail's chair. Dimitri looks at me with a frown.

I pull back to give Elias a pleasantly shocked expression, then lean back in. We continue flirting harmlessly throughout the dinner. I favor the wine a bit more tonight, wanting to drown out the smidge of jealousy that nips at me every time the velvet red-haired woman moves. I catch her hands slipping to his crotch at one point. It wins her some pain as Mikhail digs his fingertips into the weak part of her wrist. Her pout gets her nothing but an angry sigh.

After the food has made its course, I elect to dance with my newfound partner, receiving a delightfully supportive smile from Aiza. Her face warms in response to Elias's polite compliment on her flowing gown.

"Alright," I sigh dramatically. "You win brownie points for complimenting her."

"While most definitely a bonus, it was not my original intention."

His dance movements are somewhat stiff, though it does nothing to distract me from the fun of spinning and stepping around the floor with him.

"I do find that *so* hard to believe, Elias."

His hand presses to his chest, "You wound me Kali."

"My most sincere apologies, I wouldn't dream of doing such a thing."

Naturally red hair flashes in the corner of my eye. I tense at the looming presence.

"Need a rescue?" my dance partner asks sensitively.

"Yes," I keep the smile on my face, never looking at Mikhail. As a hand reaches out to grab my shoulder I'm spun away to the other side of the crowd. We both exit gracefully off of the dance floor, slightly out of breath.

"I think I'd like a cooldown walk before I go to bed, care to join me?"

His arm, swathed in white fabric that glistens with gold, offers an escape from the heated room.

"Have you visited before?" I start my own line of questions, trying to figure out his real end goal.

"No, I've been to other territories. Nothing nearly as exciting as this however."

I smack his arm lightly with my free hand, the other still resting on his forearm. The dim hallway gives way to a night sky once we're in a different courtyard that I had been training in. I had no need to be in the place spent in extreme proximity with *that* man. This courtyard has a fountain in the center, four rectangular pillars narrowing to a point high in the sky. Despite the frigid temperatures water still runs down each pillar, filling the pool below it.

"I didn't know until I came here how much the world had changed. Both physically and otherwise," I comment.

"Yes, we've been wondering why you took so long to show. Most of us popped up within the first year."

"It takes time to reach perfection," I squat down onto a bench placed near a wall.

"You clearly took enough time."

"Oh stop, you're embarrassing me," I actually blush, but try to hide it by turning my face away.

Ease of conversation pulls at the tension in my chest, reminding of my relationship with Jakir. It makes the Bond throb in anger. I realize suddenly that I would need to get to my room quickly, before the medicine wore off. Wanting to make a situation I can escape, my brain decides mouthing off is the best option.

"Enough of the game, Elias, what's your angle?" I deadpan at him.

His eyes go wide at being stunned by my approach. With incredible agility his body language goes from the playful friend, with his shoulders angled down and jaw slack, to a domineering man. His torso straightens, jaw setting, eyes hooding slightly. I rise, slowly, not allowing him to control the tempo.

"I have an angle, but not what you think," his voice isn't as light now. It has an age to it that doesn't match his face. "I want an ally."

"And who exactly are your enemies?"

"Smart one. I see the legendary Aiza's been teaching you."

"You know her?"

"Enough to know she knows what she's doing. I know she works with information."

"What exactly do you think I work with, then?"

"Power."

I blink at the blunt response.

"You want me for my power."

"I want you for what power you can hold. From what I understand," he rests an ankle on his knee. "You now hold one of the largest territories, close to Mikhail, Gallyan's, and mine. You have land, you also have a vote."

"I see. So you think that me making the number of Samle leaders odd is going to do something for you?"

"I think it will when you see just how much you're going to need someone like me."

I'm growing really bored of all the over-confident men clawing for control.

Neither of us says another thing, waiting for the other to reveal a new piece.

"You will not like Gallyan, he has a twisted mind with no regard for people. He'll do anything to stay on top."

"So I've heard." I cock an eyebrow at him. "And staying on top entails what exactly?"

"Controlling every single Samle on this damn planet, killing anyone that doesn't agree with that."

I sourly consider why Mikhail hasn't brought this up to me before.

"What do you have against him?"

A touchy subject apparently, because Elias tenses. He looks at the fountain, refusing to meet my gaze. The air around us shifts to an unpleasant one. I sit, knowing that literally looking down on him is the exact opposite of what I need to do. My leg brushes his, drawing him back out of the hole his mind was in.

"What do you have against him?" I repeat, any condescending or pointed attitude gone. He breathes in, closing his eyes.

"A fiancé. She survived with me, wasn't a dragon but survived. Was stronger, faster than us in human form," his hand drags down his face. A shadow peeps out from a tucked away spot. I wave them away discreetly. "All of that did absolutely nothing when Gallyan had her taken while I

272

was on a trip to meet with Sean. I found out three days after she was taken. Two days after that, I got her body dumped on my bed."

I settle my hand on his knee, wanting to comfort him. He doesn't shove me away.

"He hates how much we have, my Samle, wanted it all under his control. When I refused to bend the knee, killing her was his response."

"You have my condolences," my fingers press into the side of his knee.

"I appreciate it, as I would appreciate it if you did not tell anyone about the details."

"It's not my story to tell."

His face eases at that.

"Everyone lost something, Kali. Whether it was a home, a life, a person, everyone lost something. I don't know Mikhail's story, but I do know Addison's."

"You don't seem to get along with her," I test the waters, knowing perfectly well that earlier his complete ignorance of her was deliberate.

"I think choking the life out of her might do me some good," he shrugs. I wonder at his violent thoughts.

"Are you two...are you Suitors?"

His laugh makes me jump, he keeps laughing until tears start to form in his eyes. Once mostly calm he addresses my concern.

"God no, we're not Suitors. I just know she's a slimy, two-faced cunt that has some pretty close standards with Gallyan. Now her and Mikhail on the other hand," he looks at me with a face clearly assuming I know something.

"How much do you know about it?" I pretend to understand.

"Everything, I know they didn't even test out the fighting waters once they knew. Decided to jump right to sex. Risky if you ask me, Suitors sleeping together is one thing, a Dronning and Konge sleeping together that are Suitors is another."

"I mean," I fling a hand around is dismissal.

"You're telling me you have no issue with the fact that they had a pregnancy scare? The man clearly wants to put a baby in you more than he did her, I'd be worried."

I bite my tongue at the upending information. Not knowing a single bit of this makes me feel like a complete idiot. I'd had enough in the past year of feeling below another.

"You're assuming I'm even attracted to him."

"Ah, fair enough," he nods. We both watch the stars dance above, content in the silence. Pain ticks under my sternum, warning me to rush back to my room.

"I need rest, especially if more will be here tomorrow," I say, rising again for the final time.

"I agree."

Walking inside, I go to turn away to the hallway leading to my room. Elias stops me before I go too far by grasping my shoulder.

"It's been so wonderful spending the day with you, Kali. I'd like to continue this relationship with you," his face turns sly. "Whatever that relationship may be."

"Keep those little looks up and it might get you somewhere," I toss my brown hair over my shoulder as I spin away.

I'm nearly around the corner when he calls out one last time.

"And Kali," I turn back to him. "If there's something you plan on hiding from Addison, a conversation with Mikhail might do you some good."

I give nothing away, simply turning for my room. Senka practically pops out of a wall, giving me updates about what Aiza has been doing this entire time. Along the way, I whisper to Sayah to walk with me. He mists into existence immediately.

"Tell me what you know about Mikhail and Addison's relationship," I bite out.

He spills the information out without hesitation. I can't pull any joy to my face, even as he describes the pissed-off look that glued itself onto Mikhail's expression all night after I left with Elias. With a bid of goodnight, I nearly explode into my room in search of the medicine I so desperately need.

Pain starts to build exponentially around my spine, making it hard to move. Frustration at the man supposedly a Suitor to both me and Addison coils up tightly next to it. I gasp in a breath of air as it brings me to my knees. Senka opens the door, calling out to me.

"Get out," I seethe. I don't want her to see this.

"Kali-"

"Get. Out," I flare my command into my eyes, willing her to leave. She bites down on her lips, backing out while cursing my name.

I hear a heated debate in the hallway, then silence.

I'm left to fight the wheezing breaths slowly managing to cease completely, while considering how easily I can rip Mikhail's throat to ribbons.

Chapter 27

Jakir

I watch Ellie swipe sweat from her brow, exhausted from a day of farming. Crops are already growing out of the enriched soil. Corn, green beans, wheat, plenty of herbs, even a few flowers for medicinal purposes stretch to feel the sun. After convincing her to stop until tomorrow, she sweeps Lilly into her arms to bathe the mud off her skin in the lake.

"I think eventually that won't be a lake if Lilly keeps up like that," I humorously tease. She rolls her eyes as Lilly screams in delight at a worm stuck in her chubby little hands.

"Jakir," Jacob pulls my attention to him. Harlow is still working on the surprise for Kali. Day and night she spends either studying or building. Not a single day has passed where she didn't exhaust herself. The same goes for Jacob.

"Yes?"

"I have the plans completely done, and we have the entire area ready to lay foundations. Eventually we'll have to figure out how to carve into the cliffside."

"That was quick," I don't bother hiding the surprise. It makes him preen slightly. "You started the basement too?"

"Obviously, and we're digging it to be bigger than the frame of the part that's above ground. She'll figure out a use for it. Actually maybe she'll use most of it and then use the room for something else. Although she should like the ceiling."

I let him trail off in a self-discussion of what Kali might use various parts of the house for. In the time he spends monologuing, I look over the plans to find an intricate house with multiple rooms meant for a variety of uses.

"I don't think she's the type to want a log-cabin feel," I bring up gently, not wanting to insult any plans he might have.

"Dude, seriously, I'm not dumb. We'll manage to get stone from somewhere."

"My apologies, master builder," I give him a friendly look, then turn to see Harlow walking towards us.

"Jacob," she gives him a look down his body that has us going our separate ways. The compliments he doles out as they walk into their temporary single bedroom home has heat crawling to my cheeks. Very vulgar.

I walk towards my tent, being the last to be sleeping in one. I recall my argument with Filo, demanding that he take the next ready home to sleep in. Curling up in dragon form every night is the only way to keep him convinced I want nothing to do with sleeping indoors. The only thing I want nothing to do with anymore is the lonely nights without Kali around. Her breathing so deep next to my head enters my dreams occasionally, doing nothing to soothe me.

My abdomen tightens as I allow myself to think about her, the Bond finally receiving a chance to lash out in anger. Closing myself off from it had only done so much. Now with it so sensitive all it takes is a thought to have it bringing me to the ground. I manage to call out for help as golden daggers slip out of my hands.

"We got ya buddy, just hang on," Harlow says, her arms wrapping to support me as her, Jacob, and Filo bring me to the lake. It takes all three of them to unsteadily carry me, once again to ease the pain. I groan out, unable to control the utter agony. The other end of the bond flares as well, only a week and three days of her being so far and my body is already bending. Fire scurries down my spine, settling to burn brighter above my tailbone. My clothes come off quickly.

Red fire turns to white hot pain just before they all lower my body into the cooling water. Ellie is shortly behind them with a small portion of herbs from her windowsill plants. I grit my teeth as I scream, not wanting to wake the small girl I know is already asleep.

Wood slides into my mouth once I open it to take a deep breath in. This time my teeth don't crackle at the pressure of slamming them together when the pain rides through me again. A tear slips out, not at the pain, but at the ache in my chest at not being around that beautiful woman.

I don't say a word. I don't beg for them to bring her back sooner, I don't demand that she end her only opportunity to make a place for us.

Memories of her broken body come into focus. It's a clarifying image, to remember her arm hanging from a chain at an odd angle. The seeping red cuts pulling her skin in different directions. The grayish hue glazed over those amazing green eyes. It fortifies my endurance.

Cool mint brings down my rising temperature, hands on my neck and biceps keep muscles from spasming too much. I'm not quite sure how long it happens before finally ending. Too weak to clean the sweat off of my skin, Ellie washes me down with a towel. Her thin hands clean off most of me leaving the sheen to be water instead of salty sweat.

"Thank you," I rasp out.

"It's been two weeks, how long could this last?" Harlow's body is tense even as it moves shovel after shovel of dirt.

The border of the extreme manor is slowly coming together, now nearly dug out to form a basement. Her shoulder muscles flex and stretch with every movement. I find myself being surprised, even now, at how her tall, muscular figure could move with such ease.

"He wanted her there early, we have no idea how long the actual meeting will take. I know this is painful having her so far away," she winces at my use of words. "Perhaps not painful."

"I just…here we all are worried and anxious to have her back but you're sitting there with low grade back pain all day every day. It must be miserable having the Bond stretched so thin."

"It is troublesome, but I'm lucky to have you all to help me."

"Don't brush it off like that," she stands back to admire the deep expanse of a hole she's now finished to create a basement.

"I'm not brushing it off, merely acknowledging that we each have our own pain with her being gone," my Bond pulls at my center, wanting to attack again. This time, I feel a sense of warmth come down to me. So faint yet enough to know it's from her end. I force every bit of comfort I can back to her. Hope for her success blooms in me. "She's doing okay."

The shovel drops as she turns to me to look at me eye-to-eye.

"You felt it? She's okay?"

Harlow grabs my arms, searching my eyes for the answer before I can even open my mouth. I rest my hands on hers, my skin standing out starkly against her white skin. She gives me a suffocating hug only she could manage, then turns back to her work.

"Yes, she's okay," I give her a grin that's instantly returned.

"This day," she slides down into the hole below her. "Could only get better if my sweet little Suitor could return right about now."

She'd taken to using the word often once I explained that the strange attraction between her and Jacob initially is actually a telltale sign of compatibility. I thank my lucky stars when the information given to me by the Whispers Konge enlightened rather than enraged them. Not everyone takes kindly to the idea of predetermined people one could have a child with.

"Even if she is placed in any danger, I have a feeling Sayah and Senka wouldn't let a hair on her head be out of place."

"Senkyah," Harlow gives me a funny smile at the nickname she's created for them. "Are extremely territorial according to Ellie. A few rumors apparently reached the Midlans about a pair of siblings with a taste for violence."

"That's not very hard to figure out."

"I know, but before they got tossed out they were known for developing strong possessive tendencies over people they liked."

"Interesting, I wonder what belonging to a Samle finally will do to them."

"If I had my guess, I'd say leave a trail of bodies."

My forehead crinkles at the blunt statement. I'm not really sure how to take her flippant assumption at their violence. Fast approaching wings drown out my feelings. The thumping sound of air being pressed away from a green dragon has me helping Harlow out of the hole. Multiple tree trunks, having been cut down from the edge of the Dead forest, slam into the ground. He lands next to them to shift. She grabs a change of pants and loose sweater for Jacob as his human skin returns.

While he dresses, I'm absorbed by the unnaturally worried look on his face. They speak between one another though nothing about it is relaxed. Harlow's face changes from content love to one of worry. She leans down to press a kiss to his lips before guiding him over to me.

"Jacob…" I say wearily. "If the Dead Forest is becoming too much we can send Filo or Harlow to go-"

"No, Filo and I will go as a team from now on. It's not safe."

I cross my arms, staring at him for explanation. Harlow rubs his shoulder to encourage his response.

"It's okay," she comforts him. The smile he turns his head up to give her isn't a happy one. He breathes in deeply, then explains.

"I think the same people Harlow and I saw before, maybe even the same ones Kali encountered, are edging into our territory."

"How close?"

"A few miles on the other side of the forest, just a bunch of human men talking. It looks like they might have some people chained up but I couldn't get close enough to tell."

Harlow frowns, "How close did you get, Jake?"

"It was at nighttime, and not while human. They couldn't see me, but I had to walk away so they didn't hear me take off."

I consider the area he tells me they currently camp in. They're not too close, but three more weeks will have them on our doorstep.

"How many?"

"Maybe three hundred? They've clearly found more people," Jacob clears his throat. I close my eyes, willing the nerves to settle. "They're strong too, and fast. We aren't the only ones that got a few perks from the change."

"What do you mean, strong?" Harlow turns him to face her.

"Uh, like strong strong. I think they could be really dangerous, we should prepare."

"That doesn't answer her question, Jacob," I press. Filo is now next to me, taking in the information silently.

"I watched one of them flip an old, beat up car when he was drunk. He definitely didn't struggle. He just kinda," he scoops air with his hands to show a flipping motion. "Ya know?"

All four of us look at one another, unsure of what to do next. Jacob tells a bit more, explaining how much ground they cover as a group. Mostly they're slowed down by the captives. Individually they can either run forever or sprint faster than humans ever did before. He bites his lip when he tells me they can heal as fast as we can when in dragon form. I grit my teeth. Combinations of strength and speed are deadly. We might have the ability to heal faster than before, but nearly as fast as them in this skin. Harlow makes a point that their tendency to harm people could be worse, and with the healing abilities, they'll be even more difficult to beat. She argues for a minute to rescue whoever they have captive, but Filo ends the debate with a short line.

"With only four people?"

It's a bitter feeling, knowing that I'm relieved none of those people are Kali. My decency says that those people could be suffering endlessly. My Bond says the only thing that matters is Kali is nowhere near them. Then my dragon, content that its people are under safe care.

We agree that the manor still needs to be built, everything must continue as normal. Filo and Jacob will continue to retrieve materials to build, simultaneously scoping out the moving group of humans.

Around the bonfire, once work for the day has finished, I explain to Ellie what's going on. Lilly takes her mothers distraction as an opportunity to play with Filo's long beard.

A plan is put into place for safely getting us all out of here with enough food to get us to the shore. Ellie makes a list with her notepad she keeps in her apron pocket. I marvel at the lack of fear in her eyes.

"You shouldn't have to be so used to this," I try to understand how she looks so calm.

"I'm not used to it. Just thankful for what I have now. Our home is big enough that even if we have to hide for a bit, we'd be safe. I haven't had that kind of security since I found out I was pregnant with Lilly."

"We'll all keep her safe, she's going to be fine with us her entire life."

"In that case, perhaps I should start teaching her to be calmer," she laughs, warmth spreading in her cheeks when Filo looks up to the pleasant sound.

Warmth wraps at my spine again, I shut off my part of the Bond. I feel Kali do the same, wondering how she's managing the pain. I worry about how hard she'll fight to hide it from everyone, especially Konge Mikhail.

A few stories are passed between us all, Harlow talks about how close her and her mother were. Ellie asks about her father causing those blue eyes to shut down. Her brief explanation is that he hit her. Jacob steers the conversation away to talk about his family. I understand his experience in all the things about building a house now that I know he did it to support the struggling parents. Another five siblings on top of that meant long hours for him after school, never going to college.

"I actually went to trade school for a bit, got really into being an electrician. Definitely not worth my time," he laughs at his own joke. The rest of us can't help but laugh with him at the wild turn his career has taken. Filo is pressed by Jacob to give a story about his childhood.

He politely declines, not enjoying being in the spotlight. As Jacob pushes again, I step in.

"I traveled a little, mostly backpacking around various places. Learned a lot about myself."

"Explains the 'I am peace with universe' attitude you have," Jacob wiggles his head at the fire, then peers up at me to see if he's touched a nerve.

"Partially, I didn't have parents growing up. I mean I did, but there were too many foster parents to count. I met this person in France who lived out in the country by herself. We spent a summer together, me helping her with fixing up parts of her home. I had to leave because my time was up, but I'll never forget her. I thought maybe she could have been my soulmate. I thought about her every day, always wishing I had never left. I met Kali just under two years after the end of the world. To be honest," I shift uncomfortably in my seat, the burning starting to build. "Kali's brought a lot of life to me."

"You're just a tiny bit biased, being Bonded and all," Harlow uses an iron rod to shift some of the wood around. We didn't dare use wood from the sick forest, unsure of what it could release.

"Perhaps," I smile widely, missing Kali even more.

There's a deep kind of pain that comes when your body can no longer handle what you've chosen to ignore. It comes back with a vengeance after sitting in a corner to rot. I imagine that darkness in Kali is much the same. Waiting for its opportunity to strike once it's strongest.

I cry out as I fall to the ground. I at least managed to ignore it for a much shorter amount of time as compared to the last time. Stories were being passed around, much like the night I had explained a small chunk of my history. Everything had been so calm, peaceful. Stars over us only to be occasionally covered by a small cloud. Moonlight brightens any dark corners the fire doesn't reach.

Now, all of that is gone. My vision sees nothing but agonizing fire that burns white-hot around the length of my spine. Pain spreads through my core like an anxious colony of ants trying to escape the inevitable.

Distantly a feminine voice calls out my name. Probably Ellie trying to assess how much I'm hurting. I can't even get a breath in to tell them. I watch her command Jacob, who swings a crying Lilly up into his arms. They disappear into Ellie's small home.

Hands wrap under my arms, around my ankles. I'm being carried to the lake again so the water can take some of the heat from my skin, taking the pressure off my joints. Each inch aches from day after day of hard labor to build homes and till soil. It does nothing to help distract me from this.

I try my best to shut off the Bond so as not to spread anything to my Bonded, or to endure more pain than I can handle. To my dismay, I can tell she's in the same amount of pain as me. Twice I had felt her, even at such a distance. Now, I know that the debilitating feeling had to be bringing her to the ground with how strongly I can feel her side. She's trying too, to shut off the Bond, failing just as I am.

"Breath goddammit!"

I don't know who speaks, just follow their command. Small sips of air manage to be pulled in. That's the last oxygen I feel before struggling again.

"He's too hot, put him under," Ellie examines me, feeling my hot skin.

"He could drown!"

"I hope he does," she looks at Harlow with fire in her eyes.

Thin lips open and close, trying to comprehend what she wants to happen.

I have to make everything stop Harlow, just do it.

"Factory reset," Filo says, his voice still calm as always.

"You have to shitting me," she gasps.

Language.

Filo puts both hands on my chest, then shoves me down. Muffled screaming starts above the water's surface. Harlow's hands shove down as well, keeping my body from fighting them both. Ellie wades in deeper to stand behind my head. She digs her fingers into the back of my jaw forcing my mouth open. Freezing cold water tumbles into my mouth to begin its attack on my lungs.

I finally manage a breath of shock. I forget that I'm underwater.

My chest feels cold, tight. Consciousness starts to slip away, begging my body to fight back. I grab someone's throat. Blue talons dig into my forearm to pull me away from their owner's throat.

Like falling asleep, I black out.

I have no idea how long I'm out. I wake up to grass tickling my neck. My eyes are open before my first breath. The world tilts as I launch my torso up, then cough out water onto the rocky shore.

"Jakir?" Ellie comes into view. "How do you feel?"

"It's still," I cough up more water. "There, but I can shut off the Bond for now."

"She better get her ass home soon," Harlow kicks a pebble. Jacob is holding her hand.

"You could just say 'butt'," I offer, still coughing.

"Okay he's clearly fine he's corrected language again," Jacob waves me off as he pulls Harlow away.

Filo says something to Ellie, then retreats as well.

Finally getting a deep breath I lean back on my hands.

Ellie squats down next to me.

"We'll try everything we can, but that is an absolute last resort."

"I wasn't in that much pain."

"Hah!" she flicks my temple. "You were screaming so loudly you had Lilly screaming too."

"I'm so sorry, is she afraid?" my heart sinks a little at her being so scared where she's supposed to be safe.

"She's asleep," she breathes out a laugh. "Kids are resilient, I'll explain what happened tomorrow and she'll be fine."

I nod, not wanting to put any more weight on the mother's shoulders about my well-being. With a pat on the head she leaves me on the shore.

A tear slips down my face once I'm alone.

Kali is suffering too. Not knowing if she has the amount of help I do nearly has me spiraling. I let the idea that Senkyah have everything in their arsenal to help her calm me down. I send a prayer to the moon above that she'll be home soon.

As if in response from the word itself, Feathers lands in front of me. I blink multiple times to see if he's real or not. He pecks at my soaked clothes, pulling them up then letting them splat down.

"Useless!" he squawks out. "Why wet!"

"I was dirty," I settle him on my shoulder, making my way back to the tent for the night.

Chapter 28

Kali

"Get the fuck out of my room," I growl.

"Told you so," Senka brags.

"Senka," my eyes brighten drastically for my command. "Go."

I want to tell her to stop worrying too, but I can't manage more than what I've already said. Pain spreads throughout my torso in such a strong tidal wave all I can manage is a high-pitched whine out of my closed mouth. It pairs with the soreness already present from my recent combat training, heightening the agony.

"Dear gods," Elias is kneeling next to me. "If this is how you treat your guests I may very well leave tomorrow."

"Please, I'll show you the door," Mikhail mirrors Elias on my other side.

"She comes with me if I do," there's a disturbingly playful note to his warning.

"Elias, play this game right now and I'll have your general tossed off the highest ledge."

"So touchy," Elias picks up my head, getting a pulse. "Perhaps you should be nicer from now on. I can tell that the Suitor attraction is...stronger."

He snaps out a warning, clearly not wanting me to know about any other possible Suitors. Or Addison.

Red hair flares out as he spins away into a standing position, walking quickly to the nightstand.

Suddenly, the pain subsides. I manage to get one breath in before it wooshes back out in a blood-curdling scream. My mouth is buried into the chest of Elias - cutting it off. He's fast enough, because Senka and Sayah don't come running in.

His spiced scent fills my nostrils, strong enough to distract me out of the scream. As it finishes off with a sob, he lets me fall away. Still in his arms I look up. My eyes are still glowing.

"How strong is her dragon essence? That glowing is intense," his eyes stay matched with mine. Calloused hands rub on my heated cheeks.

"She outweighed mine when she got here," Mikhail drops back down, ignoring the wild stare from Elias. His eyes flick up, then back down to me.

As Mikhail smears the balm on my spine, then sternum, he catches my eye. For the first time I experience Mikhail being fearful. His full lips are pulled downward, eyes dull.

Pain pulls trembling from my feet to my chest. I look back at hazel eyes, not entirely sure who they belong to. Another beautiful man, just as muscular, a bit shorter, is holding my face.

There is literally no way I got into heaven with my track record.

Cold, then heat travels around my skin where wetness is covering my back. The dark-skinned man looks up, then transfers me to be held by the one with fiery hair. I think I hear the one holding me now, thanks him.

"Kali, you have to open your mouth. I need you to swallow this," he begs me. I want to obey him so badly; I just can't get anything in my body to function. I want to do anything he asks just to have those lips on mine. They look familiar. Maybe I've kissed him.

A small, pitiful breath is pulled into my lungs. It leaves too soon.

I can't breathe enough

My vision closes out, then reopens to a warm hand on my jaw. Looking down I note a pale, muscular forearm laying over my thigh. It curves around my body to hold me close to someone warm.

"Kali," my head whips to the man with glowing eyes. If it weren't for the utter command in them, I'd look away from the intensity. "Open. Your. Mouth."

I'm having an out of body experience, or a ghost has taken over me because my mouth that I couldn't open on my own swings wide. My eyes aren't glowing anymore.

"Swallow it all," those eyes command me. The voice is raspy, making it feel eerie. He sounds like cinnamon smells. I swallow, doing nothing of my own accord to make the action happen. An extremely bitter tincture is poured into my mouth. I want so badly to fight it, even the scent is curdling. My brain fights, causing me to choke on a sip. I then return to drinking it all. Until the last drop.

The first thing to come back to me is self-awareness. I know I'm on the floor because the Bond had a moment. My body aches from the days of sparring with Mikhail. It's nothing compared to what I just went through.

I suddenly look to Mikhail. Intense emotions flex between us. I just breathe, trying to decipher them.

"I'll leave you two alone," a man – no, Elias – says as he walks out.

My bedroom door shuts, leaving me alone with the other Konge. My eyelids swoop down, blocking out the soft fire in the corner of the room. I don't remember it being lit. He moves the hand holding my head close to his chest to be under my back instead. With incredible grace, he slowly stands up. In his arms I feel the room spin.

"No," I can barely move my limbs, I'm so weak. My head falls to his chest, that crisp scent of snow calming the stress.

"I know it hurts, I know. We're going to bed."

Old me, the me before I became this thing, comes out. The old Kali is weak, ignorant. I hate her submission to being taken care of by him.

He lays me down on the bed and surrounds me with carefully placed pillows. His lips gently touch my forehead before he turns to leave.

"Stay with me," I reach out a hand to him. He doesn't even hesitate to take it and climbs in bed next to me. Pillows are moved until he has me securely laying on his chest.

I'm exhausted enough to pass out, yet my body is still coming down from the adrenaline rush. We breathe together for a while before he finally speaks.

"I want this," his hand traces calming patterns on my hip. "Being with you."

I don't respond in hopes he thinks I'm still too weak to say anything.

"I've admittedly had a Suitor before, just so you know. It didn't feel like this. The pull is stronger, yes, but I'm not just interested in that."

"Mmm," I play into the tired feeling just wanting him to stop talking. It's not my concern what he chooses to tell me about his past. I'm no better.

"You won't be healthy enough to get out of bed until the morning after tomorrow. Your body will still be recovering," his breath pushes some of my dark brown hair over my neck. It tickles my sensitive skin that's tingling after burning up from the episode.

Through the night I wake up to find Mikhail always next to me, even if I've shifted away. Any other time where I wasn't in my current state, I would have taken the opportunity to wake him up. A missed chance, certainly not my last.

I consider how much I want to give into the Suitor attraction. Addison surely still has feelings for him with how much she touched him at dinner. Her lips came dangerously close to his skin too many times to count. I only saw him pull away once.

Waiting for the morning gives me just enough time to consider my remaining questions about the idea of Suitors. How long did the attraction last? Does it stop once one gives in, or does it keep pushing until it gets what it wants?

I answer my own question about the possibility of varying strengths. Of course, Mikhail may actually feel it more with me than with Addison, it's simply because of genetics. Him and I would make a much stronger kid than he would with her.

Having kids. An idea I had once considered. One I now stand aggressively against. Bringing a child into this world while in my position would be cruel. I decide then to never do that. At least not until I can assure they'll have everything better. No child of mine would have that for a long time. My people will always need me first, understanding that came with being their Dronning. Whatever or whoever chose me to do this, chose Jakir and I to do this together, knew. They knew we'd see what needs to be done.

Only a thought. The Bond demanding its payment for being ignored results in me being bedridden. The benefit is the forced slow down of the world around me. Laying here unable to move has now forced me to really look at what I've been handed. A chance. It's a chance for me, Jakir, and everyone in this situation with us, to have a life. Healthy, safe, happy. Especially the people I'd pulled out of the miserable conditions to call my own. They all deserve everything I have. I'd make sure of it. Only a thought, to finally realize that nothing about the old version of the world matters.

I pull in the deepest breath since arriving here. It feels as if a weight has been lifted from my shoulders.

Mikhail whispers in my ear, "Your people have been doing well, though I've heard they'd like more interaction from you."

I recall the large number of people I forcefully pushed into Mikhail's home.

"I was giving them space. I don't want to overwhelm them."

"Stressing them out is the last thing your presence will do. Go see them," he runs a finger down my cheek sweetly. "Or I will."

I tense at his threat. He doesn't want them here. This meeting needs to happen soon or I could be putting their lives at risk again rather than helping them.

"I would stay, but I have to be there for other arriving Konge's and Dronning's," Mikhail whispers, his eyes still closed while he riles himself awake. I can move more now, not enough yet to stand on my own. I shift my hips to be closer to him for warmth.

The sun isn't the only thing telling me it's morning.

"Or," I turn around to face him. With every ounce of energy I swing a leg over his hip, then push myself over him. Straddling his lap has his hardness pressing into the softest part of me. "You stay here for a little longer."

"You need to –"

My lips cut him off, pulling him into the same heated thoughts I'm having. Instantly his hands grab my hips. I feel freer than ever having emotionally stepped into my role. Power has me tingling with excitement as I dig my fingers into his scalp. He groans in response as I tighten my hold on his silky hair. The ends get pulled back over his shoulders by both gravity and my hold on the roots. He sits up, one hand still an iron grip on my hip, and scoots back to lean against the headboard.

Our tongues dance together, sliding around one another in a frenzy built up from waiting so long. I grab his bottom lip with my teeth and bite down. Not enough to draw blood, enough to have him fisting my hair at the roots and yank my head back. With my throat exposed he goes for the sensitive part of my neck he'd found earlier in the week. I moan softly when his teeth scrape down my skin then clamp down. The pain has heat blossoming in my chest all the way down to my core. I try to close my legs to ease the ache, forgetting that his body is in the way.

That beautiful mouth works the nerves in my neck to bring out another squeeze of my legs. He chuckles against my hot skin making little bumps rise up. One hand tilts my head down to kiss him again, while his other hand slides between my legs. Only a thin pair of shorts is separating his fingers from touching me. I know he can tell how turned on I already am.

"How long have you been thinking about this kitten?" His voice is cocky. He thinks I'm turned on by grinding myself on him, having no idea I'm instead turned on by my own power and control over my life.

"Stop talking," my muscles are getting weaker, so I stop rolling my hips. I still want more so I reach a hand down to grab him. Through his thin pants I can feel how big he is. My own hand has to slide up and down his length to feel everything, making me breathe faster. I feel my body starting to slip into dangerous territory of being exhausted. I ignore everything except what's in front of me.

A knock on the door has him removing me from his lap. I narrow my eyes slightly at his unwillingness to have us seen like this.

"We aren't doing anything wrong," I test him.

"No, but you need to heal. I shouldn't have let that happen," he doesn't even look me in the eye as he slides out of the bed. I keep my mouth shut until he has his shirt on.

"Come in!" I call, pulling my hair into a loose bun. The Nightmares walk in, both fully dressed and ready for the day. Mikhail throws his chest out a bit at the glares they give him. I enjoy the bit of discomfort I catch in his face, he can't hide everything. "I don't need you here anymore, you can go."

Simmering eyes snap to me. He doesn't move at first until Senka hovers a hand across his chest while walking by. Her talons are out to play, but they never touch his skin. He staggers back at the blatant disrespect.

"Never put your hand near me like that again," hazel irises glow with the force of his *essence*. Senka's face tilts down as her lips curve up into a dangerous smile. Her hand flashes out to hover over his bicep, proving my command still holds against his.

"You can go," I repeat. That violence between us is back, neither of us unwilling to bend to the other. Another knock makes him turn to leave. Aiza exchanges places with him, walking to the bed where now Senka has her head in my lap.

"I'm going to greet the others on my own, if that's alright. We don't want them thinking we're hiding. I'll inform them you're handling a situation with Elias," Aiza is quick to sweep out the awkwardness.

"You'll need him in on that," I point out. My hand threads through Senka's thick black hair. Sayah checks the various medicinal mixtures, applying one of the balms to my chest. Once he's done, Aiza continues.

"He stopped by my room last night, asking me to do this. He seemed genuinely concerned for you," she eyes me suggestively. "Making quick on the alliances, are we?"

"Friendship, actually. I have a good feeling about him."

"That's the best thing I could have heard from you. He's one of the most powerful Konge's from what I understand."

My memories go back to the utter ease he commanded me with, despite my body fighting my own will to simply breathe.

"His Samle is larger?" Sayah wonders, opening up the balcony doors so I can have some fresh air.

"No, it's smaller than Mikhail's. He just has that much essence," Aiza's deft fingers drape over her crossed arms.

"I just heard that word for the first time last night, is it basically how much power you have?" I look down at Senka, who's now lightly snoring.

"It's how much power you have as a Konge or Dronning, but yes basically."

"Good to know," I consider the level of power I sit at between the two men.

"I know telling you to stay in bed until tomorrow morning is useless, so I won't. I will, however, tell you that coming down to greet the others and mingle while unable to endure at least a dinner and dancing could destroy any chance we have of making a strong mark," Aiza's eyes are filled with concern and warning. Her brain must be spinning at full speed trying to piece together a plan to give the best shot at coming out on top of this meeting.

"I'll wait," is all I give her. She doesn't look convinced but relents away. "The two of you," I look to Sayah, and tap on Senka to wake her up. "Will do the same thing. Out of sight completely, however you do it, and will update me on who arrives, what they do, who is friendly with who. I don't need Aiza disappearing enough to make them wonder what's going on."

I get a nod and grumbled response before being left alone for a couple hours. Sleep finds me occasionally, still difficult with the low riding pain of a too-strained Bond. Each time one of the twins return I add a new leader to the list of those who have arrived. With Addison and Elias having arrived yesterday it leaves seven more to arrive. First is a group of three having traveled from the Southwestern continent. Dominé and Hendrix, who reside on either side of the Gem Samle, are friendly. They apparently try to step over the Dronning, though Senka gushes about how she actually leaves them scrounging for ground to stand on. I write down her name on a scrap piece of paper for later.

Sayah comes in with a bitter look a couple hours later, explaining that Sebastian of the Hellish Samle has arrived. His comments on how overly dressed he is has me needing to steer him back to more pertinent information. Sebastian is polite, reserved, giving nothing away other than a greeting or two. I send him away with a request to specifically keep an eye on him. Neutrality does nothing except make me uneasy.

They both return a handful more times to tell me about Dominé and Hendrix making a point to be placed in quarters across from one another, while their neighboring Dronning chooses a room in a lower level. She's either isolating herself or is being isolated by the others. Elias greets her pleasantly, sans the flirting, which is greatly returned to my relief. Another possible ally.

Having had enough of waiting around for small reports I finally heave myself up out of bed. For a moment, my legs shake under the weight of my body. Faster than expected, I'm able to stand on my own. The holes in my thigh are also completely healed now so a wrap is no longer needed. I grimace at the clean holes that splatter across the other cuts on my thighs.

Senka walks in with perfect timing as I yank off my clothes.

"Are you sure?" is all she says to check. I nod, moving to find a dress out of the bag of them I picked up from the people on the shore. I cycled through a few of them, choosing to wear the black one with chains again. Cool metal slips over my thighs in a delicious way that settles me into a state of calm. I slip on the same heels, simple look completed.

"Let's go," I follow her out of the room, well aware of her hawk eyes watching for a sign I'm about to go down.

"I have an addition for you, wait here."

She slips into her room, returning with a palette in her hand.

"Makeup? Where did you find that?"

"I keep it for special occasions," she smears a coal along my eyelids, creating a smoked-out eyeliner effect. Highlighter is rubbed into my high cheekbones, then she hands me mascara. Her hand grabs my wrist to pull me into her room, which is similar to mine but much smaller. A mirror is mounted beside her door.

I swipe the mascara wand across my lashes, careful not to use too much. When I pull away, I note the naturally vivid green of my eyes is emphasized with the charcoal eyeliner and mascara. To add just a smidge more, I sweep a thin layer of highlighter under my eyebrows.

"Thank you," I press a kiss to her cheek. She smiles proudly at my gratefulness. We exit to see Sayah waiting beside Elias in the foyer. Elias is dressed in a long maroon formal shirt that extends to his lower thigh. His gold pants are slim but loose, making him look regal yet relaxed. Sayah directs his sister to wait beside him.

Elias's ocean eyes sweep over every inch of open skin, I don't feel the heat that Mikhail's stare gives me. I do a small twirl to let him see the back. He extends a bent arm out for me to wrap my hand around. I grab it without hesitation.

"You could try and give the women a chance to not pass out, you know," I tease him. I give an exaggerated look over him as he does the same. I'm grateful he hasn't mentioned the scars.

"You could try and give everyone a chance to not fall to their knees," his smile creates one on my own face.

"Elias," I playfully cover my chest with my hand. "You act like I'd do that on purpose."

"No, I would never think such a thing of someone with delightful legs like those."

We reach the bottom of the stairs as I laugh at the playful banter between us. Aiza and Elias's general are waiting, conversing politely behind us once we pass them. Crowds of people are filtering into the grand hall. All kinds of conversation varying from who will dance with who to who might be here reach my ears.

"You know," I put my free hand on Elias's arm lightly. "In all my life I never once thought I'd have to deal with court gossip in my early twenties."

"I never thought I'd be able to be a dragon at thirty, so you're telling me," he looks sarcastically dreadful to me.

Joking back and forth about various tragedies of being pulled into a world of court politics makes the time go by so fast I don't remember entering the hall. The u-shaped table, created with three rectangular ones, is set back so as to accommodate all leaders. Mikhail stands at the center, with Addison on his right. On Addison's right are two men, one with curly black hair the other with a shaved head. As she speaks to them they both turn their heads towards us, completely ignoring whatever she's saying.

Immediately, their eyes catch my arm entwined with Elias. Walking in with him is a statement. The curly haired one drags his eyes down my body in a way that has my gut screaming to let my talons out. The other male looks over, though clearly unfriendly, does it more to size me as another leader. Addison's hand is curled into the top of the table. I lift my face to stare down Mikhail, who is now blatantly drinking me in.

His hand lifts, settling on Addison's back. Elias continues to walk me towards the pedestal. Her gaunt face turns to me with a smug grin, I return it with a heated gaze that intentionally makes her uncomfortable. My companion doesn't miss the heavy look on my face at her.

"Consider me surprised that you'd be interested in screwing her," he whispers, leading me to my chair.

"I'm not," I turn to his ear now. "I just like watching her lose her footing."

"Evil woman," he jokingly shames me.

He pulls out the chair at the corner of the table, leaving an empty one between Mikhail and me.

"Careful Elias, you'll make him very angry," I pout, earning another laugh.

Another male walks in the door, boasting loudly to whoever walks next to him about some successful hunting trip. I glance at him, taking in the patches of dark and white skin that are splayed like puzzle pieces across his exposed limbs. His dirty blond hair is shorter on the sides, curly and long on the top. I only meet his gaze for a second before we both go back to our own conversations.

"Sebastian, the Metael Samle," that warm voice explains. He pours a full glass of red wine for me. "Nasty man with a taste for killing."

"Sounds like another Konge," I mumble, watching his traveling companion split off to the table full of the other guests brought from various places. Aiza sits amongst them, handling bouncing discussions well.

"Him and Gallyan agree on most everything, it's disturbing to see that two people like that are capable of the things they've done."

I raise an eyebrow.

He sighs, takes a deep sip of wine, then continues.

"A few rumors have spread that they've both terrorized the remaining humans into extinction. I cannot say that's true because I don't know the depth of it. I am certain, though, that they've boasted about killing plenty of rogues and dissenters."

I swallow down my anger, meeting his eyes.

"Disgusting," is my only commentary.

Sebastian sits between Addison and the other men. His body language reeks of vile male dominance. Graciously, Elias keeps up appearances as I watch the people on the far side of the table interact.

They all suddenly laugh at a joke the curly haired one makes; Addison reaches out to touch Mikhail's hand. I watch his body freeze up. It's not in fear but it is from extreme discomfort. A part of me wants to watch him suffer with her. Partly for my low-level hatred for their relationship, partly for my never-ending craving to end his life.

The last to enter is a woman that has everyone looking over the same way they did me. Mikhail stands to greet her, offering the chair between us. She offers a greeting then turns to me.

Her hand, covered in oversized rings with a variety of colored jewels, reaches up to push her bangs out of her eyes. I look down her body, trying my best not to linger on her wide hips that are accented by the cutout dress she's wearing. We both look over one another appreciatively. I realize she has no hesitation on staring at my chest, so I don't either when looking at her. She flaunts her thick curves as she sits, letting her ass push out a bit.

Her teeth have a space between the two front ones, making her face look younger.

"Janét," she reaches out one of those heavily jeweled hands. The lilt to her voice suggests English is one of many languages she speaks.

"Kali," I return with my own name. The red lipstick she's wearing further intensifies my own attraction.

At least I don't want to slit her throat.

"Elias," she looks around me to greet him. "It's wonderful to see you again."

"The same to you, though I have a feeling we may not be speaking as much this time."

"No," she glances appreciatively at me. I return the same look. "I'd like to get to know the stunning new Dronning tonight."

Chapter 29

"**M**y people live between the Slips and Rain Samle's," she gestures to Dominé and Hendrix. "You should come visit some time; we have nearly all of our cultures remaining. Dancing, food, wine, all of it."

"From?" I ask, unsure of where exactly her and her people are from.

"South America," she winks.

"Sounds like you're trying to convince me to move there instead."

"My bed is big enough to share."

I nearly choke on my mouthful of soup, managing to get it down with mild grace. Laughs come from either side of me. I look back up at her to teasingly shake my head, only to find Mikhail glaring at the back of hers. Wanting to further upset him I lean into her space to talk with her. Elias watches humorously, enjoying the interaction between Janét and me. Mikhail's eyes cut down furiously as I place my hand on top of hers.

"I'll take you up on the offer sometime, but beds aren't always necessary," I say, loud enough for the man behind her to hear. Matching his stare, I give him a wicked smile. Janét turns to look between us. His jaw sets angrily. "Apologies, just tired of men who can't make up their mind."

"No, please," she dabs at her mouth. The red lipstick doesn't budge. "I'm all for bruising inflated egos, so let's play."

We both deviously look at each other. Her exaggerated wink brings a laugh to Elias, inciting a dark one from me.

I take a moment to take in the other leaders in the room. Sebastian watches us carefully, I stare him down - dark eyes clashing with mine -

until he raises his glass to me, then looks away.

All three of us converse, telling one another about our homeland. Janét's Samle, as well as the surrounding ones, are all varying Hispanic cultures rich with traditions from the Old World. Some new ones have come about from the shift in people's forms, mostly becoming about the praising of being dragons. She explains with light in her eyes that they've rebuilt many towns and are currently building a far reaching city that can support many.

"They came together so quickly after everything collapsed," the Dronning brags, proud of her people's achievements. "Even the group with nothing in common just...got along."

"Is there any divide at all between your people and those not inherently a part of it?" I ask both of them.

"No, surprisingly," Elias steps in. "There's no divide. Some chose to live further out on their own with less, others chose to live near her with plenty to go around. Having rich sources of precious gemstones doesn't hurt either."

"Can't say the same for others," Janét mumbles, giving Elias a look.

I wait patiently, confusion evident to the both of them on my face.

"Both of them have created their own class divide, it's revolting," Elias's mouth is bitter at the comment. "Anyone that's his own is treated well, any rogues have either become slaves or cast out and made to rot away in subpar conditions."

"Actually, most of them have done that. They think if you're not a dragon, not part of their flock, you don't belong," Janét is looking at Elias now, updating him since whenever their last meeting was.

"I figured as much, once Gallyan started it they all did."

I consider the alliance group across from us, clearly all people of the same beliefs. Belong or be cast out. It puts an ache in my stomach that doesn't sit well. Briefly I consider asking the natural redhead sitting quietly how he could ever consider being so generous. I hope, for his sake, that he does it to cover a minimum level of politics.

"Anyways." She raises her glass, "We're incredibly fortunate to have that as well. We're far enough along rebuilding and being one whole people that I've spoken with my council, and we've decided to extend a couple trade agreements. All because we're doing so well."

"Ah, I get the name now," it clicks why hers is the Gem Samle. "Wait," I lower my voice so as not to embarrass myself. "Is everyone's Samle named for that reason."

"A couple, but not all," she thankfully speaks in the small bubble the three of us form. "Hendrix's people live mostly in a wet area, lots of rain forests, and beautiful land - despite their Konge."

"The Rain Samle," Elias tosses in.

"Dominé lives in a very strange area, constantly a depressing drizzle. Lots of rocky terrain that's fairly unforgiving."

I clear my throat, wanting as much information as possible before interacting with the others, "What about the rest?"

"Sebastian makes weapons, lots of them, and he trades with the others for whatever they've agreed upon. It's all sword, shields, battle pieces you'd see in history books. From what I heard, he tried making guns and could never figure them out," she pushes her plate away, most likely having lost her appetite.

"Gallyan doesn't produce things, he produces people," Elias is looking between both of us. "He very rarely shares them."

"These people they...?"

Janét sighs, her oval face appearing shadowed.

"Slaves, Kali. He grabs people - his own and others - and forces them into slavery. Most are human, some are rogues, a few are dragons."

I want to drop my jaw so badly but showing anyone that I've suddenly heard anything less than positivity could give away our discussion. Elias is confused by my smile at him, then quickly realizes what I'm doing it for. I pick their brains a bit more in hope of better information that doesn't make me feel hopeless. Our conversation is ceased as conversation in the rooms drops off of a cliff.

"Speak of the devil and he shall come," Janét adjusts something in her boot that reaches incredibly high under her snug dress.

Observing, never moving, I watch a man enter the room with two people flanking his side. The one on his right is an average looking woman, with dull eyes to match her paper thin skin. The blue hue of them is stunning, but they lack life. Her frame looks rectangular, though I can't tell if it's from the ill-fitting clothes or lack of proper nutrition. She takes in the room quickly so she can move to scan the table. Starting at Sebastian she looks nervous. Her gaze pulls from her left to her right to finally land on me. I don't like the twitch her right eyelid makes. Her head tilts slightly as she starts to make her way immediately to me. I see a shadow move in the impossible height of the ceiling. One of the twins is ready to break their cover to keep her away.

They know her, I realize. Nobody else sees Sayah move so I make sure to not look up at him.

She's stopped by an arm that swings out in front of her.

"Mikhail! Have you gotten fatter?" Gallyan calls out. Mild conversation starts up again, giving the Konge a chance to lean into the woman's ear to whisper something. I can't see his face or lips, but whatever he says makes her turn around and exit the room promptly. No one is brave enough to speak over the newest guest. "Covering up that double chin with a grown out beard is certainly the way to go."

Long legs carry a large frame up the stairs. I lean back in my chair, letting the fabric of my dress fall between my legs. Janét braces besides me, her chest rising and falling with controlled movement.

Gallyan isn't muscular, but he's large. His body is clearly one that carries strength in functional muscles rather than visible ones. His golden blond hair is swept into a roguish style. High, rounded cheeks still make him look younger than he most likely is. I sweep my gaze down him, sizing up the way he moves as he extends his hand out to yank Mikhail into a rough one-armed hug.

Gallyan greets the other men much the same. He reaches Addison, his hand engulfing her frail one. He places a slow kiss to the veins sticking out along her tendons while creating an uncomfortable silence.

"Stunning as always, dear Addison," his voice is meant to be sultry, yet it comes across as greasy instead. Her cheeks flush red, her free hand coming up to cover her gloss covered lips. The strange interaction makes it seem as if she's completely forgotten that the man standing next to her exists.

I decide to stand before he turns to me. I don't want him to think I'd stand for him. My movement seems to catch his eye. Thin lips spread to reveal nearly perfect teeth. Beady eyes a strange shade of green drag down me to catch on the open slits teasingly revealing my thigh. Chills run down my spine, feeling similar to the ones I felt when Kent touched me. I shake off the memory to confront the Konge.

Not a muscle moves on me as he stops in front of me. The room is deadly silent in the wake of us staring at one another. His sick grin spreads even wider when he realizes I'm forcing him to make the first move. Small sparks of anger have his lips twitching.

"I presume you're the new Dronning," his hand extends out palm up. I place my hand in his, rotating the connection so as to enforce a firm handshake, rather than feel his curved lips on my skin. His face falters slightly.

"I am, I presume you're Gallyan?"

"Very smart girl," his words are not complementary.

"Very smart boy," I return shamelessly. My mind starts to turn towards its darker half. I feel giddy at the muscles in his face tightening at my use of the word 'boy'. He drops the equally pressured handshake. More examining of my body, I look over him with a very realistically bored gaze. I finish my inventory quickly, bringing my eyes up with an uninterested flick. Any closer and I would have to tilt my head back slightly.

His next move is a little unexpected. Those dull eyes start to glow with his essence, challenging me.

Mine remain unlit. The intensity flares out, it's nearly as strong as Elias's. Maybe more so.

Janét shifts uncomfortably next to me, looking in another direction.

I don't break eye contact. Instead, I stare directly into his eyes while letting a small amount of that creeping shadow slip its claws over my head. Keeping half of my mind sane, while letting the other start to roll in violence proves to be enough of a distraction. My eyes beg to return his challenge, but I don't let even the smallest spark out. His smile falls.

Embarrassing him by not returning the challenge slams the first nail in the coffin.

"Are you alright?" I feign a concerned tone. My head tilting slams in the next one.

Like a page turning, his eyes return to normal. That smile that had slipped off so suddenly is back. His posture is more fluid now, instead of unearthly still.

"Fabulous, thank you for asking," he blinks, then turns to sit at the end of the table next to Dominé. Both immediately begin whispering to the other. Normal sound returns to the room, washing away the tension created from Gallyan and I's standoff. In a free moment, I find Mikhail watching me. Two kinds of heat pin me in my seat. One of them is rage, I'm not sure at what. The other is an unbridled lust that will clearly have one of us paying the price later on.

"I think you and I are going to get along just fine," Janét lightly elbows me.

"Might as well tell me your ring size now," Elias says as if it's obvious what our next step is.

"I don't know if I should feel torn or not," my words have him giving me a reassuring look that says all he wants is to flirt. Janét's response about not minding another has heat rushing into my cheeks.

Dancing with her induces the same reaction again, her hips move with a sensuality I'm not used to. We stayed pressed up against each other, her plump body is distracting for many of the males. I pride myself a bit on the fact that she chooses to continue dancing with me anyway.

"We're going to make everyone jealous if we keep at this," I whisper to her. I lead us around the floor based on the movements I picked up recently. Dropping my hand to the lowest part of her back sends a heartbeat to a sensitive area. She feels something similar, because her hand on my shoulder drops enough to tease the swell of my breast.

"We can always move elsewhere."

I raise my eyebrows at her suggestion.

"Might I cut in? For purely political reasons of course," Elias sweeps her away from me to start the harmless flirting with her. I make my way out of the crowd dancing so lively to the string quartet. Mikhail is coming down the steps with a line of sight pinned on me. I turn to avoid him, only to be caught by Gallyan sweeping me back to the floor. He looks at me, only a few inches taller than me at this proximity.

Might as well, if I want a chance at figuring him out.

"Sure, I'll dance with you Gallyan. Thank you so much for offering," I dryly say.

"Nobody likes an overly confident woman."

"I beg to differ, you're the one who grabbed me like I was the last box of candy on the shelf."

"That mouth of yours is going to get you exactly what you're asking for," he grabs my other hand to begin our own path along the smooth stone. Neither of us look at the other as we speak.

"Please tell me, Gallyan, what exactly it is that I'm asking for," I dig my fingers in to squeeze his hand. He does it right back.

"To be put in place," his voice is too low for anyone to hear. I slam my jaw shut to keep from sinking my talons, which have now edged out of my fingers, into his neck.

The feeling of being watched creeps around my neck. Darkness threatens to swell over the rest of my brain. Images of his blood covering my arms flit behind my unfocused eyes. Kent's face and his blur on top of each other.

"Has anyone ever told you you're no fun?"

"No, usually they're dead before they can insult me."

I pull my head back to look at him, we both give a death stare that could fold armies in half. I go to pull away from him and am instead trapped by his arm wrapped around my waist. I press the tips of black claws into his skin.

"Easy there, wouldn't want everyone to think you're new at this."

"I don't give a shit what people think," I'm losing my temper quickly. Gallyan knows it too, because his eyes flare in excitement as he gets under my skin.

"I think you will when I have you on your knee. Which you will eventually do once you learn you're not the strongest here."

That's where I have him. I've already been clawing to keep my head above water. Survival can be so fatal when tested.

I relax my hands, leaving the long black talons to drape over his skin.

"What's your homeland like?" my sudden change in attitude catches him off guard, he only gives me a mildly condescending look before answering.

"We have the finest buildings, the finest weapons courtesy of Sebastian over there," he nods to the other Konge, who raises his glass delightfully at Gallyan. "We also have the finest soldiers. I'm unchallenged you see. People have come to understand that I'm at the top of the proverbial food chain. I have a lot to offer - should you make the wise decision to follow me."

"I didn't ask."

He continues as if I didn't speak. I let him finish.

"I can provide a better world this time around, especially when people start realizing that."

I'm now looking over his shoulder at absolutely no one. He follows my gaze multiple times to try and figure out what has my attention.

"Dronning Kali, did you hear what I said?"

I smile at him innocently, pretending to force my eyes back to him.

"Mm? Oh, no I didn't hear a word you said. Stopped listening after the first word, I believe."

I drop my hands from his body, give him an amused once-over, and then walk back to where Elias and Janét are currently speaking with Aiza. They're standing near the table we'd eaten at. All three are slightly wide eyed as I walk towards them.

Aiza looks concerned, she places a light hand on my arm.

"What did you do, Kali?"

"I played a game."

"Who's game?" Elias asks, watching the large man I'd left on the dance floor. I catch him announcing to Mikhail that he wishes to go to his rooms.

"Mine."

"That looked an awful lot like a contest of who could smile nastier," Janét glances down at her wine. Her eyes gaze up at me through her thick black lashes.

"If it was, then it's a shame Gallyan lost the first round."

"Kali," Aiza warns.

"It's fine. I'm fine. He wants me to bend the knee to him," I watch her face go through multiple emotions.

"That's faster than expected, and extremely unfortunate," she tugs on the fabric of her pink Hijab. "He'll want his answer by the end of the week."

"I gave him my answer."

"He doesn't care," Elias turns back to me. "If it's still a no by the time we all leave, he'll have you on a hit list faster than you can shift."

I feel my heart kick up in excitement at the possibility of having an actual reason to hurt him.

"Let's not make such assumptions yet," Aiza sees right through my calm exterior. She knows I'm looking for a fight with the irritating Konge. "I'd like to bring you back to Jakir and the others in one piece."

For the second time tonight I'm grabbed by a man.

"Walk with me," Mikhail's voice is tight.

"No thanks," I snap my forearm out of his grip just as he had taught me. Janét and Elias attempt control over their laughter.

"My house, my rules, let's go."

"My body, my rules. Don't touch me like that again."

Everything around us disappears. Conversation becomes a lull, movement is formed into never ending blurs. Those standing not three feet from us don't exist as Mikhail and I challenge each other. It's not a challenge of who can bend the others will first. No, this is who will drop the façade first so they can wrap themselves up in lust.

My body begs me to give in to the lips that my eyes are fully trained on. My own part in awe at the utter domination he holds over my body's reaction. His eyes sweep down to catch the movement of my slightly fuller bottom lip being relaxed. That grip on my arm changes from one type of firm to another which holds promises I want to experience.

A throat clears to my left. I realize we're still standing on the edge of the crown in the throne room. Aiza has walked away to escort herself to her room. My two newest companions watch between Mikhail and I with fascination. A jerking motion stops my breathing once I realize we've just given the two of them everything they need to know. To anyone else, it looks like a control battle between two alpha personalities.

"What a fascinating turn of events," Janét eyes me.

"You should pray to the moon Gallyan doesn't figure this out," Elias has his hands folded behind his back, examining me as well.

Light flares in my eyes, catching Janét off guard. Elias smiles a bit. I know my order will do nothing to him, yet I hope the newly blossoming friendship carries enough weight.

"All of you come with me," Mikhail says, appearing next to me.

I feel guilt at the uneasy step the caramel skinned woman takes towards me. For now, I can't be sure if she'll use the information against us. Elias schools neutrality onto his face before we begin our slow exit.

Once out of sight we follow Mikhail to the courtyard.

"Not a soul comes out here or watches us," he commands a man sitting near the entrance of the battling area. He nods, moving to command two more sentries standing nearby.

Silence thrums against my hearing until our small group stops.

"Kali," Janét's voice is a bit strained.

"I'm sorry I had to do that, I can't trust if you'll spread that to him."

Her hand stops me from going any further. She breathes in after the command releases.

"First, that essence is a threat to your own life."

"She out commanded me when she got here," Mikhail is watching me, arm crossed over his chest while he leans against the mountain wall.

"Essence grows with time, none of us have been alive long enough to witness a drastic growth, but two years was enough for me to figure it out," her eyes are clouded with an unreadable feeling.

"I'm the only one who can command over Gallyan," Elias has the same pose as Mikhail, except standing up straight. "You could be stronger or weaker than him."

"Only one way to find out," I shrug, a bit careless of the effects of my decisions. "If I need to order you not to breathe a word I will."

"You had my alliance the second I met you," Elias clears up any confusion immediately.

"While not immediate for me," Janét lifts up her chin a bit. "You have my alliance purely based off of your instinct around those vile people."

We stand eye to eye. I feel myself become much more interested in the energy she's giving off. She picks up on my shift in interest, jutting her chest out barely while letting her eyelids lower mildly.

"Enough," Mikhail severs the connection between her and I.

"Sore loser, I find myself being entertained by them. Two women with their looks playing together," he whistles. "I think even Linius would fall to his knees at that."

"Let's touch on that, actually," Janét looks directly at the redheaded man.

"I thought you'd want to touch on something else," Elias wiggles his eyebrows at her. "I wouldn't mind taking her off your hands."

I tilt the corner of my mouth up, "She did mention sharing, you know-"

Mikhail's patience runs out, because he pulls me to him. My ass presses against him making it clear he's both territorial and turned on. I fight the shiver crawling up my spine.

Janét doesn't bother to wipe the sensual look from her mouth.

My brain panics about her seeing this, the dark part of me coming out to play for a second time tonight. I let my eyes begin to burn with my glowing essence. I don't use it, but I show it as a warning. "Janét, I assume you won't say anything but I'll go ahead and make it clear. You will never breathe a word about Mikhail and I being Suitors to anyone else. Tell anyone and I'll shove my tail through your spine."

An appalled look touches both of their faces. The last of that awful part of me goes back to sleep. Mikhail gives a dark laugh that has his hardness pressing harder into my back, I arch my back just enough to tease him.

"I had no idea you were that creative."

I nearly flinch under her lingering gaze on the scars that stand out under the moon's bright light.

"Somebody got creative with me when I got dumb. It was a while ago," I explain wanting to get the attention off of my skin.

"Not that long, because any damage like that would have been healed by you changing from human to this. You got those after you woke up."

She doesn't miss a thing.

"Was it another dragon?" the Desert Samle male makes a quick guess.

"No," I pull away from the heat at my back, not wanting to feel more vulnerable. "Humans. Boys, basically. They're fast so they caught me."

My thought process battles on whether or not it's worth it to tell them the full truth. Telling them could bring me to a stooped level where they pity rather than respect me. On the other hand it could shift me into a much stronger position in their minds. I decide to wage on the latter hope.

"Jakir found me with them. I was chained up and stripped nearly naked. I'd killed three of their little pack. I don't remember anything but when I found them the next day their bodies were puzzle pieces." I feel a bit of terror run through me at the pleasure in remembering their bodies. "Eventually when they got their hands on me, they decided forty slices with a couple different blades was enough to start out."

"Forty?" Elias lifts his hand like he wants to hold me.

"To start?" Janét shares the same disbelieving tone.

Mikhail says nothing. He just stands with his hand propped up on a rough ledge of the wall sticking out. I hate the tenderness in his eyes. I don't want to be the person chained up or fighting to survive. I have to be the one that came out winning.

"I got out, now I'm here. End of story."

"Sounds more like the beginning of your story."

"Beginning or not, Elias, I shared it so I'm not such a stranger to you all anymore. You've given me plenty about yourselves, about being found by your people so quickly and what your homes are like."

Hazel eyes still stare at me. His gaze promises my hope and fears for whatever it is between us.

Two shadows dance along the edge of the walls, both wanting to reach me. I make another rash decision hoping it'll earn trust fast and hard. I extend my hand past Elias. Curling my fingers towards me has the Nightmares covering the distance. Even Mikhail is confused until both siblings step out of the shadows.

"What the fuck."

"My gods."

"Where have the two of you been?"

Senka and Sayah merely offer my Suitor an empty look.

"None of your concern," I answer for them. "Janét, Elias, I'd like to introduce Sayah and Senka."

"Hello," the twins say in unison. They feed off of the shiver Elias gives, the nervous energy Janét has.

"What is their purpose?" she asks. She continues to examine them while they stand eerily still next to me

"Whatever I need them to do."

"We protect her," Senka's eyes widen with excitement. To me, she looks sweet with how excited she is. To them, in all likelihood she looks psychopathic. Janét turns to me, then goes to step towards me. Her eyes never leave the twins.

Senka moves quickly, putting herself between us in the blink of an eye. I peer over her shoulder to Janét.

"Interesting," is all the Dronning says.

"You won't see them much after this, but they'll be around. I'll give you whatever information they feed me. Understand please, that they only answer to me."

I receive nods all around.

"How did you find places to hide," Mikhail's eyes tighten at Sayah.

Senka's giggle sends a live wire down my neck. Neither answer him. He looks to me for one, I shrug in honest innocence.

"You can't control them, Nightmares aren't meant to be controlled," I brush my hand down Senka's back to ease her guarding posture.

Chapter 30

"Then let's hope you have a sufficient amount of sway over them," Elias eases the conversation with his warm voice. We all begin to relax once I send the twins to go spar in human form.

"I originally wanted to bring Kali here to spar," Mikhail's long fingers drag through his thick hair. I watch the long ginger locks fall back around his face to frame the strong muscles in his jaw line. He moves away, beginning to warm up with moves similar to what Dimitri had taught me recently. His body repeats the motions over and over seamlessly.

"I don't believe we use the same methods, but I'd be more than happy to join in," he calls out. His head turns, and he catches me watching him. I clench my jaw at the smirk he gives me.

"Where did you learn such things?" Janét's suspicion has my own rising at the details of the men's past.

"I was enrolled in various classes on self-defense and fighting, it was for my own protection," Mikhail explains, continuing his warm up.

"Rough life?" I guess.

"Politics could be brutal on families in Russia," my heart softens a bit. Most people that survived the end of one era seemed to have done so bitterly.

"Class hierarchy in India was...testy. I learned a bit from family, then the rest I've learned from my own dragons," Elias kindly puts in his own experience. He begins to take off the long dress jacket. "Capability like that is going to be the difference between us," his voice drops so only we can hear. "And those who side with Gallyan."

314

"You seem so sure that he won't compromise at all," I let my dress slide off so I can change into one of the many outfits provided for dragons shifting back to human form. Heat from both Janét and Mikhail has me feeling slightly conscious about my marks and body. Elias has no interest, continuing the conversation at hand.

"He's been in power for two years," dark olive skin is revealed once Elias rolls up his sleeves. "He's done nothing but prove over and over again that he will continue to do whatever is necessary to gain control."

"I have a theory," Mikhail completely removes his shirt. I bite down on my tongue to keep myself from reaching out to touch him.

"You have enough information to have one?" Janét's black eyebrows raise in confusion. She changes her clothes as well into comfortable pants and a cropped shirt.

"I've met with him enough, sat next to him plenty to be able to tell he doesn't just want control. He most certainly has some distasteful ideas, I just don't think that's it. His version of control seems to be just killing people, instead of keeping them alive. There's some strange sort of attraction he has to people dying."

"You're saying it's not about gaining control over all of us?" I grab a long pole made of dense wood. Mikhail questions my choice, having not seen me during the hours I'd spent training with the twins and Dimitri.

"It is, but I think it's because he genuinely believes he knows what's best."

"Being an old white man doesn't help with that," Janét loudly whispers as she moves to a different circle to train with Elias. Torches light along the walls by Dimitri, who is apparently the only other person allowed to be out here.

"He's not that old, upper forties I believe."

"Older than most that survived. The fact his body can withstand changing at that age surprises me," Elias starts slow movements with his partner.

"Hold on, does it get harder to change as you get older?" Mikhail smacks my side with his foot at the end of my question. It knocks the breath from my lungs with the hit. I glare at him.

"None of us have been alive long enough to know what age does, but I can confirm that the older you start out at, the harder it is on your body."

"I would like to make a note that we don't even know if our life spans have been affected by all of this," rings flash in the light as Janét holds up her hands.

Barely into a training session and we're all stopped. Dimitri practically has smoke coming out of his ears at the gears turning in his head. I can't even hear everyone breathing.

"We could have a handful of years left," Mikhail tugs at his beard.

"Or a thousand," I stare intently at the pole in my hands.

"Guess we'll have to find out," Janét shrugs, going back to a now surprised Elias.

No one says anything for a bit other than mild corrections on stances or technique. Dimitri continues to step into the circle with Mikhail and I to make corrections to me. Eventually the Sekund frustrates his Konge into saying something.

"Why are you making so many corrections to her? She's been training with me, not with you ya' jackass," his breathing is nearly as fast as mine.

"Wrong," I correct him. "While you've been off distracting yourself I asked Dimitri to teach me. He obliged."

"I still think I'm much better to train with," the Konge seems injured at my choice of trainer.

"That's incorrect and you know it, jackass," Dimitri gives him a droll look. The banter turns competitive between the two men.

"Fine, then she fights with us both. Whoever loses is the worst one," his teeth flash in eagerness. Dimitri simply shrugs off his shirt. "I'll go first," that eager look turns to me. "That way you have a shot."

The man with a receding hairline steps back out of the circle. I point the staff at him.

"You knew exactly what you were doing," I let annoyance fill my words to the brim.

"Perhaps, but you should be fine."

"Be fine?"

My next words catch in my throat as Mikhail swings his own staff at me with the force of all his body. The end catches my hip hard enough I feel a bruise start to form.

"I'd prefer her skin it's regular shade when I get her in my bed the first time, Mikhail," Janét yells out. I hear Elias chide her for not being focused.

"Only inexperienced people need a bed," his staff swings under mine, knocking it to the side. I bring the side tucked close to me out and into his shoulder. He pulls that side back which opens up another swing that lands to his bicep. Breaths hiss in through his teeth. He shakes out the numb feeling I've experienced multiple times courtesy of Dimitri. I throw a half grin at the Sekund, who's eyes watch the blow that folds my right leg down.

You're being too confident.

I reel in any semblance of confidence. If it can get me taken down it can get me killed. Especially around people like Addison or Gallyan.

I have to throw my torso back to dodge the wooden pole swinging at what would have been my cheek.

"That would have been my face you moron, you like your women banged up when you fuck them?" I snap at him as he tries to jam the end of the staff into my calf. Swinging my other leg around I knock his feet out from under him, only causing him to stumble. I continue to spin, this time whipping the pole into the side of his thigh, then immediately pull back to slam the tip into his sternum.

"Being behind you can fix that," he wheezes out, still thriving off of an inflated ego.

Dimitri's lessons ring bells in my head. He'd spent every day I wasn't busy with recovering or Mikhail, drilling instincts into me.

I consider the first lessons with him as I allow Mikhail to gain strength in his leg back. Hitting him when weak wouldn't be enough to satisfy me.

"Mikhail said he would train me," I yawn, still tired from so much occurring in such little time.

"Yes, and he's nothing but busy. He's expressed multiple times how important

he believes it to be that you learn how to defend yourself."

"He cares enough to believe that?"

Dimitri drops his shoulder down to look at me funny.

"You asking that proves how little the two of you talk."

"We don't ever get the chance to do much talking," I grumble.

"You do, you just choose to fight or mess around instead."

"He asked you to do this?" I change the subject, uncomfortable with pressure about our interaction from Mikhail's closest friend.

"No, I decided to do this on my own."

"But you don't like me," I argue.

"I apologize that that is the impression you've received but it is not true. Mikhail has been through much just as any Konge or Dronning has, I simply wish to protect him," he urges me towards him with his hand. I walk forward, stupidly without a guard up. "You threatening me simply to protect your own people's feelings showed a lot."

He swings a punch into my jaw. Nothing hard enough to damage, still hard enough to snap my head to the side. I frown angrily at him.

"Showed you you're an ass?"

He shows me how to properly carry my body through various types of punches.

"No, showed me that you, Mikhail, and I are all on the same page. And that you just might be willing to go even farther than him to protect those who deserve it."

"You got all that from a small amount of interaction."

I repeat the steps he's showed me so many times I lose count. Once my movements are satisfactory, he begins throwing slow punches and movements for me to counter.

"You learn very quickly, I'm glad. And yes, if you pay close enough attention, you'll learn a lot more."

Our practice picks up speed along with my increasing comfort with the new movements. I'm humbled multiple times by how little I actually know about fighting. I leave the courtyard later on with sore spots all over my body.

I'm ripped back into the present just as Mikhail steps forward. His weight is distributed well over his feet as he leans into the dangerously charged swing. Not wanting a broken rib, I pull myself up by grabbing onto his weapon, arcing my own to slam into his knee. A crack rings out followed by a smacking sound. His momentum pulls him forward allowing him to throw a punch into my back where my kidney sits.

I grunt at the weakening feeling running down my hip. His chest presses into my back now, his forward momentum causing me to put a foot out to catch us. In a split moments notice I bend at the waist to throw him over my back. His staff drops with a clatter just before his back collides with stone. I swing my staff around behind me, grasp it with both hands, and slam it down. The entire length causes his arms to fly up in automatic defense. His legs immediately clamp together once his body realizes that the end of the staff has left a mark on the sensitive area between his legs.

Dimitri chuckles along with me. Using the staff to balance myself, I crouch down above his head. I spread my thighs so I can see his face roll up towards me.

"That was dirty," he groans.

"So's my mouth but you never complain about that baby," I laugh, breathless from both the fight and the fire spreading in me. We fall silent, his face still tight in pain, my face wildly victorious. His eyes fall back to look at the place I feel warmth starting to pool. Dimitri is grabbing a staff much larger than mine, and the other two are still dancing around the other loudly mocking their styles.

I slowly drop my knees to the ground along with the staff. Controlled movements keep the wood from being loud on the stone. Mikhail's eyes glow just a bit, enticing me to swing my head down to his.

Our lips touch, light at first. His hand swiftly tangles into my hair to tug my mouth down completely. My lips part to let him in immediately. I suck in air through my nose. It's fire against fire as our mouths slide against each other with fervor. He drags my lip between his teeth so hard a small sound escapes me. My breath is still rapid, just not from the fight. His smile spreads against my swollen lips. I feel agitated at his arrogant attitude. I pull away, swinging forward to drag my breasts across his face as I stand up.

He flips himself, cringing at the leftover pain between his thighs. I throw a smirk at him over my shoulder.

"You look good crawling towards me like that," I look at Dimitri but he knows I direct my statement elsewhere. I ignore the name calling at my back.

"We have every right to have you whipped for saying something like that," my next sparring match warns. He's leaning so carelessly against the staff I wonder if he's even ready to fight.

"You won't."

"If that's a dare I'm more than happy to oblige."

"Careful there, you sound like you might be flirting with me," I walk around the edge trying to gauge the Sekund's first move.

I'm begging to get my ass beat at this point.

"There's a difference between pretending to be big and bad," he doesn't even turn his head to follow me. He's probably listening to my steps stalking behind him.

I lunge out to drive the end directly into his lower spine. He slides out of the way with ease. Faintly I register the other three gathering against a heavy table to watch me. I step back, continuing my predatory observation of him. I jab again at his knee. Miss.

Anger starts to build in me at the general ease he carries himself with. He looks bored as I come around to his front. Still posing with his staff in a nonchalant way, his face is a rage-inducing mockery at me.

I feign going for his shoulder but he catches my plan the second I move. Movement blurs as attack after attack reigns down on my body. I only catch one or two of his swings. The rest land relentlessly along exposed parts of my sides. He gives a bit, finishing his turn with a swing to my gut. I bend over heaving in air to catch my breath

"And actually being big and bad."

For once, I keep my mouth shut. This man is not playing games with me. At least not my game, because I'm clearly playing his. I lick the corner of my bottom lip and pull myself back up. Again, we swing the staffs with primal precision. This time around our hits are equal. Vigorous training has made me much stronger than I had ever been. Thick muscles in my legs had bulked into strength. My upper body had bulked minimally, more so becoming corded and toned. My broad shoulders looked powerful instead of just wide. It still isn't enough to overcome Dimitri's experience.

His leg forces my hips back causing my torso to twist away. Wood slaps his exposed side caving in his ribs temporarily. I see an opening and pull myself forward to do the same on the other side. He bends over the new place I've hit. His face now at a much easier angle to hit I drop my hold to swing up an elbow into his jaw. His head snaps back exposing his neck and belly.

Stupidly, I think his vision being off of me means I can do whatever I want.

His knee comes to his chest in what looks like a move to ball up in pain. Instead, his foot kicks out directly into my sternum. My chest folds around him to meet directly with his staff. My nose cracks loud enough to echo in my head. All the air spills out of my mouth finishing with a grunt as I land butt first onto the ground. My back bounces off of the stone. I reactively keep my head up to keep it from being seriously injured as the Sekund drilled into me over and over.

I'm suddenly thankful for learning how to fall.

My vision is blocked out by him standing over me, staff in my face.

"Yield?" he asks.

I choke on my blood that runs to the back of my throat, "Yield."

He extends a hand out to help me up. We grip each other's forearm until I'm done coughing blood onto the ground. His eyes look at my mouth covered in blood. I give him a genuine smile.

"Next time," I warn cheerfully.

He shakes his head, laughing. We both walk to the rack of weapons to set the staffs down. I turn around and am greeted by Mikhail's upper chest. His hands grab either side of my face to turn me to look.

"Knock it off, if I was seriously hurt Sayah would have his ass."

"Let's get you cleaned up," Janét wraps her hand around mine. We begin to walk away once he reluctantly lets go of my face. "That might be the hottest thing I've seen since the all-female orgy we had a bit ago at home."

I stumble for a second at the image.

"You're lying," I wipe blood from my nose under the back of my hand. Senka's face pops out so small I nearly miss it. Imperceptibly I jerk my head in the direction of my room. She disappears again.

"To you? I would never."

Sparks light up my belly at the roughness in her voice. I look at her fully, then decide to hurry. I tug her hand behind me as I speed up through the halls. Male voices speak in hushed tones behind us. They disappear quickly as we put distance between us.

I keep an eye out around us, making sure we aren't being followed by anyone.

"How do you feel about friends with benefits?" I ask, keeping my eye on the stairs before me. I have to keep my body leaned down, as her slightly shorter frame tugs at the hands clasped between us. My door is open slightly, a warning that one of my companions is in there.

"I feel like I have interest in nothing more than that with you."

I toss a teasing beam to her as I slip us into the room. Unsurprisingly, both of the twins are waiting. Senka walks to leave the room, giggling as she leaves.

"You can set it, clean it, then leave," I order them. Sayah looks at our hands between us. I lift an eyebrow at him. His cheeks suck in as he fights a smile.

Small hands latch onto my face so suddenly I don't have time to react. Senka shoves my misaligned nose back into place. She had not been leaving apparently, just sneaking up to reset my nose.

"I'll clean it up," Janét starts to push me to the sitting area. Once she's in front of me I give Sayah a warm confirmation that I'll be fine. Finally, alone, she points to the couch. I probably look like a mental case as I flash my bloody teeth at her.

"How many bloody noses have you had to clean before?" I plop down, getting a view of her full body standing before me. Turning she picks up a wet cloth out of a bowl of steaming water to wring it. Her body slowly faces me again. She suddenly looks a little hesitant. I pat my lap. She doesn't move. I reach forward to grab her hips and tug her down. She straddles me with a sharp inhale. I ask again, "How many have you cleaned before?"

She clears her throat, it's cute how much her flawless skin flushes, "Plenty, my Sekund and advisor like to get into brawls." Her hand slowly wipes blood that's beginning to dry on my face. I rest my hands on her thighs, marveling at the softness. I slowly slide my hands up to the swell her hips, massaging along the way. Her eyelids flutter shut at my touch.

After a moment she continues to clean off my face carefully. I have my eyes closed but open them to ask a question. That question flies out of my mind the second I see how close her chest is to my face. She pulls back with her eyebrows pinched.

"Did I hurt you?" She scans my face for injury. I force my attention to move to her face instead of her chest.

"No," I squeeze out the answer in a low tone. Her lips part. That red paint is so distracting I don't catch the next thing she says.

"Have you been with a woman before?" she repeats. I squeeze the fleshy part of her hips where her thighs bend. It takes every bit of restraint to not start sliding my hands elsewhere.

"I have. Not in a long time though. I was busy being in a coma."

She laughs nervously, "Have you been with someone my size?"

I can't help the confusion written on my face. She's an incredibly attractive woman with a body that in my mind, would have the majority of people on their knees.

"What do you mean 'my size'?"

The towel gets dropped into the bowl. Blood darkens the water a bit.

"I figured you being so quiet has to do with either me being a woman or my size."

"Guessing the woman part is fair, but the size part is completely wrong. Your body is beautiful, hey," I gently guide her face to look at me. "Where is this coming from?"

Her legs start to unfold and slide back. I hook my hands behind her knees and firmly plant her back down onto my lap. Her breathing hitches, making my pulse race.

I gently take her hand and slide it to my stomach, even with all of the scars and the folds from slouching, I feel raging confidence at how eager she is to touch me. My low self esteem evaporates as her hand slides beneath the stretchy waistband of my leggings. She gives a questioning look, I nod in consent.

I have to grit my teeth to keep from moaning as her warm fingers touch the sensitive bud between my folds. I release a tight breath as she starts to work her fingers in smooth circles.

"Does that feel like I'm anything but extremely attracted to you?" I ask her. Our eyes meet. She bites her lower lip before leaning down to touch my lips to hers. At the first touch I bunch her shirt in my hands. I want so badly to slide my own hand in between her legs, but I want her to be comfortable first.

To my surprise, she drags my hand up to her chest to press it against the small handful. Moving our lips against one another in such a slow passion has my hips lifting slightly to meet her hand. I slide my hand down her torso, across her full belly, then under her shirt. Slowing down my movement, I'm amazed at how flawless her skin is. I tilt her head with my free hand so I can reach her neck. Those full lips leave mine too soon, but I find the spot just below her ear to smooth the empty spot.

"God, Kali," she moans. I drag my teeth down her neck to bite down on a lower part. The little sounds she makes has me reaching up to pinch the tight peak of her breast between my fingers.

I want to hear more sounds from her. I want to have her shaking above me.

Her fingers have other plans because she slips one into me pulling a moan from my own lips. I whisper her name as my eyes close. One hand still toying with her chest, the other moves down to the apex of her thighs.

"Should I make you wait?" I watch her round eyes open, so large they look like they're not real.

"Not unless you want to go another bit of time without a woman."

324

I hum in response, sliding my own fingers to feel how wet she is.

"Janét, fuck, you're soaked."

Her wide hips grind down onto my hand. I waste no time sliding a finger into her while keeping my thumb pressed against her clit.

Another of her fingers slide into me, pulling a shiver out of my body.

"Kali, I think," she swallows, trying to control another noise. I press against the bundle of nerves to pull it out of her. Her mouth opens as a higher pitched noise spills out. "I'm close."

Her head drops to my shoulder, fingers still curling inside of me. I press against the ridges with my fingertips with every movement. I start to feel her tighten around me. Her fingers stop moving, pulling out of me swiftly to dig into my shoulder. The scent of myself hits my nose, making me work harder to make her finish.

She does. Hard.

I completely forget about my own orgasm, reveling in how her eyes roll back and her hips settle onto my hand. Her torso shakes a bit, muscles squeezing around my fingers until she finishes the high.

We both stay there, catching our breath. Her head pulls back to look at me.

"You didn't-"

"I'm fine, it was small. I had way more fun watching you finish," I look up at her through my lashes.

"You're not expecting any sweet kisses or for me to stay the night here, are you? No offense, but I have absolutely no interest in that with you."

I throw my head back and laugh, she laughs with me as she stands up. I hear her walk to the bathroom to clean herself.

"For the record," she says coming out of the bathroom as I get up from the couch. "You are still one of the very few people I'd like to call a friend."

"You've known me for less than twenty-four hours," I deadpan.

"And? Who says there has to be a time limit on friendships? Not many of those to go around these days anyway."

I consider her words.

"Show me at the meeting, and you have yourself an alliance."

"Fair enough," she waves her fingers at me, walking towards the door.

"Oh, and Janét," I step back from the entrance of the bathing chamber. "I don't give a flying fuck who knows about this."

She takes my hint well, leaving with those perfect red lips upturned.

Chapter 31

"She's getting stronger," a black-haired woman throws sticks into a fire.

"Good."

"How long until she visits?" another person, neither feminine nor masculine wonders.

"Could be months, could be centuries."

"And we'll survive that?" the black-haired woman speaks again.

"One of us must, or this world won't survive its next apocalypse," words spoken by a silver haired person whose eyes stayed closed against the bright light of the moon. They breathe in the smoke of the special wood that burns in the forest. A burning sensation pulls at their lungs, eventually giving way to a new breathing. This breathing is rhythmic. Intentional. Controlled.

The other two watch as smoke unfurls then is sucked back in their leader's body. Moonlight seems to dance over their skin, making them look even more ethereal. After another silent moment they speak.

"Has Talia returned?"

Black hair swings with a shaking head, "Not yet. They sent word for more time. Needs more information."

A sigh.

Wood crumbles under the devouring flame.

"We cannot make the first move," the slim figure remarks. "To do so would throw the balance into a spin."

"A death spin, for sure. No, we cannot interfere. She must come to us first," the white haired one agrees.

"And then?"

"And then, we create gods."

Chapter 32

Kali

Sleep isn't easy with so many leaders here at the same time. I roll out of bed to pull on my shoes. Quietly I leave my room to journey down to the rooms where the rogues are sleeping alone. A little shuffle is more of a polite announcement than a mistake. I smile at the silhouette of the female twin that follows me.

The rooms are below the main floor, and are being kept warmer than everywhere else so it's far more comfortable. None of the bedroom doors are closed, letting me peek in to see everyone spending time in their own groups. I pass the room with the two females that I carried on my back. They're whispering with bright looks on their faces until they see me. Embarrassed to be caught snooping I move to walk away.

"Dronning Kali, wait!" the dark blond introduces herself as Laura, spreading her arms out to hug me. I awkwardly debate how comfortable I am with that. "It's okay to just ask for a handshake."

She laughs as she extends her hand. I grasp it gratefully. "This is my wife, Theri."

My chest stings knowing that the couple had practically nothing left but their love for each other as they were withering away in the forest.

"Thank you," Theri speaks up, a genuine look of appreciation in her eyes. I see others lean out of their rooms to watch us. "We didn't think we were going to make it out of there."

She rubs her hand over her shaved head nervously. A bit of the sting eases.

"I will give you everything I have so that you never have to go through that again," my hand unconsciously reaches out to touch her arm. I faintly feel that eerie familiar feeling, though not as strongly. I frown in confusion.

"Is-is everything okay?" Laura asks. I reach out for her hand again, wanting to see if I missed it in her, too. At the contact of skin, the feeling echoes a faint call. I consider how I could have missed the connection that they're mine before.

"Did you know you belong in my Samle?"

They both look shocked.

"You know that certain people belong to a specific Samle, yes?"

They both nod, others in the hallway creep closer.

"As your Dronning I can feel when someone belongs with us. In my limited experience it's been rather strong, though I think with all the problems at hand, there's a lot affecting that."

"Like?" Theri leans against the door frame.

I turn my body so that I'm not excluding anyone from the conversation. So many eyes on me, so many people waiting to understand what belonging means.

"You also are recovering from lack of proper nutrition. You're not in our Samle's territory. Each of you has enough mental and emotional stress to take down an elephant. It could be any of those things. It could just be that the connection just isn't as strong. I honestly don't know so all we can do is wait until we get home."

"When will that be?" Brawn is at the end of the hallway. His glasses catch the light off of one of the torches making it easy to spot him.

"The meeting between all of the Samle leaders will start in the next day or two. Hopefully that won't take long. For now," I change my voice to have a bit of natural command, trying to instill confidence in myself. "All of you need to eat, build up your strength, just don't overexert yourselves."

"Can we train?" Laura asks.

I feel excitement bubble up that she is already prepared to make herself stronger.

"Absolutely, if anyone says you can't train, come to me. Just promise me you'll still take care of yourselves," I stare at all of them, a serious look conveying the severity. A nod from everyone, including a vigorous one from Nelly. His curls bounce as he hurriedly returns to his room.

I stay for conversation with everyone. Most of them have questions about where we'll be going and how we'll get there. I offer a bit, not wanting them to get too wrapped up in planning anything. Once they're content with the answers I've given, doors start to swing closed as people climb into bed. Brawn approaches me last.

"I apologize for not having come down before," I cross my arms in front of me.

"No one is bothered, we know you're busy. We've seen you at dinner speaking non stop with one person or another. I just wanted to let you know about something."

"Oh?" I loosen my arms, the way he speaks now seems different.

"I'm not a genius by any means, so please don't think I'm trying to push you around," he nervously shoves his glasses by the corner back up using his palm. "I just want you to know that I read, or I used to read, a lot. I liked learning. Still like it. A lot. I stick to more tangible science now, which I'd like to start doing if you have anything I can work with back home."

"We'll figure something out."

"Right," he shifts on his feet. "I did learn a bit about psychology so I know about people. I'm not very good with people but humans have tendencies right?"

"Brawn," Theri gently catches his attention. "You're rambling."

"I-I'm sorry. I d-d-didn't mean," he stumbles over his words frustratedly.

I guide his hand away from picking at his eyebrow, "It's okay, you have a thought process you're trying to get out. Maybe slow down, it might help."

Laura and Theri smile at me as if I've handed over gold to him. I force my eyebrows not to pull together.

"Try again," I encourage him.

331

He takes a deep breath, then speaks again with a world of confidence, "I watched Konge Elias, he seems good. Very good. You should keep him around. His body language conveys honesty. Dronning Janét is good too. Though, apologies for the assumption but I think she has a particular interest in you."

His cheeks flush red, the couple next to me embolden him to continue.

"But Dronning Addison's body is very hostile. She's defensive about something. She's jealous for some reason."

I tuck that away in my quickly building mental notebook about her.

"I assume you saw the same in the others?" my head tilts to catch his gaze from looking at the wall. He glances at me uncomfortably then looks away.

"Except for Konge Gallyan I believe they just have some type of hostility towards you. It might be the power dynamic between you all. I'm not sure how normal behavior has changed since the world ended."

I consider his words. It's not new information, but it's still interesting to hear someone else witnessing the same body language. I bite the inside of my cheek. He tugs at his eyebrow again. "You don't need to worry Brawn, I not only believe but more than appreciate everything you've given me."

His hand drops from his eyebrow to show the pleased look on his face. I curve the corners of my lips up gently. Without another word he turns and goes back to his room.

"That was…"

"Abrupt?" Laura finishes for me. "He tends to leave all his conversations like that."

"Probably cause there's so much going on inside that big brain of his," Theri jokes.

"How big?"

They both stare at me.

"Seems strange how much he can figure out," the blond one starts.

"He'll know absolutely nothing about a subject. Give him a day to read, explore, whatever, and he'll talk like he's had a lifetime of experience understanding it," the other finishes.

I look back at his now shut door, considering Brawn. The couple leave me alone in the hallway to return to their room. I slowly walk out, wondering exactly how much has changed in the world.

It's here. I can feel it. The original reason I dragged myself across that nauseating ocean is here. Sometime during the small, possibly final, training session I held with Dimitri the last two remaining Konge's arrived. He had to leave quickly, explaining that his job is to set the meeting room up to accommodate everyone and determine a time to congregate.

He sets the bow and arrow down. I wince at the pain in my back and chest from constantly pulling it taught yet never firing it.

"Should I expect someone different in there?" I call after him.

He stops, knotting his hands behind his back while turning to me. Looking thoughtfully at me, he gives a rare smile. A part of me settles in my nerves at that smile. I feel my breath hitch thinking I won't like his answer.

"You can expect us all to be different people. That comes with putting the most powerful people in the world in a room together," he starts to turn but stops himself. "But the trust between you and I, has no reason to be different."

Air jerks free of my lungs. I don't particularly like that I may very well be on my own, however I'm grateful to know for sure that there will be another outsider I trust in that room.

I see shoulder length black hair move in a small notch near the entryway back into the castle. I make direct eye contact with Sayah hoping he understands that I want to speak with him.

I shoulder off the thick coat I'm wearing, needing the cold to freeze my skin so I can't feel the nerves lighting up. Every breath of wind, touch of snow, has my senses rattling. The pressure of completely understanding what is about to transpire sits like hot oil across me. The stone archway reaches me. It feels like a gaping mouth ready to swallow the last bit of me that's left.

Strange shifting noises come from behind me. I whip around to scan the courtyard, only seeing the usual early morning groups preparing to spar. Snow slides off the top of one of the mountain walls that protect the open area. A few people turn to look, immediately discussing between one another. I watch hard chunks of snow crash against rock and shatter into delicate pieces. Seeing nothing out of the norm I turn back to enter the gray castle.

Aiza is at my side instantly, speaking in a hushed voice about the proposed list of topics for today. Territory lines and definition thereof, rules surrounding visitations, even how to deal with crimes committed by a dragon in a foreign Samle. I stay silent, letting the intelligent woman next to me drive the course of discussion into my head.

"There's a lot. We won't get through it today so prepare for this meeting to drag out," she follows me into my room where the twins wait. I quickly disappear behind the cover to switch into the outfit Aiza picked out for me earlier. "Make sure you wear what I selected."

"I know, it makes a first impression," I shed off the warm leathers. "How did you get more clothes here anyway?"

"I might have sweet talked a few ladies into letting me have some fabric."

"In exchange for what?" Sayah's face drops into concern.

"Nothing of consequence."

"Sure," he drags out slowly, teasing her. She throws a pillow, with excellent aim, straight at his face. He catches it with one hand. "I guess that training is really paying off. We'll be able to fight back the clouds in no time."

"I hope you slip and fall on black ice," she retorts. Senka snickers at the bickering, only encouraging more insults being tossed back and forth.

"I'll do it in front of you, so I'll fall on you," he scrunches his nose at her.

"You'll crush me."

"That's the point."

"Good enough?" I step out from behind the panels to let Aiza examine me.

The red shirt is long sleeved with a bottom that stops above my waistline. Both sides of the shirt extend to create two panels that flow down to the floor in a cape-like effect, lengthening the look of my now very muscular legs. My collarbone is exposed to let the sharpness of it add to the look. The skin on my back is a bit cold, since a strap of the cloth extends down my spine. Two horizontal straps keep the front snug against me. Thankfully my upper body doesn't suffer too much because the black leggings are warming. It's a loose, but controlled look.

"One more thing," Aiza goes to a box I didn't notice sitting on the couch. She pulls out a pair of heavy duty black boots with belt buckles strapped all over. "You could use a break from the heels."

"Oh my gods," I sigh, quickly yanking them on over my thick socks. "You're the best advisor ever."

She smiles and flicks a fold of her fabric over her shoulder, "I know."

"Probably the one with the biggest head too," Sayah goes to flick her head but she darts away, reminding him not to touch her. "My bad," he mumbles.

Again, Senka giggles, finding his forgetfulness funny. I give her a pointed look that means absolutely nothing because she smiles wider at me. Her tongue drags over her teeth in a playful threat. I simply point my finger at her in an attempt to be serious.

I take a deep breath in as the twins file out to slip into whatever horrible spots they've found. Comfort at knowing they'll be in the room helps me not feel so weighed down. I mentally reach down to my gut to wrap around the Bond throbbing at my spine. Needing a bit of confidence, I try to convey the feelings that are kicking at my heart. I nearly pull away, thinking it's too weak, but I'm rewarded with a glowing confidence. Not nearly strong enough to push into my own feelings. Just enough to help me walk towards the first step at making my place in this world.

"Sean and Linius are the two that arrived last night, you'll want to greet Linius first. He's much more likely to be an ally since he's practically our neighbor."

"I find it mildly interesting that two Samle's never once explored the possibility of coming to help me. They had to have felt me," I muse, walking with Aiza amid conversation is helping to narrow my focus.

"You may have managed to stay just outside their boundaries. Either way, try to go in with a neutral mind. Coming at them already angry will just make it harder to get through this."

I sigh heavily through my nose, "Alright, I'll do my best. Who do they bring in there?"

"I know for a fact everyone will have either their advisor or general in with them. There may be a few guards but I'm not sure. For the most part, the advisors have mutually agreed to leave the talking to you all."

We reach the hallway that leads to the massive room I was in when Mikhail asked for my help. My mind wanders to the danger of having the open balcony over a cliffside in a room full of dragons. I pull my thoughts back towards the task ahead of me, taking in my surroundings to reacquaint myself. I spot a head of red hair in front of me.

Addison is ahead of us. She hears us walking and stops to turn and look at me. I eye her dress that hugs over the bones protruding from her hips and ribs. Small streams of fabric trail down from her shoulders like a mockery of a cape.

"Kali dear," she purrs. I hide my disgust at the term of endearment. "You look...nice. I'm sure Mikhail will give a pity compliment."

I stop a few feet before her. I stay back far enough I don't give her the satisfaction of tilting my head up to look at her. From the sound of it, nearly everyone is already in the room. Her companion - with her hair still in a tightly wrapped bun - stares between Aiza and I.

"Thank you," I return the deadly grin. I wave out a hand. "Please, you enter first."

She tilts up her nose, choosing to look down it at me. Just as she walks in the door, I give one last compliment loud enough only she can hear.

"I personally prefer to save the best for last anyway."

She doesn't look back at me, though I'm pleased to catch her shoulders stiffen. Gallyan greets her in the same slimy way as he did at dinner. I send a silent prayer out to whoever is listening that he doesn't try to touch me. Aiza walks through the massive metal doors beside me, never faltering in her smooth steps. All eyes stop to look at me. Gallyan is scanning my body with oil in his gaze. I nod at him once his eyes stop lingering on my chest.

I can feel Mikhail staring at me from the edge of the table closest to the balcony. My eyes skip over his face slow enough to make it clear I have no interest in playing games. This is the time for giving my Samle what they need, not giving in to what I want.

Two new faces step forward to greet me. I keep a neutral face, not caring if it looks emotionless. The first to greet me is a lanky man with short black hair. His eyes look tired even as he forces a half smile onto his face.

"We haven't met yet, I'm Sean. Of the Midlans Samle," he merely dips his head. No handshake, which I prefer.

"No, we haven't. Kali," I dip my head in return. That's all he says before returning to his seat.

The other new face stays at the table, simply staring at me. His pale face is drawn into one that conveys nothing. His dark, almond shaped eyes are the opposite. They seem to see everything on me or about me. Those color of his eyes looks even darker with the hair framing his face. It's so dark it almost has bluish hue to it. I feel pressured to stand straighter as he continues to stare. To cover the feeling, I walk to the last chair, placed between Elias and Janét. Each companion stands or sits directly behind each person. Aiza pulls out a notepad and pen from somewhere, enticing all the other advisors or generals to do the same.

I rest my arms on the sides, folding my leg to prop my ankle onto my knee. Sitting next to me, Janét turns her head to smile at my body language. I feel like a student placed in between her friends because Elias does the same.

"Well, good morning everyone," Mikhail begins. Dimitri steps forward to place multiple papers on the table, then returns to the desk still sitting in the corner from last time. "I'm glad you all could make it."

"We're lucky to have such a generous host," Addison has her hands folded into her lap attempting to press her chest up at him. Mikhail gives her a tight smile.

"Yes, I'll have to agree on that one. Though the weather could be better," Gallyan's voice grates on my nerves. Janét's hand clenches in her lap. "Maybe next time we'll have this meeting at the Hellish Samle."

Mikhail clears his throat, bored, and moves on, "First order of business, we get down the boundary lines of each Samle. We'll need to start building a map of the new world if we want any hope of navigating it."

"A suggestion, if I may," Elias tosses up a casual hand. "We each have a person from our own draw out our land, then send it here to help with the full map. Then you can make copies and have it sent back to each of us."

"What, so you can know every detail of our land for when you stick your nose in our business? Not a chance," Sebastian scoffs.

Here we go.

"Believing the intentions are hostile is what makes them hostile," Janét offers in a smooth voice. "Let's try to not start this out at each other's throats."

"Then perhaps start asking for things less suspicious, *Janét*," Addison stares her down, leaning forward in her seat to emphasize her bite.

"Enough," a deep voice, Linius, comes from the other side of Elias. His face, a thin scar across his cheek, silences the argument. For now. He motions for Mikhail to continue.

"Can we at least do the borders and shapes of continents, so we can avoid trespassing?"

Everyone seems to agree on that much thankfully. Around the table we go over and over, trying to decipher each of the continents. We conclude that four land masses now sit in each corner of the world. Moving on to borders is the step that it becomes messy. The Northeast and Southwest continents, despite their hostility, easily agree upon the lines to be drawn.

Once Sebastian claims the entire Southeast continent as his own I feel suspicion poke its head up. Careful not to draw attention I drop my hand to convey to Aiza to make a note of that. Later, I'll ask the twins who they saw move or speak about it both here and in private. Their positions in the room let them see everything they need.

"You have the entire continent? No contenders?" Mikhail questions the Metael Konge.

"Save for a few pesky rogues and humans, I do. Do you have a problem with that?"

"I never said I did."

We move to my continent last. Addison stands up, using the long skinny rod to point out her boundaries. I watch carefully to see where she draws it. Her pointer slides past her own line towards the Dead Forest.

"Don't get greedy, Addison," I stay seated, keeping my posture relaxed.

"What do you mean?" She plays innocent. Gallyan's beady eyes hungrily look between us.

"That forest is mine, as is a bit of the land before it," I rise up, keeping my movements calculated. I lean over the table to slide the map towards me slightly. "This," I draw the line around where my boundaries lay. From the halfway point of the northern coast, down to curve around all of the Dead Forest with some of the mountain pass in it. The line dips down to include a small section of the southern coast. "Is mine."

Dimitri looks to her with his eyebrows raised in question. Addison considers me, opening her mouth to argue. I cut her off before she begins.

"If that was your territory, you would have felt me moving through it, would you not?"

Silence is louder than the banquet hall.

"Because I was being chased down by a large pack of rabid humans, so if that's yours, you openly admit you left another Dronning you didn't even know to danger? How careless, Addison."

Her jaw locks, nostrils flare out. Another beat of silence before she continues.

"My hand must have slipped, my lines are here," she drags a line again. Dimitri looks to me for confirmation of my boundary lines.

"Then we have unclaimed land," that deep voice that sounds a millennia old comes across the table again. "My boundaries are here."

Dimitri finishes out the lines for the Whispers Samle. He pulls the huge map to look at it and remarks, "There are two sections of land remaining unclaimed."

"I'll take the southwestern section," Addison points over like she's choosing the next toy.

"No one will take anything; we wait and see what's there. Each of you can send people to look together. That way, there's no shot of dishonesty," Mikhail expertly navigates through the tense waters that ripple between the three of us. I glance at Linius, trying to depict what his angle is. Still nothing.

The conversation moves along the topics Aiza mentioned earlier. Once the sun has risen enough to bring a sad amount of warmth to the room, food is brought in by two women. They generously dish out lunch to everyone, leaving immediately after. Clanging sounds out over conversations as the doors lock shut again. Janét and Elias converse across me, leaving me alone after I don't answer them the first two times. I watch the others closely. Linius eats his food in silence, only nodding or shaking his head every now and then in response to the whispers in his ear. His eyes catch me staring, I don't drop my gaze.

Linius finally tilts his glass of water at me. Though possibly the smallest motion in history, it's still progress in my book. I do the same, immediately sweeping my stare across the table to see if someone noticed. Mikhail catches my eye.

His legs are spread out, body slouched in the chair. I can tell that playing referee is taking its toll on him. He stares me down with a bit of an edge in his eyes. My core wants me to smirk at him. To play the game Suitor attraction is so angry at me for not playing. That same thing also dares me to sink one of my boots into his chest to break a rib. Or two. Or three. Flicking my eyes down his body clad in a fitted suit, I feign distaste. The clenching of his jaw sends a thrill down my neck.

Chapter 33

Lunch dishes get left on the table to be carried out later on. More discussions about dealing with criminals. Each territory can carry out their own justice system with the rule that if at least six other Samle's deem it to be corrupt it must be taken down. The location of the crime or infraction is dealt with in that territory. Neutral land places the handling of a broken law in their home Samle. Personalities peek through in arguments revealing who has their ethics twisted and who doesn't. With little to no sway on any of us controlling another, the majority rule is used for much of the new decisions.

Ties aren't a concern. Then they are.

"I'd like to discuss outlawing slavery," Janét speaks up, staring blatantly at Gallyan.

Gallyan quirks a brow, giving her a sick smirk. His perfect teeth flash.

"Sure," he says. "We leave it up to the leader. That's not an international concern."

"I beg to differ," Elias stares him down.

Sebastian turns his head to him, "Stop turning your nose up. We need the workforce for keeping our people alive."

"Then pay them and treat them for the work they do," Janét says with deadly calm. "What makes them deserve being enslaved compared to the rest of your people?"

"They are lesser," Gallyan explains calmly, his grin still plastered to his face. "Those with smaller dragon forms, weaker human forms, no connections to a Samle? All weak. All of them can water down our race."

"They can add diversity," Elias. "Or are you afraid of people who might be different?"

Sebastian scoffs. Dominé rolls his eyes.

"Fine," Gallyan stands, putting his fingertips on the surface to hold his weight. "We put it to a vote."

I look around the table, seeing Mikhail looking down at the table. There's a murmur of discussion that I ignore. I feel eyes on me, and I flick my gaze to Janét. Her eyes are filled with worry, and she turns to stare at Mikhail as well.

I return to staring at him until he finally picks his head up. He makes eye contact but immediately pulls away to watch the others. I clench my jaw, unsure of what direction he'll go. People are speaking to Gallyan, who's watching me now. I ignore him, not needing his overly confident gaze.

"You can't be serious," Elias leans over from my right. "Would Mikhail really do that?"

"You saw that too?" I turn my head slowly to lean towards him.

Elias nods, "I did. And I honestly can't tell which way he'll go. He could try to please his continent neighbors, or stand on his own two feet."

The murmuring calms, and Elias and I lean away from one another.

Gallyan straightens, looking around as he begins the vote. "On the topic of forced servitude. All against?"

Janét, Elias, Linius, and I immediately raise our hands. Everyone watches Mikhail. His jaw works as he turns his face to me. I keep my expression guarded. We watch one another for a few more beats, something warring inside of him.

Gallyan makes a sound as he begins to move forward, but stops as Mikhail raises a hand while looking at the standing Konge. I let my eyes soften in silent appreciation before he's fully turned away.

"All for?" Gallyan stares down the Shadow Samle Konge furiously. Those of us with our hands raised drop them. Addison, Sebastian, Hendrix, Sean, Dominé, and Gallyan all raise their hands.

"Bastards," Janét hisses.

"Then it's decided. It's legal, and up to the individual Samle's to decide," Gallyan's grin widens as he sits again. I take in every hand that falls from their vote supporting the enslavement of people.

The rest of us simmer, unsure of how to handle this new decision.

"Anyone who voted for this is no longer welcome within my territory. Step foot inside my home, and you threaten war on your people."

"Same for me and my people-" Elias starts angrily.

"Enough," Linius stops the conversation at the first sound from Sebastian's mouth. "We will get nowhere except the beginning of a war. Clearly those who voted for do not agree nor like those who voted against. Leave it at that for now, we have other laws that need placement."

There's a pregnant pause, and then Mikhail continues the meeting.

Discussing the overarching laws is a large obstacle, taking up more hours than any of us anticipated. Fortunately, it's the last topic. Unfortunately, people's nerves are beginning to wear.

"I don't agree with the others, but as long as it's humane, trying to dictate minute laws is overreaching," I offer. A few looks from the opposite side of the table narrow on me.

"And who's to determine if it's humane?" Janét turns her head to me with a bit of sass.

"If the question of that is brought up, we use the majority vote to determine it," I reply.

"Then we use that," Mikhail sighs. Gallyan tips his head back, using his feet to tip the chair back. We all snap our heads to him as his chair legs slam down into the stone.

"Is the noise really necessary?" Elias rolls his eyes so hard I'm surprised they don't fall out of his head.

Gallyan leans forward to rest his forearms on the table. Staring directly at me, he clasps his hands together. I match his stare with an irritation that's had all day to build up.

"I didn't realize you decided to bring the Devil and Lilith incarnate," his face looks unsteady, wild.

"Excuse me?" I raise a single brow at him. I know exactly what he's referring to.

"You brought a psychopath into this meeting," he hisses.

"I brought my guards, just as you all brought yours," I gesture to the handful of guards standing behind a few of the leaders.

"Sayah and Senka are not guards," his voice raises a bit as he stands up, hands pressed against the table.

I sit down, annoyed with the conversation. My boots swing up onto the table where I cross my ankles.

"That's not yours to decide, is it?" I fold my hands behind my head.

"I've seen those fucking demon children, they're evil."

I nearly laugh at the irony in his statement.

"They're trained, not evil," I reply monotone.

"Trained enough to kill you the second you turn your back."

No one dares to say a word between Gallyan and I.

"They wouldn't harm a hair on my head," I flip my hand around in front of me to stare at my nails. I contemplate how fast I can shove out my talons should he continue to speak poorly about them.

"Just you wait until they kill you and take your Samle down with them," he spits as he speaks.

"The day they kill me is the day I've done something horrid enough to deserve being killed. I care for them just as I care for the rest of my Samle."

"Oh? If they care so much for you, where exactly are they?" he sneers.

I know he wants me to call them both out, so he can pin them down. He must have seen one in the rafters of the room, which is why he started this fight.

"Well, one is in the rafters," everyone looks up. I shove out my talons while they're distracted. At least, everyone but Mikhail who's watching me. Sayah is crouching above me. I look up in time to see him smirk and disappear into the shadows. "The other is somewhere, she'll be found when she wants to be."

A dainty laugh echoes from all corners of the room, the acoustics of it making it difficult for even me to pinpoint exactly where she is. I let a cat-like grin smear across my face, knowing she's watching me.

Such an amazing piece of art, I proudly think. Once everyone is looking back at me, Mikhail's face becomes dismissive. I shiver at the silence, knowing both of them have found another hiding spot. The knowledge that they could kill everyone, even me, is like ice water on an already freezing day. It brings a sense of delight, making me consider for a second that letting them loose would be a sufficient reward.

I reel back the thoughts into their tucked away place.

"Find something else to be bitter about, Gallyan," Elias backs me up. His comment inflicts multiple glares in my direction. I ignore every single one.

Later, I'll get the information from the twins about what all people said about Elias standing up for me. For now, I watch Addison lean over to whisper something in Gallyan's ear. Whatever it is, has him leering at me. I keep my boots on the table, enjoying the comfort of stretching out my legs. Janét leans back, crossing her legs towards me. We make eye contact, but it's not pleasant. I hope that it's not, though I can't ignore the small hint of fear in her eyes. Not wanting to deal with her being upset at me I swing my feet down.

"I believe that's enough for today," Mikhail announces. "We've accomplished much, but there is still two-thirds of this list to get through."

"Let's hope we can finish soon, then," Addison steps back making her way towards him. Her hips swing in an unnatural rotation, a poor attempt at seduction.

"Wait until they're all gone," Aiza whispers into my ear. I watch Addison's Sekund stare at us, then look between the two on either side of me. Her eyes look strange, glazed over. My gaze doesn't leave her until she catches me staring her down. Her head jerks a bit, surprised at my intense look, though she finally looks away.

I glance up into the rafters, barely catching a shadow. Sayah knows I want his attention. Placing a hand on the table casually, I lift my index finger towards her while turning to look elsewhere. When I look back up, I don't see anything.

Addison drags a hand down her prey's chest, making him step to the side surreptitiously to avoid contact. Her turned face shows a pout pulling at her thin lips.

"We can have a private dinner," she offers. "We haven't had alone time since-"

"I'm fully aware of how long it's been," Mikhail's voice drops, he leans towards her. He must be completely unaware that the three of us still remain. "A thousand years couldn't be enough time away from you."

Her frail hand flies up to slap him. It never makes contact. His large hand wraps around her wrist tightly, causing her to drop that side of her body in pain.

"Mikhail, you're hurting me," she whines. It grates on my nerves. The sick part of me wants to see her suffer. I retract my talons in, hoping for some pain. I'm so used to it, it doesn't even register. He drops her hand, looking sorry.

"I don't mean to hurt you," he sighs. She rubs her wrist, smiling with sickening sweetness at him. "You should go."

"Darling-"

"Don't," his teeth clench. "You had your shot. This," he motions between them. "Is done. I've had my fill of you, let Gallyan have his."

Her little gasp has me smiling. I begin to tell myself that smiling is cruel. Then I remember how fond she is of befriending someone that forces his own people into slavery. My smile turns venomous.

Addison spins away from him, staring at her Sekund, "Let's go, Alastira."

Washed out brown eyes meet mine. I keep the smile on my face. She immediately stops rubbing her thin wrist, attempting to look more put together.

"Your devil children should be careful," she croons. "Or they might end up as one of Gallyan's playthings."

Regretfully I drop my smile. I'm too angered by her statement to feign a smile or throw back a nasty threat of my own. Both of them walk out with their heads held high.

Elias comes to stand next to me, "Will you be joining us for dinner?"

"If 'us' means just you and Janét, then of course."

"Excellent, I'll have Sai escort you from your room when you're ready."

I nod, standing to leave.

"Kali."

My body tenses. The ugly part of my attraction to him rises, wanting nothing but to break the jaw of the man who let another woman touch him. I start to walk away but stop when he calls my name much more firmly. I motion Aiza to go, commenting loud enough for the siblings that one of them will walk with her.

"I'm not one of your dragons to order around."

"No, but you are a valuable person in my life."

I turn back around to walk slowly out onto the balcony. Blistering wind tugs at my braided hair pulling a small strand free. Mikhail smartly keeps his distance. My body aches to be closer, to let him lean me against the rail as he presses into me. I stomp the urge to go to him down.

"You did well today," he starts.

"I listened and spoke when necessary. That's not some magical feat."

"You should speak more."

"I will, and I have an advisor to tell me these things."

"I just want to help."

I consider a certain Dronning with flaming hair, the way she clings to him every moment she gets.

"Then stop letting Addison touch you. She's allies with Gallyan, the same man that hurt my Nightmares, the same man with a taste for human slavery, the same man that I have a feeling isn't content with what he has."

"Kali, I'm hosting a meeting of some of the most powerful people in the world. I'm just trying to keep things from blowing up."

"Right, because upsetting the woman who almost had your child would be disastrous."

He freezes from playing with something in his pocket. I turn to him, wanting to see what emotion his body betrays him to. Snow melts on the tips of my ears.

"Who told you?"

"What you should be more concerned with is why they told me."

"And why is that?" His grin is dripping cruel sarcasm, waiting for me to throw another dagger at his ego.

"They assumed I knew, so correct me if I'm wrong but I think everyone knew but me," I lean on an elbow against the stone railing. "Which means you made a point not to inform me even after Addison arrived. In my opinion, you still have an emotional attachment to her."

"I have no attachment to her, so your opinion is incorrect," he takes a further step towards me.

"Fine," I flick a hand towards him. His lips tighten at my dismissal. "It's your choice to tell me whatever you want about your past and the other Konge's."

"Glad you see that," he continues to close the distance between us. There's a heat in those hazel eyes that swirls with both lust and hatred. My body reacts by taking a step closer to him.

"However, it's my choice to choose whether or not I can trust you because of that."

Within an arm's reach, he stops. I consider asking why he didn't tell me. Perhaps not telling me was his way of easing me into the world of these people. It can be as easy as that. It can be as easy as trying to keep me in the dark to satisfy that craving we both have. His face looks how I feel trying to determine what to say next.

"I knew you'd ask more. More you might or might not have understood. I was worried you'd put a wall between us because she's a Dronning."

"That's a powerful tie to someone. A child between the two of you could have tied together your Samle's."

"I know," his eyes are frantic.

"How did you find out she wasn't pregnant?"

A low feeling pulls at my gut.

"She was pregnant. I had Nina put together some tea that aborted the fetus."

I straighten as I step back from him from the shock. So many new bits of information unfold in my head. He didn't want the tie, knew that the child would have had to be with only, or both. It might have been the responsibility he was afraid of, or even how it might limit his people. I realize that the reasons are all selfish, none of them being for the child's sake. If he was blind enough to sleep with someone so mentally skewed he most likely still can't even recognize it. I reel back at how self-centered he is – then it hits me.

"She has no idea it was you," my mouth remains open after the last word.

Mikhail tugs at his beard, then turns away to explain, "I couldn't risk the attachment. I knew exactly what she would demand. Kali I couldn't risk that when everything is still so new."

"You made the choice to stick your dick in her without thinking about the consequences. And then made the choice about losing the baby *for her*," I shake my head, turning to leave. "Protecting your Samle is one thing, making decisions about another woman's body is another."

"You've felt the pull of a Suitor attraction, Kali. You know what it's like trying to resist it."

Fair.

"Fine, you both couldn't help fucking. That doesn't make your other actions excusable."

His chuckle has the hairs on my neck rising.

"You wouldn't understand, you've barely been at this for what, a few months?"

"Yes because a few months is so different from two years."

"It is when it comes to this," he yells at me past the large doors I walk through. I give him no answer. Tucking my hands into my pockets I walk down the snug hallway. Senka pops up next to me, looping an arm around mine. I bask in the comfort of being near one of my own.

"I can hurt him for you," she says gently. I look at her without turning my head.

"No, little Nightmare," I blow out a heavy breath. "He might still be a solid piece to have on my side of the board."

She stays at my side, now unconcerned with hiding since all of the ten leaders know about the presence. We pass Dominé in one of the larger hallways, who's busy toying with some female's hair. His head pulls up to stare at us.

"Done fucking your master?" he sneers.

Senka moves to slide her arm out from mine to retaliate but I stop her.

"Done fucking yours?" I throw back. We don't stop to give him the courtesy of conversation.

"He belongs to Addison," he continues. "Just like you'll belong to Gallyan."

I let Senka slip her arm out this time. She doesn't move from my side. I realize she's waiting for me to give a command.

"And what makes you think that Dominé?"

He drops the piece of hair of the woman, pushing from the wall to face me. I catch her relieved face as she scurries away.

"He's got the biggest Samle, biggest form I've seen, he's got Konge's like me," he points to himself, sure of his worth. "He was the first one to wake up, send out kallet. He's always gotten what he wants."

"If he has everything, why would he want me?" I test the waters, seeing how much information this gossiping chess piece will give me.

"He collects useful things, Kali."

"I'm honored to be considered useful," I roll my eyes.

"Not taking a knee to him is only going to make it difficult. Don't make it so hard on yourself."

"You act like me bending the knee will happen no matter what."

"It will, I've seen his abilities. He's practically a god."

Dominé shrugs as if referring to someone as a god doesn't make him sound clinically insane. Without another word, I continue my walk with Senka back to the room. She turns and sticks her tongue out at him.

"Fighting it makes it hurt more, you know."

"Good thing I'm a sucker for pain," I practically sing the words at him. Senka beams at me excitedly.

We walk further, finally reaching our rooms. I don't change since the outfit is so comfortable.

"Where's Sayah?" I look at Senka. She points over my shoulder just as a male voice comes from behind me.

"Right here," Sayah takes a step closer. I jump a bit, caught off guard by him suddenly appearing behind me.

"Jerk," I mumble. His lips pull into a mischievous smile.

Once Aiza joins us, I relay an undetailed explanation of what Mikhail and I talked about. Mostly to Sayah and Aiza, since Senka clearly had lurked nearby to watch me. Aiza starts writing down more notes, then begins to pace as she thinks. Sayah places his own pieces on the table about what the others talked about.

"I can't move as freely, since they know we're here. But Sebastian did speak about something strange with Gallyan after the meeting. Something about using their pets in the right phase? No idea what that means, but they seemed extremely secretive."

"The right phase?" I knit my brows together, trying to figure out what they could have meant. Any possible meaning is completely lost on me.

"That sounds...ominous," Aiza comments. I nod, agreeing with her. Nothing about such a little statement like that sits well with any of us.

"Keep an eye on them, the others as well, but mostly them."

We all sit in silence as daylight fades out. I sit down on one of the chairs facing the dimly lit fire. The fireplace keeps a warm glow to the room casting shadows along the walls. Those shadows make me feel like I'm being watched as thoughts of today's meeting pass through me. I catch pieces of Senka explaining to the others what happened in the hallway with Dominé. Tilting my head back I rest my head on the back of the seat cushion. My eyelids close. Not in exhaustion, but in deep thought.

Gallyan and Addison have both been making clear efforts to establish some kind of position of power. They already have it with the way the others follow so closely behind. Nothing has conveyed how much either of the two holds. Addison wants power, easily expected of a person like her. Logical parts of my brain tell me there must be a reason. The Dronning in me knows that no matter the reason, she's not one to play friendly if I have something she wants. I settle my worry at the consideration that if she wanted something specifically from me, she would have given hint to it.

Gallyan, on the other hand, is a mystery that is quickly proving to be dangerous. He plays nicely, only letting the mask he wears slip every now and then. Talking out of turn, in his opinion, seems to be a weak spot. As is being so brash. He felt power in the meeting, when he found one of my cards peeking its head out. Instead of attempting to rip down my own standing, he instead argued about the danger of having my Nightmares so close. He wants nothing but for me to cast them out, punish them. Simply because they have a tendency towards violence.

"Sayah," I tilt my head up. They cease the discussion, looking to me. "Why did you let Gallyan see you? Was it an accident?"

His cheeks tinge with red slightly, "No. I'm sorry, I wanted him to see me over him. Wanted him to know that we hadn't died when we escaped."

I blink rapidly at the word, "Escaped?"

The twins look at one another.

"He had us chained up for a long time. Liked to hit us when we made him angry. Always kept one of us locked up so the other would behave when they went out."

"Went out for what?" I look between them. Anger starts to build in my chest.

Sayah tugs on the roots of his hair, Senka rubs at her collarbone.

"When people…upset him…he sent us out to kill them. Liked to give us directions on how to leave them," her hand rubs slower on her collarbone. "We hate killing like that."

Aiza is staring at the floor. Out of the corner of my eye I watch her head drop into her hands.

Red hot anger blooms in my chest. I dig to find any semblance of emotion from them. When I start to look I find that I can feel their pain at the memories surfacing under those dark eyes. I curl my hands into the cushion to alleviate the tension in my next words.

"I'm sorry."

"It wasn't your fault. None of that was so don't apologize for it."

"It never would have happened if I had woken up sooner," I flew out my hands only to dig them in again. Fighting the talons threatening to come out is difficult, but I don't want them to see how upset I am.

"There's nothing we can do to change that, so get over it," Sayah assures me. His own talons are out. I delve into their pain, letting it lick at my emotions like a dog seeing love for the first time.

"How about," I cross one leg over the other slowly. I know I'll regret finishing this statement, but I let my anger control me anyway. "You go play."

Senka's face pauses, then skitters into a grin. Her pearly white teeth flash at me. Sayah looks hopeful. Neither move yet. They're waiting for confirmation.

"Kali," Aiza starts. I raise a lazy hand draped over the back of the couch to cut her off.

"Toe the line, but do not cross it. I still have another meeting tomorrow."

In a flash, they disappear out of the room. Guilt starts to flood my thoughts. I shove it back down aggressively.

"This could end badly. Being the bigger person is the best way to keep us out of trouble," she folds her arms across her stomach.

"You know what's done is done. They won't do anything rash. Both of them deserve to get a little bit of vengeance."

"I hope for your sake, it's worth it."

"Honestly? I don't really care right now if it is or isn't."

I stand up from the couch, leaving a distressed Aiza to go over her notes. A dinner with Elias and Janét is much more preferable to enduring my poor decisions.

"What did you and the sex depraved man talk about?" Elias plucks up a piece of strong cheese from the food he had brought up. The entire top of the coffee table in his room is covered with various salted or dried meats, cheeses, fruit and vegetables.

Janét is plopping grapes into her mouth, mildly trying to throw seductive glances my way each time. I throw amused looks back at her, enjoying watching her be playful. The change in emotion from her fear in the meeting is a relief.

"He just complained about me avoiding him," I let the lie roll off my tongue too easily. "Expected from him."

"Have you fucked him yet?" he asks.

"Elias!" I throw a strawberry at him. He catches it and plops it into his mouth.

"She certainly didn't the other night, she was too busy with me," Janét sucks another grape into her mouth. I give her a warm look.

"Yes, yes, I know you two went at it. I want to know if you've given in to the Suitor attraction yet."

Janét's hand stops before dropping another piece into her mouth.

"You know," she looks up at the ceiling. "I definitely should have pieced that together."

I glare at Elias for revealing it, he shrugs completely unbothered.

"No, we haven't," I smear goat cheese onto a thin slice of dried beef.

"Why not? He might be a little overly-masculine but at least he's hot." Elias tries to swipe my food, but I plop it into my mouth too quickly.

"We've been busy. Why are you so concerned about my sex life?"

"Come on Kali, I'm sure you've noticed that dragons are a little more inclined to jump into bed."

"I hadn't really. Now that you mention it, it makes sense, but I haven't exactly been around enough of our kind yet to tell."

"You could go right now, I'm sure he wouldn't mind a little drop in visit from his favorite Suitor," Janét gives me a considering look.

I don't look at them. My mind goes through my previous conversation with him. The positives and negatives of sleeping with him tick off in a list.

"What's there to lose?" Elias asks. "Wait, are you a virgin?"

"No," I groan. "I lost that one a while ago."

"Holding out on yourself like that has to be stressing you out," those tanned fingers covered in rings reach for blackberries. "Do it for you. There doesn't have to be any emotion if you don't want there to be."

"I've been a little too preoccupied to feel sexually frustrated."

Darker fingers rest against mine lightly, Elias seems to stare straight into my soul as he speaks, "You're a Queen, if it doesn't harm your people why not be a little selfish?"

I maintain a steady conversation with the Konge and Dronning for the rest of our dinner, despite going over that question over and over internally. Why should I hold out on doing something for fun?

Because it might not be for fun, you moron.

I bite my cheek hard enough I nearly draw blood. Even with such a primal attraction to him, I know that wanting to give in to my hormones is more than that. It's an attraction from being in such proximity with someone in the same position. That battle continues, at least retreating to the back of my mind while I walk down to spend breakfast with the group of rogues. Some of Mikhail's people give me warm smiles with a pleasant greeting as I pass. I return them honestly, glad that his people show a welcoming attitude. Especially with so much tension in the air.

"Dronning Kali!" a voice booms down the hallway. I stop mid-step to find Gallyan storming towards me. His face is covered in thick blood that looks like it's been poured from over his head. I bite my lip, doing very little to fight off the laugh bubbling up out of me.

"Konge Gallyan, you seem to be covered in blood."

Chapter 34

"Your little twisted devil children did this."

"Did they?."

"I want them whipped," Gallyan's talons are out, silvery in the morning light.

"What's it like to want?" I go to leave yet stop when I hear a screech coming at us. I lean to one side around the older man to see Dominé speed walking at me. He's also covered in blood; it steams off of his head into the cool air.

"If you cannot teach those worthless pieces of trash self-control then I will!" he screams. He reaches me, not stopping soon enough. I thrash out my talons and put all four into his chest. Gallyan stares at mine, clearly a bit longer than his.

"I will speak to them myself. If you touch a single hair on their head, I'll rip out your spine and use it as a necklace."

"You couldn't if you tried," Dominé grits through his teeth.

I stare at him unblinking, "Hm, yes it may not make much of a necklace anyway."

He steps towards me, forgetting I have my talons poised to dig into his pectoral. I push them in a bit, pulling a hiss from his mouth.

"Dominé, enough. We don't need to worry," Gallyan settles a hand on his shoulder. "I forgot that we've established rules for this just yesterday. Konge Mikhail will handle this appropriately."

I drop my hand as the childish man steps back.

"Awfully embarrassing for you to come out of your room looking like that. And then only to forget laws that were established less than twenty-four hours ago," I fling my talons, spraying blood onto the stone. They both look back at me with so much venom, only for me to return it with a smile.

I turn away from the conversation, bored of it. I find Brawn standing at the entrance of the hallway that leads to the rogue's rooms, clearly having watched the interaction. His eyes jump back and forth between me and behind.

"A-are you o-okay?"

"I'm fine Brawn, don't worry about it," I guide him to walk with me down the hallway. "I was hoping I could spend this morning having breakfast with you all."

He shoves his glasses up his nose with the palm of his flat hand, "Oh we'd like if you aren't too busy. Everyone really liked getting to see you the other night."

"I'm glad, though I apologize for being so busy. The meeting went all day."

"I heard," he turns into a room with a few tables. Most of them are sitting down already eating a spread of breakfast foods. "We were wondering if something was wrong when they didn't open the doors until late afternoon."

"It's going to be like that until it's completely done. Hopefully we can leave within the next week," a few whoops are let out at my words. "You can all eat in the dining hall if you want."

"We're good," Nelly joins the conversation as I sit down on a bench opposite him. "We're not big fans of the red boy's Samle."

I chuckle, "Fair enough."

I'm served a heaping plate of food, told by Laura that I don't have enough meat on my bones. I look down at the muscular thighs and more naturally full stomach I had accumulated recently. Her response is to smack me on the shoulder with a wooden spoon and plop grits onto my plate. I mutter a thank you as the others laugh at her behavior. I can't help but join in since they make me feel so comfortable.

More chatter with those sharing a table with us has my time ending sooner than I would have liked. The three children brought in the group rush the door to a pleasantly dressed figure. I spot Aiza standing there, waiting for me.

"That's my queue," I sigh. I shovel the last bite of egg into my mouth before standing up to go. I shoo off the children from asking Aiza a million questions. She looks at me gratefully before leading me through the castle to the same room as yesterday.

"Addison was practically screeching about you at breakfast. You have her and Gallyan with their little posse all riled up."

"I bet I do. Gallyan wants the twins whipped."

She flinches.

"That's his go to, I'm afraid. I've heard confirmed reports of him whipping a slave so hard he severed the man's spine."

I swallow hard to remove the lump from my throat.

"What are you going to do?"

"Whatever I need to do to keep you all safe," is all I answer before we step into the room. Commotion makes it impossible to hear my own thoughts. Linius steps in behind me. He looks down at me with what faintly looks like a smile.

"I heard about what you did," he says, his deep voice coming through the noise.

"What was done? I didn't do anything," I give a little white lie.

"Ah, right. Well, whoever did it has my utmost respect. It's dirty," he steps forward. "Harmed egos, instead of people."

He breathes in deeply, then commands the room to silence. My eyes widen at how loud his voice is. Mikhail takes the chance to gain control.

"The laws created yesterday state that crimes committed against a Samle in their own territory are punishable by that Samle's Konge or Dronning. This is no matter the victim, perpetrator, or visiting guests."

"Correct, so you'll punish the twins accordingly."

"I propose an addendum to that law, actually two," I walk to my seat at the table.

"Oh please Dronning Kali, do tell us your wonderful idea," Addison places her bony hands on the table. Her lips curl up in overconfidence.

"Should they choose, their respectful leader may take their place in the punishment," I state. Aiza chokes behind me.

"Done."

Addison, Gallyan, and Sebastian all speak the word at the same time. Dominé and Hendrix follow strongly. The last to speak is Sean, who says his weakly. I look behind him at the woman with shoulder length brunette hair. Janét bites her lip as she looks down at the seated Konge with a weight on his chest.

"All in favor?" Mikhail stares me down. His anger curves its claws against my skin, raging with a fury that just might be more intense than the punishment.

"One more thing," I say.

"Good gods you're capable of more than one thought?" Addison taunts. The Konge's around her titter.

I ignore her comment to continue, "If requested, the perpetrator may choose to fight for themselves. In dragon form."

"An old way for such a young Dronning," Gallyan's voice in full of bloodlust. "I agree, let the little hatchling fight."

I bristle at his words. Deep breaths pull my emotions back in on a tight leash.

Mikhail still hasn't broken eye contact with me.

"All in favor," he says. "Say aye."

All but Janét and Elias agree. The former is staring at me, trying to get my attention. Aiza tugs on my wrist.

"Kali, what are you doing," she whispers. I move so no one can see her tug at me.

"All against," Mikhail repeats. "Say no."

Janét and Elias object to the law.

"So, what will it be, Dronning Kali," Mikhail asks me. My title is dredged up in his words like a weapon.

"I will take the place of the Nightmare's. And I choose to fight."

"Then we'll fight."

"This is going to be *so* exciting," Addison squeals.

"It'll be interesting to watch you lose," Gallyan reminds me of a snake. I roll my eyes.

"I agree," Sebastian says. I eye the Metael Konge heavily trying to determine his angle. "I'd like to see her lose an eye, or a wing. Learn her place."

I stare him down, still allowing anger to show on my face.

When I turn back to Mikhail, understanding passes between us. He knows my size alone can bring him within an inch of his life. Nothing comes out of his mouth about it.

"Animals, all of you," Janét shakes her head.

"After we finish our business at hand, we will finish the rest," Mikhail establishes a time for it. Not a single mouth opens to object.

The day's meeting finally begins. Back and forth we talk. Establishing laws from as menial as leaders being forbidden from unjustly killing another ruler, to as complicated as how to limit global power. Food is brought in, causing us to pause until the doors have been sealed and locked. Oftentimes at least one person is getting a breath of fresh air on the balcony while another paces the room. I feel time slip from me as we jump from topic to topic. Finally, it ends.

We repeat the meetings just as I repeat my routine. Wake up, breakfast, meeting, breaks, dinner, socializing, training, sleep. It's thankfully too busy to be monotonous. I switch between having breakfast and dinner with the new members, or Elias and Janét. Linius ends up joining our little group as well.

"I'm tired of the drama during mealtime. I wish to eat in peace," he tells us.

The days allow us to become comfortable around him, and he with us. He occasionally complains about the others until Elias comes out with the honest question.

"Have you allied with them?"

We fall silent.

"No. I thought my decision to select you lot as allies was clear when I separated myself from them."

With that, we return to eating and casual conversation. Linius stays quiet most of the time, only speaking every now and then.

Finally, after six total days of meeting together, everything is done. So much about the future of this world, packed into six days of speaking.

I'm standing in my guest room, preparing to go downstairs for the trial. The twins are waiting idly. Aiza is on my bed, lost in thought. My thoughts turn to the fight, the volatile position I've put myself and Mikhail in. I cringe inwardly at the awful setting I've created. I'd carelessly put an already unpredictable relationship in an even more unpredictable situation.

Everything about this fight will determine how generations of people will behave. We may not have electricity anymore and may never have it again if people don't try to bring it back. We might never have completely just laws. At least, with these rules in place, people can have a chance.

My clothes come off, to be replaced by the tying slip. I breathe in deeply just as a knock at my door sounds. Before I answer I whisper to Sayah to deliver a message to the rebels that they can join if they wish. He nods, then leaves. Three figures step into the room.

Linius stands in a position that would be awkward for anyone else, commanding the attention of the room. Janét plants a kiss on my cheek, then a light kiss on my lips. I tilt my forehead against hers, reveling in the closeness of a fast friendship.

"You know, no one ever clarified the end," Elias says, pouring himself a glass of vodka from the cabinets. I pull away from the Dronning, watching him pour with finesse. He offers me a finger of it.

"I did," I take the offered glass from him. "I said until one person couldn't get up."

I swig back the burning liquid, wincing a bit at the burn. I extend it out, and Elias gives me another pour, but heavier.

"That means many things, Kali," Linius speaks up. I meet his eyes. His narrow face and high cut cheekbones make him look even more serious than he already does. "You never clarified if it means the person is unconscious, exhausted, injured, or dead. Which tells me that you are, in fact, trying to find a way to seriously maim or kill Konge Mikhail."

I nearly drop my glass to the floor. Before setting it down I swallow the entire heavy-handed pour. A burn rolls through my chest.

"I told Linius about the predicament between you and Mikhail," Janét says. Her voice is soft, tender.

I look to Linius as he speaks again, "That problem will either save you, or kill you. Depending on how you use it."

I thank him for the insight. The need to slit his throat will only appear when I'm near Mikhail, so I wait to start letting that part fester. I say nothing as one more knock comes to the door.

"Kali," Dimitri's careful tone comes through the door. I ignore the adorned hand that comes from Janét to brush against my lower back. "It's time to go."

The others all leave first, heading down to the courtyard. I exit the room last, walking next to Dimitri.

I reach for the Bond, so carefully buried deep within me to avoid a lash of pain. Red anger flashes at me from it at being ignored for so long. It's not Jakir's anger though, just a rush of agony from the Bond itself as if it has its own life. I push a warning, a deeply connected feeling of love to Jakir. Knowing too much will raise a panic for everyone back home, so I bury the Bond again as I walk to the courtyard.

Elias touches my shoulder as the three of them walk ahead to join the others. Chairs have been placed towards the entrance of the expansive area. Addison speaks, looking clearly bored and Dominè and Hendrix talk to her. On her other side, Gallyan already sits with a snake-like grin as he speaks to Sebastian. He hasn't seen me yet.

Janèt, Elias, Linius, the twins, and Aiza take seats far away from the others. I notice the newer members of my Samle streaming out into a standing area. Mikhail's people are also here to watch.

And their Konge is standing nearby in the open space. His hands clasped behind his back. I stare at him, finally fully taking in that I'm about to fight him for the safety of my Nightmares.

"After this," Mikhail walks up to me. "Once you're healed, we're not waiting anymore."

An absolute betrayal to the violence rising up in me at his voice, my core tightens at his promise.

"If you live," I feel the darkness sweep over my mind. It's just a thin layer, testing the waters. I control how heavily it takes over, not wanting to completely forgo my control. Winning this will take tact.

"There's no need to kill," he slips off his loose pants. Now completely naked he edges up to the area visible by the crowd. I spot the group of new additions to my Samle, hoping they have the decency to leave.

"We never specified what being 'unable to get up' meant, Mikhail."

Dimitri snaps his face towards me. That head of orange hair sweeps to cover his upper back as Mikhail walks away. I fight the urge to follow so I can sink my claws into his neck.

"Kali, you can't," Dimitri begs. I clamp down my jaw, irritated by his begging.

"I can, and will, do what I need to."

"You don't *need* to do this."

"Need, feel, want. Who keeps track these days?"

Horror pulls at the features on his face. He looks away so he can cover the emotion. I follow him as he walks further out onto the silent courtyard. We pass Mikhail standing with his back to the castle. Dimitri simply points to the other end. I reach a far enough point so I can shift. Despite my want to train the pain of shifting out of myself, I know that showing what I can do will be offering a secretive hand.

"Dragon form only, until one of you cannot get up. Stay below the furthest height of the mountains, do not go past the end of the ravine."

Dimitri's voice echoes against the freezing wall. My mind faintly recognizes him, only just able to place his name. People along one side are familiar to me, my mind marks their location. Tingles race along my skin as I start the change. The one across from me, Mikhail I think his name is, starts the shift. I control mine. He should see me as slow, think

364

I'm not as used to this body. Whoever he is. I know I have to fight him.

Red scales slip out of his skin to form a body with wings and a tail. Talons tip the folding top of his wing. I'll stay away from those. I register at a low level that he's a possible Suitor. My changing nose picks up on his attractive yet infuriating scent. Rage lashes in me, wanting to kill the one in front of me. He's a threat to my own existence. A somewhat near equal that shouldn't be challenging me. He's below me.

My own snapping bones distantly reach my ears as my line of sight rises to be above seventy feet. I take in the thin fin that runs along his tail forming needles with webbed skin between them. Makes it difficult to bite down, not difficult to injure.

My mind isn't completely mine anymore. I have enough control to pull myself back, I just don't want to. The remaining human part of me hopes deeply that my words have angered Mikhail enough to make this real. Allowing that corner of me to take control has been agonizing. Feeling it slowly sink into me to remove any emotional attachment from those around me is a process that isn't pleasant. I consider a thought that perhaps just like shifting, I need to begin learning how to control whatever this is inside of me.

The red dragon steps forward, his growl comes out in a strange beat. I've heard alligators in a distant life, he sounds like one of them making a territorial warning.

My shifting finally stops. The feeling of the warm sun on my freezing scales is pleasant. I've missed this body. My tongue licks out at one of the fangs hanging down over my bottom lip. I suck in air through my nose, picking up so many scents at once it has me blowing the air back out harshly. I stare down my opponent, returning the sound with a much deeper vengeance. Something, maybe fear, flits through hazel eyes. The vertical slits in his eyes dilates. I pull my lip back at the small victory.

"Don't take this too far Kali, we can always make up after this," a voice rings in my head. I yank my snout away from his direction, upset at the intrusion of his offer.

"You sound afraid,," I curl my words at him. His eyes widen while I hear

365

his heart rate pick up.

A human coughs down on the ground, I snap to look at them so fast one of them screams. A female with hair similar to the other dragons' scales nearly tips her chair back. Her face is full of surprise. She clings to the arm of a man who looks older than the rest. Intelligent green eyes take in everything about me. None of it is fearful. To my disgust, the dark blond looks as if he's examining a soon-to-be purchase.

There's a growl from my opponent who's approaching me quickly. He leaps towards me. I open my jaws, and am promptly smacked so hard in the side of my skull my head lashes to the side. While not the most brutal weapon, the bone of his wing makes my cheek throb momentarily. I swing my sight to stare him down at the same time I pull my head back, and dive for his unguarded wing. My teeth clamp down around the bony structure, piercing through the meat and tendon surrounding it. Without realizing it I'd accidentally bitten around one of the sharp points on his wings, so it pokes at the roof of my mouth, causing me to begin bleeding.

I clench my jaw closed harder. Feeling the creak of bone and coppery taste of blood, I groan in pleasure. There's a wildly bitter side to the taste of his blood, driving the predator in me even crazier. In my peripheral, I see his head swinging down to bite onto my wing. I let go of my hold on his fragile limb, rearing up on my hind legs to try and shove him away. He rears up as well, managing to pull his head back from its course to latch onto me.

The crowd far from us lets out a collective roar. There's a mix of astonishment and cheers for more.

Our paws swipe at the other, our heads jerking around as we both try to find an in to gain an advantage. I lean into him with my front paws, pretending that I'm focused on getting my teeth around his neck. Instead, I bring up one of my hind paws to press into his stomach, trying to rip him open. I don't feel any liquid seep onto my talons or toes, so I know despite the pressure I'm placing on him I've yet to break skin.

Frustrated, I pull back my weight for a moment so I can shove at him with greater force. He takes advantage, seeing my plan before I can enact it. With an open mouth growl he slams into me. I begin to twist my body to avoid falling on my wings. As I land, his body stumbles past me with his own momentum and his tail slings from one side to the other. He successfully slicks that sharp fin under my body, slicing open a line diagonally from my stomach to lower chest.

I can tell from the tilt of his tail that he'd purposely avoided doing as much damage as he could have.

Stupid.

I finish landing on all four paws, bringing my head down at the same time. With a cautious twist I angle my head to clamp down around his tail - avoiding the fin going into the roof of my mouth. I bite down, feeling the sharper teeth in my mouth cause more of that delicious blood to spill.

At the contact, the crowd - now behind us - yells. Some in shock. Some in fear. It makes my blood thrum through my veins.

The dragon I have captive by his tail growls in pain, shaking the appendage to try and dislodge it from my maw. His body turns awkwardly, trying to avoid more damage. I don't let go, too blind by the crowd's roar and taste of his blood to notice his paw coming around to slam into my head. He shoves me into the stone tiled floor.

My head cracks as it meets the ground, but I still don't release his tail.

Frustrated with letting myself get distracted, I focus on holding onto him while also keeping my wings away from his gleaming teeth. Standing over me, he lurches repeatedly at my body, trying to bite vulnerable parts of me. Between my legs and tail, I manage to keep him from getting a successful hold on me but the focus makes me loosen my hold on his tail. He whips it from my mouth without my teeth dragging the puncture wounds open further.

I notice the wing I'd bitten earlier is limp at his side, barely managing to fold properly against his body. I'd bitten right at the largest folding joint. An idea pops into my head.

I snap my teeth together and curve my body at my ribs, bringing my tail up close enough to get my extremely long tail close to his face.

He dodges once.

Twice.

The third time, I manage to slice open his cheek. Not as deeply as I wanted, but deep enough to make blood drip down. The taste was one thing. The sight?

Far more potent.

I feel my eyes dilate to the extremes. The Konge notices, pushing away suddenly, back towards the castle, while swiping at me to keep me back. In my rage I leap at him, noticing too late that he's turning his body to sling his tail at me again. I stop my forward motion to move back quickly. His tail is turned for a more damaging attack this time. I yank my leg away only with enough space to warrant a slice rather than a gouge. The edge of the courtyard is at my back paws. I can feel the sharp corner under them.

He stops his turn, spinning back to face me. The red dragon growls. I return it with my own. He reaches for me with both paws, pushing his weight to his back paws to spring from. My torso turns away to the right to dodge, tail coming up to slap him in the neck with the broad side of the middle section. I dive over the ledge towards the far away bottom of the ravine.

"*Kali!*" the male screams.

My vision swims for a moment, forcing me to flare out my wings and catch myself on the jagged surface of the cliff face. I look up, realizing that he's diving after me. And the crowd is gathering at the edge. I swing my body out of the way, making him miss me.

His halt is far nastier, just as I'd planned. With one wing barely useful, he's forced to stop himself by twisting like a cat and digging so hard into the rock face that his talons begin shattering. He does manage to stop though, looking up at me with those furious hazel eyes.

"*Kali, stop it! You're going to get us both killed!*" he screams into my head.

"*Stay down then, and don't call me that.*"

He pauses for a moment; his grip slips so he hurries to climb up towards me. His eyes flare open in realization.

"*I see,*" his voice is taunting. "*You let* her *have her way with this.*"

I bellow out a roar that shakes off some loose rocks. He dodges them by leaping up the side of the wall diagonally, still managing to close some distance between us. I still can't let go because my vision is trying to right itself.

"You thought I might actually try and end you," he realizes, eyes flaring open.

I purposely yank down pieces of rock at him, managing to slam one small one into his head. He shakes it off, continuing to close the distance between us. I readjust my back paws for a far better grip on the ledge. My front paws strain to keep their hold, however.

He speaks again. *"Too bad I like you too much to kill you."*

"Too bad I can't say the same for you, worthless animal."

Too late I realize that he's close. Too close. His tail can swing out and knock me off balance. He realizes it too and makes a move to do just that. I launch off my back paws with a forceful thrust, speeding for the top with strong pumps of my wings. The muscles strain with how hard I flap them down, fold them in slightly to bring them up, and then swing them down again. I hear a sharp cry that snatches my attention.

The crowd watching over the ledge all stumbles back as I career over the ledge.

For a moment, everything slows.

Two people, both with dark olive skin, black hair, and dark eyes are on their knees. Similar, but not identical. I may not remember their names, but I know exactly who they are. My eyes track them as I continue to gain altitude in slow motion.

Reality speeds back up as I try to climb close to the top of the mountain range and position myself back over the courtyard.

I'm only a couple hundred feet over the open area when I'm forcefully jerked back down. Teeth clamp onto my left back leg, hard enough to make me release the tension in it to avoid worse damage. His damaged wing struggles, but he manages to use minimal effort to stay up. I realize that he must have swiftly leapt climbed from the ravine after me, only to jump as high as he could with minimal use of his wings to reach me.

I push him with my other back leg, only managing to make him clamp down harder. I let out a deep yelp mixed with a growl. His teeth are too close to the bone. One wrong move and I could lose use of it for far longer than I can afford.

"Let go of me!" one of the dark haired twins calls out. "Kali!"

I zero in on the voice, seeing that the female is being roughly restrained. I move to dive for her despite the grip on my leg.

"Finish this, or I will," that male voice tells me.

My other side is unleashed some more.

I stop pumping my wings to try and escape him, allowing my body to fall back down. It causes my leg to twist at an awkward angle in his mouth while also putting pressure on him. I keen out shortly at the flush of white hot nerves firing so strongly I can feel it in my spine. To avoid being crushed under my falling weight, he uses his wings to pull himself out of the way. I fall past him, allowing my head to pass his leg. He's already begun to roughly sink back towards the ground, his wing clearly straining to perform its intended job.

Simply to return the favor, as I pass I reach out with an open jaw and clamp down on his leg. My back paws touch the ground as my teeth sink through flesh and muscle. With a wicked snap of the length of my neck, I slam his figure down from the air and into the stone floor. He adjusts as he crashes, avoiding landing awkwardly on his wings or tail. I use extreme force, and hear the crackling of a bone beginning to fracture under the pressure.

I hear a sharp yelp, looking back towards where two of my Samle are still bound. One of them gets a kick delivered to her ribs, the other shouting at the man who does so.

Distracted, my opponent has a chance to knock me down. One of his paws puts pressure on the laceration he'd delivered to my chest and belly. His teeth clamp around one of my horns, his head snapping to the side to slam my skull into the stone. My ears ring, vision spinning out of control.

Without hesitation my full essence flares into my eyes, making them burn brightly. It catches him off guard, making him jerk back. I shove with all of my remaining strength, causing him to stumble back.

The crowd of people, both enemy and friend, are far off to the side. I barely manage to catch the mix of expressions as I start toward the two taken prisoner. I let my essence gutter out.

"Stop her! Now, dammit!"

I look at the mostly bald headed man who'd called that out, and bare my teeth at him. In the corner of my eyes I notice the blazing red dragon storming towards me. I turn to him, swinging my tail up and off the ground. Arching it up, I spear the dagger-like end towards him and through the thick hide of his wing. I slam it through so hard that the tip embeds slightly into the stone below us. His outer eyelids flutter shut, then both his inner and outer eyelids close as he loses consciousness. Cries come from the crowd.

The man who'd called out lets his jaw drop, struggling to determine if he should come closer or not. Someone else stops him, whispers into his ear that he cannot interfere. He looks at me, blue eyes making contact with my green ones. I tilt my head, regarding him for a split second before making my way back towards the twins. I yank my tail out, causing the tear in the male's wing to split a little more. I can hear it tear.

I waste no time turning back towards the two men holding my people down and let out a chuffing roar. Their hair is blown back from their faces as my hot breath and glowing eyes demand they submit. Dropping their holds and weapons immediately. I faintly recognize the mature looking man standing between them. He regards me with a cool look, challenging me.

He smiles at me as the twins break from their restraints and rush towards me as I close the distance to them. I curl a wing over them on one side, turning my body to raise my tail in threat. I'm careful of my body as I continue to stalk towards him, not wanting to hurt the precious cargo under me.

"You don't want to do that," his voice has a tremor only I can hear. Even for me, it's faint. Everything else about him is too stern, too confident for my liking.

"Oh, but I do."

"Gallyan," a female voice hisses. He snaps up his hand to stop her.

Addison, I recognize distantly.

I stay in my current form even though I know he can't hear me.

"Well, there's someone to stop you, so if you're going to kill me, better do it now."

I give him a rolling growl as a warning. I don't want to kill him. I haven't done that yet, I don't know if I can. But I do know I've also gotten myself into enough of a predicament for now.

"You'll regret letting me live," Gallyan smirks as if he already knows my decision. "Because I'm going to have you. You're going to be mine. I will break you, because if I can break you-"

Just as I give up on restraint and begin to bring my tail down, pink flashes in front of me. A small, petite human dressed in pale pink stops me from slamming my tail through the torso of Gallyan - who's now hurriedly walking inside.

"Kali, they're safe. Sayah and Senka are safe," Aiza tells me.

I lower my head to sniff her too, fretting at the scent of blood.

"It's not mine, I just stepped in some," she waves me off, pointing to the stain of blood on the bottom of her skirt.

I sniff again, recognizing the sour mix of mine and Mikhail's blood. Panic starts to crawl up my throat as I fully come back to myself, realizing what I did. I look back over to Mikhail, who's just beginning to regain consciousness. Dimitri is in his dragon form, nudging at his Bonded with his nose. Mikhail's chest rises and falls in short, pained breaths. I begin to limp towards him, allowing the twins to walk close to my side but no further. My heart drops at the sight of how damaged he is.

"You did what you had to do," Aiza says quietly, trying to comfort me. She stays close, walking beside me.

Sayah begins to run off from me and I react, snapping at him then curling my head in front of him to stop him. He slips under my neck.

"Can someone please get us some medical supplies?" he calls out, walking back into the perimeter I feel I can protect him in. I can't trust what anyone will do right now.

"Here," Nina and a few others drop a whole tub of medical supplies. "They'll have to stay in this form until they're healed."

"How do you know?" he asks.

"Better to be safe than sorry," Brawn scrambles over with Nelly right behind him. "Shifting could bring the injuries down to scale, but our human forms can't handle this kind of damage. This is nothing, they'll be fine after a few hours or so."

I keep my distance from Mikhail. Watching eyes could blow the secret between us at the wrong move.

"Kali please," Senka is pushing against my front leg. I suddenly realize she wants me far away from him. Aiza comes up to me.

"Gallyan might have been rightfully afraid, but unfortunately that little demonstration just made him covet you."

"Meaning what?"

"He'll do anything to make you his."

Chapter 35

Aiza drops the conversation, refusing to answer any more of my questions while Sayah and Senka work on my leg. I'm unable to fold it in a position that makes it easier for them so they're forced to climb onto me. Brawn works on the opposite side where my armpit was sliced. He cleans it with herbs quickly, packs it with more herbs, then steps away. I look at him with my head tilted.

"Your dragon body will pull that together on its own. Might leave a very faint scar, but you won't be able to tell once the scales fix themselves."

I lean down to press my snout gently against his chest in thanks. He awkwardly pats it, then comes around to help the twins.

"We have to reset it, it's already starting to heal wrong," Brawn says worriedly.

"On three," Sayah says. I feel multiple hands grab onto various places on my massive haunch. Senka comes around to my face as Aiza walks to the injured leg.

I breathe in Senka's scent, the smell of fear still around her. Her hands push my mouth to face the other direction, I allow her to guide me. A small sting has me twitching. She nearly stumbles at the movement of my head, so I lay my head down. Her entire body leans against my cheek.

"One, two," Sayah counts, but his count stops a crack sounds from behind me. My eyes widen as my nostrils flare in pain. I don't move my head for fear of hurting the one leaning against my face. My jaw clamps down hard to mask the small sound of a cry.

"Shh," Senka attempts to ease me. Her hand runs along my black scales, cool from the winter air.

It takes longer than expected, Mikhail is awake before they finish patching me up. I feel cool soothing herbs start to seep into my bloodstream under my arm.

"Kali," Brawn catches my attention. "Don't shift until we clear you please."

I close my eyes slowly at him in acknowledgment. Aiza is covered by a few females holding up the privacy curtain as she shifts back down to human size.

A grunt brings my gaze back to Mikhail, who is now watching me curiously. The hole in his wing is no longer bleeding, possibly even slightly smaller. The very thin strip I'd created under his tail is already scabbing over.

"*You're in worse shape than I'm in,*" he teases.

"*And yet I still won,*" I throw back, bored. His face shifts as much as it can, showing tension.

"*You tried to kill me,*" he growls with his words.

"*I did.*"

"*That's all you have to say for yourself? I thought we were beyond that.*"

"*It needed to look real, not letting that part of myself take over would have let Gallyan see everything,*" I look away in case unsavory eyes are watching. While I sniff over Aiza as she walks by, perfectly clothed in her pristine garments, I continue. "*Now that we've established the law, we have more freedom. The lot of them would have requested a change in the law or some kind of specification between Suitors if I hadn't done that.*"

"*Fine, but next time, I get to know the plan.*"

"*Perhaps,*" I now move to sniff over the twins, who have acquired bedrolls.

"*No, you either give me the respect of keeping me in the loop or you don't have an ally.*"

I fight not to swing my head up at him. Instead, I blow a frustrated breath out that has Sayah checking my leg.

"*What would you even do, run back to the woman you nearly got pregnant?*"

"Ever hear about the country Switzerland?"

My wing comes over the Nightmare's, creating a large space warmed by my excessive body heat. I hear them talk about the events of the fight as the rest of my body curls into a knot around them.

Mikhail grows frustrated by the minute. I can hear his heart rate picking up the longer I take to answer. I want to have the upper hand.

"Fine, as long as my people won't suffer you have yourself the rights to be informed, Konge Mikhail."

"Then you have yourself an ally, Dronning Kali."

He curls into a ball as well to sleep. We stay there through the night, a ball of red and black fury sleeping soundly. The twins don't feel any of the snow that collects on me, too protected by my body to know. Each snowflake helps to keep my injury from being too swollen so I don't mind the chill.

I sleep with one figurative eye open through the night, never feeling comfortable enough to truly let myself rest. Exhaustion from physical injuries, the fight, my strained Bond, days of political debate and discussion, has worn on me. I settle at the fact that once I'm healed, we'll return home.

Occasionally pains from my leg throb like growing pains in puberty. The smell of herbs from my armpit disappears by morning as the slice stitches itself closed. All that's left is for scales to grow back in that area. Nina returns to check on Mikhail. Giving him the all clear, he shrinks back to human form in all his naked glory. I watch him for only a second, taking in the bulky muscle that lines his body with strength. His wink has me turning away to wake up the twins. I gently unfurl my body from around them so that the temperature brings them to. I feel my lips curl at the ends slightly. I had never seen them sleep so deeply before.

Senka stirs first, sitting up suddenly in a mild panic. I huff warm air to get her attention, easing her into her usual alert self. Sayah wakes up the same way, more on guard than panicked. Once they're both up they immediately start inspecting my leg, telling me that I'm not ready to shift back yet. Mikhail catches wind of them remarking that the puncture holes are nearly sealed and comes over to look. Nervous that the wrong person could be watching, I drop my head in front to stop him. His eyes dart to the teeth that stretch far down from my gums. A growl edges out to warn him away.

"Kali no one cares if we care about each other," he tries to reach out a hand to touch me.

At the same time my teeth snap together loudly, Senka appears.

"Stay away from her," she bites out.

Mikhail looks at me, frustrated. I pull my head back to sniff at the remaining injury. His footsteps grow farther away as he goes to eat some of the food brought out.

"Probably about twelve more hours and you should be good to go," Sayah pats my side. I growl in annoyance only to get a chuckle from him.

"Umm, I brought some food," Brawn's voice reaches my ears. I stretch my neck as high as possible, eyeing the plate of fruit and cheese he's brought out. The twins thank him then return to their bedrolls to eat. "I don't have any food for you 'cause I couldn't find anything big enough. But you'll be fine."

I relax from the stretching to curve up a lip at him. Nelly and Brawn check my leg as well, agreeing with the twins that I need more time before I can shift. Part of me is glad I don't have to talk for once, I can sit here in silence without being entirely helpless.

"Also hope you d-don't mind the company, the rest w-wanted to be around you for a bit," Brawn nervously motions to the three kids from before peaking around the corner. I move my front legs from being crossed over one another to being straight out in front of me. The children take the invitation and don't hesitate to run at me. Their hands touch everything they can reach, climbing over my front legs to touch the large scales that blend seamlessly together.

"You're so dark, where's the shiny bits?" one asks.

"Maybe she's made of nighttime," the only little girl wonders aloud. She tries to lift up one of my claws that is longer than she is tall. Laura steps up to move her.

"Don't worry," Senka places a hand on Laura's arm. "She likes being near us."

Laura's eyes line with liquid at the words. Her smile nearly breaks my heart until I realize it's because they've never belonged somewhere before. She looks at me, staring straight into my eyes. I dip my head while blinking slowly to confirm the twins' words. Laura pulls away from the little girl who promptly begins trying to lift my talon again. I look between her and the child multiple times.

Is she yours? I wonder quietly.

"Oh," she gets the hint. "Theri and I took her in when we found her alone after the new world started. Her name is Danny."

I sniff at her, curious about how well my nose can memorize scents. For the time being, it seems to pick up every unique trait about her. The other two boys, one younger and one older than Danny come over to try and pick up my talon as well. It doesn't budge. I watch Laura and Theri go to sit with the Twins and Brawn over breakfast. The other new members sit around as well, everyone somewhere in the half crescent space my body is creating.

"Hey, stop it," Danny says. She stumbles back from one of the boys shouldering her out of the way. It's not mean, though a bit pushy. I get my eye close to the boy and snip my teeth together. He seems to have an understanding of me because he apologizes to her and hugs her.

Danny looks at me and smiles. I'm glad I'm not human right now because I don't feel worthy of the pure look on her face. I just beat another Konge into unconsciousness and *enjoyed* it, how could I deserve her kindness?

She grabs ahold of my black claw once more. This time, I lift it ever so slightly. She squeals in delight as the two boys complain about her victory.

Movement by the archway into the castle catches my attention. Gallyan is standing in a field of range only I can see clearly. He leans against the wall with his arms crossed. Beady eyes take in my body, appraising each piece with that oily stare only he can manage. I force myself to stay completely relaxed in case the twins or the kids pick up on anything. My head lifts a little higher to emphasize how below he is. Those teeth expose themselves to me in a wicked grin.

"Mine," he mouths. I simply stare him down. He stays another moment, finally dropping his arms and walking away.

Aiza walks out, looking over her shoulder as he passes her. Her face turns sour after noticing what he was doing. I feel little feet move along my body then hear them slap to the ground. Little paces make their way to my wing. With a gentle lift, I pick up Danny to let her crawl around on my back.

"I've spoken with Dimitri, he's going to get us a bigger boat. Has to speak with Mikhail about it first though. We might need two, and they're not the comfiest in the world," she looks around for the source of the noise. Spotting the people around my side she makes her way to join them. Voices clearly pleased to see her make her walk just a tad faster towards them.

I spend the day watching everyone around me, listening in to conversations, learning about the new people that would be returning home with me. Eventually the kids all join the group of people sitting around a makeshift fire built near me. I let them sleep under my wing for a while after playing for nearly four hours. No one questions how I work with them, how I manage their playing or watch them. I feel a sense of guilt at the trust they've placed in me.

As night falls, people start to get much more relaxed. Conversations turn hushed, dinner makes for a good reason to smile. Brawn finishes his small meal and stands up again. His long legs carry him to the large muscle now completely healed over. His eyebrows furrow as he looks at the new scales that have grown back.

"Uh, Sayah could you," he jerks his head to motion to the injury. Sayah quietly gets up from his conversation to check my leg.

"Interesting," is all he says. I huff at them, wanting to know what the issue is, eager to shift back into human form so we can prepare to go home. My Bond perks up at the excitement of going home. I flinch at the pain that threatens to rise up.

"Your scales grew back somehow even darker than before," Brawn explains, using his palm to push his glasses back up. I can't help but agree with Sayah at the strange revelation. While they blended with the night before, they seem to be able to blend just a bit better.

"Okay you oversized Queen, let's go," Senka smacks my shoulder. "We have packing to do."

Lifting my wing I allow for the parents, including Theri and Laura, to pick up their napping children. Once everyone is far enough away, I force my body to forgo its comfortable size. My leg stings a bit at the change after having just healed but gives way once I continue to push the change. The more my scales disappear the more the cold winter seeps into my delicate skin. Cracking reverberates in my skull as my snout gives way to a human nose and mouth.

Standing in only my skin now, I take the chance to look at my leg. Only the faintest scar, so light I almost don't see it, remains on my leg and armpit. Four circles and a line to add to my collection of stories. Sayah throws a cloak lined with fur around my shoulders. I walk in with everyone, more than ready to start the journey home.

Chapter 36

"You have to be kidding me," I drone to Dimitri. I found that after my last encounter with Gallyan everyone but Linius and Elias had gone home. Janét had received word from her own messenger that her return was crucial. A quick goodbye and peck on the cheek is all I got from her before she hurried out of the castle.

"I'm not, take the deal or find another way home," he says with that aged look in his eye.

"So, the only way you and Mikhail will let us use your largest vessel is by bringing him and some of your people with us to visit?"

"That is correct."

"That is ridiculous."

"There's plenty of room on it. We hosted you, the least you could do is return the favor."

"The least you could do," I mock in an annoyed tone. Dimitri frowns at me. "Fine."

"We leave tomorrow morning," Aiza steps up from behind me. I'm grateful for her presence in handling the coordination of getting everyone ready to go. With a nod, Dimitri leaves my room to convey my answer to Mikhail. I wonder how he's doing after such long weeks spent hosting. I feel heat pool in a sensitive area at the thought of his promise before we fought. My body wants to push him, test just how serious he was about us finally giving in to the Suitor attraction.

I shake off the thoughts of him to focus on what's in front of me. There's not much to pack except the few extra items that were offered to me.

When Aiza attempted to return them, the kind woman simply shook her head and smiled. I stare at the bag of clothes, already dressed in the loose dress I'd be putting away in the morning to fly.

I find that sleep is still restless, mostly due to the Bond heating up at the base of my spine. It aches to be near Jakir again, having already been ignored for so long.

Time blurs until finally everyone, including the group of new additions to my Samle, are standing at the bottom of the steps. Mikhail waves Dimitri off after giving him a firm hug. A handful of the people from the Shadow Samle wait for Mikhail to shift.

"Ready?" I ask him.

"Shouldn't I be asking you that?"

"I think you should start getting used to not being in charge now, so it's not so shocking when we reach my territory."

He rolls his eyes, "I haven't been that bad."

I look at him in disbelief. The Twins drop their bags down and immediately undress.

"Laura, Theri, you and Danny will ride with me," I tell them. I point out those that will be carried, leaving most of the group to change forms.

"I can carry them, it's fine," Laura argues.

"No, you haven't made this trip before. I'm not comfortable with you trying to fly while worrying about Theri and Danny."

"This is the last time," she warns. "Once we're home," she hesitates at the word. I nod, smiling to encourage her use of it. "We'll do as we please."

"I'm sure you will," I respond.

Getting up into the air with bags in our talons and people on our back is smooth. Mikhail refuses to fall back, choosing instead to fly next to me. We travel in silence through light snow that drifts across our wings. I glance to his wing to see if any mark remains from my tail. Smooth, leathery skin is all I see on the wing closest to me. On my left side, Senka flies close, her eyes moving like a hawk to keep an eye on our surroundings.

The couple and Danny on my back stay protected in the pocket between my shoulder blades. I know even with the thick blankets around them and my body heat to warm them, they'll eventually become sick again from the wind chill. I push myself to reach the coast.

A familiar village comes into view. The only change being a large boat styled after the Viking era sitting a few miles down the shore.

"Start loading everyone onto the boat," I look to Senka, and her brother on the other side of her. *"I'll drop the two on my back off."*

"Where are you going?" Mikhail begins to slow his speed to match us.

"Private business."

"On my territory?"

He hesitates as I take off again from dropping off the others, wanting to follow. I shake my head slightly.

"This is for me, and me alone," is all I say before heading down.

Magda's form is waiting for me as if she already knew I'd come. Snow flurries up around me as my feet touch the ground. Completely undisturbed, she stands still with the other elders of their town behind her. Wordlessly, I shift to follow her. She hands me a thick coat that swings around to drape over my shoulders.

The medium sized house she brings me to is warm, as if the raging winter outside doesn't exist. I question how the small fire in the kitchen oven could be keeping such a place so comfortable.

Still in silence, the two older women then followed us to sit at the table. One motions for me to take a seat with piping hot tea already placed there. Magda sets a kettle on the center of the table, then takes her own seat.

"Thank you," I clear my throat. "For the clothing. It was extremely kind of you."

"Take more before you leave," the one with a silver bob says.

"I couldn't-"

"We don't have time to play pleasantries. Take the clothes," Magda waves her knobby hand at me.

"And some extras, we have plenty for you to take. Your people will need them," the other one, with thinned hair that gleams white, tells me. She sips her tea without bothering to look at me.

Silence again. They're waiting for me.

"Why did you tell me those things before I left? What's the golden star? Who are you?"

"So many questions," bob-cut mutters.

"So impatient," white-mane sighs.

Magda takes a rattling breath in that pulls a dry cough from her. I watch as she takes in my changed figure, now fit with strong muscle. Not a single emotion passes over her face as she considers me.

"You fought Mikhail, strange," her raspy voice feels like it reaches something private within my mind. I knit my brows at how she knows, perhaps from gossip.

"A consequence of my actions."

"Indeed. Was it worth it?"

I don't know if she's referring to the fight or what led to it. My answer is the same for both.

"I wouldn't change a thing."

"You'll change so many things," Magda's brow lifts just barely. She sips her tea again. "Won't she, Mairi."

Mairi, the one with the bob cut, grins at me, "Aye, she will."

"What?"

"So much pain, so much change to come," the other adds.

"Too far, Maura," Mairi chides. They share a strange glance.

"I don't understand what is this coming from?"

Magda reaches across the table to grasp my hand. Her skin is so cold I feel a shock of prickling race up my skin. I stare into those gray eyes, the exact same as the other two. I feel uneasy suddenly in the shift of the room. Pressure bears down on my back pushing me to lean forward. My finger tightens around hers so much I fear hurting her.

"I've told you what you will do when you need me. You should go home," they all stand at the same time. Their tea is barely touched while mine is completely gone. "We'll meet again, little Goddess."

I'm too confused and stunned to ask any more questions. Any of my previous questions resulted in more confusion, so I wouldn't want to if I could. Magda leads me out of their home. They allow me to pack three large bags of clothes from the storage building before guiding me away.

Wild thoughts tumble around in my head as we walk back to the circle I'd landed in. Unlatching the cloak from my neck I hand it back.

"Ah yes, you'll need this again."

"You know the cryptic lines are really just overdramatic at this point."

They all laugh, not a fake laugh, truly laugh at my words. Tossing the bags to the side I quickly grow into a body much better suited for harsh weather.

Not even a wave from them as I grab the supply of clothes. I reach the boat to find the Twins anxiously pacing on the deck.

"Maybe a warning next time?" Senka says through her teeth.

"You were gone for more than an hour," Sayah leans in to look at me. I look at how much the sun had moved since I greeted the ladies waiting for me.

"I didn't realize it was so long," I mutter. I thought I'd only been in the little cabin for maybe twenty minutes. My brain struggles to wrap around how time had slipped from me like that.

Mikhail stares at me with his head tilted as the Nightmares leave to get the boat pulled out.

"What?" I cross my arms to ward off the intense glare from him.

"Nothing, you just seem…"

"Seem?"

"I can't put my finger on it."

I throw up my hands and roll my eyes. His face should concern me more for how much he seems worried. I brush past him to go to the lower decks to join everyone else. Eventually he stops looking at me strangely, yet I still feel the aftereffects of speaking with those women. Women who seemed to know more than this world presents.

Chapter 37

Without fail I puke on the first morning at sea. Breakfast was already an unsteady affair so this is nothing short of expected. Senka claps me on the back and leans over the railing to watch me puke.

"I think I just saw a piece of bread," she giggles.

"Fuck off," I groan. I rest my head on my forearms dangling weakly across the intricately carved wood.

A suddenly cool feeling touches my neck, contrasting with the warm salty breeze. I turn my head to see Brawn smearing a gel that smells strongly of peppermint and ginger.

"This will help, as well as keeping your eyes on the horizon," he explains.

I pull my hair up into a quick bun to keep it from getting stuck in the herb-filled gel. My body temperature cools slightly, allowing the nausea to recede enough to be manageable. The waves become much less terrifying when my eyes aren't rolling around my head with them.

"Bad enough to fight a dragon the same size but not bad enough to take on the ocean?" Mikhail's feet carry his weight easily across the deck to me. "How unfortunate."

I blink at him, unwilling to argue as another wave of nausea overcomes me.

"Keep making the snide comments and next time, I'll use my tail to shred your wings to pieces," I snarl. Feeling much better, I'm able to stand and face him. Every ounce of humor splays across his face. As does a respectable amount of fear.

"So violent," he mutters, leaning his forearms against the railing next to me. I eye up the muscle that bunches as his arms support his weight. His back presses against the railing allowing him to slouch.

"So idiotic," I mutter back. He tosses his back slightly in a laugh, easing my bristling towards him.

"Brawn seems to have quite a few tricks up his sleeve," the ginger comments, looking towards the nervous wreck of a man flitting about. He occupies himself by tending to people whether they be sea-sick, tired, or still recovering from caloric deprivation.

"He does, doesn't he?" I watch Brawn flit about again in the most nervous way possible, trying to tend to bruises on the Twins from their early morning sparring. They both wave him off, wanting to return to the game of cards they're deep in.

"Seems a bit unnatural, like the kid has something else going on."

I narrow my eyes at him as I match his stance. Back against the railing I return, "When your own intelligence is so low anything can seem amazing."

"Someone's a bit snappy today."

"You would be too if you just undid your entire breakfast."

He chuckles, causing me to do so with him. My thoughts drag back to Magda and the other elderly women. Not a single question of mine was answered. In fact, I walked out of that time consuming house with even more questions than I had walked in with. One of my biggest fears now being why they felt the need to tell me they'd be there when I needed them. How would they know, and what would be so drastic they'd have to offer in advance to help me?

I didn't even tell the Nightmares what had occurred. The only reaction out of them would be to worry. They'd had enough of that for a while.

I watch their heads bob as they play the strange game only they had ever heard of. Complicated flips and turns of cards that seemed to involve a series of mathematical calculations and guessing. Their moves are as precise as their fighting. Senkas' look blunter and crueler while Sayahs' are slick and precise. Watching them is almost better than letting Mikhail run his hands over me.

"They love you," Mikhail speaks, startling me out of my silent chaotic thoughts.

"What did you say?" my brain hitches on a single word.

"I've heard the stories of how careless they are. How reckless they've been with everyone around them. Whatever their story was, it certainly didn't include love. Yet they do so fiercely with you."

"You're deranged. Their natural dragons that belong to my Samle, of course they have affection for me."

"You misunderstand how the pull to a Samle works then."

"Enlighten me," I dryly say. He continues as if I never spoke.

"The pull is uncontrolled. Sudden. It's simply an attraction to the leader that will protect and benefit you the most. It also guides you to the one you can make stronger. Plenty of people hate their Samle, only staying because leaving is too much work."

"Or too dangerous."

He winces, "That too. But the emotions, those are completely up to the dragon."

"I've barely known them long enough."

"And? I'd go so far as to say you care for them more than they do you."

"I find you incessantly annoying sometimes," I pull my arms to cross in front of me. My body reels from the topic regarding emotions. Do I love them? Of course. I'd kill to keep them alive just as I would any of my people. Do I want to feel that feeling on my skin every hour? It's not necessary, so it'll stay buried where it needs to be.

"I find you to be a tease sometimes," his eyes are lingering on my chest that's been pushed up. Warmth spreads down my body causing my thighs to squeeze together. He notices, a smirk pulling at his lips in satisfaction.

I walk away quickly before he starts something I won't be able to stop. I search for distraction. Laura and Theri are swinging Danny back and forth in a makeshift hammock. Her squeals remind me of Lilly.

"There's a little girl at home, about half her age, but I think they'll like each other," I swing Danny for a few turns.

"I'm gonna have a friend," Danny sings to herself.

"You're gonna have a lot more than that," Theri pinches her thin thigh, pulling a sweet giggle from the little blond.

"We should be about three days out, according to the Twins and Mikhail. It won't be long before you're back on land," my eyes catch Laura's pale face.

"Please tell me you have food other than charcuterie there," she looks at me in a mock beg.

My lips tilt up, "We do, there's a farm with a wide range of vegetables and a herd of super-sized bison. There's a lake, but we haven't figured out how to catch any fish."

"I'll do it, since I can't eat the bison anyway."

I look at her quizzically.

"She pescatarian, a strange choice for a person who's been forced to eat nothing but red meat for the past two years," Theri doesn't even look up. Laura's jaw drops and she smacks at her wife's arm. I leave them to playfully bicker as my Bond clenches around my nerves tightly.

The closer we sail, the more I feel it coming out of its cave. The ache to be near my Bonded grows every day. Such excitement bubbles up with each wave. At the same time, the pain grows ferociously. I crawl up onto a flat surface that lips over the front of the boat. Just large enough I can fold my legs up under me, I place myself there. Eyes snatch on my skin. Not a chance in hell the twins wouldn't watch my every move.

I close my eyes, inhaling the salty air as I'm lifted up then dragged down in the rocking of the boat. Thankfully my stomach doesn't twist once my eyelids shut. I allow myself to delve into the connection between Jakir and I that wraps thickly around my spine. Looking inside myself for the first time I imagine a gold thread that starts in my spinal cord, branching out to entangle itself with every nerve. I flinch as it flairs in pain slightly wanting to be let loose. So much control for so long has made it thrum with a need to punish me. Invisible hands sooth the swelling of anger to a manageable irritation. For the rest of the pain, I let slip into my very bones. It stings, like multiple hornets have sunk their stingers into my muscles. My lungs expand quickly to accompany my increasing heart rate.

Pain echoes further to bite at my muscles pulling a flinching motion from my core. I hunch over as it threatens to throw me off the ship.

"Kali," Senka's voice comes from behind me. I hold up a hand, keeping her at a distance.

I force my mind to find comfort in the uncomfortable searing spreading across me. In the midst of it all I'm still diving into the Bond. Diving down until I finally see his end, where the smoky black takes over the shining gold. There's a shimmer of his personality, whole and calm. I reach out that invisible hand as far as I can. Just as I'm able to touch his mind with the excitement of my return, my body snaps itself back through the pain and out of the Bond.

My body unfolds suddenly, falling back off of the ledge. Warm air sweeps around me as my back careens down to slam into the deck. My fall stops suddenly. Tanned hands catch me with ease keeping me from an unpleasant end to my mediocre meditation attempt. Senka checks over my body quickly to keep from drawing attention.

"What were you doing up there?" she asks.

I want to tell her that pain can never cripple my mind again. I want to submerge myself in that pain, in any pain. Jakir must feel the same, suffering all while having to stay put. Its slow burn has worn on me over the weeks of being so far. Letting that control me will be exactly what Gallyan needs and what Addison wants. I never want to feel it control me like it did when my arms hung above me. I think of Kent's face sneering at me while his knife drips with my own blood. Next time, it will be my knife. The blood will be everyone he cares for. Then him.

"Adapting," my voice is hollow, the opposite of my mind.

The rest of my day, just like the others, is filled with distractions. Most of them involve training with either the Twins or Mikhail. A few of the new additions watch, two brave ones taking my spot when they grow bored of watching. I feel proud as they grow in ability. Others are offered to join, mostly too weak still to begin training. I give them each a look that encourages their response, telling them I support their smart decision.

Every break I watch Mikhail sweat against the humid air. Though cool temperatures are crawling back, his skin drips with moisture. I shamelessly eye him up as a drip falls down the path of the muscled V leading beneath his pant line. Bulky abdominal muscles contract in his heavy breaths making my eyelids drop down. Strong fingers rest on his thin waist. My eyes slick over his arms to catch the tendons in his lower arm ripple while his fingers tap against pale skin.

My green eyes meet his hazel ones. Small blushes touch my cheeks at the prideful look he gives me. Despite wanting to drag my claws down his cheek to pull the arrogance off his face, I feel a stronger urge to drag him down to one of the three private bedrooms below deck.

"Keep looking at me like that, and I'll rip those leggings off of your body faster than you can get those pretty claws of yours out."

I hold his gaze a moment longer, letting it slowly drip over the growing bulge in his pants. Most people have dispersed to wipe themselves down or eat some food.

"You *did* make me a promise," my words are only loud enough for him to hear. In two short strides he's in front of me and standing between my thighs. A boldness takes over my next words. "We wouldn't want everyone thinking you're a liar now, would we?"

His hand wraps around the base of my throat, palm resting firmly on my collarbone. I dart my tongue out to wet my suddenly dry lips. Hazel eyes catch it, making me slow my motions. A gentle squeeze from his hand receives the same gesture from my thighs.

"Gross, get a room," Nelly's lip is pulled up to showcase his teenage disgust at our public display. Embarrassed of my lack of control I push Mikhail back enough to slide out from between him and the column holding up the sails.

"I'm going to bed," I grumble, slipping away. Too frustrated with the need between my legs and homesickness in my chest I skip dinner. The door to my private room, forced upon me by everyone else, creaks open loudly. The slam of it closing eases the tension lining my shoulders.

A rough scrub of my skin with a coarse washcloth pulls off the sticky feeling of salt temporarily. I dry off with another washcloth, then climb into bed in nothing but an oversized shirt I picked up from the freezing village we left from.

Rocking back and forth calms my nerves yet does nothing to drag me under into the deep sleep I so desperately need. Daylight falls away to a pristine night of stars, visible through the small window placed above my bed frame. Wild waves crash against it most of the time making it near impossible to view the constellations. I force myself to be grateful that I can see them at all.

A light knock taps on the heavy door. I sit up slightly.

"Who is it?"

No one answers, most likely Sayah wanting to check on me. A typical silent answer from him.

"You can come in," I let my body drop back down. The shirt is cool against my body, laying like liquid on my heavy chest and full stomach. I brace for the ambush of reprimands as the door swings open. "Let's hear it, I know you're pissed about earlier."

More silence. I rub my forehead with my fingers anxiously. I drag my hands back to plant them next to me, slowly raising myself up. I dramatically drag my head from hanging back to snap up.

"Not a single man I know could be pissed after seeing you lay there like that," Mikhail's eyes are pinned on the apex of my thighs.

The edge of the shirt is bunched up, showing the bone of my hips as well. I brush my fingers across the seam to cover myself. His eyes shift down, scattering across my scars.

"You never told me how it happened."

"Why do you want to know so badly?" I swing my legs over the edge of the bed. I grab a pair of shorts to slip on.

"Don't bother with those," Mikhail's voice is like rocks tumbling over one another. Only because of what lies beneath his tone do I toss the shorts back down. My arms fold in a small act of defiance.

"I told you before, humans are fast and I got caught."

"Caught for what?"

I sigh, running a hand through my hair, "I killed a few of them because they chased me down. I did nothing but try and stay away."

"I'm surprised you didn't kill them all."

"Hard to do when you have over forty cuts, multiple bruises, broken ribs, and a dislocated arm. To name a few things."

I can visibly see his skin pale as he processes my words. His hand on his hip clenches.

"I would help you kill them, just say the word."

"They're not worth my time. Even if I did ask you to do that, Jakir would be the first to do so. Not you."

"Have you slept with him?"

I balk at the brutally pointed question, "You have to be kidding me. No, I haven't fucked him. He's my Bonded, that's disgusting."

"You seem to be so enamored with him, I was just asking," he shrugs. It's not casual, it's stiff and angry. I can tell he's jealous.

"Let me make this very clear, Mikhail," I push my shoulders back. His eyes darken at the sound of his name on my lips. "My Bonded has not only saved my life, but he also gives me a reason to keep it. No matter what happens between you and I, he will *always* come before you. Never ask a disrespectful question like that again, or I'll pull your tongue out with my bare hands."

My eyes are glowing slightly, talons out to match the anger in my voice. I can feel my muscles quake with anger at how low his question is. The pull of sinking blades of bone into his gut is so tempting I step around the end of the bed. He watches me wearily, taking in every predatory movement. His hands slowly come up, no red talons to be seen.

"Alright, I apologize for asking such a thing. It won't happen again."

"Good, now get out," I place a knee on the bed to climb back in. He moves towards me to leave out through the door behind me.

"No," hands settle on my hips. I throw my hips back to remove them, only to end up pressing myself against his hard member. With my knee still on the bed he has a vantage point over me. One push and my face will be against the mattress. My body can't tell if I want to let it happen or not.

"No?" I clench my jaw. My mind struggles to decide if I want to tease him or hit him.

"No," he repeats. "I made you a promise. A promise you made a point about less than an hour ago."

His hands slide up under my loose shirt, trailing cool sensations everywhere they go. His head dips down to the crook of my neck. Soft lips touch my skin gently. I gasp in a small breath of air at the contact. I try to turn around but can't as his arms have me pinned to his chest.

"I've gotten one taste of you; I haven't stopped thinking about it since."

I let my head fall back to rest on his shoulder. His lips take the invitation, opening so his teeth can press into the sensitive spot on my neck. I reach a hand around behind me to touch him. His hips angle into my touch. The sound of his groan pulls out my own breathy moan. My body is already singing for him, already begging me to give in to what he wants. It takes every ounce of control not to give in.

"So impatient," he chuckles, the low vibrations of it reaching my spine. My core tightens at the sound of my fingers managing to undo his pants zipper. I start to slip my fingers into the waistband of his briefs just as he stops me.

"For once, could you try to not be in control of something?" I whisper. As his hand travels up my torso, his arm has my shirt riding up to let one of my hardened nipples show. Those lips continue their assault across every inch he can reach. He nips at my skin, soothing the small bites of pain with his tongue. Sparks fly at each flick against my hot skin. My hips roll in the rhythm of his teasing. Like some reward he finally slides his other hand up to cup my breast. His fingers pinch the bud roughly, making me moan louder than expected.

"If being in control means hearing that sound again, then no," his low voice directly in my ear has me shuddering in pleasure. I roll my hips again, pressing into him gently. My shirt slides up further, so I raise my arms to let him take it off. I twist to turn around, but instead a broad hand suddenly braces between my shoulder blades. He shoves me down so quickly I don't have time to consider fighting it. With a soft thump, my cheek hits the mattress.

"Fuck you," I move my arms to get into a kneeling position. I'm shoved down again so harshly my hair whips across my face. "You're sick," I groan.

"I won't argue that, kitten," his voice drops as he lowers behind me. I angle my head to watch his face greedily take in everything bared to him. My core tightens as he pulls his bottom lip in with his tongue. Hands slide up the back of my thighs to grab the rounded muscle.

I wiggle my hips impatiently, wanting nothing but for him to touch me where I want it most. A crack rings out as his hand comes down on my ass. I bite back any sound threatening to come out of my mouth. Still, a small noise escapes me as he does it a second time.

"Instead of begging with your hips, beg with your mouth," his finger trails around the wetness starting to gather. I rock back to try and make his fingers touch the sensitive bundle of nerves. "Tell me what you want Kali, and I'll give it to you."

"I hate you," is all I can manage. My thoughts are scattered beyond recognition. This man has done everything to warrant me climbing away from him yet his voice has me pinned like he's tied me up. "Stop playing with me."

One finger slides between my folds, dragging the slick feeling of pleasure the entire length of my swollen arousal. I flex my fingers outward, pulling my talons back in to keep from shredding the mattress. His finger slides back up making lazy circles around my clit. I shudder out a whimper in response to his agonizing teasing.

"Kali, it's not that hard, just-" one finger slips into me, nearly bringing me to the edge from that small movement alone. "Tell me what you want."

"I want you to stop playing around and let me finish, I don't care how you do it. Just stop acting like a shy virgin that doesn't know how to-" I'm so loud it's practically a scream that comes out of my mouth at the feeling of Mikhail slamming himself into me. He stops for just a moment to let me adjust.

"Don't," I grit out. "Don't do that."

"I'm trying to help you," his hands grab at my waist, pulling me against him so his cock is fully seated inside me. Before he can react, I pull away from his grip. He slides out until only the tip is touching my entrance. "Fine, have it your way."

His hand slides up my back slowly, fingers lightly skipping across my skin. I feel his frustration lash out as he curls my hair around his fingers, gripping most of it close to my scalp. He pulls my body up by the grip against my head until his lips are touching my ear. He flexes the tip still inside me, then whispers, "Remember, this is your way."

Wild pride swells in my chest at the control I have over this, over him. Even with my body in a position for him to do whatever he wants I still have the ultimate say. A different type of pleasure rips through me at the same time he slams into me.

Sounds of skin against skin slapping at a wicked pace fill the room. Mikhail moves in a way clearly meant to take. I let him rock his hips into me over and over, sliding my own hand down to toy with myself. He doesn't stop me as I gently move my fingers around the aching bundle of nerves. Almost immediately I feel my body start to tighten around him repeatedly. He feels it too, making his movements rougher as he keeps his pace.

"Fuck, Mikhail," I breath out, moaning his name loud enough to feel him shiver. "Don't stop."

My skin starts to burn as his hand repeatedly slaps against my rear. Warm pain blooms across every mark he leaves. It tips me over the edge, finally giving me the rolling waves of climax I'd wanted for so long. My eyes roll back as I feel my body get jerked forward through the last moments of Mikhail's thrusting. Stars speckle across the back of my eyelids in rhythm with my muscles contracting and relaxing. His body pulls back suddenly so he can finish onto my ass still in the air. My body feels cold at the sudden loss of contact. I shove the need for touch down before I do something I'll regret.

We're quiet for a bit, nothing but our heavy breathing between us. I point lazily to the still damp washcloth hanging over a chair in the corner of the room. He goes to wipe himself off, but I snatch it out of his hands.

"Rude," I shake my head as I wipe off my backside. After cleaning me up, he wipes himself off. I notice his movements are slow, careful. His face is lost in thought. "What?"

"Did you...?" he looks at me from under deep orange eyelashes. I laugh lightly, climbing into my bed.

"Yes, I did."

"Be honest, because if you didn't, I'll change that," he tosses the washcloth onto the chair.

"I'm being honest, Mikhail. If I hadn't, you wouldn't be cleaning yourself up right now," I lift an eyebrow, interested by his sudden concern for whether or not I had an orgasm.

"Why are you looking at me like that," he sits on the edge of the bed after pulling on his pants. "Have you never had someone ask that before? Wait, are you a virgin – were you?"

I laugh again, louder this time, at the poorly hidden horror on his face. My laugh sounds twisted, like it's not mine.

"A little late to ask, but no – I wasn't. You just didn't seem to care if I did or not in the middle of it."

"You weren't exactly asking me to be nice," his own eyebrows lift at me.

I tilt my head with my shrug, "Fair, glad you got the hint."

Mikhail doesn't respond. His eyes settle on the window above my bed. I pull my shirt over my head before I flop back onto the pillows.

"Would you like me to stay?" he asks.

I breathe in deeply through my nose, my finger pinch the bridge of it.

"And do what? Cuddle? So we can be a romantic couple out in the middle of the ocean?"

"We could figure something out, it doesn't have to be lonely our whole lives."

"And what is our whole lives? We have no idea how long we'll live, so why would I commit myself to this right now? I've had this life for just over a year now and you're asking me for this?"

His hands rub at his face angrily, "You're taking this the wrong way. I just wanted to offer."

"What are you offering?" my voice rises, just as the anger at him does. The attraction between us is sated enough I no longer feel the need to crawl on top of him. This anger is purely my own, nothing about Suitor's to do with it. "For me to stay with you? Is that what you want? For me to live with you as your live-in whore? Or would you be so kind as to make me your Dronning?"

"You're not a whore," his teeth grind together. I note his refusal to answer my last question.

"Clearly you think I'll bend to your will like one."

"I never said that."

"Then why do you keep pressing me to stay with you?"

"Because we have something."

"We have a nature-made attraction between us. It's purely based off of survival, nothing about this is meant to find long-term partners. You know that."

"What's the harm in you staying with me?"

"Where would my people go? Do I force them to follow me away from the home we just found?"

"We can find space for everyone, expand as necessary," he stands suddenly, pacing the room.

"Okay, so we have room for everyone. Would I be your equal?"

His mouth closes, slapping me in the face with his repeated lack of response. I stare him down, my eyes flickering embers.

"I'm done, you can leave now," I point to the door.

"Kali, don't be ridiculous. You barely have any experience and I can help you with that."

"You can help by leaving," I pull back slightly as he steps towards me. "Don't make me call the Nightmares in here."

His lips thin.

"That nickname is going to be exactly what they turn into for you," he whips open the door.

"I think our definitions of what a nightmare is are very different."

The door slams behind him. His curses follow him on a heavy breath. Out of a need for isolation, I lock the door and return to staring out my window.

Chapter 38

Aiza

I watch Kali closely from the second she reaches the deck early in the morning. Having a room near hers meant hearing a few hints at what occurred last night. I blush again as I remember the words exchanged between them. Shaking my head, I look at Senka waiting for my go ahead. I look to Mikhail who's staring with a strange mixture of longing and hatred at the brown-haired woman next to me. My gaze shifts back to the female twin. With a dip of my head, she moves to put herself between them. The self-centered man would no longer come near her without explicit permission.

"You're quiet today," I keep my voice low to maintain a private conversation.

Kali glances at me with those bright green eyes that look just a tad darker today.

"I don't know if I regret it or not yet. The only thing keeping me from starting a fight with him is how much I can feel the Bond healing."

"We're only a few hours out," I gently touch her shoulder. She tenses, eventually relaxing against my hand. "What's done is done, instead of reconsidering the past, try focusing on the future."

Her face fights a small smile, making the tension in my chest ease. Always resilient, no matter the obstacles thrown her way. I stay next to her, wanting to give her my presence. Each time I shift around to a new sitting position she tenses. I know she expects me to leave, but I make it clear that I'm staying with my body language.

We cover a large distance in a much shorter time than expected. Shouts begin as some of the newer members start to feel the sensation of being home. It's a warming feeling I know myself and the twins feel as well.

"He's waiting for me," Kali whispers. The look on her face tells me she can feel how close she is. I envy the closeness she has with him. I look back at Sayah, standing against the railing nearby. He looks at me with a grin as she speaks again. "Once we're close enough, you're in charge Aiza."

"You go see him," I look back at her. Peace starts to ease her shadowed face. "We've got them."

She doesn't respond. I don't need her to. We have an understanding I've never had before. One that runs thick with trust. Perhaps I don't need to be envious of the Bond when I have my own with her. I feel proud of her willingness to place the care of our people under me. Every action of hers has been nothing but to protect her people. I think on her brutal victory over the simmering Konge on the other side of the ship. Senka still stands at the halfway point, ensuring he has no way of getting to our Dronning.

Land appears quickly, the raised valley of land becoming a shining beacon for the ship. As we close in, Kali stands up. She leans over the rail to peer into the water.

Nearly to the point of the water being too shallow to move any further, she walks to the center of the boat. She whispers into Senka's ear, then strides quickly to the side. Her clothes quickly come off. Mikhail makes his way to me, keeping a large distance between himself and Senka.

"There's not enough room to shift on this ship," his tone is snippy. Sayah hears it and steps to stand next to me. "I'm not going to touch her Sayah, knock it off."

"I'm not concerned about that."

Mikhail pulls his attitude back in, looking over the water to the land that's closer now. His eyes take in the vibrant beauty of it all. Something in the distance appears, multiple shapes rapidly approaching us.

"What is that?" Mikhail's body becomes defensive. I can feel Sayah's demeanor shift into an excitedly anxious one. We're all aching to get home.

"Not what," I smooth down the wrinkles on my flowing shirt. "Who."

I twist my head over my shoulder to look at Kali, who's eyes gleam with happiness. I can't stop from smiling so wide my cheeks hurt. The Konge next to me notices my stare, then spins to look at her.

She starts to shift.

Cracks sound as she sprints across the deck, her body snatching itself into a new form. Skin tears and heals, bones snap and reform, legs and arms begin to lengthen. Without faltering she manages to reach the other side of the ship still changing. Her body leaps up to plant a foot on the railing, lifting her up and over the edge.

Barely a splash sounds as she dives into the water.

A few people run to the edge, looking over into the clear water to watch her.

"Pull her out!" Mikhail commands his people.

"You couldn't," I say, calm lining my words. In my peripheral vision I see his mouth gape at me. Ignoring him I walk to the bow to watch out over the water. A shadow twists and spins in the depths below. Blackness expands into a body with wings. Stillness.

With an intense speed the dragon moves through the water towards a ridge. One swift movement forces water out of the way, breaking way to a dragon darker than a moonless night. My eyes track her as her tail snaps around to push the rest of her out of the water. Wings crack furiously against the air, creating small waves of water to run away from her. Silence is heavy on the deck. Not a breath is too loud as she climbs higher above us all.

A gleam pulls a few heads down to look out at all but one figure landing on the beach. Sunlight reflects off of golden scales so brightly I have to shield my eyes from it.

In a dive, Kali begins a small descent to match the altitude of the one flying towards her. Sun casts shadows beneath her, making a mirror image seem to race beneath the waves. Anchors splash loudly to hold us down.

They race at one another so fast my own heartbeat starts to beat in time with their wings. Oversized wings work just as hard for the golden dragon as the wickedly shaped black ones do.

Distance closes, both still stretching their necks out at one another. They may very well crash into one another.

At the last second, before their bodies collide, they both angle up into the sky. Twisting their necks together they climb. Black and gold spin and dance in the clear sky together, balanced to near perfection in size. Even with Kali being bigger than Jakir, she does everything to match him.

Whooping starts with Sayah. An excited sound that brings chills to my neck. Senka copies him, her own excitement bubbling over. It spills into the chests of the rest of the other dragons, except for Mikhail's people who remain silent. I can't hold back the deep laugh at my own excitement.

"I don't want to leave for a long time," Senka's voice comes from behind me. "I missed this place."

"Is that Jakir?" Mikhail's sour tone does nothing to put a damper on our mood. Sayah grins at him, it's a dark one that has me looking away.

"Who else would Kali be so desperate to be near?" Senka leans around me to look at him. It's a low blow to such a fresh bruise on his ego. I don't see the need to correct her for it.

Kali and Jakir are still flying around in the sky. Clearly the time apart will make it difficult to separate from one another for some time.

I grasp my hands behind my back as I face those waiting for what to do. "Lower the boats, get ready to leave."

Kali

My spine is thrumming as the Bond practically beats to the rhythm of

Jakir's wings.

"I missed you," he tells me. I can feel the warm glow of happiness spilling through from his end. With every mile the Bond had grown stronger, less irritated or strained. I could feel him growing closer, knew he was coming for me just as fast as I was for him.

"I figured," I tease him. A chuffing sound comes before vibrations from his chest. Practically purring he brushes his wings against mine to be next to me. Together we reach the boat where smaller boats have been lowered with people in the water. Mikhail is in the last one with the twins and Aiza. He glares at Jakir,

"You smell like him, why?"

I look at him with the eye closest to his face. I feel no shame at what I've done, but telling Jakir is like admitting something stupid to a friend who told you not to do it.

"I'll explain another time," is all I give him.

I can tell the twins are itching to get out of their human skin by the way their bodies won't sit still. Aiza is the ever calm presence keeping them from leaping into the crystal clear water. Their eyes track me as I sweep down to pick up a large crate from the deck of the larger boat. The masts have somehow been folded down to stay out of the way, more than likely planning for occasions like this. I fly past them, needing to drop the heavy crate quickly. Blue and green forms twist at the shore. I watch Jacob wiggle his butt around as I draw near, Harlow nipping at his wing. Jakir and I fly over the rest of the crowd heading in the same direction.

I can't stop looking at him, at the wings hanging over mine. His horns that sweep back so elegantly over his head, scraping at his neck as he tilts his head back. Golden lids flutter shut while he breathes in the crisp air rushing past us. A small black form levels between our heads.

"I think he just collectively ruined my homecoming," I groan.

"Ugly bird, 'ery ugly," Feathers screams. My ear drums shake at how loud he is.

"He's fond of you, you should stop being so mean to him," Jakir doesn't look at me.

I snap my teeth at the bird, he swerves to avoid me. Tilting back to fly next to my head he clacks his beak at me.

"I should eat him."

Rough grunting from him makes my lips pull back in a twisted smile.

"You're back! Okay. I have a surprise for you but you have to close your eyes. It's really cool you're going to love it," Jacob is walking in circles around my body. Nearly tripping me as I land in front of Harlow.

"Jacob, let her relax a bit before you bombard her," his beloved touches my snout with her bright blue one. I inhale her scent, enjoying the feeling of being so close to familiars again. *"I see the twins have only gotten wilder,"* she lifts her nose at them behind me.

I watch them help Aiza out of the boat, the second her feet touch course ground they shift. Running towards me, they take off into the air.

"We'll be back. Want to see something," Senka tells me.

"Tell me what your Dead Forest has when you get back," I respond, knowing exactly what they're heading for. Jakir's body crackles as his human skin begins to take over again. *"Tell Konge Mikhail he is not to shift."*

Jakir looks at me suspiciously, too far into being human to respond. I feel curiosity spill from him, I ease it with promise. Golden eyes look to the tall man with orange hair.

"Konge Mikhail," my Sekund extends a large hand. His muscles have grown, a thing I thought impossible with his size before I left. Those rounded shoulders are larger, stretching his shirt to its limits. Mikhail takes it in as he shakes hands with the man. He's dwarfed by Jakir's size, even having nearly a head over me is nothing compared to him. "Welcome to our home, we're pleased to have you."

"I'm not, not yet anyway," Harlow stands next to me. Her voice in my head is tense. *"I'm not going to trust him just because you slept with him."*

"I don't expect you to. And how did you know I slept with him?"

"You smell like him. I smelled like Jacob so heavily the first time we slept together I wasn't sure if I was going crazy. He left to get food and I thought he had hidden in the room."

"Good to know everyone can tell."

405

Keen eyesight watches pale hands clench too tightly around the contrasting dark skin. I lift my lip at Mikhail, warning him away from the act of aggression. It has no effect on Jakir, who simply frowns slightly in confusion.

I point out who loads onto who, making Harlow and myself carry most of the weight. With four people on my back, six on Harlow's, we're barely able to carry the weight of the two massive crates. Jacob takes a few more people.

Brawn shifts, his brown body matching Jacob's size exactly. Carrying Laura, Theri, and Danny is all he can do. A year of starvation still affects his body.

I have to push everyone to take off, most of them unwilling to go before me. Jakir and Mikhail speak on my back, exchanging casual conversation of light-hearted experiences. I'm grateful for not having to talk finally, days of speaking in meetings and dinners has mentally worn me down. I let myself delve into the Bond, which still lashes out in pains similar to a cramping muscle. I let the pain flow out from my center while still keeping level flight.

Feathers occasionally dips down to fly directly next to my face. Our eyes meet for a moment, almost convincing me he might understand how weary I am.

"Why is that bird following her?" Mikhail asks Jakir.

"He's fond of her. Been with her since she woke up."

"He seems intelligent."

"He is, very much so."

Nothing else is said as we make our way back. It takes most of the day to return to the tree overtaking a huge area. So long, that the sun has dipped well below the horizon. Clear skies let the stars dance brightly above us. It's so much light with the moon that it practically looks to be daylight to me. The temperatures have dropped enough that frost is beginning to coat the tall grass swaying beneath us.

The leaves on the tree haven't moved, just shifted to a strange mixture of yellow and orange. It doesn't move. Not a bit of breeze moves in the night. My landing is rough once we reach the tree. My body struggles to maintain composure as my paws dig into the rich earth below me. Shakey, I let those on my back climb off.

"Go lay down, I'll be over to sleep with you soon," Jakir smooths his hand over my scales. I twist my neck as I curve it, wanting to be close before he begins settling people into multiple houses that had been built in the area. Each one is in a line, varying sizes mixed together. I smile internally at the work they've put in to build a place to live from nothing.

"I have a feeling you'll be in the form until tomorrow," Lilly walks up to me. A large chunk of meat is dragging behind her. Filo follows, pulling two more pieces of meat behind him as well. "Eat, you'll be ready to shift back to being human by tomorrow afternoon."

They lay down the pieces in front of me, I hesitate at the amount of food. It might be delving too much into the herd.

"There's enough," she says. "A few had calves recently, and Filo went with Jacob to round up another herd."

I huff out a warm breath to thank them for the effort. She lightly touches my nose between my nostrils before walking away. Filo's hand brushes against Lilly's so fast I nearly miss it.

Interesting, I drawl. I leave in a corner of my mind to ask about later.

I watch from afar, thankful for Jakir's energy. His willingness to put everyone in either a house or tent while clearly wanting to be elsewhere brings me shame. I should be the one helping, even with how sore my body is. A week of travel finished by hard flying to reach the heart that calls out to me has worn me down. My wings throb tenderly as I let them splay out lazily on the ground. I can't even manage to lift them enough to tuck them in.

I rest my head down on my folded paws. Cooling ground brings my body temperature to a comfortable point where I'm no longer struggling to feel at ease.

Finally, he makes his way to me. Confident strides cover the distance between us. Long legs covered in bulky muscle flex as he walks to me. His body becomes barren of clothes just before shifting.

Golden scales slither against distant firelight. I can't lift my head to greet him, I'm so tired. Concern ripples down to me, his steps are frantic.

"Next time, speak up when you're hurting."

"I think the Bond did that plenty while I was away. You felt it too, yeah?" my eyes roll around to watch him. His mouth gently picks up my wing by the thick bone at the front. He folds it in so it's tucked carefully against my body. Doing the same with the other he makes it so the muscles are able to relax fully.

"Better?"

"Still sore, but not from that."

His body angles so his head can rest next to mine. The combination of cool ground on my belly with warmth on my side from Jakir has my eyelids fighting to stay open.

"I felt every time you suffered from the strain. Kali, I'm so sorry I had no idea being separated like that would do such awful things to you."

"To us, I'm not the only one that suffered. I know you felt it too, could feel you screaming through it."

"We know now. We don't have to be apart for the foreseeable future."

"As long as no one else appears on our shores telling me I have to go."

"Then I go with you."

"You know one of us has to be here-"

"They can handle themselves. You have to learn to let go of the control."

I feel myself drift off slightly, coming back just before final sleep.

"We have a lot to talk about tomorrow," I manage.

A gold tail wraps around my black one, the shine I know is so strangely contrasting with mine it would make one think the gold is wrapped around nothing.

Finally, sweet sleep like nothing else pulls me down. My body feels heavier than my eyelids as if I might sink beneath the ground itself.

Chapter 39

Harlow stares at the ground, her face caught between concern and consideration. After telling them everything that had transpired in the Shadow Samle territory her, Jacob, and Jakir are silent. Aiza looks to me with an encouraging face.

"And now everyone is expected to follow those rules?" Ellie continues as she combs out Lilly's hair, who sits completely unaware of the conversation. I reach out a hand to smooth a finger over her cheek. Lilly smiles at me.

"Laws, and yes. Everyone decided with someone finally claiming the last bit of land, it's time to start doing so," I keep my eyes on Lilly, who's now touching the numerous raised lines on my arm. "Whether or not people are actually going to obey them, I don't know."

"It's up to the individual Samle's how they decide to enforce their own laws," Aiza steps in. I let her explain the gray area of how punishment can be doled out by other leaders should things transpire within their boundaries.

"And that's why you took the twins' place in the fight," Jacob concludes. "Not gonna lie, that was pretty cool."

"Jacob," Harlow sighs and smacks his arm. Jacob smiles and drops a kiss on her cheek.

"Gallyan has a vendetta against the twins because they got away."

"I don't like the way this man comes across. It's unnerving," Jakir looks out over the water just as Harlow does. My leg is against his to keep the Bond from being angry. Each time I had stepped away from him since waking up my spine threatened to fold. It wanted absolutely no distance between us. I wonder how long it will take for it to be calm.

"You'll love the little quirk he's got then," I watch Jakir's eyes flick to me. "He seems to think that when he wants a person, he can have them. Like property. His Samle has…slaves, that they don't seem have any shame about."

Jakir stills, the horror peeling through his body so much I can feel it through the connection between us. My fingers wrap through his, holding his hand tightly as his chest shudders.

"Is there anything we can do?" his voice is deeper than usual, pained.

"For now, keep our ears to their walls. Attempting to change something in his territory would risk us too much."

"We're not strong enough to do anything right now," Harlow's knuckles are white as her fists clench on top of her knees.

"I know," Jakir says. "But it won't be like that forever."

I don't say anything, unable to truly understand the pain he's in. I settle for holding his hand in my lap.

"He wants me."

Jakir's hand grips mine so tightly all of a sudden I nearly pull back.

"What?" he breathes. "Why would he want you?"

I look back behind us at Mikhail, off in the distance with a group of his own people. He looks over at us occasionally, too far for him to hear us by the water. I turn back to the group circled around. My lips part to spill the more detailed story of my fight with the red dragon. Jacob and Harlow look proud as I explain the violence that I let take over my actions. Aiza looks past us at the people moving about between homes, most likely considering what she might have done differently on the other continent. Ellie becomes distraught though she tries to mask it by interacting with Lilly. I watch Filo, still speaking to them of Gallyan's behavior, calm her tense body with a light touch.

He turns away abruptly once he notices I'm looking. I knit my brows together, not understanding why he would be so shy.

"Don't go near him, don't let him in," Harlow lays out her words as if it's some simple plan no one had thought of.

"Right," I roll my eyes, shifting to lay on Jakir's lap. His back rests against a large rock. Thick fingers wind through my hair to untangle it. "He doesn't seem like the type to hold back on his word."

"We can keep an eye on him, I'm sure plenty will start to move about between Samle's now once we have them mapped out," Aiza pulls a rolled-up piece of paper from behind her. Laying it out in the middle of the circle we'd formed, she weighs down the corners with stones. Harlow helps with the other side since Aiza can't reach it. As my advisor pulls back the draping fabric of her dress drags with her to reveal the hand drawn map that had been made to match the first one.

"Though there might be some faulty lines, we know generally where each one lies," Aiza's voice falls to a dull murmur in my ears. Jakir has tapped on my stomach, urging me to follow him. Quietly we rise up to walk down the shore.

The lake is silent, not a single wave curling up to touch the rough rocks around it.

"I know it's bad news, you're not doing a good job at hiding it," my steps are twice as fast to keep up with his, even with his slowed pace.

He takes a swift breath in, then ends my relaxed mood.

"There's a large group of men skimming our borders outside of the Dead Forest. For now, they're to the west."

I stop dead in my path. My skin flushes with ice as each ragged scar on my body seems to swell.

"Tell me it's not them," I whisper.

"Then I'd be lying."

I want to sink into the ground, disappear into the mountain ranges, lose myself in the towering black walls in the north. Anything but knowing how close those men are again.

"There's more."

"Of course there is," I bite out. My words are venom yet have no affect on him. Nails drop to the ground as black talons slowly edge their way past skin that barely bleeds at their arrival now.

"Jacob and Filo both went to look a few times. They kept their distance," his hands reach for me, holding my face in his hands to help me keep my cool. "Kent is alive, missing a few fingers and an eye, but alive."

"He's mine," I nearly growl the words. I wrap my arms around myself as I turn away from both the circle of close people speaking, and the village of people working.

"There's no need to kill, Kali. You could try a warning."

"A warning? You have to be kidding me. The man strung me up like a doll and sliced every inch of my skin for a *lesson*. He was going to *rape me*, Jakir. If you hadn't found me when you did, I'd be dead, or worse."

Golden eyes fill with pain so much I have to push comfort to him through our connection. I sigh, battling the urge to shift and fly off. My fingers burn to be covered in blood. Images of dragging Kent through each ounce of pain he put me through flashes across my mind.

"They have prisoners, mostly women."

Another punch to the gut. Do I save the women? Exact revenge? Can I manage both?

"You could try to have both," his hand brushes against my cheek. "But it would risk the women's lives."

"What are they keeping them for?" I croak out.

"You and I both know the answer to that, love."

Beats of silence push at us both before I turn to him.

"I spent months escaping them, finally found my home, only to leave for another continent. I get back and the first thing I have to do is leave again?"

He pulls his full bottom lip in, considering my words.

"I don't know, but if we don't do this now it will only take longer to change."

"And who says it will change?"

"Who says it won't?" His smile is tinged with sadness. I grab at the place in my mind where the gold and black thread binds us together. Mental fingers wrap around it for comfort. For who, I'm not sure.

"We give them tonight," I say as we both begin to walk back to the village where the others have returned to greet two gray dragons landing. "A happy thing before violence."

"And a dinner to match," his arm slings around my shoulders.

"It's nowhere near being done but we weren't sure when you'd be back," Jacob beams at me. The tall blond next him tussles his hair lovingly.

"It's huge," I respond. No other words come to mind at the sight of it. The plans lay out an already enormous level to be built, allowing later floors to be stacked on top. Levels carved deep into the cliffside make it a castle Mikhail would be ashamed to have his next to. Deeper back from the front facing parts of it are hidden rooms and tunnels. I look at the dug out foundation that goes right up to the edge of the ledge.

"I thought this could be the dining room, we'll figure out a kitchen here," Jacob walks me around the edge to show me each location. "Those empty spaces at the top with the white rocks are courtyards. You'll have an office looking out this way," his arms spread to show me the view will include an overlook of the land that dips down into the lower valley. "Plenty of bedrooms for whoever you want in the house."

"And my bedroom?"

"Oh," his grin is devilish. "You don't get to see that yet."

"We all agreed it should be a surprise," Jakir cuts in to stop my argument for seeing it.

"Fine," I grumble. "I guess this isn't too bad of a homecoming gift anyway."

Jacob jumps at me to hug me, his arms wrapping around my torso. I pat his head awkwardly. Unbothered by my stiff return of affection he pulls back.

"Could I make a request?" I ask.

"Of course, I just can't promise I'll be able to do it," his grin hasn't budged.

"A laboratory, could you add a laboratory to it? And a greenhouse?"

Jacobs' long hair falls across his face to expose the shaved side of his head as it tilts. I look over to Brawn and Nelly looking at the plants shaped like cones we use for soap. Brawn pushes his glasses back up, his shoulder flexing to show the bit of muscle that had been gained since being here for a while. His curiosity had only grown with the new animals and plants he could watch here, no longer limited by the nearly lifeless tundra.

"Brawn needs a place to work, and I need him to do so freely."

"I'll get on the designs before dinner."

Flames lick up higher than anticipated from the wood that's been piled higher than Jakir's head. The twins walk next to me, chittering between one another. After returning they once again stayed by my side to wait for a free moment. With only Jakir and I in ear shot as we drag large pieces of bison over they reach out their conversation to us.

Senka looks at her hands while using them to talk. "Not even the Dead trees still thriving will catch fire - we tried. We blew flame at it, only for it to evaporate."

"Did you see any of the animals living there, if any?" I consider the image of the deer with half its face missing they'd found before.

"Anything that lives isn't normal. The air feels...wrong. It's exciting, but unnerving," Senka's hands pause in her description, mouth hesitating. "We saw the men, one of them went into the woods. I think he was drunk, so I'm not sure if the alcohol killed him or the air did."

I put my hands on my hips, sharing a glance with Jakir.

"What was he doing when he died?"

"Pissing. Then," she puts her hands to her throat pretending to choke herself. "Bye bye boy."

"It must be the air keeping them out, they can't breathe it," I face Jakir slowly. "They've been trying to find a way in."

"I smelled it when we flew over it the first time. It was quite pungent

414

so I wouldn't be surprised if humans can't handle it."

"His face got black lines all over it," Senka sighs while twisting her black hair around her finger. "I wish I could do that."

I give a shake of my head at her, "Did you happen to notice anything different about them?"

I want to see if accounts of their unnatural strength and speed are a result of Jacob's exaggerated stories or truth.

"They can move a lot more than they should be able to, but they don't look any bigger than what humans normally are."

I wave them both off, Sayah choosing to stay within close range rather than socialize like his sister. His body isn't nearly as tense. At least until Mikhail walks over to join us.

"We'll discuss a plan in the morning," Jakir puts his hand on my shoulder, nearly covering the whole thing. I begin to argue but stop as the man with ginger hair reaches us.

"Don't stop the conversation on my account, please," his teeth show in that overly confident smile. My mind flies to the memory of those lips on mine.

"It's nothing you need to worry about," Jakir waves him off. Mikhail's jaw clenches. His eyes dart to Jakir touching me, enticing me to place my hand on my Bonded's.

"Actually," my mind switches gears into a more political mode. "We could use the help, if you'd like to."

Jakir immediately opens to the idea by supporting me internally. Sayah's olive skin tightens across his face with his body. I suddenly wish for a connection strong enough with him to ease him.

"Ah, now you need my help," Mikhail snipes.

"I never said *need*, Mikhail. We're perfectly capable of handling our own issues without having our people killed or slaughtering innocents," I say through my teeth.

"I'm missing a bit of the story, I believe," Jakir tries to intervene in the boiling violence between the Konge and I.

"I was trying to protect my people," the Konge argues.

"You were ready to kill outsiders who simply wanted to survive rather than help them to ease the problem," I retort.

"What's done is done," Jakir slips his hand from me to step in between us. "Kali's taken the problem off your hands, you've been provided an opportunity to learn."

Mikhail opens his mouth prepared to spew venom. Jakir's eyes glow slightly, though his step forward is what makes the Konge's mouth slam shut. I feel my morals slip slightly at the sight of Mikhail being forced to look up at Jakir.

I guess he looks good looking up at both of us.

"You have your own problem of rogue's now?" he retreats verbally, body still tense. My fingers twitch to reach out and slap him.

"No, we have humans who've apparently developed their own abilities. They want into our territory."

"Why not let them in?" his smirk makes my arm twitch.

"Because they want their toy back," I watch the words sink in. Jakir is visibly calm, holding back anger on the inside. Sayah pulls out a dagger to start flipping around his hand in complex movements. "You can come with, though we're going to try Jakir's way first."

"And what is your way, Jakir?"

"We talk first, rescue the captives they have."

"And if talking doesn't work?"

"We do it my way."

Hazel eyes stare me down. They mirror the stubbornness that I hold in mine. A cold heat shares the same space, telling me his lust is just as strong right now. Uninterested in playing games I move away to the house Jakir and I currently share.

"He wanted to protect his own people."

"By killing those who were suffering. I found them in the middle of a snow desert, they had nothing," I pull on a loose dress that only has enough fabric to cover my breasts. Flimsy material lays lazily over my body letting the cold air pimple my skin. "He could have given them a home, or at least left them alone."

"This isn't the same world, love," he opens the door for me to walk outside. "I'm not saying I agree with it. Things are going to be very different since people can change into fairy-tale creatures."

I look at him, pull my braid around to the front, and take in his words.

I wrap my hand around Jakir's bicep to walk us towards the festivity around the dancing fire. Though bigger now, it still has no chance of reaching the first branch of the tree. Its heat is enough to warm me through the thin material of what could barely be called a dress. As we approach the large group, I catch Sayah already shifted into his gray form.

"No socializing tonight, little nightmare?" I drag my hand down his scales as I make my way past him. He catches my eye, snorting heavily as if to say 'absolutely not'. I chuckle, "Fair enough."

Jakir removes his shirt, already overheating from the proximity to the flames licking out. Muscles in his back shift like tidal waves as he grabs meat from a roast over a much smaller fire.

I lose myself in eating and talking. The people who were once rogues no longer show such drastic signs of starvation. A small smile stays on my face, never dropping into the emotionless look that had become normal. Jacob pulls out multiple cases of liquor that I don't bother asking how he acquired. His innocent face feigns confusion at Harlow.

"There is no way you just happened to find this," her hands plant firmly on her hips. "You specifically went looking for this, didn't you?"

"Harlow," he gasps, placing a hand on his chest. "I would never do anything like that. You told me to stay away from the city so I did."

I reach around him to grab a bottle of whiskey, "I call bullshit."

"No," Harlow grabs his chin to tilt up his face to look at her. "I think he's telling the truth. But I still believe he went out of his way to find this much."

I cock my head at him as I pop off the cap. His eyes dart between the two of us. A hand comes up to grab Harlow's arm. As her face swings down to look at it, her pale hair falls in a curtain. Feeling the tension rise between them I slink off to go sit with Jakir and Mikhail, speaking idly.

A few hands touch me in passing, gentle reminders of thanks or just

417

simply a wish of connection.

Deep in my chest, a small piece of me gets put back together. The crack remains, but I'm no longer scrambling every second for survival. Even with houses still to be built and people to home I can feel the change. It startles me enough that I catch Jakir checking in on me. I sit between his legs with my bottle of whiskey.

"Want some?" I swing it up to him, starting to feel the intoxication running through my head.

"I don't drink, but thank you," he squeezes my shoulder.

"You're no fun," I grumble.

"One of us has to be sober."

"I would like to vote that it *not* be Kali, I have yet to see her drunk," Mikhail's eyes look brighter in the firelight. Their hazel color is leaning towards a green tonight.

"Nobody asked you, ginger," I can feel words starting to become more difficult to annunciate. Tilting the bottle I take another long swig.

"I've decided to grace you with my opinion anyway."

I lay my head back against Jakir's torso, he holds himself up to support the weight.

People begin to dance around the fire to a song belted out in some language that sounds similar to Russian, though I can't be sure. Laura grabs Theri, leaving their daughter to play with Lilly. Theri's blue eyes are bright against her dark skin, they sparkle at me. With a wave she begs me to join her.

"Go," Jakir's smooth voice rumbles in my ear. I shove him away with a lazy hand.

With grace, courtesy of my Sekund's strong arm, I stand on wobbly feet. I use the now half empty bottle to point at Mikhail.

"You're next, man whore."

I spin away into another body. I look at the face to find Brawn with eyes as glassy as mine most likely are.

"I-I'm sorry Kali. W-wasn't watching where I was going," his palm goes to shove his glasses, which aren't there. I giggle at the habitual movement.

"Did I do something w-wrong?"

"No," I let out a soft burp. "I was rude."

I watch his teeth start to show in possibly the most lopsided smile ever. We help to keep one another up, dancing awkwardly. My muscles relax so much my back adjusts while twisting around. Another person grabs me to spin me around, stomping to the beat of the throaty song.

Heat grazes my skin every time I swing closely to the fire. Flames lick at me, nearly burning me until I snatch myself away at the last moment. The mix of reality with blurred images has me humming along with the new song. Repetitive beats from stomping feet all around shake my very bones. I throw my head back while another pair of hands grabs at my waist. My body warms slightly at the touch. Vision completely upside down I catch Jakir smiling so widely at me it pulls my own lips up my back.

I want to stay there, watch the perfect teeth gleam at me. In a swift motion I'm swung back up to a standing position.

"I've never seen you like this, it's nearly as intoxicating to me as that whiskey to you," Mikhail's lips drag down the sensitive part of my throat.

"And you're nearly as annoying as my bottle being almost empty."

"Ah," his hand slides down to my rear. "Even angrier when you're drunk. I like it."

"You also like killing innocent people."

He pulls back, undeterred by my snapping tone. I watch his lips curl, heat curling along with it between my thighs. A heavy breath escapes my lips at the feeling of the Suitor attraction pulling me to him. My hand on his chest digs into his skin, talons begging to come out and sink into him.

"Do it, Kali. I know you're itching to bury those pretty little daggers of yours into my chest," his mouth is next to my other ear.

I squirm in his grasp. My body wants to walk away to a darker shadow for privacy. My mind wants to watch him beg for breath.

"If I didn't know you any better I'd say you're asking for it like a desperate puppy."

Immediately his hand guides me to leave the circle. I touch Jakir's shoulder on the way past, assuring him silently that I'm choosing this. Almost missing my hand, he breezes his own across my fingers.

My legs struggle to keep up with Mikhail's striding through the short grass. I look back over my shoulder at the fire slipping further away. My dress drags behind me across the top of grass, occasionally snagging.

"I never agreed to this," my words are becoming clear again. A bit of the haze clearing as panic sets it. We stop walking. Mikhail turns to face me just as I see a large figure stand by the fire. His face twists in confusion.

A grumble comes from over my shoulder.

"I didn't mean to make you feel forced."

I snort, "You couldn't force me to do anything with you if you tried. Luckily for you, I think I might be a bit more of a heavyweight than before."

"Before?" his hand drops from mine. I can feel Sayah still behind me, watching the interaction. His sensitive eardrums I know are picking up every kick of my heart against my chest.

"When I was human," my vision clears up completely, my thoughts now much clearer. "I wasn't a lightweight by any means but this," I motion to the bottle with only a third of its contents remaining. "Is-was, a lot."

"I'm sure the muscle you've packed on in the past weeks has helped plenty," his eyes appreciatively run over my legs.

I smack his arm hard enough to knock him off balance.

"Guess we better figure out how to make something stronger," I grab his hand to continue leading us behind a small house.

"Are you sure?"

"Are you, coward?" I snark. His eyes flash in irritation. In one swift movement my back is against the wall. The bottle drops from my hands with a thud to the ground, allowing me to thread my fingers through his hair.

Chapter 40

There is nothing gentle or sweet about the way Mikhail's fingers slip under the flimsy material of my dress. Soft skin glides to the burning apex between my thighs.

"Still so ready even when that wild head of yours wants to kill me," his lips move in a feather-like way across the shell of my ear. I shiver at the path his hand leaves on along my thigh up to my hip. My head drops back in pleasure letting him have access to the soft skin of my neck.

I feel my nail beds burn briefly, the pain pulling me further into the oblivion I so badly want. He grabs a thigh and tugs firmly, hooking it around his waist.

"I have sleep to get," I curl my hand over his shoulder to press my talons into his back. "Make it quick."

"And since when did I want your demands when it came to this?" his other hand frees his swollen member from his pants. "Put your talons away."

I don't like the slight bit of defensiveness I hear in his voice.

I dig into his back angrily, "Since you decided to step onto my land."

We stare into each other's eyes, a stubbornness fueling both of us with wildfire. I feel the skin of his back start to give way underneath sharp points. In one swift movement he buries himself inside me.

"You're arrogant," he bites down on my shoulder after lashing his words at me. I slip one hand around the back of his head to bury his face into the crook of my neck, keeping the other one pressured against bunching muscles that hold me up against the wall. His pace is wild and harsh, meant for him to release the anger built up.

"I am," a moan slips out from me as the more sensitive part inside me is brushed against after he shifts the angle of my hips. "Because I have you begging for me."

"If it wasn't for keeping you pinned on this wall," his voice drops with bitter anger. "I'd correct that mouth of yours."

His pace picks up even more, forcing my shoulder blades to start bruising from being rocked into the wall behind me. I sink a small amount of the points in the muscle of his back. One powerful dig and I could have his heart screaming for mercy. He must notice it because his face shifts just enough I can catch it in the shadows. He's on edge, fully aware of the hold I have on his life right now. I feel myself become slicker where our bodies are joined at the realization.

My core shakes, then clamps down repeatedly before finally bringing me over the edge. Mikhail still moves, his hips rocking in jerky movements. I rip my hand from his back causing a hiss to spill from him. He pulls back from me, dropping my legs so I stand on my own. I watch Sayah - just out of ear shot with his back to us - sit down to wait for me.

I lean to Mikhail's ear, able to reach it since he's bending over from the shock of senses to his body.

"That, my friend, is for being so rude on the boat."

Not a word comes from his mouth. I smirk at the pain he feels in two separate parts of his body.

"You didn't even let me finish," he yells at me. I swear as I walk toward the gray dragon, I hear it laugh. Black talons shrink back into my body, the muscles in my forearm rolling as they're reabsorbed.

Sayah walks with me, his pace slow to keep from passing me. The rumbles of his paws against the ground comfort me. I look up to see him watching me.

"Don't judge, I'm allowed to have my play time," I rub his shoulder. It seems to push him off of staring me down.

Jakir knows through the Bond what I return from doing, though he does nothing but smile. His arm wraps around my shoulder offering me some vegetables from the large garden.

We watch the fire slowly fall asleep, its embers encouraging people to leave for sleep. Orange hair flashes in my eye as Jakir and I walk towards the house closest to the tree where we'd first slept. I catch Mikhail's glare while the man in front of me dips down through the door frame. A raised eyebrow is all I return before shutting the door behind me.

* * *

Sayah's nose flares to drag in the bitter air to his lungs. Next to him Senka completely stills, nearly convincing me she's stopped breathing. My sensitive hearing picks up her heartbeat just to check.

"They don't know we're here, so we have the element of surprise," I say to them all.

"Surprise will only go so far with people like them," Harlow's voice is bitterly short. Her blue eyes stare down the human men adjusting themselves in their pants. *"I still say we end them, all of them."*

"No," Jakir's voice is a calm for everyone. Even Mikhail, who stays further back behind the five of us, eases. *"Going in violent could risk the lives of the women they have captive. We try diplomacy first."*

I nod, then pull my body back down to its small frame. The sound of reshaping myself catches the attention of the group past the edge of the woods we currently hide in. Shouts ring out tinged with fear. Human men scramble to grab weapons, mostly ones with sharp edges. I flinch as the last of my dragon body disappears.

I grab the clothes we brought in a small bag to pull over myself. My top covers my chest, the tight leggings sitting low enough that the scars across my body catch the sunlight. Pulling on the black boots I turn to Jakir. His head comes down so I can rest mine between his eyes. Hot breath dances around my legs as he breathes.

"Not into the woods you idiots!"

That voice. A voice carved into my memories from nights of being strung up for carving. I pull on the strength of Jakir's support from our connection hoping it steels me enough to face him. My feet carry me past the massive large gray trees that emit such a bitter odor. Once past it, I feel the difference in the air shift to a more natural one.

If unclean men and blood could be considered natural.

"Holy shit boys," Kent drags on a cigarette. "I think somebody missed us."

I snap my gaze to him to take in the damage to his face. A scar drags raggedly across one eye, blinding him according to the gray color of his iris. Two of his fingers are missing on one hand, gnarled stumps replacing them. His free hand has to use a cane to support a mangled leg mostly hidden by his jeans.

It hits me very suddenly that this is Jakir's doing. Ever calm, never angry, meditative Jakir. I smirk at the damage done. Pride warms my chest at his capability.

"Bring her here!" Kent screams, spit flying from his mouth. I shove out my talons quickly in anticipation. My temples flare in warmth, fueling my eyes to glow brightly. The handful of men racing towards me skid to a halt. I feel my mind start to slip into a dark place, only to be controlled by Jakir's hold on my emotions. Invisible fingers wrap around the base of my spine, ready to choke out the red hot violence if necessary.

"Ah ah ah." I suck the back of my teeth. "I'll rip their throats out if they take one more step."

They wait, one of them looking back at Kent for his next commands. I watch the muscles in the man's neck strain as he swallows. Motion comes from another one of them, edging me to a point of almost begging for them to run at me.

"You heard what I said," Kent takes a step forward, his cane wobbling from his anger.

Clearly taking my words as a challenge, only one of them steps forward. His pocket knife is gripped tightly in his hand.

One more step, and I let go of the human part of myself.

His arm arcs out to cut me across the gut. I dodge it, feeling the brush of air scrape past my skin. In another move he manages to scrape my shoulder with the edge.

"Dragon bitch," he seethes.

"Human man," I throw back. I continue dodging him, trying to spot an in. Jacob was right, these humans are much faster, recovering just as quickly as they run. But speed does nothing against trained anger.

Slipping into his blind spot I drive my hand into the back of his neck, cutting his spinal cord. Gurgling comes out his mouth in an attempt to scream. I rip my hand away, spin him to face me, only to dig my claws through his throat so far they stick out the other side of his trachea.

Sloppy noises that sound like suction cups being removed fill the silence between myself and Kent. I yank as hard as possible, bringing the chunk of throat with me. My stare matches Kent's as the body sways, then drops to the ground. I feel my lips tug uncontrolled into a wild grin at his face making a poor attempt to hide the horror.

"I knew you were a freak," another one of the men in front of me goes to step forward. I don't move as Jakir steadies me. His disappointment in the blood doesn't bother me, though I feel his protective tendency leap out. The man stops suddenly, spotting what's causing the ground to rumble behind me.

"Son of a bitch," another mumbles, stumbling back. Gold takes up the majority of my left peripheral vision. I don't move as dark gray scales move like water next to me.

"What do ya' want, then?" the half blind man says, the twang in his voice irking me.

"You have prisoners, I want them," I shrug casually.

His lips pull into a sneer at me, "Why would I let go more of my women when you already slipped through my fingers. If you had stayed I wouldn't have had ta' find more."

Guilt pulls my mind back into a shadowed corner, huddling down for safety. Perhaps staying would have kept them interested enough that they wouldn't find more. I process through all the possibilities of how I could have prevented them trapping more women. Every inch of violence that Jakir has a hold on in me starts to fight to be let out. I feel myself warring on whether or not I should kill him for insulting me. I struggle against the shame and guilt of being the one to survive, the one to get out of Kent's hold. I have a family, these girls have fear.

Jakir fights back, his heart rate picking up as his side of the Bond starts to beat back the urge to spill more blood. Finally I manage to pull out the words I want.

"Don't make us kill anyone else, Kent," my voice is saccharine sweet. "Either you give me every last one of the people you have captive, or I let my little Nightmares shred you."

Both of the twin's growl in response. It's a low noise that carries on with promise.

"And I get what in return?" his eyes watch them carefully, still speaking to me. I feel my hold on Senka start to slip as her craving for a fight increases tenfold.

"Your life, and the lives of your little bandwagon."

He considers it, taking too long so I speak again.

"Why have you been sitting outside of my territory, Kent?" I tilt my head to the side. His demeanor is shifting, becoming nervous. "We have laws now, us dragons. Laws that give me every right to kill you for threatening us."

"I don't abide by y'all's stupid laws, I'm not some ungodly creation," he shouts at me, trying to mask his nerves.

Both of the twins snap their teeth together at him, telling me their patience is getting too thin. I look up at the sky to take a deep breath in, almost choking on the stench of men.

"Fun fact, Kent, you're the minority now. I know your puny little man brain has trouble understanding that so let me explain," I take a few steps forward. Sayah and Senka step with me. "These 'ungodly creations' behind me barely scratch the surface of the amount of us in the world now. Which means you don't run this show. Not anymore. One word to let them go is all it takes. I will have every single one of these little

426

groupies slaughtered and leave you as my fun little toy to bring home and string up. You might be stronger as a human now, but you're at the bottom of the food chain now my friend."

His jaw works as the wheels in his head turn. Looking like he might snap back, Sayah opens his mouth in a warning growl, saliva dripping from his mouth.

"Take them, and don't come here again."

"I won't need to, as long as you don't pick up any more women against their will."

"That's none of your concern."

I move through his people with two gray dragons following me. Senka moves past me to start sniffing at their tents. I stop as I reach Kent's side.

"It will be, if you do it again. And next time, I won't ask," my eyes glow at him. I start to feel the cracking of bones as my body threatens a shift. With combined control from both Jakir and I, I manage to stop it before it gets too far. The painfully human man steps back, immediately putting distance between us so that Sayah can stay next to me as we walk.

A rolling noise comes from Senka, who's standing by the tent that reeks the most of human filth. I reach, pushing back the curtain to reveal more women than there should be in this size of accommodations. Each one reacts differently, most flinching back away from the now open flap. Restraints that have clearly created deep injuries keep them all bound by wrists and ankles. Their clothes, those lucky enough to have them, are torn and dirty. Some caked in blood, others in their own bodily fluids.

One gets on her knees, seeming to protect the rest of those behind her. I watch her keeping my own face emotionless.

"Who the fuck are you," she croaks out.

"The person who just negotiated your release, can you all walk?"

"We don't know you," she spits on the ground, her dark blue eyes burning with hatred.

Senka nudges me to the side, wanting to peer into the tents. I notice her breathing is halted as she looks around.

Screams from the women have my ears ringing. I gently guide Senka's head away from being between myself and them. She huffs out a breath as she rises to her full height.

"Give me the key," I demand of the nearest person. Face full of disgust he hands me a single key. "I hope this unlocks every single one of them because if it doesn't I'm feeding you to her," I point at Senka.

"Them first, they can walk but just barely," the appointed leader states firmly. She ushers a few women forward who have to crawl on their hands and knees to get out of the tent. One by one I unlock the chains binding their feet and ankles. Hesitantly they move to stand between the Nightmares who have formed an area to protect them. Only the last one remains.

"I suppose you're going to be the person they listen to?" I ask her as I undo her bindings. Like all the others before her she doesn't even rub at the skin because of how open and infected it is.

"Maybe."

"Look," I sigh. "We're going to take you all back, restraint free, and get you cleaned up. After you've had a few days of rest you can decide what to do from there."

"How can we trust someone who might be trapping us?"

"You can't, really. But I can promise you that if you think you'll survive a single day without getting caught or killed by these people," I gesture widely to the men boring holes into my back. "You're either stupid or stubborn."

She looks from me to the large group of women huddled together. They look pitiful the way they stand, surrounded by gray bodies more powerful than they realize.

I can tell the humans are getting antsy while she considers their options. I step forward, ignoring the smell of urine that stings my nostrils.

"I'm fully aware of your fear. Kent had me too, gave me these scars after I killed three of his men. I was petrified when I woke up to my Sekund having rescued me. It takes time to heal from this, I still haven't from my own experience. But risking the lives of twenty-something women who cannot fend for themselves right now will leave a mark on your conscience you will never recover from. Make whatever decision you'd like, but make it now."

"Fine, what do we do?"

"I just need them to get on our backs."

"Our, you're..."

"Correct, I just needed to be able to speak stupid to smooth brain over there."

I swear I see her lips twitch at my name calling.

"Are they okay with flying on males? That gray one," I point to Senka. "And the blue one are female. The others are male."

She speaks with them softly, asking who is comfortable enough to ride on the gray, gold, or red dragon behind me. Only ten are willing, so we divide them to be carried then ease them up into the riding dips. Situated so they don't fall I send Jakir, Mikhail, and Sayah to begin to journey back.

"Your name?" I ask her as she lifts another person onto Harlow. I watch awe on the face of them as they nervously touch the rich blue scales.

Her curly black hair is matted, but she pushes it out of her face. Her nose has a graceful curve to it that I note as she turns to the side.

"Oriana, it's Oriana now."

I nearly ask if it wasn't her name before but decide against it for now.

"Oriana," the name rolls off my tongue delicately. "My name is Kali."

She doesn't shake the hand outstretched to her. I smile as I drop it, understanding her unease at physical touch currently. The last six follow, led by Senka with four already on her back. They have to hug each other to fit in the smaller space. I watch carefully as the five on Harlow's back yelp in surprise as she lifts from the ground.

"That forest smells hideous," Oriana says, wrinkling her nose in distaste.

"That's because it's constantly rotting or dead." I shuck off my clothes as Senka watches my back. Oriana's dark brown eyes take in every one of my scars. I feel a sense of gratitude for having them now. Being able to show that none of them are alone in this brings me a twisted sort of relief.

"If you ever miss it, darlin'," I clench my jaw at Kent's jab. "I'll have my knife and cock waiting for you."

I spin around, body completely on display. Only for a moment is he able to greedily take in my body before it begins cracking and stretching. My bones ache with a pain that eases my vexation at him. Continuing the walk towards him my vision starts to lift from being just below his, to finally standing well over him. Horror, true undiluted horror, pushes his body back until he falls on his rear. I lower my snout until it's hanging over his prone form.

I feel my saliva glands work over time as I crack open my mouth. Teeth too long to fit expose the dripping wetness. I let a dribble of it slowly come off my tongue to fall onto his chest. A low rumble climbs up through my neck to blow hot air across his face.

"*Pathetic,*" I say, only Senka around to hear me. She lifts up Oriana and the other five women onto my back. Being the weakest out of the group it takes much more care and effort to situate them so they won't fall out. Simultaneously the female twin and I push off from the ground to carry the survivors back over the Dead Forest. The entirety of the flight I hear Oriana comforting the others, telling them that she wouldn't let anything happen ever again. I smell the stench of more than just blood and urine. The scent of what was done to them is so strong I nearly hurl stomach acid onto the forest far below me.

"*I smell it too,*" Senka says. "*Smelled it on every single one that came out of the tent. I think some might have been from this morning.*"

I bite back the urge to snap my teeth, knowing sudden noises like it could scare them. Ellie is already running around mothering the women as much as they'll let her. People are moving out of the homes built to make room for the newcomers. My stress levels lower knowing that the people I've brought home are so accommodating. I wait until all of the riders on me and Senka are on solid ground. Senka remains in form, sticking around to keep an eye on everyone.

"Did you ever consider how many mouths we have to feed now?" Ellie scolds as she throws clothes at me.

"Did you ever consider how many people I have to build an army with?" I toss back at her. The attitude doesn't work well because she stretches up to lightly smack me on the back of my head.

"You better find another herd of bison, or some kind of meat source. Not enough calves have been born to keep up with this."

"I'll figure it out Ellie," I grasp her hand. "I appreciate your kindness to them."

"They've done nothing to deserve otherwise, you're the brainless one," she scowls playfully. I give her a wide grin before walking over to address Oriana.

Not a single woman has entered one of the houses cleared out for them. All of the men but Jakir have been ushered away to begin helping the tasks required to expand our supplies and capabilities.

"And who are you?" Oriana's arms are crossed, her stance defensive as she tilts her head back to look at Jakir. He remains passive, keeping his arms down and palms open towards her.

"My name is Jakir, I was the gold colored dragon you saw at the campsite. I'm Kali's Sekund."

"That's not a real word."

"It is, it's just from another language. You can consider me her right hand."

"Why would she choose a man?"

"We didn't exactly have a say in the matter," his smile is kind though it does nothing to ease her tension.

"He'll leave you alone if you ask," I step into the conversation with ease. "He only wants to help."

"And how can I believe that?" she snaps at me. The women behind her shift together, standing so close they move as one.

"Because he found me the same way I found you."

Our eyes meet, her proud nose tilts up as she looks through me. It must be sincere enough because she finally drops her arms.

"He can be around, no one else. They need food first, then a bath, then clothes."

Harlow walks up with Aiza in tow behind her, "Can the food wait? It's cooking currently and the bison takes a while to be done."

Oriana twists to get confirmation from the rest, all of them agreeing to a bath first. They hesitate at the idea of being nude in front of so many people once they reach the water.

"Squeeze these and they'll produce soap," Aiza empties a bag of the red pinecone shaped plants onto the shore. "Senka will lay here to shield you from the men."

"We can too," Theri and Laura walk up, beginning to pull off their clothes. I nod my thanks.

"This is Theri and Laura," I introduce them. "They came with me from another continent."

"She saved us, is more like it," Laura corrects me. I grimace at the idea of being some kind of hero. "Otherwise Konge Mikhail would have had us killed."

"I'm learning to dislike him more and more," Oriana's face becomes one of distaste. It falls away into a matching one of awe as Laura shifts into a pale green color, nothing like the vibrant purple color of her wife. With Senka, they lay down to form a long wall tall enough to offer privacy to those bathing. I shed my own clothing, needing a bath myself.

Harlow helps other women from the collection of rogues to pick up the shredding pieces of clothing no longer usable. As suds build up in the water more clothing is brought for each person to sort through. I catch a few scars on some bodies, most of them bruised more than anything else.

Oriana stays close to the handful of women who aren't comfortable enough to go near anybody else. Their fear of any sudden noise fuels a low burning fire in me. Jakir feels the simmering anger though he remains on the other side of Senka. His soothing calmness brings my body to a point of being able to move freely rather than remain frozen. We communicate with emotion as I scrub off the oily feeling from my skin that had accumulated while being around Kent. The combination of the cool water and distraction of monitoring the survivors cleanses me.

Oriana shows the others it's safe by walking out first, hesitantly drying off with the offered towel, then picking up a warm pair of leggings and a sweatshirt.

I watch the other twenty four frail humans repeat her motions. They do the same as they're split up into the now empty homes. With food brought to them by only the women in the Samle, I finally settle in a small circle with the closest of my people. Other circles have various volumes of conversation while people eat at the dripping meat and cooked vegetables.

"There's another large herd north, towards the mountains," Jacob wipes the fat dripping down his chin. "Filo and I can go get them, bring them here."

"Is there another somewhere?" I ask. Feathers flits over to peck at my ear. I hand him bits of my food, letting him eat while sitting on my shoulder.

"There is, you want them too?"

I shake my head, "Not until we know it won't drain their numbers. Filo you'll take a few new people from the other continent with you," he nods as he hands Lilly a small piece of meat to chew. "Jacob you can take some with you to go get more seeds for Ellie."

"You're not going?" Jakir elbows me gently.

I shake my head again, "I've had enough traveling, there's things I need to take care of here."

Jacob gets distracted annoying Harlow by flirting with her. She rolls her eyes at his attempt to convince her to take a bath with him in the lake.

"My love, the water might get too cold soon we have to take one now," he begs.

"Actually that water hasn't gotten any cooler or warmer in the past couple months," Aiza tugs her blanket around her shoulders at the bitter winds that rushes through.

Jacob gives her an annoyed look, "You're not helping me get laid here, Aiza."

"Like I would ever help you with that," her lips pull down.

"Aiz come on, learn to give to charity," I watch her face fight back a laugh.

"The only charity Jake needs is for his height," Harlow's silky blond hair covers Jacob's face as she kisses him on the head. His cheeks flush red at the affection.

"My height is perfectly fine, you're the odd ones," he points at Jakir, who only shrugs.

Chapter 41

I watch two forms fly south, heading towards the Whisper's Samle to request the presence of Linius and then south to retrieve Janét.

"I could have done that," Mikhail's smooth voice makes the muscles in my neck tense up.

"Could you? Sure. Would I accept it?"

"Of course you would," his face becomes overly confident with his smile.

"You stand corrected," I frown at him, bored of the conversation.

"Why do I feel like we're fighting yet there hasn't been an argument between us in weeks? Or any other satisfying interaction," his fingers brush a strand of brown hair behind one of my ears.

I smack his hand away from me, "Because I haven't had a need for it since then."

"Finding it elsewhere?" he follows me as I walk through the newest section of houses. These are homes that will have at least three bedrooms in them, rather than the one or two in the houses closest to the manor. "Perhaps from-?"

I swing around, bringing my fist with me. My knuckles collide with his jaw hard enough to send a wave of pain ricocheting down my arm. Red talons rip through his hands, matched by my own black ones extending out. I feel the suitor attraction whip out angrily. It's desperate for another fight.

A handful of people move towards us, one of them is Harlow who looks ready to kill.

"Unnecessary and disrespectful," Mikhail seethes. His hand darts out to wrap around my throat. My body is sluggish having only trained a few times since returning, but the intense lessons from Dimitri return quickly.

"You're lucky you stopped before you finished that sentence," I slam my fist against his face two more times, just as his claws pull red from my bicep. "I promised I'd rip out your tongue the next time you did that."

His foot lands in my gut, only to be removed immediately. His body slams into the dirt as Harlow buries her shoulder into his stomach. A deep sound reverberates from the ground at his rough landing. He struggles against her but stops once he realizes that she's the same size.

I tilt my chin up, looking down at him while fighting the urge to curl my lip up at him. I allow myself to watch the pure force of her make Mikhail struggle for air for a moment before calling her off. His face has streaks of soil and his hair is tousled into tangles.

"Enough, Harlow," I blandly say. Jakir's body heat warms my back in the frigid air. The Bond thrums as he checks it to make sure I've not been injured. With an invisible hand I brush against his mind gently.

"You should apologize, in fact I recommend it, Konge Mikhail," Jakir's thick voice permeates the tension in the air. Mikhail's people cluster behind him facing my own, ready to defend their Konge. "It's uncouth to disrespect a Dronning on her own land, punishable by temporary imprisonment if I recall the laws recently created."

Mikhail pulls his talons back in to wipe the blood from his face. It only serves to smear into the dark lines of dirt also on his pale skin. He stares down Jakir, then looks at me with a cold steel in his eyes. My own warm in a dare to him to take another swing at me – physical or verbal. Keeping my nose higher in the air than normal, I tilt my head as I wait for him to speak.

"My," he breathes in. "Apologies, Dronning Kali."

My title is bitter in his mouth. I simply raise an eyebrow before turning away to face the twins directly behind me. Both of them are in their scaled forms – they seem to be more comfortable in them lately.

"Bring me Brawn and Ellie, I have things for them to do," I ask Jakir.

He nods, turning to fetch them from the construction of the new homes. The Nightmares follow me closely, refusing to leave my side. I attempt dismissing them firmly, only to be ignored with a click of teeth. I sigh, making my way towards the manor, the surface level nearly finished. Ellie meets with me briefly to update me on the process of pregnant bison. She runs off again, unable to spend much time away from her duties.

The outside walls are complete since the entirety of the inside has been framed out and lined. Long curved hallways and stairs give way to massive rooms that will become bedrooms, an office, even a kitchen. Somehow Jacob had figured out during the weeks of building the framework how to combine the use of trees from the Dead Forest, which could never catch fire. Useful considering a few dragons had accidentally lost control of their own fire during training.

"Kali," Brawn catches up to me as I make my way down the longest part of the house. "You asked for me?"

"I appreciate your time; I need to ask a favor."

"Anything," he shoves his glasses back up his nose.

"How long would it take you to become familiar with herbal medicine?" I walk through an entryway made of stone from the walls on the northern shore. Glassy black rock glimmers in the sunlight, brought here by Harlow's direction. Those that went with her to retrieve it still speak of how odd the parallel walls were.

"Maybe a day or two to get the basics, about four or five to be confident enough to administer it to people. Why?"

"Because we have no one who understands medicine, and the women I brought here aren't recovering fast enough," I drag my hand across the wall as he follows me into the courtyard already primed to hold various flowers and trees for Ellie. Sayah lands at the other end of the courtyard, curling up to rest in the sun. I catch Senka flying in circles high above. "One of the wings of this place will have a large enough space for you to use as a lab. For now, you'll have to make do with the house you have."

"I, I don't know w-w-what to say. You don't have to," his eyes flit around, clearly uncomfortable with eye contact I attempt.

I wave his words off, "I do actually. In exchange for the lab, you'll study medicine as well as dragons. I want to know everything there is about us. How long will we live? What's our health like? Our weaknesses? I want everything, and then some. I want to know more than the other Samle's."

He calms, already running through my questions in his head.

"That," he smiles, looking at Sayah picking at a talon with his teeth. "Is a fair trade, I think."

We walk together through the wing that stretches out from the main building towards the west. Adding sections had practically doubled the original size. None of it bothered Jacob, only increasing his energy for planning out what sections would be for. Through the rest of our meeting, we speak about the questions needing answers along with how Brawn would find said answers. He eventually leaves to begin the long road of studying. I return to the courtyard to sit on a bench near Sayah's form. His scales are warm to the touch, cooling due to the dropping sun. Jakir joins me quietly situating himself behind me so I'm nestled between his massive thighs.

I drop my head back against his chest. His breathing is slow but deep.

"I can feel your mind racing even without the Bond, talk to me beautiful," he whispers.

My words feel like they tumble out of my mouth uncontrollably. Every thought running through my mind comes out before I finally reach what I'm truly wrapped up in.

"Linius and Janét should be here soon, I want more than just a one time meeting between us all. We need allies - soon. There's this bad feeling in my gut about Gallyan and the others."

"How bad is this feeling?" his fingers play with my hair that brushes over my waist. It's become thin and brittle at the ends from growing uncared for for so long.

"The kind of bad that tells me he meant what he said. He wants me, wants control over me."

"He could have anyone else, why you?"

I shrug a shoulder, "He saw my dragon form, so he knows I'm not on the small side. I'm convinced he wants me as a symbol of power. He wants the Nightmares back under his hand where he had them before. It would tell everyone else that he can have anything he wants."

Sayah stirs sharply, his lips pulling back to show his grayish teeth. I put out a hand palm down to motion to him to calm down. He does so reluctantly despite the memories I know that are crashing down on him.

"You believe we can trust Janét and Linius?"

"I do, I'd ask Elias too, but he's got Gallyan and Sean eyeing his every move," I recall the quiet conversation before he left, warning me to only send for him in dire need. Otherwise, I was to go to him. "So, for now, we invite those two. Aiza wants the alliance to be made stronger."

"Wise of you to listen to her," he chuckles. It makes his chest rumble against the back of my head. I smile faintly at the feeling of warm happiness spilling into the golden cord connecting us.

"Am I doing it right?"

His fingers continue to play with my hair, prickling my scalp in a relaxing way.

"Doing what right?"

"This dragon bullshit-"

"Language."

"With all the leading and being a *Dronning*, the protecting and providing. I'm not even doing half of it honestly. Ellie and Harlow, Filo and Jacob, Aiza and you, the twins, you're all taking care of things while I'm sitting here doing these menial tasks yet just demanding more every day."

"You're building a future Kali. It's called delegation, it's what good leaders do. You'd be horrible if you tried to do it all yourself. Jacob understands how to plan and construct buildings because of his past. Aiza learned from her experience as a human. You got lucky with these people, I think it's karma for having come so late into this world."

"Karma also must have felt bad about killing my family," I mutter. I don't feel the usual pang of sadness at the memory of their dead bodies in so long. "Or maybe it feels guilty about letting Kent play surgeon on my body."

439

His arm tightens around my torso in response, calm slithering over my own angry feelings. I allow it to control the flare of it all. His emotions are so sure, so firm against my own that run rampant in my own body.

"I think you want karma to be sentient enough to do so."

"I want someone else to suffer like I do."

"You don't need to do anything for that to happen, their time will come." He pauses, slowly taking a deep breath. "People like the twins have suffered in ways similar to you. I think that's one of the reasons why those like the twins feel so drawn to you. We've practically collected the outcasts of every society, and yet each one has a talent that benefits this samle."

"I get it I get it," I groan, covering my face. "I should be grateful for all the talent and skill my people have."

"No, well yes," Jakir's hands engulf mine, pulling them down to my chest. "I'm more trying to convince you of why you shouldn't be so focused on your past. It brought you to me. For that, I am grateful."

I peel open an eye to look at his golden ones hanging above me. They catch the gleam of the moon and stars above us. Slight glowing brightens their color into molten gold. His forehead comes down to touch mine sweetly. I bathe in the heat from his body, forgetting how cold the temperature is.

A small spot of cold touches my skin, warming immediately after it reaches my senses.

"What was that?" I pick my head up, automatically putting my hands out in front of me. Humor flits from Jakir. "What are you laughing at?"

He throws his hands up in mock defense, "I didn't say a word."

I poked his abdominal muscles, "I can feel you holding it back."

Another biting sensation touches my nose. My eyes cross as I try to see what it is. Suddenly it clicks what's happening.

"Oh my god," I stand suddenly. Sayah tilts his head at me. "It's snowing. This is snow?"

Flurries come down at an increasing pace around us. Sayah's gray scales become wet as the snow melts on his heated body. He rolls his tongue out to catch a few.

"Have you not seen snow before?" Jakir asks, standing up to be next to me.

"I have, when I traveled with my family," that's the second time tonight I remember the human family I once had. "But I wasn't sure it would be cold enough to snow here."

"Our perception of what is cold, I believe, is different now. Probably below forty out here, if not colder."

"Brawn is probably already asking people questions-"

"I already did actually," Brawn walks back into the courtyard with a notepad in hand. "Already had the question down about why it would be winter, and people wouldn't feel the need for warmer clothing. Started snowing, I realized that our body temperature is most likely much higher than it was as humans."

I don't even question his words, unable to deny the snow falling onto my skin that immediately melts. Jakir and I make our way down a roughly carved path towards the growing cluster of houses down below, where Brawn begins discussing the layout of them.

"They're too easy, eventually this will grow into a city. Barring any awful attacks where we're slaughtered, and our home is destroyed."

I turn my head to him, giving him a look that questions his sanity. He simply looks at me, smooths his hand over his coarse short hair.

"Out with it Brawn, just tell me what we should do?"

"You can leave the current design, the two winding roads that curve through the houses. But everything else? Expect the worst. Design so if we were to be attacked, we'd have every chance to slow them down or stop them before reaching the manor."

"You're assuming the manor would be the highest point of the city. I'm sure plenty of the city will eventually be built behind us."

"It makes sense that it would be. But the Manor is where you, the Dronning, and your court will reside. Putting you at the highest point is not only expected from nearly everyone but symbolic. We would just mandate that nothing taller be built behind it so we can maintain visuals."

441

"Symbolic of what, exactly?" Jakir picks up materials as we pass to add fuel to the large bonfire. Harlow and Jacob invite us over with a wave of their hands. Ellie sits between Filo's legs, watching Lilly play tag with Danni around the fire. I catch Theri's ice blue eyes catch mine, the beauty of them against her dark skin throwing me off for a second.

I hear Brawn explaining the importance of my home being at the center of our territory, using the drone of his voice to enjoy the relaxed air around me. Mikhail wisely stays with his own people only looking to me to nod is a pathetic attempt at an apology.

"If we're going to make the layout of the city that complicated I'll need you to do most of that," Jacob leans into Brawn, a bit intoxicated from the liquor in his hands. "But we can do it. Good thing you said it early enough."

Brawn chuckles but leans back to maintain his own space. Harlow pulls her Suitor back to enforce some breathing space.

"We'll be fine with as many additions to the herd we have now, Filo found some wild pigs towards the south, a few cows," Ellie catches my attention. I watch Filo start to pull away from being wrapped around her. I place my hand on his, shaking my head with a smile. He looks between me and Ellie, who's still watching the girls play. "I just have to ration out food until the breeding season is done."

"Fine, I trust you to handle it."

"I know, but you also have a responsibility to know what's going on," she looks at me pointedly.

"Mmm."

I lean into the daily reports from each of those close to me, Jacob and

Brawn work closely to plan out the city. They show me the additional plans I request for security.

"This goes nowhere. I'll pick who builds it. I decide who knows about it."

Jacob clears his throat, "Harlow-"

"Will know nothing," I finish. "Us alone. No one else."

They look at me, to each other, then again at me. That ends the conversation. I pull away, pulling on a light jacket to protect me from the biting wind. A snow storm is near, causing the everyday flurries of falling snowflakes to begin morphing into sheets of ice layering the ground in white blankets.

In my chest, a shift occurs. Like a strange breath that wasn't quite full enough to satiate my lungs. Instinctively, I know something has come into my territory. I take in a physical breath to alleviate the pressure in my chest. Jakir looks over at me from lowering a piece of granite into the manor from the ceiling. His head swivels to me, eyes catching me every time his wings flap. Clicking his teeth, he motions to Harlow that the piece of rock is in place.

Snow escapes his body as he lands. White winds blow my hair back over my shoulders. Cracking sounds until his body is back to being covered in rich dark skin.

"They're here, give it a couple days and they'll be in the vicinity."

"I felt it too," Jakir brushes a hand across my neck. "You seem excited."

"I mean, once you see Janét you'll understand why. Woman is *every* reason to hop into bed with her."

He cringes, "I don't need to know your plans ahead of time to bed her, love."

"Again. To bed her again."

He chokes a bit on the water he was sipping down. I bite down on my lip to avoid laughing at him. A withering look repeats itself at the later comments from the Nightmares on whether or not I'll need "a private moment" with the Dronning when she arrives.

Just as the snow storm begins to hit the ceiling on the massive building meant to be the center of it all is finished. Jakir and Harlow had worked tirelessly to place multiple pieces of granite too large for humans to carry into various rooms. I never receive an answer from Jacob as to what they are for. On my last try, he forbids me from going inside until it's done.

Mikhail eventually returns to working next to me each day, getting over the shame of being pummeled into the ground.

"Would you mind keeping your tongue in check while Janét and Linius are here?" I ask him.

"Yeah, don't ruin her chances of getting laid again by a real adventure," Senka teases him. I balk at Mikhail's reaction.

"What?" his voice drops, guiding me away so his body hides me. I look around him to see Aiza patiently looking to the south.

"What are you asking about?"

"What did Senka mean by that?"

"I'm not sure what you find confusing, Konge Mikhail," I use the title hoping it will distract him.

"Oh there's nothing confusing about it, kitten," his fingers brush my hair from my face. "I just want to know why you decided to sleep with someone else in my own damn castle."

"You weren't exactly playing nice."

"You just don't know how to play with me," his fingers grip my chin harshly. I reach up to wrap my own around his wrist.

"Actually, she just knows how to play my *game* a lot better."

"Not nearly as satisfying as with me, I'm sure," his eyes search my face for a sign of weakness.

"Sure, if doing chores is supposed to be satisfying."

"Bitch," he seethes.

"Careful Mikhail," I peel his fingers away by twisting his wrist violently. "Your jealousy is showing."

Brushing past him I reach Aiza's side. Looking over at Mikhail I watch him slowly stalk towards me, an anger echoing in every step he takes until standing some distance beside me.

"Where's Filo?" I ask her.

She frowns, "I actually haven't seen him today, must be taking a while to take down some more trees from the forest."

I shrug, glancing at Mikhail one last time.

His gaze gets pulled to Senka, who grins at him wildly. To others he looks calm. I don't miss the bit of uncertainty that pulls at his lips.

A pale green dragon, its scales tipped with pale blue as though they'd individually dipped into a bucket of paint, lands with grace. Its eyes tell me who it is before they pull down into a human form.

I eye the curves and full stomach of Janét before she slips on clothing. Her hips sway, teasing me until I look into her brown eyes. I see Linius shifting down from his burnt orange form, nodding at him once.

"Kali," Janét purrs. "I know this is diplomatic but it's hard to think you aren't asking for more by calling me here."

"I know exactly what my face is telling you," I step forward, brushing my lips against her cheek. I place my mouth next to her ear as I speak again. "There's enough room in housing for you to sleep elsewhere, but the invitation to my own bed remains open."

"It would be my pleasure, Dronning Kali," her red painted lips curve into a wicked smile that has my thighs tensing. We pull away so I can greet Linius.

"Kali," his eyes narrow as he smiles faintly. I take in his form, trying to gain an idea of his current mood. "I appreciate the invitation, and I'm honored to be so warmly welcomed into your home."

"As an ally, you're both always welcome here, for any reason."

"And as our ally as well, the Whisper's Samle always welcomes you," Linius dips his chin in respect.

"Well," I clasp my hands together. "Let me show you your accommodations for the time being."

Chapter 42

"Try to convince him to ease up," I tell Ellie. Her face is slightly twisted with concern about how busy Filo had been recently. "He's worried, which I understand, but he shouldn't be out there for that long."

"I'll try, but he's really concerned about Addison pressing in, or even the Skin Carvers," Ellie rings her hands, looking off behind me where her Suitor sits.

"The who?" I ask.

She flicks a hand at me, "Heard the women calling them that."

"I can try as well, let him know things are going smoothly for now," Aiza offers, trying to ease the tension in Ellie's shoulders.

They both nod, returning to tend to the greatly expanded farm that's only surviving due to the large fires encompassing it, as well as some new vegetables clearly not affected by the weather. Some of the women from the group brought here weeks ago bathe in the waters again. Every morning since recovery they'd demanded lessons on fighting, combat, and survival. Harlow, Senka, with a few female rogues had taken up the chore without hesitation. I watch from a few yards away, enjoying the progress they'd all made so quickly.

Noticing my glance, Oriana dries off and walks to me. Her body is muscular now, nearing one that demands respect from anyone who gazes at her. A few other women notice me, waving shyly. I return the gesture with a genuine smile.

"Everything alright?" she asks, stopping to look between me and my point of focus.

"Better than, I'm glad you all have begun to heal."

She places a hand on my shoulder, the physical touch from her makes me want to fall to my knees. Such a difference from the frail, frightened woman covering up her trauma weeks ago. I feel blessed to be trusted enough by her that she trusts me. Not wanting it to end, I say nothing of it.

"We finished healing a while ago, physically. It's the mind we're strengthening now. Never again will I let them be forced into that position."

"Do you have everything you need?"

"Mostly, though we'd like to have a few words with the Gem Samles' Dronning," she looks back to Janét who's offering advice to people decorating the houses.

"May I ask why?"

"No," she looks at her, more analyzing rather than sexually. "But we've spoken. We'd like to see you at our morning practices."

I breathe in through my nose, considering the early mornings they have.

"I'd enjoy that."

She nods, dropping her hand, and returns to the women now completely dressed. A flash in the water, much closer to the other side of the lake, catches my eye. I walk towards the shore hoping to see if the fish from further north have traveled towards this end. Strange ripples pulsate from the source of the original motion. I narrow my eyes at it, suspicious of how strange the movement was. Another movement, much farther under the surface.

While fish scales would catch the sunlight, I notice this looks to have its own light source. There is nothing reflecting. Instead it emanates from whatever is moving.

"What are you looking at?" Janét stops beside me, her arm brushing against mine.

"I thought I saw something in the water. It looked like light," I respond, still watching to see if I can catch the form again.

447

"I don't see anything," she squints out at the water, her long black lashes nearly brushing her cheek. "Maybe it's an animal we haven't seen yet. My people still find new species every week in the surrounding rain forests. We found a type of alligator with shark skin just the other day."

I turn to her, surprised by her story.

"I swear," her accent is thicker than I remember in Mikhail's castle. "The birds are twice the size they were before. But the leaves, oh the leaves, everything is greener. The forest thrives now."

"I'm sure not having nearly as many humans on the planet to ruin it all helps."

"I'd have to agree," she chuckles. Her hand wraps around my bicep, letting me lead her back to the long table surrounded by the others.

Filo ceases the conversation with Linius to acknowledge my arrival into the grand hall. I bend a leg up in front of me to rest it on the table. My other thigh leans against the thick gray wood. The smell of rot finally disappeared a time ago, allowing Jacob to find a way to seal it. It hadn't moved from the spot he built it at until just before the ceilings on the manor had been closed up. Jakir managed to move it himself, with a bit of help from me to guide it. Being nearly twenty-four feet long made it awkward to place.

"I was just discussing your border protection with Filo," Linius ceases all conversation by speaking up. Such a deep tenor demanded attention from everyone. His fingers sweep through his short jet-black hair that falls heavily over one side of his forehead.

"It's lacking, but so are my numbers," I cross my arms.

"Not quite. I've drawn out various sections that you could assign to three or four dragons at a time," he pushes a rough map of the territory towards me. I scan over it to get the gist of the three sections. "You'll see I left only two to guard the southern tip."

"I'm assuming the large section you left open is facing your land?" Jakir adds in.

Linius leans on the table while staring down the map, "It faces towards us, but this large section," he circles an area pinched between the peninsula of mine that stretches down south and the eastern side of his. "Is unclaimed. I tried to push into it, but it wasn't right."

"I don't think anybody would care if you took it, morals don't really apply here," Harlow shrugs.

"They very much do," Aiza looks disappointed at the warrior blonde. "But I don't think that is what he's saying."

"It's not, we've had our moments in the Gem Samle with the same feeling," Janét sighs. "But it usually happens in caves."

"There's something *wrong* about the land. It's like stepping into a bubble of air that doesn't want to be breathed in," his dark eyes look up to me. I tighten my lips at his words. "I sent a few of my own into it, only for every single person to come back as if they'd seen ghosts."

"Maybe they did," Jacob looks excited at the prospect. I shake my head at him.

"No, they saw nothing but untouched perfect land. It's what they felt. Said the place pushed them with their own fear, made them more fearful for every step they took."

I stare down at the lines drawn around the expansive area, burning to know what the land holds.

"I'd send my own," I start.

"But you don't have the people, you need to focus on protecting your borders first, Dronning Kali," Linius pulls us all back into the conversation. I turn to see Mikhail walking towards us. He hesitates for a moment at the death glare the twins serve him. I jerk my head to motion him over without bothering to pull the chain on the Nightmares.

"Scouting your borders?" he asks, his fiery hair falling over his shoulder as he leans forward to look at the detailed map.

"Protecting them, you should have interest in doing so as well if you'd like to continue boasting about being her first ally," the Whisper's Konge stares down Mikhail with such power I nearly giggle at the rush it gives me. Biting back the inappropriate response I continue talking.

"There are some people I brought with me that were part of the rogues surviving out in the land, I'll ask who all would like to volunteer."

"I've already heard some who wish to live out on their own, they're just as trained as anyone else here," Harlow shifts her weight to motion to a few groups standing on their own. I see the handful of trios sitting alone to work on their chores. "We can ask, but I assure you they want nothing more than to live alone."

"Is there something lacking here for them?" I ask, worried I've missed something. "Is it those who aren't naturally my own?"

"Surprisingly it's those who are, they just want peace."

"You've done everything right, Kali," Jakir eases the worry in me. "What's happened to this world affects everyone differently."

"I've had a few dragons do the same, who now live on my borders. Most of the time, they were too afraid of insulting me to ask," Linius places a notebook in front of me. "I've done the grunt work of asking who would like to leave to live along the fringes."

I look over the paper, finding four groups of either three or four. Inhaling a steadying breath I nod at Filo, who seems more comfortable than any other time I had known him. He squares his shoulders, knowing what I'm about to ask before I do.

"You've seen nearly every inch of our borders, yes?" I toss the notebook to him. He nods, sure of himself. "Then I'd like to ask you to be my Head of Guard." I feel those around me still unsure of my next move save for Jakir. "I can't be caught up in worrying about every group protecting our borders, and this land is too big to do so. If you'll take it, you'll be the first in this position. It'll set a precedent for every Commander to come after you. So make sure you make it what you want."

I watch a genuine smile cross his face as he picks up the notepad. For a moment I wonder if there is a more formal way to appoint him into the position. Making a mental note to find a way to do so, I allow him to step with Ellie to say goodbyes. He wraps a firm arm around Ellie, pressing his lips to her forehead. His beard tickles her face, making her laugh.

"They'll leave tonight then," I decide. I still watch the two of them interact while finding Lilly. A question of if they're Suitors or not crosses my thoughts, but I brush it away thinking it doesn't matter.

"I'll make copies of the housing for each of them," Jacob tugs at Harlow, who refuses to budge, still looking at me.

"Adjust them to be built in the trees if they want, they'll figure out the rest. I want updates once every few days," I catch Linius nodding, encouraging my demands. "Filo," I call after him. He spins to look at me, jogging back towards me. "I want to talk to them before they leave."

I walk past Linius, his head turns to follow me back towards the nearly finished row of houses.

"You'll be better off sending them out rather than keeping them here," his dark eyes glance down at me, though not by much since he's only half a head taller than me. "I hated sending my own out, it made me feel helpless. It gets easier as you realize those people are happier being alone."

"You didn't speak this much at the meeting, why?"

His thin lips lift at the side, making his high cheekbones pinch.

"Sometimes, Dronning Kali, not saying anything is more powerful than saying anything at all."

"Not saying anything wouldn't have every person there keeping a wide berth between you and them."

"You don't have one yet, but your Samle will eventually gain its own name. Just as mine did. And it will gain it for a reason."

I recall the seemingly harmless name of his own people.

"And you gained yours by being so quiet?"

He chuckles, a sound that makes me want to sit by a fire with a cup of tea.

"To be completely honest, in an act of trust between allies, I'll give you the truth," he helps me sweep out the dust and dirt from the first finished house. "Most know the basics, that I found and spilled secrets about Gallyan."

"Which I'm sure he has plenty of," I roll my eyes. Linius waits, conveying he just wants me to listen.

"He had a wife before we all changed. She survived with him as a dragon. Unfortunately, in a fit of Suitor attraction he lost his temper and killed her."

I pause in my own sweeping, while the Konge continues as though nothing had been said out of the ordinary.

"I hear interesting things. Most of the time I wonder why I even hear them. Either in the right place at the right time, or I chance meeting someone who has the info. Like the slave who managed to escape, found his way to Elias's territory whom I was visiting at the time, spilled his secrets as a house servant, then promptly died."

My movements are robotic as I wipe down surfaces of the dining room table, the windows and countertops in the kitchen. The oven is cold, never being lit until the first person moves in to put wood in it and warm this place. The temperature feels colder as Linius spills the heavily weighted secret.

"I could tell who already had themselves wrapped around his finger, those who truly agreed with his enslavement of humans and rogue dragons. The rest, Janét, Elias, and Mikhail, I branched out."

"I know the first two must have believed you, but I find it hard to believe Mikhail did it blindly."

"He took some convincing, but eventually when I pointed out the other secrets like Gallyan being so possessive over everything he could get his talons into, the off feeling being around him, he finally believed me."

"But you never told everyone about him killing his wife."

"No," he pauses, resting his hands on top of the broom. "I just told them about the slaves. That was enough to divide everyone. I also didn't tell them what Gallyan mentioned to Addison at the meeting we all convened at."

"Addison is wildly in love in Gallyan, or obsessed."

"Addison is in love with power, obsessed with achieving it. Gallyan has her convinced she'll have Mikhail back, she'll have this entire continent under her control, and nothing to stop her."

I strongly debate giving him my secret that Elias had given me, and decide to hold off until a more appropriate time.

"Mikhail has no interest in her anymore, except for keeping things peaceful."

"I'm sure he does, after forcing her through an abortion without her knowing."

I spin on my heel toward him, wondering how in the world he could have known what Mikhail had only told me. My hands wring around the damp cloth as I wonder if holding back will earn distrust.

"I would never expect you to openly admit that to me, so I hold nothing against you."

"But how could you have heard that?"

"It's both too complicated and irrelevant," he returns to sweeping. I walk around to check that each room is ready. Walking out with him I shut the door behind us. "It stays between us. Should I catch wind of you spilling anything, I'd be forced to break this friendship."

I give him a smirk, enjoying that someone finally returns my own aggression, "I wouldn't dare. Not with so few people liking me anyway."

Those sent to live at the border send no word except for their weekly reports, I lower it to biweekly after the first three reports. Too much travel could wear them down, after discussion with Filo. He spends most of his time flying between the four groups, the additional one being placed on the eastern shore to watch for those coming in from the water.

Most of the reports remained quiet. A few sightings of animals too large or too small than their previous forms. A couple reports found new plants that after some study from Brawn, ended up being powerful medicinal plants. Those were brought back in bunches, then used to help the women still healing from their brutal experience.

Their bodies fill out exponentially in the midst of intense training with Harlow and Senka. Janét agrees to send her own people, a mix of men and women but majority female, to live here with the others. Her men had come from being enslaved, the women from the same hideous past living under Dominé and Hendrix. Her offer to Oriana for them all to live with her had been brutally turned down.

"You live in a place caged in by rapists and slavers, why would I force them to be in a more dangerous place than here?" Oriana had said. A few females standing behind her had nodded their heads, agreeing.

"I simply wanted to offer," Janét replied.

"I appreciate the hospitality, but we have our lives here. This is our home now," the group quickly returned to their combative session. I hadn't missed the title she'd placed on this place, hope bleeding into me that they'd truly started to recover.

Shoving the thoughts aside I refocus on Harlow smearing a blend of herbs onto my back. Sparring with her early in the morning had resulted in my back being nearly covered in bruises. While Dimitri's fighting had been like a dance, hers was a game of survival. Using the mock swords she'd scavenged ensured my sides, arms, and thighs had also been covered in welts.

"Why didn't you pick me?" she breaks the comfortable silence. This method of putting the herb on one another had become routine. I enjoyed being able to be silent around her for so long. We never spoke about Samle issues, only the possibilities of our future.

"What are you talking about, Harlow," I spin, gripping my shirt that lays in my lap as I do. The soft bra she wears expands as she inhales sharply.

"You chose Filo to take control over the border patrol, I'm the one that had a military family. You knew that, knew I'd grown up understanding this shit, still studying it so I can help, and you decide to pick him?" her fingers dig into a particularly sensitive bruise.

I smack away her arm, eyes glowing with the command to take control of her temper. She attempts to stare me down, giving in to the glowing green essence of my own stare.

"Why would I put you, with the expertise I'm very much aware of, into a position where it goes to waste?"

"Watching our borders to make sure Addison or Gallyan don't infiltrate is exactly what I can do."

"Wrong," I pull my shirt on. "What you can do is help keep this Samle alive once they decide to invite themselves in."

"You *expect* them to get through? I'm sure keeping those men alive that hurt you doesn't help."

"Until I find a way to protect every inch of our boundaries I do. Having those dragons there will give us enough of a heads up to do something. And no, it doesn't help but killing them would have risked Oriana and the others."

She stays silent, waiting for the explanation of what I want her to do.

"Harlow," I exhale her name. "I had no reason to ask until we needed one - but with one power-crazed Dronning on one side and a Konge wanting to put a collar on my neck - eventually, I might need you to help me navigate it all."

"You're asking for a war general," her mouth stays parted in her shock.

"I don't need you being caught up in guarding when the time comes."

"You're saying that a fight is inevitable."

"Assuming it isn't would be stupid," I leave her to consider our conversation. Feathers lands on my shoulder. His beak messes with my hair, untangling a small knot in it.

"Enemy here," he croaks out.

"Not yet, Feathers," I rub my fingers down his chest to calm his anxious flitting.

"Yes yet, yes yet, idiot."

I freeze, looking at the beady eyes on my shoulder.

"What did you see?" I whisper, my chest feels wrong. The base of my spine heats as it reaches out to Jakir to wrap around him. I can feel his concern grow as realizes the panic I'm in.

"Jacob gone, you see?"

I wildly search for the familiar face, calling to him loudly, "Jacob? Jacob, where are you?"

"Kali?" Harlow runs to my side.

"Where's Jacob?" I demand. She turns frantic, trying to remember when she last saw him.

"He left to go with Filo, helping one of the couples at the boundary settle. Kali" she grabs my arm firmly. "What is it? Tell me what's wrong, what do you know?"

I dig the heel of my hand into my chest to alleviate the pain. Nothing works to remove the uneasy feeling. I feel Feathers dig his claws into my shoulder, it keeps my mind from succumbing to the wild rage that begins.

Loud screaming sounds come from him, signaling to everyone. Shortly, I'm surrounded by people.

"Look at me, love, look at me," Jakir's hands wrap under my chin. In his eyes I see my own glowing. I can barely breath enough to get out words of explanation. My knee drops to the ground.

"The western border," I groan. "There's something there."

"Someone bad, darlin'. Someone bad," Feathers hops onto the ground in front of me. "Go now, I say now."

It clicks then. Feather knew something was coming towards us, headed for me to warn me. He knows the heavy weight on my chest is the warning to what's happening.

"The rest of you stay here," I sweep a finger across everyone. Lucius holds Janét back from walking towards me.

Jakir and Harlow follow me as I push myself from the ground into a sprint. Leading them I force my body into the change. Pain snaps out at every snap of bone. Adrenaline pumps through my veins, fueling the anger I feel slipping over my mind.

Two gray forms swoop down low, their wings spread out to cast a shadow over me.

Oh my sweet friend, I think. I don't bother controlling it as it wipes away any semblance of mercy. It doesn't feel like me anymore as the sun warms my scales under the flurries of snow. Land flies under me. Briefly my eyes catch the glistening gold on one side, blue on the other. Further ahead I watch the Nightmares start to descend.

"Rip them apart," I tell the two ahead of me. Their tails flick down as we reach the vicinity of the newest outpost. My lips pull back in a feral snarl at the sound of a human scream. Wet sounds touch my sensitive eardrums, skin tearing and muscles shredding.

The violence feels familiar. Comfortable. I want more of it. More of my own. A gold snout snaps at my wing, getting cracked away at a whip of my bony structure. Sparse foliage, much healthier than that of the distant Dead Forest, stills as I dive into it. A wide opening lets me spot

Jacob, bloodied but fighting. The twins sprint through, taking off once it's too snug to chase the others to their death.

My throat shakes as I slam down into the ground. In the midst of a roar loud enough to shake the very ground beneath me, a human slams a massive sword into my side.

"Fuck you, ungodly monster," he bellows.

My paw swipes down his weapon into the ground. His shout tells me he must not expect my tail as it slices at his arm. A forearm with the hand connected drops to the ground. Ribs are exposed, unable to escape the slash. For a moment, no blood drips from the new wound since the adrenaline is keeping his muscles contracted.

"Kali I can't shift, not while they're fighting!" Jacob yells over his shoulder. His face has scrapes all over it marring the features that distinguish him. Harlow knocks away two of the men cornering him, wrapping her tail around his body. Her front claws sink into the back of one man. Three more men rush her, blunt weapons with crude sharp objects impaled on them ready to damage. Her long jaw opens wide to blow hot blue flame at those rushing to her. I notice her holding it back, not letting it touch them just yet.

"*Stop holding back, they deserve none of our mercy,*" I snarl.

"*They deserve a chance to earn it,*" Jakir attempts to sate some of the craving for violence. I snap shut the Bond, only keeping enough open to feel his life.

I don't respond to him. My body twists and curls to keep them from reaching Harlow's open side where she cannot defend herself. My tail slices down on the man with a lost arm. He slowly reaches for a weapon only to have his chest crack when my tail pierces it.

Harlow roars, high pitched and in pain.

"Harlow!" Jacob cries.

I turn to see multiple weapons sticking out of Harlow's body. She's too afraid to set the land on fire to use the full force of her fire.

Ridiculous, I grit my jaw. Slamming a human body back into a tree trunk so fast I hear his spine shatter against the wood. *Just end them.*

One of them steps back, dropping his weapon. I snap my teeth at his body, just missing him. My neck curls back to reach the blue and white dragon, yanking out as many of the crude spears and daggers buried in the softer parts of her body. They angle so they can slip under her scales, making it difficult to grab them.

Another weapon flies past my face, narrowly missing my nostrils.

Without hesitation I close my jaws around the thick body. Clamping down spurts blood into my mouth.

I moan silently, wanting more of the taste. Bones snap into pieces with another firm clench of the muscles in my mouth. Spitting the body back out, I don't even stop to look at the damage done.

A contraction clamps down on my chest, knocking the air from my lungs.

Harlow bellows, only the sound never reaches my ears.

Jakir slams his head into the last person, hooking their body on his horns to toss them over his body.

Jacob collapses, holding what's left of his leg.

I feel time slow as I swing my head around. My ears strain to hear any signs of humans or their weapons. Leaves dance in the breeze of our movement.

Another man moves in the thicker part of the woods. His pale face and dark hair peek out from a tree. I step forward to chase him down. His feet scurry to a further tree, too hidden for me to reach.

Harlow pulls her body down to hold Jacob in her arms. I hear her scream a plea but I can't make out the words. Blood floods my nose as time speeds back up. Bodies lay across the ground. Weapons broken, shattered, pitiful, lay strewn about the bodies. Most are no longer intact. Those that are are now barely recognizable in the midst of missing chunks of flesh.

"They're lucky these trees stopped us from moving as freely," I snarl with my words to them.

"Kali," Harlow's voice is shaky. It rocks me with fear. "We have to get him back, please."

Her words are a sob. Rightfully so. I dip my head towards Jacob, the echo of pain he feels nearly forcing me back to human form. I whine lowly, hoping she'll force him up to move him. With a nod, she picks him up in her arms. The movement of Jacob's leg, slowly starting to seep dark red blood, pulls his eyelids down into unconsciousness.

Watching them both suffer such thick suffering shoves the darkness in my mind back to its wretched corner.

"Jakir go," I reopen the Bond, letting him search me for injury. He aids the calming of my mind before I continue. *"Warn Brawn, we're going to need everyone."*

Jakir's golden scales are gone before I start helping Harlow onto my back. Her brown eyes meet mine. Filled with tears she begs me again to go. Using my tail to push her as far as possible into the rider's dip on my back.

My body works itself into a frenzy. With speed built from more than a year of constant demand, I fly towards the only chance Jacob has of survival.

Chapter 43

I watch Brawn work silently. The second I land; he begins work on Jacob. A tourniquet is immediately placed above where his knee should have been. Carrying him into one of the rooms of the manor, a table is brought in.

"Can't we make him more comfortable?" Harlow smooths the hair back from her Suitor's face, tears dripping onto his face.

"No, I need him on a surface he can't move as much on," Brawn is the calmest I've ever seen him. Face focused, warm brown eyes dark with focus and concern. "Do you want him comfortable or dead?"

"Brawn, easy," Jakir warns. Looking genuinely confused, Brawn returns to cleaning out the wound.

"Start the fireplace, get it as hot as possible," he commands the extra hands here to help. "Bring me clean water from the lake, towels, and a saw."

"You can't be serious," Harlow's face pales. She looks sick with her hair limp from the travel. Brawn doesn't answer her, only finishes cleaning out the debris from Jacob's leg. Jakir helps Filo get the fire started, the large inset in the room quickly removing the chill. Once burning so hot the room becomes uncomfortable, they both return to us.

"Can I help with anything?" Ellie says from the doorway. Lilly squirms in her arms.

"Keep everyone away," I walk to her, placing a hand gently on Lilly's head. "This will not sound pretty."

I return to the table in the center of the room, Brawn still hunched over

Jacob's leg. He sets down a blade while tracing his fingers around the pieces of dangling skin.

"Hold him down, and put this between his teeth," Brawn reaches for the saw he brought. I grab the strip of thick leather. Gripping Jacobs jaw I look down at his soft face before opening his mouth wide enough to fit it in. "He might be unconscious, but if he wakes up any movement could force us to remove more. Or kill him."

I catch the horror on Harlow's face, correcting Brawn, "Tell her only what's necessary. Keep the rest to yourself."

"How can you be so sure?" Harlow's cheeks glisten with tears. Her voice is shaky, nothing close to the usual deep tenor.

"I've been doing enough research within the medical field as Kali asked," he cleans a saw, sharpened to a deadly glistening. "The rest is common sense. Hold him still."

Jakir helps to hold him down across his chest, the twins grip his waist and remaining leg. I wrap my arm around the free limb.

Grinding begins once Brawn starts. It's only moments before Jacob wakes again. Immediately he looks down to see the saw working off the shattered bone protruding from his thigh. Screams tear from his mouth. Each one of them never truly conveying how much pain he must be in. The screams sear into my mind, marking a sound none of us will ever forget.

His body begins to flail, but the four of us holding him all grip tightly, managing to keep his body still.

"Kali," Brawn commands,keeping focus on his task. "Grab the vial of pale green syrup. Pour one third of the bottle down his throat."

I do as he tells me, Jakir having to help me shift Jacob's jaw open to make him swallow it.

"Baby please," Harlow keeps the leather in his mouth. "I know, I know baby you have to lay down. You have to stop moving."

She continues to coo until he passes out from the pain. With no more screaming all I can hear is bone being sawed through. He awakes to scream and passes out twice more, his eyes becoming heavily hooded.

Each of us are breathing heavily as we continue to fight his body. The whites of his eyes turn red, and his pupils dilate. Finally, the sounds stop. Brawn's hands work quickly, smearing herbs and medicine over the fresh nerves and flesh.

I don't notice the sun completing its path until he steps back.

"It looks like it may actually already be healing, but I'll need to check it every day, make some adjustments. " He picks up the side of his mouth briefly at me. Harlow glares at him. "I suppose that would be something we can confirm at the end of this process."

With a pat on Harlow's shoulder he cleans his hands and leaves. She doesn't move, only smoothing her hand over the shaven sides of Jacobs head. Occasionally her fingers twist in the center section of hair that's long enough to brush his neck.

"We have to clean his hair, he hates having messy hair," she mutters. I bend slightly to press my lips to her head. Closing my eyes I allow myself a moment of peace before pulling away. Her lips let loose a shuddering breath as she breaks into tears.

"Get her a bowl of water and some soap to clean him," I jerk my chin at Nelly as he brings in more wood for the fire. His eyes dart to the body on the table behind me. I move to block his vision, not wanting his mind to be haunted by the image.

"Did he hit his head?" he asks timidly.

"No," I can't bring the energy forward to lie, but I cannot tell him the truth. "Go get the water, make sure it's warm, knock when you come back."

He nods, setting the wood down by the fireplace.

"And Nelly," I call to him, my eyes burn with the command as it leaves me. "Do *not* set foot in or around this room unless explicitly told to do so by me or Jakir."

His eyes cast downward, pulling at my chest. I know his curiosity will do nothing but hurt him, though forcing a command on my own hurts less.

Jakir steps in front of me before I'm able to leave the room. I motion to the twins behind him to leave.

"Where are you going?" his voice is low, trying to avoid disturbing Harlow.

"One of them survived, so I'm going to find him."

"With the Nightmares?"

"Obviously."

"They'll kill him."

"They won't. They want blood just as much as I do, but they're not impulsive."

"Kali-"

I move around him, pushing open the door with both hands.

"I can feel it, Jakir," my eyes meet his somber ones. "They have more reasons than just trying to find me. No one without some motive would go to these lengths."

I don't let him finish before I leave. I ease the door shut behind me.

"Let us kill him," Senka's accent is bitter, heavy with her Russian heritage.

"It'll be slow," Sayah twirls a knife against his pointer finger. He licks away the dot of blood that appears.

"It'll be when I decide to do so," I remove my clothing swiftly. Folding it, I leave it on a short stone wall on the side of the manor. Simmering anger bubbles up in my chest. Everyone is angry, their emotions mix into my own.

"What do you want then?" they both ask.

I make my way through the shadows, avoiding the firelight. Mikhail's home has a candle lit in it. My hand raises, keeping the dark haired twins outside.

"Get up," I walk in. His eyes take in my nakedness, narrowing at me.

"You're not here for sex, are you, kitten?" his voice drips with lust.

"I'm assuming you heard."

"I heard Jacob was hurt."

"We had to remove what was left of his knee."

"Will he make it?"

I pause, lip trembling. Clenching my jaw I grip my fear so tightly it turns into a craving for revenge.

"You want them dead, don't you? You want revenge for what they did to your people?" he asks. There's a tone in his voice that's mocking my train of thought. "I wouldn't do it on your own if I were you."

"The Twins can help, but they won't stop me from killing him."

"They couldn't if they wanted to," his eyebrows climb. "Ah, I see. You want a leash."

"I hate you," I seethe at the image of him in my head, holding the end of a leash clasped to a collar on my neck.

"You can thank me later," he pulls off his shirt, abdominal muscles flexing in the movement. He rubs his beard, completely covering the lower half of his face now that it's grown out. Heat builds between my legs.

I shoulder check him on my way out the door.

Senka and Sayah follow closely behind. Neither of them mentions the extra guest with us. Each of us make our way through the tall grass to put distance between our snapping bones and those around the nightly bonfire.

The only sound in the night, other than our beating wings, is an occasional wolf howling. It comes from all directions, multiple packs announcing their attendance. I briefly wonder at how we covered so much distance in such a short time, the normal day and a half trip took much less time.

The threat of losing Jacob must have been enough adrenaline, I consider.

It takes only two days to reach the healthy trees that expand to eventually border the gray decaying ones. Though just barely in sight, the wind carries the faint scent of death from them. Again, the wolves are howling across the land.

"Find him, do not kill him. Bring him to me."

Gray heads shake off the snow that had formed in the heavy downfall. Like silver bullets in the night, they slink off into the trees to find the last remaining man.

"How can you be sure he's still in these woods?" Mikhail sniffs along the ground, walking slowly so as to avoid shaking the earth below us.

"They can't walk through the Dead Forest, he's most likely trying to find a way to the other side."

"How did they get through in the first place?" his horns brush his neck as he swings back his head to look at me. I make eye contact briefly.

"That's something I intend on asking once I have him."

"Perhaps they dug a tunnel."

"No, the twins dug down when they came out here. The rot is too deep."

"So how?"

"Either they found a way in, or they were brought in."

He stills, watching me move through the trees.

"She wouldn't do that."

"First off, I never mentioned her; you're the one who assumed. Second, you sound like you still have feelings for her, Mikhail."

"Addison might be loyal to Gallyan, but she's not stupid."

"Might be? Don't be ridiculous," I catch the scent of sweat, picking up speed through the trees. *"His essence is probably what has her and the others cowering. Everything about him says he wants more than what he has. Addison wants a piece of it."*

"Are you jealous of her behavior in my home?"

I have to clench my jaw to keep from snapping at him, *"Why would I be jealous of what's below me?"*

I stop before setting my paw down again, hearing breathing further away. In the night, my eyes pick up a slight break in a branch nearby. I feel the other side, the side that wants to feel this man's head crush between my teeth, swallow any sense of control.

"Found you, little mouse."

I push off the base of a tree with the back of my foot. My neck bends around the corners of thick trunks. Small human feet pound through fallen leaves as he tries to run. The light snow from weeks ago has made the floor of the open woods muddy, causing him to slip. Just as I slam a paw down he darts away again.

My jaw unhinges to release a roar loud enough I feel my own ears shutter closed. Red scales slip past me to herd the male out of the tree line into open land. High pitched roars respond to my call, along with the sound of a couple trees shattering.

His arm catches a sharp bush in his next attempt to escape. The smell of blood permeates the air making me salivate. Snapping my teeth together I chuff as he slows. The human's body is thin and worn, clearly running off of fumes. Breaking free of a maze of trees he runs unknowingly in the direction of our home.

I lift off the ground slightly, letting my wings carry me a short distance to catch up. Without the trees to slow me down I finally end up next to him. His head turns, fear crossing his eyes once they finally focus on me. I know his human eyesight makes it hard to see me on such a dark night, so spotting my eye next to him nearly makes him fall again.

Disappointed that he stays upright, I pump my wings once. With a thrash, my tail slams into his body rewarding me with a crack.

"*Kill him,*" Senka's smile is clear as day through her voice.

"*Kali,*" Mikhail lands with a heavy thud, having dropped from the air above me. "*Remember those answers you want.*"

"*Do I really need them though?*" I walk over him, placing my talons around his body. They sink into the ground successfully putting pressure on his chest and caging him in.

"*You do if you want to prove me right about Addison.*"

That makes me stop the increasing pressure. Below my paw he struggles for air, the sound of his pain confirming that I've broken a few of his ribs.

"*Don't make Brawn focus on healing someone as worthless as him,*" Sayah's nose pushes on my cheek. His gentle voice pulls me from my stupor. Walking away, he leaves with his sister at my command to be ready when I arrive.

Mikhail steps into my vision, drawing my attention from the now passed out human male. His eyebrow is pierced, as is his lip.

"*Do you want me to carry him?*"

I look up. The red scales look like poinsettias at night, such a rich vibrant red.

"No," I inhale through my nose. Cold air calms my nerves. *"I want him under my watch."*

With a heavy thrust of our wings, we pull ourselves into the air. Closing my talons I yank the body up with me along with the dirt beneath him. The strain of knocking my wings against tree trunks to hunt is evident in the throbbing of bone. Each time my wings come down the soreness fuels my anger.

Janét stands with Linius, waiting for me to land. Other people watch from a distance, some closing in to get a good look. Oriana's eyes bore into me, even at the lake I see her lips pull into a snarl at the form in my claws. I drop the male in my hold from a height hard enough to hurt, but not too high to damage him any further. Mikhail reaches his snout towards me to nuzzle my neck.

My teeth close down around his sensitive nose. He releases a sudden rush of air as my teeth pierce into the bundle of nerves inside his nostril.

"Let go," he starts to jerk his head back but stops before it forces my teeth to rip through his septum. Dropping my jaw open I lick at the tiny amount of blood on my teeth.

Back in human form, he brushes past Linius angrily saying, "Careful, she's in a foul mood."

I catch his glare as he looks over his shoulder, nose bleeding heavily. Linius stares me down as he removes his clothing. Quickly his dragon form takes over.

"Tie him up," I tell the twins, enjoying the way they roughly handle our new captive. *"I'll meet you in the basement."*

The Konge's scales remind me of hot embers in the fireplace of the manor. Jacob had insisted upon having a massive inset for one in the common area.

"*I understand your anger, but you have to control it.*"

"*What would you know about this, Linius?*"

"*I know that I was furious because Addison visited me and started a fight with a teenager simply because he didn't bow to her.*"

I walk with him towards the manor, spotting Jakir waiting patiently by the door. He brushes an invisible hand down me to check for injury. Wordlessly he moves back inside to disappear.

"*I'm sorry that happened.*"

"*So am I. I'm more sorry that I let my anger at them being harmed turn into another thing entirely. A few of my own were so terrified of me that they wouldn't look me in the eye.*"

"*How did you fix it?*"

"*I apologized, but it did nothing except exacerbate the idea that I'm a ruthless Konge to even my own people.*"

"*Maybe that's what I want,*" I feel my shoulder blades crack particularly hard as they reset into their smaller shapes.

"It's not. Having your enemies fear you is one thing. Having your own people is another. Don't push them into the arms of a dragon that won't care for them."

I close the distance between us, getting in his face for my next words.

"*Never insinuate that I'd willingly push my people to one of them, again.*"

"Then don't give me a reason to," his hand splays across one side of my head to press the side of my face to his. His lips near my ear, his shoulder bent slightly to match my height. "I see through it, Kali. I see through the anger and the violence. If I'm going to have you as an ally, then expect me to be the one person that will never take your bullshit."

His hand drops from my face. I watch his back until he leaves the house.

His words bother me. I can't decipher if he wants to bring me to heel or might truly be a friend. I process our interactions, deciding to assume he finds me to be a close friend. Believing the former option weighs too heavily on me.

The door to the isolated basement is well hidden, tucked away by a small closet. No light streams in since it's buried within the cliffside. Opening the door I push gently at one of the shelves to unlock the wall. Smiling to myself I consider the humor of how sweet Jacob was so proud of considering a basement, only for it to be used to torture a hostage. Closing the door, I move the wall back to its position of being simply a wall of shelves. A whoosh of air blows at my face as the passageway goes dark.

The sound of skin being slapped echoes in my ears. I let my boots fall heavily to warn the Twins of my arrival. Lessons from them had given improvement to my stealth greatly, so making myself loud had become a sign of trust to them.

"He's awake," Senka announces as I round the corner from the stairs. I glance at Sayah for any progress, who shakes his head.

"Well then," I tip his head back with my pointer finger against his forehead. He groans when his head is upright. "What's your name?"

"Fuck you," he spits blood onto the floor.

I sigh, "Okay little human, I'm going to ask again. This time I really want an answer because killing you is supposed to be the last thing I do."

His brows lower, pinching in the middle. A shift happens in his eyes, then he answers.

"Fin, my name is Fin."

Senka pokes at his side, forcing him to hiss at the pain.

"Fin," I ignore her playing with the bruised parts of his body. "I'd like to be as nice as possible, but there's only so much I can do to control my little Nightmares here."

"Do what you want, I don't care," Fin's eyes close, the pale blue disappearing until he opens them again. "You'll just force me like the others did."

Senka stills behind him for a moment. She looks at me confused. I keep my face neutral as I take the chair offered by Sayah.

"The others?" I ask. I straddle the chair, folding my arms on the back of it to rest my chin on. "What do you mean?"

His eyes look to the floor, most of the fight in them gone at my questions.

"All of you dragons, you're all murderers. Addison seemed different. She seemed better."

I tilt my head at her name, face still unmoving. It's a struggle not to run to Mikhail and prove my point, or to immediately lash out at my gut feeling being proven correct. Curiosity is tangible in the air with myself and the twins wondering at Fin's past.

"Unfortunately you bumped into one of the worst of us. What did Addison want with you?"

He hesitates, watching Senka continue to make a prowling circle around him.

"A little cut here," she points at his cheek. "A little cut there," she giggles at him, flinching away from her dancing fingers on his neck.

Fin looks between us, lingering on me as if to ask for help. I play his game, wanting to see how easily he'll trust.

"Leave it, Senka," I say softly. She pouts but continues her antsy path walking around him. I note the tension leave Fin's shoulders slightly. "What did Addison want?"

"She had a deal with Kent, I think. All I know is she asked us to find a way in here, find you all, then go back and tell her everything. Said if we got into a fight, make sure no one made it out."

"That didn't go so well for you, did it?"

Those pale blue eyes meet mine, defeat evident. I struggle to hide the smile that threatens to creep up, instead choosing to force a look of pity.

"No," he sighs. "I didn't want to but Kent doesn't let us live if we argue. Every time he finds someone it's kill or join the killing."

"That must have been a difficult choice, Fin," I reach out, placing a hand on his knee. He stiffens at first, then relaxes into my touch. "I'm sorry that you were forced to do so. I see why you ran now."

I watch the realization dawn on Senka's face finally at what I'm doing. They're hesitant, but they don't argue. They look curious more than anything.

"Can you untie me now?"

He thinks I'm playing into his game.

"Can you tell me why you didn't run sooner? Why it took me trying to kill you for you to run?"

"You," he looks behind me to Sayah in fear, then back to me. "You're the big one, the one with the black scales."

I only give him a feral smile.

"I told you Kent made us fight."

"Yeah but," my fingers burn as matte black talons extend out from them. "You tried to fight first, managed to even get a weapon into one of us."

"I know," his head hangs, making me wonder how much of his regret is real. "That's what made me run. That's the first time I've ever actually hurt a dragon."

"It'll be your last," Sayah warns. His thick accent bleeds into his words, most likely to disturb Fin.

Linius's message repeats in my head, making me lean towards a merciful choice. My decision clicks into place in my head. I steady myself for the blowback.

"At least it should be if you want to live," I hold a lazy hand up at Senka's surprised reaction. "You'll stay in a room for tonight. You'll follow any rule myself or my Sekund gives you. If anyone comes to harm because of you, whether directly or indirectly, I'll let Senka break every bone in your body, then Sayah will put it all back into place. Then I'll rip your little human heart out."

Fin's body relaxes at my judgment though still clearly weary of us.

"Guest room?" Senka asks, still staring down Fin.

I stand up, dusting off my pants. Moving the chair out of the way quietly I step towards him. With a jerk of my chin Senka removes the bonds from his wrists and ankles.

"Thank-"

I slam my fist into the side of his head, dropping him into being unconscious.

"Not fair! I've been wanting to do that!" Senka whines.

"Even though you already did it multiple times?" Sayah asks as he lifts Fin over his shoulder.

She gasps, placing both hands on the side of her face, "Sayah I would never do that."

"Yes, you would, Senka," I give her a bored look. She giggles and skips out of the room. Shaking my head I follow Sayah out of the basement through the passage that leads into the kitchen.

Chapter 44

Jakir lifts his eyebrows as Sayah passes him to take Fin to his room.

"Showing a bit of mercy, are we?" he asks.

"I'm trying something new," I shrug.

"And you're sure he won't be an issue?"

I worry my bottom lip while watching the hallways Sayah had gone down to deposit him.

"He was forced to join Kent, just like Harlow and Jacob said. He didn't make all the scars, he just got the experience."

Jakir leans against the massive island in the kitchen, pulling me to lean back against him. I let him wrap his arms around me, sinking into the comfort of his strong body. The Bond surges with warmth as Jakir soothes the tension racking me from such an eventful day.

"Though I support you being kind-hearted, I still want you to be careful. We don't know what his motives are."

"No," I tilt my head back to rest it against his chest. "But we know that Addison is the one behind them."

Jakir's thumb stops the circling motion it had been tracing on my arm. Muscles bulge and roll in his arms as I feel him immediately beginning to plan.

"You're sure?"

"Completely, he mentioned her name without my prompting. He also mentioned Kent, but he's clearly falling to his knees for Addison."

"I was hoping it was merely two personalities clashing at the meeting," his lips drop to rest on my forehead briefly. "But I believe you're right.

Addison must have known you were in her territory. If she's bold enough to send people in-"

"Carry them in, they couldn't have gotten through unless they went all the way north and came down."

"Fair, which means she's invested."

"Yes, but invested in what? Does she want our Samle or does she want me dead?"

"The two are not mutually exclusive, my dear."

"We don't know what killing a Dronning or Konge would do to a Samle, she can't possibly be willing to risk losing everyone here."

"I'll make a note to Brawn about that, in the meantime I think we need to speak with Linus and Janét," he squeezes me gently before allowing me to step away to face him. "If you truly want their trust you need to be open with what's happened. I doubt they'd appreciate being blindsided by a consequence of her actions here."

I nod, "I'll bring them into the office. Meet me there with Filo and Aiza."

"What about the twins?"

"They know," I look into a dark corner of the kitchen. Senka slips her hand into the light before disappearing.

It doesn't take long to bring everyone together into the large room in the southern wing of the house. A massive floor to ceiling window lets me see the lake and tree a good distance away. Beautiful gray wood marred with claw marks makes up the desk situated in front of it that I lean on at the front. Once I gathered the visiting dragons they berated me with questions, which I deflected until the others entered.

"Harlow staying with Jacob?" Filo asks, sitting on one of the long couches creating a sitting area in front of the desk.

"She doesn't need to be involved in this, she has enough weighing on her."

"And that's for you to decide?" Mikhail tosses out the accusation at me lazily. His ankle rests on the opposite knee creating a dominating air around him.

"It is when I know her judgment would be clouded."

"Bold of you to assume."

"Not as bold as killing the innocent."

The blow lands directly on his ego. Watching the muscles in his jaw brings a satisfaction to me that only insulting him could do.

"I think you hurt the baby's feelings," Janét sneers at him.

They toss insults at each other until Linius sits down next to Janét.

"Quite a collection of books you already have," He adjusts the dress coat he's wearing, perfectly matching the dress pants.

"We had a lot to learn," I stare him down, pointedly remarking on his earlier words to me.

His lips barely move, the movement so small I barely catch it before his face returns to his serious expression.

"There is an issue you all need to be aware of," Jakir remains standing close to me. "I'm sure you were made aware of the attack that recently occurred."

"At your border, in what you call the Dead Forest, correct?"

"Why *do* you call it that?" Mikhail asks me.

"It smells like rot, as you experienced. Every animal in it looks half dead or ready to make another animal be so."

"It's also not possible, or at least extremely difficult, for humans to walk through even with how quickly they can heal. The Twins watched a few men try to enter it, only to become sick and delusional," Jakir's eyes look to the Nightmares sitting at a table situated under the second level walkway. Sayah nods to confirm the information.

"It was men that we found. And we only found them because Jacob happened to be gone just a bit too long," I unfold my arms, needing to carry the weight of Jacob's injury against the desk. The golden rope inside of me glows, a steadying presence that keeps my knees from buckling. "I've had interactions with them before, all unpleasant."

"The same men you pulled Oriana and the others from?" Janét's eyes are uneasy, filled with worry. Her bright red lips thin in her concern.

"The same men that sliced you to pieces?" Mikhail asks. Slowly, I slide my gaze to him to pin him with the fury I feel. I hadn't wanted pity, though

I knew bringing this to the others might require some back story. His lips turn up, enjoying the anger he's sparked in me. Attempting to hold myself back from ripping one of his eyes out, I look to Linius. Thankfully, not an ounce of judgment is on his face.

"I was slow, they were fast. And mean," I draw out. Linius doesn't say anything, helping me to ease back into conversation. "Now they're fast, mean and helping Addison."

Janét chokes on air, leaning forward suddenly to catch her breath. She says what sounds like they might be a few choice words in Spanish.

"I knew that bitch wouldn't sit back and relax when she found out you and Mikhail were fucking," her smile is contagious, bringing one to both my face as well as Senka's.

"We need to tread carefully in these next steps," Aiza places herself on the armrest of the couch closest to me. Linius respectfully pulls away his arm to give her room. "Thank you. While what she did is inexcusable, there are laws now. It's crucial we follow them. Otherwise the people coming after us will never follow them either."

"Aiza you realize that since humans can't make it through those woods alone, she had them carried in?"

"Or they found a hole, which I'm working on right now," Filo tugs at his beard, the length touching his chest.

I nod at him, "Tell us the second you find something. For now, the concrete information we have is that Addison is working with the humans. Information gained from the human we found yesterday."

"And where is this human, exactly?" Mikhail asks.

"In a room, he'll be closely watched, but not held captive."

"You're letting the man who cut off Jacob's leg run free?" Filo's voice is firm, holding back anger at my words.

"He wasn't the one who did it, I killed that one."

"How can you be so sure?"

I glare at him. My thoughts spin, trying to remember every detail of the fight, which man I crushed in my mouth. Suddenly, I'm not so sure I remember who swung the blow at Jacob.

Jakir steps forward, dropping his arms from being crossed over his chest. Like mint on one's neck on a hot day, he breaks down the tangible cord of strain in the room, "We found him because he ran, he was forced into that group. It's not the first we've heard of it, it's unfortunately common. The humans controlling that group hold no morality in this world."

Oriana walks in, shutting the door gently behind her. "Fucking Skin Carvers aren't humans."

"I'm assuming playing with knives wasn't a special treat for me?" I raise an eyebrow at her, she maintains eye contact while flopping into a loveseat. Mentally I note to include her in these from now on, wanting all aspects of this Samle involved would only benefit me.

"It was, they only used it as a threat most of the time. They preferred to carve out chunks from us when we misbehaved," memories flit behind her eyes, haunting us both despite the outward appearance of being fine. "I caught pieces of their meetings with Addison when it was my turn with Kent."

I'm an idiot for not having her here from the start, lesson learned.

A few faces in the room, mostly Jakir and Janét, turn solemn at her words.

"How often did they meet?" I ask, knowing she wants nothing of pity at her words. It's a fact for her, just as it is for me.

"Not often, but she had her Sekund there with her every time. She never stopped looking at people, always bouncing back and forth."

"Did she ever say anything?" Linius tosses in.

"When she did, she was careful to whisper it. I caught her staring at people's chests, then whispering in Addison's ear a lot. Everything about her was off," Oriana says the last part in thought, almost as if trying to process it now.

"Interesting," Linius mumbles. I look to him curiously. "Alastira knows people, Addison rarely travels, meets, or moves without her. I noticed the same things when visiting them for the first time."

"I barely noticed her at the meeting," I push myself away from the desk, moving behind it to grab paper and pen. "She made herself quite small."

"Or you were too distracted elsewhere," Mikhail raises a hand to stop me from biting his head off. "She keeps herself small purposely, you had a lot going on so naturally you wouldn't have noticed anything out of the ordinary."

"She has a secret, Alastira does. I have a feeling that it's only helping Addison's plans," Linius works his jaw in irritation.

"For now, I believe the primary issue at hand is not only Addison, but Gallyan," Aiza adjusts the tan cloth covering her hair to sit flatter on her shoulder. "He made it very clear that he has an interest in Kali."

"But why, it's more than just the size of her as a dragon," Janét crosses her legs. "I saw how he looked at her. You're an hors d'oeuvre and he's a starving man."

"You also have one of the largest territories between all of us," Linius nods at the other Dronning and Konge, who tilt their heads in agreement. "Controlling you, or getting rid of you, could prove fruitful for anyone."

"And Addison?" I drop the pen and paper, having written down the reminders I need later. "What does she have to gain?"

"Killing off competition," Mikhail shrugs, causing his hair to fall over his shoulder. "Or what she thinks is competition. As well as earning some sway with a Konge who clearly wants to control more than his own Samle."

* * *

Jakir

Kali's end of the Bond is riddled with emotion. I feel her anger at the humans, her struggle to ignore the attraction to Mikhail, the fear for the Samle.

I have to restrain myself from wrapping her up in my arms. She would be furious about such a public display of affection. For now, I do as much as I can by keeping most of her emotions down until she can deal with them alone.

"Can we find out more before doing anything?" Kali looks to Filo, but it's Linius who answers her.

"We can, give me a few days."

I look at him, wanting to know why he of all people would be able to gain information in a matter of days.

"Will you be visiting her?" I ask him, wondering what his plan is.

"No," he pulls himself up from the couch, buttons his jacket, then leaves.

"That man has never made sense to me," Janét watches him as he goes.

Kali just looks at the door closing behind him. She knows something, I can see it in her eyes.

"You'll see the human, Fin around," she says to the Dronning. "Keep an eye on him. I don't fully trust him, nor do I trust his background."

The curvy Hispanic woman nods, dropping a kiss onto Kali's cheek that lingers a bit. She catches me looking at her. I smile back playfully, wanting her to understand I know she means well with my Bonded.

"Mikhail," I turn to him, still shocked by the fiery color of his hair every time I look at him. "Might I have a moment with Kali alone please?"

Mikhail tries to give me a hard look. I hold his stare, putting ire into my eyes until he backs down and leaves, as do everyone but the twins. Senka has slipped into one of the many hiding places I'm sure, Sayah moves along the railing that's closer to the top. Even six floors up he still concerns me with the way he moves.

"Everything okay?" she asks me. Always so cautious of everyone's feelings but her own.

"I'm fine, you're not," I brush the backs of my fingers down her cheek. A small bit of the stress eases in her. "What can I do to ease it all?"

She smiles, a rare sight on her. Yet not so rare around me. I feel my own happiness grow at the look on her face.

"Keep your eye on Fin, keep me in check."

I chuckle, "Keeping you in check is easier than breathing."

She lightly smacks my chest, rolling her eyes. I search her face and the Bond, spotting the other emotion quickly.

"You have a soft spot for him?" I ask.

She looks at me, bored, "What do you think? I'm self-aware enough to know when I'm sympathizing. He was trapped just like I was, he just got a different deal because of what's between his legs."

"I'm glad you can recognize it. But if you can do that, why can't you stop yourself if you go too far with it?"

"I don't know if I'll be able to tell before it's too late. I feel for him, I really do."

"I promise to keep my eyes on both of you."

"Thank you," she breathes out, smiling at me again. The slightly crooked tooth next to her incisors makes it even more adorable. "I think I'm going to go talk to him, see how he's doing."

As she walks away she points up, right at Sayah and says, "You can look, not touch. I can handle myself."

I hear a huff from him. Waiting a moment I collect myself with a breathing exercise. It brings my heart rate down enough I feel confident to return outdoors to help with the building.

With the cold setting in and becoming deeper, a large dining hall had begun to be constructed to hold everyone. Our growing size and various tasks to be completed means not everyone could join for dinner each night. Despite that, I'd started the project so that the building could be converted for other uses once we became too large.

I pass Kali speaking with the human man on the way out. I give her a smile, but the second she turns her head I press as much essence into my eyes as I can. He might be human, but the glowing would be enough to scare him. With every ounce of anger stored inside me I threaten him. His eyes widen in fear as Kali's head is turned away, speaking about a chore he can help with. My lips spread, pulling into a dark smile that has nothing pleasant about it.

Continuing to walk past him, I wave with my talons out. The gold gleams at him, forcing his eyes to widen more.

He moves his mouth to speak, instead having to follow Kali as she snaps at him to follow. With a look from him, I head my own way.

My only issue with his look, is that it's one that conveys both fear and hostility.

Chapter 45

Kali

F in seems comfortable in the house. He's nervous once I enter his room, but comfortable. It's not until I turn back around mid-conversation that I notice he's acting scared.

"What is it?" I drop my hand from pointing at the dining hall.

"Nothing," he brushes it off.

I roll my eyes, "I won't ask again. I can tell you'd like to say what's on your mind. Don't expect me to care more than I already do."

"That's a bit harsh," Fin picks at a scab on his arm.

I lift an eyebrow at him, "So is trying to kill two of my dragons."

He physically shrinks back, deterred by my words. I close my eyes for just a second to collect myself.

"I'm sorry, that was harsh," my hand lightly rests on his bicep, it's a struggle for me to touch him even this much. I imagine how I'd felt when I woke up to Jakir, it seems to work.

"I get it, they're your family."

"And I get it for you, you were just trying to survive."

He smiles, unfortunately warming my heart to him just a bit more.

I keep him by my side, unwilling to release him amongst my people while the anger about what happened is so fresh. He's compliant with everything both myself and others ask of him.

For a few days we work with Ellie to tend to the now massive farm. She barks commands like a general in battle. Even with the harsh winter she manages to force multiple types of vegetables to grow. It's never enough for her, she tells me, always needing to grow more food just in case.

I enjoy the hard labor after morning training sessions with the twins. It eases the ache in my body. The bruises, minor cuts, and stiff muscles are well worth it. No longer does my body struggle under starvation. It doesn't need to focus on recovery or surviving either.

I notice during one of the days of work, that Fins' body doesn't struggle at all to recover. The humans ability to now recover faster than us makes me anxious. It has me pondering why his is slower than I thought it should be. I pull myself into different thoughts, not wanting to increase my distrust in him for no reason.

Taking note of the rigid muscles underneath his long sleeved shirt my mind starts turning before I can stop it.

"What type of leader is Kent?"

Fin pauses, using the shovel to lean on heavily. He isn't looking at where he leans though, and his arm slips, sending him stumbling to the right. His cheeks flush as he struggles to right himself, and then lean on the shovel without missing it. He stares at me, not saying a word about his reaction.

"Unforgiving, not many slip ups in the group."

His answer doesn't ease my questioning of how healthy he seems. Not only physically, but mentally he only took a day to recover before seeming genuinely fine.

"You seem to have made it out relatively unscathed," I keep my tone neutral, trying to betray my doubt in his story.

"It was either eat or be eaten, so I did everything I could to make sure I wasn't eaten."

I look at him, expecting more to his story. Brushing it off as him not being ready to speak more about it I return to my own work.

"What about you?" he tosses the question back at me. His tone is honestly curious, though also hesitant.

I flip my braid back over my shoulder, still working on clipping dead leaves. Clearing my throat I respond, "I got my ass handed to me."

"You pick the fight?"

My eyes narrow at him.

"No," I don't miss the minute surprise he quickly hides. "But I got out."

"How?"

Why I choose to lie I don't know, but I do.

"I fought back."

"That's a nice way of saying you killed one of them," his face is light, I force myself to let his emotion put my distrust at ease. Having been in the same position as him, I can understand his desperation to feel normal again.

"You said it, not me," I force a smile back at him. Suddenly he throws his head back laughing. It's loud enough to draw attention from some of the surrounding people helping out.

"That is the most forced smile I think I have ever seen," he continues laughing.

Muttering to myself I turn back to my work, focusing on it with a renewed vigor. Fin nudges my shoulder gently while his laugh calms down. Out of the corner of my eye I catch Aiza moving quickly towards me. Dark blue fabric flutters around her with the wind.

"Kali," her voice is calm and rushed at the same time. "Jacob is awake."

Dropping my tool instantly I move towards the manor. Footsteps behind me make me look over my shoulder.

"Fin, no," I place a hand up. He still follows. "I said no!"

He shrinks back at the increased volume. His behavior irritates me, making me wonder at how horrible of a person I could be to be bothered by his fear.

"I just want to see how he's doing," he says quietly. Wearing his heart on his sleeve I can see the guilt eating at him.

I bite the inside of my cheek, "I'll tell you later how he's doing. Please go back to work."

Thankfully he walks back towards the field to pick up the shovel.

"He seemed genuinely concerned," Aiza remarks.

"He did, but Harlow doesn't need to see one of the men that attacked her in the same room while she's on edge."

"You think she'd try to hurt him?"

"I don't know what she'd do right now, she's only let Brawn in regularly. The sole reason Jakir and I could see her is because she's known us the longest."

"We'd never do anything to harm her though," she looks hurt at my words. I brush a hand over her shoulder.

"It's not that. She doesn't trust her own reactions right now."

Aiza's face relaxes once we cross the threshold of the front entrance. Walking under the stone overhang we push through the front doors leading out to one side of the manor. More people litter the hallways now bringing in furniture to their respective rooms. Whether built, found, or refurbished the entire Samle had managed to come up with enough to create a unique space in every room. It has an old feel to it, bringing in a comfortable space.

"How is he?" I ask Brawn, who's standing outside the door with Jakir.

"The leg needed to be cleaned up a bit," he looks down at his notes. Shoving his glasses up with his palm he continues, "But the large majority of the healing seems to be when he's awake. I induced much of his sleep to keep him from being in too much pain."

"Will he be able to get up and move around? Can we find some sort of prosthetic?" Jakir crosses his arms over his chest.

"I can start working on that, sure. He has to take this incredibly slow for now, I have no idea what the ramifications of a dragon losing their leg could be," he turns to walk away. "And no shifting until I say otherwise!"

I frown, wondering why shifting would even be an issue when Jacob has only just woken up. Easing the door to their room open, I walk in to see Harlow smiling at Jacob's bedside.

"How'd you get this bed?" he asks me, a large smile on his face.

"Hello to you too," I say, grinning at his positive mood. I glance down at the end of his leg to see no blood. Only bandages and medical tape.

"It's fine really, I can't believe Brawn managed it," Jacob goes to move, only for Harlow to jump up from her chair.

"What? What do you need? I can get it for you." She hovers over him, ready for anything.

"Low I'm fine, I was just sitting up," he pushes his torso up as she adjusts the pillows behind him.

Enjoying Harlow being a mother hen, I answer Jacob's question, "I had them find it and bring it here. This is the first fully furnished room."

He pumps his fist in front of him, "Hell yeah, we get the best room."

I fold a leg up to sit on the edge of the bed.

"Seriously, how are you doing?" I'm aware of how gentle my tone is, as if speaking too loud will bring him pain.

"Tired," he shrugs. "There's obviously a bit of pain, nothing compared to what it could've been. Could be dead."

He finds the last part funny, Harlow does not. Tears well in her eyes.

"Harlow," I whisper. My decision about keeping Fin here rather than another option becomes questionable suddenly.

"I'm okay, I'm alive. I'm more than alive," Jacob cups her cheek. "I just need some time."

Swallowing, I start to move, afraid I'm interrupting a private moment.

"Let me know if you need anything," I offer.

"No, no, stay," Jacob pats the bed again, grimacing at a flare of pain. He hides it before she sees. "Tell me everything that's happened. Good, bad, and the ugly."

I breathe in deeply, then start the explanation of everything from the buildings both finished and started to the pregnancy announced by a couple last week. They both find some joy in that, giving each other a hinting look until I continue.

"There's one more thing, it's not easy, but we need to talk about it."

I drag in a lungful of air, bracing myself.

"I know it's hard, but we don't know who did this to you. Even if it was Fin…"

"He was just trying to survive, like the rest of us," Jacob finishes for me. I nod. "Brawn says once the pain subsides I can move around on some forearm crutches. I'd like to meet him once I'm up."

"When you're ready," I grip the duvet cover, then stand. "I need to get back out there. Just send for me if you need anything at all."

"Kali," Harlow calls my name just as I step out of the room.

I don't respond in fear of upsetting her more than she already must be.

"Why did you let him live?" tears well in her eyes.

I take her hand in mine and smooth my thumb over it. Aiza steps up next to her, touching her arm gently.

"I can't end every person that looks at me wrong. There has to be mercy somewhere in this world."

"It doesn't need to be the man that cut Jacob's leg off," she bites back.

Patiently, I try again, "I don't think it was him. I'm fairly certain Jakir speared the one that did."

Her lids flutter closed at the same time she takes a deep breath in.

"They were moving so fast I just couldn't see anything."

"Neither could I, that's their advantage. With enough of them working together their speed and strength might be able to take one of us down."

Her face turns thoughtful, almost absent.

"Let me know if anything with him changes," she says, dipping back into the room.

Standing at the end of the hall is Fin. His face falls at the clear anger on my face. Aiza follows my gaze, becoming stern.

"Didn't you tell him to stay away?"

I don't answer her. Moving quickly I walk towards him. His feet stumble, carrying him backwards from me. He rounds a corner in the direction of leaving the house.

"Fin!" I call. Once I make my way around the same corner he's gone. I search, finally catching him further away from the house than he should be. Thinking he must have run, I start following him again.

He's already picked up some materials to carry once I reach him.

"I told you to stay away," I grit my teeth so hard it feels like they might crack.

"Is there something you're not telling me? You're lucky I let you live," I grab a fistful of his shirt, pulling him close to me. He has to hunch slightly to avoid his shirt being torn. "When I give you a command you follow it.

Disobey me again and I'll rip your heart out and feed it to the Twins."

Nodding he starts to speak before I can stop him.

"I just want to tell him I'm sorry," he pauses, breathing shakily. I watch a tear fall down his face. "I won't do it again."

Rather than giving in to his pity, I let go of him with a shove.

"I hope not, it would be a shame for you to ruin it for any other survivors."

Jakir finds me later in the day sitting in the large dining hall, bringing me a plate of food. Sayah and Senka are right behind him, choosing to sit right next to me.

"I don't like him," Senka garbles through her mouthful of bison. Sayah nods his agreement.

"I get it, guys, he came from a bad place. That doesn't mean he's a bad person."

"Give it time, love," Jakir sits next to me, letting me lean against his side while we eat. "Nobody has ever had a reason to trust people like him."

"You mean humans," I pick at steaming vegetables. They're spiced with some of the herbs Ellie had recently been successful in growing in her new greenhouse.

"Sure."

"Speak of the devil," Senka mutters. Scarfing down their food, the Nightmares slink off into the shadows. Moments later, Fin appears with two plates of food.

"Hey I brought you some, oh," his face falls at the sight of my food. Looking between Jakir and I he falters in his steps. "I'll find another place to eat."

"It's fine," I say, glancing at Jakir. He nods encouragingly. "You can eat with us."

Fin smiles as he sits. I grab the extra dish of food to replace it with my now empty one.

"Where are you from, originally?" Jakir makes his attempt at breaking the awkwardness around us.

"Northeast, all over there."

"How'd you end up with the Skin Carvers?"

He chuckles, "Who's calling them that?"

"Everyone," I toss in, not bothering to look up from my plate.

"Bit of a rough name, don't you think?" he looks around the room, looking at everyone but us.

Jakir and I both pause in our eating to stare at him.

"I think it's appropriate enough for a group of rapists," my response has him looking uncertain.

"I guess so," he looks down at his food. His thoughts travel elsewhere, making his face vacant.

A thought suddenly occurs to me.

"Did you ever touch one of the women?" I deadpan. A mixture of shock and fear crosses his face. Jakir stills against my back.

"What?" Fin's voice is barely above a whisper.

"Did you rape them, the women?"

He stutters out his answer, "N-no, I'd never do that."

Taking his blush for being either under stress or extremely naïve I drop the subject.

"So, like Jakir said, how did you end up with them?" I leave out their title, not wanting another distraction from the answer.

"I was trying to find some food in a grocery store in some city, not sure which one because everything is so destroyed now. They caught me trying to hide in a freezer after I heard them."

"I take it you didn't escape?" My dark humor puts a small smile on both of the twins' faces. A somber weight settles on Fin in the quiet. He looks up at me shyly, then at Jakir, then back to his plate.

"I need some more food," my Bonded stands, squeezing the back of my neck assuredly. "Be back in a bit."

Leaving us in silence I branch out again to try and get an answer from Fin.

"How long were you with them?"

"I honestly couldn't tell you," he shrugs, seeming tired. "Got so focused on surviving I lost track of time."

Gentle warmth flits across my skin. Behind closed eyes I watch the memories of pushing Feathers away before Kent found me. Grant's face flashes angrily at me.

"What problem do you have with Addison?"

His question has my eyes flying open. I wait, staring at him until I've carefully created a response.

"I don't, she has one with me. Dropping multiple people into my territory with a directive to cause harm gives me legal rights to demand repayment."

"Why haven't you?"

I eye him suspiciously, "Why are you asking?"

"I just don't get all this dragon stuff. You guys seem so violent but also so protective of your own, it must be nice having that kind of thing. We...I never had that with the guys."

"It's not a good idea right now. I'd rather try and avoid losing any of my own people."

"You seem like you're holding back, why isn't Addison?"

"Because she wants more, having her Samle isn't enough," I purposely leave the details out, still distrusting.

"Is there anything I can do to help?"

His offer clears my suspicion of his questions.

He's just trying to help. The guilt must be making him feel like he owes us. He's human, he doesn't understand our world.

"For now, just stay out of trouble. I think most have been easing up since you haven't tried to kill anyone," my lips turn up slightly, attempting to ease Fin's distress.

"Yeah I guess that would help put people's mind at ease usually," he chuckles, the sound light.

I feel warmth touch my chest again. It spreads, making me feel an inclination to lean towards him. I hold back, suddenly irritated at the feeling. The realization hits me suddenly.

Fuck.

"Excuse me, I need to go handle some boring old politics before I go to bed."

"Alright," he smiles up at me. "I'm just going to finish eating here, if that's alright."

"Yeah," I grab my plates.

"Goodnight, Kali," his dark blue eyes look nearly black in the night.

"Goodnight," I mumble.

Hurriedly I return my plate to the eating hall, dodging the pull of conversation from various people wanting me to join them for drinks. I make my way through the house area, slipping quickly into a single bedroom home. My heart rate climbs so high my hands start to shake.

"Mikhail," I breathe out, releasing the tension in my chest. For a moment, I'm distracted by the sight of him shirtless. Water drips down his chest towards the belt line hanging low on his waist.

"Kali," his voice is rough, bringing shivers up my spine. I lick my lips that are suddenly dry at the sight of his pants tightening on him. "You either speak now or we won't be doing any until I've finished inside your mouth."

My eyes snap up to meet his, the hazel color dark with lust. His facial hair has grown out heavily, making him look more mature than he did in the castle. His step towards me has me clearing my throat to speak.

"Is a Suitor attraction between a dragon and human possible?"

Any sexual tension evaporates into thin air. His mouth opens to speak multiple times, no words ever coming out. Running a hand through his hair I have to force my eyes not to travel down to the flexing thighs covered by cloth. His face turns away, hiding any emotion he may be feeling.

"Why are you asking?"

I ignore the jealousy in his question.

"Just answer the question," I'm unsure of what to do with my hands, deciding to rub my collarbone with one.

"I've only heard of dragons having a Suitor attraction with other dragons," he splashes water on his face. I drop my shoulders in relief, only to tense them back up at his next words. "But the first dragon woke

491

up three years ago, there's nothing saying that one with a human isn't possible."

I sag into a chair unsure of how to take everything in.

"Tell me who, we can figure this out," Mikhail crouches down in front of me. Resting his hands on my thighs puts my mind in a state of war trying to decide if I should distract myself or not. Pulling his hands to hold mine I work on calming my heart. "Kali, tell me."

I stare into his eyes as if the answer would appear if I just look long enough. He murmurs my name occasionally, placing his forehead against mine. Taking refuge in silence for only a moment longer I finally tell him.

"It's Fin."

Chapter 46

His entire body stills for a second, before suddenly pulling away. "You must be mistaken."

"You just said there's nothing saying it's not possible."

"I was confused."

"Bullshit."

We hold each other's stares, neither of us moving except to breathe. I'm the first to break eye contact, reaching for the door.

"Don't," he grunts. "I didn't mean to come across…"

"Like a possessive caveman?" I plant a hand firmly on one hip. "Having sex with me doesn't constitute playing a pissing game every time another man threatens you."

"It's quite literally not my fault," his eyebrows pinch at the same time his head tilts to the side.

"Then why was I able to let go of my jealousy over Addison so quickly?" I mimic his movement, trying to annoy him. My fingers are itching to start a fight.

"Be honest with yourself Kali, we both know you hated her the moment she looked at me a little too long."

Too stubborn to admit that he's right, I clench my jaw. He chuckles humorlessly.

"It doesn't matter anymore-"

"It doesn't as long as you're not looking for reasons to go after Addison."

"*Looking* for reasons?" I say in disbelief. "She's handing them to me left and right. You saw how friendly she was with Gallyan, who clearly wants a new pet named 'Kali'. She sends humans into my territory that cut off Jacobs' god damn leg! She didn't even have the wherewithal to help when I was being chased down by them. Addison knows what they did, knows I got my pretty little fucking pattern from them slicing me to pieces because I killed three of them. Killed them for trying to take me down out of a tree with a knife lodged in my ribs. I got away, don't even remember shifting, found their bodies torn apart like puzzle pieces, and they hunted me down for *weeks*. *Weeks*, Mikhail. I've been coming and going from my own damn territory so much I've missed nearly everything happening here. You have a castle to protect your people, walls to hide them behind if you're attacked. I have *nothing* to defend my people with other than some sick," I jam a finger into the side of my head. "Twisted," I step towards him, he steps back. "Part of me," I keep stepping towards him. "That I have to fight against every damn time I shift because she wants to taste blood no matter who it comes from."

I realize my eyes are glowing, so much that Mikhail is starting to bend under my essence coming out of them.

"Do you know what it's like, wanting to let the Nightmares go? Let them shred anyone that puts a finger on me I don't like? Do you understand how difficult it was not to rip out your fucking throat when you laid there on the ground with my tail in your wing? God, I wanted to feel you squirm as I tore your wings from your back," I laugh, but it's dark and unnatural. I recognize concern flickering down the Bond as the other side of me keeps its ugly head reared. One slip, and I'll no longer be in control. "All I want, is for my people to be safe. To never experience what I did again. I'm doing everything I can, and it still feels like it's not enough. Best part of it? I didn't even get to choose this."

Heat in my eyes dims to a cooler temperature, taking the glow of the light with it. Without realizing, my talons had come out in the middle of my venting. I pull them back in slowly.

"I'm sorry," is all he can get out before the door bursts open. Jakir ducks his head as he steps into the house.

"What's going on," he demands. Those golden eyes look between

Mikhail and I feverishly until I step forward. In the Bond, I grab the golden string tightly, reaching out until the gold starts to turn into black. Holding onto it until I feel calm.

"I'm okay, everything is fine."

"It's clearly not," Jakir is speaking to me, but staring Mikhail down. Surprisingly, I feel anger start a flame in Jakir.

"I'm concerned I might have a Suitor attraction with Fin."

That pulls his eyes to me and extinguishes the flame in him. He doesn't ask for an explanation, only looks to Mikhail to ask if it's possible.

"I told Kali that I don't know. We've only been around as a species for three years. I've never seen it before, but that's not to say it can't happen."

"I'm worried it might be clouding my judgment," I splay my hands out at my Sekund. He closes the door behind him, pulls me to the table, and sits me down next to him.

Him and Mikhail toss ideas back and forth on why such a thing would be possible in the first place, and the reasons it would happen.

My own mind spirals, wondering how I could have been put in such a precarious position. A man, not even a dragon, trying to survive this new world, only to end up in the hands of what he thought was the enemy.

Maybe he still does.

"Would he be able to feel it?" I ask.

"We don't know, a lot of things that affect us as dragons are most likely caused by the fact that we're interacting with our own species."

"Or being connected with our own land."

"Exactly, but how does a human play into that?"

"Perhaps being on our territory means someone your body wouldn't recognize otherwise is now easier to pick out," Jakir sips from the glass of water Mikhail hands him.

They continue discussing how such a thing could be both possible and not. I think back to the fight, trying to remember if I felt anything. I felt the violence, the need to harm, but I was also in the middle of defending two of my own. I just as easily could have been feeling the attraction without being able to distinguish. It could have gotten Jacob killed.

"Is it possible for a dragon to tell if a person could be a Suitor to another?" I stare at a scratch in the wood, struggling to comprehend my own words.

They both stay silent, unwilling to answer a question suggesting Addison's part in this.

"This isn't me saying Addison has some weird ability to tell, I'm not looking for reasons to go after her," I look pointedly at Mikhail, who winces under Jakir's glare. "I'm just saying we have concrete information saying that she's the one who sent them in. I watched her drool over Gallyan at the meeting so she's probably playing into his game, and now this? That's no coincidence."

"If it is, it's a poorly timed one," Jakir sucks in his bottom lip.

"Or a perfectly timed one if you think about it," I trace a pattern in the table. Fins' guilty face stares back at me in my head. The flinching and fear of a reaction that's too loud or too sudden. How he follows every command down to the tiniest detail, no matter who gives it to him. All signs of previous abuse from Kent.

"I'd keep it between us for now, don't say anything to him just yet," Jakir stands from the table, offering a hand to help me up.

I wait in the door as Jakir steps out, looking back at Mikhail.

"You need to either come clean with Addison, or let go of the guilt you have about the baby."

"I don't know what you're talking about," he doesn't even have the audacity to look ashamed.

"Protecting her like you do, arguing that she's an innocent, is only going to put you in a tight spot."

"I don't need advice from a Dronning who's only been so for half as long as I have."

I flinch at the verbal slap across my face. Mikhail's face drops in realization of what he's done. Anger flares up inside of me, lashing out to Jakir for stability. His form fills the doorframe behind me, a solid anchor in the turmoil of my feelings.

"Get out," I say calmly, the complete opposite of the emotions raging inside me. A bit of betrayal enhances the edge to them.

He sighs, tugging on his hair, "Kali I didn't mean-"

"You have until tomorrow evening to gather your own people and get out," I step outside.

"Don't be-"

"You heard her," Jakir's emotions start to turn defensive. "Leave."

Mikhail moves to step towards me aggressively, his fingers dropping nails to the floor.

"I'm allowed to stay until I no longer agree with you?"

I clench my fists, fighting the urge to give into his fight. He doesn't stop with that.

"I offered you safety with me, you and I could be safe together. You're not strong enough yet without me helping you."

Heat flares so quickly in my eyes that a tear threatens to fall down the outer corner. Hazel eyes glow in response, trying to bite back at the force pushing out from me. Jakir moves so quickly I almost don't see it. Mikhail is blocked from my view, then slammed into the wall outside of the house.

People heading into their homes take notice, pausing to watch. Mikhail's small group of people start to move towards us. They stop as Jakir tightens his death grip around the Konge's neck. Choking sounds send a thrill through my body. No one moves further.

"Even if she wasn't strong enough to hold her own," his talons are shimmering at night, lit by the torches fueled on the dirt path between houses. "She always has me," the huge golden daggers touch the pale bare skin covering abdominal muscle.

Pale skin turns a shade darker as the blood and air become lacking.

"I don't enjoy taking lives," his broad nose flares, inhaling deeply. "But I will for her."

The truth in his words drops like an anchor in still water. Never had I seen him so violent towards anything. I feel it in the deepest parts of him that he means every word. Fearful of just how close he is to tipping over that edge I place a firm hand against one of his shoulder blades. Bulky muscles relax in reaction, Jakir drops his hand from Mikhail's throat. I watch his ginger hair fall over his shoulders as he's brought to his knees gasping.

"Consider your place," I squat down in front of him and pull his face up to meet mine with a finger. "I will not give up my throne for a man."

I'm unsure of what pushes me to press my lips to his. I chalk it up to being the physical want after violence, as the pattern between us has occurred before.

"Are you guys okay?" Fin walks up to us as we pass the last grouping of houses. His hands wring together nervously. "I just caught the last part, is something wrong?"

I stare, trying to sift through my feelings of how I feel about him. Faintly I hear Jakir tell him how it was just some territorial behavior between dragons. Fin's arms flex, his biceps bulging then relaxing as his fingers dance. I realize how much I'm staring, finally pulling my eyes up to his. His smile is knowing, sweet. Disgruntled with being caught staring I look away.

Stupid, don't show him you're shy.

"Aren't you supposed to be working on one of the farms right now?" Jakir asks.

"Oh I finished the work super early, being able to move faster and all tends to help," he grins. "But are you okay, Kali?"

"I'm fine, thank you," I softly respond, too emotionally wiped to fake any interest in seeing him.

"Well, I'm gonna head back to my room," he doesn't stop smiling at me, so I offer a small smile to him. We watch him walk away, waiting until he's out of ear shot to start walking again.

Feathers flits over my head, landing on my outstretched arm.

"Please no more bad news, I can't do it right now Feathers," I plead.

"Bad man?"

I bite the inside of my cheek, not wanting anyone to see my smile at his words.

Leaning in I whisper to him, "Just a little testy, still a good man."

Jakir grunts, "We'll see about that."

"He is a good man, at heart. Just a little wrapped up in his emotions," I let Feathers rub his beak on my cheek, then play with a few strands of loose hair. "I've never seen you that angry."

"I'm sorry, love. I don't like being like that, he's just gotten too out of hand here. Too territorial."

I follow him to his room where Feathers takes up a space on top of a shelf. He removes his clothing, changing into sweatpants. Picking up his shirt I change into it, needing to be as close as I can be. His arms open once he's in bed. Crawling onto the mattress I curl up into his side using his pectoral as a pillow. Deft fingers trace the patterns on my back, easing me into the most peaceful sleep in months.

In the morning, I inform Fin that he'll be moving into Mikhail's house at the end of the day.

"Are you sure?" he scoops a spoonful of black beans into his mouth.

I nod once, "Yes, it was temporary while he visited anyway. The only permanent ones are for those staying."

"Whoa, didn't think we'd be talking about me moving in so soon," he wiggles his eyebrows at me. Rolling my eyes I turn to Lilly, who's decided to sit next to me every breakfast.

"I have my own room, Mama said I'm too big to sleep with her now," she crams a fistful of grapes into her mouth.

"Lilly, easy," I mutter, pulling two grapes out of her mouth by pressing on her cheek. She giggles and kicks her feet hanging over the bench.

"Wow, you have a room all to yourself?" Fin uses his spoon to point at her, making her smile.

"Yes, all mine. I keep my toys in there too," she crawls up onto her knees to grab more grapes. "And snacks too," she whispers. "But don't tell mama that."

Fin looks genuinely concerned at me, trying to figure out if what she's saying is a bad thing or not. Laura leans over from feeding her own daughter to explain in a whisper.

"Ellie knows, she just likes to pretend she doesn't so that she doesn't have to fight with Lilly to get her to eat."

Relief washes over his face, making me laugh.

"I think that was the most stressful thing I've experienced in the past three weeks," he says, exasperated. "Other than being hunted down by a dragon."

"I'm a dragon!" Lilly stands up, making an attempt at growling noises with yet more grapes in her mouth.

"You're a child," I frown, setting her back down on her butt. She finds my words funny, holding my hand as she laughs. I switch to my left hand to eat to allow her to keep holding it.

The conversation in the room dulls at the entrance of Mikhail. Looking up I see him staring at me, a dull sadness in his eyes. He looks to the empty seat next to me, which is immediately filled by Sayah.

"Ignorant bird," Theri wipes her mouth, turning from staring him down over her shoulder.

"I take it word has spread," I place my elbows onto the table, lacing my fingers to rest my chin on.

"We knew about his self-centered temper before," her eyes are icy, stiff with the grudge her and all the other previously rogue dragons hold.

"He d-did t-try and k-kill us," Brawn speaks up as he scoots down to make room for Ellie. "I-if it hadn't been for you, w-we'd all be dead."

"Dead as a doorknob," Feather screams, landing on the table. Joyfully Lilly reaches to grab him, setting her and Emma into a chasing game with him.

"Brawn," Ellie starts sweetly. "Please try to word things a little more sensitively around the little ones."

He apologizes, even offering a brief grin to her.

"Then why is he here?" Fin pulls us back to the conversation at hand.

"Allies matter, even the stupid ones," I respond.

"But now he's not?"

I search for the right terms to describe my relationship with him without giving away the small parts. Janét and Linius join, taking the empty spots created by the two girls running off.

"Mikhail cares for his Samle just like I do, we just have different ways of doing so."

"He seems to have a way to care about you too."

Conversation drops in the small section of the table. Laura and Theri tense, continuing to eat without looking up. Sayah pins Fin with a glare, who returns it with a bold aggression that catches me off guard.

It's Janét who breaks the lull.

"We dragons aren't particularly shy about physical relationships like you humans. It's either that or violence."

"I noticed the second part," Fin teases.

Glad of having avoided a complicated answer involving politics I finish up my plate quickly. I stand up, reaching to grab it only for Fin to pick it up first.

"I got it for you."

"Uh, thank you," uncomfortable with the forced kindness I turn, tapping Sayah as I do. He nods, finishing up his food quickly to follow me. "We'll be helping with some of the heavy lifting for today. I know you're a human, but with your extra strength you can do some of the minor stuff."

"I don't mind working on the farm," he rubs his neck.

"I know, but we need you inside helping to move and hold materials."

He looks worried as I move to take off my clothes. Those sweet blue eyes track over my scars briefly, fighting not to stare.

"Staring is rude," I tease him, trying to lighten the mood.

"I'm sorry," he mumbles. "Could I work on the farm again? I really liked it there."

"Tomorrow, I promise," my heart aches a bit at the pleading in his voice. "I really need your help with this today."

Walking away before he can argue more I force my body through the change, walking smoothly through it until I'm at full size. Fin's groan is humorous as he walks in, sounding like a moody man. I spot a man with short brown hair and olive skin moving about with an unsteady gait.

"Jacob," I say surprised, to Harlow.

"*I'm only letting him walk around for a few minutes at a time.*"

"*I don't doubt it,*" my lips pull into the strange smile my leathery lips can manage.

"He's healing well, Brawn's already working on a prosthetic for him because he's moving along so quickly," she picks up a bag of tiles with her mouth. Setting them down in front of the outline that would eventually become the first shops, she turns back to me. *"How's it going with the human?"*

"His name is Fin, and he's getting better. Still a bit jumpy but I was too when Jakir found me."

"Hmm, yes I distinctly remember you looking like you wanted to end me. In a church of all places. How unholy of you," she laughs.

I nip at her neck playfully, she does the same then bumps under my chin with her snout.

"I'm the last person you should think of when it comes to being holy."

"I second that," Aiza squeezes between us, pulling a cart full of nails, screws, and wooden pieces that would lock the walls permanently into place.

"Ganging up on me is entirely uncalled for," my wings pull to hover over the ground. Carrying myself to a pile of wood, a man with short cropped black hair directs me which ones to pick up.

"And having a crush on a human man you captured only weeks ago isn't?"

"How did you know?" My question is sarcastic, bored. *"You both know me too well, leave before I have to end you."*

They chuckle, tossing a few more teasing lines at me. Our banter stays lighthearted even as Jacob barks directions at people. Harlow keeps her eye on him, sniffing him every now and then to check.

A loud crash comes from one of the shops, followed by a scream. My neck curls backward before my body does. Trying to see what's happened I lower my head.

Fin is on the ground next to someone who's holding their arm. His face is contorted into extreme panic. Hurriedly shifting I yank on a sweater and shorts nearby. They must be Harlow's because the shorts fall off, forcing me to find another pair.

"Dammit dammit dammit," I mutter to myself. People move out of my way, creating a path for me to reach the injured man.

"Please," he whines. "Stop touching me."

Fin looks up to see me, now looking hurt.

"I don't know what happened, it just fell," he whispers.

"You dropped it," the man, who I recognize as Anahl from Mikhail's territory. "I thought humans could hold that weight."

I crouch down to look at Anahl's arm, "One of you go get Brawn."

Another person dashes out to retrieve him.

"Ow," Anahl, tries to move his arm from me.

"I'm so sorry I didn't mean to," Fin steps back.

"Wait outside," I say shortly. "Don't go any further."

He leaves, passing Brawn on the way out.

"Let me see," Brawn gently brushes me aside. Stepping back I give him room to get Anahl up on his feet. Immediately the work picks up again, this time with some hushed conversation about Fin's mistake. I look over to the slab of stone that had been cut from a mountain in the north. While incredibly difficult to handle for most, I wonder what would have caused it to drop like it did.

Outside Harlow is curled around Jacob. She glares at Fin from her position. I walk outside, breaking their staring contest.

"Dropping a stone slab is a mistake, but staring her down is a death wish," I motion for him to follow me. We walk in silence to his house, giving me time to ease Jakir's curiosity before stepping inside. "What happened?"

"I don't know, I really don't," he sits down, wringing his hands together.

I go to comfort him but hold back. Thoughts of how the Suitor attraction could sway my judgment stop me from easing my tone. Maintaining the firm exterior I push forward.

"I've seen the strength humans have, the speed too. If that rock had slipped, which it shouldn't have in the first place, you should have been fast enough to move Anahl out of the way."

"Who?"

I frown, "Anahl, the one who ended up with a broken arm. You were working with him."

His eyes drop from mine, boring into the floor beneath him. I lean against a door frame with my shoulder, arms crossed to contain my emotions.

"Kali I'm trying my best here," he shudders, tears lining his voice. "I don't know why you'd automatically blame me like this. I thought you were kinder."

I jerk, the words hitting me like a hot brand. My mind doesn't know how to take his words.

"Excuse me?"

"You've been so patient, and I really appreciate that. I just don't get why one mistake gets me in trouble like this. I got distracted," his hands stop twisting around one another. He looks up at me with tears in his eyes, a look of sorrow on his face. "I think about what happened sometimes, I forget where I am."

Guilt racks me suddenly. He's a survivor, just like I was, and my pushing him isn't helping.

"I'm sorry," I shake my head as if I can shake the frustration from it. "I wasn't trying to push. You just seemed comfortable and ready to do more after a few weeks of healing."

"It's okay Kali, everyone makes mistakes," he smiles slightly, the tears finally disappearing.

"Take a day or two off, let me know if you need anything."

I don't say another word as I leave. My head feels foggy like I've just woken up from a nap. Leaving his place I head straight for the manor to check on Anahl. I shed my clothes to shift once clear of the housing area. I land next to a side door that leads into the wing Brawn's area is in. Pulling on my shirt I walk alone down the hallway. The double wooden doors to Brawn's office are open. A strong herbal smell wafts out of the long room.

"Gods, Brawn, what are you using?" I wave my hand in front of my nose, trying to get the stinging smell out.

"Capsaicin, cat's claw, and peppermint. It's not that hard to figure out," he sits on a stool, his legs spread so he can reach Anahl, who's reclined on a medical chair.

"For you it's not."

"Of course it's not."

I lean over him, examining Anahl's arm that's now much straighter. Braces are on both sides of his arm, stabilizing the bone.

"How are you feeling?" I ask him.

Weakly his lips curl, "A bit woozy, but doctor Brawn here definitely knows how to fix this."

Brawn moves to a workbench where he sets down his now dirty tools. Anahl swings his legs over to stand up.

"Anahl, could you tell me what happened?"

He hesitates, looking away in thought.

"I asked him to pick it up, knew a piece that size shouldn't be too difficult for him. Being human and all you know?"

I nod, encouraging him to continue. I sit down on Brawn's stool, who walks further back towards a collection of plants to give us privacy.

"He argued against doing it, saying he was tired," he continues. "I told him if he was then after this he could head home. Looked mad but he picked it up anyway. Next thing I know we're setting it down, it starts to fall, then my arm's hurting."

"Alright, thank you."

I start to leave, only pausing to catch his last words.

"He must be exhausted, he struggled to pick it up until I helped..." he mutters a few more things to himself I don't bother sticking around to hear.

Chapter 47

Mikhail leaves in the evening quietly. His people are packed, most of them shifted to fly back to the shore.

"I'll send a boat back for you."

"How kind," I say dryly. My dark look disappears for a moment as I shake hands with one of his guards.

"I'm truly sorry about how I acted, it wasn't necessary."

"It was uncalled for."

"I feel no different about you."

Annoyed, I lift a brow at him.

"And how exactly do you feel about me, Konge Mikhail?"

"Stop with the title, it's passive aggressive."

"It's meant to be aggressive aggressive."

After a pause of silence, we both laugh.

"I can understand your guilt, but I will never understand the supporting of someone clearly ill-fitted to be a friend."

"Our....discussion, helped me see a bit clearer on the subject. I still consider you a close friend, Kali."

He hugs me tightly then puts distance between us. His mouth opens to speak, closes, then opens again.

"Out with it," I motion him to speak.

"I had a gut feeling I need to go home anyway. I will say this, no matter the time and place you have my support. Whether it's people, food, or anything your puny heart desires," he laughs when I smack his arm. "You have the Shadow Samles' support."

"And you have the...you have our support."

"You'll find your name one day. Maybe you'll find a reason to stay with me one day too, when you're ready for more."

I breathe out heavily, "Mikhail, the only way that will happen is if you move everything here. I won't give this up, won't do that to my people."

"My offer still, and always will, stand."

I watch the small group leave. Relief floods through me once I feel the presence of another ruler step off my land.

Days roll into one another with no more unfortunate events. While Linius, Janét and I meet often there is still no word of any movement from other Samle's. We begin to assume that most have decidedly settled into staying within their boundaries until Linius hears a concerning word from a newcomer. Groups of them had begun to appear soon after Mikhail left. Most were here of their own free will, allowed to leave by their rulers. A group from the Desert Samle brought a message from Elias.

"He wanted us to tell you he misses your sweet face, and that he'd like to see you again some time soon," the man, named Bassam, told me. With a blush he finishes by leaning in to whisper. "He also said his bedroom isn't difficult to find once you arrive."

Linius spent time sending for anyone of his own people that wished to come here, having been moved by *kallet*. Only a small handful moved here, both of them speaking in heavy accents that Linius helps me understand.

"Their accents are interesting," I comment.

"They were originally from Norway," he bows slightly to them, a custom he had explained earlier that they use for respect in his home. "If my timeline is correct, I believe them, along with a few people spread about, were the first to wake up after the end of it all."

"So, they coined some of the terms?"

He confirms it, restating he isn't sure still.

"While I enjoy talking about the possibilities of our history, I'm afraid I have some unfortunate news. I spoke with the survivors that escaped from Gallyan."

Muscles along my spine tense, making me reach out to Jakir.

"Jakir is on his way, is this something you'd like to share with Janét?"

"In terms of our alliance to her, and your relationship with her, I believe it is a piece of information crucial to her awareness."

"You could have just said yes," I groan slightly, making my way towards my office.

I catch the twins toying with a few weapons, sparring against one another. They follow us in, closing the doors and latching them once everyone is settled. I nod to Oriana, who only blinks in response.

"I don't like the *vibras* in this room," she says, sweeping in elegantly to place herself on her usual spot.

"You're going to love the news then," I lift myself onto the desk. Jakir leans against it next to me, placing a steadying hand on my thigh. I glance up at him, calming at the sight of the golden hue of his irises.

Linius clears his throat then begins.

"I'm not going to waste time making assumptions before conveying all the information to you, so just allow me to finish before speaking."

Oriana, sitting opposite of the Dronning, looks at her pointedly. Janét raises her hands in defense, then pretends to zip her lips closed.

"As you've seen, there have be two groups that recently fled the Hellish Samle. They both conveyed to Kali and I that an underground group has begun attempting to free the slaves under his control."

"I assume it's painfully slow, but they have to be otherwise they'll lose their progress."

"Or their lives," Linius ends the off-track discussion.

"But we knew about the slaves," Jakir's other hand is a fist, the one on my thigh tight. I wrap my hand around his as much as I can, pushing comfort and calm to him.

"What we didn't know," Linius folds his arms over his chest. It makes his slim figure look sharper. "Is where he started. He came out from his begravelse last, until Kali of course."

"Begravelse is the sleep we all went into before waking up as dragons," Jakir whispers to me, feeling me trying to decipher the word.

"I figured."

"He wasn't alone when he came out," Linius paces as he speaks. "He had a Suitor, his wife, who survived as well. The details get muddy from there, but clear up right around the time he mistakenly took her life. In a fit of Suitor driven rage, he ripped her throat out. In death her body never shifted back. He carried her out to a pyre and burned her with his own flame."

He lets it sink in for us, then continues.

"For an unknown reason, that warped him far enough to believe that he's the sole savior of this world. Thinks some dragons are just meant to be at the bottom of the totem pole, while others belong at the top in complete control."

"Holy hell," Janét rubs her forehead, stress evident in her body language.

"It explains his mindset for slavery, but not wanting Kali," Oriana holds her hand out at me, waiting for him to correct himself.

"Gallyan thinks Kali is powerful enough, based on the size of her dragon, that having her means having more power. She's got the bark to match her bite, which she proved in the fight with Mikhail."

"He wasn't looking for real revenge on the twins," I realize out loud. "He was looking for insight."

"I can promise you he wanted revenge on the twins, but only slightly. By letting everyone know what happened, risking his own reputation, he knew there was a chance you'd do what you could to save them."

"Isn't any other ruler just as capable as her?" Jakir rubs his thumb on my knee absently.

Linius shakes his head, still slowly pacing the room, "Even if they were, no one has demonstrated the sheer size and violence that Kali has. In his mind, she's a weapon. A means to an end."

"And this is all from people who escaped the forced labor?" Oriana stares at Linius, who seems to falter for a moment at the freezing look she gives him. "How would these people have heard so much?"

"I think you'd understand, considering the place you were rescued from only a few months ago," he throws back. Her stare is just as freezing, yet the look in her eyes shifts to show a modicum of respect. "People talk, especially people in that situation. People forget they're living breathing people, and say things they wouldn't around guests."

"Did you happen to ask them if they'd heard about Addison?" the Sekund considers, his face thoughtful.

"It only confirmed our previous ideas, that she's working with Gallyan."

"What does she have to earn from it though? She's strong, but not powerful," I list off names on my fingers. "Elias, Mikhail, me, you," I gesture to Linius. "We all easily outrank her in that regard don't we?"

Linius nods, "We do, but she isn't the weakest."

"Who is?" Oriana shifts her legs to cross over one another. I catch Janét staring at the exposed olive skin of her thigh.

"Sean, he's by far the smallest Konge."

I bite the inside of my cheek, "That's why he was so hesitant at the meeting. He's under Gallyan's hand."

"Sean has never been exactly social and visited other territories," Janét pulls out a pack of cigarettes, a rare commodity she'd made a point to have found while here. "Even with Gallyan around, he acts like a beaten dog. I don't think his bending the knee is by his own choice."

"Gallyan has either threatened him or scared him into being a good little boy. So, what do we do?" I look at Linius, his mind processing our conversation. He paces further, drawing us all into silence. Janét blows out smoke towards the tall ceiling. I follow it up, catching Sayah and Senka leaning over the railing whispering to one another. Senka catches my eye, grinning at me with a wave. "Bring Aiza and Harlow here."

"You trust them with this?" Linius questions me. The twins climb down to slip out of the room.

"I trust them with my life, so yes."

"Might I ask what exactly gave you a reason to trust them?"

"Oh just Harlow putting up with me, Aiza giving me nothing but sound advice and guidance while supporting me even if she didn't agree with me."

"*Kallet* must have been strong," he says.

Both women enter, complete contrasts to one another. Harlow's height makes Aiza's frame look even smaller. Aiza seems to float in despite wearing heels with her pants.

Linius retells the information, then I bring them up to speed on our thoughts so far. Harlow is silent, mostly absorbing information. Her first words don't shock me.

"This should be grounds for war," she spreads her arms out, confused as to why we haven't already decided this. "If he's that twisted over losing his wife because of his own lack of self-control that's on him. Bringing people into slavery? Forcing other rulers into submission rather than alliance? Too far. Who else is going to stop it?"

"Not us," Aiza holds her chin, looking to me. "At least not yet. Starting a war as the most recent Dronning to come into power will destroy our standing with anyone that might be on the fence."

"Seemed to me like Hendrix and Dominé weren't exactly being forced into their friendship with him," Senka's voice is light, nearly fairy like. She climbs back into the third level of books along the wall.

"Rulers will do a lot to make sure their people are safe. Even Gallyan cares for his own people," Linius looks at her.

Aiza moves towards a window surrounded by books, "I say we hold for now, focus on training for the possibility of war-"

"You mean certainty," I slide off the desk, moving to sit on one of the couches.

"Either way, we prepare. Harlow and Filo can meet with you to discuss how to improve our security."

"You should do that soon, if not now," Linius turns deadly serious. "Because the last piece of information I received is that Gallyan plans to

511

arrive here with Addison, within five days, if the timing I've considered is correct."

"Motherfucker," I bite out. My fists curl, I forcibly open my hands as my talons shred out.

"Language, Kali," Jakir rubs my shoulder. His hand falls away once I step out of reach.

I breathe in deeply through my nose, running both hands through my hair. My scalp tingles at the sensation of sharp points scraping along it.

"Why?" I nearly growl.

Linius is calm, stern as ever in his response.

"Because he can."

Aiza offers a more sensible reason, "Most likely because he wants to prove to you he can. Wants to scare you at how easily he can show up unannounced. He also knows that if you do one thing out of line to disrespect him or turn him away, it's ammunition."

"Ammunition," the Dominican Dronning joins. "That he can use to convince others to go to war with you as well. If they aren't already convinced."

"This is ridiculous. I'm supposed to host the creepy man that wants to put a collar around my neck and host his side piece all with a smile on my face?" I sink my talons into the surface, thankfully unable to penetrate the dense piece of gray wood. Jacob must have known this thing would need to take a beating.

Janét smiles sympathetically, "Welcome to being a Dronning."

"While I greatly appreciate our time together," I track the Konge as he straightens his purple tie that stands so heavily against the charcoal gray suit he wears. "I do believe that having Janét and I here when they arrive would only cause you more issues."

Panic settles in my stomach at having to handle both Gallyan and Addison without them at my back.

"I agree," Aiza stands, catching the hints from them about leaving. "We also appreciate your time here. We'll be sure to visit some time soon."

"I have someone lined up as an ambassador I'd like to send here," Janét brushes off her pants once fully standing. "Send word when you're ready to receive them."

Jakir reaches through the Bond, grasping tightly onto me. He ushers them out, promising my attendance to see them off.

"I'd like to speak to you tonight," those red lips move tantalizingly in front of me. She reaches up to brush my shoulder inconspicuously. Her rings flash brightly in the sunlight streaming through the windows. "Alone, if you wouldn't mind."

In my mild panic, I notice the hinting look in her eyes. Smirking, I squeeze her hip. She turns, swaying her hips as I watch her leave. Jakir is the only one left in the room, the Twins having run off to go visit the southern parts of the Dead Forest.

"That was a lot," his voice tugs on me the same way he does to the Bond. "I know you're scared, but it's going to be okay."

"Will it, Jakir? How do we know?"

"Gallyan, even with his horrid tendencies and ideas, has yet to do anything directly at you. He might just be trying to scare you into obeying him."

"With the two of them leaving to go back home how am I supposed to deal with not one, but two people who despise me?"

"You don't, *we* do."

I lightly hit his chest with the back of my hand.

"You're ridiculous," I feel the crushing fear lift, making it easier to breathe.

"Your emotions don't seem to think so," his arm wraps around my shoulders, drawing me into the warm scent of him. "Make sure you're up early tomorrow, I have a birthday surprise for you."

I stop dead in my tracks.

"How did you know when my birthday is?"

"Found it amongst the random notes you like to write down, might have been confirmed in one of your drunken monologues you like to have when you come home from the weekly bonfires."

Blushing furiously I bite my lip, "I don't drink at every single one."

"No," he grins, the color of his eyes contrasting heavily against his dark skin. "Just the one's you don't remember."

"I can't believe it'll be January twenty ninth tomorrow," I groan. "How long have we been at this?"

"A while," he laughs. I groan again, walking with him to the kitchen for dinner.

* * *

Now that the Samle is comprised of so many people, dinners have turned to be private between families. Those who were independent having chosen their family long ago made it so no one is left alone for a night.

Dinners with my own family now brings a light to my life, I realize, as we sit around the kitchen, eating soup made by Aiza.

"I had no idea you could cook," Jacob says, using the back of his hand to wipe his mouth. He sits on the counter, swinging his leg back and forth.

"Nobody got away with not learning to cook in my family," she points using her spoon. "Except my cousin, she was a horrible cook. Burned water somehow."

She shakes her head, smiling while the rest of us chuckle. Jacob moves to get more but Harlow stops him by putting a forearm against his torso. Sitting on the counter allows him to be only a couple inches shorter than her, making his attempt at frustration more legitimate.

"Just ask, idiot," she rolls her eyes. I grab his bowl, filling it with more soup to hand back to him.

"Only the weak ask for help," Senka stick her tongue out at him from the other side of me, sitting cross legged on the counter. I flick her nose.

"So," Jakir sets his bowl down. It looks like a child's bowl in his hands. "I'll make breakfast tomorrow."

"I'm making the cake," Aiza's cheek pinch with her smile.

"You have to be kidding me," I lower my bowl to glare at my Bonded. "You told them?"

"He mentioned the birthday, I pulled the date out of him," Sayah gives an evil grin, twin to his sisters.

"We didn't even have to cut it out of him!" Senka playfully looks to Jakir who gives nothing but a gentle look of happiness.

"And," Jacob finishes his third bowl of soup, finally setting the bowl down. "We all have a big surprise for you tomorrow."

"Well," I grab the empty bowls, placing them in the sink. "I like happy surprises."

"How old will you be?" Ellie's leaning into Filo, happily finishing her bowl after returning from putting Lilly to bed.

I pinch my eyebrows together, trying to remember how old I am.

"I remember my last being twenty-two I think."

"Aw Kali," Jacob places his hands on his cheeks. "We're the same age."

"You might be the youngest here," Aiza raises her eyebrows, lips pull down slightly.

"Nope," Senka pops her mouth on the end of the word. "She's got us by a year."

"You make it seem like she's got more than that on you," Harlow teases.

A knife flies out of Senka's hand, caught by Harlow who finds it quite amusing.

"You're going to play with those knives and hurt yourself one day," Ellie shakes her finger. "Lilly is starting to pick up a liking to them because of you."

"Please," Sayah drops his head. "Let's not have another one of her."

"Alright," I step away from the sink, walking towards the door. "I need some sleep, but I have to check on Fin first."

"The human is still here? And alive?" Harlow looks genuinely surprised.

I let the laughter trail behind me on my way down the hall. As I pass the open courtyard while heading towards the front door I spot Fin. Silently, I creep up on him.

"You don't sleep here anymore."

Scared by my sudden presence he falls forward from the bench. Scrambling away he turns around with an infuriated look. I tilt my head, wondering why he's glaring. Just as I'm about to ask why he looks angry he speaks.

"Kali, it's just you," he pushes his hands behind his back to prop himself up. "You scared me. You shouldn't do that, it's a bit rude."

"I guess you don't get anything else other than speed and strength, huh?"

"No not quite, wish I did. How are you?"

"Why are you in the courtyard? You don't sleep here anymore."

"Oh," he looks around him while standing. His hands stay propped on his lower back. "I just really like the flowers here, it was the first place I saw when I got here."

"You were knocked out when you got here," I narrow my eyes with a smile. He looks mildly uncomfortable and nervous. It's adorable.

Rolling his eyes he laughs, "I meant when I was let out of my room."

"Fair," I step towards him, unsure why I feel drawn in. "Is your back hurt?" I point to his hands awkwardly placed.

"No, not at all," he drops them. "Just felt nervous about being found looking at flowers."

I tilt my lips up slightly at his nervous chuckle. He notices, looking down at my lips.

"I, um," he blinks rapidly. "You look happy, anything happen?"

"Just some calm, taking it in before the storm."

"Storm?" his demeanor changes, more interested in my words than my lips now.

"A couple visitors from other Samle's," I rub my collarbone trying to calm myself. "Addison wants to make an appearance."

I catch the realization hit him the same time it hits me.

"Addison is going to be here?" his voice is so low I struggle to hear him.

"She is, but Fin," I reach out, placing my hands on his biceps. I run my hands down to catch his own to hold tightly. "You can stay inside for the day. There's no need to come out. I understand the fear."

I don't really. He's safe here. Does he not feel safe?

"Why would you invite her here?"

"I didn't invite her," I gently clench my fingers around his. "She's basically invited herself. Turning her away could put my people in danger in the future. It's just politics. She'll be gone after a day or two."

"Why would you let her come here? You know I'm terrified of her finding me out and sending me back to Kent," he swallows audibly. "Or just slicing my throat open for betraying her."

I pull him to sit him down on one of the benches in front of a water structure. Four pillars stand slightly apart, to create the appearance of a singular pillar with clear sections of water.

"Fin, this isn't a meeting I'm going to enjoy," I gently guide his face to look at me. "You don't even have to look at her. She'll never find you, and there's a lesser chance of her recognizing you. If I had the choice I'd turn her away, but that will do more harm than good. Please be understanding of that."

"You're not exactly giving me a choice," his hand trembles, then stills. "I'll just deal with it."

A strange hurt makes it feel like there's a knot in my chest. I rub my collarbone again to soothe the static sensation. Threats of violence boil up, ready to fly out of my mouth like Senka's knife did at Harlow. We're quiet again. Fin stares at the water fountain for a moment then finally turns to look at me. His eyes drop to my lips, then down to the cleavage exposed by my tank top. The violence dims, turning into its heated counterpart.

Maybe he does feel the Suitor attraction.

My lips part under his heated gaze. One of his hands raises to cup my cheek, pulling me in slightly. Our mouths are inches away. I feel his breath brush across my lips for a moment before he moves.

His lips crush against mine feverishly. In a state of shock it takes my brain processing that he's kissing me for my mouth to move in response. I press close to him, wanting to feel the same heat I did with Mikhail. His hand slides down to wrap under my jaw. Tilting my head more I place a hand on his chest, curling my fingers into the soft muscle.

Fin's tongue darts out to swipe across my bottom lip, tasting it before biting down. I force my lips to move with his even with my body hesitating in confusion.

Just as I reach a point where my body starts to listen to me, he pulls back. He smiles, brushing a piece of hair back from my face.

"I just...felt the need to do that. You're special to me, you know that?"

I pull my lips up enough to please him further.

"I need to go to bed now, Fin."

He frowns slightly, "Did I do something wrong?"

"Not at all, I'm just exhausted. I'm amazed you aren't, with lifting all day."

Confused, he simply stares at me.

"You're still working with the buildings right? I haven't seen you around at all since I've been busy but I figured you were there these past few days."

"Oh, no I went back to the farm. Figured it was too much to be near people who already have a prejudice."

"They're fine, you just have to talk to them."

"Please stop pressuring me, I'm not ready to go back yet," his eyes turn dark. "I don't appreciate you trying to control me."

Mental whiplash keeps me from responding. I start to turn to walk away, stopped by him suddenly grabbing my arm. My eyes glow dimly at him.

"Do not grab me like that again, Fin. I'm not sure what your issue is but speaking to me like that won't work."

He throws his hands up in defense, "Alright, let's just agree to forget about the arguing. I think we're both tired, right?"

I nod, telling him goodnight and watching him leave out of the front doors.

Chapter 48

Nearly asleep, a knock on my door wakes me. I call for them to come in, and see Janét.

"You look surprised, did you forget I told you I wanted to see you tonight?" she smirks, walking towards the bed.

I groan and fall back against my pillows, "I'm sorry, I did forget."

"It's fine," she climbs onto the bed straddling me. I place my hands on her wide hips, enjoying the heat her body gives off. "At least I didn't forget."

She leans down to brush her lips against my neck. I tilt my head back, trying to enjoy a moment with no expectations. It's a matter of seconds before she stops, pulling back.

"What's wrong?" I press my thumb into her hip.

"I should be asking you that. You're off."

"Rude," I tickle her thigh. She giggles and climbs off of me. Laying next to me she props her head up with her hand.

"Tell me."

I close my eyes, body still confused from the kiss with Fin.

"I kissed Fin."

She gasps dramatically and pinches my arm.

"Why didn't you tell me? That's gossip right there. Dronning saves human guy and falls in love," she looks away dramatically.

"I'm not in love, I think it's a Suitor thing."

"Why do you say that?"

"I feel so close with him sometimes, other times I want to punch him to knock him out."

"I mean, isn't it like that with all men?" she gives me a pointed look.

"It's like that all the time for me," I roll, facing towards her. "I always feel a little violent."

"With what you've dealt with – what you're dealing with – you have a right to."

"That's besides the point, I don't know what to do about him," I stare at the bed sheets as I fiddle with them. "Can Suitor attractions be weak?"

She considers it for a moment before answering.

"I've felt enough to say that I don't think so. They're typically strong enough to drive you crazy. That's the point, push buttons until mother nature gets a baby out of us," she gently pokes my abdomen hanging slightly. "This is also the first time I've heard of a human and a dragon being Suitors."

"I know it's hard to believe, I just don't know what all I can deem true and untrue. We went from being human to suddenly being able to shift into dragons. Who's to say anything's impossible?"

Janét doesn't answer, only waits for me to vent again.

"I'm so tired of having to deal with external factors. Why, of all times, would Addison and Gallyan choose now to show up?"

"Who knows, but all you can do is deal with it."

"What if I don't want to?"

"You mean what if you don't want to be a Dronning?"

I stare at her intense eyes, reflecting on what my words really mean.

"Why did we get picked?"

"I don't think that's an answer we'll ever get. However, I think there's a reason everything happens," her black hair glistens in the moonlight that shines through my window. Shadows across her face paint her in a beautifully dark picture. "Otherwise we wouldn't be sticking around like we do."

"I think you're sticking around for more than just being a Dronning," I lick my lips slowly, tracking her gaze at it follows my movement.

"I'm here for building an alliance. Reaping the benefits for my people."

"Ah, so very noble of you," I lift my self until I'm on top of her.

I exhaust my body until sleep is no longer a choice. She slips out as my eyes close, gently pulling the door shut behind her.

Her and Linius leave late in the night, only waking me to inform me of their exit.

"Happy Birthday! Wake up wake up, happy birthday!" I'm jostled awake by my bed being shaken violently. Peeling one eye open I mistakenly catch Senka staring at me as she jumps on the bed. She flops down on top of me, crushing the air out of my lungs. Feathers lands on the window open on the side of the room, staring at me.

Oriana is the last to walk in, giving me a smile only for me to see. I lift my lips at her.

"Oh gods, Senka," I groan, trying to shove her off of me. She latches on tighter, squeezing me in a death grip hug.

"Happy birthday Aunty Kali," Lilly says sweetly. Senka rolls to allow her to climb up with Ellie's help. "I got you a present."

"Really? Lilly that's so sweet, let me see," I hold out my hands, grinning like a mad woman once Lilly places a little origami swan in my hands. I gingerly cup it in one hand as I place a kiss on her cheek. Her laugh, like bells ringing, puts a smile on Ellie's face.

"Sayah and I got you something too!" Senka dives off the other side of the bed. She disappears as she wiggles under it.

"Let me get up first," I push myself into a sitting position. Senka jumps back on the bed with a squeal, sitting cross-legged next to me. She holds out a rectangular shape wrapped in black velvet. It's heavy and weighted strangely.

"Open it," she says. I look to Sayah who is just as pleased, even grinning ear to ear about the gift. He tells me to open it.

Lifting the black velvet cloth back carefully, I gasp once I see it.

It's a dagger with metal that seems to come alive in the swirling pattern. The tip is so pointed it's nearly impossible to see where it truly ends. Edges so sharp they flicker in and out of sight travel down, flaring out twice near the broadest part to create two more points on each side. It's a dark color, but not as dark as the handle. Made of wood so dark it almost absorbs the light, the intricately laid carvings create the texture of scales. The pommel is light but brutal, rounded more for impact than holding.

"This is beautiful," my voice is hoarse. "I love it."

Senka and Sayah both beam with pride at my thanks. I brush my fingers on Senka's cheek, making her lean into my touch. Filo hands me a sheath that will holster the dagger at my thighs. The tip of it is metal, the only thing capable of containing the sharp point of the knife.

"Alright everybody find your seats," Jakir walks through the doorway with a large serving plate of food on it. Jacob and Harlow are in tow, each carrying smaller plates of food. There's excited commotion as food is doled out for breakfast. Most find their seat on the bed, Lilly specifically requesting to sit in between my legs. Leaning against the headboard I offer her pieces of my egg and dried meat.

"You spoil her," Ellie swallows her food, looking playfully at Lilly.

"It's my birthday I can do what I want," I shrug.

"We can do what we want," Lilly repeats it over and over until Filo quiets her with some more food.

Finished with my plate, I set it on my nightstand.

"Thank you all, this means the world to me. I'd almost forgotten I even had a birthday."

"We know," Jakir places a kiss on my forehead. He steps back to pick up other plates. "Don't worry we won't ever forget, we'll remind you."

I roll my eyes, "Well how about your birthdays? I want to know them," before anyone can fight, I pull out the ultimate argument. "They're important to me and I'm demanding it as a birthday present."

Senka speaks first, excited to tell me theirs is August tenth. Jakir bends to my birthday wish, mentioning the date of February twenty-second. The others are more difficult, only Jacob and Harlow giving in.

"March fifteen," Lilly crawls up leaning into my face.

"Fifteenth," Ellie corrects. "You need a bath, and to go get ready for daycare. Don't make Auntie Laura wait again."

She pulls her from me, but not before Lilly plants a kiss on my cheek. Watching them leave I begin to get up as well. Filo hands me a robe to slip on before leaving with them.

"We have one more gift for you," Jacob is grinning ear to ear, making me nervous at whatever he has planned. I narrow my eyes at him.

"I couldn't trust that grin less if I tried," I pull on thick pants and a bulky sweater to protect against the freezing temperatures outside.

"You don't need a jacket," Harlow locks her fingers through mine. "It's in the manor."

I look to Oriana, who's beginning to slip out of the room.

"Not a chance," I stop her with my words. "You're a part of this circus now, come with us."

She looks uncomfortable at first, then gives in by following us out of the room.

The Nightmares move to disappear into a wall, making their way around the house for the morning rounds they had become used to. I grab Sayah before he slips into a dark section of the large hallway.

"Keep an eye out for Fin," I squeeze his forearm. His thin lips turn down at my words. "I don't want him walking in here all the time, even if it's because he feels safe. We can't have everyone feeling uncomfortable."

He nods, slipping off to do as he pleases. I walk down towards the kitchen, suddenly being halted by Harlow as we reach a picture frame.

"What was that about?" she asks, watching Jakir run his hand down the wall.

"I was telling Sayah to watch for Fin," I respond. Jacob looks at me uneasily. "I found him in the courtyard last night. Said it made him feel comfortable."

"He was a prisoner with the humans, shouldn't the home where he wasn't bound make him feel better?"

I crack my neck before responding, "I don't know."

Jakir pulls back the picture frame to reveal a door, barely outlined at the top by a thin line of space. Harlow steps in front of me, sliding back a thick panel that disappears into the wall. They all watch me, eager as I step forward into the dark hallway.

With plenty of space they all crowd in behind me. A bit of light illuminates the hallway from a square panel every six feet.

"Mirrors, they catch the light from the roof and bring it down a narrow tunnel," Jacob explains, moving past me on his forearm crutches. "These little levers," he grabs one next to a mirror inset in the wall. "Will completely shut the pathway. Water tight seal."

He pulls on it, dropping the light in the passageway drastically by closing it off.

"So when it rains someone needs to rush in and close these every time?" Oriana challenges him, just as interested in the light system as I am.

"Not at all," he shakes his head.

"What about at night?" she scans the wall. "Unless she tried to shift, which her back leg would be the only thing to fit in here, human eyes can't see well in the dark."

"Right, which is why all it takes is a match to light the torches set deep in here," he lifts a stone object shaped like a jar cork from a well-hidden hole in front of the angled mirror piece. I move to stand next to him, spotting a pipe. "Brawn figured out a flammable mixture that we pour in here. It runs in small pipes under every single one. Doesn't evaporate almost at all, burns forever. You cover them all up to extinguish it."

"And the heat build up?" she asks. I look at her over my shoulder, pleased by the questions she's asking. She catches my eye, trying desperately to hide the slight pride that crawls her lips upward.

"Vents that lead to the fireplaces, either warming the manor or leaving outside."

She grunts softly, motioning for us to continue. We walk towards a circular set of stairs that twists upward drastically.

"Now there is something you need to decide on how many people know," Harlow stops at the base of the stairs. Her face is grave as she turns to me. "We made sure there was a way to get out in case anything happened. Jacob, Jakir, and I know them because we planned and built them. No one else."

Her and Oriana stare one another down, a strange communication happening between them I don't understand. After a moment they both look to me.

"Oriana has given me no reason not to trust her. With everything happening she understands, just as much as you do, the risk we're at currently."

"The risk *you're* at," Oriana tilts her head down, looking a bit violent in the strange light of the stone passage. Harlow agrees with her, only to be supported by the two men. I continue, not arguing with them.

"I trust her. Hoping it never happens, if she and the other women needed to get to me, she needs to know where to lead them."

My recognition of the women's progress has Oriana bringing her head back up, pride splashed across her stern features.

"Alright then," Harlow points behind her to an empty arch that looks tiny, being lined with shelves. "This is the first route, it goes outside. Just push the shelves to leave. Easy to get out, takes four people minimum to get in."

"Why?" my surprise is evident in the way I pull back.

"The door is extremely heavy, and the mechanisms are built to be easy to go one way, nearly impossible to go the other without help."

"This is feeling a bit somber," Jacob starts to hobble up the stairs. "Let's go see the happy place."

Harlow scoops him up, cradling him before he can go too far. I laugh at his annoyed face tossed behind her. Sticking his tongue out at me makes me continue to chuckle. My heart squeezes at the care she shows for Jacob in carrying him so he wouldn't have to struggle up these stairs.

A doorway finally appears, set into the wall where the stairs end at a platform just big enough for a singular person to stand on. I reach for the handle, hearing Jacob squeal excitedly behind me. Harlow sets him down once he firmly demands it.

Opening the door floods cool air towards me in a rush that knocks the breath from my lungs. Still walking into the room I manage to inhale again at the sight before me.

A glass dome created by glass panels welded together creates an ethereal light in the morning. Gray wood – from the Dead Forest more likely – makes the floor seem old but strong. I walk across it, amazed by the smoothness on my bare feet. Looking up I try to figure out what the walls are made of, how they're so dark without paint.

"We sanded them, then used some plants to dye it," Harlow speaks softly, afraid to disturb the delicate silence.

A large bed rests against the wall across from the room. I turn to the right to walk towards it, noting the size of the room. My mind compares the height similar to Mikhail's castle bedroom, triumphantly noting that my room feels larger.

Bookshelves made from stone curve along a large majority of another section of wall. Fictional stories of all types fill them, a few titles I recognize from a life forever ago. Still moving around I finally notice that multiple portions of the wall across from my bed is entirely made up of floor to ceiling glass panels. Beyond them is a balcony that curves around the diameter of the room, allowing me to look towards the sunrise over the lake, the sunset over the dying trees. Even the mountains to the north stand proud as if they want me to see them. Between some of the bookshelves are windows, giving a nearly complete circular view to land around the manor and beyond.

Jakir is ecstatic, unable to contain his happiness from lapping at me in waves. He moves up behind me, placing a hand on my back.

"I told them the ceiling had to be glass, so you would never feel trapped in here," he says in my ear. I stare up at it directly above me, faintly aware of him watching me with that beautifully full smile of his.

I close my eyes to reel in the wild emotion. My eyes sting as tears well up behind them.

Jacob hobbles past me, so I open my eyes to watch him move towards a window. Harlow helps him, undoing locks from the top down to the bottom where two panels meet. Oriana steps forward to help push the panels back, sliding them until a large majority of the balcony leads into my room. Freezing winds caress my face, instantly cooling the skin until it starts to blush.

"You can close them, I know you're all cold," I laugh, grinning at them all.

"Oh thank god," Jacob mutters, shivering.

They're silent again, Oriana still inspecting various parts of the room. She reaches the bed, noticing something that has her pointing out the escape hatch.

"Ah yes," Jakir moves towards her. I follow, watching him open a panel of floor on the side of the bed opposite from my door. "This leads to the kitchen, but only for emergencies."

"And if I want to sneak a snack in here?"

"You're the Dronning," Oriana rolls her eyes. "No one is going to stop you from doing what you want in your own castle."

They laugh, enjoying my slight look of embarrassment. It dies down again as I continue to walk around, enjoying the hanging lights that hold candles.

"You're fairly difficult to surprise, you know that?" Jacob points a crutch at me.

I turn to him, folding my arms over my chest, "How did you manage to hide this? It's a literal dome on top of this place?"

"Easy to do when we just keep you busy enough," Jakir lifts his eyebrows. "Always made sure during the day you were either over by the houses or inside. Never outside too long during the day without one of us distracting you."

"It's also just barely hidden by the taller parts of the library and entrance, if you're standing close enough to the building."

I realize how wrapped up in my own world I had been the past weeks to notice so little. An entire room, its own glass dome on top of the castle being built into the natural wall defending the city, and I had missed the entire process.

Of course people would be testing our borders if I'm this oblivious.

"I don't think I can thank you enough," I breathe, still enraptured by the darkly themed room.

Harlow hugs me so tightly I feel my spine pop into place. Jacob attempts to do the same instead managing to smack my thigh with a crutch; to his amusement.

I spend the rest of the day around the Samle. No other gifts are shoved in my face, just large amounts of food from each family. I take only from those who have managed to properly feed themselves into health. Dishes have begun to evolve into more complicated ones with the new spices grown in windows. I savor everything, the talks especially making the day that much better.

In the evening, I manage to escape the massive feast held around the bonfire still placed under the tree. Filo follows me after I wave to him purposely. We stop by one of the newly built shops to speak, out of ear shot from most of the celebration.

"You wanted to speak with me?" His face gives me pause. It's always so serious with some underlying hint of mischievous thought. I collect myself, switching back from my celebratory mindset.

"How are the borders, other than the nagging from the humans?"

He rubs his beard, looking off behind me.

"Still coming, I've kept you updated for the most part. They seem to be trying to find a way in. Sully and his husband in the south told me they had to shift to scare off a few bold ones."

"And they've calmed?"

"Quite the opposite, they've gotten bolder. One did try it himself, drunk, but the poison of the forest sent him screaming."

"So they really can't go in there alone," I murmur, gently touching my collarbone. "Addison must still be pushing them."

"If she is, it's not very much. They went nearly silent for the past few days, likely due to her arriving here so soon."

"Good timing with one of them losing their minds trying to get in. Any others try?"

"A couple of 'em tried it further north."

I nod, "She's pushing Kent to find a way."

"Even if she does, they'll die."

"The forest produces a gas, but I didn't think it was toxic."

"It's not," he spreads his feet apart, taking a relaxed stance. "All the animals are predators. Eventually, they'll find the humans and eat them."

I look to the ground for a moment in thought, then back to him.

"Ask around for more people who want to move. Our numbers are growing, we can afford to put more people out there. I trust you'll know how many to put."

He tilts his body forward in a slight bow before walking away in long strides. I step back from the side of the shop, eager to get to my office to make notes.

My body is nearly knocked to the ground from walking directly into a wall. Except it's not a wall, it's Fin who's rushed around the corner.

He nearly fumbles the basket of bread into the ground. A few rolls slip his fingertips.

"I'm sorry Kali, I wasn't looking where I was going," his fingers struggle to pick up the bread, shaking every few seconds. "I'm not making a good track record for myself."

I stand above him, not moving. Guilt wants me to help him. Anger wants me to rip his teeth out of his mouth. He straightens from picking it all up. His eyes turn soft once he realizes I'm staring at him with nothing on my face.

"Kali, you can't possibly be mad at me, right?"

I shake it off, suddenly feeling more guilty about standing over him.

"No, I," I put my hand to my forehead. He steps forward, placing his hand on my cheek. His thumb brushes over the skin, a prickling sensation washes down my neck. "I'm just tired."

"All good, you need to watch where you're going though."

I go to pull away, only to freeze at him leaning in. His mouth brushes mine, then comes back full force. Small thumps at my feet sound as the bread falls from the dropped basket.

"You should come with me," his lips brush my ear. I shudder, pulling away.

"I have a few things to do before sleep," I tilt my head back as he drags his mouth down my neck. I feel frustrated, wanting to give in, but wanting sleep more.

"Put them off until tomorrow, you can sleep in," his hands pull me against him. His hardness presses into me, his hands pressing my lower half against him firmly.

"My work doesn't stop just because of a celebration."

"Clearly, can't even stay away," he bites down on my shoulder. Through my sweater he grabs a handful of my breast and squeezes. A sharp bite of pain radiates from his fingers finding my hardened nipple and pinching hard. "You spoke with Fiko, that's enough work for tonight."

I force my lips to curl enough he can't see my frustration. Even with my nonexistent response his hands still grope at me. Not entirely unpleasant, yet I feel so distracted by everything else.

"You mean Filo," I correct, he pulls back to look at me for a moment. "And I thought you were just coming around the corner?"

"I was," he leans in, staring at my lips. "Anyone can tell you're working when they see you, you never stop."

"Which is why," I pull back. "I need sleep."

His jaw muscles bunch. Immediately he relaxes, reaching out to grab my arm.

"I've been really lonely," his tone is a strange attempt at lust. Fearing embarrassing him I only give him a sweet look. "I'd really like you to come back with me. It's the least you could do, you know," he raises his eyebrows up and down. "Kidnapping me, scaring me, all that."

My lips fall, unable to keep up the smile. I lift an eyebrow at him.

"Letting you live, showing you mercy, all that isn't enough?"

"You did kiss me," his emotions change again, looking fragile. "You're starting to really confuse me Kali. I already have a lot on my shoulders, especially being afraid of Addison and all-"

"Which is why the second she gets here, you need to stay in your house," I feel myself take a physical stance that replicates the mental one. "That's an order. You need to be safe, away from her. We don't need her seeing you and trying to hurt you."

His grin is tight in his annoyance at me switching the topic.

"I can do that," he says dryly.

"I'll have food brought to you, and anything else you need."

I feel the twins sticking to me like a shadow once I leave for the manor. They both pester me for what's dragging my mood down, dropping it eventually. I attempt to send them off to go find another person to avoid. Senka chooses to stick close anyway, sleeping next to me all night.

I'm thankful for the familiar presence. Especially with the hair on the back of my neck standing straight up.

Chapter 49

The long coat I'm wearing almost drags behind me while I make my way through the curved, open hallway surrounding the courtyard. Earlier in the morning my Nightmares had already snuck into every room to wake each person up. I sent them immediately afterwards to fetch Oriana, wanting her nearby to keep an eye on the arriving guests.

Feathers is on my shoulder, having pecked at my window to be let in while I dressed. After disappearing for a few days, he had returned to announce Addison having crossed the boundary. My gut tells me that Gallyan won't be far behind. Aiza verbalizes it though, and is nearly as nervous as I am.

"How does he know so much? Know what to relay?" Oriana asks, trailing directly behind me. She's carrying a bow on her back that makes me proud to see her carry a weapon so confidently.

Feathers and I stare at each other as I walk. The black buttons that shine back at me rotate around my face. Eerie intelligence winks back at me.

"I don't know, just know the idiot found me when I woke up."

His beak taps at my skull. It's slightly painful though I show no sign of it. He reaches out a wing to flap it against my skull, stirring my loose hair into my face.

"Idiot," he says.

"Jerk," I snipe back.

"Bitch," he squawks loudly, flapping his wing again at me.

"Enough, there's no need to do that," Jakir holds open the front door of the manor for me. "Not today."

"Her fault," Feathers shakes his head. I reach up to touch his head in an attempt to calm him. He leans into my hand to nuzzle it.

We quickly move towards the expanding cluster of homes and shops.

"Saykya," I mix the two names up into one accidentally in my nervousness. "Shift. We're going to meet her far out enough that she can't see any details about our home. She'll just run to the others to tell them."

Instantly their bodies snap into their more lethal forms. The dirt road created to make travel between the manor and the village is muddy from the snow. Made more so by their paws walking along it to stir it up. Sayah lets out a sound similar to a deep purr in my ear, just slightly sharper.

Feathers lets out a shriek at being nearly knocked off his perch. He promptly situates himself on my other shoulder, glaring at Sayah.

I see a faint group of dragons approaching us from the direction of Addison's territory. Senka makes a chittering sound. I silently hope that word has gotten to Fin for him to stay inside. I climb on to Sayah's back, flying out with Aiza and Oriana on Senka's back, then Jakir behind us a few miles west. Just far enough she can't see what the cliff is hiding.

"Tell them they can land in the field out west," my voice is stronger now. I feel irritation at her arrival more than nervousness. "Landing anywhere else will get them imprisoned."

"Easy, Kali," Aiza whispers. She adjusts her flowing dress once we come to a stop in front of the large training pad.

Addison, who I pick out purely based on the way she holds herself, gives a lingering look to the manor in the distance. My upper lip twitches to fight the snarl forming. Another dragon, much smaller than the twins, is next to her. It's a strange lavender color, with membranes stretching across the wings so tightly it looks as if it'll tear.

The Dronning lands softly while staring me down. I keep my eyes pinned to hers even through her shift into human form.

"Dronning Kali," her smile reminds me of a snake. "It's a pleasure to see you."

"Addison, welcome," my arms widen to present myself in an open way.

"I suppose since you sent Janét and Linius off before my arrival that this is no surprise," she looks around while speaking. I show nothing but a polite smile on my face.

"They had business to attend to in their own homes, and I'm no one to keep them from that."

"So kind of you," she turns to the lavender dragon that's now standing next to her. "This is Alastira, my Sekund."

Alastira gives the same impression a chipmunk would. Soft rounded cheeks with an average full body. Except with her, the smile isn't sweet and kind. It feels inhuman. She glances at my chest, then around to others.

"I remember us meeting in Konge Mikhail's territory, I'm sure you both remember Aiza."

Aiza glides forward by a step to greet them. I watch Alastira stare intently at each person surrounding me. Her gaze lingers in strange amounts of time bouncing between everyone, but always coming back to me to look a little longer.

"Using titles with him now?" Addison tilts her head sideways. "Did he get bored of you?"

I breathe calmly.

"That happens," I shrug, placing my hands in the pocket of my jacket to hide my fists. "You would know all about him getting bored, correct?"

That gets me a small reaction. I feel guilt knowing that it was much worse than boredom that made him shun her, but I keep my lips sealed. It's only her lips dropping for a second that I catch, but it's something. Her Sekund's face twitches as well.

I continue, "All good, I generally find men like him purely entertaining."

They're both confused by my words. It probably seemed like I could be trying to earn her support or insult her.

"Fair point," she concedes. A couple men behind her are standing with crossed arms and blank faces. I look at them interestingly, wondering if they're guards or something more. "I see you've noticed our weapons.

Konge Sebastian was kind enough to have a large batch forged for me."

"I see where his Samle's name comes from," Jakir joins the conversation. Relief floods me in his support.

"Exactly," she drags her eyes down his body. Though he doesn't feel repulsed by the type of attention, I do. "Lots of material to be found in his land. Gallyan's quite powerful for having such an ally."

I pull on the knowledge Aiza had fed me months ago while traveling across the water, "I'm sure with Konge Sean providing as much food as he does, Konge Gallyan is fairly comfortable."

Her shoulders push back trying to show how confident she is. In what, I can't tell.

"He is, you'd be smart to join him. Gallyan has plenty to offer you, as do I."

"Let's walk," I turn around to start walking along the lake. She joins me, along with her two male guards. "They can stay, Oriana will have some water brought for them."

The lines of required hospitality under the laws we both helped create blur at this point. We both know I'm required to house them should they stay longer than half a day, and that I'm required to supply them with sustenance while here. She knows, ready to use it against me.

Jakir follows far enough behind to allow Alastira to walk in front of him. Oriana directs the remaining guests to be seated on a bench while a few of her subordinates fetch water.

"I appreciate it. We'll be-"

"Oh," I cut her off before she declares her own length of stay. "And you'll have to leave before sunset. We just don't have the room for you all. I wouldn't feel right making you sleep outside."

"That large house," she points to the manor. "Seems large enough. You wouldn't kick us out that early would you?"

Internally, I bristle.

"I wish I didn't have to, but it's only fair for me to ensure you aren't held here in less than favorable conditions."

She can't argue. Doing so would only risk her making it clear she has distaste for me, forcing a stay here might risk exposing herself.

"Right, I'll make sure we don't get too comfortable. Gallyan might not appreciate having to leave so soon."

I know she's watching me for a reaction, hoping that I'll be surprised by her announcement. I give her nothing. Alastira is looking up at Sayah and Senka flying in a broad circle above us. Her gaze seems unfocused, like she's under the influence of something.

"Is your Sekund alright?" I ask Addison, who pinches her. She comes out of her stupor with a flinch, looking apologetically at her Dronning.

"She's fine," her teeth are clamped. "Just always has her eyes elsewhere. I take it you're doing alright here? Looks like you have the beginning of a city underway."

It's nothing close to a city, perhaps a large town, but not a city. She's looking for a weak spot out of bitterness.

"We are. Are you offering help?"

"I just thought you might have been struggling, with the humans at your border and all."

I pause for a moment, cursing my body for betraying such a reaction. Her smile widens and her eyebrows climb.

"They're in your territory technically, I thought you would have been aware of everything in your area?"

"I am," she lifts her chin, her ego getting the best of her before she realizes her mistake.

"So they're a part of your samle?"

"They're guests."

She knows she can't claim being unaware.

"Guests you've allowed out of your sight that are now pushing into a neighboring Dronning's land. You saw it yourself on your way here. Why wouldn't you stop to handle that?" I want to wrap my hands around her tiny neck and strangle her until her lips turn blue. She's so blatantly against me yet not smart enough to play the political game. "If they're your guests, allowing them to do such a thing would constitute freedom on my part to enter into your territory and end them. With no consequence to me."

"I'll be sure to speak with them about it. Though they haven't left the protection of my boundary."

Aiza is strangely quiet next to me. Her footsteps are always light, but there's thoughtfulness to her eyes making her seem out of it.

"Right," I feign genuine agreement.

Jakir warns me in the Bond, knowing I'm treading on dangerous territory here. I don't dismiss him.

Addison doesn't show a hint of knowing what happened with Fin. She only agrees then explains how she'll ask them to cease their efforts. I think again of him being hidden away inside. Picking up on my worry, Jakir dismisses himself to take care of checking on him. Addison's Sekund is staring at him with that glazed look again.

In a break in her talking I throw in another rock to disturb the waters between us.

"You seemed to so strongly dislike me at the meeting," I brush my hand down against my thigh to check that my new dagger is still strapped there. "Now you're suddenly inclined to visit. May I ask why the change of heart?"

I know expecting a blatant answer of her wanting to gain insight, or admitting her dislike of me is a long shot. I still wait, knowing whatever she does give me will only help my understanding.

"You just seemed too unnecessarily confident over there," she digs under her perfect nails with her other hand. "I wanted to see if you had calmed a bit."

"What's that like, being jealous of someone else's confidence?"

Too far. I've pushed too far with her. Her body tightens at my words. Aiza breathes in just a second longer than normal, telling me I've smashed any chance of getting more out of her.

"On second thought, I think I'll leave my guests to do as they please."

I turn my head to look over the lake. Sunlight glitters off of the still water.

"Do as you please," I don't look at her, but I feel Aiza slide closer to me.

Alastira tracks her, bouncing her sight between us. "But the second they step foot on my land, their heads are mine."

"Killing them will be an act of war, they're my guests."

"I'll do you one better, if they cross that line again, or if you decide to have them carried into my territory again, *that* will be an act of war. Once they're on my land, their blood is *mine.*"

Her dyed red hair gets flung back over her shoulder aggressively. I feel the thinly veiled anger get released, none of our previous façade to be seen.

"Such a blood thirsty little girl. Since you don't want to play this the easy way I'll go ahead and lay it out for you. Gallyan favors me, he's promised me your land should you and your Sekund happen to...disappear. I was trying to offer you an alliance to ensure such a tragedy doesn't happen."

"How considerate," I sneer as I roll my eyes at her. She either doesn't care or doesn't notice, because she continues on.

"Should you choose to, you have the opportunity to bend the knee to me. Otherwise, Gallyan fully plans on having you as his little pet," she leans forward, stooping slightly to be level with my face. "Taming a wild little bird like you is exactly what all those other rulers need to see."

"What they need to see is you beaten down a few notches," my voice is dark. Crawling sensations across my brain start the downward spiral. I desperately reach out to the Bond, holding to keep myself from slipping.

"You're so new to this world, so immature compared to the rest of us. Yet for some ridiculous reason, you've got some of the most powerful rulers looking at you like a snack. That used to be me," she curls her lip in disgust at me. "They'll get bored, they did with me when I didn't fawn over them."

"Good thing I don't get on my knees for other people's attention."

She takes the innuendo like a slap. Her hand reaches up, tracing a thin cold finger down my cheek. I notice one of the twins dive down towards us. The ground beneath our feet trembles under Senka's landing. Addison drops her hand, glaring up at the female dragon hanging her head over me.

"Nasty weapon you have there," she remarks. Senka drops her mouth open slowly to expose the two rows of teeth I know are gleaming.

My hold on the Bond slips a bit, Jakir reaches out, holding on to me tightly. It feels like his hand is wrapped around the base of my spine itself. I so desperately want to lose myself in shredding Addison to pieces.

"A weapon is controllable," I let the rest of the sentence be implied. The Dronning drops her gaze to me, calculating her next words.

"You'd be wise to treat Gallyan with more care. Once he has a goal, he'll stop at nothing to get it."

"You were easy enough. He didn't even have to pause for you to give up your power."

She leans forward again, but instead stumbles back from Senka's snapping jaws. Alastira is staring wildly at us while she shucks off her clothes to shift. It doesn't take her long to reach full size. Her shoulder barely touches five feet from the ground. She has to crane her neck to keep her eye on the wild one behind me.

Sayah lands behind them, his knife-like tail swaying in anger. Looking behind her, Addison keeps a straight face while stepping away from me. I feel the craving for violence recede in my head. Jakir ushers it back with steadying waves.

"I'm afraid I need to cut my visit short, Kali," she begins peeling her clothes off as well. Her thin frame looks weak despite the way she holds herself. "It looks as though I'm no longer welcome here."

I catch Harlow and Ellie waiting in the distance. Ellie nods at me.

"I'm glad you figured that out. You're men have been fed, and there's a small snack waiting for you and your Sekund should you choose to take it."

"Tell Gallyan he's more than welcome to come visit a friend after dealing with you."

Looking down her nose at me, she shifts. She's a bit taller than her Sekund and built with short back legs that tilt her body naturally. With a snap at Alastira they lift away. Two males follow after them, pumping their wings expediently to catch up. I wait, sending the twins after to ensure they cross the border.

Reaching Ellie and Harlow, Aiza finally speaks.

"Kali you know that was exactly what we didn't need," her cheeks look so pale compared to their regular dark tone. Her lips are stretched into a thin, impatient line. "Any hope of keeping the peace with her is gone."

"Aiza be realistic, that hope was gone the second Jacob lost his leg."

Harlow flinches, looking out at the shrinking forms.

"She wanted a reason to come after you, she'll claim you insulted her, claim you kicked them out," she's strangely flustered.

"She can claim what she likes," Oriana holds up a hand. "Coming here wasn't political. I can promise you she was scoping you out."

"What do you mean?" Aiza turns from her anger for a moment to listen. "Meeting with other Dronnings and Konge's has been how we've established trade between them, how alliances form."

"Those alliances formed at that meeting you had," she rests a hand on her wide hips. Her eyes bore into me for her next words. "Fin already told you she was behind the attack. They wouldn't still be so bold to try getting through those woods if they didn't have her to back them. This was a scouting mission to see how defenseless you are, to see how much you know."

"Then why offer the alliance with her and Gallyan again?"

"Last grasp at gaining control the easy way. She knows making an enemy out of you is going to make her life much more difficult," Harlow drags her hand down her face.

I start playing out scenarios in my mind, voicing the first one of concern. "You think she's likely to attack soon?"

They all pause, thinking over their own scenarios.

"She won't do anything drastic, since you're both at a stand off currently," Harlow says thoughtfully. "She'll start small, test your boundaries."

"Which are what exactly?" Oriana look from Harlow to me.

"I told her if she or her human toys crosses that line their heads are mine."

"Kali..." Aiza whispers.

"No, Aiza, I'm not going to start this Samle's history with being terrified of another one. I refuse to subject these people to centuries of violence due to my own cowardice."

"We never said you were a coward," she says pleadingly.

"But she will be if she lets this all go without punishment," Harlow argues. Aiza doesn't argue against her.

I suddenly start moving towards the shops, one of which is now a blacksmith. Towards the back is an open area where the owner works on cooling projects. The three women behind me follow, asking where I'm going. I don't answer. Freyr, the man who owns the shop looks up at me.

"Kali, good to see you," his voice is gruff, as if he can never completely clear his throat. "You like the dagger you got from the Nightmares?"

I smile, "I did, beautiful work."

He grunts, turning back to work on another dagger in front of him.

"You're not here for givin' me compliments though, are ya'?"

"Unfortunately no," I keep my distance from the still glowing weapon. His son, who I recall arriving as an escapee from Sebastians' Samle with Freyr, steps outside to grab one of the dangling tools. I watch him as I speak. "You won't be doing commissions or projects for a long time, I'm afraid."

He stills suddenly. Gungnir drops the tool he was grabbing, apologizing.

"Go inside, boy," Freyr's voice isn't wobbly, but I hear the realization dripping from it. We wait in silence. I catch Aiza shifting uncomfortably.

"Freyr, I know you just got out of Sebastian's hold."

"You know," he pulls a flask out of his pocket, taking a swig of it. I know it's not alcohol from the smell. The scent of turmeric, ginger, mint and garlic spills out until he closes the bottle. "I was one of his best blacksmiths. Learned it before this world ended, never knew I'd actually end up needing to know how to. Or improving the skill so much, for that matter."

"I don't like that I have to ask."

"But it's why I came here, to help fight for a better cause," he grabs a cloth, wiping the sweat from his bald face and head. "I don't like creating weapons specifically for war, but if I have to, I'm gonna do it for the right side."

With Harlow and Oriana pitching in occasionally we discuss the numbers needed. Knowing nearly nothing about weapons of war I feel surprised at just how many they plan to have. Oriana asks to have a cart of them delivered for the human women to begin training. Harlow steps inside to be measured with her for armor. I leave to find Fin.

He's sitting inside his small single bedroom home. A glass of water is in front of him, untouched.

"She's gone, if you'd like to come out now."

He jumps at the sound of my voice.

"Did you not hear me come in? I practically slammed the door because of the wind."

"I was out of it," he shakes his head, like he's getting cobwebs out of his hair. "I felt like I couldn't breathe the entire time."

Chapter 50

"You'll all be traveling north to the mountains here," I point out the northern section of the territory. The large range of cold, unforgiving mountains is sketched out to show just how expansive they are. "A handful will fly you to the Dead Forest."

Oriana steps forward to explain the rest to the twenty-four women listening intently.

"Only one dragon will be with us, Senka," she nods to the twin who waves eagerly from the back. "We will be moving through the forest until we reach the mountains, where we'll start the climb. Once we reach the top, we'll light a fire with one of Brawn's mixtures so that the boundary guards can spot us."

I raise a brow, "The forest? You know the hallucinogens in the air and plant life will drive you mad? Could even have you fearful enough to make your heart stop? Not to mention how little we know about the wildlife in there."

Oriana shakes her head, "We'll go through the thinner parts. But it's going to add to the training for resiliency. If we're going to live here, we need to be able to manage the threats as well as dragons."

"Senka will be there, if anyone is in life-threatening danger, let her pull them out."

"Agreed."

Whispers put an annoyed look on Oriana's face. Her jaw twitches as she clears her throat, successfully pulling everyone's attention back to her.

543

"What's the point?" Ashley asks, a curly haired ginger with a lithe body that had been morphed into a weapon just as the others had.

"The point," I step forward. "In complete honesty, is that I need a large majority of the Samle out of sight until Gallyan leaves. I need him to think we're weaker and smaller than we actually are."

"Why," Ashley pushes. She was one of the most terrified out of all of them. Today, she's becoming the one always asking questions and pushing Oriana's patience to the limit. I relax at her tone, remembering she's the best swordsman we have thanks to her fencing in a previous life.

"I will answer that question as soon as you sit down and stop trying to test my limits with you. Oriana has much more patience than I do, Ashley."

Saying her name seems to shock her enough she plops down onto the bench.

"Addison isn't my biggest fan, she's testing limits with pushing the Skin Carvers more everyday towards us. Gallyan wants a pet, I'm currently his primary focus. Showing our hand when everything is beginning to tip the scales towards all out war between the Samle's would be poor planning. So I'm making good use of you all having to disappear, and sending you to train."

"So wait, the Dead Forest isn't poisonous?" Phedran, a woman with pale skin and eyes that tilt gently up. She brushes her long ponytail over her shoulder.

"Sort of, to humans. It will induce hallucinations, could put you to sleep, might even make you ill. It won't kill you if you know to stay calm. Should any of you become unable to make it through, like I said, Senka will carry you out."

"We'll make it out," Phedran says proudly. They all voice their agreement.

I smile, feeling excitement swell at their strength and resilience.

"I hope so," is all I say.

Oriana explains what they should pack, nodding to me in thanks as I leave the hall. Harlow and Senka stay, listening to the rest of plan. I ask one of the delivery people nearby to find out where Fin is and have him sent to me so I can check in on him. Afterwards, I'm immediately pulled to the side by a heavily breathing Filo.

"Catch your breath," I say calmly.

"One of the humans got through this time, they almost missed him. Said he almost appeared out of nowhere," he wipes his brow. "They tied him up, I brought him here as fast as I could."

I straighten, "Where is he?"

"Sayah has him, said you knew where he'd be."

I send him to get food and water before leaving, excusing myself immediately. My legs burn at how fast I move into an area large enough to shift. It's not a long flight, though it gets me there much quicker than trying to do so on foot up the stairs or a sloping side of the crescent shaped landmark.

I check my surroundings before slipping into the manor quietly, letting Jakir know I'm calm and need some peace. I close down the Bond tightly, leaving enough open for him to push through if this turns ugly.

I look around another time just as I slip into the entrance to the basement. Confirming that no one is around, I close the door behind me.

Muffled screaming throws my heart rate into an excited pace. I pinch my inner bicep to calm myself.

"What do we have here," I say, not attempting to cover the beam spread across my face. The Skin Carver sits tied up, just as Fin was before him. His legs are individually tied to the chair legs, his arms tied down the arm rests. Even his torso is bound against the back of the chair.

"I'm sure Filo told you," Sayah ruffs out. Standing against a pillar behind me.

"He did," I drag a talon down his cheek. "And I couldn't believe that I got a present from Addison this early."

The man thrashes his head around, trying keep me from touching him. I wrap my hand around the bottom of his jaw, sinking sharp tips into the side of his face. He stops moving, eyes going wide.

He mumbles incoherently around the gag in his mouth. I roll my eyes, ripping it out. He says it again.

"You're the dragon bitch."

I slap him so hard I hear his neck crack. Sayah chuckles at the sob that comes out of him.

"Don't call me that it's rude," I straighten up from leaning over. Moving to grab a knife from the floating shelf on the adjacent wall. "And what do you think Addison is?"

"Let me go, Addison is gonna know. Kent is-"

He screams at the knife suddenly lodged in his shoulder.

I look over at Sayah, who's now frowning deeply. He looks at me and shrugs.

"I don't like that name," he reasons.

"Fair," I nod my head in a tilt. "What's your name, human?"

"Why, you're just gonna kill me, aren't ya?"

I pick up a curved knife, then a serrated one.

"No actually, not if you comply."

He eyes me suspiciously.

"Ralf."

Stupid man.

"Look Ralf," I grasp small shoots of gray wood that had been shaved down to thin, sturdy strips. "I have this issue with your people constantly trying to find your way in. If you tell me what Addison wants out of you, I'll let you go."

He shifts, as much as he can, in the metal chair.

"I ain't tellin' you anything."

"Damn shame," I twist my lips to the side. I zero in on his fingers, pleased that Sayah knows to place his hand on top to hold him down.

I hum to myself while shoving the wood underneath his nail, far past where the nail bed ends. Ralf screams so loud I temporarily lose some of the hearing in my ears. Blood pools under his nail, creating pressure.

"Please," tears spill down his face. He looks through them at his pointer finger, angry and swelling.

"Tell me why, Ralf, and we can stop," I explain, like it's a simple game.

"She wants you dead, that's all I heard. She started tellin' Kent to go to specific places, said she had better information now and was promised your territory and any survivors."

"For?"

"Probably livestock," he shrugs.

"When was this?"

"I don't know, maybe a week ago?"

I look up at Sayah, who's angular face stares down at me.

"What else did she say?"

"That's all I know, I don't know anything else," his strength is returning in his voice. Sayah shakes his head at me. I step back, letting him place the next splinter of wood.

"You're lying, Ralf. How can you expect me to let you go when I know you're lying?" I sigh, disappointed. Black crackles over in a trickle. I control it, letting it peak its ugly head out.

Just a taste.

I want to test it, see if giving in just a bit will keep it from fighting to get out every chance it gets.

It seems to be satiated, not fighting any further. I know it's a part of me, but I can't help seeing it as some deep thing that isn't.

"We know that she wants me out of the way, but we don't know exactly why. I know for sure she wants the people, the land, under her control. Numbers are everything."

Sayah listens intently. His face splattered with blood makes him look more menacing.

"She's probably listening to Gallyan," Sayah rubs his neck, spreading more of Ralph's blood around. "She may just be doing it under his direction. Or as a volunteer."

"But then how can we stop her from listening to him? She thinks he has this whole world figured out, thinks he's going to be the Konge of everything."

He sucks in his lower lip, releasing it with a pop.

"Not everyone's mind can be changed. She showed nothing but utter confidence in him while here. Addison is blind to all else. Humans are of no consequence to her."

"That would suggest that we won't make our point until the Skin Carvers are all dead."

He looks at me, not arguing at all. I lean back against the sink, tilting my head back.

"We're missing a piece," I start, my eyes closed. "I can feel it, we're not seeing the whole picture of Addison. He mentioned she had more information before coming here."

"Perhaps she's making her own trips we're not seeing."

I look at Ralfs' dead body, still dripping blood onto the ground where I'd let Sayah shove his talons into his corpse. If the bleeding out didn't kill him, his shredded organs did.

"What if Linius or Janét are feeding her information?" I feel panic rise in my throat. "What if I've been blindly trusting them this whole time?"

Sayah wipes his hands before placing them on my shoulders.

"Senka and I would have seen through it with how much they were around, so would Aiza and Oriana. Even Jakir would have. They're our allies."

I breathe in the scent of blood, distracted by the stir it causes in me.

"You're right," I let out a whoosh of air. "Maybe she just had new ideas, and she is in fact making her own trips."

"I'll let Filo know," he cleans off most of the blood in the shower, even with his clothes on. He pushes me out to take care of the body.

I take my own bath in the lake. Grateful for the concealment of the night I run my hands over my shoulders quickly to get out of the water.

Even with the freezing temperatures, it's remained warm enough to use.

I catch movement disappearing under the surface. With such little moonlight my eyes can't make out what it is before the ripples its caused disappear.

"How did the interview go?" Jakir's voice pulls my attention. He's standing at the shore with a towel in hand. Walking towards it I grab it, thanking him.

"That's what you're calling it?"

"I'm certainly not going to call it work."

"We didn't get much, other than that Addison is crazy enough to do the dirty work herself. I think she's making trips out there to figure out the woods, even carry some of them over."

"Bold."

"Exactly. What I don't get is how he managed to 'appear' out of nowhere. Filo said those that caught him didn't even see a dragon fly over."

"That's concerning, although maybe she's sending one that's small enough to miss."

"I doubt it," I pull on thick loose pants. "I think we're not seeing a piece of this. She's got something on me."

"It's not our allies, I can promise you that."

I hook my hand around his arm, walking with him back to the manor.

"That's what Sayah promised me as well. It doesn't help my anxiety with thinking I'm not thinking of the right thing."

"It'll come to you."

"Sure," I reach for a cabinet, grabbing a bowl to heat soup in.

"I heard you were looking for Fin, did you find him?" he reaches above me, grabbing two of them and waving me off to sit down.

"Actually no," I frown. "I never saw him. Did you?"

He shakes his head, "No, tried looking for him all day. Saw him dragging his feet into his room later."

"How late?"

"While I was walking to the lake to find you, seemed exhausted."

"He must have been working all day then," I watch the element on the stove heat up from being exposed to the furnace beneath it. "I thought word would get around enough that someone would send him."

"People are getting busier in their own lives. We're not a couple of shabby houses anymore," he stirs the soup, watching me. "Shops are opening, people are beginning to trade. Some are talking about heading out a bit to have room for their own farms."

I smile to myself, "I'm proud of them, for surviving."

"I am too, but it's you who's given them the opportunity to live, my love."

I lean back in the chair, resting my feet on the counter. Jakir shoves them off, smacking me in the shin before doing so. He points at me in a mock threat.

"I refuse to take Ellie's scolding when she sees dirt on these countertops."

I don't sleep that night, even when I crank closed the panels that drop my room into complete darkness. Watching them slide up and over the glass ceiling only reminds of an eye blinking. Of my own eye closing to what must be right in front of me.

I let one candle glow on the opposite side of the room. Pulling the blankets up over my head so that only the faintest shadows can be seen above my headboard. Behind closed eyes I remember the terrified look on Ralfs' face when Sayah shoved his hand into his abdomen. Not a sound came out of his mouth until his breath. It came out more like a whimper than anything else.

It doesn't disturb me, only frustrates me that so little results came out of so much effort.

I toss and turn all night, never feeling any ease to my distraught thoughts. Jakir walks in once the sun is up, his face holding the news I don't want.

"I hate him."

"Yet we both need to greet him. Aiza's throwing a fit right now, she's worried you'll upset him."

"She should be more worried about him upsetting me," I grumble, throwing back the covers. He walks to the large crank, opening the metal sheath around my room. Early golden light streams in, not burning my eyes.

"Get dressed quickly," he tosses me a long pantsuit with half a skirt attached around the back of it. Red designs crawl up from the bottom of it crawling around to curl up and around one breast. Shaking out my hair I yank on heeled boots angrily.

I let him calm me, settling into the Bond deeply to ground myself amongst all the emotions. Once strong enough, I leave with Jakir in tow.

With Oriana gone to the Dead Forest, multiple families sent away to hide amongst various places, our numbers are low. The town looks pitiful with such few people bustling through it. They've even played the part of looking somber.

Aiza stops me before we're within earshot of Gallyan, patiently waiting under the massive tree.

"Addison was one thing," she grasps my hand tightly. "Gallyan is entirely different."

"I know," I squeeze her hand back. "I'll keep this short, and as pleasant as possible."

"I'm right here, just rub your pointer finger and thumb together when you need me to take over for a bit."

I feel empty without Harlow behind me. She'd chosen to leave with Jacob towards the black cliffs on the beach, worried that his missing leg would entertain Gallyan far too much. Her eyes looked at me sadly before the white underside of her wings flashed as she flew off.

Filo left immediately after with a crying Lilly who clung to his neck. Ellie remained, her nerves of steel pushing her to stand with me. Her gentle kiss to Filo's cheek had me turning away.

Both Senka and Sayah elect to remain in human form, wanting Gallyan to be upset seeing them alive. Aiza and Jakir had both tried to convince them otherwise to disappear. They look at me one last time, I ignore their pleas to control them.

"Let them play," the Nightmares perk up. "Only like this, for now."

Feather settles on a branch far above, not making a sound.

"Kali, you look good," Gallyan's voice is smooth. It's one a crowd of people might push each other to the floor just be close enough to hear every word. "Glad to see you're thriving here. Hello Senka, hello Sayah."

They stare, saying nothing.

He looks around, and I can't tell if it's in genuine interest or distaste. He looks healthier, his hair no longer looks greasy. His eyes are bright instead of the dull beady look they had in the Shadows Samle.

I switch myself into a different persona. It feels like water running over my head.

"What brings you here?" I ask him, still watching as he takes in the town off to our right, the water behind him, the open field to the left.

"I wanted to check in on you, since the last I saw of you was recovery after that brutal fight," his smirk is dangerous, even attractive. I stare at him without any emotion on my face. "I know how being new can be. It's lonely, even with people claiming alliances."

"And you speak from experience?"

"I do," he clasps his hands behind his back, making the rectangular shape of his body extreme. "Did you know I was the last to come out of my begravelse?"

I feign my mild surprise.

"I didn't," I turn to walk towards the village. I want him to see the emptiness, the hope for more to come. "But I'd like to know about it."

"I figured, you like knowledge. Always watching people's movements. I've even seen you watch the way a person's mouth moves to decipher their words. What did you learn from watching all those Konge's and Dronning's, hmm?"

"That I'm more aware than they think I am."

"You think you're better than all of us," his shoulder brushes mine. It elicits goosebumps along my skin. I'm thankful for the thick coat I have on.

"Do you think I am?"

He chuckles, sounding like rocks in a velvet bag.

"I think you're more capable than you'd like them to know. You want them to think you're overconfident, that you can't back those vicious words you toss out so freely," he shoos off his singular guard. I notice that the woman who attended the meeting with him is not present for this trip. "You have a violence in your temper that could be molded into a force of nature."

"Why would I want to do that?" I send one of the twins off with a flick of a finger, not trusting even a single guard of Gallyan's not to go sniffing around.

"I won't go snooping into your home without an invitation," I let an eyebrow twitch at the sincerity in his voice.

"You want that," he leaves out the word defining the possibility of my question. "Because this world isn't the same one we lived in before. There are no leaders of countries, massive governments and regimes to battle with. It's a new world. One that must be carefully crafted."

I read between the lines, Linius and his words flashing a warning at me in my memories. Laura and Theri walk past, pretending to look at Gallyan with confusion.

I play into his lead, "If it has to be crafted, then I suppose it needs to be taken care of. I say let people figure it out, the world will form itself."

"I'm guessing that's your humble abode?" he motions to the manor, which can be seen through a gap between two homes.

"Perhaps one day," I say wistfully. "Still much to be done."

He takes my indirect answer with narrowed eyes.

"You have plenty of homes to go around, not many people to fill them. Send them away?"

I scoff, "If you're going to insult the size of my Samle, do it with Addison. I have every right to punish you if I find your disrespect to be too much."

He pauses, searching my face for any hint of dishonesty. Grasping desperately onto stillness I wait for him to call out my lie. I place my pointer finger and thumb near one another.

"So hopeful for more," his says, fascinated. I nearly sigh at him taking the lie.

"I'm sure you were as well," I drop my shoulders to imply relaxation. I place my hand into my pocket, hiding my fingers. Aiza stays behind us, walking next to Jakir. Gallyan looks back at them as we reach the dining hall, then gives me a hinting look. Senka picks up on what he's asking and takes a step closer to me.

"Strange, how attached they've become to you. You sure you can handle such nightmares on your own?"

Senka stiffens. Her hand moves to her knife.

"I find myself more comfortable in nightmares than in dreams," I hold up a hand, opening a half door with the other. They each stare at me, looking fearful. Except Jakir, he passes support to me in a grip on my spine. Closing the doors plummets me into the tense air of being alone with Gallyan for the first time.

"Kind people you have supporting you," he sits on a bench attached to the table. Opposite of him, across a wide expanse between the two tables, I sit on the tabletop.

"They can't hear you," I place my forearms on my knees. "You can stop with the political speak."

He throws his head back in laughter. The cords of muscles from his shoulders to his throat flex. I take him while I can, noticing that he not only carries power but he holds it too. Once he's done laughing he brings his head forward again, staring at me with a gleam in his deeply green eyes.

"It's refreshing to be speaking with a ruler who's so unabashedly blunt. I like you, Dronning Kali."

I don't speak, hoping he'll fill in the silence like he did in the castle.

He leans back, resting his arms next to him on the table. It makes him look casual, even displays how in shape he actually is.

His eyes start to glow, brightening with his essence. It's powerful enough I sense it plucking at the cord of control. I fight it, unwilling to bend to his demands.

"Is that how you got the others to submit to you? Commanded them to do so?"

He lets the light extinguish.

"They follow of their own free will, because they believe in what I'm doing."

"And what is it, exactly, that you're doing?"

"We let the world shape itself before," he folds a leg up to rest his calf on the opposite knee. "Yet it became starved, overpopulated, controlled by those who had no real appreciation for power. We were blessed with a blank slate."

"Who is this 'we' that you keep bringing up? I'm not stupid enough to believe that you find Sebastian or Sean to be your equals. Especially not Addison," I bend my hand at the wrist to lazily point a finger.

Gallyan rolls his eyes, shaking his head as well. He catches me off guard in saying, "Addison is a pawn. Sure, she's a nuisance. She's also one more knife guarding my back rather than trying to stab it. I'm talking about you and me, the two of us," he motions between us. "I saw everything I needed to in that fight with Mikhail, who I thought was the largest dragon I'd seen. I was delightfully wrong. You move as if you were meant to be a dragon when you were still human."

"That doesn't answer my question, Gallyan."

"It does. You don't just want to know what 'we' meant, you knew the answer. You just want the 'why'. Because we're both survivors. Half of the people look to you as the ruler among us, the others look to me. Some just need a bit more guidance in the right direction – don't look at me like that," he sighs. "Kali there are people who will never be good enough to belong, those people are meant to serve or die. The rest of us are responsible for creating a world where we don't get tied up and sliced to pieces by human garbage."

I physically flinch at his words. Him knowing that history of mine makes adrenaline drip into my veins.

"Where did you hear that?" I grind my teeth together.

"If you're going to work with me, you'd be smart to not ask questions like that."

"Good thing I won't be working with you."

He frowns. Deeply.

"Kali, you're smarter than this. I know you're a bit riled up from

Addison's petty behavior during her visit, don't let that cloud your judgment."

"You want to guide people, you think there are those who just have to die, have to be slaves. What of yourself? Where do you fall?"

"You and I have both been put down, stepped on, and left for dead. We've experienced more than any other ruler could handle. It's made us strong," He shakes his fist slightly at me. "I've had my own experience, you're the only one I know of who's had anything close to mine."

Being sliced up isn't the same as killing your wife in a fit of ill-handled rage, bastard.

"It's hard, you have no idea, being the only one to see what the world needs. Comparable to a parent trying to bathe their child, it's difficult but it's good for them."

I catch his comparison to a child, wondering how close to being a parent he was. Or is.

"Either you work with me willingly, or I have to collar you. You're too much to be let loose," he continues. "I didn't have to give you this opportunity, I could have just put my foot on your neck."

I laugh one time. A single chuckle.

"You plan to control me either way?"

His eyes are pained, genuinely pained. I almost lean in to get a closer look, trying to see what he knows and I don't.

"I have to, I have no other choice," his voice is torn. Without any earlier context of our conversation one might believe that he could be speaking about ending a close pet's life, or jumping from a cliff. "Without my guidance, this world will tear itself apart bit by bit. We'll return to centuries of war, starvation, poverty, illness. The cycle will never end."

I flick my gaze around his face, taking in every detail of the man demanding I let him put a collar around my neck.

"You're wrong, Gallyan. Being given a blank slate is enough to make people try to be better. There's better ways to teach them humanity if it isn't."

I stand, attempting to leave to avoid lashing out in anger. He grabs me by the waist, pulling me into him so we're chest to chest.

"Don't make me do this, Kali," his warm breath washes across my face. I tilt my face up to stare directly in his eyes.

"Do what?" I challenge him to hurt me. My mind craves the violence, remembering the blood coming out of Ralfs' fingers isn't enough. I'm not satiated any more by those memories. Red hot anger swells at his dream of hurting innocents. I want to end his life before he can end innocents. It consumes my gut, warming me from my stomach down to my legs.

"There it is," he murmurs. His lips are close to mine, nose flaring as if he can taste the anger bubbling up my chest now.

I feel my talons unsheathe themselves.

In response, Gallyan's do as well. I consider briefly it might be in excitement rather than defense.

"You should leave," I grind out. My voice isn't completely mine, it feels like it belongs to another woman. A beak pecks at the door.

"One last chance, should you choose to go against me," his gleaming, pure white talons slide down my arm to brush against my black ones. "I won't kill you, no. I need you alive. I'll just chain you up."

Chapter 51

"With what power?" I seethe, stepping back from him. Gallyan opens his mouth to speak, only for it to promptly shut when the door to the hall slams open.

"I believe we've much to take care of," Jakir smiles at me, then nods partially to the Konge. "Konge Gallyan," Jakir walks briskly towards me. "My apologies for the interruption but I'm afraid you need to leave."

"I was just telling dear Kali goodbye," he looks down at me, an odd look passing over his face.

"There are people to escort you to Dronning Addison's territory," Aiza directs him outside of the hall, casting a concerned glance towards me.

Fin walks around the door, entering quickly. He stares at Gallyan walking by, the color draining from his face. My stomach drops, realizing I'd forgotten to tell him to hide. I beg silently that Gallyan doesn't recognize him.

The Konge stares, taking in all of his frame. He sniffs once, says "Interesting," then moves away. Fin rushes to stand near me.

"What happened," he tosses his eyes between Jakir and I.

"Nothing of your concern," Jakir dismisses.

I walk outside, following Gallyan. His dirty blond hair shifts in the breeze that blows at him. Flurries of snow start to come down. They drift onto Feathers wings, who is cautiously following me by flitting and hopping around my feet. His guard hastily stands, staring at him for a moment then flicking his eyes to me. He starts to glare at me venomously. I flare my essence at him, making him flinch.

558

Gallyan looks over his shoulder, realizing what I did.

"Such a shame I'm going to have to put a muzzle on a creature like you," his eyes rake over my body.

"Or," I stop a few feet from him, Jakir sticking by my side. "You simply keep to your own Samle and keep your nose out of everyone else's. Carrying the weight of the world is self-imposed."

"Only the blind would try to shed such a responsibility onto others."

I can only stare at him in slight disbelief, even disappointment, as he sheds his borrowed clothes to change forms. I hear Aiza suck in the smallest breath as Gallyan's white form is exposed. He's large, making me question if he might be just as tall, or taller, than I am. The bright white of his scales makes him blend in through the snow coming down, the gleam. A small part of me aches to drench him in his own blood.

While I feel built like a monster, pieces of anger and weapons thrown together to create what is meant to kill, he's art. His legs are long and graceful holding up a body that looks as if it could fly for hours on the lightest wind. His neck cranes down to meet me, the slits of his pupils narrowing then blowing out. I watch the fin that runs from the tip of his head down to his tail snap upright, the supporting bones extending past the membrane creating needlepoints.

I can feel the bitter thoughts streaming from his head. Hot air blows from his nostrils, waves of heat melting the soft snow in the bubble around us.

He has fire, I realize. I hope that he hasn't been gifted with a white flame hotter than Harlow's blue one.

"Such a shame I'll have to destroy a piece of work this beautiful," I whisper to him. Jakir grasps onto the Bond the moment my emotions shift. His emotional hold on me is so strong I can't reach for the knife strapped to my thigh. I've never felt him hold onto me so tightly through the Bond.

Gallyan looks over my shoulder as he steps back. Fin comes closer to stare him down. Just as I glance between them Gallyan lifts his body up with the most graceful movements of his wings. As soon he's long out of sight heading towards Addison's territory. Jakir lets out a shuddering breath. My knees give out, slamming into the ground.

A wave of pain washes over me, but it's not mine. I turn back to look at Jakir. His forehead is on the ground, muscled back expanding through his long sleeve shirt with every agonizing breath he takes. I reach inwardly, grasping so far down the Bond that I'm touching the black rope within him. I can almost see it, how tightly pulled it was.

"What did you do?" I crawl to him, placing my torso over his. Letting my body heat and weight wash over him to calm him.

The twins have shifted back, lurking carefully around us. They know not to touch us now.

"I can feel it, I know the signs now," his breathing calms. "That part of you that takes control started to fester while you were inside with Gallyan. I held it down, felt like I was absorbing it."

"Jakir," my voice shakes, I start tugging on his exhaustion to be washed into my body. He fights me at first, but a brisk hand over his emotions allows me to remove it.

"There we go," I murmur. I look up, seeing Fin staring out to the sky where Gallyan's white form has disappeared.

"What was he doing here?" he asks.

I narrow my eyes, "You know him."

He flushes, shaking his head, "No not at all. He just…seemed important."

Not in the mood for dealing with him I don't push on the subject. I let Jakir put a bit of his weight onto me as he stands. I'm still absorbing the aches of his pain, letting it fuel my hatred of Gallyan and his twisted mind.

"Let me help," Fin reaches for Jakir.

"Don't touch him!" I snap, my eyes flaring so bright tears threaten to well up. I have to fight against my burning hands so I don't harm Jakir. Fin takes another step forward.

Suddenly his back is thrown into the ground by Senka. Placing her foot on his chest she growls out Russian insults. Her bitterness behind her words is tangible.

Sayah steps between myself and the human, "Go take care of him."

I don't hesitate to move my Sekund to the manor. Feathers follows, flitting to be ahead, resting every few feet until I reach him. I consider telling Senka not to hurt Fin, though his childlike behavior has irritated me beyond that.

Tugging on both Jakir and the Bond I manage to get him up to my room. My body is humming with energy from feeding on all of the pain in him. Instead of shrinking back, the darker side of my mind is drinking in every bit of it.

He crawls onto the bed, reaching for me. I change into shorts and large shirt knowing that his body heat will have me sweating if I don't.

"It's okay," he croaks out. "You don't have to take it all."

"Actually," I climb into the bed, curling up into his chest while facing him. "It satiates me."

He grunts in response.

I force my body to rest. My thoughts might not allow me to sleep, but my body can relax from the stressful encounter. I slip out once he's asleep to grab paper. He wakes up halfway, moves to place a pillow on my lower legs, then falls back asleep. I write out the details of my interaction with both rulers, my thoughts on them, and plans for readying for their inevitable attempt to gain control. Copying the letter three times I finally fold up each of them.

Jakir sleeps for nearly twelve hours, not even moving to eat or use the restroom. Ellie brings up food for me, sitting with me until I eat. She looks at him with a look in her eyes only a mother could muster.

"He loves you, even without the Bond," she tells me.

"I know," I place the plate of food down on my nightstand. "I don't think I could care for another person more than I do him."

"Maybe not more, but caring in a different way is possible."

"You don't have to check on me every few hours, you know."

"I don't have to make my food delicious either," she flicks my leg. "But I do. And don't put your feet on my kitchen counter anymore."

"How do you even - never mind that. That's actually my kitchen counter, technically," I argue.

She moves to leave with my empty dish, "You couldn't cook to save your life, Kali. I've tasted your roasted bison, made me want to remove my ability to taste."

I throw a pillow at her on her way out. She dodges it.

Sayah and Senka sneak in through the balcony doors later. Jakir stirs, his body beginning to wake. I hand them the letters.

"Once enough people return, I need you two to get these to Linius and Janét," I hand them two of the letters, sealed with wax. "These two need to go to Mikhail and Elias, but I don't trust anyone else to carry them."

They realize my intention before I get it out, Senka throwing hers down.

"No," she shakes her head harshly. "We aren't leaving you here. Not with Addison and Gallyan acting so idiotic."

I brace myself for the argument ahead.

"You know I would never ask you to do something you're incapable of," I stand, grasping the hand of each. "I need these letters delivered quietly, and I expect Gallyan is waiting to see if I do do exactly this. You'll take them, keep your presence hidden, and report back here immediately. I want reports on the health of their Samle's as well, especially Elias."

"Don't do this Kali," Sayah's narrow face looks intense, violent. "There's people just as capable."

"There isn't," I walk to the balcony doors. They don't move from the center of the room until I stand straighter. "You know how dangerous it is, anyone else could expose us. You're the only two people I know who can get in and out unseen."

"Us leaving exposes *you*," Senka closes the distance between us. Her hands drop the letter to grasp the front of my shirt. "You're all Sayah and I have."

I realize that even with the others, Harlow, Jacob, Aiza, Ellie – they'll only ever love me. Two of the most dangerous people in this world are attached to my life. I take in their faces, both so beautiful with their black hair and tanned skin. Their broad noses make them look stronger, fiercer than they already do.

I bend, picking up the letter from the floor. I tuck it into her leather vest that matches her brothers. Pulling her head towards me, I place a kiss on her forehead. Her hands clench tightly. I wave Sayah closer, pulling his head down to do the same. Coming down from standing up on the balls of my feet I look at both of them. A tear rolls down Sayah's cheek. My chest tightens, not from my own feelings of sadness, but from theirs.

"It won't be long, you'll be back before you know it."

I watch them walk over the threshold, slipping down the roof. They both break off into a jog to find people to send the other two letters with. Minutes later, two gray scaled beasts fly out over the lake. Both turn their heads back to look at me. Even though I can only make out the motion from this distance, I wave my hand above my head.

Heavy hands rest on my shoulders, spinning me to face a very broad chest. Jakir tugs me in, wrapping one arm around my middle back, the other curling to place his hand around the back of my head. I shudder into his chest.

"You made a good decision. Those letters will only benefit our allies."

"I hope so."

In a strange brush of coincidence, I receive two letters the next day. One from Mikhail, mentioning a brief meeting with some old ladies on the shore of his home continent. He mentions them asking after me, wondering what I've done to achieve such an interest from 'old, cranky women'. In the last part of the letter, I nearly crumple the page at his boldness. His wax seal, made of a single castle tower casting a shadow over a mountain, bends in my hand.

In true Mikhail fashion, he explains the power he holds, the opportunities he presents, the interest in me he has. He then asks me again for a more permanent alliance, practically my hand in marriage.

"He's after the sex, and my power," I toss it onto my desk.

"You are in fact Suitors, compatible ones from what I've seen," Jakir sits on a nearby windowsill. He looks like a normal sized person in front of such a massive window.

"They are, but that drive could also be what would make them awful as joint rulers," Aiza fluffs out the green fabric of her hijab. "Neither of them would bend to the other, it's not in their nature. Better to remain allies."

"I couldn't agree more," I mumble. She smiles pointedly at Jakir, who concedes with her.

I pick up the second letter, nearly choking once I read who it's from. Aiza waits patiently, scanning my face.

"My love?" Jakir leans his torso towards me.

"It's from Sean," I don't hesitate to use a letter opener to get to it. The wax seal of a four leaf clover being held up by a talon falls away.

I read through it once. Twice. A third time. I drop the letter onto the desk, a whirlwind of planning and thought spurring me to pace the room. I hear Aiza get up from the couch, picking up the letter to read it. Rubbing my hand across my collarbone I look at her.

"You can't be serious," she says. Still looking at me she hands it to Jakir, who reads it faster than both of us.

"He did seem scared of Gallyan, respectful, but scared," I bite my lower lip.

"How twisted is this man to hold another Konge's son captive?" Jakir sets the paper down.

"We don't even know if he's alive."

"Aiza," I frown at her. "If he killed his son, Sean would have no reason to obey him. This is a cry for help."

"Or a trap," Jakir says. We're all silent. I suddenly wish desperately for the comfort of the twins lurking in the shadows.

I think of Lilly, scared and helpless in the hands of a Samle she knows nothing of. Her big doe eyes spilling over with tears as she cries for her mother. Aiza lists off the possibilities of this letter, looking at it from all angles.

"He must have sent it either right after Gallyan left the continent, or right as he did, otherwise he risks him seeing it."

"In open water like that?" Jakir questions.

"You can see plenty out there, another ship traveling the same direction at the same time is cause for concern on his part," I reason. They look to me, waiting for the answers I'm not sure I have. "So he must have sent this covertly, otherwise Gallyan would know."

"Well, the two letters have nothing to do with one another so we can be rest assured that Mikhail and Sean did not work together on this," Aiza considers.

"Mikhail wouldn't anyway," I lighten my fingers on my collarbone, tracing them lightly. "He doesn't like Gallyan either. May not go about it right, but he isn't a fan of his practices."

"At least there's some decency to him," my Sekund mumbles. I smile at him, enjoying his humor more after such a long time watching him heal.

"We don't have enough people to send help, and you going on your own is out of the question," Aiza sits back down on one of the couches.

"Why?" I slap my hands down onto my thighs, leaning against the desk.

She shakes her head, "It's too close to Gallyan, too much of a trap. We wait it out for a few weeks, then we can consider the risk of sending him a response."

I drop my head down, knowing that her response is fair. She's logical, understanding of a cruel situation, but logical.

"Alright," I concede. "We wait."

In a short time, the snow begins to fade away, but it gives way to another season similar to autumn, rather than spring. It was strange watching the leaves turn from the green of spring time, into the colors of autumn, only to revert back to the colors of autumn after winter. In speaking with Brawn about it, he explains that like the animals had been affected, so had the seasons. We may only experience what we would once consider a very wet season of spring for the majority of the year, rather than any hot summers.

Oriana is the first of the women to return after the last snowfall. I greet her at the training rings, along with the rest when they arrive, a proud look on my face.

"So you not only chose to make your own way all the way back, not a single one of you needed to be brought home early?"

I glance at all of them, their bodies slightly leaned out from the survival on nothing but what they had on their packs or what they could find. A few have received dark bruises that look painful, but they show them with pride. Some even have healing wounds that will certainly scar.

"That we did," she gives a rare half-smile to the women around her.

"Do I have a reason to believe I have a group of women I could ask to ride into a war?"

"You have a group of women that will do just about anything to defend their Dronning."

I still, "Their Dronning?"

"Don't get so emotional about it," she says dryly. "But yes, we all agreed once we reached the top of the mountain that we've accepted being a part of this Samle."

"I'm honored," I extend a hand out to shake hers.

"On one condition," she holds up a finger. I drop my hand.

"What."

"You refer to us as Varangians."

I lick my lower lip, dragging it into my mouth to bite gently and hide my smile. I fail miserably.

"Sticking with the rest of the terminology?"

"Sort of," she lifts a shoulder. "But from some of the text I've read, it only seemed fitting."

"Deal."

She sneaks an arm out incredibly fast, reminding me just how quick humans can be. Suddenly I'm wrapped in a hug, smelling the scent of oak and spice.

Just as quickly as she hugged me, she lets go. Dusting herself off, Oriana walks away to begin giving orders for the Varangians to clean up. Shaking my head I direct my attention towards a waiting Harlow and Filo. Filo looks like his usual grim self, but something is off.

"You know one day, I'm going have a day that's not filled with some kind of bad news."

"That's what birthdays are for," Filo grunts at me.

"Fine, what is it?"

Harlow answers, "While I was coming back from the mountain base I saw three men running through a field towards the Dead Forest. They were clearly running for cover."

"Did you bring them here?" I grit out, moving swiftly out of hearing range. Fin starts to approach us from my right. I shake my head, pleading for a moment. He backs off patiently.

"Him," Filo corrects. "She roasted the others alive."

Surprised, I search Harlows' face for confirmation.

"The last time I let people live my partner lost most of his leg. I didn't leave it burning, the land is too wet to hold a fire anyway."

"Good, bring me to him Filo. Harlow, go check in with Freyr."

"Kali," Filo says hoarsely. "We lost someone, she was one of the rogues from Mikhail's territory."

I'll slaughter everyone Addison cares about.

"Bring her, we'll burn the body. I think it's what a dragon should have rights to.

Well on our way towards the manor I speak lowly to Filo.

"You're going to hit him hard enough to knock him out. Then you're going to go see Ellie for a day before flying back out to the borders."

"If you're trying to keep me from seeing the torture you don't need to. I don't mind being there, I just don't want to do it."

I blink rapidly, "Alright, it's your choice. You can't speak about where we go to anyone."

"I won't," he promises.

Once the man is down in the basement, tied to the chair, and awake, I begin. It's much more difficult with this one. He doesn't give in until all ten of fingernails have wooden slivers under them. Only then do I get his name. Ike.

Carefully I balance between having him in excruciating pain enough to pass out and being in enough relief he thinks it's almost over. I break him down, piece by piece.

At one point, I reach a knife towards his crotch area. He begs and squirms until he realizes I'm cutting away his pants. Relief washes over him, only for him to panic again at me unlatching the bottom of his seat. Ike looks down below him, seeing a large hole under his legs and part of his butt. He's still supported, so he's confused.

Filo keeps his face passive, completely in control of his emotions until I unhook a large loop of rope from the wall. At the end, a large tied knot drags behind me on the ground. That's when I see surprise for the first time on his eyebrows.

I faintly hear the begs and screams of Ike for me not to swing that heavy knot at the underside of his seat.

"I won't do it, if you tell me where every man is that's trying to get in here. Where does Addison have them?"

He stares, trying to be brave. I roll my eyes.

"Becoming a dragon did not mean I became patient. In fact, the opposite."

"You've found us all, I'm the last."

"Liar."

I swing the rope to hit him from under the chair.

It continues like that, me switching from one method to the other until I finally find a useful piece.

"She said she had a connection, got some kinda way in you don't know about. That's how Kent told me the way to go," Ike's breathing is labored and shallow.

Knowing that's truly all he has from the way he speaks I stop sliding the knife under his knee cap.

"You'll let me go?" His eyes aren't normal. One is swollen shut, the other surrounded by a bruise.

"I will," I say gently.

CHAPTER 51

I shove my talons into his temple.

Chapter 52

There's practically no time between the attempts to cross the boundary anymore. They happen no less than three times daily, dragging me down with everyone. More people move out to cover the border until another method of defense is created. Thankfully it balances the numbers here at home while more people still show up from other Samle's. The influx has slowed, allowing Jacob to catch up with building places to live.

"You're still building more shops along with the housing?" I ask him.

"Correct, with people moving in here it's becoming much more a necessity that they have the ability to function like this," Jacob sits on a bench, immediately handed water to him by Harlow. Aiza sits next to him, enjoying her own drink.

"I'm glad they're so self-sufficient," I say honestly.

"I actually heard some of them talking the other day," Harlow joins. "They wanted to have an audience with you to see about moving out further."

I furrow my brow, "Why would they need to meet with me to do so."

"Respect," Aiza puts her drink down. "You're the one who gave them a home, so they believe they owe you the respect of asking your permission before leaving."

"They don't owe me-"

Aiza holds up a hand, cutting me off, "Let them. While you may not need to do so, the generations of rulers after you will benefit from such a tradition. Eventually the population here will grow too large for you to have a direct connection with them."

"Sounds like I need to plan a throne room, along with a few other things," Jacob's smile is devious.

"Yes," Harlow says, her own smile matching his. "I think she needs just that."

Jacob doesn't let a moment slip by without putting his thoughts into drawings. He even mentions working in a pulley system on the outside operated by some type of steam or fire so that people aren't forced to climb the now broad steps dug into the side. Even with the high walls keeping people from falling off, they're a hazard. I point out where we can expand the face of the manor looking out towards the city, while also marking where it might be a better idea to dig deeper and spread out the rooms. We form other plans, ensuring the safety of all residing inside should anything happen.

The funeral for Theo and his husband Parker are that same day. Their bodies are tightly wrapped in black cloth to hide the brutal wounds. Never having the time to shift put them at the disadvantage when the humans attacked them. I can smell the heavy scent of decaying flesh as I near them, towering over their bodies as a dragon. Lifting into the air, I grab them in my talons and set them down gently onto a raft made of wood from the Dead Forest. I fly the short distance back to the lake shore, where Jakir waits for me. His scales gleam in the colors of the sun setting behind us.

He wraps his tail around mine, intertwining gold with black. It comforts me.

"*Harlow,*" I call her out of her unfocused look. She glances at me. With an inhale so deep she whines, blue fire blasts from her open maw. The surrounding dry grass that creates a bed under the couple ignites immediately. Their bodies, wrapped in the cloth dipped in flammable liquid, begin to burn. None of the Dead Forest wood catches, only holding their bodies on the water so that they may rest.

Some have chosen to stay in human form, others pushing their bodies as we walked to the lake to be in their predatory one.

One of the survivors from Gallyan's Samle leans forward, pulling my attention. He too breathes in, just as Harlow did. His neck stretches out to release a deep, painful sound. I recall his name briefly, letting it flit away to instead recognize his sorrow in this moment.

Another joins him, and another. Soon, most of them gathered are bellowing into the painted sky, the sound shaking our very bones. Oriana and the Varangian's step forward, and begin a shrill cry that makes my scales flutter. There's a soulful anger in it, one that demands retribution for one lost. Still screaming her cry, with lines of anger on her face, Oriana looks up to me.

I join them, letting out the rage at everything into the air. In my hopes of letting it go, I feel it amplify instead.

I rush back to my room, landing heavily in front of the manor. Jakir follows, staying close behind. I snap back into my smaller form, briskly walking inside. I don't even bother with clothes until I reach my dresser. I move to slam the door, breathing too heavily, my head becomes light. The bodies of Theo and his husband burning scald my eyes, I can't stop seeing the fire in front of me. Just like the fire Kent tied me up in front of.

Jakir holds it open, barely trying as he stops me from closing myself in. I look at him, losing myself.

No, no no no, please no.

"Easy, beautiful," he steps in, closing the door behind him.

I step back, tripping on a rug. It brings me down to the floor so hard my tailbone bruises.

"I can't, I can't," I hear my fingernails drop to the floor. My black talons scratch along my frail human skin. "When does it end?"

My vision is blurry as I feel the rope tie itself around my wrists. I'm sinking back into the fire, the twang of male voices is all I hear. Someone, I can't tell who, tries to reach out to me.

I scream at them, telling them to stop.

Darlin' darlin' darlin'

Forty to start

Dragon bitch

I sob at the last thought. It must be raining. I think of the open windows of my room, needing to close them but unable to move. Every scar burns in my skin red hot. I rock, tucking my legs into my chest in hopes that if I make myself small enough, the memories will go away.

I hear a deep voice in my ear. I cry out, wanting desperately to latch onto something other than the memories of being a toy for a spiteful human.

Soft material goes around my shoulders, and the ground disappears under me. I'm flying. Or floating. Either one, but I'm not sitting still. I want to lash out again, I want to carve Kent to pieces until he's begging for me to end him.

"You're safe, you're safe with me," that voice of a thousand drums beats at the flashes of pain. A cold feeling touches my back. It's thin, tracing intricate marks along my back. I'm in a bed.

When does it end I need it to end

Jakir

She mumbles incoherently, whispers of words thrown at her like daggers. I trace the pattern on her back until it's too deep. I move the knife towards another open area, carving again.

Kali starts to ease in her anxiety, the Bond reopening from when she closed it after the funeral. I felt it as she did, but wasn't able to slip inside her grasp fast enough.

I hear her take a deep breath, one of the first signs of her coming out of this dark hole. I don't stop my knife work, knowing it has to continue until she's completely out or she'll fall right back in.

"That's it, my love," I whisper in her ear. "Come back to me, you're safe here."

Her breathing evens out until it hitches once. I immediately set the knife down on the nightstand, cautious not to be too loud. Her green eyes look up at me through her wet lashes. I continue telling her she's safe, describing the room as she looks around so she knows this is real. Each time she swings her eyes to a new area I describe another object.

Finally able to fully grasp the Bond at the base of my spine, I shove calm feelings down into her. Immediately she relaxes, muscles becoming shaky from the tension held in them so stiffly.

I hold her tightly for a moment, turning my head when a knock sounds at the door. Ellie pokes her head through the opening. She glances between us, and with a nod disappears.

When she returns, she brings in a bowl of warm water and a cloth. She starts to clean Kali's back, gently wiping at the blood seeping down her back. She's so tender in her movements that I feel my eyes pinch shut.

My Bonded hisses when Ellie smears a salve over the open wounds. I murmur into her ear, calming her. Ellie's narrow eyes look to me for permission to continue. I nod.

Once down, she wipes her hands and smooths back her shortly cropped hair. She drops the tin of salve into her apron, leaving the bed.

"Not a single person other than you or I can come up here," I inform her. "She needs time."

Nobody would try and fight her anyway, just as no one would dare fight their own mother.

"She has to sleep, and eat. Or those won't heal properly, you're lucky the others did," she says. Her brown hair blows as wind whips into the room. I watch her close the doors to the balcony, then leave me with Kali.

I brush my hands through her hair. It's thinned from all the stress she's endured, all the responsibility she's internalized. Her breaths slow once she slips into a deep sleep next to me.

I leave her for a bit, knowing she won't wake for at least half a day. The Bond thrums, maintaining a steady flow of calming aid to keep her at ease.

"Jakir," Filo catches me watching the construction of the new wing.

"Good morning," I greet him. He remains serious, like Kali so often does.

"Morning, where's Kali?"

"Resting," is all I answer. He doesn't question it and continues speaking to me.

"I'm heading back out to the border. Going to check on our weak spots. Fin wants to join, thinks he might be able to call some of them out. It's up to you."

I pull my hair up into a ponytail. Cool air kisses the back of my neck. I let myself think it over for a moment, weighing the possibilities.

"Sure, just keep a close eye on him."

"I can do that," he leaves, cutting off the conversation from unnecessary small talk.

A large beam is being moved, two people struggling to lift it in their talons. I shift to help them move it.

Kali

Ellie walks into the room just after I wake up, some strange sense probably telling her I'm awake.

"I'm sorry about that," I say shamefully. I keep my face down low so she can't see the blush. She flicks my earlobe, though it's gentle.

"We all have our past, you more than any of us, bottling it up does you no good."

I don't argue with her as to why I should be controlling it more. I feel responsible for letting it get to me, as though there's nothing worse than a Dronning who can't control her memories. Thoughts of war spill through the cracks of my fractured mind. It's injured, needing to heal just a bit more before being able to avoid a breakdown like that again.

I can't help the images of dragons fighting for their lives on open plains, slanted mountains. Blood flies behind my eyelids, teeth and talons ripping at one another. In a moment's notice I might be needed to fight to defend my people, and I could be rendered useless by a mental instability. One caused by the very man himself leading it all here.

"Thinking of it like that won't do you any good," she finishes making my bed. I turn to her from the emerald green velvet chair I've planted myself in. She puts a hand on a hip, wagging a finger at me, "Get up, sitting here will do nothing but make you feel worse."

I look over at the bedside table for my dagger. It's there, safely in its sheath. Next to it is a perfectly cut stone made of a strange milky white color. Shaped in a gentle curve, like a dried bean, it sits as if the air itself carries it.

"Ellie," I pick it up. A little shock zaps my fingers. "Did you set this here?"

She comes to my side to look at it, reaching out a finger to touch it.

"I would have noticed it. I didn't, Jakir didn't."

"It shocked me," I note.

She shrugs, "Didn't me, perhaps you should stop dragging your feet around on the rug."

I set it down, restraining myself from tossing it at her in playful annoyance. Aiza enters after a gentle knock and me inviting her in.

"You were asleep a long time," she smiles, handing me a paper with notes on it. All updates on what happened while I was asleep.

Ellie glares at me, daring me to apologize again.

"I was," is all I say. Aiza digs deeply into every word shared between Gallyan and I, her smooth, perfect skin turning a pale shade with every word.

"This isn't your fault," she crosses her arms, tapping her foot restlessly. "He really is twisted, and I don't think he's going to change. He'll do anything to save the world in his image."

"You know, even if he kept to his own Samle I'm sure plenty of rulers would have their own issue with the mistreatment of people."

"But this is another situation entirely," Ellie pushes me into a chair, dragging a comb through my knotted hair. "If he has another man's child held against his will, slavery to operate a Samle, and a belief like you say. He's nowhere near the mindset of keeping it to himself."

"We can't go after him, not yet," I turn my head, only for it to be turned back by her firm hands.

"For now," Aiza takes the papers. "What do you want to do?"

"I've already sent out letters to our four allies," I'm finally allowed to stand after Ellie finishes tucking my hair into a braid that sits on top of my hair, hanging down to my back. "We may need to make some visits to them soon, see what they have to offer in training us. Or even showing us how to defend ourselves."

She nods, "I'll start laying out plans. Also, Filo is back with Fin and wants to speak with you."

My stomach tightens out of habit, the news from our defenses never being completely good. I realize the other part of her statement as we travel down the stairs.

"You said he's back with Fin?"

Aiza nods, looking back over her shoulder at me briefly.

Ellie picks up her speed down the steps, letting me reach the bottom quickly. I reach out in the Bond, letting Jakir know that I'm awake and back on my feet. He shows relief mixed in with happiness.

He meets me at the large hall filled with people eating their lunch between work. Filo is sitting at a table, looking annoyed as Fin asks questions. They both stand once they see me approaching their table. I glance at Fin briefly, then give Filo a questioning look.

"Said he wanted to come, could help point out weaknesses," he responds, spooning food into his mouth. Fin looks nervous, staring at anything but me. I brush a hand over his, easing out the nervousness from his body.

"And did he?"

"Not particularly, it was nice not flying alone for once," Filo doesn't look up from his meal. "Also nice when I wasn't the only one fighting off the Skin Carvers yesterday."

I refocus on him, concerned about the latest attack.

"What happened?"

"They got in, the people directly west missed them. Got caught off guard somehow. They nearly made a solid distance into the territory."

"They nearly let in humans because they missed it. That doesn't make sense," I shake my head. "At least one of them is supposed to be in dragon form at all times."

Filo swallows, "I know, I asked them why they were both in human form and they said they were fixing multiple traps in the woods. Animals must have messed with them."

My heart picks up pace, feeling that something is off.

"They haven't messed with them before," I deadpan. Filo picks up on my irritation, setting his spoon down to address me directly. Without moving his head he flicks his eyes to the side, towards Fin. Who's falling asleep, not noticing.

Keeping up the conversation I continue, "Those animals aren't normal. They live in air saturated with poison, perhaps you should tell them to start hiding traps better. And from now on, I don't care if a trap has a human in it. Every pair or trio has at least one shifted dragon at all times. No exceptions."

Fin's head falls forward, almost hitting the table. Filo doesn't break my stare, intense focus boring into me. Anxiety stirs in my chest, it's not mine. I stand up, Aiza following me. I open my arms for a hug. Surprise crosses her face but she hugs me anyway.

I whisper into her ear, causing her to tense up. Fin stands, rubbing his eyes blearily.

"Thank you for the talk," I tell her, pulling away. "I do feel much more relaxed."

"I'll head back out, update them on the guidelines," Filo tells me.

"I'll go with you," Fin moves to follow him. I hook my arm through his, stopping him.

"Actually," I give a soft curve of my lips. "I wanted to spend a bit of time with you."

He turns his head towards Filo, who's already leaving the hall ahead of us.

"I think I need to go with Filo, so he's not so lonely."

I chuckle, "Hate to break it to you, but Filo is a loner. Only really likes spending time with Ellie. He was being nice."

Fin blushes, rubbing the back of his head in embarrassment.

"Kinda makes me look like a fool."

Not you, I think bitterly.

"Don't worry about it, he's a difficult man to work with. Always has his head in work."

We walk down one of the larger streets lined with shops. Smells of meat cooking fill my nose, then hot melting metal, then flowers.

"Where are we going?" Fin asks, his face twisted in confusion.

"It's a surprise," I grin. I catch Harlow walking on the opposite side of the shops, a space between buildings every now and then showing me flashes of her face. She has a large sword strapped to her hip now, courtesy of Freyr.

We reach the training circles, stopping in the middle of the largest one in the center. White sand creates a reflective surface that makes it more difficult to see in the daylight. In the surrounding circles of assorted sizes, the Varangian's practice with their weapons. Their movements are slow, methodical.

"I don't know how to fight Kali," Fin says, his eyes skittering around him.

"You can learn," I take the staffs handed to me by Oriana. With my back to Fin, I stare at the rope dart hanging from her thick belt for a long moment. I blink, bringing my eyes to hers. I watch her eyes shutter.

Oriana moves around, leaning in to criticize each woman's stance or methods.

"She seems stubborn," Fin comments, taking one of the long heavy staffs. "You don't think she'll start to resent you at some point?"

"She owes me her life," I respond.

"Right, but all this training, only to still be under someone else's control?"

I ignore his statement, coming at him fast. He doesn't catch my movement in time, so his legs are swept out from under him. I stand back, waiting for him to get up.

"What the hell, Kali. I told you I can't fight."

"Even so, humans are fast enough to dodge that kind of swing."

His face turns angry, "You're being ridiculous. You saw me falling asleep at that table, I'm tired."

"Being tired doesn't override this," I spin the staff, swinging it up over my head to crack it down. He holds his with both hands, catching my staff with his. His arms shake as I bear down with a large portion of my strength.

"Stop it," he grits through his teeth.

"You should be able to fight back, Fin. I've seen how strong the Skin Carvers are, they could fight me off in human form a lot better than this," I snap out my foot directly into his ribs. "You dropped a piece of stone a human would have been able to carry."

"Why are you doing this?" his eyes well with tears.

I still suddenly, my head cocking to the side in a predatory manner. Claws sink into my mind, inching its way over my thoughts.

"I should be asking you that question."

"You know I've been through a lot, you're being cruel," he winces, standing back up.

The Varangian's are at a standstill, watching his every move with dangerous precision. They're monitoring him.

I step towards him, closing the distance. I force my body to look soft, similar to a surrender. His face drops slightly, becoming sadder. It nearly makes me question myself.

"Why were my people having to reset the traps, Fin?"

"I don't know, Filo and I were already leaving when we heard the shouting."

"Filo seems to get plenty of rest on his trips, maybe a missed bit of sleep, but nothing even Lilly couldn't handle."

I feel that monstrous side of me bare its teeth at his jaw tightening. My fingers are burning, itching to come out. I let them.

"Dragons are a different breed; humans struggle to keep up."

I feign utter confusion, "But you're always tired. Gone for hours supposedly off helping others, only to be found once you're going back into your house. No one ever sees you helping, Fin."

Every time I say his name his fists tighten.

I start my attack again, swinging the staff to hit him in multiple places. I don't stop advancing on him. He backs away, only staying defensive while I continue to knock him to the ground over and over.

"Tell me Fin, where do you go all the time? Why do you always show up in places you shouldn't be? Are you looking for something? Secrets? Information to hand over to Addison?"

"I would never give her anything, I'm loyal to you. I'm grateful for you showing me mercy. Where's the person that showed me mercy?"

I laugh, a bit hysterical as my temper fluctuates from his lies. I feel Jakir grab ahold of the imaginary hand I hold out. He's watching, thanks to Aiza retrieving him as I'd asked her earlier.

Fin falls back on his rear, inhaling sharply as the ground makes harsh contact with his tailbone. I swing back a leg, then slam my boot into his ribs. He rolls over, coughing.

"Please, why are you doing this?"

If physical approach won't work, let's try mental.

"Showing them how weak you are," I grab his arm, my talons digging into his chest as I yank him up. "You're useless, everyone has noticed it.

Can't do anything without ruining it or hurting my own people."

"I *am* your people," he wheezes. He weakly swings the staff at me. I dodge it, circling him. The tip of my own weapon drags in the sand behind me. He's limping, so I go for the injured knee.

He cries out at the snap of his leg breaking.

"You're weak," I spit on the ground next to his face. "You're useless. I should have killed you the day I met you. Should have ripped your puny throat out and fed it to the Nightmares. From day one you've been nothing but a clingy, whiney, weak, selfish, arrogant little bitch who doesn't know his place."

I pause, letting him crawl away from me. He stays on his back so he can keep his eyes on me. His leg moves around in a strange manner, the broken knee rendering it impossible to use. The women standing around the ring don't let him leave. He looks around frantically, trying to find a place to run.

"You don't deserve these people," he says.

I slam the staff into the side of his head, making him gasp. His eyes roll back. I grab his face, shaking him back into consciousness.

"Time to show yourself, little liar."

I rear my hand back, talons poised to drive straight into his heart. The blue of his eyes darkens in both fear and anger. He grasps the ankle of the foot pressed on his chest. I bear down with all my weight, crushing the already broken ribs. His mouth opens wide as he screams in pain.

Finally, his talons shred through the tips of his fingers.

Chapter 53

Triumphantly I kick off his hand before he can sink them into me. I stare down at the sickly green color. They're not very long, only about an inch out from the tips of his fingers.

Violent curses fly from the mouths of the women around me. I notice other people have gathered. Most likely from seeing Jakir rush over. I glance at Harlow, who immediately begins working with Jacob to herd everyone back into town and away from the training area. Feathers lands on Oriana's shoulder, she looks at him and begins to remove him. He snaps at her, intently watching me while remaining on her.

Fin stands himself up, dusting the sand as best he can from his clothing. His demeanor is different now, menacing.

"You were willing to take a beating for that long, just to hide it all?" I scoff, looking away for a moment. "I'll give you credit for that."

He takes a defensive stance, not picking up the staff on the ground next to him. Not that he would be able to use it properly.

"Fine, you've proven I'm not human. Now leave me alone," he spins around to leave. Weapons come down in front of him. Ashley holds out her sword to cross with Jamari's ax. Jamari hisses at him, her final warning.

"I mentioned every single one of the things you've done to pull suspicion out of me, and you still deny being a traitorous son of a bitch?"

His shoulders tense, hands curling tightly. I watch him, leaning heavily on my staff. He breathes in, chest expanding slowly.

"She'll come looking for me," he says over his shoulder.

"Who?" my grin could be compared to that of a snake.

"You know exactly who."

"Say it," I lick my lips in anticipation. I want everyone to hear his admission.

His lips follow the motion. He looks back up.

"Addison will kill you for this," he steps towards me. The sounds of swords being unsheathed rings out, a bow is pulled taught by Phedran. "Are you going to let your new slaves do the dirty work for you?"

"I saw him a few times, enjoying himself amongst the other Skin Carvers," Clovis says. I glance at her, recognizing her messy, prematurely gray hair. She flips knives in her hands, countless others hanging from her body, "Never saw him shift, only saw him when he looked at us like his next toy to break."

"Shut your mouth," he snaps. A vein pops out in his neck.

"Bad bad boy," Feathers chuckles after his words. I see a few women smile.

I lean forward, still using the blunt weapon to lean on.

"Ah, see now I really can't let you live. You blatantly disrespected a member of my Samle."

"They're human," he scoffs.

"They're mine," I growl. I sling out the staff, he dodges it once. I continue to swing eventually hitting him in the other leg. I take my chance at hitting it again, effectively taking him down to his remaining knee.

"This will start a war," he argues.

"You think you haven't started it firsthand? You came into this place knowing the truth. Were lucky enough to receive my mercy. And you shoved it in my face." I drop the staff smoothly sending my talons to pierce his shoulder with my left hand. "Beg for your life."

He inhales sharply, most likely noticing it so starkly against the rest of the pain he'd become used to.

My essence flares brightly, not demanding the action, but only intimidating him. I want to truly feel him beg for it.

He considers not doing so, thoughts warring in his head.

"Let me live, I'll give you information about Addison. I'll tell you everything she has planned with Gallyan," he grabs my wrist, trying to pull my talons out. I curl my fingers, twisting them in his muscle.

"Liar liar, dirty lair," the black feathered bird squawks. I glare at him, effectively ending his commentary. He stays to watch.

"More," I demand. Heat builds, then ebbs in my eyes.

"You'd feel guilty, you'll never recover from this. I know you figured out we're Suitors, you can't kill me. You'd be a monster in their eyes. "

No one flinches at his words, no one cares. Some of the Varangian's curse at him, tell him he's not worthy. I feel angry, wanting to rip his throat out for attempting to place the blame on me. My hands twitch, wanting to end his life.

Not yet.

"Get up," I snatch his throat, pulling him up. He struggles, his body untrained to deal with this amount of agony.

Fin swings out his talons, unexpectedly catching my ribs. It's a shallow cut, stinging as blood wells. Two women step forward, grabbing his arms. He fights against their hold.

I fling my talons out to spray off the blood dripping from them.

"How much information did you feed her?"

"Guess you'll never know," he smirks.

I give an over exaggerated frown, "That hurts, Fin."

"So does killing a Suitor," he throws back.

"I don't think so," I tap my finger on my chin. "I think it's going to feel so good I wish I could do it again."

I flick my hand downwards, they shove him to his knees. The broken one grinds as bone grates over tendon. His breath catches, unable to stay silent. Their hands keep his shoulders still so he can't move forward. I step towards him, crouching in front of him.

"Look around Fin, I've got everyone here because they're loyal to me. Not out of fear or manipulation, but pure loyalty. Oriana," I twist my torso towards her. "Do you want to leave? Or fight me?"

"Only in good fun would I fight you, Dronning Kali," her eyes are glittering from the white sands reflection of sunlight.

"Hear that?" I use a talon to tilt up his head. He tries to reach for me, earning a deep gash down his forearm.

"I hear how lonely you'll be when Addison shreds everyone of these dragons to pieces, after she lets Kent fuck his way through these whores," spit flies from his mouth in the last word.

To their credit, none of the women move. Feathers flaps his wings a couple times before settling again, he stares down Fin. Jakir is nearby, keeping a loose leash on me. I shudder as my mind twists, melding slightly with the monster. My head jerks slightly, more of a twitch. I close my eyes for a moment, reveling in the darkness that slips over any coherent thought. It wipes out the glowing from my eyes. The heat of their glow vanishes into a cool wisp.

"Kali," Fin's voice is nervous.

A part of me considers for a moment, just a moment, that these women may run after they see this. Too late to care I grab both sides of his head. My thumbs drag down the sides of his face, carving through to the bone.

"I'm going to watch you bleed," I pull a thumb away to lick it. Warm coppery flavors burst on my tongue.

It tastes so good

"Leave him to me," I hear myself say. They drop their hold on his shoulders, joining the expanding circle. I hear Jakir give them a warning not to let me out.

"Kali."

The name makes my eye twitch.

My thumbs hover over his eyes, talons shaking to dive down into his head.

"I have a better idea," I whisper to myself.

I yank him up, tossing him into the center of the ring. He immediately rolls to his stomach, trying to get up on his semi-good leg. I step quickly, grabbing his shoulder to shove him forward. Reaching down I thrash my hand across the back of both legs, severing his Achilles tendons.

His screams make adrenaline flood my body. I laugh, the sound seeming too shrill to be mine. Fin starts begging, truly begging, for me to stop. He makes promises, offers faint strings that I might have once stopped to listen to.

Another voice begs to Jakir to help. Not Fin, they want him to help me. A man, shorter than me, tries to reach in. Jakir calls to Oriana, who commands the women not let him in. I snap my head up, spotting the short man. Jacob. I wait, wondering if he'll enter. I don't trust myself not to kill him.

Turning my attention back to Fin, crawling away from me with his arms. He reaches for an ankle, I kick him in the hip. The thud makes the black mist covering my mind shudder in pleasure.

He sounds so good being broken

"Don't run away, I'm not done playing," I snap, grabbing a foot and dragging him towards the center. His foot moves strangely, most likely from me nearly severing it. I grab him by his hair instead, tossing him onto his back. His face is red, tear coating his cheeks. The blue of his eyes is brighter from how red lines the whites of his eyes are. I squat next to his head, examining them. He stares at me, mouth struggling to put out any words. It's disgusting.

"I'm...sorry..." he chokes out.

I scoff, "You're sorry you got caught."

I stand, switching to straddle his beaten body.

"Betraying me is one thing. You put the lives of my own people on the line multiple times, then you insulted my Varangian's. Every mark on your body is for them. But this," I trace a talon down his throat, my pupils expanding rapidly as he chokes further. "Is for me."

I bring my arm back, elbow towards my hip, spreading my fingers out to form a circle of talons.

His eyes become wild, realization setting in.

You never thought I would do it I want to do it always wanted to do it

I stare at him. Never breaking eye contact.

I drive my hand up at an angle under his ribs. Wet gushing sounds make bumps raise on my skin. His chest cracks under the sudden pressure. I hear bones grinding as the pieces of ribs slide against one another. Finally, I grasp the beating muscle in his chest. Enclosing the black shards around it I yank. Again. Again.

With a sucking sound, I extract my hand from his chest cavity.

His heart weakly struggles in my hand. I break the eye contact to watch it die in front of me. I like the blood dripping down my forearm.

Looks so good covered in red like that

I drop it down onto the ground next to him. My senses start to dull out a bit. Jakir, I know it's him, pulling back the shadow like a tired animal that still wants to chase. Slowly, I come back to myself. Colors settle, sounds aren't so sharp anymore. I feel calm stretch out over my body. I'm not tired at all, instead I'm invigorated by the smell and taste of blood.

I look to Oriana, "Sorry about ruining your sand."

She laughs, a full blown laugh. As do many of the women, others shaking their head with a smile. I find myself smiling as well. Their happiness from their strength giving me the last bit of courage I need to stand in my decision.

"Harlow!" I call out. "Take the body, bring Filo as an escort. Drop it well over the boundaries for Addison. She can have her pawn back."

She steps back only to shift immediately. Her lips curl in disgust, revealing sharp teeth. Oriana commands the women to step away from the ring. They follow her command, eyes watching the blue and white dragon on awe.

I watch his lifeless body, pulling my talons back into my hands. The blood slips out onto the sand.

"Good for the next generation to see," Oriana claps me on the back.

"Wait," I tell Harlow. I grab his heart from before she picks him up. "Now go."

Jakir waits for me. I walk towards him, limp heart in hand.

"Consolation prize," I shrug.

He hums, putting a hand on my back to guide me towards a much needed bath in the lake.

"You feel better?" Jakir asks, rubbing the blood from my face. I'd long given up trying to scrub it off with water alone. His face doesn't have it's normal slight happiness to it. There's a sadness that hurts me to see.

"Are you disgusted by me?" I return. I can't look in his eyes, fear of what he might think or say holding tight. I can already feel the disappointment in the Bond. He isn't closing it down completely, but I can sense it there.

He tilts my face up, using a washcloth to remove some of the splattered blood on my neck. His eyes look over my face to search for any remaining spots. Satisfied, he gently dips me below the surface to clean off the soap. I start considering what exactly he might think of me. There's concern swirling in him, probably at how violent I was. I can even feel disappointment eating away at my elation from ripping Fin's heart out.

"I could never be disgusted by you," his eyes sear into mine. "I'm just disappointed at how he turned out. I'd hoped he'd give you a reason to believe in showing mercy. But I also wish you'd found a different way to punish him."

I blink rapidly, surprised by his answer.

"C'mon now, you literally have access to my emotions."

"Which is why I'm worried you're pulling away," I drop my head to watch my fingers play with the water.

He smooths my wet hair back from my face, "Kali, I'm not pulling away. I accepted the violence in you a long time ago. While I may have done it differently myself, I understand why you did that. It wasn't just for you."

"It was entirely for me."

He shakes his head, "You did it for Oriana and the other women. You did it for your Samle. I could feel how upset you were about being betrayed. But the fury you held once you realized the danger your people have been in, the insult he delivered to the Varangian's by saying what he did, that's justified. There's a reason you were selected as Dronning – because we need someone that will tread through the morally gray for us. Without those choices, we will never cease being a target."

"What if I lose control?" I whisper.

"You won't," he places a gentle kiss on my forehead. "Should it come to that, I'll take your life myself to protect our people."

I can still feel the way he feels about what I'd done, but I know that nothing I say will change that. There's enough comfort knowing that he doesn't hate me, so I have to make myself be okay with it since I wouldn't change a single thing I did.

"You're a goddamn liar."

"Language, please. It's so unnecessary," he frowns lightly. I reach forward to tickle his abdominal muscles, earning myself a splash in the face.

I gape at him, playing insulted.

"I can literally feel that you're planning to splash me."

"I would never."

I sling my arm towards him, cupping water up into his face.

Harlow

I wait for Jacob to pull off his pants on his own.

"I can help you," I say quietly. He hates needing help. Hates not being entirely independent.

"If I have any chance of being able to function on my own," he yanks them from his legs, shivering in the slight chill of the air. "I have to do this kind of stuff on my own, Low."

I sigh deeply, annoyed with his insistence on struggling.

"You'll always have me, what's the point?"

He stops once he's lifted himself up to stand without the help of his crutches. The look he gives me haunts me. It's stern and cold, so unlike him.

"I won't. We both know that."

My eyebrows pull together at his words.

"Look at what's happening around us. Kali is actively having weapons made to supply an army. That army is growing by the numbers of people flocking here to either find home or escape. One day, you're going to be out there," he motions to my sword laying on the ground. Its leather holster makes it look so unassuming – even useless. I know just how dangerous that sword has become with my capabilities. He drops his hands to his side, "I'll be able to help, but not next to you. You'd be too distracted protecting me."

"You'll be safe inside wherever we hide the rest of those unable to fight," I try to slyly convince him of it every time we have this conversation. It never works.

He clenches his jaw, breathing slowly to calm his frustration.

"I won't be with them; until my last breath I'll be doing what I can to make sure this place doesn't return to the dark ages. This is going to be a city one day. It can't be that without people, it certainly can't be that without building more, and it most definitely won't be that without every able dragon helping to defend it," he grabs my hand, tugging me down to gently press his lips to mine. My stomach twists as he regains his balance.

We both look out at Kali, her green eyes catching ours for a moment before turning away to avoid a splash of water. Her laughter feels like a gift after watching her let out so much anger.

"Do you think she'll ever get to just be her?" Jacob asks, still watching her.

"You mean do I ever think she'll stop being a Dronning?"

"She would never stop doing that, whatever picked her clearly did so for a good reason. I mean do you think she'll ever get to have more than just...that?"

"Maybe, but she won't have it without us getting her there."

"I wonder what happens to a Samle when they lose their ruler," his words snap me out of my consideration of Kali's future.

"Why would you say that?" I lean away from him, trying to see what's wrong for him to ask such a thing.

"Low, be honest with yourself. If this does turn into some full blown war at least one ruler won't make it through. She has this weird connection that lets her feel our pain sometimes. Who's to say we don't have the same connection to her?"

I don't answer. I'm uncomfortable with how little we know about our own species and how it works. My mind turns to another subject to escape the weight of this one.

"When is Brawn going to have your prosthetic ready?"

"Whenever he finishes it," he cheekily says. I wrap my hand around the back of his head, locking my lips with his. Playfully nipping at his bottom lip, I feel his body shudder.

Kali calls out at us, begging us to come into the water with her. Jakir lifts her out of the water, her underthings completely soaked from being submerged multiple times, and throws her back under. I like seeing the way his face lights up when they're together.

"You can pay for that smart comment later," I tell him, before stripping down to my own underthings to join Kali.

All the blood on her body is gone, washed away by the always pure turquoise lake. It's still cold enough outside that the lake feels warm. I know I'll have to run with Jacob to the house before we both get too cold. We'll be wrapped up in nothing but a blanket in front of the fireplace in our bedroom.

He's thinking the same thing with the way he grins at me. I splash water at him before wading towards Kali.

She leaps at me, catching me off guard and pushing me under the water. Bubbles rush up past us as her hands push down on my chest. Kali laughs, more bubbles rushing her mouth. I laugh too, getting my knees under her and shoving back. We wrestle for a bit, finally coming up for air together.

"You can sort of hold your own against me," I shove my hair from my face. "It's because my hair got in the way."

"Right," Kali rolls her eyes. "Not because I've actually learned some things about fighting."

I tap my chin, faking deep consideration. I look up, shaking my head briefly, "Nope not it."

"So you done being murder mittens for a while?" Jacob pokes at her side.

She raises one of those perfectly poised eyebrows, "Got any reason I shouldn't be?"

Jacob flushes, looking slightly afraid for a moment.

"I'm kidding," she calms him. "I've for sure learned a lesson on trusting outsiders."

"What about the people still showing up on our shores?" I ask her, catching Aiza playing with Lilly at the shore. She struggles to keep the little one from running into the water fully clothed. Filo strips to briefs, walking in holding Ellie's hand.

"The ones that are confidently mine wouldn't destroy their home," she notices Ellie and Filo coming out, looking blissful together. "The others are seeking refuge. Both groups have reason to protect this Samle."

"Those on the border that have chosen to live on their own have only grown more defensive," Filo holds Ellie to his chest. It makes me pull Jacob into mine.

"I'm sure they will be nearly unstoppable once they hear of this," Ellie comments. "And Aiza's mind is already spinning across all of the ramifications of what's to come of this."

"She doesn't need to," Kali's face has dropped, the conversation turning into entirely different one. "This is going to light a fire under Addison's ass. She'll declare war, I'm sure of it."

"We don't know that," Jakir speaks soothingly, not wanting the careless Kali to disappear just yet.

"We do," I'm honest with them, ignoring Jacob's tight squeeze on my waist. "War is the only way to truly end this; it'll drag on forever otherwise."

"On the former, I can't disagree," Filo shakes the long hair back from his face. His hands smooth over the shaved sides of his head. "But on the latter, it will end. It's just a matter of who outlasts it."

Kali looks out over the lake towards the sun setting behind the rising skyline of the town. Her thoughts are distant, drawn into her role again as Dronning. I watch her leave the lake alone. Jakir watches her with pain in his eyes.

"How is she, truly?" Ellie asks. Her thin lips are tight with concern.

I watch our Sekund breathe in steadily. It's one of his calming techniques I see him often use when Kali is experiencing duress.

"She's not considering war at this point, she's planning for it," he says.

Chapter 54

I can't stop playing the bloody images of Fin's body breaking in my mind. Every crack, tear, and snap echoes in my memories. There is no second guessing myself, only the satisfaction of pulling his life from him. I briefly grasp how serious it is that I'm excited by killing rather than horrified. Rather than linger on that, however, I decide to analyze what I missed.

Gently closing off the Bond so I can process in peace I lay across my bed. I play over Fin showing up in the manor, being in the courtyard. Him coming around the corner after a brief conversation with Mikhail. Each and every detail I missed slams into my mind without reprieve. It's all so clear now that I've looked at it through a different lens.

"Idiot," I mutter to myself.

I only get up in the night to crank shut the cover over my room. It blocks out the morning light, allowing me to gain a couple hours of sleep. I crank it back open the moment I'm up again.

A knock sounds on the door moments later.

"Yes?" I call, flipping my covers back.

Ellie steps in, staying in the doorway, "I'm surprised you keep this as neat as you do."

"What does that mean?" I convey mild offense with a hand on my chest.

"You're brain is everywhere all the time," she looks bored at me. "Hurry up and get dressed. You're not going out for training anymore until you've eaten."

I cross my arms in defiance, "I've been just fine eating brunch."

"Wrong, I can see you losing weight. Get down here."

I look down at my thighs, the muscle creating a curve that extends out. A dusty mirror is next to my door, surrounded by emerald green painted wood. I look, seeing a thick build to the muscles in me legs. I pull my shirt up to see the muscle in my back flex.

"Stop checking yourself out and come eat!" she yells. A mild blush rushes my cheeks. I drop the hem of my top, pulling on thick boots before leaving.

Ellie crams so much food down my throat I feel overly bloated as I leave. She looks proud of her work, cleaning up my dishes with a smug look on her face.

I don't hesitate in leaving, making my way slowly through the courtyard to enjoy the pool at one end. As I leave, one of the Varangian's appears in the corner of my vision.

"Hi," Maia pushes away from the wall next to the archway. Her wavy black hair flows down her back, tied up in a ponytail.

"Hi," I slide my eyes to her, eyeing her spear. "Can I help you, Maia?"

"Oriana wanted me to ask if you'd be training with us today," her long strides help her keep up with my quick pace.

"That's the plan."

"She says you have a plan for us."

"I do."

Maia groans, slamming her spear into the ground a few times as we walk. I smile briefly, trying not to irk her.

"We don't like surprises," she tries a different angle.

"You may not like them, but you should be prepared for them."

She huffs, taking to silence until we reach the rest of them. A few new women have joined. I note the looks on their faces, similar to the ones the trained women wore when I first brought them here. I catch Brawn set down a pack on a nearby bench, Harlow and a handful of others behind him.

Oriana leaves her sparring with two other women to greet me. I put up a hand, stopping her question before she asks it.

"They're going to learn an important lesson today, a few hopefully."

"Fine, but not the new ones," she motions to the women being trained by one of the more gentle Varangian's, Owena. "They need time."

"Of course," I dip my head in respect to her demands.

I wait for them all to gather around me. Oriana only has to nod at them all for them to listen to me.

"Unfortunately, I don't think Dronning Addison is going to take me killing one of her people very well," I smile, they chuckle at my words. "Which means we're another step closer to war. This isn't going to be some mostly political mess like the old world. There won't be meetings to stop it. There's already plenty of dragons that want it. Eventually, that means you all will be fighting for this Samle's life."

I pause, letting my words sink in. I continue, wanting to drive the point home.

"You'll not only be expected to train the rest of those in this Samle who are able-bodied, you'll also be expected to lead them. Furthermore," I take a deep breath. "I expect all of you to have a deep understanding of dragons. From our weaknesses, to our strengths, to how to ride with us."

Eyes go wide, shock rippling across all of them. The new trainees seem shaken, unsure of how these women could be so excited.

"Where do we start?" Oriana asks.

I begin taking off my clothes. Though nudity had long since become normal occurrence for these women to witness, they still take in the scars littering my body.

"Myself, along with those standing near Harlow," I point to her, she begins taking off her clothes as well. "Will shift multiple times today. Every one of you will watch us. I want you to know what the weak points are as we shift, especially what it looks like. Learn how our bodies move individually."

"Split up," Oriana's voice carries, a firm rock for her group to depend on.

"You'll be with me first," I tell her. "Once we get to learning how to ride-"

"I'm your rider," she cuts me off. Her confidence astounds me. "Surprised?"

"Didn't think you'd already considered it in such a short time."

She shrugs, "It only makes sense."

I crack my shoulders and neck, watching Harlow shift first. The Varangian's surrounding her move around, watching her body change.

"Typically I make everyone move while doing it," I step away from the women surrounding me.

"Makes for a much more mobile dragon, though painful I'm sure," Maia leans on her spear.

"Very," I look at her seriously. "We're breaking our bodies and rebuilding them every time we shift. Which is why you'll have another set of dragons doing this every day."

I pause, looking around me. I have to use my diaphragm to be loud enough for them to hear me.

"Be prepared to move back some more."

"I don't recall you being that large..." Ashley trails off.

Oriana swings her head at her, daring her to say another word.

My knees give out first, the tendons expanding so rapidly that the bones feel tangled in them. Cracks happen in succession throughout my body. It pulls me back, causing my back to arch. I nearly begin to move forward, but have to force myself to stay still. My eyes begin to change letting the pupil elongate into the slit that gives me better vision. Oriana's mouth tightens, her mind probably flashing back to the day I pulled her from Kent's campsite. I marvel at the difference in her body as my face stretches out, jaw unhinging then realigning to pop back into a different setting. Any thoughts of Fin disappear in the comfort of being back in my safest form.

No more skin and bones now, are you little Varangian?

I know she'd kill me if she heard the nickname I'd called her.

"We can't c-c-communicate with humans in dragon form, but w-we can c-communicate with each other," Brawn explains to them. Others have chosen to stay in human form, helping to explain our species to each group.

"How do they communicate?" Oriana reaches a hand up, I lower my snout so as to allow her to touch my face.

"Mind to mind, it's the same as speaking. The further you are, the harder it is to hear. Same effort as speaking," he reaches into his pocket. Pulling out a few vials. Their smells make my lip curl.

Oriana and Maia snatch their hands away at the sight of my teeth.

"It's still Kali, she's n-not going to bite. She just doesn't l-like the smell of some of this stuff. Sensitive noses you wouldn't believe," he says. He pulls out a few syringes, stepping towards me.

"What are you doing?" Oriana seems uneasy. She looks into the eye staring down her and Brawn. I hear her heart rate pick up as I make eye contact with her.

"Taking blood, I need some for studying," he mumbles, his demeanor is confident as he pats my lip for me to lift again. I lick my gums with my tongue, annoyed at his pace. He quickly sticks a needle into my gums, with drawing blood multiple times. Once satisfied he pulls out some of the awful-smelling vials.

"I swear this man tests my limits every day," I growl.

"I'm not jealous of you being his test subject today," Harlow laughs at me. I lift my head quickly to full height, snapping my teeth at her. She shakes her head and neck, like she's physically shaking off my attitude. I return my attention to Oriana and Brawn's conversation.

"Their bodies automatically know how to communicate physically. Some of their movements and such are because it's ingrained into them," he says. I lower my head down, only to growl and snap it away at the vial he holds near my nose. I almost swipe at him.

"She clearly loves that," Oriana drags a hand across my nose. I breath in her scent, taking the time to memorize it should I need to find it. Her hands are comforting on the sensitive part of me, calming from growling at the man near me. Brawn writes down notes.

I shift back down, forcing my body to slow down enough that the women can see what's happening. It's much more painful slowing it down, taking more energy out of me.

"I wasn't done," Brawn frowns, he shoves his glasses back up with a flat hand. "Shift back."

I look at him sternly, "I'll shift back when I'm ready Brawn."

Completely in his element he brushes me off, continuing to write notes down.

"Harlow has fire, what about you?" Ashley asks me, pausing her pacing around me.

"I don't, not all of us do. Harlow's is too dangerous which is why she rarely uses it."

"What makes it so dangerous?"

"It's incinerating, only a white or violet flame is hotter than hers."

"We'll keep that in mind when matching her with a rider," Oriana taps her chin, already planning out who will become riders.

I shift back again, still feeling the need to walk. Brawn waves more smells in front of me, none of them as mad as the first. I shift a few more times until I can't take standing still any longer.

"I'm going to move as I shift now, which might change some of what you see," I tell them.

"Walking as your body breaks apart? Are you a masochist?" Maia shakes her head, but she's smiling.

I smirk, "Absolutely, considering most of us can run while doing it."

"Actually why do you choose to do that? I've never understood the reason."

"Because you never know when you'll need to do it on the move. I've made it practically law that everyone learns how to. At some point," I turn to face Oriana. "You all will need to learn how to get yourselves onto us both still and moving. We can help some, but not all tails are helpful."

She only nods, watching me grow as I walk through the grass. The rest follow suit, each group moving back and forth as their respective dragons allow them to view and touch. Many of them call out strengths and weaknesses that occur during the shift, helping us to see what we should be careful of.

While the back is one of the first to be covered in tough skin and scales, the armpit remains vulnerable until the front legs have fully formed to bend back. Even then, it's still a soft place to be struck.

The neck is an easy place to take us down, if you can get high enough and swing at a very specific spot in a matter of seconds before it become too tough to slice through. I converse with Harlow about all of these and what to do.

After a few days of consideration, we both walk to Freyr's blacksmith shop. Feathers is with me, eyeing everyone that walks by with his beady look from my shoulders. Most people simply ignore him, used to his strange mannerisms.

"You realize making a suit of armor for one dragon alone could easily take me four months, even more if it's you, Kali," he says, rubbing his bald head.

"Can you try and recruit more people?" I lean against his shop counter. "Plenty are coming in, they need work."

"The work force is the easy part, it's the fact I don't have enough space for making it all."

"What if you had a place the size of a mountain?" Harlow interjects. I slowly turn to face her, unsure of where she's going with this. She looks at me, "There's already places in the mountains that are caves. Enough mining and digging and we can use them as large places to make the armor and weapons needed."

Freyr looks down at his hands, considering. Feathers jumps from my shoulder onto the table, his feet tapping along the surface as he struts in front of me. I smooth my fingers over his head.

"Freyr," I grab his attention. "With enough people, can you manage building a secure place that's big enough in the mountains?"

He nods slowly, "There's a lot to be done. Building to casts, measuring you lot out, carving out pure stone to build to system we need. We'd be starting from scratch, but we can do it."

"I'll send you the number of people we can spare you, you ask for that number and we'll send you with as many supplies as we can afford."

He thanks me nervously as I leave, though I catch a glint in his eyes at having such an opportunity.

"Think he'll be able to actually do it?" Harlow looks up ahead at the street full of bustling people. Dipping into and out of shops people move about, using copper, silver, and gold that had been reformed into coins.

"I do, but I'm not sure if it'll be done in time," I walk with her, heading back towards the manor. "Could take years to even build the size of the place he needs."

"You better hope that war can wait years then."

I bite the inside of my cheek, already aware that war would wait for no one.

I take another night to myself, worn from so much shifting and interaction. Jakir is just as busy, offering to be one of the dragons shifting for the Varangian's. I meet with the Varangian's for training each morning, though it's the longest amount of interaction I get during the day.

Barely any of us are able to maintain long talks. Not between Ellie making trips with Filo and Lilly to help those further out start up their own food supply, Jacob quickly expanding the build of the town in taller buildings, Aiza visiting Linius and Janét.

I wait anxiously for the Twins to return, knowing that getting across the water takes a week alone. The journey into each territory to reach Elias and Mikhail taking even longer if they wish to stay undetected. No contact with them is still making me nervous not having my Nightmares in my shadow constantly.

Moving slowly through the courtyard I use the evening to relax. I follow the path through multiple fountains, pools, and statues with small steps.

A young willow tree rustles in the gentle wind that manages to crawl through. It's leaves rustle, like whispers in my ear. I sit below it on a stone bench. The dipping branches barely manage to touch the top of my head. Closing my eyes I breathe in the smell of flowers starting to bloom.

Spring started only three days ago with the turn to slightly warmer weather, but flowers took the opportunity to explode immediately. It's the first true Spring I'd seen since waking up from my begravelse. I reach out to touch a large flower, its petals being sucked into the tubular stem as so as my skin comes in contact with it. I smile to myself in the growing darkness of night. Faint glowing on the other end of the courtyard begins; the only glowing water plant that Ellie had found opening. I chose to stay, not wanting to leave the cover of the willow tree just yet to go see the flowers up close.

A sound pulls my attention to the open hallway on my right. I peer into the darkness, cursing my human sight as I struggle to find the source.

"Jakir?" I call out, wondering who had made it back so late.

No one answers, so I brush off the sound.

Except I can't.

The hairs on the back of my neck stand up as another scuffling sound echoes against the stone walls. I still completely, unsure of what to make of it.

No one good would be trying to play a joke right now.

I stand, immediately reaching out to Jakir. His emotions are dulled out by his sleep, making me hold off on stirring him. Moving silently through the courtyard I keep my ears open to any other sounds.

Suddenly footsteps sound behind me, nearly silent. I catch them, turning at the last minute to see a large figure bringing down the blunt edge of a knife handle towards my face.

It nearly catches my cheek, avoided by my dips away. I grunt out, unable to call for help once the air is knocked from my lungs by a foot slamming into my chest. Deprived of air I struggle to regain control of the fight. My body is worn from so much shifting during the day that I can't move as quickly as I normally do. A few hits land on me, much more than the ones I'm landing on my attackers.

It's too damn dark, of course it's a new moon tonight.

Another person grabs my arm from behind, attempting to wrap rope around my wrist. I maneuver away, spinning and twisting to try and put myself in a better position. Hands fly towards me with weapons in hand. I hope silently that the clanging of metal on the ground will wake someone.

Distantly I feel Jakir start to stir.

At the same time, another body comes behind me.

"Enough," he says, his voice sounding dangerously irritated.

As I turn around to run out of the manor, away from the three figures raining down hateful blows, I almost run into another.

My head jerks sideways at the brute force that slams into my temple.

Already passing into dangerously unconscious territory, I'm hit again in the back of the head.

Blackness washes over my mind just as I watch the ground fly up to me.

Chapter 55

"Talia's news isn't good, it's incredibly concerning."

The woman with red hair smooths it behind her ear, "That depends entirely on how you're looking at it."

"We convened month ago, now we meet again only for you to tell us she's been taken into the wrong hands?"

"Eina, enough," the silver haired one commands down the argument before it begins. "We don't know all of the plans, only our part in them."

"Who's to say what's to be assumed and what's to be taken literally?" a curvy, red-haired woman speaks.

"I agree with Surtr," Eina nods, looking towards the opposite side of the stone table.

A sigh from that side.

"She'll make it out, that's when we reach out. We cannot step in too quickly or we risk our survival."

"For now, we just allow this to happen? Who's to say she won't be broken?" Petrichor's face is concerned, shadowed by worry.

"We certainly aren't," another, one with smooth blue hair that falls against their chest.

Eina rolls his eyes, placing his hands flat on the table, "You all should pray this doesn't kill her or her spirit. Find me when it's actually time."

The group slowly disperses, leaving the tall one with silver hair to look out over the waterfall. Mist from the water rises to touch their face, gently coating it in a shine.

"Breathe, Kali," they plead into the night sky. "Just breathe."
Their whispers carry on the wind, straining to reach her ears.

Chapter 56

Jakir

What wakes me is a sharp rise in panic, then absolute silence through the Bond. I sit up in bed, immediately reaching out to sense Kali. The only certain thing I feel is that the Bond is still there.

A strain thrums down, like the one I experienced when she left for Mikhail's territory. Throwing back the covers I rush to Aiza's room. After a sharp knock I hear her bed creaking.

"Aiza, get up," anxiety fills my gut. "It's Kali."

The door is thrown open, her head haphazardly covered in fabric.

"What do you mean?" her eyes are bleary, still recovering from sleep.

"Something is wrong. Did she tell you she was going anywhere today?"

She frowns, "No, her plan was to help with more of Jacob's new project."

My heart skips a beat, stops, then picks up a wild pace. I almost fall to my knees at the gut feeling.

"Jakir," she reaches towards me, her voice filled with the same panic I feel. "What's wrong, tell me what's wrong."

"Get dressed now and find Filo," I don't wait for her to respond. I feel a pinch of guilt at being so rude in waking her up only to disappear.

Sprinting down the halls I come around the corner, nearly running into Harlow.

"Jakir what are you-"

"KALI!" I scream, my voice cracks at the end of her name. I struggle to open the door to her room, not enough light from the sun filtering into the hallway yet. The torches are all out.

Harlow helps me, slamming open the door. We both sprint up the stairs as quickly as we can. Nothing is touched, not since the night before last. It feels stale.

"No," I mumble. "No no no no no no no."

I open the windows, stumbling onto the balcony to look out over the land. My talons curl over the stone, causing divots to be created.

"Jakir," Harlow grabs my bicep firmly, spinning me to face her. "Where is she, what happened?"

"I can barely feel her," I clutch at my chest, fingers curling and uncurling in hopes I grab onto the sliver of feeling I have of her life.

"Maybe she closed down the Bond for some privacy," she pumps her hand in an attempt to soothe me.

"She wouldn't do this, she wouldn't close it down."

"Maybe she just-"

"Someone took her!" I scream. My voice carries down across the still morning.

Harlow pulls back, dread washing over her face. She doesn't have time to absorb the information before I rush past her into the bedroom. Kali's knife is sitting on her nightstand, not strapped to her thigh like it is every day.

"She wouldn't have left without this," I grab it, showing Harlow. "You know she always wears this unless she's here in the manor."

"I know," she whispers, voice strangled through fear.

"Shift, sound the alarm," I demand. "Find her."

Harlow doesn't waste time, launching herself over the balcony railing to slide towards the ground. She lands, immediately beginning to shift. Her jaw unhinges, bellowing out a roar that shakes the very ground beneath her. I rush back inside, Kali's knife still in hand, to take up my own search with Aiza inside of the manor, finding nothing around. Room after room I find nothing, every empty space compounding the empty hole in my chest.

Two large thuds bring my attention outside, causing me to walk towards the entrance.

The Nightmares are looking over towards the town, dragons flying out in every direction. Sayah shifts, looking angry.

"Where is she?" he demands.

I don't even question his sixth sense of her knowing that something is wrong.

"She's gone," I clench my fists. He looks down, wild shock filling his face. In a flash, both of them leave, flying in a direction different from others to cover ground.

Aiza walks up next to me, her hands shaking.

"What do we do?"

"We reach out to our allies, carefully report her missing."

"How do you know they didn't do it? We can't be too careful," she looks up at me.

I glance down, taking in the black shirt with flowing sleeves that pinch at her wrists. The fabric of her pants is also black, matching her hijab.

"I know who did it," my nails dig into my palms, eventually being ripped away by golden talons making an appearance.

"Jakir," she cautiously says.

"I'm going to fucking slaughter those that took her," I grit out, my anger becoming a hot wave over my body. Aiza's mouth drops open in shock. "And then I'm going to drown Gallyan in their blood."

Kali

My first instinct is to immediately lash out at whatever might be near me, but I know that won't do any good. I take in the sounds I hear first. All I hear is the shifting of feet.

The Bond flutters, weak from such distance from Jakir. It isn't painful yet, though I know with enough time it will morph into excruciating pain.

Slowly opening my eyes, I take in the dim light barely allowing me to see. There's not much except for plain stone walls surrounding me that seem to thrum with energy.

I pull my legs up to stand, surprised by the sound of metal dragging on the floor. I snap my eyes to look, finding my ankles bound by thick cuffs attached to a large chain. My chest clamps as I follow the chains a short distance to where they've been firmly attached to the concrete. My fingers fumble over the lock, knowing it's useless but still wanting to hope that there's an easy way out of this.

Nothing budges, only grinds against the bone of my ankle.

I begin to consider shifting, but realize that the cuffs may cut through my limbs instead of breaking away from my skin. Even if I break through, I could be risking crushing myself to death if these walls won't give. I huff, concluding that shifting isn't an option.

Rising, I walk to the edge of the lightly colored circle on the floor. I'm contained within it by my restraints, unable to stretch even a finger outside of the boundary. Beyond that line is a darker material, where it stretches until only the wall meets it.

I don't allow myself to panic despite the relentless fear of being chained down after I'd been knocked into unconsciousness. My chest expands with the deep breaths I take, slowing until I've eased my heart rate.

"Is she awake?"

The voice that responds is the one I'd heard before they'd slammed something into my temple. I remain silent to hear as much as I can before anyone walks in.

"I think so, I'm not sure," another voice, clearly uncaring.

"Go check, I'll be back with him shortly."

The one that sounds uncaring sighs, now very much annoyed that he has to check on whether or not I'm awake. A lock clicks open, allowing the door to swing wide enough for him to fit through. I still don't say a word as the man steps in, locking the door behind him. He turns, looking at me distastefully.

"Guess I didn't need to check," he gruffs.

"Where am I?" I croak out. My throat feels like it's cracking from being so dry.

"Not my business to tell you," he says, readying to leave the room again.

I pause, deciding in only a second on how I want this to go. I'm fuming, and that's clearly affecting my thinking.

"Makes sense that they would put someone as useless as you here with me," I sneer at him.

It gets me the reaction I want, because he spins around with a violent look on his face.

"What did you just say to me?"

"Oh good, you're deaf too. I said-" I start to exaggerate my words until he storms towards me. I scan him quickly for keys, seeing them on his belt.

"Shut your mouth, or I'll put a boot in your stomach," he points a finger at me, his toes just over the line crossing into my little circle.

Just a little further.

I dramatically throw the back of my hand to my forehead, "You're so terrifying. Please have mercy!"

He drops his hand, knuckles turning white from how hard he clenches his hands. I watch him decide whether or not he wants to risk crossing the line completely to hit me. The monster inside my head perks up, excited at the idea of him getting close enough to hurt.

"You're not worth it," he mumbles, turning to leave.

"You must hear that a lot, pants look a little snug, you know?" I motion to his crotch, successfully turning him back around.

"What does that mean?"

"Exactly what you think it means," I look again, lingering at the apex of his legs, then giving a disappointed look.

Take the bait, take the bait.

"You don't know jack shit," he snaps.

"I know enough to know when a man has a small penis."

A sound outside of the room brings my attention to the door.

"You deserve exactly what you get from him," he spits at me.

"You haven't turned away, tell me you like this kind of talk. Bit of a momma's boy, are we?" I cock my head, watch his face burn.

"Fuck you," he steps inside the circle, cocking his hand back to hit me. I pretend to flinch, waiting for him to get closer. Now within arm's reach, I dive out and grab his ankle. My other hand wraps around his knee, pulling it out to force him down. His knees hit the ground, just as the door opens. He attempts to fight back, only to be knocked back in a daze once I slam my fist into his nose. He groans, rolling his head back and forth slowly. The smell of blood becomes pungent, making my pupils dilate in the dim lighting.

I look up to see Gallyan walk in with another man. He frowns at the man under my knee. I clench my jaw, feeling a sudden need to go after the Konge.

"Jeremy, I thought you wouldn't be stupid enough to get near her," he says, those green eyes taking in my body.

I glance at the man behind him, who's standing relaxed. His hands are in his pockets, defining the v-shape of his body. His dark, upturned eyes don't budge to meet mine. They stay pinned to Jeremy.

"She came after me," he groans from the pressure I'm putting on his sternum.

"She wouldn't have been able to if you'd stayed out of the circle," Gallyan pulls out a cigarette, lighting it with a match. "Let him go Kali."

The man behind him flicks his eyes up at me, but I'm not looking at him anymore. I curl my fingers around Jeremy's shirt, yanking him up to stand. He sways on his feet, taking a moment to put his back to me. I look to Jeremy quickly, staring at his neck. Gallyan raises his eyebrows in challenge.

"Let me go," I say calmly.

He stares me down. The tension is thick in the room, Jeremy still trying to fix his nose.

Gallyan's eyes widen in slight surprise. Jeremy takes a step forward, his next step is his last. My talons rip out quickly, slamming through his neck to sever his spine from his skull. Blood seeps out, then runs down my arm. I yank away my hand, causing a suction sound as the four holes in his neck are left empty.

Jeremy's body falls to the ground, sans the keys previously attached to his waist. He gurgles, struggling on his last breath.

"Interesting," Gallyan steps forward, crouching just outside the confines of my reach. "You're not as good as you pretend to be."

I don't waste a moment, reaching for my ankle restraints to unlock them. Just as I insert the key, I'm knocked back onto the ground. I sit up and reach for the keys, my wrist being pinned down by a boot. Looking up, I see the stranger that had come in with Gallyan looking down. His face is void of any and all emotion, his body completely relaxed as he crushes my wrist under his boot.

I grab his ankle with my other hand to pull him down as well.

He's clearly much faster, one of his hands coming out of his pocket to grab my throat. He lifts me up, staring at me. My feet dangle off the ground as he brings me up to be face to face with him. I grab his wrist with both hands, trying to pry him from me. Heat flashes in my eyes, prepared to command him to drop me.

I freeze, caught off guard by the two differently colored eyes. One iris is so white it almost blends into the rest of his eye, the other so dark I wonder if it's actually black. His full lips create a face that in another life, I might try and carve it out of stone. I look down his jawline, wondering at how such sharp cheekbones and angled lines that outline his face could be bestowed on someone aligned with Gallyan. His long nose accentuates the features of his face, making him even more distracting.

I bring up my foot to plant directly in his chest. It misses as he drops me to the ground, the keys now in his hands.

"Bring them in, Ares," Gallyan is standing again, watching my every move. "Since she can't behave herself."

Ares walks away from me, leaving the room to retrieve whatever Gallyan has requested.

"I told you not to make me do this Kali, but you forced my hand," the Konge shakes his head. "Once I heard you'd killed a Suitor I knew I had to act. You're getting out of control, I need to put a leash on you."

"I'm not your pet," I snarl.

"You are, in case you missed the chains."

Ares walks back in, massive chains causing his biceps to strain with the weight. I fight him as he grabs my wrists, locking the clamps around them tightly. He refuses to look me in the eye as he restrains both of my arms just as my legs are.

"At any point should you wish to do this the easy way, you can give in to me," Gallyan's eyes glow, his essence attempting to pound into my resolve. "But until that point, I am going to break you down to your barest structure, then I'm going to rebuild you the way you should have been made."

I fight him, allowing my own eyes to glow angrily at him. The silent battle only stops once he lets his eyes cool down to their non-glowing look. I let out a heavy breath, already exhausted.

"When I get out of these," I lift my chains, letting them drop onto the floor. Ares moves towards me, grasping my hand and sliding covers over each finger. I attempt to release myself, only earning a sharp stab into each finger as he locks it in place. I hiss through my teeth once he's done. Every finger encased in some strange feeling metal, a sharp needle holding them down by piercing through me. I start to grow out my talons, "I will slaughter your entire Samle."

"I'd be careful letting your talons out," Gallyan warns, nodding towards my attempts. "The pins embedded in your fingers will drag through your skin and muscle, practically reducing your fingers to useless ligaments."

Uncontrolled horror drains my face of warmth. Being unable to use my talons anymore makes my hands feel cold, lifeless. I look up at him as he steps inside the ring, I don't move. His hand guides my face up to look at him, those perfect teeth smiling down on me.

"I've got a muzzle too, so watch yourself," he angles my head and looks down at my torn shirt. "Tempt me enough with that attitude of yours, and I'll take other liberties for myself."

I flinch away, crawling backwards from him as far as the chains allow me. He laughs once, then turns to leave.

"Find some competent guards this time, Ares," is all he says before walking out.

Ares stares me down, an unreadable expression crossing his face. I feel anger surge to sink my claws into his eyes but do nothing in fear of the muzzle Gallyan spoke of.

I feel my Bond to Jakir struggling. The base of my spine twitches as it begins to deteriorate into a much more aggressive reaction at being torn from him. I watch them leave, footsteps echoing down a hall growing fainter by the second.

They slam a door behind them so far away I nearly miss it. I breathe in, then out. Again. I try to grab onto the fringes of the Bond. I play images of my family, wondering if they're safe or captured like I've been. Nothing works.

I scream, the sound full of pain and promises of violence.

I scream over and over again until my throat is raw.

Then I let the darkness wash over my mind, taking all of myself into a deep, dark corner to survive.

Earth - Post Apocalypse

Acknowledgments

Salmah. My biggest cheerleader, marketer, advertiser, honest feedback giver - everything a wonderful friend and an amazing beta reader can be. Thank you for everything you have done and continue to do for me. You were the driving factor to me self publishing, because you showed me how much I could give to other readers out there. If you're an author, I hope you find you a Salmah because *damn* - you are one of a kind, you beautiful woman.

Simon, my critique partner who gave me the verbal lashings I needed when I talked poorly about my own work. And for also doing so when I was a little too far over the writers ledge. Now that I'm published, I can finally breath (the misspelling is intentional everyone, I swear) thanks to you. And another thank you for designing that super cool scene break image.

Emily B., Casserole, and Kaitertot for being such wonderful beta readers and cheering me on to finish this book. The reactions and feedback I got from you all are priceless.

Brock, my husband, for fully supporting my dream of being an author. Thank you for listening to me ramble for all those hours about my plans and ideas for becoming a writer. Every time I got excited you got excited with me, and that means more than you know. I am so lucky to have you. I love you.

My gaming bitches - you know who you all are - for hyping me up, answering every question, giving every opinion I could ask for, and being such wonderful people. I'm lucky to call you all my friends.

Adrian, for putting up with all of my complaints, stories, ideas, and constant distractions when a dog walked by as I was talking. Thank you for your patience and friendship.

Allison, thank you so much for putting up with listening to some of the most gruesome ideas, despite hating anything very dark. And for being so aggressively and genuinely loving when I went even remotely close to second guessing my ability to do this.

Kamryn (especially for those late night questions during school) and Ash for being excellent soundboards when I just couldn't figure things out. And for telling me I was, in fact, not as crazy as I thought.

The reader, for giving my very first book a shot. I see your need to escape into a new world, to pretend that things are different, or better, or easier for a bit, and I get it. I will do my best to continue to write stories that give that to you all. Now stop clenching your jaw and go drink some water. Not coffee. Water.

I hope we meet again.

CPSIA information can be obtained
at www.ICGtesting.com
Printed in the USA
LVHW090929140723
752259LV00002B/12